Approach to

Practical Pediatrics

Approach to

Practical Pediatrics

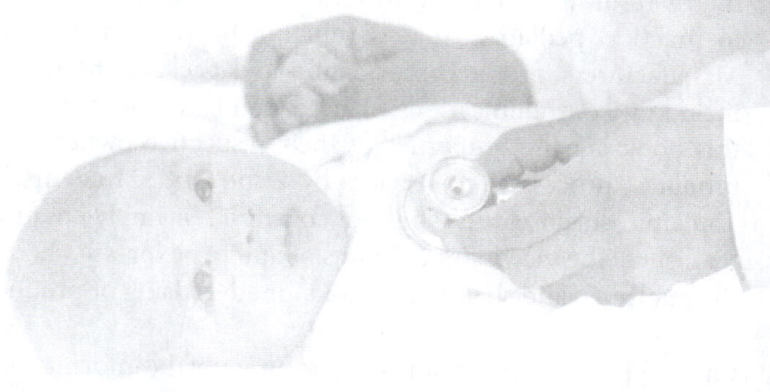

Niranjan Shendurnikar MD, FIAP
Consultant Pediatrician
KG Patel Children Hospital
Vadodara

Paresh A Thakkar MD, DCH, DNB
Associate Professor of Pediatrics
Medical College Baroda & SSG Hospital
Vadodara

Wolters Kluwer

Publishing Manager: Dr Vandana Mittal
Senior Production Editor: Nayan Gogoi
Assistant Manager Manufacturing: Sumit Johry

10th Floor, Tower C, Building No. 10, Phase – II, DLF Cyber City
Gurgaon, Haryana - 122002

ISBN: 978-93-88696-43-2

Published by Wolters Kluwer (India) Pvt. Ltd., New Delhi
Compositor: Design Modus, New Delhi (www.designmodus.in)
Printed and bound at Sanat Printers

For product enquiry, please contact – Marketing Department (marketing@wolterskluwerindia.co.in) or log on to our website www.wolterskluwerindia.co.in.

Dedication

This book is dedicated to those individuals who have greatest influence on the life of the authors and their approach to the science of Pediatrics.

Notable among them are their students who are and always will be their asset and best teachers in the continued learning of Pediatrics; revered and respected late Professor Arvind R Shah who lived and breathed the art and science of Pediatrics and affectionately helped his students learn and practice the medical science with empathy; Dr YK Amdekar, Dr Jagdish N Patel, Dr Sudarshan Kumari, Dr Ashok Dutta, Dr Vinod Jain, and Dr Somnath Banerjee who have guided and helped them to strive for continued love and learning for children and child health.

Dr Niranjan Shendurnikar also dedicates this book to the dynamic lady, spouse, and love of his life, Preeti, for her support and never ending love toward humanity and selfless service; and to Nidhi, Tushar, and Rohini.

Dr Paresh A Thakkar also dedicates this book to his revered parents, Amritlal and Manjula Thakkar, for their blessings. He is also grateful to his wonderful wife and soulmate, Ukti, for her constant and unconditional support and his kids, Kavina and Avit, for teaching him subtle nuances of pediatrics and complementing his life with their purity and innocence.

Foreword

This book is a testament of the fulfilment of the dreams of two astute clinicians, academicians, and teachers who have devoted themselves to the cause of child health and medical teaching over the past several years. A need was felt for a book which would help the undergraduate students learn an approach to clinical methods in pediatrics, help them practise their skills, sharpen their acumen, and guide them to reach a systematic and logical interpretation in their bed side learning process. In the present times, when the art of clinical diagnosis is getting diluted by laboratory and imaging diagnosis, it is prudent that clinical examination must remain indispensable in the art and science of medicine.

Writing and editing a book is a lengthy and herculean task. Right from conceptualization of the subject or theme of the book, selection of the topics, and assigning them to the authors, editing, streamlining, and setting proper flow is a meticulous process. I am convinced that this book has the potential to be of great help to the undergraduate students as well as postgraduates and clinicians in practice to enhance their knowledge and master the art of practical pediatrics. The contents of the book include essentials of physical examination of the children as well as relevant topics and aspects which are closely linked to practical examinations in pediatrics such as child development, infant feeding, childhood immunization, and clinical case scenarios. All such inclusions would assist the students to prepare for relevant and logical clinical preparation and presentations.

The highlight of this book is its relevance in the Indian perspective. The authors have taken great pain in writing the chapters and giving clinical pearls by fishing them out from the ocean of published knowledge which is exponentially increasing day in and day out. I sincerely feel that this book is set to offer enormous benefit to the students of pediatrics interested in mastering the clinical skills and sharpening their clinical acumen.

I would like to express my pride and happiness in getting associated with this book which I can aptly describe as reader friendly in simple and lucid language bringing out the essentials of practical pediatrics. The text and the points should help and guide the students to learn, practice, and remember important facts during their day to day clinical postings in their colleges and institutions. This book would become a practical and useful tool in the students' pursuit of learning practical aspects of clinical pediatrics. I take great pleasure to recommend this book as a clinical and bed side companion to the undergraduate students to help them during their vital learning period.

Dr Raju C Shah
Former Professor and Head
Department of Pediatrics, GCS Medical College, Ahmedabad
National President, Indian Academy of Pediatrics (2005)
President Pediatric Association of SAARC (2005-08)

Preface

In spite of burgeoning advances in the medical sciences, history taking and a thorough clinical examination still remain the corner stone of clinical learning and pediatric practice. With an expanding battery of newer and sophisticated investigations, it is likely that the focus on the clinical examination and the diagnosis may become diluted. However not forgetting an old adage that it is ultimately the student's ability to learn the art of history taking, conduct a thorough examination, and distil the information and the facts, which form the central core of learning during the initial years in clinical pediatrics.

With these objectives in the background, it has been our earnest endeavor to bring out a book for the undergraduate MBBS students to help them learn the basic aspects of history, clinical examination, and relevant practical aspects with which the students need to equip themselves during their clinical postings in pediatrics. Once the students initiate to devote themselves toward this essential and continued clinical learning process, we assume that they would have set their minds on the right track to enhance their clinical pediatric learning sans any short cuts. A thorough history, meticulous physical examination, a logical inference, and the conclusion form the whole exercise to strengthen the core of practical and clinical pediatrics. Comprehending the needs of undergraduate students with particular relevance to the basic concepts of clinical examination and pediatrics, an attempt has been made to facilitate this process in a clear, concise, and illustrative manner.

Like any other medical subject, pediatric literature too has seen a vast expansion during the last few years and the books tend to become more and more voluminous. However, with our objective of keeping the text simple, easy to read, follow and understand to the felt needs of undergraduate students, we have resisted the use of complex jargons and made best attempts to present the clinical and practical skills in a simplified manner. Such a work cannot be accomplished without a collaborative effort; hence the diverse and contributory authorship of the book reflects the growing dependence upon the eminent contributors from far and wide who have whole heartedly done their best to make the project what it actually is.

The text is purposely designed to assist the students understand, grasp the logic, and learn clinical pediatrics as relevant to the clinical postings, internal examinations, and as a quick revision guide to the practical examinations in pediatrics. With this reference the adequate emphasis has been directed toward history and the essentials of physical examination in children. Besides other aspects of child health which are closely linked to practical pediatrics such as drugs and dosages, clinical case scenarios and radiological imaging are included to supplement the learning process in MBBS curriculum and initial phase of pediatric postgraduate training program. However the book is not a replacement for the text and the theory in the field of pediatrics.

We have been consistently guided and helped by the Team of Wolters Kluwer (India) led by Dr Mahesh Inder Veer Singh (Vice President, Health), Dr Vandana Mittal (Publishing Manager), P. Sangeetha (Senior Publishing Manager), Nayan Gogoi (Senior Publishing Editor), and Shruti Sharma. Their efforts have contributed to significant improvements in the final drafting of the book.

We gratefully acknowledge the constructive contributions and inputs to the book by Dr Anand Naregal, Dr Hiren Bhatt, Dr Prashant Dabhi, and Dr Vivek Jain. We are privileged to have an eminent academician, pediatrician, and a popular teacher Dr Raju C Shah to have written the foreword for the book.

We would welcome feedback and responses from the students which would help us to know our shortcomings and thus the ways to improve upon in our future endeavors. We earnestly hope that with our efforts we are able to fulfil the students' needs and expectations.

Niranjan Shendurnikar
Paresh A Thakkar

Contributors

Abhishek Kulkarni MD, PDCC
Pediatric Endocrinologist
SRCC Children's Hospital
Mumbai

Anand Prakash Dubey MD, FIAP
Professor of Pediatrics
ESI, PGIMSR, Basaidarapur
New Delhi

Bakul B Javadekar MD
Professor of Pediatrics
Medical College Baroda & SSG Hospital
Vadodara

Bakulesh M Chauhan MD, PGDAP
Consultant Pediatrician
KG Patel Children Hospital
Vadodara

Baldev S Prajapati MD, FIAP, MNAMS
Professor of Pediatrics
GCS Medical College
Ahmedabad

Bhavna Dhingra MD, DNB
Additional Professor of Pediatrics
All India Institute of Medical Sciences
Bhopal

Divya Dave MD
Associate Professor of Pediatrics
GMERS Medical College
Vadodara

Fagun Shah MD
Pediatric Nephrologist
Child Kidney Care Center
Surat

Gaurang Upadhyay DNB, IDPCCM
Clinical Fellow, Pediatric Intensive Care
Great Ormond Street Hospital
London

Ketan Shah MD, DCH
Consultant Pediatrician
Ketan Children Hospital
Surat

Habib Bhurawala MD, DCH, FRACP
Senior Consultant in Pediatrics
Nepean Hospital
Sydney

Mukesh Agrawal MD
Professor of Pediatrics
Seth G S Medical College
Mumbai

Mukesh K Singh MD, DNB, FNB
Pediatric Cardiologist
Kailash Hospital
Vadodara

Niranjan Shendurnikar MD, FIAP
Consultant Pediatrician
KG Patel Children Hospital
Vadodara

Pankaj Agrawal MD, MMSC
Associate Professor of Pediatrics
Harvard Medical School
Boston

Paresh A Thakkar MD, DCH, DNB
Associate Professor of Pediatrics
Medical College Baroda & SSG Hospital
Vadodara

Piyush Gupta MD, FIAP, FIMSA
Professor of Pediatrics
University College of Medical Sciences
New Delhi

Pratap Kumar Patra MD, PGDHM
Associate Professor of Pediatrics
All India Institute of Medical Sciences
Patna

Raghvendra Singh Kachhwaha DCH, DNB
Consultant Pediatrician
Ekta Institute of Child Health
Raipur

Rajal Prajapati MD, D Ped
Professor of Pediatrics
NHL Municipal Medical College
Ahmedabad

Rinki H Shah MD
Assistant Professor of Pediatrics
Medical College Baroda & SSG Hospital
Vadodara

Sanwar Agrawal MD
Consultant Pediatrician
Ekta Institute of Child Health
Raipur

Sarah Morton MD, PhD
Attending Neonatologist
Boston Children Hospital
Boston

Sheela Bharani Chawla MD
Consultant Pediatrician
KG Patel Children Hospital
Vadodara

Sheila Aiyer MD
Additional Professor of Pediatrics
Medical College Baroda & SSG Hospital
Vadodara

Sumaira Khalil DNB
Pediatrician
Safdarjung Hospital
New Delhi

Tushar P Shah MD
Consultant Pediatrician
Navkar Children Hospital
Vadodara

Uma S Nayak MD, D Ped
Professor of Pediatrics
Parul Institute of Medical Sciences and Research
Waghodia,Vadodara

Vaishali Chanpura MD
Assistant Professor of Pediatrics
Medical College Baroda & SSG Hospital
Vadodara

Vijayashree Mishra DNB
Junior Consultant
KG Patel Children Hospital
Vadodara

Contents

CHAPTER 1

The Art of History Taking in Pediatrics

Mukesh Agrawal, Niranjan Shendurnikar, Gaurang Upadhyay

History taking in pediatrics is an art that can be perfected only by practice. Despite all the advances in the medical sciences, a comprehensive history and a thorough clinical examination remain the cornerstones of a good clinical practice. While the broad principles and the format of history taking in children are the same as in adults, three important differences are noteworthy:

1. Pediatric history is generally dependent on a third party such as the parents or relatives and it may be influenced by their own concerns, beliefs, emotions, and attitudes toward the child.
2. Childhood is a dynamic phase in life and history taking in children must be tailored according to their age with different areas of emphasis for different age groups.
3. History taking in children should also include additional components of perinatal, developmental, dietary, and immunization histories, as these are important external determinants of child health.

History forms the plinth for building a clinical diagnosis based on which the need and extent of physical examination and investigations must be determined. It also provides an opportunity to build rapport with the patient and parents. Although no cast iron protocols may be used in pediatric history taking, this chapter outlines broad guidelines within the semistructured format.

Essentials of History Taking

A good history needs the selection of a reliable informant, development of a good rapport with the child and the parents, appropriate questioning techniques, correct interpretation of responses, and proper documentation of information for future use. Some important prerequisites for obtaining a good history are being discussed next.

Setting

History must be recorded in a quiet and comfortable environment to ease the anxiety of the patient and parents with due concerns to their privacy, especially in case of adolescents. Adolescent girls must be interviewed only in the presence of a parent or a female nurse. The room should have adequate and, if possible, an informal seating arrangement without unnecessary barriers such as a large office table and other distractions.

Rapport Building

Development of a good rapport with the child and the parents is vital to gather reliable and complete information. Useful strategies to establish a rapport include:

- Greeting and introducing yourself
- Addressing the child with his/her name
- Establishing good eye contact
- Conversing in an empathetic and concerned manner

- Listening attentively to the initial narration of history without unnecessary interruptions
- Avoiding distractions, e.g., phone calls, during history taking
- Assurance regarding the confidentiality of information

Choosing the Informant

Children are often accompanied by both parents and at times with many relatives who are all eager to provide their own versions of history that may be markedly contradictory.

A good history is often influenced by intellect and emotions of informant as well as actual awareness of the problem. A mother is the most reliable informant in most of the cases and must be given preference for obtaining the history. The males of the family can be dominating sometimes while providing the history and override the mother and thus should be handled tactfully.

- In absence of the mother, history may be obtained from the father, grandparents, or other household members who reside with the child and have first-hand knowledge of the problem. If necessary, history may be cross-checked with the other parent or relatives.
- Parents, in particular the mother, are perceptive observers of their child. However trivial it may seem, their narration must not be dismissed or ignored.
- Children above the age of 7 years often provide good history themselves with minimal assistance, especially for presenting complaints; therefore, they must be made the primary informant or contributors. However, other aspects of history, e.g., immunization and developmental history, need to be obtained from the parents even in cases of older children.

Questioning

The inquiries for history must preferably be in a conversational manner rather than in an interrogational manner.

- Begin with open-ended questions, e.g., "What is wrong ...," and allow the informant to narrate the history in her/his own words without unnecessary interruptions. Open-ended questions also allow parents to reveal their perceptions about the child's problem. Avoid double-barreled questions, e.g., "Since when is the child having diarrhea and vomiting?"
- Subsequently, identify the points that need clarification and use close-ended questions to get the desired answer, e.g., "Is it the first time ...?"
- Ask about each complaint separately to ensure accurate response. Involve older children and adolescents in the process and offer them an opportunity to discuss their concerns, privately if necessary.
- Choose the language best understood by the parents/child. If you are not fluent in the family's language, use a mutually acceptable interpreter.
- Follow the broad sequence of history taking, as outlined in this chapter, to avoid missing the important information or repetition. However, move over to the next question if the child/parent becomes agitated or upset in response to some questions, especially if the information is not needed immediately.
- In case of chronic illnesses or illnesses associated with relapses or intermittent exacerbations, parents may know the disease and the diagnosis, e.g., asthma, nephrotic syndrome, and drug allergies.
- The students must remember that they have limited time to take the history and then conduct the physical examination. The history and the presentation should be succinct and in logical sequence with a stress on positive information and relevant negative information.
- Thus, in summary, the assessor should remember the "ABC" of history taking: *a*ccurate, *b*rief, and *c*lear.

Assess the Response

Responses from the informants to questions asked in the history are often influenced by their intellectual level, awareness of the problem, and emotional reactions.

Listen carefully to the informant's narration of events and answers to close-ended questions. Also, observe his/her behavior and nonverbal clues, e.g., hesitancy, avoidance of a certain question, change in tone or attitude, or lack of concern. Avoid argument, embarrassment, or laughter on his/her answers.

Documentation

It is essential to maintain records for future reference and for legal implications. The following points should be taken care of:

- History should be recorded in a prestructured format, as soon as possible though preferably after the interview is complete to avoid interruptions in the process of narration.
- All answers must be entered as told by parents, regardless of your own opinion.
- Avoid abbreviations and medical jargon as much as possible and use diagrams to depict pictorial information, e.g., distribution of rash. Record and present the history as much as possible in parents' own words.
- Date and time of history taking must be clearly stated on the document, along with the name and signature of the interviewer.
- During the interview, it is important to convey to the parent your interest in the child and the information provided by him/her. The parent should be allowed to talk freely and express concerns in his/her own words. The interviewer should intermittently look directly at either the parent or the child and not only at the writing instruments. A sympathetic listener who addresses the parent and the child by name frequently obtains more accurate information than a harried, distracted assessor. Careful observation during the interview frequently uncovers stresses and concerns that otherwise are not apparent.

Closure

At the end of the interview, ask for any other concern that the parents have, although it may not be related to the medical problem, and appreciate them for their cooperation toward giving a detailed history and their initiative to seek medical attention. Answer their questions regarding the child as truthfully as possible.

Components of History Taking

Although the emphasis and sequence may vary in individual cases according to the clinical problems, a general protocol of history taking in children should include 13 major steps:

1. Demographic data
2. Presenting complaints
3. History of present illness (HPI)
4. System review including negative history
5. Past history
6. Antenatal, natal, and postnatal history
7. Family history
8. Developmental history
9. Dietary history
10. Immunization history
11. Personal history
12. Socioeconomic history
13. Environmental history

It is useful to observe/look toward the child before the beginning of a formal interview and history taking. This observation can provide helpful information about the child's general well-being, severity of the sickness, and the behavior in general. Keeping some age-appropriate toys and interesting play items can make the child comfortable, thereby assisting in a good history taking.

Demographic Data

This is essential not only to establish the identity of the patient but also to assist in differential diagnosis of the clinical problem and follow-up. A record of the correct demographic data is also essential for medicolegal and insurance purposes. Important components of demographic data include name, age, sex, religion/caste, and residential address.

- *Name* is the most commonly used indicator of identity and must be recorded correctly to avoid later hassles. Addressing the child with his/her name also helps to develop rapport with him/her and the parents.
- *Age* must be recorded in completed time units appropriate for that age, i.e., in hours during the first 3–5 days of life, in days during the neonatal period, in months till 1–2 years of age, and in years thereafter. In case when parents are uncertain about age, information may be obtained in relation to important events such as festivals or family functions.
- Apart from being the indicator of identity, age also assists in differential diagnosis as many diseases are more common in specific age groups. While congenital anomalies and genetic disorders usually manifest in neonatal period or early infancy, infections and injuries are more common in toddlers. Connective tissue disorders such as systemic lupus erythematosus (SLE) are uncommon before early adolescence. The common age-wise distribution of a few childhood illnesses is shown in Table 1.1.
- *Gender* or *sex* is another identifier and must be recorded carefully, especially in cases of newborns, to prevent complications at a later stage. In cases with ambiguous genitalia (also known as disorders of sexual differentiation [DSD]), sex should be assigned only after thorough investigations.
- Gender is also important in suspecting or excluding a clinical diagnosis as many diseases that present during childhood have a distinct gender bias. X-linked recessive disorders, e.g., Duchene muscular dystrophy or G6PD deficiency, almost always manifest only in males with females being asymptomatic carriers. Other examples of X-linked recessive conditions in males include hemophilia A and B, fragile X syndrome, and Hunter syndrome (mucopolysaccharidosis). Collagen disorders such as SLE and rheumatoid arthritis (few forms of juvenile idiopathic arthritis have female to male ratio of 5:1) are more common in females than in males.
- *Religion* and *caste* information, though being a sensitive issue for some, helps in considering the possibilities of diseases common in certain ethnic groups. The examples of such diseases include sickle cell disease in tribals and thalassemia syndromes in certain communities.

TABLE 1.1 Age-Wise Distribution of Childhood Illnesses

Disease	Age
Febrile seizures	6 months to 5 years
Bronchiolitis	1 month to 1 year
Infantile tremor syndrome (ITS)	6 months to 2 years
Kawasaki disease	Below 5 years
Minimal change nephrotic syndrome (MCNS)	2–8 years
Rheumatic fever	5–15 years
Wilson disease (metabolic liver disease)	Above 5 years
Slipped upper femoral epiphyses	Adolescents
Systemic lupus erythematosus (SLE)	Adolescents

- *Residence* must be recorded in detail. The complete postal address along with contact phone number is helpful for following up the case. Permanent address, if different from the present contact address, must also be recorded, especially in migrants. Many diseases have well-defined geographical distribution, e.g., visceral leishmaniasis (kala-azar) in Bihar, and residential information helps to consider those possibilities during differential diagnosis. Correct address is also helpful for public health authorities for taking necessary disease containment measures during outbreaks.

Presenting or Chief Complaints

The chief complaints form the basis for clinical history and convey the main cause for seeking medical attention. Important aspects of writing the chief complaint are as follows:

- All presenting complaints must be recorded in the chronological order of appearance along with the duration of complaints.
- All major complaints that have developed after the onset of an illness must be included, even if some of them may have been resolved, either spontaneously or after treatment.
- To limit the number of complaints, those that are incidentally discovered and unlikely to have a diagnostic significance, e.g., lethargy, may be overlooked in this section.
- All complaints must be recorded in a list form, including brief telegraphic description along with duration (Box 1.1). A short adjective to convey the character of complaint, e.g., acute, progressive, and severe, may be added to the description.

Box 1.1 Example for writing presenting complaints

- High-grade fever for ... 14 days
- Persistent cough for ... 10 days
- Progressive breathlessness for ... 7 days
- Generalized convulsion once ... 2 days back

- Duration must be calculated from the day of interview rather than from the day of admission if different.
- Each complaint should be recorded in the exact words of child/parents and not in medical terms or interpretations, e.g., write bluish discoloration rather than cyanosis. However, description may be truncated for the sake of brevity.
- In cases of chronic illnesses, e.g., cerebral palsy or nephrotic syndrome, chief complaints may be structured to include the whole duration of illness, rather than listing only those for which the patient has come. It is acceptable that in a child with a chronic disease, the presenting complaints/symptoms may overlap with the past medical history. An effort should be made to avoid unnecessary duplication.
- A known diagnosis from the past should be included before listing the complaints to assist in the analytic process. For example, begin with "A known case of nephrotic syndrome, presenting with ... ." However, any diagnosis told by parents but not substantiated by documents must not be included to avoid bias. Thus, in chronic diseases that begin insidiously or have intermittent exacerbations (e.g., epilepsy, chronic arthritis, nephrotic syndrome, and asthma), the child may be brought due to an acute episode or an intercurrent illness. Here, the presenting complaints should be structured in such a way that the presentation conveys the onset and the total duration of illness.

History of Present Illness

This includes a detailed description of the current health problem/problems listed in the section "Presenting or Chief Complaints." In addition, it also includes a description of complaints considered not very relevant in the previous section and the important negative histories to exclude associated health problems or complications of presenting complaints.

TABLE 1.2 Key Points to be Recorded in Relation to Complaints in History of Present Illness

Key points	Defining variable
Type of symptoms	Fever, cough, diarrhea, weakness, seizures
Onset of illness	Sudden, acute, or gradual (state date and time of onset if possible)
Duration	Days/months or from … years of age
Severity	Mild, moderate, severe, incapacitating
Course	Progressive, static, improving, episodic, or waxing and waning
Aggravating/relieving factors	Effect of posture, meals, cough, etc.
Interventions	Medications, investigations, hospitalization

Important aspects of writing the HPI are as follows:

- HPI should be written in a concise manner but connected in a story-like format.
- Begin with a statement depicting the onset of the first complaint, e.g., "Baby was apparently alright till … days back (or till … years of age)."
- Elaborate on each complaint with special emphasis on the (i) mode of onset, (ii) duration of symptoms, (iii) characteristics, e.g., severity or localization, (iv) clinical course over time, and (v) aggravating or relieving factors (Table 1.2). Ask leading questions related to the symptom under evaluation to clarify the history or detect associated problems.
- Describe each complaint separately in a clear, concise, temporal sequence and chronological order.
- Details of any investigation or treatment received during the course of illness must be included, preferably after checking with records. However, any information prior to the onset of first complaint must be recorded in "Past History."

System Review

This is the fishing-out expedition to search for missed complaints, considered as too trivial by the parents as compared with the presenting complaints and omitted unintentionally. A quick system review helps to identify involvement of other organs/systems as either an incidental associated problem or a complication of presenting illness. Important components of a system review include the following:

- It should be relevant to broad differential diagnosis based on the HPI.
- It should be quick but comprehensive, covering common complaints related to various organs/systems, other than those already revealed in HPI (Table 1.3).
- Any positive complaint should be recorded in detail. Negative histories must also be recorded but only if relevant to exclude associated problems or complications.
- The HPI should be revised based on the system review.

Before the HPI is concluded, it is important to include relevant negative history to help analyze the nature of the disease process and the possible cause, and narrow it down to a probable clinical diagnosis. Such a systemic inquiry often helps the student to make an approach to determine the system that is likely to be affected.

Example: A 5-year-old child presenting with fever, abdominal pain, and loss of appetite for 20 days may seem to be a case of enteric fever or acute hepatitis. However, a negative history of bone and joint pains and any bleeding/purpuric rash in the skin would reasonably help to exclude conditions such as acute leukemia and sickle cell disease.

TABLE 1.3 System Review

System/organ	Common symptoms
General	Growth, development, appetite, behavior, sleep, activity, school performance
Head	Head injury, headache
Eyes	Vision problems, squint, redness, injury
Ears	Hearing problems, pain, ear discharge
Nose	Runny nose, stuffiness, epistaxis
Oral cavity	Swallowing difficulties, ulcers, sore throat
Neck	Pain/stiffness, swelling, restricted movements
Skin	Rash, itching, injuries, bruises, hair and nail changes
Gastrointestinal	Vomiting, diarrhea, abdominal pain, constipation, jaundice
Respiratory	Breathlessness, cough, wheeze, chest pain, recurrent respiratory illness
Cardiovascular	Breathlessness, palpitation, cyanosis, pedal edema, fainting spells, feeding difficulties, recurrent respiratory illness
Neurological	Altered behavior, seizures, fainting spells, weakness, abnormal movements, problems in gait or balancing
Genitourinary	Dysuria, oliguria, frequency, hematuria, nocturnal enuresis, urinary stream, urethral/vaginal discharge, menstruation
Musculoskeletal	Injuries, deformities, joint pain/swelling, muscle pain/swelling, weakness, restricted movements
Hematologic	Pallor, mucocutaneous bleeds, transfusions
Psychiatric	Temperament, behavioral problems, drug abuse

Past History

This must include details of all significant health-related events prior to the onset of present illness with special emphasis on (i) major illnesses or infections; (ii) hospitalization, medications, or transfusions; (iii) injuries or surgical interventions; and (iv) allergic or other adverse reactions following any medication. Attempts should be made to strengthen past history while keeping in mind previous health records, prescriptions, laboratory reports, or hospital discharge summaries. If possible, check partly used drug containers or tablet strips to verify the history.

Many of the childhood morbidities have an important correlation with the past history. A child presenting with a convulsion may have had a prior history of febrile seizure or head trauma. A child presenting with a history of recurrent chest symptoms may have had a past history of failure to thrive (cystic fibrosis) or foreign body aspiration.

History of contact with tuberculosis is an essential component of history taking in pediatrics. It is considered to be positive if the child is in contact with a person who is an open or unresolved case of tuberculosis, is on treatment with antitubercular drugs, or has completed the treatment within the past 2 years.

Antenatal, Natal, and Postnatal History

The aim is to correlate the HPI with antenatal, peripartum (perinatal), or early postnatal events. It is more relevant in cases of infants and young children with congenital malformations, developmental delay, or unexplained chronic diseases.

Antenatal History

This must include information about:

- Maternal age, nutritional status, and pre-pregnancy health problems, e.g., fever, lymphadenopathy, and rash, which suggest intrauterine infections (TORCH) (advanced maternal age is associated with trisomy 21 [Down syndrome])
- Obstetric history with outcome of previous conceptions/deliveries
- Antenatal care and results of any tests done during this period
- Potential exposure to infections, drugs, toxins, or radiation during pregnancy
- Major prenatal complications, e.g., eclampsia, bleeding, and gestational diabetes

Peripartum or Birth History

This must include information about:

- Place of delivery, e.g., home or hospital
- Mode of delivery, e.g., vaginal, instrumental, or operative
- Obstetric complications, e.g., prolonged labor or meconium staining
- Apgar score or the first cry and need for neonatal resuscitation or NICU admission
- Gestational age and birth weight of baby

Early or Immediate Postnatal History

This must include information about:

- Early infant feeding
- Postnatal complications, e.g., sepsis, icterus, and seizures
- NICU admission or rooming in with mother
- Day of the discharge from the hospital
- Follow-up visits

The following examples are a few of the possible associations between the antenatal, natal, and postnatal history and their implications later on:

- *Periconceptional folic acid*: Prevention of neural tube defects
- *Small-for-date babies/intrauterine growth restriction* (IUGR): Congenital malformations
- *Delayed passage of meconium*: Cystic fibrosis
- *Delayed cry/perinatal asphyxia*: Developmental delay and cerebral palsy
- *Infant of diabetic mother*: Hypoglycemia, large-for-date baby, and increased risk of congenital malformations
- *Maternal lupus* (SLE): Neonatal heart block
- *Intracranial hemorrhage/neonatal meningitis*: Hydrocephalous in infancy

Family History

Family history aims to identify not only the genetic factors but also the shared environmental risk factors that can influence a child's health. Getting a reliable family history may be challenging as parents often tend to hide embarrassing facts and should be reassured about the confidentiality. Major components of family history are as follows:

- Record the history of similar illness in family members, which may be indicative of common genetics or shared environment, e.g., infections or toxic exposure.
- Search for infectious illnesses not only in the family but also in other household members in the present or recent past, especially tuberculosis.
- Assess the psychosocial environment of the family with special reference to marital conflicts, psychiatric illnesses, substance abuse, and child rearing practices.
- Consanguinity should be inquired as it is common in few communities and poses an increased risk of transmission of genetic diseases. The degrees of consanguinity are shown in Table 1.4.

TABLE 1.4 Strength of Consanguinity

Strength	Relationship
First degree	• Sibling and sibling • Parent and child
Second degree	• Uncle and niece • Aunt and nephew • Stepbrother and stepsister • Grandparents and grandchildren
Third degree	First cousins

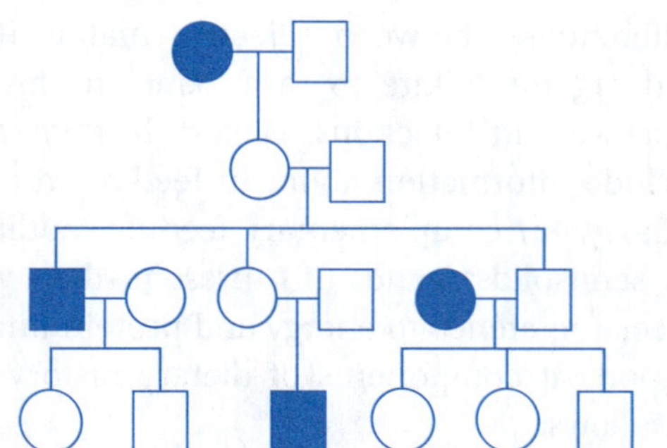

Figure 1.1 Pedigree chart: Vertical lines connect children to their parents.

- Prepare a family tree or pedigree chart (Fig. 1.1) including three generations—siblings, parents, and grandparents—to assess the possibility of genetic basis and mode of inheritance.
- Pedigree chart is defined as a diagram of family history indicating the normal and the affected individuals and their relationships with the proband as well as their status with respect to a particular genetic disorder.
- All the members of the same generation (living or dead) should be placed in the same line and each generation should be denoted by the Roman numerals on the left (I, II, and III). By convention, the male members are placed on the left side of the chart.
- The commonly used symbols in the pedigree chart are shown in Figure 1.2.

Developmental History

Development is age-dependent and is more relevant in cases where HPI suggests a neurological, developmental, or behavioral problem or the presence of risk factors, e.g., perinatal insult. Important aspects of recording the developmental history are as follows:

- Developmental history must record achievement of various milestones in four major fields: gross motor, fine motor, social and language development, along with the age at which these milestones have been achieved (for details, see Chapter 4).
- Age of achievement of these milestones must be compared with normal standards to identify any deviation from normal. However, the pace of development varies widely, and

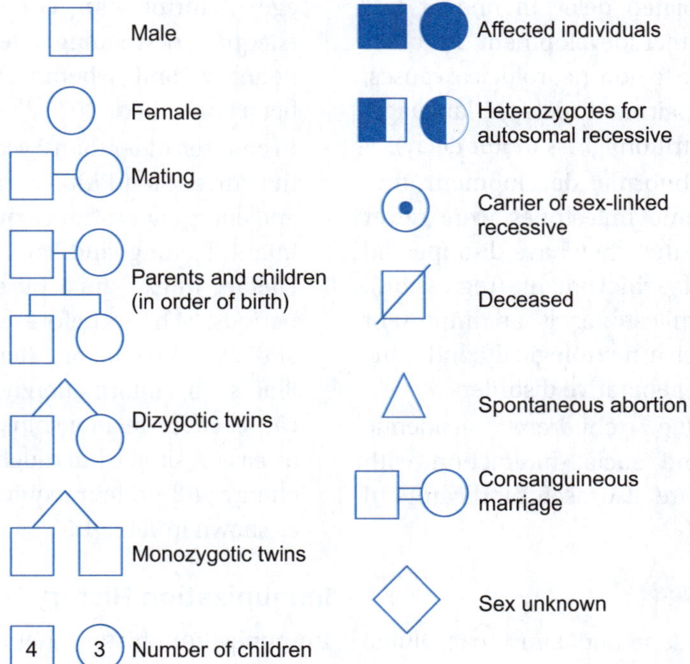

Figure 1.2 Examples of pedigree symbols.

a marginal delay does not necessarily mean developmental retardation. Parents may also be asked to compare the development of index child with that of the other siblings.

- In cases with presenting complaints suggestive of neurodevelopmental problems or risk factors, development history must include details about all major milestones in different fields starting from early neonatal period to get an idea about the age from which milestones began to falter.
- In other cases, begin with milestones that the child should have achieved by the present chronological age. If normal, then the development is most likely normal and further enquiry about earlier milestones is futile as the general order of the appearance of milestones is fairly constant. Finding out the last major milestone achieved in each field by going in backward order of development from the present age also gives a fair idea about the developmental age.
- In cases with delayed milestones, assess whether milestones are uniformly delayed in all the fields (global developmental retardation). Isolated delay in one or two fields with normal development in other fields may be due to non-neurological causes, e.g., hearing impairment (delayed language) or severe malnutrition (gross motor delay).
- In cases with abnormal development, find out whether some milestones were never achieved or whether they have disappeared after the initial achievement (regression). Regression of milestones is an important clue to progressive neurological conditions such as neurodegenerative disorders.
- In school-going children, academic performance and social interaction with other students are also useful indicators of development.

Dietary History

This is age-dependent and aims to evaluate the role of diet in causation of present illness, e.g., malnutrition. It also helps to differentiate between dietary malnutrition and organic failure to thrive due to chronic illnesses and infections. Dietary history must include information about (i) feeding in early infancy, (ii) complementary feeding (addition of semisolids), and (iii) present diet with special reference to energy and protein intake. Important components of dietary history are as follows:

- In infants younger than 6 months, concentrate on the history related to early infant feeding with special emphasis on the type of feeding, e.g., breastfeeding or top feeding, and problems encountered during breastfeeding. Find out the reasons for shifting to or adding top feeds (dairy milk/ formula feeds). If the patient was given top feed, it is important to note the mode of feeding, e.g., bottle or katori–spoon.
- In children from 6 months to 2 years of age, concentrate on the history related to weaning (complementary feeding), i.e., addition of semisolids to the infant's diet, apart from a quick review of early infant feeding, with special emphasis on age of introducing complementary foods, adequacy of weaning in terms of quality and quantity, and whether breastfeeding has been continued.
- In children older than 2 years, concentrate on the current food intake in terms of proteins and energy apart from a quick review of early infant feeding and complementary feeds. Dietary intake must be calculated for two periods: 24 hours before recording the history and 24 hours before the onset of present illness. This information helps to evaluate the cause–effect relationship between diet and disease. A simple but rough way is to calculate energy and protein requirements in children as shown in Table 1.5.

Immunization History

Immunization history helps to evaluate the role of diseases preventable by vaccination or adverse reactions to vaccines in causation of

TABLE 1.5 Energy and Protein Requirements in Children

Body weight (kg)	Requirements
Energy	
<10	100 cal/kg/day
10–20	1000 + 50 cal for every additional kilogram of body weight above 10 kg
>20	1500 cal + 20 cal/kg/day, above 20 kg
Proteins	
<10	Proteins: 2 g/kg/day
>10	1.5 g/kg subject to minimum 20 g/day

present illness. It is best recorded by the review of immunization card often available with the parents. The emphasis should be on recording the receipt of vaccines included in the National Immunization Schedule and the age at which doses were received. Later, the information may be obtained about additional vaccines the child may have received.

Information must also be obtained about any adverse event following a vaccine dose. It is helpful to look out for the presence or absence of BCG scar on the left upper arm near the insertion of deltoid. The information about the child having received oral polio vaccines on National Immunization Days (pulse polio immunizations on Sundays) must also be documented. Further details on immunization are included in Chapter 5.

Personal History

Personal history is more important in older children and adolescents and must include information about (i) eating habits, (ii) bladder and bowel control, (iii) sleeping patterns, (iv) temperament and behavioral problems, and (v) menstrual history in girls.

Social History

Social history not only aims to identify the risk factors for causation of a disease but also helps in choosing the most suitable diagnostic, therapeutic, and rehabilitative interventions that are acceptable to and affordable for the parents. Three important components of social history include: (i) parental education status, (ii) parental occupation, and (iii) family income. Kuppuswamy scale is most commonly used for the assessment of socioeconomic status as per prevalent consumer price index of 2017 (Table 1.6).

TABLE 1.6 Modified Kuppuswamy Scale

Variable	Score
A: Educational status	
1. Profession or honors	7
2. Graduate or postgraduate	6
3. Intermediate or post–high school	5
4. High school	4
5. Middle school	3
6. Primary school	2
7. Illiterate	1
B: Occupational status	
1. Professional	10
2. Semiprofessional	6
3. Clerical, shop owner, farmer	5
4. Skilled worker	4
5. Semiskilled worker	3
6. Unskilled worker	2
7. Unemployed	1
C: Monthly family income (₹)	
1. >41,430	12
2. 20,175–41,429	10
3. 15,536–20,714	6
4. 10,357–15,535	4
5. 6214–10,356	3
6. 2092–6213	2
7. <2091	1
Socioeconomic classification	
Upper (I)	26–29
Upper-middle (II)	16–25
Lower-middle (III)	11–15
Upper-lower (IV)	5–10
Lower (V)	<5

Total score (A + B + C), socioeconomic class: 26–29, upper (I); 16–25, upper-middle (II); 11–15, middle lower middle (III); 5–10, lower upper lower (IV); <5, lower (V).

Environmental History

This is intended to look out for risk factors in various components of indoor and outdoor environment including:

- Overcrowding as assessed by noting the size and number of rooms in the house with respect to the size of the family
- Air quality as assessed by ventilation, pollution by cooking fuel, passive smoke, construction activity, or chemical/toxic fumes
- Water quality as assessed by questions related to the source, storage, and purification method for drinking water
- General sanitation as assessed by questions related to the hygiene awareness and practices, especially during food preparation/consumption and excreta disposal

Practical Tips

Some practical tips for presenting the history are shown in Box 1.2.

Box 1.2 Making a presentation of history

- Keep the language simple, grammatically correct, and to the point.
- Use short sentences in a crisp manner with a continued flow and sequential manner.
- Make your voice clearly audible.
- Avoid focusing too much on negative history and include only what is relevant to that particular patient.
- Understand the importance and relevance of history for each child; e.g., in a school-going child who has come for acute abdominal pain with no past history, birth history is not needed in detail. Say that the child was a normal newborn with no perinatal complications.
- System review should be brief, precise, and relevant.
- Analyze and keep a track of time available for presentation.
- Conclude with a brief summary.

KEY POINTS

- Pediatrics is related to the health of the child starting from the newborn period till the time of adolescence or teenage, and hence the spectrum of health problems is extremely wide and diverse.
- History taking is the foremost initial step in the usual process of managing a child/patient.
- A properly and patiently elicited history with effective communication and a comprehensive physical examination is an extremely useful tool to help collate the findings from the exercise, arrive at a clinical/differential diagnosis, and formulate a plan of appropriate management.

CHAPTER 2

General Physical Examination in Children

Anand Prakash Dubey, Sumaira Khalil, Divya Dave

General physical examination in children is a combination of art and science. This chapter discusses an approach to the examination, the essential prerequisites, and how to interpret the examination findings to help reach a logical conclusion. It is ideal to practice general examination in as many normal infants and children as possible so that the student becomes well versed with what is normal, and with practice and observation, the difference between the normal and the abnormal is likely to become more obvious subsequently.

- Examination of neonates, infants, and children requires a good observation power, warm and well-lit room, and warm hands. This is important as the physical examination of a child is different as compared with that of an adult and also depends on the age and the development of the child. Due to the presence of stranger anxiety in young children and unfamiliar circumstances, the examiner must consider these issues to carry out a helpful and decisive physical examination.
- A gentle and confident approach without being dominant and threatening is likely to be extremely helpful in conducting the examination.
- While examining a child, one should begin with areas such as hands or knees/legs as this is least likely to scare the child. If the child is able enough to follow, then tell the child what you are about to do.
- Try to assess as much as you can before touching or undressing the child. The room can be made more child-friendly with bright colorful pictures and toys. The student should approach the patient in a friendly, nonthreatening, and nonhurried manner.
- Once you have begun the general examination, feel at ease, give simple instructions as and when needed to the parents, position the child appropriately, and ensure the adequate exposure of the part to be examined. As an example, if you want to examine the axillary lymph nodes, then it becomes necessary to remove the top clothing. Let the parents remove the clothing as this would avoid undue anxiety in the child. If the child is old enough to understand, he or she can be explained about the need for such an intervention and what you are going to do.
- Ensure that the examination room has adequate illumination as physical findings such as jaundice, pallor, cyanosis, and skin rashes may not be made out easily in the absence of proper light.
- Most children are likely to be examined in an outpatient care setup but now many pediatric hospitals have a triage area to determine the priority of treatment based on the severity of the child's condition. Children with emergency signs should be seen immediately and children with priority signs should not be kept waiting for a longer time (Table 2.1).
- Up to the age of 3 months, babies can be examined on the examination table or in the mother's lap.

TABLE 2.1 Emergency and Priority Conditions in Children

Emergency signs	Priority signs
• Not breathing or gasping • Central cyanosis • Severe respiratory distress (RR >70/min) • Cold extremities with capillary refill time longer than 3 seconds and weak and fast pulse (signs of shock) • Coma or convulsions • Signs of severe dehydration	• Age <2 months • Restless, irritable, lethargic • Malnutrition or visible severe wasting • Respiratory distress (RR >60/min) • Trauma or other urgent surgical condition • Edema of both feet • Poisoning • Temperature <36.5°C or >38°C • Bleeding • Pallor (severe)

RR, respiratory rate.

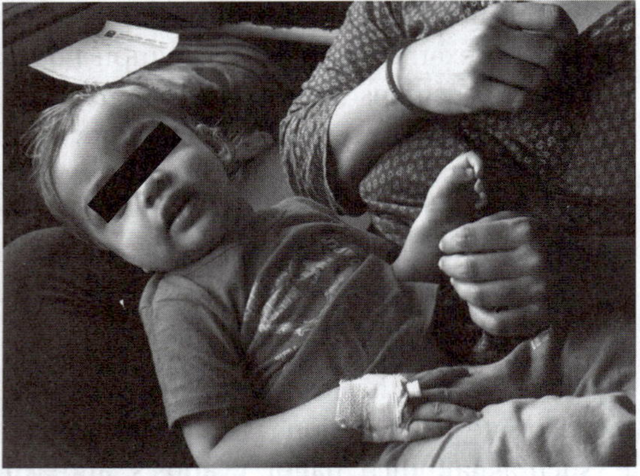

Figure 2.1 An infant being examined in mother's lap.

- For an infant, examination must be done in the mother's lap; it can be done even while the child is feeding on the breast (Fig. 2.1).
- Toddlers can be examined in a standing position or in the mother's lap. They are prone to separation anxiety from their parents by any stranger and thus adapting the examination to the child's age and the condition is needed.
- In children older than 3 years, examination can be performed on the examination table with the mother close by.
- An unpleasant procedure or examination should be postponed till the end. If a child cries during examination, wait for some time; if required, tell the mother to feed the child and then examine the patient. If it is appropriate, then difficult examination may be conducted toward the end and, if needed, use age-appropriate toys such as rattles, soft balls, and/or blocks to keep the child engaged and distract his or her attention.
- Teenage children must always be examined in the presence of their attendants or the paramedical staff. If undressing is required, then ask the attendants to perform it and cover the patient as soon as possible once the task has been completed.
- It is important first to make a visual impression about the well-being, posture, and nutritional status of the child. Determining whether the child is comfortable, sick-looking, or under any distress is helpful. The level of consciousness, attitude of the child, posture, and any gait abnormalities are significant clinical clues.
- The person examining the child must be in possession of a stethoscope, torch, fiberglass, measuring tape, spatula, thermometer, soft toy, and a red ring.

General Appearance of the Child

Careful and close observation helps to provide useful information about the following:

- *Severity of the illness*: A child may appear very sick on inspection, e.g., severe dehydration, breathlessness, or obvious bleeding, and would need priority management. This can result from either an acute or a chronic condition. Appearance of a well-nourished, active, and alert child usually rules out a serious disorder.
- *Growth and nutrition*: Does the child look emaciated and wasted with loss of subcutaneous fat? Is the child obese? Obesity may be due to overeating or due to an endocrinal or a syndromic cause.

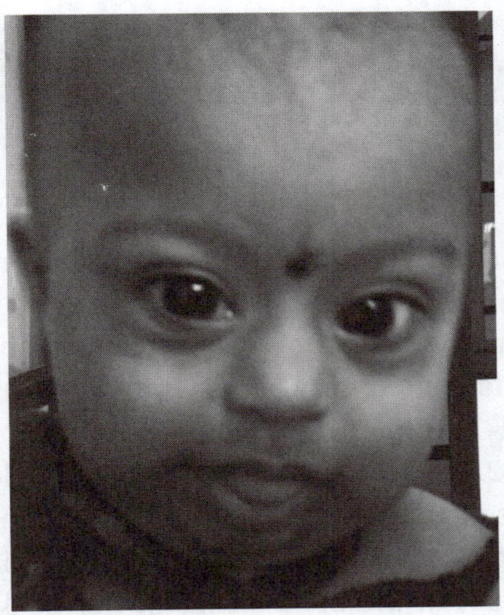

Figure 2.2 Facial dysmorphism in Down syndrome.

- *Behavior and responsiveness*: Is the child alert, apathetic, drowsy, sick-looking, or comatose? A drowsy, comatose child is an emergency and should be evaluated and treated immediately.
- *Facial dysmorphism*: Does the child have facial dysmorphism (unusual physical features that have their origin during embryogenesis)? The phenotypic features of the child point to the diagnosis of some syndromes, e.g., Down syndrome (trisomy 21) and Marfan syndrome. As an example, the facial dysmorphism in Down syndrome includes flat occiput (brachycephaly), frontal bossing, depressed nasal bridge, widely spaced eyes (mongoloid slant), epicanthic folds, protruding tongue, and low-set ears (Fig. 2.2).
- *Icterus/pallor/cyanosis*: Does the child have icterus, pallor, or cyanosis? Severity of the pallor should be assessed. Further examination is done to look for signs of congestive cardiac failure and the likely cause of anemia.
- *Hydration and skin texture*: Assess whether the child appears dehydrated or not. This can be done by checking whether he or she is drowsy/irritable (sensorium) and has dry, wrinkled skin and sunken eyes.

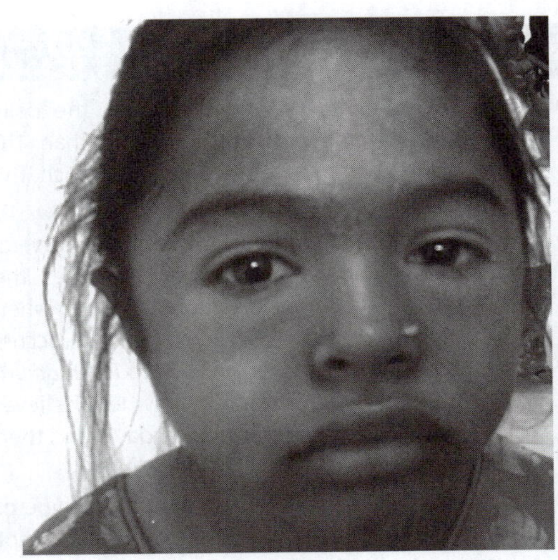

Figure 2.3 Coarse features seen in a child with hypothyroidism.

- *Other abnormalities*: These may include obvious skin rash, anasarca, posture and limb abnormalities, etc. Look for the presence of any coarse facial features such as seen in hypothyroidism. Coarse features include a combination of features such as prominent or large head, saddle-like, flat-bridged nose, coarse facial skin, large lips, and hypertrophied gums. Few causes of coarse features in children include hypothyroidism, mucopolysaccharidosis (MPS), McCune–Albright syndrome, skeletal dysplasia, and a few forms of genetic mental retardation. Figure 2.3 shows coarse features as seen in hypothyroidism.

Vital Signs

The vital signs include temperature, heart rate, respiratory rate, blood pressure, capillary refill time, hydration, and oxygen saturation by pulse oximetry.

Temperature

The normal body temperature is 37°C or 98.4°F. Body temperature fluctuates in the defined normal range (36.6–37.9°C), rectally. Fever is defined as rectal temperature ≥38°C (100.4°F). Various patterns of fever are given in Box 2.1.

Box 2.1 Patterns and characteristics of fever

- *Continuous fever*: In this type of fever, the daily fluctuation in temperature is not more than 1°C (1.5°F) and the temperature does not touch the baseline in 24 hours.
- *Intermittent fever*: Fever presents only for several hours a day and the temperature touches the baseline. The fever is called quotidian fever when it occurs daily, and tertian fever when it occurs every other day, e.g., in malaria due to *Plasmodium falciparum* or *vivax*. Quartan fever is when the fever occurs every third day (occurring on day 1 and then on day 4).
- *Remittent fever*: The daily fluctuation in this type of fever exceeds 2°C, and the temperature does not touch the baseline in 24 hours. The classical example of remittent fever in children is enteric fever.
- *Hyperpyrexia*: It is said to be present when the fever exceeds 41.5°C or 107°F. This is commonly seen in heat stroke, pontine hemorrhage, septicemia, malaria, and malignant hyperthermia.
- *Fever with chills and rigors*: This may be seen when the body temperature rises rapidly from the normal baseline levels. Chills are the subjective feeling of cold felt by the child and are accompanied by peripheral vasoconstriction to conserve the heat. Later, the excess heat production by vigorous muscle actions/contractions leads to rigors. Though common in malarial infections, these are also seen in urinary tract infections and lobar pneumonia.

The diurnal variation in temperature is usually 0.5°C. The temperature in evening is usually higher. Due to the temperature being higher in the evening, the milder degrees of fever are more likely to be recognized in the evenings and present as an evening rise of temperature. In neonates, the normal temperature is 36.5–37.5°C. Mercury thermometers as well as digital thermometers can be used. Temperature can also be measured on forehead using infrared thermometers. The various sites of measuring temperature are discussed next.

Rectal Temperature

This corresponds with the core temperature and is more than the oral temperature by 0.5°C. This is the most reliable temperature in children

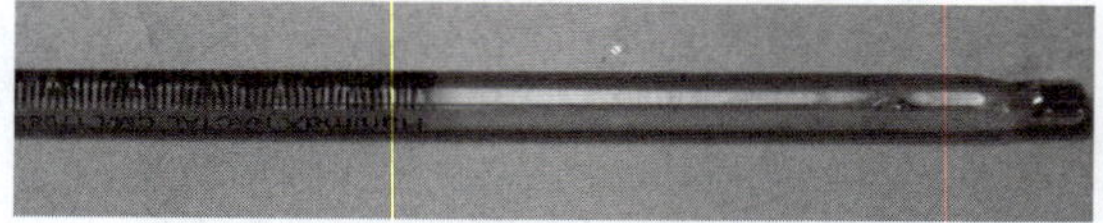

Figure 2.4 Rectal thermometer.

and is usually used in newborns and infants. Rectal temperature is rarely used in older children due to its practical inconvenience, and taking a rectal temperature requires a rectal thermometer with a rounded bulb (Fig. 2.4). The rectal thermometer is cleaned with soap and water, wiped dry, and then used. A water-based jelly or lubricant is applied on the tip. Put the baby on his or her back on a firm surface. Hold the baby's ankles and lift both legs, as if changing diaper. Gently slip the thermometer into rectum, 0.25–0.5 inch. Hold the thermometer in place till it beeps. Slide the thermometer out and read the temperature on the digital display.

Oral Temperature

The difference between oral temperature and axillary temperature normally is 0.5–1°C. Thermometer should be kept in mouth for 1 minute. This method can be used in children older than 6 years.

Axillary Temperature

Axillary temperature is 1°C less than rectal temperature. For accurate measurement of temperature, care must be taken to see that the mercury is in the bulb and axilla is dry; the thermometer is kept in the axilla for a minimum of 3 minutes with the bulb of thermometer toward the apex of axilla, the elbow is flexed, and the hand is held close to the chest wall. The thermometer should be cleaned with 70% isopropyl alcohol after each use, dried, and kept in its container. While using a digital thermometer, switch on the thermometer and keep the bulb at the apex of dry axilla till it beeps.

Heart Rate/Pulse Rate

- The pulse is defined as the expansion of the vessel wall due to the wave propagated

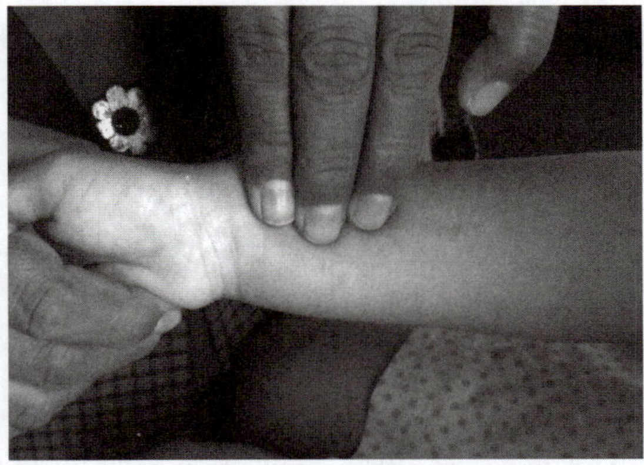

Figure 2.5 Checking radial pulse in a child.

during each cardiac contraction into the circulation.

- All the pulses should be checked for presence/absence, rate, rhythm, volume, character, and radioradial and radiofemoral delay.
- The radial pulse is assessed using the index, middle, and ring fingers with the arm in slight pronation and the wrist slightly flexed (Fig. 2.5). The pulse is best counted for complete 1 minute except in emergency situations where it can be counted for 6 seconds and then multiplied by 10 to get the rate for 1 minute.
- If the radial pulse is feeble or absent, check the pulsations in bigger vessels, i.e., carotid or femoral artery. The femoral pulsations may be diminished in coarctation of aorta or hypoplastic left heart syndrome. Pulses are weak or absent in shock, severe dehydration, cardiomyopathy, aortic stenosis, and vasculitis (Takayasu arteritis).
- High-volume or bounding pulses are felt in high-output states such as anemia, thyrotoxicosis, fever, and cardiac diseases (aortic regurgitation, patent ductus arteriosus, hypertension, and arteriovenous fistula). The volume of the pulse is dependent on the pulse pressure. Higher the pulse pressure, higher is the volume of the pulse.
- Feel for radial and femoral pulses simultaneously. The pulses are normally felt together. Radiofemoral/brachiofemoral delay is seen in coarctation of aorta.

TABLE 2.2 Age-Specific Normal Pulse Rates at Rest

Age	Rate per minute
<1 year	110–160
2–5 years	90–140
5–12 years	80–120
>12 years	60–100

- The age-specific pulse rates are shown in Table 2.2.
- Tachycardia in children is seen with fever, exercise, heart failure, tachyarrhythmia, excessive crying, and anxiety. Bradycardia refers to heart rate <60/min in children older than 2 years, <80/min in children younger than 2 years, and <100/min in neonates. It is physiologically seen in athletes. Other causes are heart block, raised intracranial tension, and drugs such as propranolol and digitalis.

Respiration

Note the rate, depth, regularity, and any specific variation of respiration. The respiratory rate must be counted for 1 full minute when the child is quiet (not crying). Normally, infants have abdominal or abdominothoracic respiration and children have thoracic respiration. Paradoxical respiration is seen in diaphragmatic paralysis. Reduced respiratory excursion is seen in children with Guillain–Barré syndrome.

Dyspnea refers to increased work of breathing leading to difficulty in breathing, while *tachypnea* refers to an increased rate of respiration. Look for signs of use of accessory muscles of respiration such as flaring of alae nasi, intercostal and subcostal retractions, and suprasternal retractions.

Age-specific normal respiratory rates are as shown in Table 2.3. However, the cutoff rates for tachypnea are different at different ages:

- *0–2 months*: RR >60/min
- *2–12 months*: RR >50/min
- *1 year*: RR >40/min

TABLE 2.3 Age-Specific Normal Respiratory Rates

Age	Respiratory rate (breaths/min)
Premature	40–60
Term newborn	30–50
1 month to 1 year	20–40
1–5 years	20–30
5–10 years	15–25
Above 10 years	15–20

Respiratory rates and tachypnea are useful signs for the diagnosis of pneumonia in children and chest indrawing for severe pneumonia in children younger than 5 years of age.

While tachypnea can be caused by both respiratory and nonrespiratory conditions (severe anemia, high-grade fever, and metabolic acidosis), chest indrawing is caused by any condition that causes either reduced lung compliance (such as pneumonia) or increased tissue/airway resistance (such as asthma).

Periodic breathing occurs normally in neonates when there are alternate periods of rapid respirations followed by apnea, which does not exceed 20 seconds and is not associated with bradycardia and cyanosis. Cheyne–Stokes breathing is similar to periodic breathing (period of apnea), but occurs in older children with cerebral edema or cardiac failure. Biot's breathing occurs in conditions with raised intracranial pressure and is characterized by apnea followed by four to five normal breaths.

Bradypnea refers to decreased respiratory rate and is seen in alkalosis, hypothyroidism, and increased intracranial tension.

Listen to adventitious sounds such as snoring, which is heard in oropharyngeal obstruction due to adenoid enlargement, and other respiratory sounds such as stridor and audible wheezing.

The respiratory rate (normal or abnormal), increased work of breathing (use of accessory muscles of respiration), audible respiratory sounds, and cyanosis can be useful pointers toward a respiratory tract involvement in the child.

Blood Pressure

The proper technique for taking a blood pressure reading in children is the same as for measuring blood pressure in adults. Most devices for measuring blood pressure are dependent on one common feature, namely, occluding the artery of an extremity (arm, wrist, finger, or leg) with an inflatable cuff to measure blood pressure either oscillometrically or by detection of Korotkoff sounds.

- Blood pressure must be taken when the child is relaxed. It is taken in both the upper and the lower limbs.
- Blood pressure may be measured in lying down or sitting position.
- BP instrument is kept at the level of the heart.
- If there is difficulty in recording blood pressure by auscultation, palpatory method may be used. It is the appearance and disappearance of Korotkoff sounds that are taken as the points for measuring systolic and diastolic blood pressure, respectively.
- The width of the bladder of the pediatric BP cuff should cover at least two-third of the length of the arm from axilla to the cubital fossa.
- The length of the bladder should encircle the arm covering at least 80% of the circumference.
- The age-wise recommended bladder sizes to be used in children are 6 cm for infants, 8 cm for children, and 10 cm for adolescents. A cuff too small spuriously can give high readings and a large cuff spuriously gives low readings.
- The cuff should be inflated rapidly and deflated slowly.

Techniques to Measure Blood Pressure in Children

- *Auscultatory method (by using a sphygmomanometer)*: The cuff should be tied approximately 2.5 cm above the cubital fossa. It should be inflated to 20–30 mmHg above the level where the radial pulse is not felt. Now deflate the cuff slowly. Auscultate the sounds over the brachial artery in the cubital fossa. For the lower limb, the stethoscope should be placed on the popliteal artery. The point at which the first sounds are heard is the systolic pressure. As the cuff is further deflated, the sounds get muffled and then disappear. The point at which the sounds start muffling (not disappear) is the diastolic pressure.

- *Palpatory method*: Feel the radial pulse as the cuff is being deflated. The point at which the radial pulse reappears is the systolic pressure.
- *Flush method*: This method is now rarely used but may be helpful in newborns and infants to measure the systolic blood pressure. This method is an unreliable method for blood pressure examination.
- *Oscillometric method*: This is a noninvasive method and uses an oscillometer to detect the flow of blood in the radial or brachial artery. It is commonly used in patients in whom long-term measurement is required. It uses an electronic pressure sensor to detect blood flow. The cuff is inflated to exceed the systolic arterial pressure and then deflated to below diastolic pressure over 30 seconds. The correct cuff size is essential for an accurate reading. This is a noninvasive method to detect the flow of blood in radial or brachial artery.

  Oscillometric method may not provide accurate readings in patients with heart and circulation problems.
- *Doppler method*: This method uses ultrasound Doppler to detect the flow in the radial or brachial artery.

Normal Values for Blood Pressure

The following formulae are devised to approximately calculate the 50th percentile of systolic and diastolic blood pressures in children older than 1 year:

- Systolic blood pressure = 90 + (2 × age in years)
- Diastolic blood pressure = 55 + (2 × age in years)
- Lower limit of systolic blood pressure (fifth centile) = 70 + (2 × age in years)

Hypertension

- Hypertension is said to be present if systolic and/or diastolic pressure are equal to or more than 95th percentile for that age and sex on at least three different occasions.
- Hypertension in children is more likely to be due to secondary causes such as acute glomerulonephritis, renovascular conditions (renal artery stenosis), coarctation of aorta, neuroblastoma, and prolonged steroid therapy, and essential hypertension is more common in adolescents.

Capillary Refill Time

It is a very useful bedside test and is also called capillary filling time (CFT). It is an indicator of peripheral tissue perfusion. It is tested by pressing a finger or thumb against bony prominences, commonly over forehead or sternum, for 5 seconds. Skin gets blanched on pressure and time taken for skin to regain its normal color is noted. If the perfusion is good, skin regains its normal pink color within 3 seconds. Capillary refill time is said to be delayed if it is ≥3 seconds. It is delayed in status of shock and in severe dehydration.

Hydration

Assessment of hydration and finding out whether the infant or child is dehydrated or not is one of the important aspects of evaluation, particularly in the presence of diarrheal illness.

- Look for sunken eyes: As the child's body loses fluids, his/her eyes may appear sunken.
- Pinch the skin over the abdomen: Locate the area halfway between the umbilicus and the side of the abdomen and then pinch the skin over it with the thumb and the index finger. When you release the skin, check whether the skin goes back very slowly (>2 seconds), slowly, or immediately. In a child with

TABLE 2.4 Assessment of Dehydration

Criteria	Some dehydration	Severe dehydration
Sensorium*	Restless and irritable	Lethargic or unconscious
Eyes*	Sunken	Very sunken
Skin pinch*	Skin goes back slowly	Skin goes back very slowly
Oral mucosa	Dry	Very dry
Thirst*	Drinks eagerly	Unable to drink
Urine output	Decreased	Very decreased or absent

Note: As per integrated management of neonatal and childhood illness (IMNCI), any of the two signs marked as "*" should be present in a child to label as some or severe dehydration.

marasmus, due to loss of subcutaneous fat, the skin pinch may be abnormal (slowly) even in the absence of dehydration.

- Dehydration is classified as no dehydration, some dehydration, and severe dehydration based on the signs, and the assessment is shown in Table 2.4.
- In no dehydration, there are not enough signs to classify as some or severe dehydration. The child with no dehydration is alert, with moist oral mucosa, the skin pinch goes back immediately, the child is not thirsty, and he/she has normal urine output.

Oxygen Saturation

Saturation of oxygenation is an important parameter and this can be assessed with noninvasive technique of pulse oximetry. This is a very useful bedside tool to assess hypoxemia in a patient. It measures the percent saturation of hemoglobin bound with oxygen in blood. If the oxygen saturation is less than 90%, it indicates hypoxemia. It is assessed with the help of a pulse oximeter machine, probe of which is applied to pulp of finger or toe or can be applied to ear lobule. Being a noninvasive bedside tool, it is very useful; however, there are certain limitations. The readings are not accurate if perfusion is poor like in case of shock, hypothermia, and severe hypoxemia when saturation goes below 70%.

Anthropometry

Anthropometric data are used to assess the nutritional status of a child. It is therefore necessary to take the weight, height, head circumference, mid-arm circumference, and upper segment and lower segment ratio as a part of general examination in every child. The monitoring of the growth is done by plotting various parameters on growth charts. The growth charts universally recommended are the WHO growth charts. Anthropometry has been discussed in detail separately.

Head-to-Toe Examination

Size of Head

Head circumference should be measured and compared with the normal values for the child's age and sex.

- Microcephaly is defined as head circumference <3SD below normal. It can be primary or secondary. The head appears small and the forehead is often slanting (Fig. 2.6).
  - Primary microcephaly is when the brain is inherently small since birth

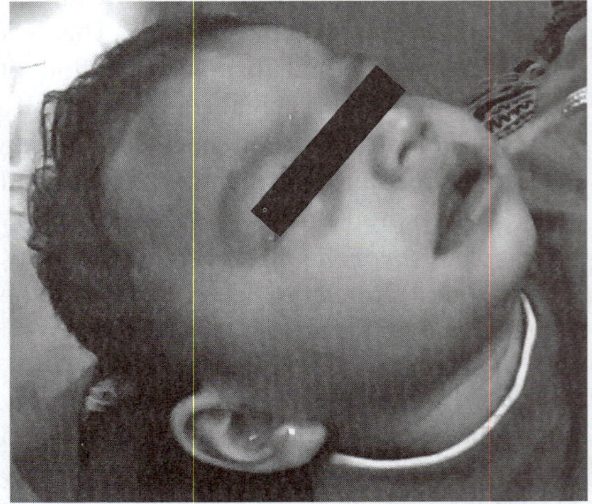

Figure 2.6 An infant with a microcephaly and slanting forehead.

TABLE 2.5 Causes of Primary and Secondary Microcephaly

Primary microcephaly	Secondary microcephaly
Familial	Intrauterine infection, e.g., CMV, rubella, *Toxoplasma*
Chromosomal disorders, e.g., Down syndrome, Edward syndrome, Rubinstein–Taybi syndrome	Intrauterine toxins, e.g., fetal alcohol syndrome, fetal hydantoin syndrome
Autosomal dominant, autosomal recessive, X linked	Perinatal and postnatal insult due to meningitis, encephalitis

CMV, cytomegalovirus.

with or without its potential of growth. It is seen in familial cases or in genetic and chromosomal disorders. In case of familial microcephaly, the child is asymptomatic with normal development.

- Secondary microcephaly occurs secondary to numerous insults to a previously normally growing brain. This is often associated with global developmental delay. The causes of primary and secondary microcephaly are shown in Table 2.5.

• Macrocephaly is defined as a head circumference >2SD above normal. Clinically, look for wide and delayed closure of sutures, sutural diastasis, bulging anterior fontanel (AF), and sun-setting sign. Examine the spine for any spina bifida or neural tube defects such as meningocele and meningomyelocele (Fig. 2.7).

Common causes of macrocephaly are listed in Box 2.2.

Shape of the Head

The shape of the head forms an important part of the examination of the head. The different types of head shapes are shown in Table 2.6 and Figure 2.8.

Figure 2.7 A newborn with neural tube defect (meningomyelocele).

Box 2.2 Causes of macrocephaly

- Hydrocephalus (congenital/acquired)
- Mucopolysaccharidosis
- White matter degeneration, e.g., Canavan and Alexander diseases
- Familial
- Neurocutaneous syndrome, e.g., tuberous sclerosis, neurofibromatosis
- Cerebral gigantism or Sotos syndrome

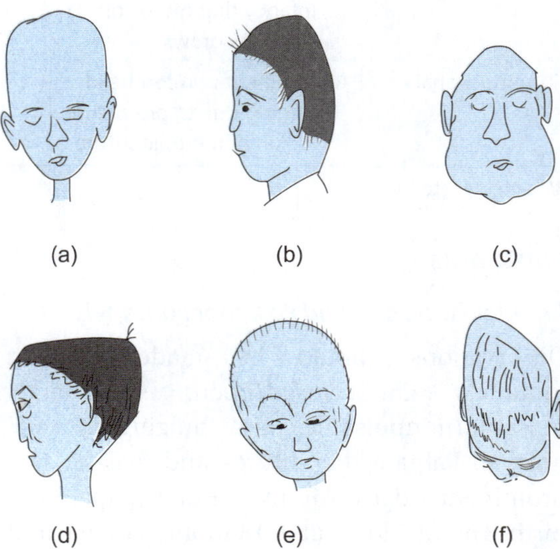

Figure 2.8 Shapes of the head. (a) Oxycephaly; (b) brachycephaly; (c) microcephaly; (d) scaphocephaly; (e) hydrocephalus; and (f) plagiocephaly.

TABLE 2.6 Abnormal Shapes of the Head/Skull

Oxycephaly (turricephaly)	Elongation of skull like a tower due to premature closure of multiple sutures. This leads to compensatory upward growth of skull (acrocephaly) and is seen in Apert and Carpenter syndromes
Brachycephaly	Occurs due to premature fusion of coronal sutures when the head cannot grow in the AP diameter and grows only in the transverse diameter with a flat occiput, e.g., Down syndrome
Dolichocephaly/ scaphocephaly	The growth proceeds only in the AP diameter due to early closure of sagittal suture. It appears narrow when looked from front and cannot grow laterally. May be seen in preterm babies and those with Hurler syndrome
Plagiocephaly	Unilateral asymmetry of head due to unilateral premature closure of coronal or lambdoid sutures. Viewed from above, it looks like a parallelogram. This is usually a postural deformity in early infancy that often corrects as the baby grows
Trigonocephaly	A prominent mid-forehead ridging due to premature fusion of metopic suture

AP, anteroposterior.

Fontanels

Anterior Fontanels and Posterior Fontanels (PF)

Observations should be made whether fontanels are closed/open, small/large, pulsatile/nonpulsatile, and bulging/sunken/normal. Palpate the sutures and feel for any prominent ridges. AF and PF are palpable at birth. The AF closes at 9–18 months of age and the PF closes at 2 months of age.

- At birth, normally, the AF measures 2.5 × 2.5 cm and is diamond shaped; the PF measures <1 cm allowing only the tip of the little finger.

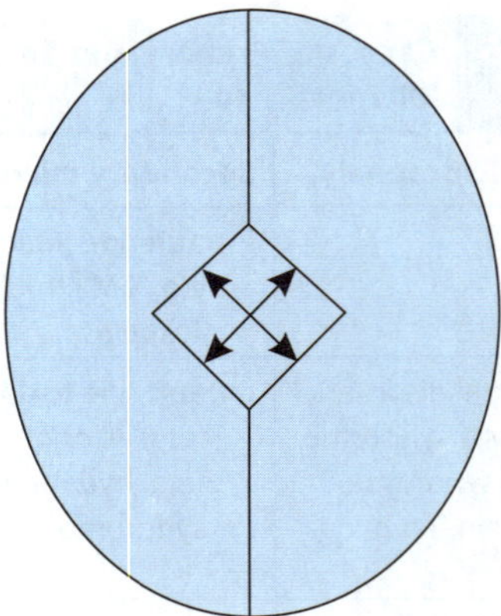

Figure 2.9 Diagrammatic representation to measure anterior fontanel.

- The tension in AF is important in deciding whether there is an increased intracranial pressure (bulging and nonpulsatile) or dehydration (sunken/depressed).
- The AF is measured by a nonstretchable tape between the two points diagonally, as shown in Figure 2.9.
- The fontanel must be palpated when the infant is quiet, sitting, and held upright with the head lifted up. A bulging fontanel in a crying infant does not necessarily mean increased intracranial pressure.
- A bulging AF in cases of raised intracranial pressure (with absence of normal pulsations) is seen in meningitis, hydrocephalus, intracranial hemorrhage, benign intracranial hypertension, etc.
- If a tense/bulging fontanel is accompanied by a large head and separated sutures, then an increased intracranial pressure is the most likely cause.
- Delayed closure of AF can occur in rickets, congenital hypothyroidism, hydrocephalus, Down syndrome, and achondroplasia.
- A systolic bruit may also be audible transiently over AF in acute bacterial meningitis.
- Small fontanel is seen in cases of craniosynostosis.

Other Noteworthy Points for Head Examination

- Craniotabes (softening or thinning of the skull) is commonly seen in rickets and preterm newborns.
- Crusts and scaling over skin of the scalp (seborrhea) (Fig. 2.10) are present.
- Color and texture of hair: The hair may be thin, sparse, lusterless, and hypopigmented with areas of hair loss (alopecia) as seen in severe malnutrition (Fig. 2.11).

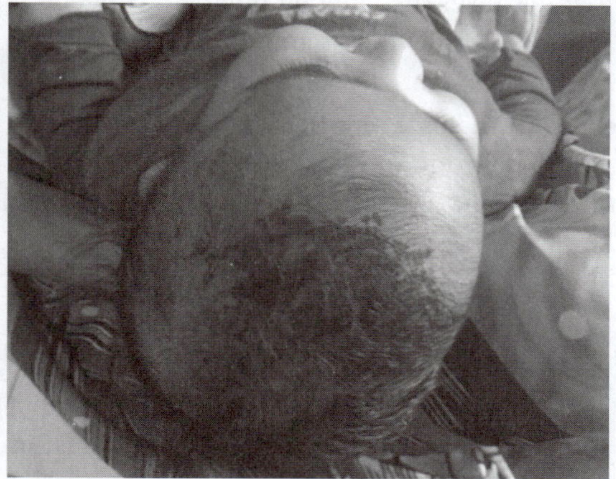

Figure 2.10 Crusts and scaling on scalp in seborrheic dermatitis.

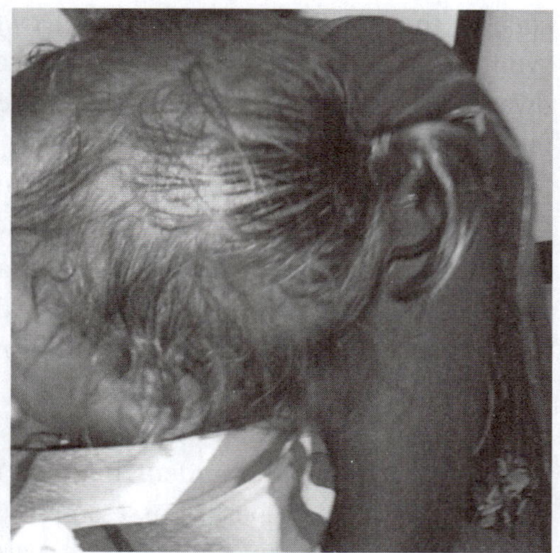

Figure 2.11 Sparse and depigmented hair in an infant with severe protein energy malnutrition (PEM).

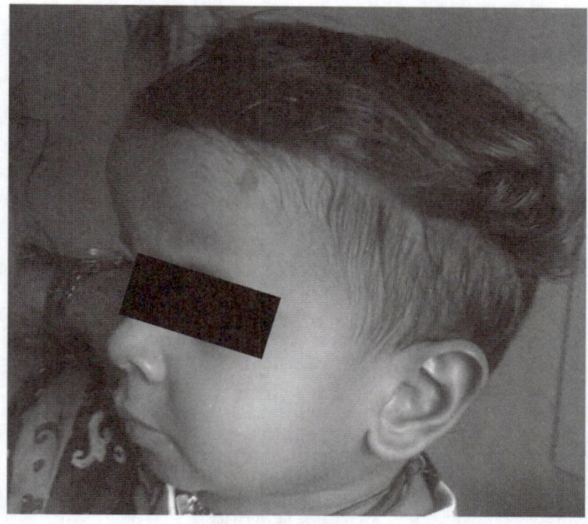

Figure 2.12 Frontal bossing in a child.

- Bossing of skull bones (frontal and parietal) is seen in rickets and thalassemia. The presence of frontal bossing is indicated by a prominent and protruding forehead (Fig. 2.12).
- Alopecia is the partial or total loss of hair. It is seen in zinc deficiency, polyendocrine deficiency syndrome (hypoparathyroidism, adrenal insufficiency, and hypothyroidism), fungal infection on scalp, and vitamin D–dependent rickets.

Face

The face offers useful clues for clinical diagnosis particularly in a child with dysmorphic features such as mongoloid face (Down syndrome), hemolytic facies (thalassemia and other severe, chronic anemias), Cushingoid facies (Cushing syndrome and prolonged steroid therapy), and coarse features (hypothyroidism).

Eyes

Examination of the eyes is a crucial part of general examination. The eyes must be examined for any hypertelorism, mongoloid slant, ptosis, strabismus, presence of nystagmus, congenital cataract, Kayser–Fleischer (KF) rings (Wilson disease due to copper deposits), and presence of any signs suggestive of nutrient deficiency such as vitamin A deficiency.

TABLE 2.7 Eye Signs in Vitamin A Deficiency

Grades of xerophthalmia	Eye sign
XIA	Conjunctival xerosis
X1B	Bitot spots
X2	Corneal xerosis
X3A	Corneal ulceration involving ≤1/3 cornea
X3B	Corneal ulceration involving ≥1/2 cornea
XN	Night blindness
XF	Xerophthalmic fundus
XS	Corneal scarring

- Subconjunctival hemorrhages are seen in children with pertussis and vitamin C deficiency. The signs of vitamin A deficiency (xerophthalmia) as per the WHO are shown in Table 2.7.
- Spacing of the eyes refers to the distance between both the eyes. It is measured by canthal index and interpupillary distance.
  - Canthal index is derived from the ratio of the distances between the inner and the outer canthi of both eyes multiplied by 100. The normal canthal index is 33–38.
  - Interpupillary distance is the distance between the centers of the pupils of both the eyes. The mean interpupillary distance is 40 mm in children and 50–75 mm in adults.
  - Ocular hypotelorism means that the spacing between the eyes is less than normal. In such cases, the canthal index is less than 33.
  - Ocular hypertelorism is an abnormally wide spacing of the eyes with a broadened bridge of the nose, usually due to maldevelopment of the sphenoid bone. In cases of hypertelorism, the canthal index is more than 38. Causes of hypertelorism include racial variation, cretinism, cerebral gigantism, craniofacial dysostosis, orofacial digital syndrome, thalassemia major, and Down syndrome.
- Mongoloid slant is a palpebral slant where the outer canthi are at a higher level than the inner canthi and is seen in Down syndrome and Prader–Willi syndrome. This may also be normal in certain races. Antimongoloid slant is seen in Turner syndrome and Noonan syndrome.
- Corneal clouding is seen in MPS and lysosomal disorders.
- Fifty percent of the cataracts seen in the infants are of unknown etiology. In addition to the idiopathic and hereditary factors, the causes of cataract include congenital TORCH infections (congenital rubella) and galactosemia.
- Exophthalmos may be seen in thyrotoxicosis and neurofibromatosis.
- Other signs that should be looked for in eyes include pallor (in palpebral conjunctiva), icterus (bulbar conjunctiva), phlyctenular conjunctivitis, blue sclera (osteogenesis imperfecta and congenital glaucoma), absent iris (aniridia), and Brushfield spots (salt and pepper speckling of iris) as seen in Down syndrome.

Ears

- Low-set ears are seen in several cases such as those with Apert syndrome, Down syndrome, William syndrome, Seckel dwarfism, trisomy 13, trisomy 18, and Potter facies (renal agenesis).
- Small ears (microtia) are seen in Treacher Collins syndrome and Goldenhar syndrome.
- Preauricular tags are seen in Goldenhar malformation, often associated with renal malformations and hypothyroidism (Fig. 2.13).
- Although ear examination with an otoscope is not expected from the student, middle ear examination forms a part of assessment of any febrile child below the age of 5 years; otherwise, a diagnosis of acute otitis media may be missed.

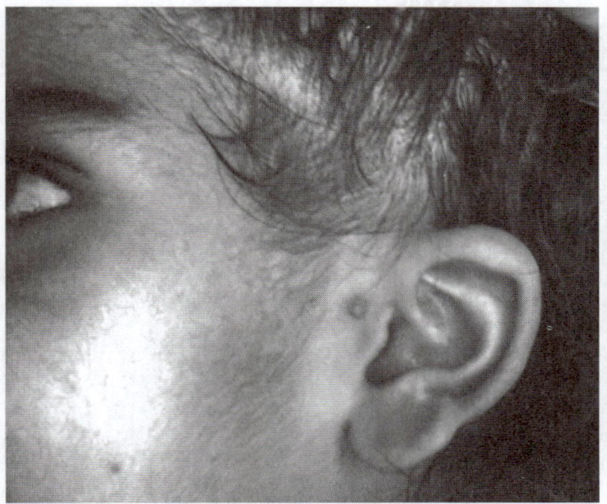

Figure 2.13 Preauricular tag.

Pallor

Pallor is the most common clinical manifestation of presence of anemia and depends on the amount and quality of blood in the capillaries. It is a common clinical finding in children and can be due to many causes such as nutritional deficiencies (e.g., iron, folate), ongoing chronic hemolysis (e.g., thalassemia, sickle cell anemia), or excessive blood loss. A poor blood flow in the peripheral blood vessels such as in shock, left heart failure, and syncope also may make the child appear pale.

The sites where pallor can be examined clinically are lower palpebral conjunctiva, nail beds, palms and soles, tongue, and general appearance of skin. The palm is compared with the palm of the examiner assuming that the examiner is not having anemia. The severity of pallor can be assessed by comparing the color of the palmar creases with that of the surrounding skin. In moderate pallor, the color of the palmar creases is comparable to that of the surrounding skin. In severe pallor, the creases are indistinguishable and lighter than the surrounding skin (Fig. 2.14).

Icterus

Icterus is the yellow discoloration of skin and mucous membranes that occurs due to excess accumulation of bilirubin as a manifestation of jaundice. The various sites for clinical examination of icterus are sclera, skin, palms and soles, soft palate, and undersurface of the tongue. Icterus must always be examined by taking the child next to the window in bright daylight. Sclera is the most common site where icterus is looked for as sclera is rich in elastic tissue and has a high affinity for bilirubin (Fig. 2.15).

- Hemolytic jaundice gives a very light and lemon-yellow color discoloration to the skin and mucous membrane.
- In case of hepatocellular or obstructive jaundice, there is dark yellow or an orange tint to the skin.

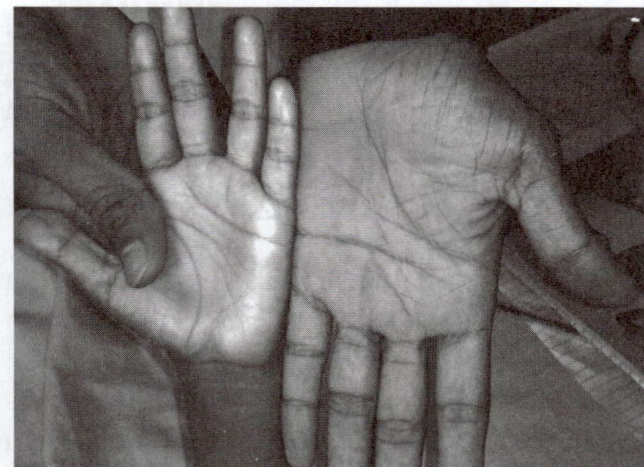

Figure 2.14 Pallor as seen and compared with examiner's normal palm.

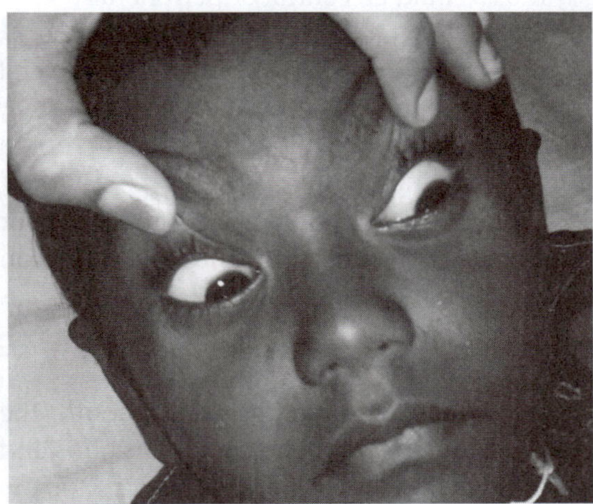

Figure 2.15 Examination for icterus in sclera.

- In case of obstructive jaundice, scratch marks could also be present due to pruritis.
- Yellowish discoloration of skin is also seen in carotenemia.

Cyanosis

Cyanosis is the bluish discoloration of skin and mucous membrane due to excess of deoxygenated hemoglobin or abnormal hemoglobin. Clinically, cyanosis manifests when the amount of deoxygenated hemoglobin exceeds 5 g/dL. Sites where cyanosis is looked for are tongue, fingers and toes, inner surface of lips or gums, ear lobules, palms, and soles. Cyanosis could be central or peripheral.

Peripheral cyanosis, also known as acrocyanosis, occurs due to peripheral vasoconstriction or diminished cardiac output, and is clinically seen in the nail beds but not in the mucous membranes.

Central cyanosis could be due to cardiac or pulmonary defects and manifests in both skin and mucous membranes (Box 2.3).

Mouth and Oral Cavity

- During the examination of the mouth, the clinician should note the dentition and abnormality in the perioral region, tongue and buccal mucosa, and posterior pharynx.
- Angular stomatitis/cheilosis: Maceration, fissuring at the angle of the mouth, and dry, cracked lips are seen in vitamin B_2 or riboflavin deficiency (Fig. 2.16).

Box 2.3 Causes of central cyanosis

- *Cardiac causes*: Cyanotic congenital heart disease, Eisenmenger syndrome, acute heart failure, pulmonary edema
- *Pulmonary causes*: Pneumonia, acute bronchiolitis, acute exacerbation of asthma (uncommon and late sign)
- *Decreased arterial oxygen saturation*: High altitude, alveolar hypoventilation, impaired oxygen diffusion, V–P mismatch
- *Excess deoxygenated Hb with high Hb level*: Primary polycythemia
- *Abnormal hemoglobin*: Methemoglobinemia, HbM disease

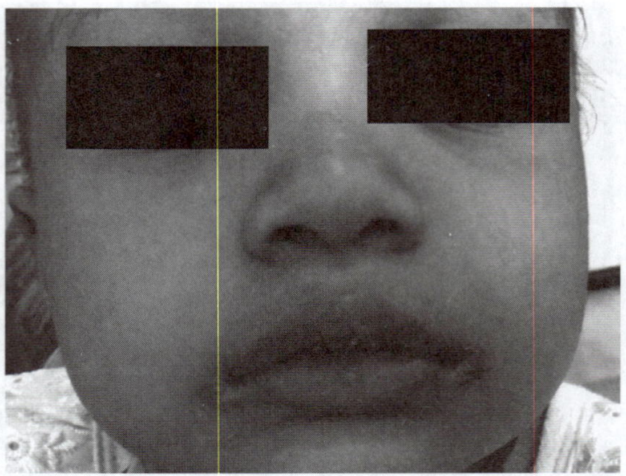

Figure 2.16 Angular cheilosis in a child.

- Buccal mucosa: Koplik spots are small papules on faint erythematous base on the buccal mucosa, seen near the opening of the parotid duct opposite to the first lower molar teeth in patients with measles.
- Aphthous ulcers are painful, recurrent oral ulcers seen on tongue, cheeks, soft palate, and the base of gums. They may be single or multiple. The ulcers may be less than 0.5 cm in diameter, with depressed center and erythematous periphery. The etiology is unknown or possibly due to folic acid deficiency.
- Thrush is the fungal infection caused by *Candida albicans*. It appears as a white, thick patch that bleeds on removal.
- Pigmentation, brown or black, due to increased melanin, is seen in Addison disease and Peutz–Jeghers syndrome.

Teeth

- There are 20 primary teeth.
- Primary dentition is complete by 30 months.
- Secondary dentition starts at around 6 years.
- Chalky white teeth are seen in fluorosis and teeth may be stained black due to excessive iron.
- Delayed dentition occurs in hypothyroidism, Down syndrome, protein energy malnutrition (PEM), and rickets.

- Teeth are absent in ectodermal dysplasia and cleidocranial dysostosis.
- Natal teeth may be present at birth. Lower incisor teeth may be present in normal babies and they do not interfere with feeding. They fall spontaneously in a few days. If they are very loose and there is risk of aspiration, they may be removed at any time. Neonatal teeth are seen in Ellis–van Creveld syndrome and Pierre Robin syndrome.
- Dental caries should be identified, and timely intervention should be done.
- Gums should be checked for any bleeding or hypertrophy. Gum hypertrophy is seen with phenytoin therapy, acute monocytic leukemia, and poor oral hygiene.

Tongue

- Macroglossia (large tongue) is seen in congenital hypothyroidism, MPS, hemangioma or lymphangioma of the tongue, glycogen storage disorders, and Down syndrome.
- Microglossia (small tongue) is seen in XII cranial nerve palsy and cerebral palsy.
- Pale and smooth tongue with loss of papillae is seen in iron deficiency anemia.
- Magenta red tongue is seen in riboflavin deficiency.
- Bright red strawberry tongue is seen in scarlet fever, measles, and Kawasaki disease.
- Blue tongue is seen in cyanotic congenital heart disease and methemoglobinemia.
- Black tongue is seen after ingestion of iron, bismuth, and charcoal.
- Red, swollen, beefy tongue is seen in pellagra and vitamin B_{12} deficiency.
- Black hairy tongue is seen in fungal infections.
- White-coated tongue is seen in typhoid fever.
- Geographic tongue is also called benign migratory glossitis and is seen as single or multiple, well-demarcated, smooth, red, irregular patches caused by the transient atrophy of the filiform papillae of the tongue (Fig. 2.17).

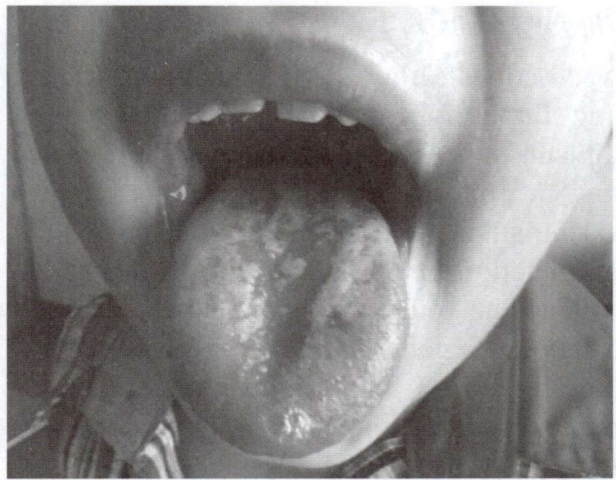

Figure 2.17 Geographic tongue.

- Tongue tie is a condition where the tongue is attached to the floor of the mouth by frenulum. If the frenulum is thick and tight, interferes with the movement of the tongue, and causes difficulty in speech, it should be released.

Palate

Cleft lip and palate may be seen isolated or together. These may be associated with some diseases such as Apert syndrome, Cornelia de Lange syndrome, maternal phenytoin intake, Pierre Robin syndrome, and trisomy 13 (Fig. 2.18).

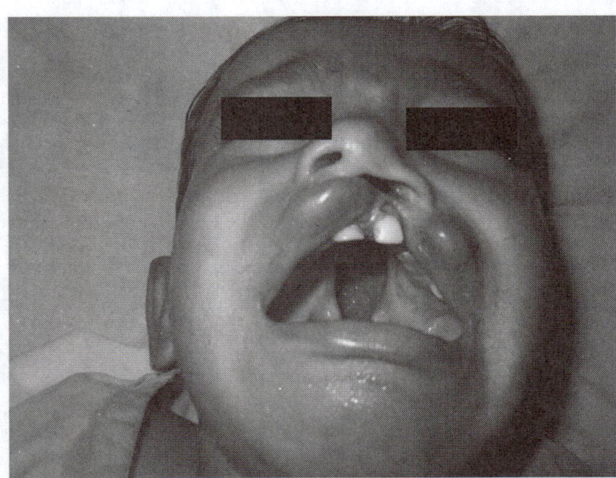

Figure 2.18 Cleft lip and palate.

Throat/Tonsils

As described earlier, the examination of mouth and throat is a potentially arduous and a difficult task in young children and hence may be performed toward the end of physical examination. Help of another person for the examination of throat and tonsils is needed to hold the young/anxious child steadily and it requires a good light source, a well-opened mouth, and a quick maneuver. Look for redness, congestion, ulcers, and exudates in the pharynx and tonsils. While examining for tonsils, it is advisable to ask the child to say "aah" and open the mouth. Look for the size of tonsils, any membrane (gray membrane seen in diphtheria), follicles, and exudates (streptococcal infection).

Examination of Skin and Nails

The skin, mucous membrane, conjunctiva, hair, and nails must be carefully examined. The color, texture, turgor, temperature, and moisture of the skin must be noted under sufficient illumination. Always examine for the presence of any pigmentation, depigmentation, rash, petechiae or purpura spots, pruritis, postpyoderma marks, and presence of scabies. The description of skin lesions is shown in Table 2.8. A few examples of primary skin lesions are shown in Figure 2.19.

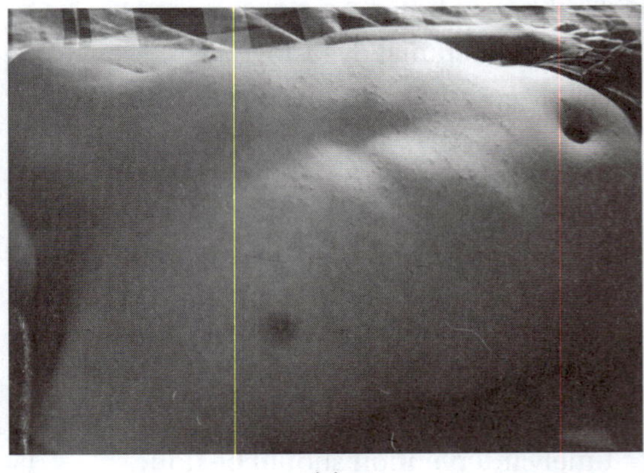

(a)

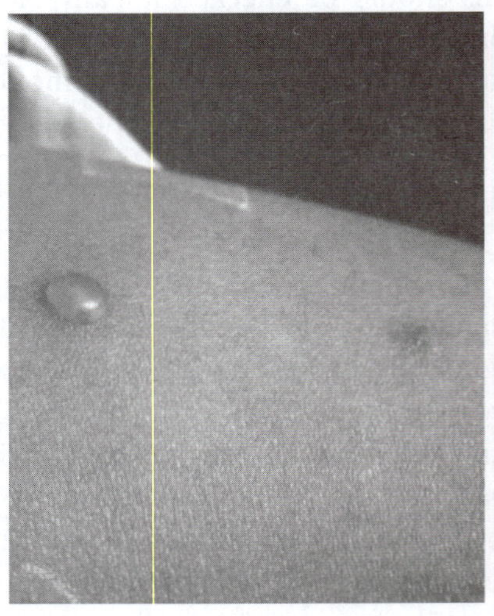

(b)

Figure 2.19 Skin lesions and rash. (a) Papular rash and (b) vesicular rash.

Changes in the fingernails and toenails also must be examined for any atrophy (seen in ectodermal dysplasia), pitting (psoriasis), or flattening and spooning (platonychia and koilonychias) seen in iron deficiency (Fig. 2.20).

TABLE 2.8 Description of Primary and Secondary Skin lesions

Primary skin lesions	Secondary skin lesions
Macule: Flat, nonpalpable, flush with surface of the skin	Lichenification
Papule: Small, palpable lesions; larger ones are called nodules	Crust formation
Vesicle: Elevated, small, fluid-filled blister	Desquamation
Pustule: Pus-containing superficial vesicles	Pigmentation
Wheal: Skin lesions that are elevated with central part paler than periphery	Ulceration
Petechiae: Pinhead-sized macule of blood	Scar formation
Purpura: Large petechiae that do not blanch	Atrophy

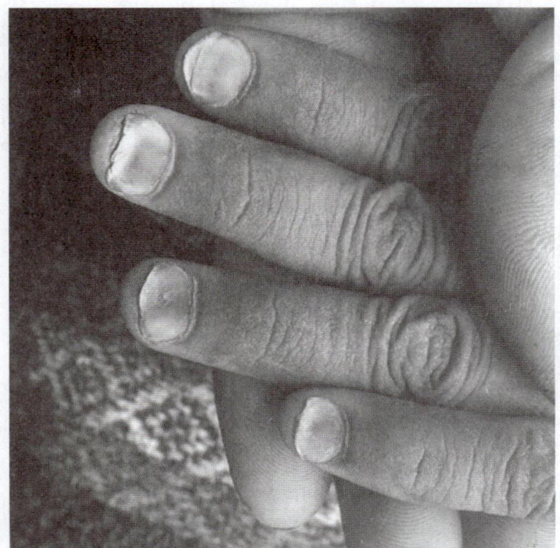

Figure 2.20 Spoon-shaped nails (koilonychia) in iron deficiency anemia.

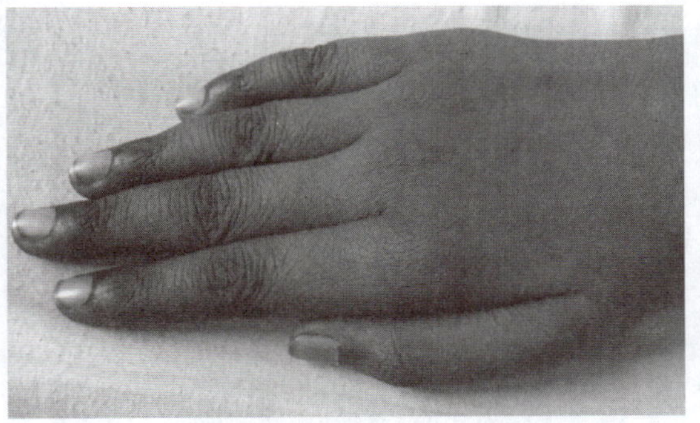

Figure 2.21 Knuckle pigmentation.

Another important aspect is to look for the hyperpigmentation of the fingers and the knuckles, which is commonly seen in megaloblastic anemia (Fig. 2.21).

Clubbing

Clubbing is characterized by bulbous enlargement of the distal phalanx due to proliferation of the subungual connective tissue in response to anoxia or other stimuli. The angle between the nail and the nail bed is lost and there is a widening of the extremities of the digits. This subcutaneous swelling involving the base of nail bed results in the fluctuation and the softening of the nail bed. The nail

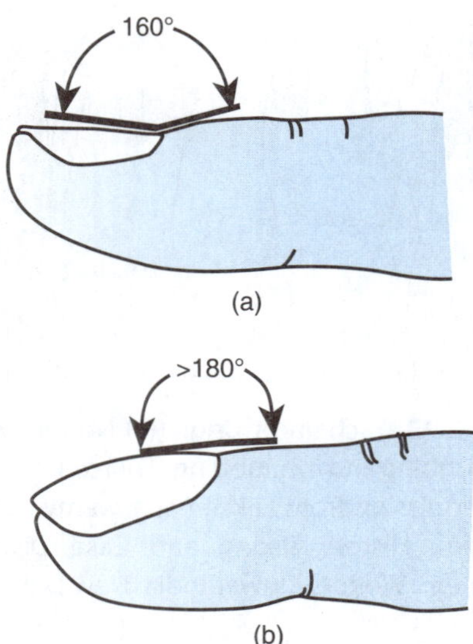

Figure 2.22 Lovibond angle. (a) Normal. (b) Obliterated. *Source*: Reproduced with permission from Lakshmanaswamy A. Clinical Pediatrics: History Taking and Case Discussion, 4th edition. Wolters Kluwer India: New Delhi.

fold angle, which in normal nails/fingers is 160° (profile angle), becomes obliterated and becomes 180° (Fig. 2.22).

Clubbing is elicited by Schamroth sign, when the two corresponding dorsal surfaces of terminal phalanges of opposite side are placed together in contact with each other. In normal fingers without clubbing, a diamond-shaped window (Schamroth window) is seen but in clubbing, this space is obliterated, and this is known as positive Schamroth sign or window test (Fig. 2.23).

The causes of clubbing and its grading are given in Tables 2.9 and 2.10.

Clubbing generally takes a few months to develop; for example, in cyanotic congenital heart disease, it takes about 6 months to develop, while it may develop acutely within 2–3 weeks in lung abscess and infective endocarditis.

Asymmetrical clubbing is extremely rare and can be observed in conditions such as anomalous aortic arch and subclavian artery aneurysm. Clubbing of the toes without that of fingers may be seen in coarctation of aorta.

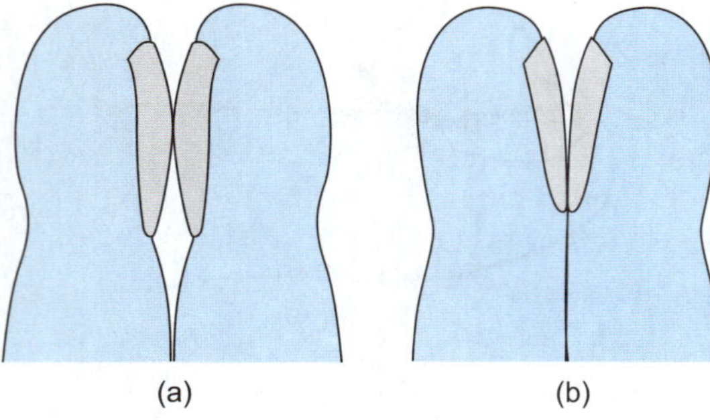

Figure 2.23 Schamroth sign. (a) Normal window in no clubbing and (b) clubbing. *Source*: Reproduced with permission from Lakshmanaswamy A. Clinical Pediatrics: History Taking and Case Discussion, 4th edition. Wolters Kluwer India: New Delhi, 2017.

TABLE 2.9 Causes of Clubbing

Cardiac	• Cyanotic congenital heart disease, e.g., tetralogy of Fallot • Eisenmenger syndrome • Infective endocarditis
Pulmonary	• Empyema • Bronchiectasis • Lung abscess • Tuberculosis in advanced stages • Interstitial lung disease • Mesothelioma
Gastrointestinal	• Ulcerative colitis • Chronic liver disease • Malignancy • Crohn disease • Cystic fibrosis
Familial	Presents rarely with other family members also having clubbing

Limbs and Joints

The examination of the upper and lower extremities along with bones and joints must be included in general physical examination. Observe the limb length and posture, and look for any joint tenderness and swelling that may be commonly observed in conditions such as acute rheumatic fever, sickle cell anemia, and septic arthritis. Look for genu varum (bowing of the legs) and genu valgum (knock knees). Check for wrist widening and double malleoli as seen in rickets (Fig. 2.24).

TABLE 2.10 Grades of Clubbing

Grade I	Softening of the nail bed
Grade II	Obliteration and fluctuation of the nail bed angle. This is clinically detected by the Schamroth sign. When the nails of both the index fingers are placed face to face, a diamond-shaped window is formed, which gets obliterated
Grade III	Parrot beak appearance. There is swelling of the subcutaneous tissue around the base and increase in curvature of the nail in its long axis. If the fingertips also get enlarged, it is called "drumstick appearance"
Grade IV	Swelling of fingers with hypertrophic pulmonary osteoarthropathy leading to pain and swelling, thickening of periosteum of radius, ulna, etc., and subperiosteal new bone formation. Rarely seen in children

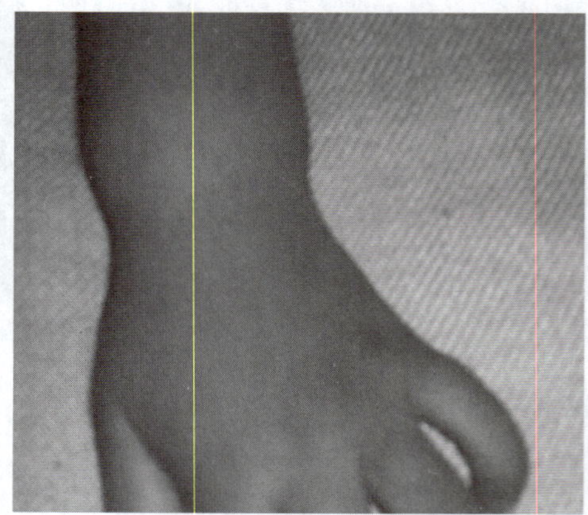

Figure 2.24 Wrist widening as seen in rickets.

Lymphadenopathy

Lymph node enlargement is a common occurrence in pediatric age group, but it is important to determine whether the enlargement is significant or not. Most children at one time or the other have palpable/enlarged lymph nodes during their childhood and one of the most common reasons for localized enlargement is an infection in the draining area. This can be seen as an infection of the scalp and can cause enlargement of occipital and postauricular nodes.

- Presence of lymph nodes and their enlargement must be noted and analyzed in the context of other symptoms and signs. For example, a generalized lymphadenopathy with weight loss and hepatosplenomegaly may indicate an underlying disorder as progressive pulmonary TB, HIV, or acute leukemia, whereas one to two small, discrete cervical nodes in an otherwise well child may not be of significance.
- Generalized lymphadenopathy requires the involvement of two or more noncontiguous areas (such as cervical and axillary). If only one area is involved, it is called localized lymphadenopathy, and if it persists for >3 months, it is called persistent generalized lymphadenopathy.
- The causes of generalized lymphadenopathy include bacterial infections such as tuberculosis, viral infections, upper respiratory infections (mononucleosis, HIV, rubella), malignancies (childhood leukemia and lymphoma, neuroblastoma), and connective tissue diseases (systemic lupus erythematosus, juvenile idiopathic arthritis, etc.).
- The important attributes of lymph node on examination should include:
  - Location of lymph nodes: Localized or generalized
  - Size and numbers (single/multiple)
  - Consistency: Soft, firm, or rubbery
  - Adherence to the underlying structures: Fixed or not
  - Painful or painless
- Cervical and inguinal lymph nodes >1.5 cm and axillary lymph node >1 cm are usually taken as significant lymphadenopathy. Even small-sized (0.5 cm) supraclavicular and epitrochlear lymph nodes should be considered significant and need further evaluation.
- The various groups of cervical lymph nodes to be examined include submental, submandibular, anterior and posterior cervical (vertical chain), posterior auricular, and occipital nodes. These lymph nodes are palpated by flexing the neck of the child slightly, either from standing behind the child with a slight flexion of the neck or from the front. The nodes are gently palpated with the pads of index and middle fingers (Figs 2.25 and 2.26).
- Axillary: The anterior group, posterior group, and lateral and deep nodes in apex of the axilla should be examined. Axillary nodes should be examined by inserting the fingers in the axillae with the patient's arm slightly abducted.
- Other lymph nodes that should be examined include epitrochlear and inguinal lymph nodes.

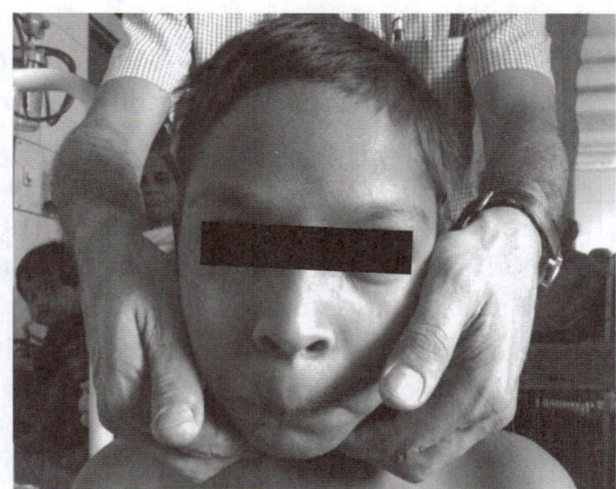

Figure 2.25 Palpation of cervical lymph nodes.

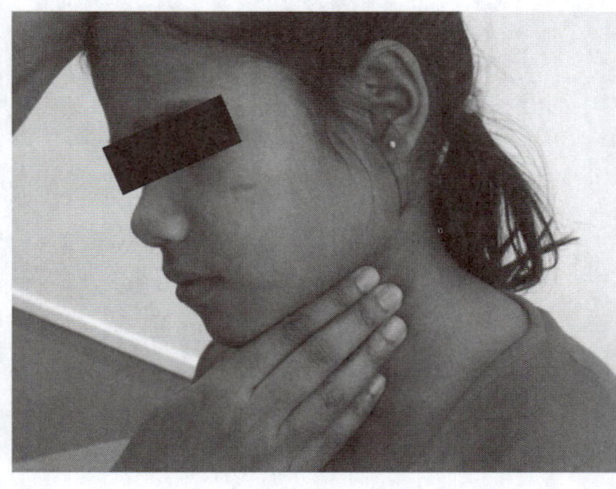

Figure 2.26 Palpation of deep cervical lymph nodes.

Edema

Edema is clinically examined by applying pressure against a bony prominence to look for presence of depression. In ambulatory children, it is done at the ankle above the medial malleolus where pressure is applied with the examiner's thumb and maintained for 20–30 seconds. If edema is present, then a pit or a depression is seen at that site in case of pitting edema (Fig. 2.27). In sick and bedridden children, edema is clinically examined at the most dependent area, i.e., sacrum. Most of the times, pitting edema is seen (Box 2.4).

Nonpitting edema is seen much rarely, e.g., in filariasis, infiltration, and hypothyroidism. Localized edema is seen in angioneurotic cases, urticaria, and cellulitis.

The causes of edema are classified according to the pathophysiological mechanisms such as:

- Reduced plasma oncotic pressure due to hypoproteinemia (nephrotic syndrome, chronic liver diseases, malnutrition, severe burns)
- Increased hydrostatic pressure (heart failure, constrictive pericarditis, acute glomerulonephritis, and venous obstruction, e.g., Budd–Chiari syndrome)
- Increased capillary permeability such as in angioneurotic edema and vasculitis, e.g., systemic lupus erythematosus
- Impaired lymphatic drainage, e.g., congenital lymphedema, filariasis, and postsurgical conditions
- Miscellaneous, e.g., myxedema and drugs such as calcium channel blockers

Box 2.4 Causes of edema in children

- *Cardiac*: Severe anemia, congestive cardiac failure, beriberi
- *Renal*: Nephrotic syndrome, acute nephritis
- *Hepatic*: Chronic liver disease/liver cirrhosis
- Severe acute malnutrition (kwashiorkor)
- *Endocrine*: Myxedema, Cushing syndrome, excess exogenous steroid

Jugular Venous Pressure (JVP)

JVP is the relationship between the venous tone, volume of blood in the venous system, and the pressure in the right side of the heart. It is expressed as the vertical height from the sternal angle to the pulsation in the internal jugular vein.

Measurement of JVP

JVP is measured in the supine position with the head end propped up at 45°, head turned away to the opposite side, and neck relaxed. The sternal angle is taken as the zero point and the maximum height of pulsation in the

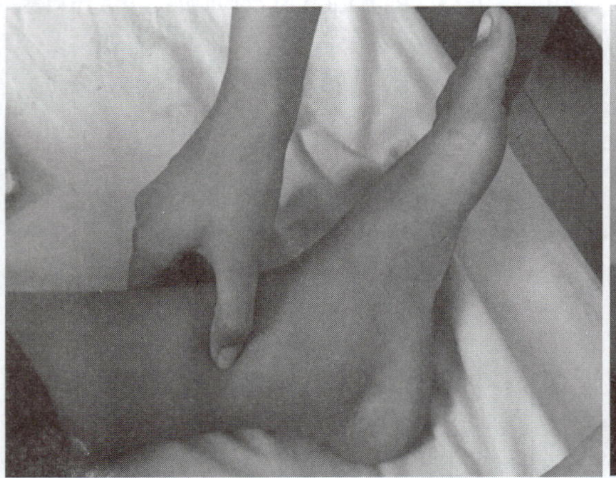

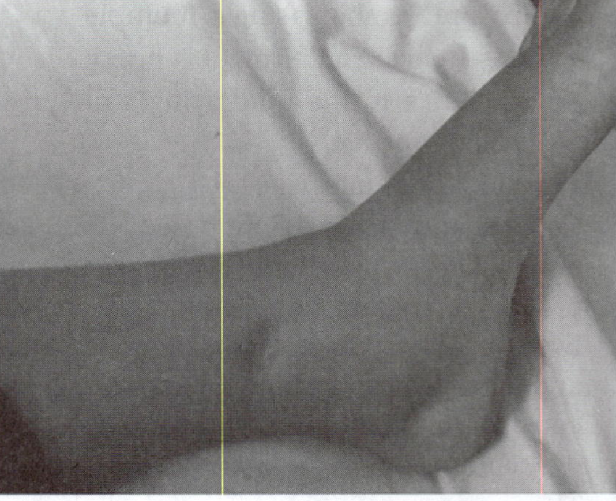

Figure 2.27 Examination for edema.

internal jugular vein is measured. JVP more than 3 cm from the zero point is taken as abnormal.

Genitalia

Though often combined with per abdominal examination, examination of genitals is an essential part of general examination. The child and particularly the male child should be examined for hernia sites, undescended testes (Fig. 2.28), testicular swelling, scrotal edema (Fig. 2.29), ambiguous genitalia, hypospadias, and phimosis.

A general guide to look out for gross congenital anomalies is shown in Box 2.5.

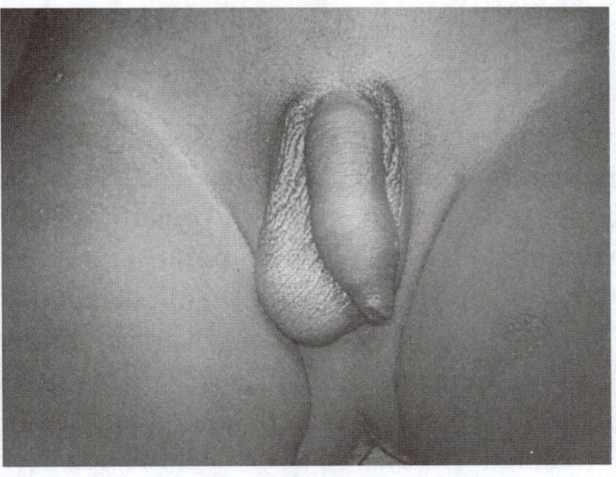

Figure 2.28 Undescended testes (left).

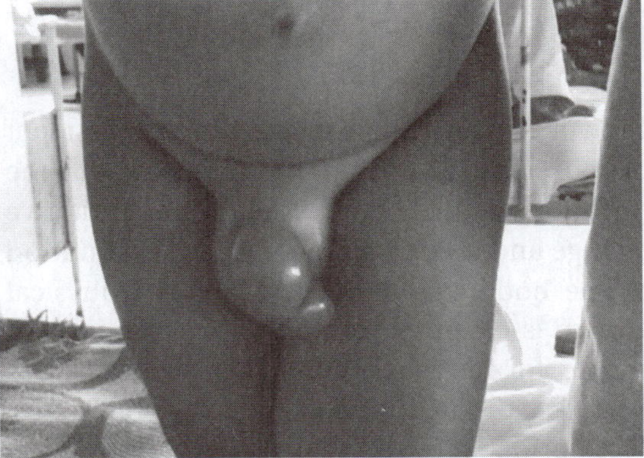

Figure 2.29 Scrotal edema in a child with ascites.

Box 2.5 Gross congenital anomalies

- *Face*: Dysmorphism, micrognathia, retrognathia, mid-face hypoplasia
- *Eyes*: Hypertelorism, hypotelorism, abnormal slant, nystagmus, cataract, coloboma
- *Mouth*: Cleft lip, cleft palate, abnormal shape of color of teeth
- *Ears*: Preauricular sinus, low-set ears, anomalies
- *Neck*: Short neck, webbing
- *Nose*: Flat nasal bridge, upturned nares
- *Limbs*: Abnormal crease, clinodactyly/syndactyly/arachnodactyly, overriding of fingers, abnormal dermatoglyphics, arches of foot, short/long limbs, broad thumb
- *Chest*: Wide-spaced nipples, pectus excavatum/carinatum
- *Spine*: Dimples, hair tuft, swelling (meningocele, myelomeningocele), kyphosis, scoliosis
- *Genitalia*: Ambiguous genitalia, cryptorchidism, micropenis, hydrocele, hernia

KEY POINTS

- As much as possible, a thorough general examination needs to be conducted in children regardless of the reason for the visit to the hospital.
- Pediatric general physical examination is an essential part of diagnostic process in newborns, infants, and children and is the venerated element of the art of medicine.
- An ability to perform a thorough general examination in children is one of the most essential clinical skills that must be practiced and perfected during the undergraduate training period.

CHAPTER 3

Growth Assessment in Children

Piyush Gupta, Bhavna Dhingra

Growth is a continuous process and assessment of physical growth is an indicator of the nutritional status of a child. It is a quantitative change and it refers to the physical maturation of the body. Periodic assessment of physical growth is essential to monitor the progress of a child, for early detection of any abnormalities and prompt institution of corrective measures. Monitoring growth velocity over a period of time and recording on a growth chart help to identify deviations from the normal growth pattern.

Anthropometry is the science of measurement of various body parts and helps in the assessment of physical growth of an individual against a set of established standards. The most commonly used anthropometric measurements for growth assessment in routine practice are:

- Weight
- Height/length
- Head circumference
- Mid–upper arm circumference (MUAC)
- Chest circumference

Other parameters that may be used in certain situations are: body proportions like upper segment to lower segment ratio and arm span, body mass index (BMI), assessment of bone age and tooth age, and sexual maturity rating (SMR).

Weight

Weight of a child is the reflection of his/her nutritional status and is the most commonly used parameter for growth assessment. It is an age-dependent parameter and the first to get affected in case of undernutrition/overnutrition. The following points should be taken care of while weighing an infant/child:

- Weight should be measured with minimal/no clothing (such as in brief and vest for a child). Newborns and infants should be weighed without the diapers. If the newborn or the baby is weighed with the diaper/nappy, then its weight should be subtracted from the baby's weight.
- Serial measurements should be done preferably on the same weighing scale.
- Weight should ideally be measured on a digital electronic weighing scale or a beam scale with minimum graduations of 100 g.
- Infants weighing up to 10 kg are placed on the pan or the bucket type of weighing scales. The infant is placed on the tray that is supported on the reading frame calibrated for measuring nearest to 10 g (Fig. 3.1).
- Use of spring balances should be avoided as they are likely to be inaccurate.
- Older children who can stand steadily are weighed using the platform type of weighing scale. All the weighing scales must be calibrated regularly with the known/standard weights.
- The infant should be placed in the center of the weighing tray for equal distribution of weight. Similarly, while observing the child's weight on a platform type of scale, the scale should be on a firm surface for the reading to be taken.

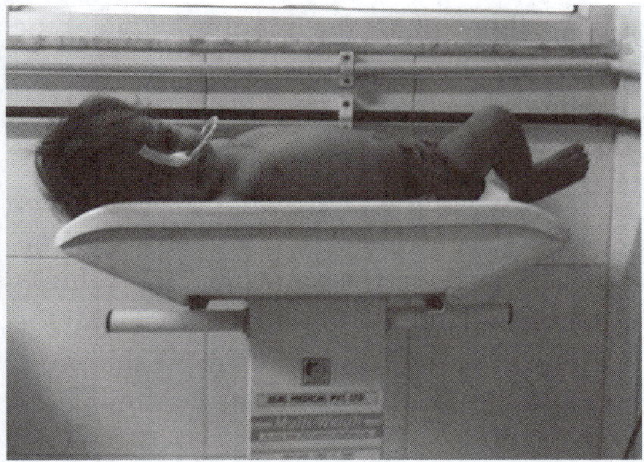

Figure 3.1 Pan type of digital weighing scale for weighing an infant.

Growth Velocity Based on Weight

- On an average, infants gain 30 g/day between 0 and 3 months and then 20 g/day between 3 and 6 months. An average normal newborn weighs 2.5–3 kg at birth, loses up to 5–10% of the birth weight by 7 days, and regains it by the 10th day of life.
- A child generally doubles the birth weight by 5 months, triples the birth weight by the end of 1 year, and quadruples it by 2 years of age. From the second year onwards, the child gains 2–2.5 kg/year till the onset of pubertal growth spurt.
- The pubertal/adolescent acceleration of growth/weight occurs earlier in girls (10–12 years) and later in boys (12–14 years).
- The expected weight can be calculated by Weech's formula (Box 3.1). Table 3.1 provides the rate of weight gain for children from birth to adolescence.

TABLE 3.1 Weight Gain from Birth to Adolescence

Age	Rate of weight gain	Amount of weight gain (kg)
Birth to 3 months	30 g/day	2.5–3
3–6 months	20 g/day	1.5–2
6–9 months	15 g/day	1–1.5
9–12 months	10 g/day	1
1–3 years	3 kg/year	6
4–12 years	2 kg/year	16
12–14 years	5–6 kg/year	10–12

Length/Height

Length or height is not affected in cases of acute undernutrition but gets affected with chronic undernutrition. Length (and not height) should be measured for all children up to 2 years of age with the help of an infantometer. Normally, there is a difference of <1 cm between the length and the height due to the presence of physiological lumbar lordosis in infants and young children.

Box 3.1 Weech's formula

3–12 months	(X + 9)/2	X = age in months
1–6 years	2x + 8	X = age in years
7–12 years	(7x – 5)/2	X = age in years

Measurement of Length

- The instrument used for measuring the length is *Harpenden infantometer*, which has a fixed head end and a movable foot end with a firm board in between (Fig. 3.2). The infantometer is marked from 0 to 100 cm to measure the supine length and measure up to nearest 1 mm.

Figure 3.2 Infantometer to measure the length of an infant.

- The head of the baby is held firmly in contact with the fixed headboard; the legs are kept straight with firm but gentle pressure on the knees, feet perpendicular to the legs, and toes pointing upwards. The mobile footboard is brought in firm contact with both the heels and the length can be measured on a fixed scale between the headboard and the footboard of the infantometer.
- The procedure is best performed with the help of an assistant who steadies and holds the child's head at the head end of the board.

Standing Height

- For children older than 2 years of age, standing height should be measured in an upright position after removing footwear and socks, with the heels separated slightly. The heels, buttocks, and back should be in line and touching the surface against which the child is standing, e.g., wall or an instrument used to measure standing height known as *stadiometer* (Fig. 3.3).
- Both the arms should be relaxed and hanging by the side; the child should be looking straight with the head in the Frankfurt plane (line joining the inferior margin of the orbit and the upper margin of the external auditory meatus).

Figure 3.3 Measurement of standing height by stadiometer.

- The headboard of the stadiometer is then moved to compress the hair over the vertex, so that they are not a source of an erroneous greater reading; the corresponding value is then noted on the stadiometer to record the height of the individual. Figure 3.3 shows the measurement of height using a stadiometer.

Growth Velocity Based on Height

- A full-term newborn measures 48–50 cm at birth and attains a length of 64 cm at 6 months, 75 cm at 1 year, and 90 cm at 2 years. Thereafter, till the onset of puberty, children gain 5 cm/year. The adolescent height spurt corresponds closely to the weight spurt.
- A formula can be used to calculate the expected height between the ages of 2 and 12 years, as follows:

  Expected height (cm) = ([age in years] × 6) + 77.

  As an example, for a 4-year-old child, the expected height would be (4 × 6) + 77 = 101 cm.

- The term "height age" refers to the age of the normal child who would have the same height as the child who is under evaluation; for example, if a child aged 7 years has a height of 100 cm, then his/her height age is 4 years.

Weight for Height

Weight for height indicates degree of wasting and so degree of acute malnutrition. It is an age-independent parameter, so useful when age of the child is not known. As per WHO criteria, child has severe acute malnutrition, if weight for height is below –3 SD and has moderate acute malnutrition if it is below –2 SD.

Head Circumference

Head circumference or occipitofrontal circumference (OFC) is recorded from birth up to 5 years, which is the period of maximum brain growth. It is measured using a nonstretchable measuring tape to record the maximum circumference of the head between the occipital protuberance posteriorly and the supraorbital ridges and the glabella in front.

Infants and young children should be placed in the mother's lap, while older children can sit or stand while the head circumference is measured.

The tape should be crossed in the temporal region while applying gentle but firm pressure to compress the hair. The lower reading on the tape should be subtracted from the higher reading at the point where the two ends of the tape cross, to obtain the actual value of the head circumference. Make sure that the tape is perpendicular to the long axis of the face and record the reading up to the nearest 1 mm. Figure 3.4 shows the correct way of measuring the head circumference.

If the head circumference is less than the normal, then palpate for any bony ridges along the suture lines and look for the abnormal shapes of the head. If the child resists or becomes anxious or is crying and is not pacified, then it is suggested to take the head circumference later, after completing the rest of the examination.

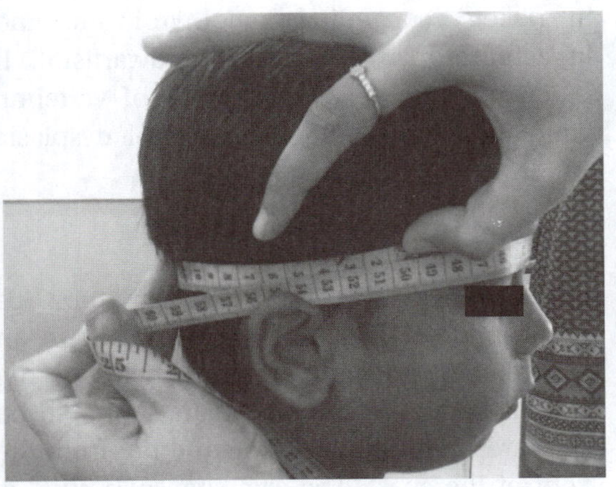

Figure 3.4 Measurement of head circumference in a child.

TABLE 3.2 Rate of Increase in Head Circumference from Birth to 5 Years of Age

Age	Gain in head circumference	Measured head circumference
0–3 months	2 cm/month	40 cm at 3 months
3–6 months	1 cm/month	43 cm at 6 months
6–12 months	0.5 cm/month	46 cm at 1 year
1–3 years	2 cm/year	50 cm at 3 years
3–5 years	1 cm/year	52 cm at 5 years

The rapid growth of brain in the first 2 years of life results in a rapid increase in the head circumference. The adult value of head circumference is reached by 5 years of age. Table 3.2 provides the rate of gain of head circumference in the first 5 years of life.

Growth Velocity for Head Circumference

The head circumference at birth is about 35 cm and increases to 45–46 cm at 1 year of age with an increment of 2 cm in the second year and 1 cm in the third year (49 cm). A formula (Dine's formula) also helps to find the expected head circumference in infants up to 1 year of age.

$$([\text{Length (cm)}/2] + 9.5) \pm 2.5 \text{ cm}$$

Chest Circumference

For children younger than 5 years of age, the chest circumference should ideally be measured at the level of the nipples midway between inspiration and expiration in supine position. The erect position is preferable for older children. In both cases, a nonstretchable tape should be used with the cross-over method.

Chest circumference is less than head circumference at birth, but it becomes more than head circumference at 6–9 months of age in a well-nourished child.

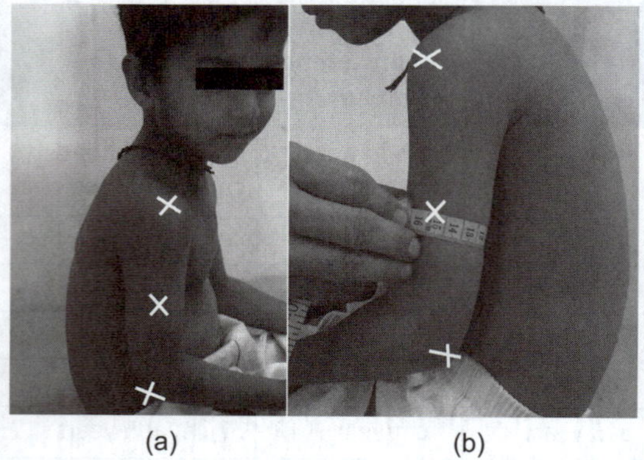

Figure 3.5 Landmarks for mid–upper arm circumference.

Mid–Upper Arm Circumference

Using a nonstretchable tape and the cross-over method, the MUAC is measured midway between the acromion process of the scapula and the olecranon process of the ulna in the left arm of the child while the arm is hanging freely by his/her side. The tape must be encircled around the midpoint on the perpendicular axis of the upper arm and the measurement noted (Fig. 3.5). MUAC is an *age-independent* variable as the value remains fairly constant between 1 and 5 years of age and is commonly used for identification of children with severe acute malnutrition (SAM). Midarm circumference at birth is 9–11 cm in a term newborn and becomes 16 cm by the end of the first year. MUAC less than 12.5 cm indicates malnutrition, while MUAC less than 11.5 cm is indicative of SAM.

Assessment of Body Proportions

It is an important part of assessment of linear growth in children and is especially useful in evaluating children with short or tall stature. Two such important parameters are upper segment to lower segment ratio and arm span.

Upper Segment (US):Lower Segment (LS) Ratio

The distance between the vertex and the pubic symphysis is the US and that between the pubic symphysis and the heel is the LS. After obtaining the height of an individual, the LS can be subtracted from the height to obtain the US value and finally a ratio of the US and LS can be obtained. US can be measured with the help of sitting height of an individual.

TABLE 3.3 Normal Upper and Lower Segment Ratios (US:LS) at Various Ages

Age	US:LS
At birth	1.7:1
6 months	1.6:1
1 year	1.5:1
2 years	1.4:1
3 years	1.3:1
4 years	1.2:1
6 years	1.1:1
10 years	1:1
18 years	0.9:1

The child is made to sit erect on a square stool kept against the stadiometer rod and the headboard is then brought to compress the hair on the vertex and the reading is noted. The height of the stool used is then subtracted from this reading to obtain the sitting height or the US. Table 3.3 provides the normal values for US and LS ratio at various ages. An abnormal ratio helps to identify cause for disproportionate short stature. The ratio is higher than expected in rickets, congenital hypothyroidism, and in achondroplasia (short limb dwarfism). It is lower than expected in cases of vertebral anomalies and spondyloepiphyseal dysplasia (short trunk dwarfism).

Arm Span

The distance measured between the tips of the middle fingers of the two arms in an outstretched position at right angles to the body is known as the arm span. It should be measured from the backside and not from the front of the chest. The arm span of a child is 3 cm less than the length at birth. The arm span and the height are usually equal by the age of

10 years and thereafter the arm span exceeds the height, but not more than 3 cm.

Arm span is useful in evaluation of disproportionate short/tall stature. It is less than the height in cases of cretinism and achondroplasia. It is greater than the height by more than 3 cm in cases of Marfan syndrome and Klinefelter syndrome.

Body Mass Index

BMI is derived from the height and weight of an individual by using the following formula:

$$\text{BMI} = \frac{\text{Weight (kg)}}{\text{Height}^2\text{ (m)}}$$

BMI is used in the assessment of overweight and obesity. Universally, BMI more than or at the 95th centile for age and sex is defined as obesity. Table 3.4 provides classification of nutritional status according to BMI in children and adolescents.

Z (SD) Score

In any population with a normal Gaussian distribution of variables, each value of the variable can be expressed in terms of standard deviation (SD) of that particular value from the median value. *Z* score is the measure of how many SDs (below or above) an element is from the population mean. It is defined as the deviation of an individual value from the median value of the reference population divided by the SD of the same reference population, and is given by the following formula:

$$\text{SI score} = \frac{\text{(Observed value} - \text{Median value of reference population)}}{\text{SD of the reference population}}$$

The advantage of using *Z* scores is that they allow comparison of observations of different variables in an individual. They also allow comparison of children with racial and ethnic differences where the expected growth parameters are likely to be different. A *Z* score value of +1.5SD means that the difference between the observed and the expected (reference median value) is 1.5 times the SD of the reference population. A positive value indicates that the observed reading is more than the reference median, while a negative value means that the observed reading is less than the expected. Table 3.5 provides the interpretation of these scores.

TABLE 3.4 Assessment of Nutritional Status According to BMI in Children and Adolescents

Nutritional status classification	BMI (kg/m²)
Underweight	<5th centile
Normal	5th to 84th centile
Overweight	85th to 94th centile
Obesity	>95th centile

BMI, body mass index.

TABLE 3.5 Interpretation of Standard Deviation Scores

Standard deviation score	Interpretation
−2 to −3	Moderate malnutrition
<−3	Severe malnutrition
+2 to +3	Overweight
>+3	Obesity

Bone Age

Estimation of bone age can be done by considering the following factors:

- Number, shape, and size of epiphyseal centers and the time of fusion of epiphysis and diaphysis
- Size, shape, and density of the ends of bones

Tanner and Whitehouse classification, which describes eight to nine stages of development of ossification centers, is most commonly used for assessment of bone age. For estimation of bone age in infants younger than 1 year of age, radiograph of the shoulder should be done. Radiographs of the hands and wrists should be done for children between the ages of 1 and 12 years, and radiographs of the elbow and hip are useful for those between 12 and 16 years of age.

Appearance of Ossification Centers

- The earliest ossification centers to appear are those of calcaneum and the talus bone between 22 and 26 weeks of gestation.
- At full term, the distal femoral, proximal tibial epiphysis, cuboid, talus, and calcaneal epiphysis are present.
- As a rule, the number of ossification centers in the wrist is one more than the age of the child in years; e.g., a 5-year-old child will have six ossification centers in the wrist.

Bone Age Versus Chronological Age

- Bone age is delayed for the chronological age in conditions such as constitutional growth delay, undernutrition, congenital hypothyroidism, hypopituitarism, and male hypogonadism.
- Advanced bone age in relation to the chronological age is seen in cases of precocious puberty, hyperthyroidism, congenital adrenal hyperplasia, and chondrodystrophies.

Eruption of Teeth

Teeth erupt in an orderly sequence at different ages and this can be used to evaluate the growth of the child and for age estimation.

Primary Teeth

The upper jaw teeth appear earlier than the lower jaw teeth except for the lower central incisors that are the first teeth to appear at 6–8 months of age, followed sequentially by upper central incisors, upper lateral incisors, and then lower lateral incisors by 10 months of age. The first molars erupt at 12–15 months of age followed by the canines at 15–18 months of age and the second molars by 24 months of age. The total number of primary or deciduous teeth is 20.

Although the eruption of primary teeth follows a pattern, individual and normal variations are often observed. Eruption of primary teeth may be normally delayed till the completion of the first year even in absence of any disease. Other causes of delayed dentition are vitamin D deficiency, hypothyroidism, hypopituitarism, and cleidocranial dysplasia.

Permanent Teeth

First molars are the earliest to appear at the age of 6–7 years followed by central and lateral incisors at the age of 6–8 years, canines and premolars by the age of 9–12 years, second molars around the age of 12 years, and the third molars at the age of 18 years or later.

Sexual Maturity Rating

The onset and pattern of pubertal development is different for boys and girls. The various changes that occur during puberty can be assessed and classified according to Tanner's stages of SMR. Table 3.6 provides the details of SMR stages.

The sequence of pubertal development in females is thelarche, pubarche, and then menarche. The onset is around 8 (10–12 years) years of age, with the approximate interval between thelarche and menarche being 2–2.5 years. For males, testicular enlargement is the first sign of pubertal development, beginning around 11.5 years (9–14 years), followed by penile enlargement and pubarche.

Growth Velocity

Measurement of growth parameters at a single time point does not reflect the rate of growth of a child and merely indicates whether the child comes within the normal range or not. It is essential to monitor the rate of growth serially to know whether the child is growing normally.

Plotting serial measurements on a growth chart (Fig. 3.6) helps to identify the time period during which the growth pattern has deviated from the normal and to pinpoint the possible

TABLE 3.6 Stages of Sexual Maturity Rating

Girls

Stage	Breast development	Pubic hair
I	No breast tissue	Same as abdominal hair
II	Breast bud, enlargement of areola	Minimally pigmented, mainly over labia
III	Further enlargement of breast bud	Darker and coarser hair on mons pubis
IV	Secondary mound formed by papilla and areola	Adult type, less distribution
V	Adult contour with projection of papilla alone	Adult feminine distribution

Boys

Stage	Genital changes	Testicular volume mL)	Pubic hair
I	Prepubertal	<4	Same as abdominal hair
II	Early penile growth, scrotal enlargement, pink scrotum	4–10	Fine pubic hair at the base of penis
III	Increase in penile length, scrotal growth	10–15	Increase in number of hair, darkening
IV	Increase in penile length and width, pigmented scrotum	15–20	Spread around thigh, less than adult distribution
V	Adult size	>20	Adult male distribution

cause for the same, so that appropriate corrective measures can be instituted to prevent growth faltering. It also provides the rate of growth per unit time and is helpful in predicting the final adult height that the child would achieve.

As any normal child is expected to gain 5 cm/year from the age of 5 years onwards, a height velocity of less than 4 cm/year indicates the presence of a pathologic cause for the short stature. The growth velocity of height also helps to predict the ultimate adult height. The target height that a child would achieve as an adult can be estimated by calculating the midparental height (MPH) as follows:

- *Boy*: {(Mother's height [cm] + father's height [cm])/2} + 6.5 cm
- *Girl*: {(Mother's height [cm] + father's height [cm])/2} – 6.5 cm

The value thus obtained is then plotted on a reference growth chart for height age of 18 years as adult equivalent. This provides an estimate of the target height for the child and the percentile that the child is likely to follow. The projected adult height is MPH ± 8.5 cm.

Growth Standards

These are the established norms for growth obtained from a representative population and depicted in a tabular or graphical manner. There are numerous growth charts available for comparing the weight with the expected weight to classify malnutrition. For these classifications, the term "expected" means the median (50th percentile) value of the reference standard. Nowadays, the World Health Organization (WHO) growth charts are recommended universally as standard reference for growth monitoring.

The WHO standards that are currently in use have been derived from children in India, Brazil, Ghana, Norway, Oman, and the United States of America. These standards are available for variables such as weight,

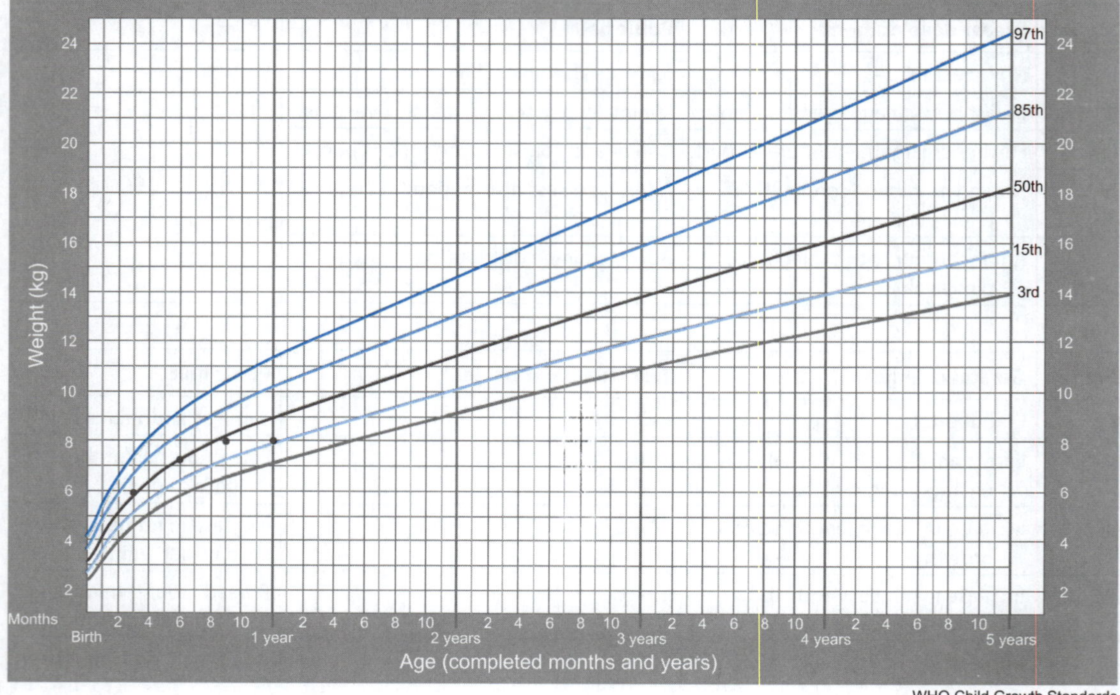

Figure 3.6 Use of growth chart for growth monitoring. *Source*: WHO.

length or height, weight for height, and head circumference separately for boys and girls from birth to 5 years of age. From 5 to 10 years of age, additional standards are available for BMI as well.

Growth Charts

- These are pictorial tools/charts that are used to assess growth over a period of time by plotting changes in height, weight, head circumference, etc., over a period of time (Fig. 3.6).
- A series of curves depicting the specific percentile of a variable, e.g., height for age and sex, is depicted in these charts.
- The values of measurement such as weight, height, and head circumference are given on the *y*-axis of the graph, while the age is shown on the *x*-axis. The readings are marked on the charts as separate dots.
- Separate charts are used for boys and girls. Serial repeated measurements for the child can be plotted on these graphs to ascertain the growth velocity and to identify any deviations from normal pattern of growth.
- The serially plotted information for an individual child gives the percentile ranking and the status of the growth of the child within the reference population. A flat or a downward line/curve on a chart indicates a deviation from the normal pattern of the growth.
- It helps in early institution of corrective measures to prevent growth faltering. The growth charts of the WHO are available at http://www.who.int/childgrowth/standards/en/. Regular and sequential assessment of growth parameters to help implement

TABLE 3.7 Recommendations for Growth Monitoring from Birth to 18 Years

Age group	Parameters to be monitored	Frequency of monitoring
Birth to 18 months	Height, weight, and head circumference	At birth, 6, 10, and 14 weeks, 6, 9, and 15–18 months
18 months to 3 years	Height, weight, and head circumference	Every 6 months
4–8 years	Height and weight	Every 6 months
9–18 years	Height, weight, and BMI	Every year

BMI, body mass index.

corrective, effective, and timely interventions is referred to as *growth monitoring*.

- Table 3.7 mentions the recommendations for growth monitoring in children at various ages.

Growth and Nutritional Disorders

If a child does not fall within the normal range of growth parameters for a defined age and sex, he/she is said to be suffering from a growth disorder. Malnutrition indicates that something is wrong with the nutrition; hence, it encompasses both undernutrition and overnutrition. Usually, the term malnutrition is used interchangeably with undernutrition. Some practical aspects of growth, its deviation, and related aspects are discussed in brief for practical purposes only.

- When the nutritional demands of the body are not met with adequately, it results in a state of undernutrition, which could be due to inadequate intake, poor absorption, or increase in loss of nutrients from the body resulting in a deficit of nutrients.
- When this deficit is of the major nutrients such as proteins and carbohydrates, the condition is referred to as protein–energy malnutrition.

TABLE 3.8 Types of Malnutrition According to Weight and Height

Type of malnutrition	Acute	Chronic	Acute on chronic
Weight for age	↓	↓	↓↓
Height for age	Normal	↓	↓
Weight for height	↓	Normal	↓

- Assessment of malnutrition is done by measurement of height, weight, and MUAC or skinfold thickness. Any child having low weight for age is *underweight*, and this condition can be seen in both acute and chronic malnutrition. Height is not affected in case of acute malnutrition.
- Any child with low height for age is known to be *stunted*, and this condition is seen in cases of chronic malnutrition.

  Any child whose weight for height or length also gets affected is *wasted*, and this condition is seen in acute on chronic malnutrition.
- Table 3.8 provides differentiation between acute, chronic, and acute on chronic malnutrition, and the WHO classification of malnutrition is shown in Table 3.9.

The WHO has recommended the use of a cutoff for weight for height below –3SD of the WHO standards to identify infants and children as having SAM. The weight for length reference cards for boys and girls are included as Appendices I and II, respectively.

Assessment of nutritional status when the exact age of the child may not be known can be done with the use of certain indicators that change minimally or very slowly over a broad age range; these are known as *age-independent indices*. Some of the commonly used indices in common field practice are as follows:

- *MUAC*: MUAC remains nearly constant between the ages of 1 and 5 years; it is also an

TABLE 3.9 World Health Organization (WHO) Classification of Malnutrition

	Moderate undernutrition	Severe undernutrition
Symmetrical edema	No	• Yes*
Weight for height (measure of wasting)	• *Z* score†: –2 to –3 (70–79% of expected‡)	• *Z* score <–3 (<70% of expected)
Height for age (measure of stunting)	• *Z* score†: –2 to –3 (85–89% of expected‡)	• *Z* score <–3 (<85% of expected)

*This includes kwashiorkar and marasmic kwashiorkar.
†*Z* (SD) score = ([observed value] – [expected value])/(standard deviation of reference population).
‡Median (50th percentile of NCHS [National Centre for Health Statistics] standards).

TABLE 3.10 Measurements on Shakir Tape

Color zone	Measured value	Interpretation
Red	<12.5 cm	Wasted
Yellow	12.5–13.5 cm	Borderline
Green	>13.5 cm	Normal

age-independent anthropometric criterion for the assessment of malnutrition. MUAC less than 12.5 cm indicates malnutrition, while a reading below 11.5 cm indicates SAM.

- *Shakir tape*: This tape has three color zones for different values of MUAC with different interpretations as given in Table 3.10.
- *Bangle test*: The child is made to wear a bangle with an internal diameter of 4 cm. In normal children, it is not possible to pass the bangle above the elbow, but in severely malnourished children, it can be passed above the elbow.
- *Skinfold thickness*: Triceps skinfold thickness in normal children up to 16 years of age is more than 10 mm, but in cases of severe malnutrition, it may be less than 6 mm.

Disorders of Growth

The common disorders of growth requiring evaluation are described in brief.

Failure to Thrive

Failure to thrive is best defined as poor physical growth diagnosed by observation over a period of time using reference growth charts. Child is said to have FTT if the following criteria are met on multiple occasions:

- Weight for age less than fifth percentile
- Weight deceleration crossing two major percentile lines
- Body mass index less than fifth percentile for the age and gender

The causes of failure to thrive could be organic wherein there is an underlying medical disorder or nonorganic wherein there is no medical condition but it is due to lack of adequate calories (nutritional) or due to psychosocial reasons or due to emotional deprivation.

Short Stature

Short stature is defined as height or length less than 2SD below the mean or less than the third percentile. It can be classified as follows:

- *Physiological*
  - Constitutional growth delay
  - Familial short stature
- *Pathological*
  - *Proportionate*: The body proportions (US:LS) are maintained, e.g., in conditions such as intrauterine growth restriction, growth hormone deficiency, hypothyroidism, and Turner syndrome.
  - *Disproportionate*: The US:LS ratio is altered, e.g., in conditions such as achondroplasia, chondrodysplasia, osteogenesis imperfecta, mucopolysaccharidosis, and spondyloepiphyseal dysplasia.

Evaluation for a child with short stature should include the following:

- A detailed clinical history and physical examination. Height or length should be recorded to the closest centimeter by the appropriate method and then plotted on the growth chart to obtain the centile or the *Z* scores.
- Estimation of target height should be done by calculating the MPH, which can be plotted as the expected height at 18 years of age, and plotting the child's current height to obtain the centile where it falls with respect to the MPH.
- Height velocity of the child over a defined period should be calculated and the child should be assessed for sexual maturity. The height velocity is not affected in physiological short stature.
- Decreased height velocity is a pointer toward pathological short stature. Height velocity less than 4 cm/year is suggestive of growth hormone deficiency.
- Appropriate investigations in a sequential manner relevant to the case may be performed while evaluating a child with short stature.

Tall Stature

Individuals with height more than the 97th percentile for age and sex or more than 2SDs above the mean are considered tall.

MPH should be calculated to identify children with constitutional tall stature. Tall stature may be seen in children with Marfan syndrome, Soto syndrome, Beckwith–Wiedemann syndrome, Klinefelter syndrome, pituitary tumor, and precocious puberty.

Overweight/Obesity

- A child having weight for age and sex between 110% and 120% of the standard body weight for age is classified as being overweight. If the weight for age and sex is above 120% of the standard weight or more than the ideal body weight (IBW) by 20%, or if the BMI is more than the 95th percentile for age and sex, the child is classified as obese.
- Various endocrine conditions such as hypothyroidism, and Cushing syndrome, and genetic diseases such as Prader–Willi syndrome, Laurence–Moon–Biedl syndrome, and Beckwith–Wiedemann syndrome can give rise to obesity.
- A detailed clinical history including medication history, dietary details, and physical activity along with meticulous physical examination is required to ascertain the cause of obesity.

Micronutrient Deficiencies

Micronutrients consist of various vitamins, minerals, and trace elements that are required in small quantities for normal functioning of the body's metabolic processes and for the maintenance of normal function of various organ systems. Deficiency or excess intake of these micronutrients gives rise to specific disease states.

Vitamins

These cannot be synthesized in adequate quantities by the body and need to be taken exogenously. They are classified as water-soluble (vitamins B-complex and C) and fat soluble (vitamins A, D, E, and K). Vitamins function as:

- Hormones
- Antioxidants
- Cell signaling mediators
- Regulators of cell signaling and growth
- Catalysts and substrates for metabolic processes

Minerals

The functions of minerals are to support various biochemical reactions in the body by being a structural component of cells and helping in cellular function, and to act as catalysts in metabolic processes and as electrolytes.

Trace Elements

These are required in very minute quantities for various body functions and act as cofactors for enzymes or are structural components of metalloenzymes. Table 3.11 mentions the recommended daily allowances and deficiency manifestations for various micronutrients.

TABLE 3.11 Micronutrient Requirements and Deficiency States

Name of micronutrient	Recommended daily allowance (RDA)	Deficiency manifestations and disease states
Vitamin A	• Infants: 400 μg • Children: 500 μg • Adolescents: 750 μg	Xerophthalmia including night blindness, keratinization, infertility, urinary calculi, impaired immunity, fetal anomalies in pregnancy
Vitamin D	• Infants: 200 IU • Children: 400 IU	Rickets, osteomalacia
Vitamin E	• Premature newborns: 15 mg • Term newborns: 3 mg • Infants: 6 mg	Hemolytic anemia, spinocerebellar disease, pigmentary retinopathy
Vitamin K	• Newborns: 5 μg • Infants: 10 μg • Children: 10–30 μg	Hemorrhagic disease of newborn
Vitamin B_1 (thiamine)	0.4 mg/1000 kcal consumed	Beriberi: Dry, wet, and acute forms
Vitamin B_2 (riboflavin)	• Infants: 0.4 mg/1000 kcal consumed • Children: 1 mg/1000 kcal consumed	Photophobia, cataract, corneal vascularization, glossitis, stomatitis, seborrheic dermatitis
Vitamin B_3 (niacin)	6.5–8 mg/1000 kcal consumed	Pellagra: Diarrhea, dermatitis, dementia
Vitamin B_6 (pyridoxine)	• Newborns: 0.1 mg • Infants: 0.3 mg • Children: 0.5 mg • Adolescents: 1.0 mg	Anemia, nerve damage, seizures, skin lesions, mouth ulcers
Vitamin B_{12} (cobalamin)	• Infants: 0.3 μg • Children: 1 μg • Adolescents: 2 μg	Megaloblastic anemia, methylmalonic aciduria, hypersegmentation of neutrophils
Folic acid	• Infants: 70 μg • 1–3 years: 100 μg • 4–6 years: 150 μg • 7–9 years: 200 μg • Adolescents: 300 μg • Pregnancy/lactation: 400 μg	• Impaired cell function, megaloblastic anemia, impaired brain and nerve functions • Neural tube defects in fetus
Biotin	0.15 mg	• Dermatitis, glossitis, hypercholesterolemia • Multiple carboxylase deficiency
Pantothenic acid	• Infants: 2–3 mg • Children: 3–5 mg	Burning feet, insomnia, gastrointestinal symptoms
Vitamin C	• Infants: 30–40 mg • Children: 40–70 mg	Scurvy: Anorexia, diarrhea, pallor, irritability, pseudoparalysis of legs, bleeding manifestations
Calcium	• Infants: 500 mg • Children: 800 mg • Adolescents: 1200 mg	Tetany, seizures, rickets, osteoporosis
Magnesium	• Newborns: 50 mg • Infants: 60 mg • Children: 200 mg	Irritability, tetany, hyporeflexia/hyperreflexia
Zinc	• Infants: 5 mg • Children: 10 mg	Delayed growth and sexual maturation, hypogonadism, anemia, diarrhea, alopecia, dermatitis, impaired immunity

(Continued)

(Continued)

Name of micronutrient	Recommended daily allowance (RDA)	Deficiency manifestations and disease states
Copper	• Infants: 0.5 mg • Children: 1.0 mg • Adolescents: 2.0 mg	Microcytic anemia, neutropenia, osteoporosis, bony changes—submetaphyseal fractures, seborrheic dermatitis, depigmented hair, failure to thrive
Selenium	• Infants: 20 µg • Children: 30 µg • Adolescents: 50 µg	Keshan disease: Cardiomyopathy, skeletal myopathy, macrocytosis, hair depigmentation
Chromium	• Infants: 50 µg • Preschool children: 75 µg • Schoolchildren: 100 µg • Adolescents: 200 µg	Glucose intolerance, peripheral neuropathy, disturbed nitrogen and lipid metabolism
Iodine	• Preschool children: 90 µg • Schoolchildren: 120 µg • Pregnancy/lactation: 250 µg	Iodine deficiency disorders: Cretinism, mental impairment, hypothyroidism, goiter, impaired development, stillbirths, abortions
Iron	• Infants: 10 mg • Children: 10 mg • Adolescents: 15 mg • Pregnancy: 25 mg • Lactation: 10 mg	Anemia; impaired mental, cognitive, and emotional development; impaired immunity

KEY POINTS

- Growth is a continuous process in childhood.
- Assessment of growth on repeated occasions over a period of time is essential to detect any deviation from the normal growth pattern.
- Accurate measurement of anthropometric parameters, e.g., height, weight, and head circumference, with correct technique is important before interpretation.
- Mid–upper arm circumference is an age-independent parameter for assessment of nutritional status in children up to 5 years of age.
- Midparental height (MPH) should be calculated in all children with suspected short stature.
- Body mass index (BMI) should be calculated for children with suspected overweight/obesity.

Appendix I

WHO Child Growth Standards

Weight-for-Length for Boys from Birth to 2 Years (*Z* Scores)

Length (cm)	−3SD	−2SD	−1SD	Median	1SD	2SD	3SD
45.0	1.9	2.0	2.2	2.4	2.7	3.0	3.3
45.5	1.9	2.1	2.3	2.5	2.8	3.1	3.4
46.0	2.0	2.2	2.4	2.6	2.9	3.1	3.5
46.5	2.1	2.3	2.5	2.7	3.0	3.2	3.6
47.0	2.1	2.3	2.5	2.8	3.0	3.3	3.7
47.5	2.2	2.4	2.6	2.9	3.1	3.4	3.8
48.0	2.3	2.5	2.7	2.9	3.2	3.6	3.9
48.5	2.3	2.6	2.8	3.0	3.3	3.7	4.0
49.0	2.4	2.6	2.9	3.1	3.4	3.8	4.2
49.5	2.5	2.7	3.0	3.2	3.5	3.9	4.3
50.0	2.6	2.8	3.0	3.3	3.6	4.0	4.4
50.5	2.7	2.9	3.1	3.4	3.8	4.1	4.5
51.0	2.7	3.0	3.2	3.5	3.9	4.2	4.7
51.5	2.8	3.1	3.3	3.6	4.0	4.4	4.8
52.0	2.9	3.2	3.5	3.8	4.1	4.5	5.0
52.5	3.0	3.3	3.6	3.9	4.2	4.6	5.1
53.0	3.1	3.4	3.7	4.0	4.4	4.8	5.3
53.5	3.2	3.5	3.8	4.1	4.5	4.9	5.4
54.0	3.3	3.6	3.9	4.3	4.7	5.1	5.6
54.5	3.4	3.7	4.0	4.4	4.8	5.3	5.8
55.0	3.6	3.8	4.2	4.5	5.0	5.4	6.0
55.5	3.7	4.0	4.3	4.7	5.1	5.6	6.1
56.0	3.8	4.1	4.4	4.8	5.3	5.8	6.3
56.5	3.9	4.2	4.6	5.0	5.4	5.9	6.5
57.0	4.0	4.3	4.7	5.1	5.6	6.1	6.7
57.5	4.1	4.5	4.9	5.3	5.7	6.3	6.9
58.0	4.3	4.6	5.0	5.4	5.9	6.4	7.1
58.5	4.4	4.7	5.1	5.6	6.1	6.6	7.2
59.0	4.5	4.8	5.3	5.7	6.2	6.8	7.4
59.5	4.6	5.0	5.4	5.9	6.4	7.0	7.6
60.0	4.7	5.1	5.5	6.0	6.5	7.1	7.8
60.5	4.8	5.2	5.6	6.1	6.7	7.3	8.0
61.0	4.9	5.3	5.8	6.3	6.8	7.4	8.1
61.5	5.0	5.4	5.9	6.4	7.0	7.6	8.3
62.0	5.1	5.6	6.0	6.5	7.1	7.7	8.5

(Continued)

(Continued)

Length (cm)	−3SD	−2SD	−1SD	Median	1SD	2SD	3SD
62.5	5.2	5.7	6.1	6.7	7.2	7.9	8.6
63.0	5.3	5.8	6.2	6.8	7.4	8.0	8.8
63.5	5.4	5.9	6.4	6.9	7.5	8.2	8.9
64.0	5.5	6.0	6.5	7.0	7.6	8.3	9.1
64.5	5.6	6.1	6.6	7.1	7.8	8.5	9.3
65.0	5.7	6.2	6.7	7.3	7.9	8.6	9.4
65.5	5.8	6.3	6.8	7.4	8.0	8.7	9.6
66.0	5.9	6.4	6.9	7.5	8.2	8.9	9.7
66.5	6.0	6.5	7.0	7.6	8.3	9.0	9.9
67.0	6.1	6.6	7.1	7.7	8.4	9.2	10.0
67.5	6.2	6.7	7.2	7.9	8.5	9.3	10.2
68.0	6.3	6.8	7.3	8.0	8.7	9.4	10.3
68.5	6.4	6.9	7.5	8.1	8.8	9.6	10.5
69.0	6.5	7.0	7.6	8.2	8.9	9.7	10.6
69.5	6.6	7.1	7.7	8.3	9.0	9.8	10.8
70.0	6.6	7.2	7.8	8.4	9.2	10.0	10.9
70.5	6.7	7.3	7.9	8.5	9.3	10.1	11.1
71.0	6.8	7.4	8.0	8.6	9.4	10.2	11.2
71.5	6.9	7.5	8.1	8.8	9.5	10.4	11.3
72.0	7.0	7.6	8.2	8.9	9.6	10.5	11.5
72.5	7.1	7.6	8.3	9.0	9.8	10.6	11.6
73.0	7.2	7.7	8.4	9.1	9.9	10.8	11.8
73.5	7.2	7.8	8.5	9.2	10.0	10.9	11.9
74.0	7.3	7.9	8.6	9.3	10.1	11.0	12.1
74.5	7.4	8.0	8.7	9.4	10.2	11.2	12.2
75.0	7.5	8.1	8.8	9.5	10.3	11.3	12.3
75.5	7.6	8.2	8.8	9.6	10.4	11.4	12.5
76.0	7.6	8.3	8.9	9.7	10.6	11.5	12.6
76.5	7.7	8.3	9.0	9.8	10.7	11.6	12.7
77.0	7.8	8.4	9.1	9.9	10.8	11.7	12.8
77.5	7.9	8.5	9.2	10.0	10.9	11.9	13.0
78.0	7.9	8.6	9.3	10.1	11.0	12.0	13.1
78.5	8.0	8.7	9.4	10.2	11.1	12.1	13.2
79.0	8.1	8.7	9.5	10.3	11.2	12.2	13.3
79.5	8.2	8.8	9.5	10.4	11.3	12.3	13.4
80.0	8.2	8.9	9.6	10.4	11.4	12.4	13.6
80.5	8.3	9.0	9.7	10.5	11.5	12.5	13.7
81.0	8.4	9.1	9.8	10.6	11.6	12.6	13.8
81.5	8.5	9.1	9.9	10.7	11.7	12.7	13.9
82.0	8.5	9.2	10.0	10.8	11.8	12.8	14.0
82.5	8.6	9.3	10.1	10.9	11.9	13.0	14.2

(Continued)

(Continued)

Length (cm)	−3SD	−2SD	−1SD	Median	1SD	2SD	3SD
83.0	8.7	9.4	10.2	11.0	12.0	13.1	14.3
83.5	8.8	9.5	10.3	11.2	12.1	13.2	14.4
84.0	8.9	9.6	10.4	11.3	12.2	13.3	14.6
84.5	9.0	9.7	10.5	11.4	12.4	13.5	14.7
85.0	9.1	9.8	10.6	11.5	12.5	13.6	14.9
85.5	9.2	9.9	10.7	11.6	12.6	13.7	15.0
86.0	9.3	10.0	10.8	11.7	12.8	13.9	15.2
86.5	9.4	10.1	11.0	11.9	12.9	14.0	15.3
87.0	9.5	10.2	11.1	12.0	13.0	14.2	15.5
87.5	9.6	10.4	11.2	12.1	13.2	14.3	15.6
88.0	9.7	10.5	11.3	12.2	13.3	14.5	15.8
88.5	9.8	10.6	11.4	12.4	13.4	14.6	15.9
89.0	9.9	10.7	11.5	12.5	13.5	14.7	16.1
89.5	10.0	10.8	11.6	12.6	13.7	14.9	16.2
90.0	10.1	10.9	11.8	12.7	13.8	15.0	16.4
90.5	10.2	11.0	11.9	12.8	13.9	15.1	16.5
91.0	10.3	11.1	12.0	13.0	14.1	15.3	16.7
91.5	10.4	11.2	12.1	13.1	14.2	15.4	16.8
92.0	10.5	11.3	12.2	13.2	14.3	15.6	17.0
92.5	10.6	11.4	12.3	13.3	14.4	15.7	17.1
93.0	10.7	11.5	12.4	13.4	14.6	15.8	17.3
93.5	10.7	11.6	12.5	13.5	14.7	16.0	17.4
94.0	10.8	11.7	12.6	13.7	14.8	16.1	17.6
94.5	10.9	11.8	12.7	13.8	14.9	16.3	17.7
95.0	11.0	11.9	12.8	13.9	15.1	16.4	17.9
95.5	11.1	12.0	12.9	14.0	15.2	16.5	18.0
96.0	11.2	12.1	13.1	14.1	15.3	16.7	18.2
96.5	11.3	12.2	13.2	14.3	15.5	16.8	18.4
97.0	11.4	12.3	13.3	14.4	15.6	17.0	18.5
97.5	11.5	12.4	13.4	14.5	15.7	17.1	18.7
98.0	11.6	12.5	13.5	14.6	15.9	17.3	18.9
98.5	11.7	12.6	13.6	14.8	16.0	17.5	19.1
99.0	11.8	12.7	13.7	14.9	16.2	17.6	19.2
99.5	11.9	12.8	13.9	15.0	16.3	17.8	19.4
100.0	12.0	12.9	14.0	15.2	16.5	18.0	19.6
100.5	12.1	13.0	14.1	15.3	16.6	18.1	19.8
101.0	12.2	13.2	14.2	15.4	16.8	18.3	20.0
101.5	12.3	13.3	14.4	15.6	16.9	18.5	20.2
102.0	12.4	13.4	14.5	15.7	17.1	18.7	20.4
102.5	12.5	13.5	14.6	15.9	17.3	18.8	20.6
103.0	12.6	13.6	14.8	16.0	17.4	19.0	20.8

(Continued)

(Continued)

Length (cm)	–3SD	–2SD	–1SD	Median	1SD	2SD	3SD
103.5	12.7	13.7	14.9	16.2	17.6	19.2	21.0
104.0	12.8	13.9	15.0	16.3	17.8	19.4	21.2
104.5	12.9	14.0	15.2	16.5	17.9	19.6	21.5
105.0	13.0	14.1	15.3	16.6	18.1	19.8	21.7
105.5	13.2	14.2	15.4	16.8	18.3	20.0	21.9
106.0	13.3	14.4	15.6	16.9	18.5	20.2	22.1
106.5	13.4	14.5	15.7	17.1	18.6	20.4	22.4
107.0	13.5	14.6	15.9	17.3	18.8	20.6	22.6
107.5	13.6	14.7	16.0	17.4	19.0	20.8	22.8
108.0	13.7	14.9	16.2	17.6	19.2	21.0	23.1
108.5	13.8	15.0	16.3	17.8	19.4	21.2	23.3
109.0	14.0	15.1	16.5	17.9	19.6	21.4	23.6
109.5	14.1	15.3	16.6	18.1	19.8	21.7	23.8
110.0	14.2	15.4	16.8	18.3	20.0	21.9	24.1

Weight-for-Length for Boys from Birth to 2 Years (Percentiles)

Length (cm)	3rd	15th	Median	85th	97th
45.0	2.1	2.2	2.4	2.7	2.9
45.5	2.1	2.3	2.5	2.8	3.0
46.0	2.2	2.4	2.6	2.9	3.1
46.5	2.3	2.5	2.7	3.0	3.2
47.0	2.4	2.5	2.8	3.1	3.3
47.5	2.4	2.6	2.9	3.1	3.4
48.0	2.5	2.7	2.9	3.2	3.5
48.5	2.6	2.8	3.0	3.3	3.6
49.0	2.7	2.9	3.1	3.4	3.7
49.5	2.7	2.9	3.2	3.5	3.8
50.0	2.8	3.0	3.3	3.7	4.0
50.5	2.9	3.1	3.4	3.8	4.1
51.0	3.0	3.2	3.5	3.9	4.2
51.5	3.1	3.3	3.6	4.0	4.3
52.0	3.2	3.4	3.8	4.1	4.5
52.5	3.3	3.6	3.9	4.3	4.6
53.0	3.4	3.7	4.0	4.4	4.7
53.5	3.5	3.8	4.1	4.5	4.9
54.0	3.6	3.9	4.3	4.7	5.0
54.5	3.8	4.0	4.4	4.8	5.2
55.0	3.9	4.2	4.5	5.0	5.4
55.5	4.0	4.3	4.7	5.1	5.5
56.0	4.1	4.4	4.8	5.3	5.7

(Continued)

(Continued)

Length (cm)	3rd	15th	Median	85th	97th
56.5	4.3	4.6	5.0	5.4	5.9
57.0	4.4	4.7	5.1	5.6	6.0
57.5	4.5	4.8	5.3	5.8	6.2
58.0	4.6	5.0	5.4	5.9	6.4
58.5	4.8	5.1	5.6	6.1	6.5
59.0	4.9	5.2	5.7	6.2	6.7
59.5	5.0	5.4	5.9	6.4	6.9
60.0	5.1	5.5	6.0	6.5	7.0
60.5	5.3	5.6	6.1	6.7	7.2
61.0	5.4	5.8	6.3	6.8	7.4
61.5	5.5	5.9	6.4	7.0	7.5
62.0	5.6	6.0	6.5	7.1	7.7
62.5	5.7	6.1	6.7	7.3	7.8
63.0	5.8	6.2	6.8	7.4	8.0
63.5	5.9	6.3	6.9	7.5	8.1
64.0	6.0	6.5	7.0	7.7	8.2
64.5	6.1	6.6	7.1	7.8	8.4
65.0	6.3	6.7	7.3	7.9	8.5
65.5	6.4	6.8	7.4	8.1	8.7
66.0	6.5	6.9	7.5	8.2	8.8
66.5	6.6	7.0	7.6	8.3	8.9
67.0	6.7	7.1	7.7	8.4	9.1
67.5	6.8	7.2	7.9	8.6	9.2
68.0	6.9	7.3	8.0	8.7	9.3
68.5	7.0	7.4	8.1	8.8	9.5
69.0	7.1	7.5	8.2	8.9	9.6
69.5	7.1	7.6	8.3	9.1	9.7
70.0	7.2	7.7	8.4	9.2	9.9
70.5	7.3	7.8	8.5	9.3	10.0
71.0	7.4	8.0	8.6	9.4	10.1
71.5	7.5	8.1	8.8	9.6	10.3
72.0	7.6	8.2	8.9	9.7	10.4
72.5	7.7	8.3	9.0	9.8	10.5
73.0	7.8	8.4	9.1	9.9	10.7
73.5	7.9	8.4	9.2	10.0	10.8
74.0	8.0	8.5	9.3	10.1	10.9
74.5	8.1	8.6	9.4	10.3	11.0
75.0	8.2	8.7	9.5	10.4	11.2
75.5	8.2	8.8	9.6	10.5	11.3
76.0	8.3	8.9	9.7	10.6	11.4
76.5	8.4	9.0	9.8	10.7	11.5

(Continued)

(Continued)

Length (cm)	3rd	15th	Median	85th	97th
77.0	8.5	9.1	9.9	10.8	11.6
77.5	8.6	9.2	10.0	10.9	11.7
78.0	8.7	9.3	10.1	11.0	11.8
78.5	8.7	9.3	10.2	11.1	12.0
79.0	8.8	9.4	10.3	11.2	12.1
79.5	8.9	9.5	10.4	11.3	12.2
80.0	9.0	9.6	10.4	11.4	12.3
80.5	9.1	9.7	10.5	11.5	12.4
81.0	9.1	9.8	10.6	11.6	12.5
81.5	9.2	9.9	10.7	11.7	12.6
82.0	9.3	10.0	10.8	11.8	12.7
82.5	9.4	10.1	10.9	11.9	12.8
83.0	9.5	10.1	11.0	12.0	13.0
83.5	9.6	10.3	11.2	12.2	13.1
84.0	9.7	10.4	11.3	12.3	13.2
84.5	9.8	10.5	11.4	12.4	13.3
85.0	9.9	10.6	11.5	12.5	13.5
85.5	10.0	10.7	11.6	12.7	13.6
86.0	10.1	10.8	11.7	12.8	13.7
86.5	10.2	10.9	11.9	12.9	13.9
87.0	10.3	11.0	12.0	13.1	14.0
87.5	10.4	11.2	12.1	13.2	14.2
88.0	10.6	11.3	12.2	13.3	14.3
88.5	10.7	11.4	12.4	13.5	14.4
89.0	10.8	11.5	12.5	13.6	14.6
89.5	10.9	11.6	12.6	13.7	14.7
90.0	11.0	11.7	12.7	13.8	14.9
90.5	11.1	11.8	12.8	14.0	15.0
91.0	11.2	11.9	13.0	14.1	15.1
91.5	11.3	12.0	13.1	14.2	15.3
92.0	11.4	12.2	13.2	14.4	15.4
92.5	11.5	12.3	13.3	14.5	15.5
93.0	11.6	12.4	13.4	14.6	15.7
93.5	11.7	12.5	13.5	14.7	15.8
94.0	11.8	12.6	13.7	14.9	16.0
94.5	11.9	12.7	13.8	15.0	16.1
95.0	12.0	12.8	13.9	15.1	16.2
95.5	12.1	12.9	14.0	15.3	16.4
96.0	12.2	13.0	14.1	15.4	16.5
96.5	12.3	13.1	14.3	15.5	16.7
97.0	12.4	13.2	14.4	15.7	16.8

(Continued)

(Continued)

Length (cm)	3rd	15th	Median	85th	97th
97.5	12.5	13.4	14.5	15.8	17.0
98.0	12.6	13.5	14.6	15.9	17.1
98.5	12.7	13.6	14.8	16.1	17.3
99.0	12.8	13.7	14.9	16.2	17.4
99.5	12.9	13.8	15.0	16.4	17.6
100.0	13.0	13.9	15.2	16.5	17.8
100.5	13.2	14.1	15.3	16.7	17.9
101.0	13.3	14.2	15.4	16.8	18.1
101.5	13.4	14.3	15.6	17.0	18.3
102.0	13.5	14.5	15.7	17.2	18.5
102.5	13.6	14.6	15.9	17.3	18.6
103.0	13.8	14.7	16.0	17.5	18.8
103.5	13.9	14.8	16.2	17.7	19.0
104.0	14.0	15.0	16.3	17.8	19.2
104.5	14.1	15.1	16.5	18.0	19.4
105.0	14.2	15.3	16.6	18.2	19.6
105.5	14.4	15.4	16.8	18.4	19.8
106.0	14.5	15.5	16.9	18.5	20.0
106.5	14.6	15.7	17.1	18.7	20.2
107.0	14.8	15.8	17.3	18.9	20.4
107.5	14.9	16.0	17.4	19.1	20.6
108.0	15.0	16.1	17.6	19.3	20.8
108.5	15.2	16.3	17.8	19.5	21.0
109.0	15.3	16.4	17.9	19.6	21.2
109.5	15.4	16.6	18.1	19.8	21.4
110.0	15.6	16.7	18.3	20.0	21.6

APPENDIX II

WHO Child Growth Standards

Weight-for-Length for Girls from Birth to 2 Years (*Z* Scores)

Length (cm)	−3SD	−2SD	−1SD	Median	1SD	2SD	3SD
45.0	1.9	2.1	2.3	2.5	2.7	3.0	3.3
45.5	2.0	2.1	2.3	2.5	2.8	3.1	3.4
46.0	2.0	2.2	2.4	2.6	2.9	3.2	3.5
46.5	2.1	2.3	2.5	2.7	3.0	3.3	3.6
47.0	2.2	2.4	2.6	2.8	3.1	3.4	3.7
47.5	2.2	2.4	2.6	2.9	3.2	3.5	3.8
48.0	2.3	2.5	2.7	3.0	3.3	3.6	4.0
48.5	2.4	2.6	2.8	3.1	3.4	3.7	4.1
49.0	2.4	2.6	2.9	3.2	3.5	3.8	4.2
49.5	2.5	2.7	3.0	3.3	3.6	3.9	4.3
50.0	2.6	2.8	3.1	3.4	3.7	4.0	4.5
50.5	2.7	2.9	3.2	3.5	3.8	4.2	4.6
51.0	2.8	3.0	3.3	3.6	3.9	4.3	4.8
51.5	2.8	3.1	3.4	3.7	4.0	4.4	4.9
52.0	2.9	3.2	3.5	3.8	4.2	4.6	5.1
52.5	3.0	3.3	3.6	3.9	4.3	4.7	5.2
53.0	3.1	3.4	3.7	4.0	4.4	4.9	5.4
53.5	3.2	3.5	3.8	4.2	4.6	5.0	5.5
54.0	3.3	3.6	3.9	4.3	4.7	5.2	5.7
54.5	3.4	3.7	4.0	4.4	4.8	5.3	5.9
55.0	3.5	3.8	4.2	4.5	5.0	5.5	6.1
55.5	3.6	3.9	4.3	4.7	5.1	5.7	6.3
56.0	3.7	4.0	4.4	4.8	5.3	5.8	6.4
56.5	3.8	4.1	4.5	5.0	5.4	6.0	6.6
57.0	3.9	4.3	4.6	5.1	5.6	6.1	6.8
57.5	4.0	4.4	4.8	5.2	5.7	6.3	7.0
58.0	4.1	4.5	4.9	5.4	5.9	6.5	7.1
58.5	4.2	4.6	5.0	5.5	6.0	6.6	7.3
59.0	4.3	4.7	5.1	5.6	6.2	6.8	7.5
59.5	4.4	4.8	5.3	5.7	6.3	6.9	7.7
60.0	4.5	4.9	5.4	5.9	6.4	7.1	7.8
60.5	4.6	5.0	5.5	6.0	6.6	7.3	8.0
61.0	4.7	5.1	5.6	6.1	6.7	7.4	8.2
61.5	4.8	5.2	5.7	6.3	6.9	7.6	8.4
62.0	4.9	5.3	5.8	6.4	7.0	7.7	8.5
62.5	5.0	5.4	5.9	6.5	7.1	7.8	8.7

(Continued)

(Continued)

Length (cm)	−3SD	−2SD	−1SD	Median	1SD	2SD	3SD
63.0	5.1	5.5	6.0	6.6	7.3	8.0	8.8
63.5	5.2	5.6	6.2	6.7	7.4	8.1	9.0
64.0	5.3	5.7	6.3	6.9	7.5	8.3	9.1
64.5	5.4	5.8	6.4	7.0	7.6	8.4	9.3
65.0	5.5	5.9	6.5	7.1	7.8	8.6	9.5
65.5	5.5	6.0	6.6	7.2	7.9	8.7	9.6
66.0	5.6	6.1	6.7	7.3	8.0	8.8	9.8
66.5	5.7	6.2	6.8	7.4	8.1	9.0	9.9
67.0	5.8	6.3	6.9	7.5	8.3	9.1	10.0
67.5	5.9	6.4	7.0	7.6	8.4	9.2	10.2
68.0	6.0	6.5	7.1	7.7	8.5	9.4	10.3
68.5	6.1	6.6	7.2	7.9	8.6	9.5	10.5
69.0	6.1	6.7	7.3	8.0	8.7	9.6	10.6
69.5	6.2	6.8	7.4	8.1	8.8	9.7	10.7
70.0	6.3	6.9	7.5	8.2	9.0	9.9	10.9
70.5	6.4	6.9	7.6	8.3	9.1	10.0	11.0
71.0	6.5	7.0	7.7	8.4	9.2	10.1	11.1
71.5	6.5	7.1	7.7	8.5	9.3	10.2	11.3
72.0	6.6	7.2	7.8	8.6	9.4	10.3	11.4
72.5	6.7	7.3	7.9	8.7	9.5	10.5	11.5
73.0	6.8	7.4	8.0	8.8	9.6	10.6	11.7
73.5	6.9	7.4	8.1	8.9	9.7	10.7	11.8
74.0	6.9	7.5	8.2	9.0	9.8	10.8	11.9
74.5	7.0	7.6	8.3	9.1	9.9	10.9	12.0
75.0	7.1	7.7	8.4	9.1	10.0	11.0	12.2
75.5	7.1	7.8	8.5	9.2	10.1	11.1	12.3
76.0	7.2	7.8	8.5	9.3	10.2	11.2	12.4
76.5	7.3	7.9	8.6	9.4	10.3	11.4	12.5
77.0	7.4	8.0	8.7	9.5	10.4	11.5	12.6
77.5	7.4	8.1	8.8	9.6	10.5	11.6	12.8
78.0	7.5	8.2	8.9	9.7	10.6	11.7	12.9
78.5	7.6	8.2	9.0	9.8	10.7	11.8	13.0
79.0	7.7	8.3	9.1	9.9	10.8	11.9	13.1
79.5	7.7	8.4	9.1	10.0	10.9	12.0	13.3
80.0	7.8	8.5	9.2	10.1	11.0	12.1	13.4
80.5	7.9	8.6	9.3	10.2	11.2	12.3	13.5
81.0	8.0	8.7	9.4	10.3	11.3	12.4	13.7
81.5	8.1	8.8	9.5	10.4	11.4	12.5	13.8
82.0	8.1	8.8	9.6	10.5	11.5	12.6	13.9
82.5	8.2	8.9	9.7	10.6	11.6	12.8	14.1
83.0	8.3	9.0	9.8	10.7	11.8	12.9	14.2

(Continued)

(Continued)

Length (cm)	−3SD	−2SD	−1SD	Median	1SD	2SD	3SD
83.5	8.4	9.1	9.9	10.9	11.9	13.1	14.4
84.0	8.5	9.2	10.1	11.0	12.0	13.2	14.5
84.5	8.6	9.3	10.2	11.1	12.1	13.3	14.7
85.0	8.7	9.4	10.3	11.2	12.3	13.5	14.9
85.5	8.8	9.5	10.4	11.3	12.4	13.6	15.0
86.0	8.9	9.7	10.5	11.5	12.6	13.8	15.2
86.5	9.0	9.8	10.6	11.6	12.7	13.9	15.4
87.0	9.1	9.9	10.7	11.7	12.8	14.1	15.5
87.5	9.2	10.0	10.9	11.8	13.0	14.2	15.7
88.0	9.3	10.1	11.0	12.0	13.1	14.4	15.9
88.5	9.4	10.2	11.1	12.1	13.2	14.5	16.0
89.0	9.5	10.3	11.2	12.2	13.4	14.7	16.2
89.5	9.6	10.4	11.3	12.3	13.5	14.8	16.4
90.0	9.7	10.5	11.4	12.5	13.7	15.0	16.5
90.5	9.8	10.6	11.5	12.6	13.8	15.1	16.7
91.0	9.9	10.7	11.7	12.7	13.9	15.3	16.9
91.5	10.0	10.8	11.8	12.8	14.1	15.5	17.0
92.0	10.1	10.9	11.9	13.0	14.2	15.6	17.2
92.5	10.1	11.0	12.0	13.1	14.3	15.8	17.4
93.0	10.2	11.1	12.1	13.2	14.5	15.9	17.5
93.5	10.3	11.2	12.2	13.3	14.6	16.1	17.7
94.0	10.4	11.3	12.3	13.5	14.7	16.2	17.9
94.5	10.5	11.4	12.4	13.6	14.9	16.4	18.0
95.0	10.6	11.5	12.6	13.7	15.0	16.5	18.2
95.5	10.7	11.6	12.7	13.8	15.2	16.7	18.4
96.0	10.8	11.7	12.8	14.0	15.3	16.8	18.6
96.5	10.9	11.8	12.9	14.1	15.4	17.0	18.7
97.0	11.0	12.0	13.0	14.2	15.6	17.1	18.9
97.5	11.1	12.1	13.1	14.4	15.7	17.3	19.1
98.0	11.2	12.2	13.3	14.5	15.9	17.5	19.3
98.5	11.3	12.3	13.4	14.6	16.0	17.6	19.5
99.0	11.4	12.4	13.5	14.8	16.2	17.8	19.6
99.5	11.5	12.5	13.6	14.9	16.3	18.0	19.8
100.0	11.6	12.6	13.7	15.0	16.5	18.1	20.0
100.5	11.7	12.7	13.9	15.2	16.6	18.3	20.2
101.0	11.8	12.8	14.0	15.3	16.8	18.5	20.4
101.5	11.9	13.0	14.1	15.5	17.0	18.7	20.6
102.0	12.0	13.1	14.3	15.6	17.1	18.9	20.8
102.5	12.1	13.2	14.4	15.8	17.3	19.0	21.0
103.0	12.3	13.3	14.5	15.9	17.5	19.2	21.3
103.5	12.4	13.5	14.7	16.1	17.6	19.4	21.5

(Continued)

(Continued)

Length (cm)	−3SD	−2SD	−1SD	Median	1SD	2SD	3SD
104.0	12.5	13.6	14.8	16.2	17.8	19.6	21.7
104.5	12.6	13.7	15.0	16.4	18.0	19.8	21.9
105.0	12.7	13.8	15.1	16.5	18.2	20.0	22.2
105.5	12.8	14.0	15.3	16.7	18.4	20.2	22.4
106.0	13.0	14.1	15.4	16.9	18.5	20.5	22.6
106.5	13.1	14.3	15.6	17.1	18.7	20.7	22.9
107.0	13.2	14.4	15.7	17.2	18.9	20.9	23.1
107.5	13.3	14.5	15.9	17.4	19.1	21.1	23.4
108.0	13.5	14.7	16.0	17.6	19.3	21.3	23.6
108.5	13.6	14.8	16.2	17.8	19.5	21.6	23.9
109.0	13.7	15.0	16.4	18.0	19.7	21.8	24.2
109.5	13.9	15.1	16.5	18.1	20.0	22.0	24.4
110.0	14.0	15.3	16.7	18.3	20.2	22.3	24.7

Weight-for-Length for Girls from Birth to 2 Years (Percentiles)

Length (cm)	3rd	15th	Median	85th	97th
45.0	2.1	2.2	2.5	2.7	2.9
45.5	2.2	2.3	2.5	2.8	3.0
46.0	2.2	2.4	2.6	2.9	3.1
46.5	2.3	2.5	2.7	3.0	3.2
47.0	2.4	2.6	2.8	3.1	3.3
47.5	2.4	2.6	2.9	3.2	3.4
48.0	2.5	2.7	3.0	3.3	3.5
48.5	2.6	2.8	3.1	3.4	3.7
49.0	2.7	2.9	3.2	3.5	3.8
49.5	2.8	3.0	3.3	3.6	3.9
50.0	2.8	3.1	3.4	3.7	4.0
50.5	2.9	3.2	3.5	3.8	4.1
51.0	3.0	3.2	3.6	3.9	4.3
51.5	3.1	3.4	3.7	4.0	4.4
52.0	3.2	3.5	3.8	4.2	4.5
52.5	3.3	3.6	3.9	4.3	4.7
53.0	3.4	3.7	4.0	4.4	4.8
53.5	3.5	3.8	4.2	4.6	5.0
54.0	3.6	3.9	4.3	4.7	5.1
54.5	3.7	4.0	4.4	4.9	5.3
55.0	3.9	4.1	4.5	5.0	5.4
55.5	4.0	4.3	4.7	5.2	5.6
56.0	4.1	4.4	4.8	5.3	5.8
56.5	4.2	4.5	5.0	5.5	5.9
57.0	4.3	4.6	5.1	5.6	6.1

(Continued)

(Continued)

Length (cm)	3rd	15th	Median	85th	97th
57.5	4.4	4.8	5.2	5.7	6.2
58.0	4.5	4.9	5.4	5.9	6.4
58.5	4.6	5.0	5.5	6.0	6.5
59.0	4.8	5.1	5.6	6.2	6.7
59.5	4.9	5.2	5.7	6.3	6.9
60.0	5.0	5.4	5.9	6.5	7.0
60.5	5.1	5.5	6.0	6.6	7.2
61.0	5.2	5.6	6.1	6.7	7.3
61.5	5.3	5.7	6.3	6.9	7.5
62.0	5.4	5.8	6.4	7.0	7.6
62.5	5.5	5.9	6.5	7.2	7.8
63.0	5.6	6.0	6.6	7.3	7.9
63.5	5.7	6.1	6.7	7.4	8.0
64.0	5.8	6.2	6.9	7.5	8.2
64.5	5.9	6.3	7.0	7.7	8.3
65.0	6.0	6.5	7.1	7.8	8.5
65.5	6.1	6.6	7.2	7.9	8.6
66.0	6.2	6.7	7.3	8.0	8.7
66.5	6.3	6.8	7.4	8.2	8.9
67.0	6.4	6.9	7.5	8.3	9.0
67.5	6.5	7.0	7.6	8.4	9.1
68.0	6.6	7.1	7.7	8.5	9.2
68.5	6.7	7.2	7.9	8.6	9.4
69.0	6.7	7.3	8.0	8.8	9.5
69.5	6.8	7.3	8.1	8.9	9.6
70.0	6.9	7.4	8.2	9.0	9.7
70.5	7.0	7.5	8.3	9.1	9.9
71.0	7.1	7.6	8.4	9.2	10.0
71.5	7.2	7.7	8.5	9.3	10.1
72.0	7.3	7.8	8.6	9.4	10.2
72.5	7.4	7.9	8.7	9.5	10.3
73.0	7.4	8.0	8.8	9.6	10.4
73.5	7.5	8.1	8.9	9.7	10.6
74.0	7.6	8.2	9.0	9.9	10.7
74.5	7.7	8.3	9.1	10.0	10.8
75.0	7.8	8.3	9.1	10.1	10.9
75.5	7.8	8.4	9.2	10.2	11.0
76.0	7.9	8.5	9.3	10.3	11.1
76.5	8.0	8.6	9.4	10.4	11.2
77.0	8.1	8.7	9.5	10.5	11.3
77.5	8.2	8.8	9.6	10.6	11.4

(Continued)

(Continued)

Length (cm)	3rd	15th	Median	85th	97th
78.0	8.2	8.9	9.7	10.7	11.5
78.5	8.3	8.9	9.8	10.8	11.7
79.0	8.4	9.0	9.9	10.9	11.8
79.5	8.5	9.1	10.0	11.0	11.9
80.0	8.6	9.2	10.1	11.1	12.0
80.5	8.7	9.3	10.2	11.2	12.1
81.0	8.8	9.4	10.3	11.3	12.2
81.5	8.8	9.5	10.4	11.4	12.4
82.0	8.9	9.6	10.5	11.6	12.5
82.5	9.0	9.7	10.6	11.7	12.6
83.0	9.1	9.8	10.7	11.8	12.8
83.5	9.2	9.9	10.9	11.9	12.9
84.0	9.3	10.0	11.0	12.1	13.1
84.5	9.4	10.1	11.1	12.2	13.2
85.0	9.5	10.2	11.2	12.3	13.3
85.5	9.6	10.4	11.3	12.5	13.5
86.0	9.8	10.5	11.5	12.6	13.6
86.5	9.9	10.6	11.6	12.7	13.8
87.0	10.0	10.7	11.7	12.9	13.9
87.5	10.1	10.8	11.8	13.0	14.1
88.0	10.2	10.9	12.0	13.2	14.2
88.5	10.3	11.0	12.1	13.3	14.4
89.0	10.4	11.2	12.2	13.4	14.5
89.5	10.5	11.3	12.3	13.6	14.7
90.0	10.6	11.4	12.5	13.7	14.8
90.5	10.7	11.5	12.6	13.8	15.0
91.0	10.8	11.6	12.7	14.0	15.1
91.5	10.9	11.7	12.8	14.1	15.3
92.0	11.0	11.8	13.0	14.2	15.4
92.5	11.1	12.0	13.1	14.4	15.6
93.0	11.2	12.1	13.2	14.5	15.7
93.5	11.3	12.2	13.3	14.7	15.9
94.0	11.4	12.3	13.5	14.8	16.0
94.5	11.5	12.4	13.6	14.9	16.2
95.0	11.6	12.5	13.7	15.1	16.3
95.5	11.8	12.6	13.8	15.2	16.5
96.0	11.9	12.7	14.0	15.4	16.6
96.5	12.0	12.9	14.1	15.5	16.8
97.0	12.1	13.0	14.2	15.6	16.9
97.5	12.2	13.1	14.4	15.8	17.1
98.0	12.3	13.2	14.5	15.9	17.3

(Continued)

(Continued)

Length (cm)	3rd	15th	Median	85th	97th
98.5	12.4	13.3	14.6	16.1	17.4
99.0	12.5	13.5	14.8	16.2	17.6
99.5	12.6	13.6	14.9	16.4	17.8
100.0	12.7	13.7	15.0	16.5	17.9
100.5	12.9	13.8	15.2	16.7	18.1
101.0	13.0	14.0	15.3	16.9	18.3
101.5	13.1	14.1	15.5	17.0	18.5
102.0	13.2	14.2	15.6	17.2	18.6
102.5	13.3	14.4	15.8	17.4	18.8
103.0	13.5	14.5	15.9	17.5	19.0
103.5	13.6	14.6	16.1	17.7	19.2
104.0	13.7	14.8	16.2	17.9	19.4
104.5	13.9	14.9	16.4	18.1	19.6
105.0	14.0	15.1	16.5	18.2	19.8
105.5	14.1	15.2	16.7	18.4	20.0
106.0	14.3	15.4	16.9	18.6	20.2
106.5	14.4	15.5	17.1	18.8	20.4
107.0	14.5	15.7	17.2	19.0	20.6
107.5	14.7	15.8	17.4	19.2	20.9
108.0	14.8	16.0	17.6	19.4	21.1
108.5	15.0	16.2	17.8	19.6	21.3
109.0	15.1	16.3	18.0	19.8	21.5
109.5	15.3	16.5	18.1	20.0	21.8
110.0	15.4	16.7	18.3	20.2	22.0

CHAPTER 4

The Normal Development

Pratap Kumar Patra, Paresh A Thakkar, Habib Bhurawala

Development is a complex process where maturation of specific functions occurs, and it is related to myelination of the central nervous system. It is intricately influenced by a combination of genetic, biological, and psychosocial factors. Children grow and develop at different rates. However, each child must pass through an identifiable skill set along the way, called *developmental milestones*; these are skills that build on each other, from simple to complex, during a predictable period. Thus, the term "child development" broadly refers to the skills acquired by children from birth to about 5 years of age.

Laws of Development

- Development is a continuous process from conception to maturity.
- The sequence of development is same in all children, but the rate of development can vary in individual cases.
- Development is intimately related to maturation/myelination of the nervous system. The normal development needs an intact anatomical and functionally normal central nervous system and its pathways. A child who has suffered from any brain insult (hypoxic, infective, or metabolic) during infancy and early childhood may have delayed/abnormal development.
- The development proceeds in a cephalocaudal direction. Thus, a child must learn to hold his/her head before he/she learns to sit/stand.
- Generalized mass activity is replaced by specific individual responses. Initially, the young infant can widely move his/her trunk, arms, and legs, and pants with excitement when he/she sees something; with time, this is replaced by merely a smile and the attempt of reaching toward the object.
- Certain primitive reflexes have to be lost before acquiring corresponding voluntary movement. A child cannot develop finger–thumb apposition (pincer grasp) unless he/she loses the primitive grasp reflex.
- The development in one field may not be parallel to that in other field(s) and this is termed *developmental dissociation*.
- Persistence of neonatal/primitive reflexes beyond the age at which they should disappear is an important predictor of abnormal development.
- Developmental delay should be differentiated from developmental regression in which the infant/child loses the already acquired milestones.

Domains of Development

Normal development occurs under the sphere of four main domains. These are:

1. Gross motor
2. Fine motor
3. Language (speech and hearing)
4. Personal–social milestones

The gross motor skills and the activities such as head/neck control and sitting are the most obvious initial areas of the child development, whereas personal/social development is a spectrum of the psychological developmental process. It must be remembered that if one area of development is affected, it may have an impact on the other field(s) of development. For example, if a child has a hearing deficit, apart from the language delay, it can also affect/delay his/her personal/social development.

The child's development is an outcome of the interaction between his/her intrinsic (hereditary) and extrinsic (environmental) factors. The hereditary factors would determine the potential of how the child develops, and the environmental factors (physical, social, and emotional) would influence the extent to which that potential is achieved. The acquisition of these new skills is referred to as the *developmental milestones*. It must also be remembered that although the developmental milestones are organized into four different domains for the ease of assessment, they are interrelated.

If a child is born prematurely, his/her corrected age should be considered while assessing development. Thus, the anticipated development of a 10-month-old baby (chronological age) who was born at 28 weeks of gestation (3 months early) is more like that of a 7-month-old baby (corrected age). This correction is not needed after 2 years of age.

While evaluating the child's development, the following points need to be considered:

- Has the child achieved his/her age-appropriate development in each/different field(s)?
- Is the sequence of the developmental process normal? Is there any skipping of the milestones?
- Is the developmental progress in each field similar?
- How does the child's development relate to the chronological age?
- Is the development normal or delayed? If it is delayed, determine whether it is a global delay or there is a dissociation between the various fields of development. As an example, a child with hearing deficit resulting in speech delay can have normal motor milestones.
- Is it developmental delay or developmental regression? In few cases, the child may have acquired initial milestones appropriate for age, and after certain age there is delay in development. This can be due to acute neurological insult or severe acute illness, or this regression of milestones may indicate a possibility of neurodegenerative disorders.

Gross Motor Milestones

Gross motor (physical) skills are those that require whole-body movements, and that involve the large core-stabilizing muscles of the body to perform everyday functions, such as sitting, standing, crawling, walking, and running. They also include eye–hand coordination skills such as ball skills (throwing, catching, kicking). The key gross motor milestones are listed in Table 4.1.

In the neonatal period, the baby lies supine in flexed and symmetrical posture and has a marked head/neck lag on being pulled up (Fig. 4.1). The motor development for the

TABLE 4.1 Gross Motor Milestones

Time	Milestones
3 months	Head control/neck holding
5 months	Rolling over
6 months	Sitting with support
8 months	Sitting without support
9–10 months	Standing with support, pivoting/turning the neck around to pick a toy without overbalancing
12–13 months	Standing to rise and walk independently
18 months	Running, climbing onto chair
2 years	Climbing upstairs using two feet per step, kicking a ball
2.5 years	Jumping, climbing upstairs using two feet per step
3 years	Riding and peddling a tricycle, standing on one leg for a few seconds
4 years	Hopping on one foot, climbing up and downstairs with one foot per step
5 years	Skipping and jumping

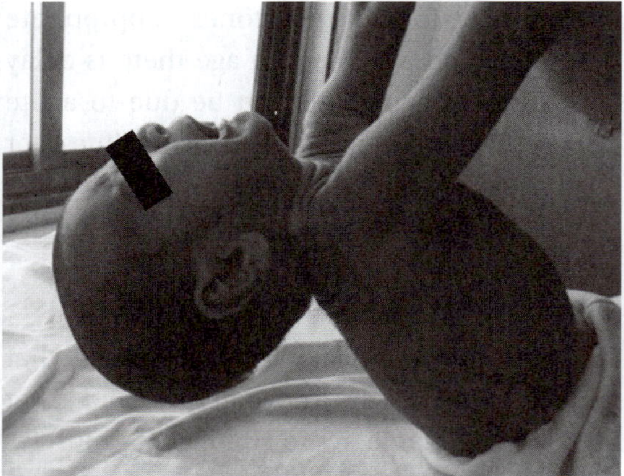

Figure 4.1 Head lag in newborn on being pulled up.

young infant in the first 3 months is tested by the maneuvers as discussed next.

Ventral Suspension

The child is held in ventral suspension in a prone position with the examiner's hand under the abdomen. At 6–8 weeks, the baby momentarily holds the head in a horizontal position in the plane of the trunk and by 12 weeks, the head is held above the horizontal plane (Fig. 4.2). This is because with increase in myelination, the infant starts to develop improved tone and head control. Starting at 6 weeks, the head control develops by 12 weeks and complete neck control is attained by 20 weeks.

Prone Position

At 4 weeks, the child lifts the chin up momentarily; by 6–8 weeks, face is lifted at 45° and by 12 weeks, the child can bear weight on forearm with chin and shoulder off the couch and face lifted up to 90° (Fig. 4.3). Between 5 and 6 months, the baby learns to roll over, first from prone to supine and then from supine to prone.

Sitting

The child learns to sit with support at 6–8 months of age. First, the baby learns to sit

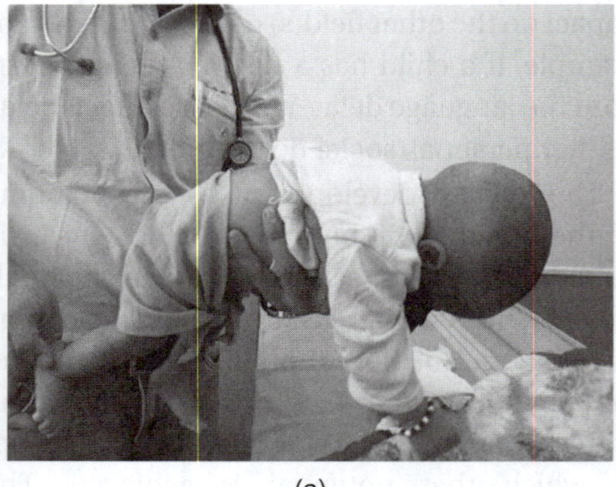

(a)

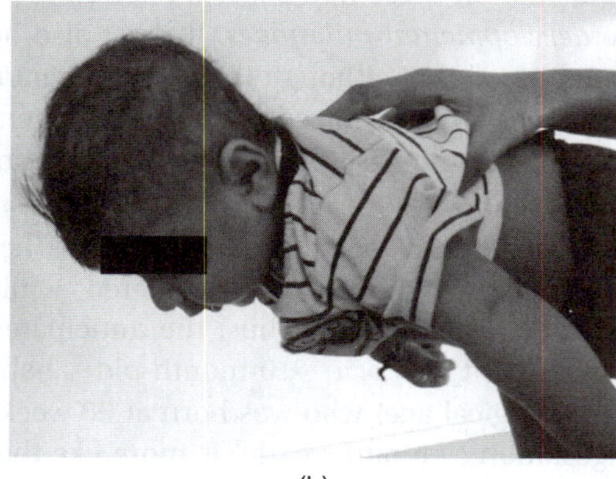

(b)

Figure 4.2 (a) Ventral suspension at 6 weeks: head momentarily held in the same plane as the body. (b) Ventral suspension in a 12-week-old infant: head held above the horizontal plain.

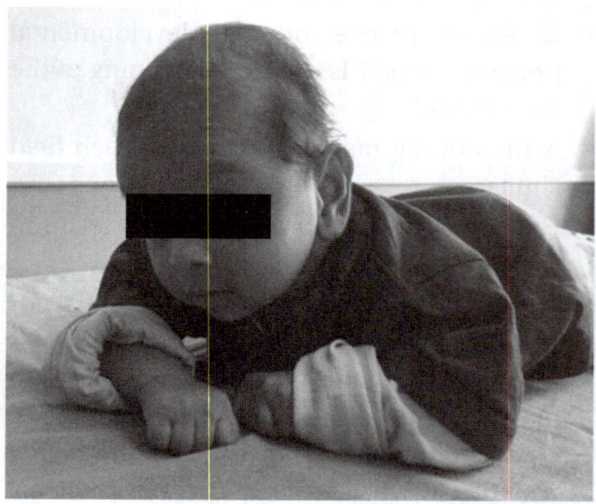

Figure 4.3 Prone position at 12 weeks: bearing weight on forearms and lifting chest/head.

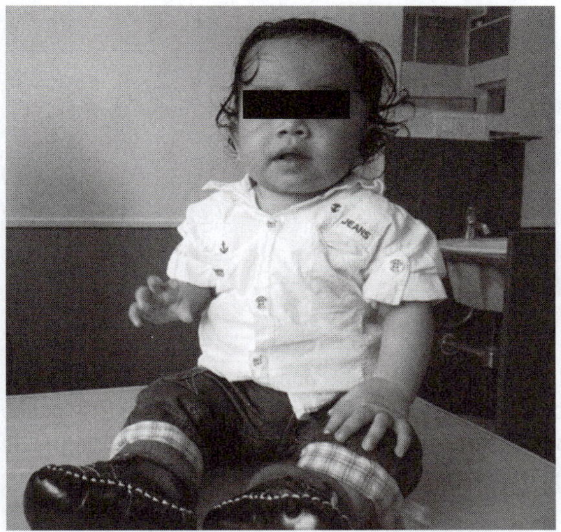

Figure 4.4 Baby sits without support and with straight back at 8 months.

with hands forward for support with a rounded back. Later, the baby sits with a straight back without support at 8 months (Fig. 4.4).

Crawling

An infant starts crawling on hands and knees at 8–9 months of age (Fig. 4.5). While a majority of children crawl before they walk, a few infants may not crawl but are bottom shufflers and then straight away learn to stand and walk.

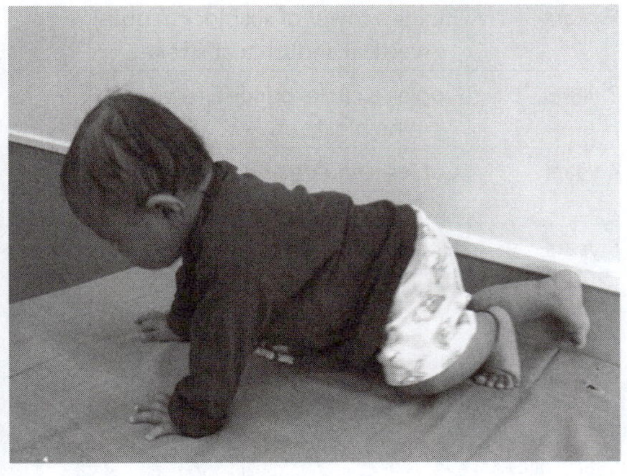

Figure 4.5 A 9-month-old infant crawling on hands and knees.

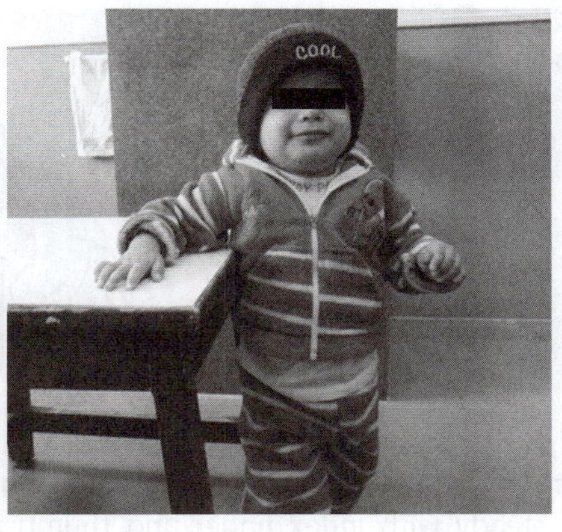

(a)

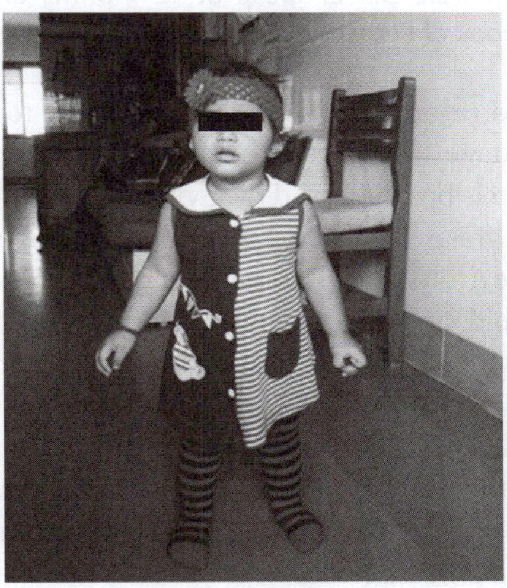

(b)

Figure 4.6 (a) An 11-month-old infant walking with support (cruising) and (b) a 13-month-old child walking independently.

Standing/Walking

Most infants learn to stand and then walk first unsteadily with their hands apart and with a broad gait by the age of 11–12 months. They also learn to cruise along, i.e., walk sideways (Fig. 4.6a), holding furniture. They can walk alone steadily by 13–15 months of age (Fig. 4.6b).

Fine Motor Development

Fine motor development mainly involves manipulation skills. Between 3 and 4 months, a baby observes his/her hands very intently

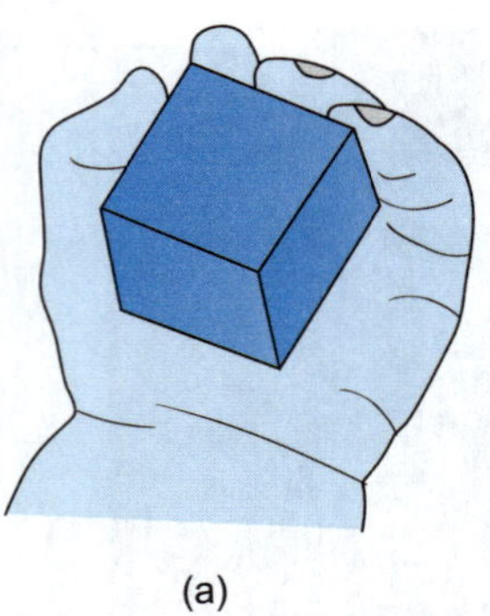

(a)

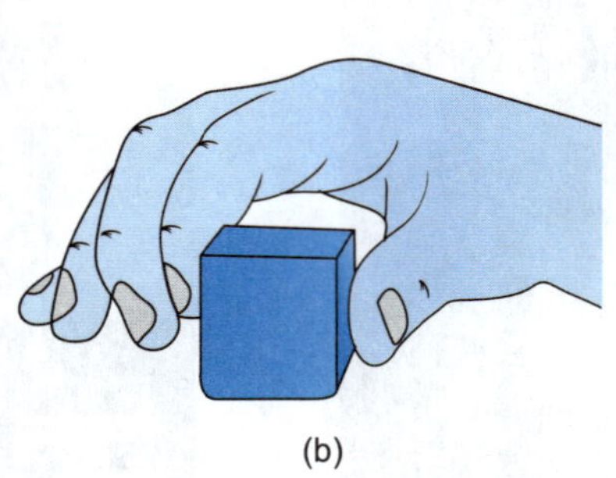

(b)

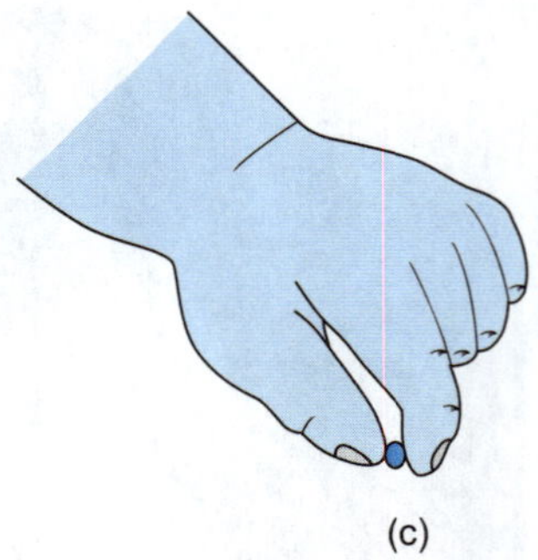

(c)

Figure 4.7 (a) Approaches cube with fingers and holds with palm at 6 months of age. (b) Holds cube steady with index finger and thumb at 9 months of age. (c) Approaches and picks up pellet with mature pincer grasp at 12 months of age. *Source*: Reproduced with permission from Gupta P. Textbook of Pediatrics. CBS Publishers and Distributors: New Delhi, 2013.

(hand regard). Subsequently, the baby reaches the stage where he/she can hold the objects. Grasp is best assessed by giving cubes. Initially, the grasp is bidextrous that changes to unidextrous and then to pincer grasp (attempt to hold an object between index finger and thumb). The pincer grasp matures at 12 months only (Fig. 4.7). By 6 months of age, the baby starts putting everything that is in his/her hand into the mouth (mouthing); this disappears by 1 year of age. The key fine motor milestones are enlisted in Table 4.2.

The child then learns to copy and draw figures, as shown in Figure 4.8.

TABLE 4.2 Fine Motor Milestones

Age	Milestones
6 weeks	Follows face in midline and turns head toward moving object
4 months	Reaches for toy/red ring or rattle in front with both hands
6 months	Reaches for objects by one hand only (palmar grasp)
7 months	Transfers objects from one hand to another
9–10 months	Pincer grasp (picks up a pellet neatly with thumb and index finger)
12 months	Casting (throwing the object away)
15 months	Able to feed self with spoon without spilling the contents
18 months	Builds a tower of three cubes and scribbles
2 years	Builds a tower of six blocks/cubes; vertical and circular strokes
3 years	Copies a circle, builds a tower of nine blocks
4 years	Copies a square and cross, builds a bridge with blocks
5 years	Draws a triangle

Personal and Social Development

The domains of social intelligence and development are critical components of descriptions of human ability and behavior. Cognitive development and understanding is reflected by attainment of milestones in this domain. The important personal and social milestones are enlisted in Table 4.3.

Toilet training is an integral part of development. By the age of 10–12 months, the infant can be placed on the baby toilet seat and is usually ready for toilet training by the age of 15–18 months. The child becomes dry by day by the age of 2 years and is dry by night by the age of 3 years. However, a small percentage of normal

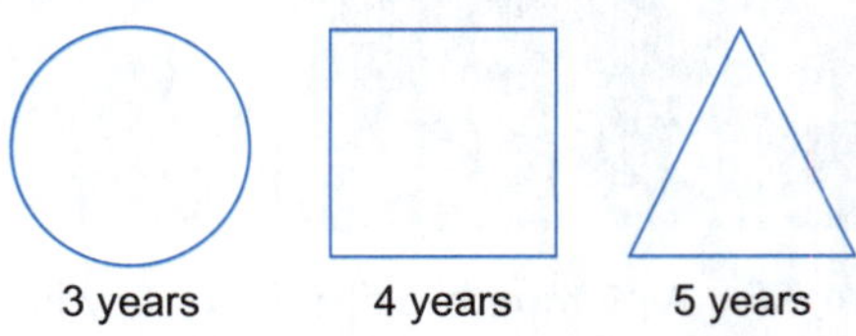

Figure 4.8 Copying skills at different ages.

TABLE 4.3 Personal and Social Development

Age	Milestones
1 month	Alert to sound
2 months	Social smile (responds with smile to social contact)
3 months	Recognizes mother
6 months	Smiles at reflection in the mirror
9 months	Waves "bye-bye"
12 months	Plays simple ball games
15–18 months	Holds spoon and feeds without spilling
18–24 months	Copies parent's tasks, has symbolic play (e.g., feeding a stuffed toy)
3 years	Shares toys and knows name, gender. Dry by night
4 years	Goes to the toilet alone
5 years	Helps in household tasks, dresses and undresses

children (up to 5%) may not be toilet trained by this age but achieve bladder control later.

Language Development

The infant has many methods of preverbal communication. The newborn and the infant communicate mainly by crying, smiling, or frowning. Thus, language development is the progressive development of the infant's ability to use language from initial simple sound production to subsequent word fluency. During the first 3 months, the baby's language development can be observed by his/her ability to vocalize, recognize the mother's voice, and smile and respond to human voices. The important language milestones are shown in Table 4.4.

TABLE 4.4 Language Development

Time	Milestones
1 month	Alert/turns head to sound
3 months	Vocalizes and coos
6 months	Speaks monosyllables (ma, ba, pa)
7–8 months	Turns to soft sounds out of sight
9 months	Speaks bisyllables (mama, baba)
12 months	One to two words with meaning
18 months	Ten to 15 words with meaning; shows two parts of the body
24 months	Uses two to three words to make phrases
2.5–3 years	Speaks in sentences, knows his/her name, and tells a story

Variations in Normal Development and Red Flags

The developmental milestones and their age of acquisition that have been described (as median ages) earlier are applicable to a large percentage of normal children, thus serving as a useful guide for developmental assessment. However, it is also possible that a small percentage of normal children may not reach a particular stage of development at an age at which most children would have.

- To obviate this problem, if a child has not reached a particular developmental milestone, the limit age (i.e., the upper limit) for that particular milestone must be considered, i.e., the maximal age by which a child should achieve that milestone.
- Use of limit age is a helpful guide to assess whether the child's development is in sync with the median age or not. If a child fails to meet the limit age for that milestone, then a further detailed developmental assessment followed by an investigation to determine the underlying cause and then an intervention is called for.
- Hence, if a child does not achieve any milestone by his/her limit age, then it is a red flag sign.
- A few developmental milestones and their limit ages are shown in Table 4.5.

Besides the few above-mentioned red flags that are likely to suggest developmental delay, parents' observation about their baby/child must be carefully considered so as not to overlook any suspected delay. The following observations need to be carefully considered:

- The baby does not smile or watch the things move or does not get startled with a loud noise.

TABLE 4.5 Developmental Milestones with Their Limit (Upper) Ages: Red Flag Signs

Milestones	Upper/limit age
Visual fixation	3 months
Head control	5 months
Reaching for toys/objects	6 months
Sits alone, with good coordination	9 months
Pincer grasp	12 months
Walks alone	18 months

- The baby either appears very stiff with tight muscles or appears limp/hypotonic like a rag doll. This is often observed while changing the baby's diapers.
- The baby does not coo, laugh, or make squealing sounds and shows no affection to caregivers.
- The baby does not play with other children and toys.
- The baby falls frequently or has an unsteady/limping gait.
- The baby does not learn gestures and point to things.

Developmental Delay

Developmental delay is said to be present when the child's performance is two standard deviations or more below the expected norms in one or more of the five domains of development.

- *Developmental quotient* (DQ): DQ is the numeric expression of a child's developmental level and is calculated by dividing the developmental age by the chronological age and multiplying the result with 100. It should be calculated for each developmental domain. DQ of 65–75 is considered as a risk for developmental delay.
- *Global developmental delay*: This term is applied if there is a delay in two or more developmental domains and it is used for children up to the age of 3 years.
- *Developmental dissociation*: It is said to be present when the rate of development significantly differs in different developmental domains. For example, in a child with mental retardation, motor milestones can be normal.
- *Developmental regression*: It refers to the loss of previously acquired milestones. Developmental regression is characteristic of neurodegenerative disorders (such as Tay–Sachs disease, leukodystrophies).

It is often difficult to make and confirm the diagnosis of developmental delay in the first few months of life but a thorough history and enquiry into maternal risk factors along with perinatal history can offer important clues to the diagnosis. The age of achievement of various milestones and a thorough developmental assessment by an expert would be essential for appropriate diagnosis and therapy. The common causes of delayed development are shown in Box 4.1.

Evaluation of Development

The global prevalence of developmental delay in children is reported as 1–3%, while the World Health Organization estimates that 15% of the world's population lives with some form of disability. The American Academy of Paediatrics (AAP) recommends developmental surveillance of high-risk children at each health visit from birth to 3 years, and a routine screening of low-risk children at 9, 18, and 24 months or earlier if concerns are elicited. There is a possibility to recognize developmental delay in early infancy. Speech impairment, hyperactivity, and emotional disturbances are common at 3–4 years of age.

Prerequisite for Assessment

Development should be assessed in a place and setting that is not distracting for the child. It is important that the child should not be hungry, ill, or irritated at the time of assessment.

Box 4.1 Causes of developmental delay

Antenatal/maternal conditions
- Intrauterine infections (rubella, cytomegalovirus, toxoplasmosis, HIV)
- Maternal irradiation, drugs
- Placental dysfunction, toxemia

Fetal conditions
- Congenital central nervous system malformations, e.g., congenital hydrocephalous
- Genetic diseases, e.g., Down syndrome, fragile X syndrome
- Extreme prematurity

Natal conditions
- Birth asphyxia, hypoxic ischemic encephalopathy, intracranial hemorrhage

Postnatal conditions
- Neonatal meningitis, hypoxia, bilirubin encephalopathy
- Metabolic conditions such as hypoglycemia, galactosemia

Other conditions
- Hypothyroidism (preventable by early diagnosis and therapy), cerebral palsy, neurodegenerative diseases, emotional deprivation, autistic spectrum disorders, hearing impairment, and neuromuscular diseases (Duchenne muscular dystrophy)

Steps of Assessment

- Obtaining a good history
- Identification of tools
- Performing an assessment including vision and hearing
- Calculation of the DQ
- Classification of development into normal or abnormal
- Classification of developmental delay into global or dissociative, and to check whether regression is present

History Taking and Physical Examination for Developmental Assessment

History taking and a detailed physical examination are very important as far as the assessment of development is concerned.

- History taking not only involves age of achievement of milestones but also includes antenatal, natal, and postnatal history that can adversely affect the development.
- Past medical history is important for eliciting risk factors including biological (e.g., prematurity), genetic (e.g., Down syndrome), environmental (e.g., lead exposure), and psychosocial (e.g., maternal education, family income, marital status) factors.
- A developmental history reviewing the acquisition of developmental milestones should be taken, evaluating gross motor, expressive and receptive language, as well as social skills.
- The developmental progress of older children is best evaluated by consideration of school performance, proficiency in games, and social behavior.
- The physical examination includes evaluation of growth parameters, including head circumference, dysmorphology, and a complete neurological examination. In evaluating growth parameters, careful attention should be given to anthropometric measurements such as head circumference—looking for microcephaly, macrocephaly, or an increased growth velocity. Dysmorphology examination should look at both major and minor anomalies that might explain the etiology of the developmental delay. A neurological examination should review strength, tone, and symmetry, and evaluate for the presence or absence of primitive reflexes.

Developmental assessment is thus a detailed analysis of developmental areas and is a part of the diagnostic process and must be followed by relevant investigations, therapy, and counseling by a multidisciplinary approach.

Bedside Tools

Simple objects and instruments are useful for bedside assessment of development. These items include a torch, a dangling ring of 6.5 cm diameter, a red ball of 5 cm diameter, ten 2- to 5-cm-sized colorful cubes, a bell, a rattle, a cup with handle, pellets or beads, a picture book, paper, and crayons.

Hearing and Vision Assessment

Failure to detect children with congenital or acquired hearing loss may result in lifelong deficiencies in speech and language acquisition, poor academic performance, personal–social maladjustment, and emotional difficulties. Early identification of hearing loss and appropriate intervention within the first 6 months of life have been demonstrated to prevent many adverse consequences and facilitate language acquisition.

Surveillance of Development

During each visit, the infant/child should be monitored for normal development and should be watched for the presence of any "red flags." The term "developmental surveillance" refers to the process of identifying potential risk factors for abnormal development. This is done by developmental screening, good history, close follow-up, recording the details, and attending to parental concerns, if any.

Developmental Screening Tools

The basic concept of developmental assessment is to analyze the child's progress on a longitudinal basis and considering each skill/development and its achievement individually, and then correlating the progress of one to other and to the child's chronological age. A thorough developmental history along with careful observation and examination generally suffices in the assessment of normal children while a detailed and formal assessment by qualified personnel is mandatory in children with developmental delay.

Developmental screening is the administration of a standard and validated test that helps in the early identification of children who are at risk for a developmental delay/abnormal development (such as extreme prematurity, neonatal hyperbilirubinemia). Infants and children who fail to pass these developmental screening tests are candidates for a regular follow-up and additional diagnostic assessment.

Finding an ideal screening tool that is easy to administer, is not much time-consuming, is sensitive and cost-effective, demonstrates strong psychometric qualities, and is culturally relevant remains a challenge. A variety of screening tests are available to choose from, many of which are completed by parents and require only a short period of time to administer and score. For example, the Parents' Evaluation of Developmental Status (PEDS) is a parent interview form that provides an algorithm to guide a need for referral, more screening, or continued surveillance. Another example is the Ages & Stages Questionnaire (ASQ), which is a parent-completed questionnaire that may be used as a general developmental screening tool for children between the ages of 4 and 60 months. ASQ can be used to screen children between the ages of 1 month and 5.5 years and can be completed in 15 minutes.

Denver Developmental Screening Test (DDST) is a screening test that was widely accepted and used in clinical practice for many years. Due to its poor sensitivity and specificity, the test is no longer recommended as a screening test for children.

Several directly administered tests for developmental evaluation have been developed in India. Phatak's Baroda Screening Test (BDST), developed by Pramila Phatak, is based on Bayley Scales of Infant Development (BSID) and is widely used for the developmental evaluation of children up to 30 months of age. The BSID is considered as a gold standard for assessing development.

Another screening tool, the Trivandrum Developmental Screening Chart (TDSC) was developed from Bayley scale (Baroda norms). It is a 17-item screening tool for children up to 24 months of age, requiring minimal training for administration. The TDSC can be done in 5 minutes and covers mental and motor milestones.

Definitive Tests for Diagnosis of Developmental Delay

The children who are suspected to be abnormal on screening tests should be subjected to detailed and definitive developmental diagnostic tests. BSID III is also used for definitive diagnosis of developmental delay in children between the ages of 1 month and 3 years. Developmental Assessment Scale for Indian Infants (DASII) is a widely used tool in India. These tests are based on the evaluation of gross motor, fine motor, language, behavior, and visual problem-solving skills.

Intelligence Tests

There are a number of tests available for the measurement of intelligence in children. The Wechsler Intelligence Scale (WISC) is used to assess intelligence in children above 6 years of age. In India, Malin's Intelligence Scale for Indian Children (MISIC) is used for assessment of children above 5 years of age; this test is an adaptation of the WISC. Stanford–Binet test is another test for IQ assess: ment.

KEY POINTS

- The child's developmental assessment is an integral part of the child's comprehensive evaluation and helps to identify normal development and to recognize early patterns of abnormal development.
- It not only includes the evaluation of children who have a developmental delay but also focuses on those who are developing normally but may be at risk of developmental disorders.
- The child with a developmental delay must be referred to a center that offers specialized services with a multidisciplinary approach.

CHAPTER 5

Vaccines and Immunization

Niranjan Shendurnikar, Uma S Nayak, Sheila Aiyer

Vaccines and childhood immunizations are one of the most cost-effective healthcare interventions over the past decades. The successful implementation of polio eradication programs across the world is a testimony of the preventive benefits of immunization. During the past two decades, revolutionary changes in vaccinology improved immunization coverage of children and the availability of newer vaccines has made this an evolving and dynamic subject. It thus becomes necessary to be fully aware of the common issues concerning vaccines and immunizations such as schedules of immunization, definitions, individual vaccines, their appropriate use, indications, contraindications, and precautions. Immunity against infection and/or disease can be acquired from a natural infection that may manifest as a clinical disease or as a subclinical/inapparent infection. Some important terms are given in Box 5.1.

Role of T and B Cells

The immune system is not well developed at birth but maternal antibodies transmitted passively across the placenta provide the newborn a short-term protection during the first few days. After birth, evolution of the stem cells in the bone marrow into T-cell and B-cell precursors assumes an important role in the childhood immunity.

- T-cell precursors differentiate into immunocompetent T cells within the thymus and are responsible for the production of *cell-mediated immunity*.
- B cells form a more important component of immune system in the body and these do not pass through the thymus but differentiate into immunocompetent B cells in the bone marrow.
- B cells have an immunoglobulin surface receptor that binds with the specific antigen present on the antigenic pathogen and thus are primarily responsible for *humoral or antibody-mediated immune responses.*

Primary and Secondary Immune Response

With the first administration/contact with the antigen/vaccine, the *primary response* takes place. The antibodies are detectable in the serum after a longer gap than that seen with the secondary response. This lag period is 7–10 days but may vary depending on the nature/dose and the route of vaccine administration (parenteral or oral). The initial serum antibody levels rise for 2–4 weeks and then may drop to very low levels. The first antibodies in the primary response to appear are IgM followed by IgG or IgA. IgM levels fall earlier than the IgG levels (Fig. 5.1).

The secondary response occurs with the second dose/contact with the antigen after the primary response. There is a rapid rise of antibodies to higher levels than in the primary immune response. This response is attributed to the persistence of antigen-specific memory cells after the first dose of vaccine or after the first contact with the agent. A larger amount of IgG is produced, and its levels tend to persist longer than in the primary response.

Box 5.1 Terminology

- *Vaccine*: It refers to a biological preparation consisting of either live (attenuated) or inactive bacteria or viruses or their fractions and needs to be administered to the recipient in one or more doses to induce the immunity against the corresponding pathogen and prevent the infectious disease or its sequelae.
- *Vaccination/immunization*: The terms "vaccination" and "immunization" are often used interchangeably but there is a small difference. Vaccination refers to the process of administering the vaccine (agent) into the body and the recipient (vaccinee) may or may not develop the protective response. However, immunization indicates the process of generating an immune response in the vaccinee against that pathogen. The immunization may be either of the following:
  - *Active immunization*: The protection and immunity is produced by the production of antibodies or other immune responses through the administration of the antigen or its modified product (e.g., tetanus toxoid).
  - *Passive immunization*: This indicates the acquisition of temporary/short-lasting immunity by the administration of preformed antibodies (e.g., immunoglobulins) particularly when the benefit of protection is needed immediately after exposure (e.g., tetanus immunoglobulin, rabies immunoglobulin, and hepatitis B immunoglobulin).
- *Seroconversion*: Seroconversion denotes the change from an antibody-negative status to an antibody-positive status after the immunization.
- *Seroprotection*: This denotes a state of protection from the disease due to the presence of certain detectable levels of antibody in the sera.
- *Vaccine immunogenicity*: It is defined as the ability of the vaccine/antigen to induce antibody production that may or may not be protective to the host.
- *Vaccine efficacy (VE)*: It is the ability of a vaccine to protect a child under experimental conditions. It is calculated as follows:

$$\text{VE} = \frac{\text{disease in the unvaccinated} - \text{disease in the vaccinated}}{\text{disease in unvaccinated}}$$

- *Herd effect*: It is defined as the reduction of the infection or disease in the unimmunized population owing to immunization of a proportion (more than 85%) against that disease. This is due to breaking and reducing the chain of transmission of a microorganism by vaccinated cohort and is thus observed with vaccines against diseases of which humans are the only source of transmission, e.g., oral polio vaccine.
- *Herd immunity*: It reflects the proportion of immune subjects in the population following a disease or immunization against that disease.

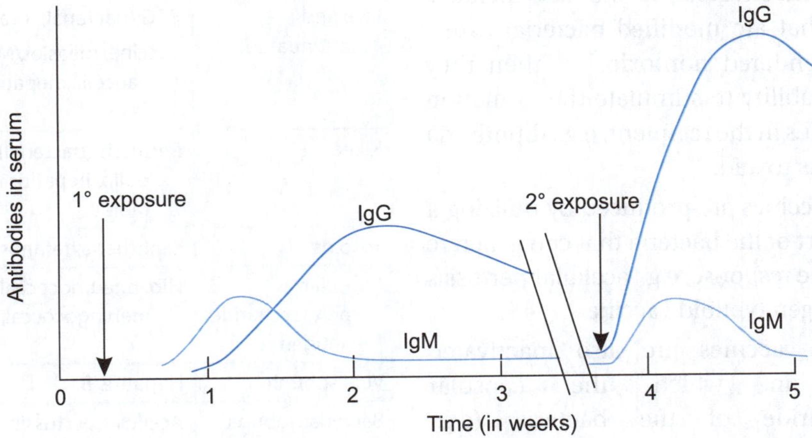

Figure 5.1 Primary and secondary immune response.

Live attenuated vaccines that are administered orally (oral polio vaccine [OPV], rotavirus [RV] vaccine) produce immunity by the multiplication of the infecting agent in the intestinal mucosa after the ingestion. The initial response locally is the production of IgA antibodies, and later the systemic production of IgG antibodies takes place.

Basic Attributes of Vaccines

Vaccines are broadly classified as either live attenuated vaccines or killed/inactivated vaccines.

- Live vaccines are attenuated products in which bacteria/viruses are subjected to processes that attenuate their pathogenicity (disease-causing abilities) while retaining their capacity to generate antibodies and produce immunity. After the administration, the microorganisms in the vaccine multiply in the vaccinee and thus generate an immune response similar to that in a natural infection.
- Killed/inactivated vaccines include several subtypes of the vaccines. These are produced by growing the bacteria or the viruses in the culture media and then making them inactive (killed) by artificial processes (e.g., whole-cell pertussis and typhoid vaccine).
- A group of inactivated vaccines also includes vaccines that are modified bacterial toxins and are rendered nontoxic but then they retain the ability to stimulate the formation of antibodies in the recipient, e.g., diphtheria and tetanus toxoid.
- Subunit vaccines are produced by utilizing a specific part of the bacteria that can generate the immune response, e.g., acellular pertussis and Vi antigen typhoid vaccine.
- Conjugate vaccines are also inactivated vaccines in which the capsular polysaccharide of the bacteria (e.g., *Haemophilus influenzae* type b [Hib], *S. pneumoniae*) is linked to a carrier protein (conjugation) to render it immunogenic, thus converting it from a T-cell-independent to a T-cell-dependent antigen to improve the immunogenicity in children younger than 2 years.
- Recombinant vaccines are synthesized by using a nonpathogenic organism (viral subunit) carrying immunogenic components to elicit an immune response, e.g., hepatitis B vaccine (HBV).
- Live vaccines must not be administered to children with significant immunosuppression whether caused by the diseases, e.g., malignancy, or by drugs such as anticancer drugs and corticosteroids. If need arises, these may be given at least 3 months after stopping the steroids and other immunosuppressive therapy.
- Many inactivated/killed vaccines are formulated with adjuvants (aluminum salts), which are potent enhancers of antibody response and immunogenic memory due to a slow release from the injection site.
- Different types of vaccines are shown in Table 5.1.

TABLE 5.1 Types of Vaccines

Antigenic type	Vaccines
Live and attenuated	BCG (bacterial), oral polio Vaccine, measles/MMR, rotavirus, varicella, hepatitis A, yellow fever
Killed	Pertussis (bacterial), inactivated polio, hepatitis A (killed), rabies
Toxoids	Diphtheria, tetanus
Capsular polysaccharide antigen	Hib, pneumococcal, meningococcal, typhoid Vi
Viral subunit	Hepatitis B
Bacterial subunit	Acellular pertussis

Hib, Haemophilus influenzae type b; *MMR*, measles, mumps, and rubella.

Immunization Schedule

An effective immunization schedule is one that is epidemiologically relevant, feasible, immunologically competent, socially acceptable, and sustainable. Various factors that need to be considered are as follows:

- Childhood immunization program is one of the key interventions for the protection of children from preventable life-threatening diseases. The National Immunization Program of India is one of the largest immunization programs in the world and a major public health intervention in the country.
- An immunization schedule is thus likely to vary for different countries and also from time to time.
- Another thing that needs to be considered is the minimal age at which the given vaccine can elicit an immune response and the number of the doses required.
- Disease severity and mortality from the disease are important considerations.
- Programmatic factors to deliver the vaccines and the coverage and timings of the visit are also essential components of an immunization schedule.

National Immunization Schedule and IAP Recommendations

- National immunization schedule consists of those vaccines that are given free of cost to all the children of the country under Expanded Program of Immunization (EPI), also referred to as National Immunization Program.
- Immunization program in India has been a part of the National Rural Health Mission (NRHM) since the year 2005.
- The National Immunization Schedule for India is shown in Table 5.2. Under this schedule (UIP, Universal Immunization Program), the Government of India provides vaccination for preventable diseases, i.e., diphtheria, pertussis, tetanus, poliomyelitis, measles, hepatitis B, meningitis, and pneumonia, caused by Hib and tuberculosis.
- In addition, the Indian Academy of Pediatrics (IAP) recommends several vaccines that are not included in national schedule but are recommended for use and are largely used in the private sector, e.g., RV vaccine, varicella vaccine, hepatitis A vaccine, and a few others (Table 5.3).

TABLE 5.2 National Immunization Schedule

Age	Vaccines
Birth*	BCG, HBV, OPV
6 weeks†	DPT (I), Hib (I), HBV (I) OPV (I) and IPV (I)
10 weeks	DPT/Hib/HBV (II) OPV (II)
14 weeks	DPT/Hib/HBV (III) OPV (III) and IPV (II)
9–12 months	Measles/MR vaccine (I)
16–24 months‡	MMR/or MR vaccine
18–24 months	DPT (1st booster) and OPV (IV)
5–6 years	DPT (2nd booster)
10 and 16 years	Tetanus toxoid

Japanese encephalitis (JE) vaccine is given in select endemic areas in 2 dose schedules (9–12 months and 16–24 months).

*At birth (HBV, birth dose), to be given as early after birth or maximum up to 24 hours after birth. OPV at birth (zero dose) maximally up to 15 days.

†DPT/Hib/HBV given as combination Pentavalent vaccine, and IPV is given as fractional dose administered by intradermal route.

‡2nd dose of measles vaccine given as rubella vaccine in the form of MR/MMR vaccine.

Additional Points for IAP Immunization Schedule

- BCG, OPV (0), and HBV should be given to babies delivered in hospitals before their discharge.
- If inactivated polio vaccine (IPV) is not feasible in the primary series of 6, 10, and 14 weeks, then it should be substituted with OPV in the same schedule.

TABLE 5.3 IAP Immunization Schedule

Age (completed months/years)	Vaccines
Birth	BCG/OPV (0)/HBV (first)
6 weeks	DPT/HBV/Hib/IPV (first)/RV (first)/ PCV (first)
10 weeks	DPT/Hib/IPV (second)/RV (second)/ PCV (second)
14 weeks	DPT/Hib/IPV (third)/RV (third)/ PCV (third)
6 months	HBV (third)
9 months	MMR-1
9–12 months	Typhoid conjugate vaccine
12 months	Hepatitis A (1)
15 months	MMR (second)/varicella (first)/ PCV booster
16–18 months	DPT or DaPT/Hib/IPV (booster first)
18 months	Hepatitis A (second)
2 years	Typhoid
4–6 years	DPT or DaPT (booster second)/OPV Typhoid booster
10–12 years	TdaP or Td; HPV for girls

HBV, hepatitis B vaccine; *Hib*, *Haemophilus influenzae* type b; *HPV*, human papillomavirus vaccine; *IAP*, Indian Academy of Pediatrics; *IPV*, inactivated polio vaccine; *MMR*, measles, mumps, and rubella; *OPV*, oral polio vaccine; *PCV*, pneumococcal conjugate vaccine; *RV*, rotavirus.

- DaPT should be preferably avoided in primary immunization. It may be used in specific situations only as an alternative to whole-cell DPT.
- No child should leave the center without IPV or OPV if indicated by the schedule.
- RV vaccine RV1 (monovalent) needs two doses only (at 6 and 10 weeks). RV vaccine RV5 needs three doses in 6-, 10-, and 14-week schedule.
- The third and/or final dose of HBV vaccine should be given not earlier than 6 months and at least 16 weeks after the first dose.
- Single measles vaccine at 9 months is replaced by measles, mumps, and rubella (MMR) (first).
- If live/attenuated H2 strain of hepatitis A vaccine is used instead of the inactivated one, then only one dose is needed.
- DaPT can be considered for use as the first booster at 16–18 months instead of DPT.
- The second dose of varicella is generally given between 4 and 6 years and can be given anytime 3 months after the first dose.
- The IAP recommends vaccines under special circumstances for a group of high-risk children (children with immune deficiencies, chronic/systemic diseases, e.g., asthma, liver diseases, and diabetes); children on long-term steroids, salicylates, and immunosuppressive drugs; disease outbreaks; healthcare workers; travelers; and exposure to pets and animals. The vaccines in these special circumstances include vaccines against influenza, meningococcal infection, Japanese encephalitis (JE), cholera, yellow fever, rabies, and polysaccharide pneumococcal vaccine (PPSV-23).

Childhood Vaccines

BCG Vaccine

BCG vaccine is at present the only effective vaccine against tuberculosis while several new vaccines against tuberculosis are in developmental phases.

- Originally derived from the bovine strain of *Mycobacterium tuberculosis* in 1921, the strain used in India is Copenhagen (Danish 1331).
- BCG vaccine does not prevent the infection with *M. tuberculosis* but generates cell-mediated immunity and provides efficacy of approximately 80% against miliary and meningeal forms of TB and 50% against pulmonary tuberculosis.
- The vaccine is a live, attenuated vaccine containing 0.1–0.4 million bacilli per dose and is supplied as a lyophilized powder (freeze-dried form) in a dark, vacuum-sealed vial (due to being light and heat

sensitive) along with the separate diluent (normal saline).

- The vaccine must be reconstituted just before use and must be utilized within 4 hours of its reconstitution.
- BCG vaccine is administered after birth and thereafter in a dose of 0.1 mL given intradermally (ID) with a tuberculin syringe and 26-G needle on the left upper arm just above the insertion of the deltoid muscle. Local antiseptic cleansing of the injection is not recommended; however, the site should be swabbed clean with sterile saline.
- The vaccine can be given anytime after birth in institutional deliveries up to 2 weeks. If delayed, it can be given at 1.5 months of age at the time of primary immunization.
- If any child has not received the vaccine earlier or has missed it, then the catch-up vaccination with BCG is recommended till the age of 5 years without any prior tuberculin testing. However, its simultaneous administration with measles/MMR vaccine needs to be avoided and an interval of 4 weeks should be kept between the two vaccines.
- BCG vaccine raises a wheal of 5–8 mm at the injection site followed by the development of a papule (2–3 weeks), pustule (4–6 weeks), and a thin scar over the injection site in 8–12 weeks. If no scar is visible at the injection site after 12 weeks, the vaccine needs to be repeated.
- The vaccine is safe, and the side effects are extremely rare such as nonsuppurative regional lymphadenopathy and disseminated BCG infection particularly in those with immune deficiencies.
- Although the vaccine should not be used in immunodeficient children and symptomatic HIV infection, BCG should be given at birth to babies born to HIV-positive mothers.
- Freeze-dried BCG vaccine can be stored at 2–8°C for up to 1 year.

DPT Vaccine

Vaccines against diphtheria, pertussis, and tetanus are most commonly available and used as a triple antigen (commonly known as DPT or DTwP), as bivalent vaccines (DT pediatric and dT as adult), and as tetanus, diphtheria, and pertussis (TdaP) for older children. There are two types of pertussis components in DPT vaccine: (i) the conventional DPT (i.e., DTwP) is a suspension of formalin-inactivated, killed suspension of *B. pertussis*; and (ii) DaPT is a component subunit, inactivated triple antigen that contains purified contents of *B. pertussis*.

- The presence of "w" with pertussis indicates that the pertussis component is a whole-cell vaccine product, while "aP" (e.g., DaPT) indicates that the vaccine contains acellular pertussis component.
- DPT, DaPT, and DT are the vaccines that are used in children younger than 7 years. In older children, the forms of these vaccines that are used are dT and Tdap.
- Tdap vaccine has been formulated for use in older children, adolescents, and adults and contains a reduced quantity of both pertussis toxin and diphtheria toxoid.
- DPT vaccine is a killed/inactivated vaccine and is given as three primary doses in the first year of life with a minimum interval of 4 weeks between the doses. A booster dose is given at the age of 15–18 months and the second booster should be given at 4.5–5 years of age. Any one of DPT or DaPT can be used to complete the primary immunization. If any dose is delayed or missed, then the sequence should be completed without any additional/extra dose.
- DPT vaccine is available in liquid form containing aluminum salt as an adjuvant and is given as 0.5 mL intramuscularly (IM) in the anterolateral part of the thigh.
- The vaccine is stored at 2–8°C and should not be frozen. If frozen accidentally, then it must be discarded.
- The vaccine efficacy is 80%, 70%, and 100% against diphtheria, pertussis, and tetanus,

respectively, after the completion of three primary doses. Immunity against all the three components tends to decline over the next 6–12 years and hence a regular boosting is required. DPT (i.e., DTwP) is not recommended for use in children aged 7 years and older due to increased risk of side effects.

- The side effects of DPT vaccine are largely due to the pertussis component and mild ones include fever, pain, induration, and redness at the injection site. These appear within several hours of injection and subside in 2–3 days. An induration can persist for several days at the injection site and this is due to sterile abscess formed by the adjuvant.
- Local and febrile side effects are less common and less severe with acellular (DaPT) than with whole-cell (DPT) vaccine.
- Serious adverse reactions have been reported with DPT vaccine but are very rare. Conditions such as fever greater than 40.5°C, hypotonic-hyporesponsive episode and/or persistent/inconsolable crying for more than 3 hours, and convulsions following DPT vaccine within 48 hours, which were earlier considered contraindications for further doses, are now considered as precautions. Such events do not recur with the further doses and have not been proven to cause permanent damage/sequelae.
- The absolute contraindications for the use of pertussis-containing vaccines, whether whole-cell or acellular (DPT and DaPT, respectively), are an immediate anaphylactic reaction and/or encephalopathy following an earlier dose of the vaccine. In such a situation, the series can be completed with either DT or dT.

Hepatitis B Vaccine

HBV is a genetically engineered recombinant DNA vaccine and contains the surface antigens of the HB virus derived from the yeast (*Saccharomyces cerevisiae*). The vaccine is available in single formulations (pediatric and adult doses) and in combination with DPT and Hib vaccine as pentavalent vaccine.

- Administration of three doses of HBV in different schedules provides a high degree of seroconversion resulting in more than 90% of recipients developing protective antibody levels (>10 MIU/mL).
- The vaccine is given as 0.5 mL (10 µg) in children and adolescents younger than 18 years of age, and 1.0 mL (20 µg) in subjects more than 18 years old. It is given IM in the anterolateral thigh or deltoid region.
- The vaccine can be given in any of the following schedules of three doses: 0 (at birth), 1, and 6 months, or at 6, 10, and 14 weeks of age. If the mother is HBsAg positive, then the newborn must receive the first dose of vaccine and hepatitis B immunoglobulin (HBIG) within 24 hours of birth at separate sites.
- Routinely, no booster doses of HBV are needed in healthy/immunocompetent children but they may be required in underlying immunocompromised hosts and those with chronic systemic illnesses when the antibody levels may drop below the protective levels.
- All children and adolescents who have not been previously vaccinated with HBV should be given the HBV in a schedule of 0, 1, and 6 months as a catch-up vaccination.
- The vaccine is safe and well tolerated, and hardly ever has any adverse effects.

Haemophilus influenzae type b Vaccine

Vaccines against Hib provide protection against severe/serious infections, such as meningitis, pneumonia, and bacteremia, in infants and young children younger than 5 years of age.

- Hib vaccine is developed by conjugating (linking) the Hib capsular polysaccharide to one of the carrier proteins, e.g., a diphtheria toxoid-like carrier protein (PRP-HBOC) or carrier tetanus toxoid (PRP-T). This process greatly enhances the immunogenic response of Hib vaccine in the first few months of life when the protection is most needed.

- Hib vaccines are now largely used as a combination vaccine along with DPT/DaPT/HBV/IPV given as a constituent of DPT (pentavalent) vaccine in three primary doses. With increasing age, if the child has not received Hib vaccine earlier, then the number of doses gets reduced (age 7–11 months: two primary doses; and age 12–15 months: one primary dose). All these should be followed by the booster dose between the age of 15 and 18 months.
- Though not given to children more than 5 years old, a single dose of Hib vaccine is recommended in those with childhood leukemia, other immunosuppressive conditions, and functional asplenia (sickle cell disease).
- Side effects are uncommon and are mild only such as transient fever, pain, and tenderness.

Polio Vaccines

Vaccines against poliomyelitis are of two types: live attenuated OPV and IPV. The use of these vaccines over the past few decades has ensured remarkable decline in the global burden of poliomyelitis and has ensured the success of Global Polio Eradication Initiative.

Oral Polio Vaccine

- This is a trivalent vaccine containing a suspension of all the three types of polioviruses (1, 2, and 3) derived from the original Sabin strain.
- OPV is stabilized with magnesium chloride and is presented in a buffered salt solution with light pink color, indicating its correct pH. OPV vials now come with vaccine vial monitors (VVMs) to indicate the potency of the vaccine and detect its temperature exposure.
- The vaccine is given orally and, to be effective, the poliovirus needs to multiply in the gastrointestinal tract. As it is a trivalent vaccine, the virus must establish an infection in the intestines (known as vaccine virus take) before an immune response can occur. This may not happen with single dose and thus multiple doses are necessary in primary immunization to ensure the take-up of each type at least once.
- The immune response and the seroconversion rates to OPV in a developing country such as India are lower (about 70%) than those in developed countries, particularly against type 1 virus. This is due to high prevalence of non-polio enteroviruses in the gut, malnutrition, and logistic reasons such as temperature and storage inadequacies. The protection conferred by polio vaccines is long-lasting due to the presence and boosting up of the neutralizing antibodies.
- Monovalent OPV (mOPVs: type 1) and bivalent OPV (bOPV: types 1 and 3) are presumably two to three times more effective than trivalent OPV used routinely. These have been used in India selectively and successfully in pulse polio immunizations to help India achieve polio eradication.
- OPV doses are given along with DPT in the primary immunization at the same visit at an interval of 4–6 weeks. Hospital-born babies are given a "0" dose of OPV at birth (and up to 14 days) to enhance the later seroconversion with the primary doses. Further booster doses are given at 16–18 months and at 5 years. In addition, all the children should receive pulse polio doses on national and subnational immunization days irrespective of their routine immunization.
- The most severe adverse effect of OPV is vaccine-associated paralytic polio (VAPP), which is caused by the neurovirulence of the replicating poliovirus in the intestinal tract. VAPP is defined as residual paralysis 60 days after the onset of paralysis in patients with acute flaccid paralysis (AFP), and in these patients, vaccine-related poliovirus instead of wild virus is isolated from the stool samples. The incidence of VAPP is estimated

to be 4 cases per million (1/1,000,000) birth cohort per year in countries using OPV.

- At the outreach facility, OPV needs to be stored at 2–8°C, while long-term storage for 1–2 years is done at –20°C.

Inactivated Polio Vaccine

- IPV is a formaldehyde-killed and inactivated vaccine against all the three types (1, 2, and 3) of polioviruses. The ones that are presently used are enhanced potency IPVs (eIPVs) that induce the development of neutralizing antibodies against all the three types in 95–100% of patients after the primary immunization.
- IPV produces excellent humoral immunity and provides herd immunity, though less than OPV.
- IPV can be coadministered along with and in combination with DPT/DaPT, Hib, and HBV vaccines without compromising the immune response or increasing the side effects.
- The vaccine has a good safety profile and side effects such as allergic reactions to trace amounts of contained antibiotics in the vaccine (e.g., streptomycin and neomycin) are extremely rare.
- Several countries in the world have shifted over from all doses of OPV to sequential OPV–IPV schedule and later will shift to all IPV schedule slowly with the eradication of wild poliovirus. In post-eradication era, use of IPV will become indispensable.
- IPV has been introduced in National Immunization Schedule by intradermal route in primary series and 6 and 14 weeks.

Measles/MMR Vaccine

Measles is a highly contagious viral infection and vaccine against measles is available as a monovalent (measles) and also as a combination vaccine (MMR and MR—measles and rubella—vaccine).

- This is a live attenuated vaccine developed from Edmonston-Zagreb strain and contains no preservatives.
- The immunogenicity of the vaccine is best after the age of 12 months when the maternal antibodies against measles would have disappeared but by then a significant number of infants may develop measles infection leading to high morbidity and mortality; hence, the vaccine is logistically given at the age of completed 9 months. During an outbreak of measles in the community, the vaccine can be given as early as 6 months to be followed by another dose between 12 and 15 months.
- The protective efficacy of measles vaccine is 85–90% when it is administered at the age of 9 months. Based on this factor and to provide protection to remaining 15% of babies who fail to respond, an additional (second) dose of measles or preferably MMR vaccine at the age of 15 months is recommended to provide possible lifelong protection.
- Measles/MMR vaccines are supplied as freeze-dried vaccines in single/multidose vials and need to be reconstituted just before administration with the diluent, kept between 2°C and 8°C, and must be used within 4 hours to avoid any contamination as they do not contain any preservative.
- The vaccine should be given 0.5 mL subcutaneously (SC) in either anterolateral thigh or deltoid in the upper arm.
- Measles/MMR vaccines are safe with few and mild side effects such as fever, pain, and mild measles-like illness (maculopapular rash) 7–12 days after the vaccination. Adverse events are extremely rare. Serious effect such as toxic shock syndrome is due to the contamination of the vaccine with *Staphylococcus aureus*.
- Measles/MMR vaccine is contraindicated in immunocompromised children.
- A second dose of the vaccine (MMR) is now recommended and implemented in a few states under UIP (routine immunization

program) that have a coverage of >80% with the first dose of measles vaccine.

- MMR vaccine is also a live attenuated vaccine, in a freeze-dried form, and has 95% efficacy in the prevention of mumps and rubella. The recommended age for its use is at or beyond 15 months of age. Rubella vaccine is also available as a single-component vaccine.
- Side effects due to MMR vaccine are mild and transient and occur in few recipients.
- MMR vaccine should not be given during pregnancy due to the risk of congenital malformations in the fetus, in immunosuppressed children, and in those who have a history of severe allergic reaction to a prior dose of MMR or its preservative components (gelatin, neomycin).

Hepatitis A Vaccine

- Hepatitis A vaccine is a whole-cell inactivated vaccine. It is inactivated with formalin and adsorbed on aluminum hydroxide as adjuvant.
- The vaccine is available both in pediatric formulation (720 EU) for children between 12 months and 18 years of age and in adult formulations (1440 EU) for subjects aged 19 years and older.
- Two doses of the vaccine administered at an interval of 6 months, after the age of 1 year, provide immunogenicity and the seroconversion rates of 95–100%. No booster is needed.
- The vaccine is given as an IM injection and can be given along with other childhood vaccines. It is not a part of routine immunization program but is particularly advisable for use in children with preexisting chronic liver disease.
- The side effects are mild and transient only.
- Hepatitis A vaccine is stored between 2°C and 8°C.
- A live attenuated hepatitis A vaccine has also now become available and is used in a single dose of 1 mL by SC route, beyond the age of 1 year.

Typhoid Vaccine

Earlier, the vaccines against typhoid fever included the parenteral heat-inactivated and live attenuated oral Ty21a vaccines but these are now not available in India. Currently available typhoid vaccines include Vi polysaccharide vaccine and Vi conjugate typhoid vaccines.

- *Vi polysaccharide vaccine*: A newer-generation, purified Vi polysaccharide against *S. typhi* has been in use and is effective in children above the age of 2 years. The vaccine is administered in a dose of 0.5 mL IM and its protective efficacy ranges from 55% to 75%. As the duration of protection of this single dose is up to 3 years, revaccination should be done once every 3 years for a continued protection. The side effects of Vi vaccine are mild and include fever, pain, and redness at the injection site.
- *Vi conjugate typhoid vaccines*: The advantages over polysaccharide vaccines are that they can be given below 2 years of age (above 6 months), they have a higher efficacy and immune memory due to T-cell-dependent response, and there is no need to repeat them every 3 years. The first dose is recommended between 9 and 12 months of age and the second dose at 2 years of age for long-term protection.

Varicella Vaccine

Varicella (chicken pox) vaccine is a live attenuated vaccine derived from the Oka strain of varicella zoster virus (VZV). It is prepared by passage through human diploid cells (HDCs) and contains a minimum virus content of 1350 PFU per dose. The vaccine also contains trace amounts of antibiotics as stabilizer but has no preservative.

- The vaccine is highly immunogenic and vaccine efficacy after the recommended two doses is estimated to be 70–90% against any varicella infection and 90–100% against moderate and severe varicella disease.

- The immunity induced by the vaccine is long-lasting and is usually permanent in majority of the vaccinees. If these children develop varicella infection, they generally have breakthrough infections (milder illness with less than 50 lesions, no or mild fever, and shorter duration of illness).
- Varicella vaccine is a lyophilized product that must be reconstituted just before its use and used within 30 minutes. It is administered SC on the upper arm or anterolateral part of thigh.
- Two doses of vaccine are recommended in children 15 months onwards and the second dose should be given anytime 3 months after the first dose but is generally given along with the other booster doses between 4 and 6 years.
- The vaccine is effective as postexposure prophylaxis in preventing or modifying the varicella disease if used within 3 days of exposure to an index case.
- Being a live attenuated viral vaccine, if it is not given on the same day along with other viral vaccines (e.g., MMR), there should be a minimum gap of 28 days between the two vaccines.
- The vaccine is not included in routine immunization program but should be offered to all healthy children, with special emphasis on children in high-risk group, for varicella and its complications. These include conditions such as nephrotic syndrome in remission, chronic lung/heart diseases, children with HIV infections (CD4 counts >15% and above the age-related cutoff), children likely to be put on long-term steroids, and adolescents/adults who did not have varicella in the past.
- Varicella zoster immunoglobulin (VZIG) is used selectively for passive prophylaxis such as in immunocompromised children at risk of varicella and in newborns whose mothers have developed varicella disease from 5 days before the delivery to 2 days after the delivery.
- The vaccine is safe and side effects are mild such as pain and low-grade fever. Systemic adverse reactions are extremely rare. The vaccine is contraindicated in immunocompromised children and pregnant women.
- The vaccine needs to be stored at –15°C and the diluent at room temperature or 4–8°C.

Rotavirus Vaccine

Diarrhea caused by RV is a common cause of morbidity in children and almost all the children get infected with RV by 5 years of age.

- RV vaccine(s) are live attenuated vaccines to be administered orally. Two types of RV vaccines are available in India: RV5 (containing five reassortant human and bovine RV strains) and RV1 (human G1P 8, monovalent) vaccines. Another RV vaccine (reassortant monovalent strain 116E) is likely to become available soon.
- RV5 vaccine comes with vaccine viruses suspended in buffer solution and is ready to use. While RV1 is provided as a lyophilized powder and should be reconstituted before use, RV5 is available as ready to use. None of these vaccines contain any preservative.
- RV vaccines provide 74–87% protection against any RV gastroenteritis and 85–98% protection against severe RV gastroenteritis. The exact duration of protection is not yet known.
- The upper limit for the first dose is 14 weeks and 6 days and the last dose of RV vaccine (second for RV1 and third for RV5 with a minimum interval of 4 weeks between the doses) can be given maximally up to 8 months. Beyond the age of 8 months, it increases the risk of intussusception and hence should not be given. Similarly, a past history of intussusception in an infant is a contraindication to its use.

- If RV1 is given in a two-dose schedule, then the first dose should be started at 10 weeks instead of at 6 weeks.
- The RV vaccines are safe and no serious adverse effects have been reported.

Pneumococcal Vaccine

Pneumococcal infections cause significant morbidities such as pneumonia, meningitis, otitis media, and bacteremia, particularly in children younger than 2 years old. A 23-valent unconjugated polysaccharide vaccine is available for many years, but as it is T-cell independent, it is poorly immunogenic below 2 years of age and is useful only above 2 years of age in specific/high-risk situations such as chronic systemic diseases, nephrotic syndrome, and sickle cell disease.

- The long-term benefit of protection against invasive pneumococcal infections at an early age is provided by pneumococcal conjugate vaccine (PCV 13), which is effective in the targeted children younger than 2 years of age. This protein carrier conjugated vaccine contains 13 common strains/serotypes of *S. pneumoniae* (conjugated pneumococcal vaccine).
- PCV 13 is available as a prefilled, ready-to-use syringe and is given IM in a three-dose schedule in infancy at an interval of 4–8 weeks followed by a booster dose at 15–18 months.
- Unvaccinated infants/children 7 months and older require lesser number of doses.
- The common side effects include fever, malaise, and injection site soreness.

Other Vaccines

Besides the vaccines described earlier, there are few other vaccines that are used in infants, children, and adolescents but are used either less frequently or in specific geographical, seasonal, or situations prone to exposure.

Meningococcal Vaccine

Its use is not *routinely* carried out in India. Two types of meningococcal vaccines are available: (i) polysaccharide unconjugated meningococcal vaccine not immunogenic in children <2 years of age, available for many years and is bivalent (A and C) or quadrivalent (A, C, Y, W 135); (ii) recently, a quadrivalent meningococcal conjugated vaccine (MCV) providing a longer duration of protection and that is approved for use in children aged 9 months and above has become available but is expensive. Meningococcal vaccines are recommended for use in high-risk group of children (e.g., asplenia), during outbreaks as an adjunct to chemoprophylaxis, and in international travelers to Haj and sub-Saharan Africa.

Japanese Encephalitis Vaccine

Viral encephalitis caused by JE is endemic in some parts of India (Andhra Pradesh, Uttar Pradesh, and West Bengal) and is associated with high morbidity and mortality.

- Although three types of JE vaccine have been used earlier, recently a new JE vaccine produced in India (an inactivated Vero cell culture derived with Indian strain) is available and is highly immunogenic and can be used in children >9 months old.
- Two doses of JE vaccine (SA14–14-2) are recommended for routine use in national schedule in selected JE endemic districts and states.

Influenza Vaccines

Influenza viruses are characterized by frequent mutations, shifts, and antigenic drifts, and with specific strains' immunity, influenza vaccines have to incorporate the prevalent antigenic strains.

- Based on WHO recommendations, influenza vaccines are updated every year.
- Influenza vaccine is recommended for children older than 6 months and is given

by SC/IM route in anterolateral thigh or deltoid muscle as 0.25 mL (for children aged 6–36 months) and 0.5 mL (for older children and adults).
- First-time recipients need to receive two doses at an interval of 4 weeks.
- Yearly/annual influenza vaccine at present is recommended for high-risk groups (e.g., chronic systemic diseases, hemoglobinopathies, and immunocompromised children and adults).
- The side effects include transient manifestations such as fever, myalgia, and malaise.
- Vaccine against swine flu is available in combination with seasonal flu vaccine.

Cholera Vaccines

The parenteral killed cholera vaccine used earlier had low efficacy and short-lived protection and hence is no longer recommended. A killed whole-cell oral cholera vaccine (WC-RBs) has been developed and is given in two doses, 1 week apart, in persons residing in highly endemic areas or traveling to areas where the risk of transmission is very high. The vaccine is not recommended for routine use in healthy individuals.

Rabies Vaccine

Three types of rabies vaccines are available for use: (i) HDC vaccine, (ii) purified chick embryo cell (PCEC), and (iii) purified Vero cell (PVR).
- All these vaccines satisfy the criteria of potency, immunogenicity, and safety, and there are no contraindications for their use for postexposure prophylaxis after an animal bite/lick/scratch.
- Along with the wound care, rabies prophylaxis is administered IM on anterolateral thigh/deltoid within 24 hours of exposure with a total of five doses (0, 3, 7, 14, and 30 days) as per Essen protocol. Rabies vaccine should never be given on the gluteal region.
- Rabies immunoglobulin (RIG) should be given at a separate site in all category III exposures.
- The vaccine is also useful for pre-exposure prophylaxis when there is risk of exposure in persons such as in children having pets at home, laboratory staff, and animal handlers. The dosing schedule is three doses (0, 7, and 21 days).

Human Papillomavirus Vaccine (HPV)

HPV is an important cause of cervical cancer in women and genital warts, and is implicated in other anogenital cancers.
- Presently, two HPV vaccines (a quadrivalent and a bivalent) with aluminum as adjuvant are available, which are manufactured by recombinant DNA technology that produces noninfectious virus-like particles (VLPs).
- Both the vaccines have two commonest oncogenic serotypes HPV 16 and 18. HPV vaccines have an excellent immunogenic and safety profile. No severe side effects are observed.
- Only two doses of either of the two HPV vaccines are recommended for adolescent/preadolescent girls aged 9–14 years.
- Girls 15 years and older and immunocompromised need to be given three doses, and the doses can be administered at 0, 1–2 (depending on the brand), and 6 months.
- For the two-dose schedule, the minimum interval between doses should be 6 months.
- Catch-up vaccination is permitted till the age of 45 years.

Vaccines Under Development

Some of the vaccines under investigation are those against malaria, HIV, kala-azar, dengue, respiratory syncytial virus (causing bronchiolitis), hepatitis C, *Shigella*, and streptococci (rheumatic fever) and the newer BCG vaccine. Vaccine development in future apart from preventing infectious diseases should also focus on chronic and systemic diseases.

Combination Vaccines

Currently, a few vaccines are available in combination and more are likely to become available in future.

- A combination vaccine is one that consists of two or more separate immunogens that are physically combined in a single preparation.
- Several examples of combination vaccines include DPT, MMR, OPV/IPV, pentavalent (DPT + Hib + HBV), DaPT + Hib + IPV, and conjugate pneumococcal (10) with nontypable *H. influenzae*.
- Combination vaccines offer benefits such as reduced number of injections/healthcare visits, reduced pain/anxiety, better compliance, and improved logistics such as fewer burdens on cold chain.
- However, these must fit into a schedule without compromising the recommended age/interval of the individual vaccines and if an adverse effect occurs, then it may be uncertain to link it with specific antigen/vaccine component in that combination vaccine.

Vaccine Administration, Practical, and Other Safety Issues

- Sterile techniques and safe injection practices should always be adhered to during immunization. Hand washing should be carried out using the WHO's six-step technique. Alternatively, an alcohol-based hand scrub may be used. Gloves are not needed while administering the vaccines.
- For multidose vials, the septum should be cleaned with an alcohol swab each time before withdrawing the vaccine. Changing of needles between puncturing the vial and administering the vaccine to the child is not necessary.
- Many vaccines are now available in prefilled syringes. For vaccines available in vials, disposable syringes should be used, preferably autodisabled syringes that automatically get disabled after a single use, thus preventing inadvertent reuse.
- Each vaccine should be filled in a different syringe. Mixing of vaccines in the same syringe is not allowed unless specified and labeled by the manufacturer.
- The length of the needle depends on the route of administration—shorter for ID and SC injections.
- A 23- to 25-gauge needle that is 0.6–1 inch in length is appropriate for IM route in infants and children.
- All vaccines should be administered by the correct prescribed route for obtaining maximum efficacy and for minimizing side effects. All inactivated vaccines are given IM as these vaccines contain adjuvants (aluminum salts) to enhance the efficacy. Adjuvants are irritants and hence IM route is used to minimize local reactions.
- Site used for IM route is anterolateral aspect (at the junction of middle and lower one-third) of the thigh in children. However, upper arm (deltoid) may also be used in older children if muscle mass is adequate. The gluteal region should never be used due to the probability of injuring the sciatic nerve. Also, in the gluteal region, the muscle is deep inside as the fat layer is abundant and an intended IM injection may be delivered SC, thus decreasing efficacy and increasing the incidence of local adverse reactions.
- Angles used for correctly administering IM and SC injections are 90° and 45°, respectively, to the injection site. During an IM injection, aspiration after a prick is not advised as no large arteries are present in the chosen sites. Aspiration would also waste time and increase pain and an IM injection would get inadvertently converted into a SC injection.

- Each injection can be spaced from the other by about 1 inch. After withdrawal of the needle, gently press/rub the injection site with a dry swab to minimize irritation and help the vaccine spread.
- Routes of administration are ID (for BCG and rabies vaccines in selective situations where IM route is to be avoided), SC (for measles, MMR, varicella), IM (e.g., DPT, HBV, TT), and oral (OPV and RV vaccines).
- Delayed visits/doses of a particular antigen/vaccine do not indicate restarting the series, but the number of scheduled/remaining doses must be completed.
- Interval between the doses of vaccines is an important aspect for the live vaccines as the attenuated microorganisms invade the host and multiply in the body to generate an immune response. Two or more live vaccines should be administered 4 weeks apart to ensure an adequate immune response.
- Injection safety and waste disposal are of utmost importance. The correct method of waste disposal should be used to dispose of the syringes, needles, and cotton swabs to prevent needlestick injuries and transmission of infections. The material should be immediately discarded; needles should never be recapped before being discarded in labeled puncture-proof containers designated for appropriate disposal.

Comfort Measures to Reduce Pain

- Decreasing pain and discomfort during immunization procedures should be given utmost importance.
- Nonpharmacological methods to reduce pain are cuddling the baby in mother's lap, breastfeeding, ingestion of sweet-tasting liquids, and kangaroo mother care.
- Pharmacological methods to reduce pain are oral paracetamol, local anesthetic sprays, and patches.
- When multiple vaccines are to be administered in a single sitting, it is prudent to give the oral vaccine first followed by less painful injections (SC), keeping the more painful IM injections for the last.

Cold Chain

Cold chain is a system of transporting, storing, and distributing vaccines in a potent state, at recommended temperatures, from the manufacturer to the point of use. The requirements for proper cold chain maintenance are:

- Storing facilities/equipment: Walk-in cold rooms (WICs)/walk-in freezers (WIFs), deep freezers, ice-lined refrigerators (ILRs), domestic refrigerators, and purpose-built refrigerators (PBRs)
- Transporting facility/equipment: Cold boxes/vaccine carriers
- Monitoring tools: VVMs, thermometers, and Freeze Watch indicators
- Trained, committed, and motivated personnel

Cold chain has a crucial role in the immunization programs because the vaccines are sensitive to heat and light and improper cold chain maintenance can irreversibly affect the vaccine potency and efficacy.

The cold rooms, deep freezers, ILRs, and domestic refrigerators constitute the *fixed components* and the cold boxes/vaccine carriers are *mobile components* of cold chain maintenance.

Cold Rooms, Deep Freezers, ILRs

- Cold rooms are available at manufacturing sites and at large distribution centers. These WICs are sophisticated and are equipped with cooling units, generators, temperature recorders, and alarm systems.
- Deep freezers are used for long-term storage of vaccines and for making ice packs required for lining ILR.
- ILR is also used for storing vaccines and is more useful at places where electricity supply is intermittent and erratic. In this situation, the ice packs lining the ILR

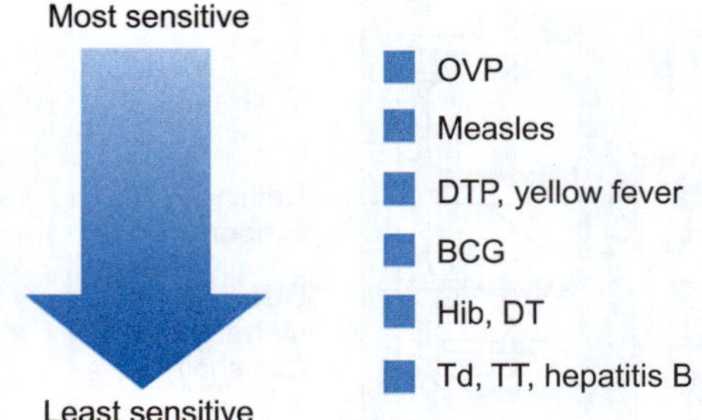

Figure 5.2 Vaccine sensitivity to heat.

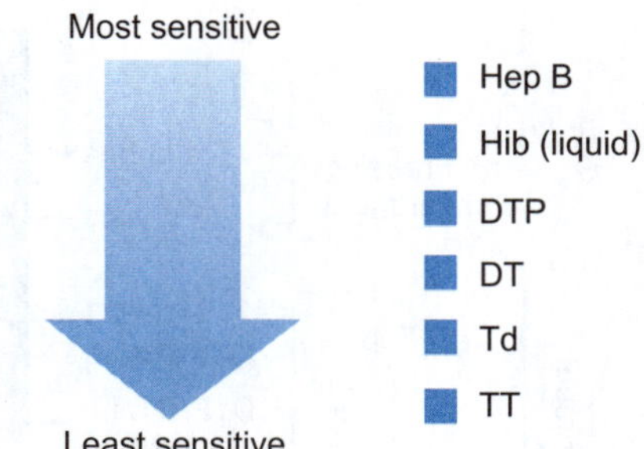

Figure 5.3 Sensitivity of vaccines to cold/freezing.

maintain the required temperature for several hours to several days.

Heat and Freeze Sensitivity of Vaccines

- As vaccines are biological products, all the vaccines are sensitive to heat but to varying degrees.
- The live vaccines are the most heat sensitive and thermosensitivity of the vaccines in decreasing order is as follows: BCG (after reconstitution), OPV, measles/MMR, DPT, BCG (before reconstitution), DT, TT, HBV, and JE vaccines (Fig. 5.2).
- BCG, measles, and MMR vaccines are both heat and light sensitive and are supplied in dark-colored glass vials to protect their exposure and damage from the light.
- Reconstituted BCG, measles, and JE vaccines are the most sensitive to heat and light. Since these live vaccines do not contain preservatives, there is risk of contamination with *S. aureus*, leading to toxic shock syndrome, and, therefore, they should not be used after 4 hours of reconstitution.
- All vaccines containing adjuvants are susceptible to damage by freezing.
- Sensitivity to freezing in decreasing order starting from the most freeze (cold)-sensitive vaccine is as follows: hepatitis B, Hib, DPT, DT, TT, and combination vaccines. If these vaccines are accidentally frozen, then they must not be used but discarded (Fig. 5.3).

Storage of Vaccines in Domestic Refrigerator

Domestic refrigerators are not the best place to store the vaccines; they are however the most common storage equipment for these products in many centers providing vaccination services. However, certain precautions must be observed and due to less temperature variations in frost-free refrigerators, these are more suitable for vaccine storage than those with manual/cyclic defrost mechanisms. Following points need to be observed:

- Refrigerator must be at least 10 cm away from the wall, to allow proper air circulation for cooling.
- The refrigerator compartment must be at 2–8°C and the freezer compartment at or below –15°C. Ice packs should be kept in the freezer along with water-filled bottles to increase the cool mass in the refrigerator. No vaccine should be kept in the refrigerator's door.
- Temperature log should be filled out twice daily and the power supply source should be safeguarded to avoid it being switched off accidentally. Avoid overcrowding of vaccines and their boxes, leaving some space between them.
- The most heat-sensitive vaccine (OPV) should be stored in the freezer or in the top shelf. However, repeated freezing and thawing of OPV damages the potency of the OPV and hence should be avoided. Other freeze-tolerant vaccines (measles, MMR, BCG) should also be kept in the top shelf.

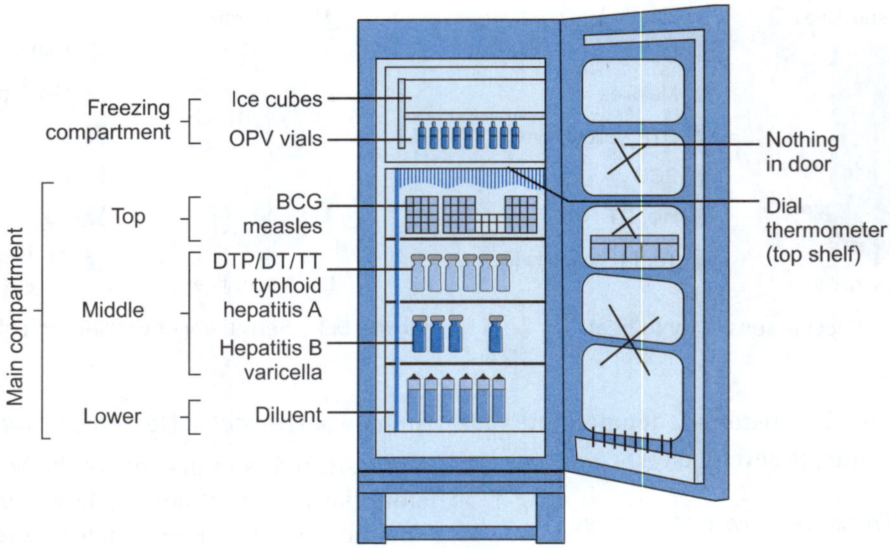

Freezing compartment
Ice cubes
OPV vials
Main compartment
Top
BCG
measles
Middle
DTP/DT/TT
typhoid
hepatitis A
Hepatitis B
varicella
Lower
Diluent
Nothing in door
Dial thermometer (top shelf)

Figure 5.4 Vaccine storage in a domestic refrigerator.

- Freeze-sensitive vaccines (DPT, Hib, HBV, IPV, and some varicella vaccines) should be kept on the middle shelf (Fig. 5.4).
- Opened vial policy means that in case of multidose vials of DPT/DT/TT, combination vaccines (pentavalent), hepatitis B, and OPV, the vials can be utilized for subsequent immunization sessions for a maximum of 1 month, provided they have been stored in ideal conditions.
- In case of BCG and measles vaccine, this policy does not hold true, and the vial, even if not fully utilized, has to be discarded after either each session or maximum 6 hours.
- Diluents must never be frozen and should be kept in the lowermost compartments.
- The recommended storage of vaccines in a refrigerator in a clinical setup is shown in Figure 5.4.

Purpose-Built Refrigerator

- This is a refrigerator built for the special purpose of storing vaccines and nothing else is stored. PBR meets medical standards. Temperature control is better than that in domestic refrigerator.
- PBR has a microprocessor-based electronic control system with alarms for maximum/minimum temperatures. The glass doors and interior lighting provide easy viewing and easy accessibility to vaccines.
- The storage space available for vaccines is more than that in a domestic refrigerator.

Cold Box/Vaccine Carrier

These are equipment used for transporting vaccines from the place of storage to the immunization venue (Fig. 5.5). Cold boxes are larger than vaccine carriers and are made of thermocol, at least 2 inches thick. Vaccine carriers are more compact and easy to carry by a health worker. The sides are lined with ice packs and the central space is used for

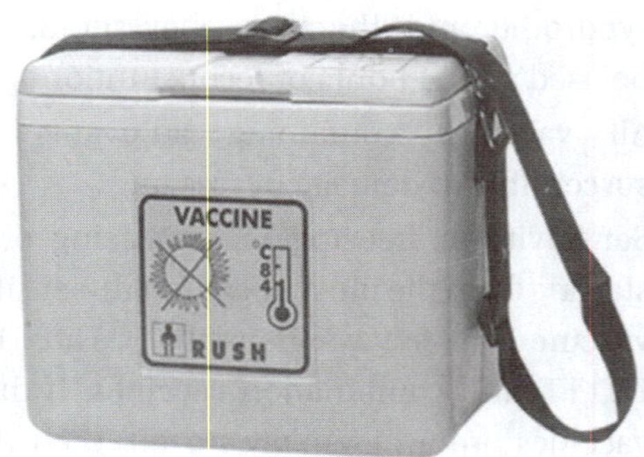

Figure 5.5 Vaccine carrier.

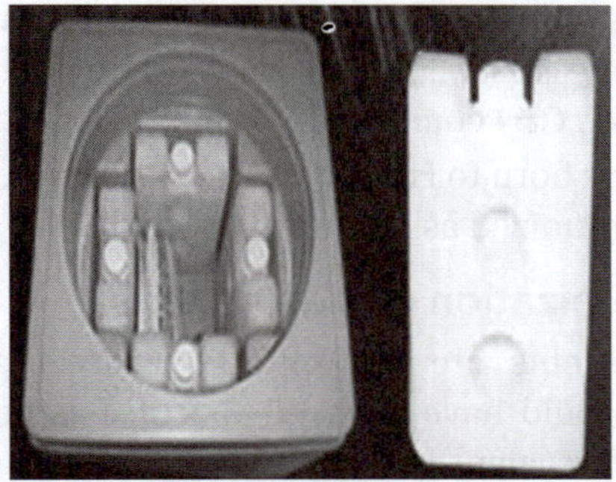

Figure 5.6 Vaccine carrier lined with coolant (ice packs).

carrying the necessary amount of vaccine needed for the day's schedule. The vaccines are packed in a plastic bag and are not allowed to come in direct contact with the ice pack. A dial thermometer is placed in the carrier for temperature monitoring. The lid is tightly closed before carrying to the outreach session (Fig. 5.6).

Monitoring Tools

- All manufacturers should provide a *VVM* on each vial of the vaccine. Decision to use or discard a vaccine depends on the color of the inner square of the VVM (Fig. 5.7).
- Thermometers are other tools available for monitoring. The different types available are dial thermometers, maximum–minimum thermometers, and electronic/digital thermometers that should be placed amid the vaccines and not in the door or near the freezer for effective temperature monitoring.
- A Freeze Watch indicator is another monitoring tool that consists of a vial of red liquid attached to a white card and covered in plastic. The vial breaks if temperature drops below 0°C for more than 1 hour. This tool is very useful to maintain potency of cold-sensitive vaccines such as DPT, DT, TT, and hepatitis B.

Figure 5.7 Vaccine vial monitors.

Immunization Under Special Situations

Certain special situations warrant a change in the recommended immunization schedule or at least a consideration toward the same. The issues at hand are immunocompromised situations (prematurity, HIV, steroid therapy). These increase chances of infections and hence there is an enhanced need for complete and timely immunization.

However, these situations lead to poor immunogenicity and poor immune response to vaccines. A vaccine strain may also lead to disease in immunocompromised children and hence utmost care and consideration is required to draw a balance and immunize optimally.

Preterm and Low-Birth-Weight (LBW) Babies

All vaccines should be given as per schedule as for term babies. BCG and OPV should be given at birth as soon as baby stabilizes or at least at the time of discharge. HBV evokes poor antibody response in babies weighing less than 2 kg and hence should be given at 1 month of age. However, if mother is HBsAg positive, the baby should receive vaccine and immunoglobulin soon after birth. No other change of schedule or lowering of dose should be done. All other vaccines should be given as per regular recommended schedule as most of the vaccines evoke good/satisfactory seroconversion rates.

Steroid Therapy

Steroid therapy is a contraindication to live vaccines *only* when child is on high-dose (2 mg/kg/day, or 20 mg/day) and long-term (>2 weeks) therapy. There is no contraindication for killed/inactivated vaccines. Low-dose, short-term, and alternate-day treatment with steroids is not a contraindication and all vaccines can be given as per schedule in these situations.

Children with Splenectomy

Children with splenic dysfunction and asplenia, either anatomic or functional (e.g., sickle cell disease), are at increased risk of infections with capsulated organisms such as *S. pneumococcus*, Hib, and *N. meningitidis*. Vaccines against these organisms need to be given at least 2 weeks prior to surgery. If not, then they should be given as soon as after the surgery once the child is hemodynamically stable.

HIV Infection

Children with HIV infection are immunocompromised and more prone to infections. Immunogenicity, efficacy, and safety are well preserved in early stage and compromised only in advanced stage. Hence, decision on immunization schedule largely depends on whether the child is asymptomatic or symptomatic. Considerations while immunizing a child with HIV infection are as follows:

- IPV should be given instead of OPV. However, if cost is a concern, OPV can be given.
- In asymptomatic children, all other vaccines are given as per schedule with extra care to see that boosters are not missed.
- In symptomatic children, live vaccines such as measles, MMR, and varicella are given only when CD4 count is >15% and BCG is avoided.
- Baby born to HIV-positive mother should be immunized as per normal schedule.

Immunization of Adolescents

Adolescents are an important target group who would have received vaccines as per the then prevalent and recommended schedule either completely or partially. All contact with adolescents in healthcare setup should be used to immunize these adolescents as newer vaccines have been added or newer schedules recommended.

- Hepatitis B, hepatitis A, MMR, and varicella vaccines should be given if not already received.
- Adolescents traveling to other countries for study purpose should additionally receive vaccines as per recommendations of the country of visit.
- Td or TdaP should be given instead of TT at 10 and 16 years of age.

Immunization and Communication

Parents must be given clear information and instructions so that timely vaccinations are completed, and they understand the benefits of immunization. They must be informed about:

- Which vaccine was given, and which disease(s) is prevented
- What the minor side effects are and how to deal with them
- When to come again for the next visit
- Keeping the immunization/vaccination card/record safe and bringing it along at the next visit

KEY POINTS

- Immunization not only protects the children against preventable diseases but also provides an opportunity to deliver other health-related interventions such as vitamin A supplementation.
- In addition, the benefits of immunization are now further extended to adolescents (e.g., HPV vaccine) and adults, providing protection against life-threatening diseases such as influenza, meningitis, and cancers that occur in adulthood.

CHAPTER 6

Infant and Young Child Feeding

Bakulesh M Chauhan, Vijayashree Mishra

Breastfeeding is the best and the ideal form of infant feeding and is crucial for the lifelong health and the well-being of the child. Among its numerous benefits, breast milk offers unique nutritional, immunological, and psychological advantages.

Scientific studies and research have established the advantages and benefits of breastfeeding not only for the child but also for the mother, the family, the community, and the environment. Thus, the breast milk of the mother is best suited to meet the biological needs of her baby. Artificial feeding exposes the child to infections and allergies and contributes to over 1 million childhood deaths per year in the world. Breastfeeding alone provides all nutrition up to 6 months of age, after which its proportion declines. It can provide 70% of the nutritional needs between 7 and 9 months of age and about 55% requirement at 10–12 months of age.

Composition of Breast Milk

- The composition of human milk is not constant. It changes with maturity, stages of lactation, with day and night, and even during the same feed in the initial and end periods.
- The milk is yellow and often thick in the initial 3–4 days, known as "colostrum," and gradually changes to the white mature milk by the 10th day.
- Colostrum is easily digestible and rich in proteins, vitamins, growth factors, and anti-infective factors. It has a mild purgative action that helps clearing the meconium and bile pigments (reducing the risk of hyperbilirubinemia).
- It contains twice the amount of protein, more minerals, and anti-infective substances that protect the baby against infections and help in catch-up growth. The colostrum is considered as the first vaccine for the newborn baby.
- Foremilk: The milk in the initial period (foremilk) has a high content of water and lactose and less of fat (appeasement of thirst and hunger).
- Hindmilk: As the feeding continues, the fat content increases; hence, it is important that the baby empties one breast before starting on the other breast. The side of feeding should be changed only after the baby has finished feeding from the first.
- Preterm milk: Milk produced by a woman who has delivered prematurely is called preterm milk. This milk has higher protein, minerals, immunoglobulins compared to term milk, making it suitable to the needs of a preterm baby.

Important Components of Human Milk

- *Proteins*: There are mainly two classes of proteins in milk—whey proteins (acid soluble) and casein (acid precipitable curd). Human milk is whey predominant; whey protein to casein ratio is 60:40 compared to that of 20:80 in cow milk. Human milk is the source of highest quality of protein.

TABLE 6.1 Gross Composition of Human and Cow Milk Per 100 mL

	Human milk	Cow milk
Energy (cal)	67	67
Protein (g)	1.1	3.2
Fat (g)	3.8	3.7
Lactose (g)	7.0	4.5
Essential fatty acids (%)	13	2
Ca:P ratio	>2	<2
Osmolarity (mOsm/L)	290	350

It contains cysteine and taurine which are essential for the development of brain and retina.

- *Fat*: The fat globules of smaller size and lipase that facilitates complete digestion of fats and fatty acids (arachidonic and docosahexaenoic) are important for neurodevelopment and myelination.
- *Carbohydrates*: Lactose in the breast milk is a ready source of energy and it is also a source of galactose and galactolipids that are essential for the central nervous system (CNS) development.
- *Vitamins and minerals*: Breast milk contains sufficient amounts of vitamin A, C, D, and B complex. Vitamin K content is less therefore a single dose of Vitamin K is given at birth. Iron content in breast milk is less; however, the bioavailability of iron is much superior. Calcium to phosphorus ratio is more than 2 (optimal), which is less than 2 in cow milk.
- *Osmolality*: The osmolality of human milk matches that of serum while that of cow milk is very high and imposes burden on the neonatal and infant kidneys. The constituents and the differences between the human milk and the cow milk are shown in Table 6.1.

Anti-Infective Factors

- Antibodies in the mucosa-associated lymphoid tissue (MALT) are passed through breast milk.
- A large number of antibodies (e.g., IgA), non-antibodies (lysozyme, lactoferrin, bifidus factor), and cellular components (macrophages, B and T lymphocytes) in the breast milk protect the infant against many infections.

Antiallergic Factors

Secretory IgA in the human milk blocks the translocation of foreign protein and sensitization of the immune system. Infantile eczema and reactive airway disease are more common in babies given artificial feeding. Prelacteal feeds (ghutti, honey, ghee, "gal-thuthi," gripe water, etc.) not only can carry infection but also may sensitize the baby to develop allergic reaction.

Initiation of Breastfeeding

- The preparation and motivation for breast-feeding should begin during the antenatal visits. Mother should be checked for retracted/cracked nipples and necessary advice should be given so that the baby does not face any difficulty during breastfeeding after birth.
- The absence of sucking difficulties during early nursing is of vital importance to establish successful lactation.
- Breastfeeding should be initiated within half an hour of birth in all healthy newborns. This is done as soon as the mother recovers from the fatigue of the labor and in case of cesarean section, within 4 hours of birth.
- Healthy babies after the delivery should have immediate skin-to-skin contact with their mothers. Mothers and babies should remain together and "room-in" the same hospital room throughout their hospital stay to initiate early breastfeeding.
- The frequency of breastfeeding should be as often as the baby wants (demand feeding) during both day and night. Early and frequent feedings are associated with increased milk production.

Box 6.1 Definitions in breastfeeding

- *Exclusive breastfeeding*: The baby is given only breast milk and no other food/drink is given, not even water. Medicines, vitamins, and minerals are permitted if indicated. An infant should be breastfed exclusively for the first 6 months.
- *Predominant breastfeeding*: The main source of nutrition is breast milk, but the child also receives other fluids.
- *Partial breastfeeding*: The infant receives the nonhuman milk, formula, or cereal-based foods in addition to breast milk before the age of 6 months.

- Adequate support, guidance, and encouragement from the family and the hospital setup are a great boost to enhance the breast milk production in the mother.
- No prelacteal feeds such as glucose water or honey should be given.
- Bottle feeds of formula milk should be totally avoided even if there is an anxiety about the lack of inadequate milk. This is so because the bottle feeds cause nipple confusion as a baby has different mechanisms to feed from the teat of the bottle and the breast. This can lead to decreased breast milk production due to reduced sucking efforts and reduced hormonal stimulation.
- In a situation of maternal separation from the infant, the mother should be counseled and taught the technique of expression of the milk. She should also be taught how to feed breast milk with cup or spoon.
- Certain definitions related to breast feeding are given in Box 6.1.

Adequacy of Breastfeeding

"Not enough milk" is a common complaint, though almost all mothers have enough milk secretions to feed their babies. Excessive crying most of the times is wrongly attributed to hunger cry due to insufficient milk. However, cry can also be due to other reasons such as infantile colic, improper clothing, and wet nappies. The following are the criteria to judge the adequacy of breastfeeding.

- When a baby is fed adequately, he/she appears relaxed during feeding and satiated after the feeding.
- The baby passes dilute water-like urine at least six times per day.
- The best criterion for the adequacy of breast milk is that the baby starts to gain 25–30 g of weight per day after the first week of life.

Technique of Breastfeeding

Although breastfeeding is naturally instinctive to most mothers, a few steps and advice help the mothers to practice breastfeeding with ease, comfort, and confidence.

- Mother should take any position that is comfortable to her and her baby. She may sit or lie with the back well supported.
- Baby should be raised up to the level of breast so that the baby's mouth can easily reach the areola and the nipple.
- The correct position is indicated if the baby's neck is straight, back slightly bent and completely supported, and baby facing toward and lying close to the mother with its abdomen touching the mother's abdomen (Fig. 6.1).
- The most common position is the *cradle hold* where the baby's head is supported by the mother's elbow, and the back and the

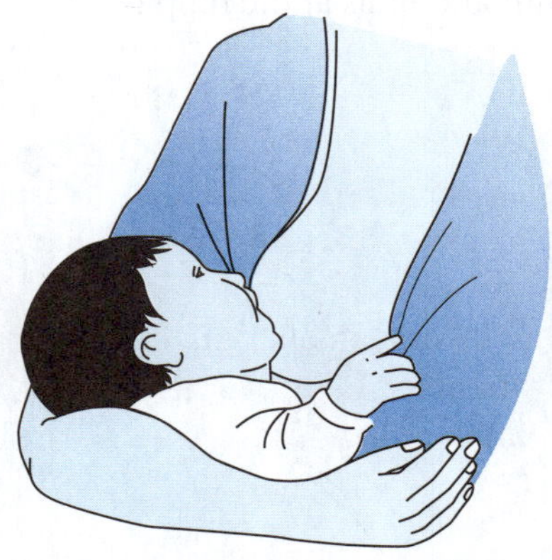

Figure 6.1 Proper positioning of the baby during breastfeeding. *Source*: Lakshmanaswamy A. Clinical Paediatrics History Taking and Case Discussion, 4th edn. Wolters Kluwer India: New Delhi, 2017.

buttocks are supported by the arm and lifted to the breast.

- Once the lips/cheeks of the baby touch the mother's breasts, he/she opens the mouth and roots toward the nipple. Then the baby should grasp the nipple and the part of areola of the breast in his/her mouth. This is called *attachment* to the breast. Good attachment or *latching* is central to proper and adequate breastfeeding.
- The *signs of good attachment* include
  - Widely open baby's mouth
  - Everted lower lip
  - Baby's chin touching the mother's breast
  - Most of the areola and nipple inside baby's mouth, with more areola visible above than below baby's mouth

  The mother feels no pain or discomfort while breastfeeding (Fig. 6.2).
- Effective suckling is indicated by slow and deep sucks, and sometimes pauses in between. One can also see or hear the baby swallowing with gulping sounds.

Poor attachment can result in pain and trauma leading to sore nipples, and breast engorgement. Poor feeding may lead to inadequate breast milk production. The poor attachment is shown in Figure 6.3. Here, the baby is shown not to have most of the areola in the mouth and pulls at the nipple.

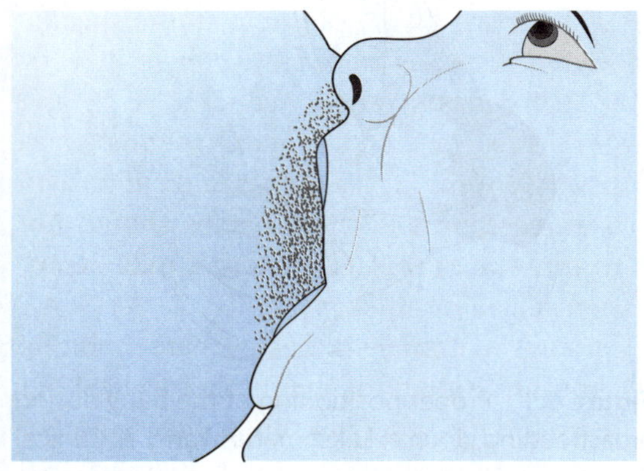

Figure 6.2 Good attachment in breastfeeding.

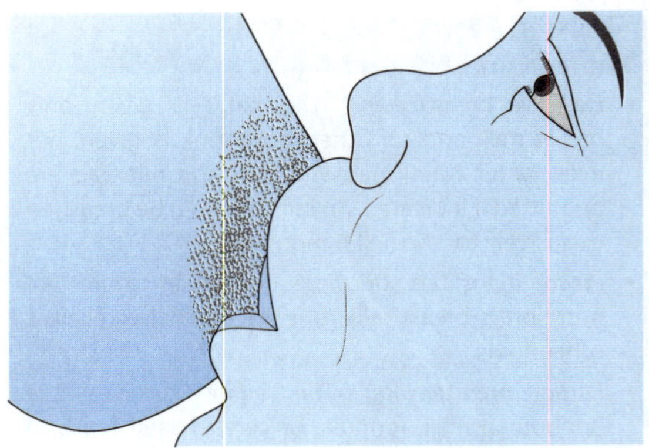

Figure 6.3 Poor attachment of the baby to the mother's breast.

Guidelines in Clinical Practice for Successful Breastfeeding

At Birth

- There should be enthusiastic support of breastfeeding by all healthcare providers.
- Recommend human milk for all infants as the first choice for feeding.
- Healthy newborns should be in direct skin-to-skin contact with their mothers immediately after birth.
- Initiate breastfeeding in the first hour of birth in all healthy infants.
- Help the mother with positioning and attaching the baby in the first few attempts.

During Postnatal Care

- Healthcare providers should be proactive and provide support for breastfeeding.
- Promote exclusive breastfeeding.
- The mother and the baby should sleep in proximity to each other.
- Observe a breastfeeding session. It involves observing and assessing feeding pattern, positioning and attachment, sucking behavior, and breast fullness.
- Implement babyfriendly hospital initiative.
- The use of commercial discharge packs containing formula or promotional material for formula milk must be strictly avoided.

- Enforce the principles and aims of the International Code of Marketing of Breast-Milk Substitutes.
- Support breastfeeding mothers and babies when confronted with medical needs that may jeopardize successful breastfeeding.
- Each mother at the time of discharge should demonstrate competence with nursing, including latching, identifying infant swallows and readiness to end a feeding, and identifying early feeding cues.

For NICU Mothers

- Early, frequent, and effective milk expression appears to be the most important factor in establishing lactation.
- When direct breastfeeding is not possible, expressed human milk should be provided.
- Personal assistance should be given that includes peer counselors, lactation specialist, or peer support for mothers with insufficient breast milk.
- There are some simple practical ways of stimulating milk production. These include: expressing milk in proximity to the infant, skin-to-skin (kangaroo) care, non-nutritive suckling at the breast, and breast massage.

At Home

- There should be exclusive breastfeeds till the first 6 months.
- Demand feeding, which is frequent and unrestricted breastfeeding, day and night, is the best way to feed a baby.
- Water and other fluids should not be given to breastfeeding infants in the first 6 months.
- Continue breastfeeds up to 2 years and beyond in addition to complementary feeds from 6 months of age.
- Freshly expressed human milk can be used safely for up to 8 hours at room temperature.

For Healthcare Providers

- Advocate, support, and promote breastfeeding.
- See the baby within 1–2 days after discharge from the hospital or birthing center, and continue frequent visits until the baby is gaining weight adequately and the mother appears confident.
- Assess for adequacy of breastfeeding at every opportunity by the infant's weight, hydration status, and the presence or absence of jaundice.
- Respond to parental concerns on feeding.
- Prevention and early help with breastfeeding problems are crucial.
- Most common infant and maternal health problems should not preclude breastfeeding, but mothers and infants will need support from knowledgeable healthcare professionals.
- Each prescribing decision should be taken after considering the risks and benefits to the individual mother and baby.
- Provide written or multimedia resources for patient education.
- Few situations and their management for breastfeeding problems are shown in Table 6.2.

Alternative Use of Breast Milk Substitutes

Almost all mothers can breastfeed successfully; nevertheless, a small number of health conditions of the infant or the mother may justify not breastfeeding temporarily or permanently. Whenever ceasing of breastfeeding is considered, the benefits of breastfeeding should be weighed against the risks posed by the presence of the specific conditions listed as follows:

- A few rare metabolic conditions in the newborns such as galactosemia and phenylketonuria are contraindications to breastfeeding and these babies should not receive breast milk or any other milk except specialized formula.
- Minor maternal illnesses are not a contraindication for the mother to feed her baby. If the mother has tuberculosis, mother and infant should be treated together and the breastfeeds be continued.

TABLE 6.2 Troubleshooting for Breastfeeding Problems

Problem	Characteristics	Management
Breast engorgement	May occur on days 2–7 when milk "comes in"; if engorgement is not relieved, milk production would diminish	• Frequent breastfeeding • Analgesia compatible with breastfeeding • Breast massage • Manual expression if necessary • Warm compresses
Sore nipples	It can be due to incorrect attachment (baby sucks only at nipple). It can also be due to candida infection. Cleaning breast frequently with soap and water removes the natural oil and causes soreness	• Correct position and attachment • Application of hindmilk over nipple • Exposure of nipple to air in between the feeds • Treatment with topical antifungal if necessary
Mastitis/breast abscess	Caused by a blocked milk duct and poor milk drainage; signs and symptoms range from local inflammation with minimal systemic symptoms to abscess formation	• Continue breastfeeding or give expressed breast milk • Use of analgesics and warm compresses to alleviate pain • Antibiotics • Incision and drainage may be needed if abscess has developed
Inverted or flat nipples	Nipple does not protract. Any attempt to pull it out shifts it further into the breast	• Teach mother to grasp breast tissue so that it forms a teat and the baby is able to suck • Manual stretching and syringing techniques are advised • For syringing, take 10 or 20 cc disposable syringe, cut the nozzle, insert the plunger from cut end, apply the other end over nipple and pull the plunger so that the nipple protrudes into the syringe. This should be done 5–8 times a day (Fig. 6.4)
Multiple births	Ongoing struggles with the sheer intensity of the process of breast-feeding	• Reassure mother that she can produce enough milk required for her babies • She can feed them consecutively or simultaneously • She can use cradle or football or combination position method • Family support is essential
Preterm baby	Co-ordinated sucking and swallowing usually comes at around 32–34 weeks of gestation, so the newborn may not be able to suck directly on breast. Feeding may also be delayed due to various morbidities related to prematurity and LBW	• If child is unable to suck from breast, then expressed breast milk can be given either as intragastric feeding or can be given with *katori* and spoon/paladey

- Severe illness that prevents a mother from caring for her infant, for example, sepsis or postpartum psychosis, justifies temporary deferment of breastfeeding.
- Hepatitis B is not a contraindication to breastfeeding, provided the baby receives hepatitis B immunoglobulin and vaccine against hepatitis B.
- HIV-positive mother should be counseled about the risk of transmission of HIV versus benefits of breastfeeding. She should be given support for deciding appropriate infant feeding practices. With appropriate antiretroviral drugs to the mother and the infant, exclusive breastfeeding for 6 months is recommended in India.

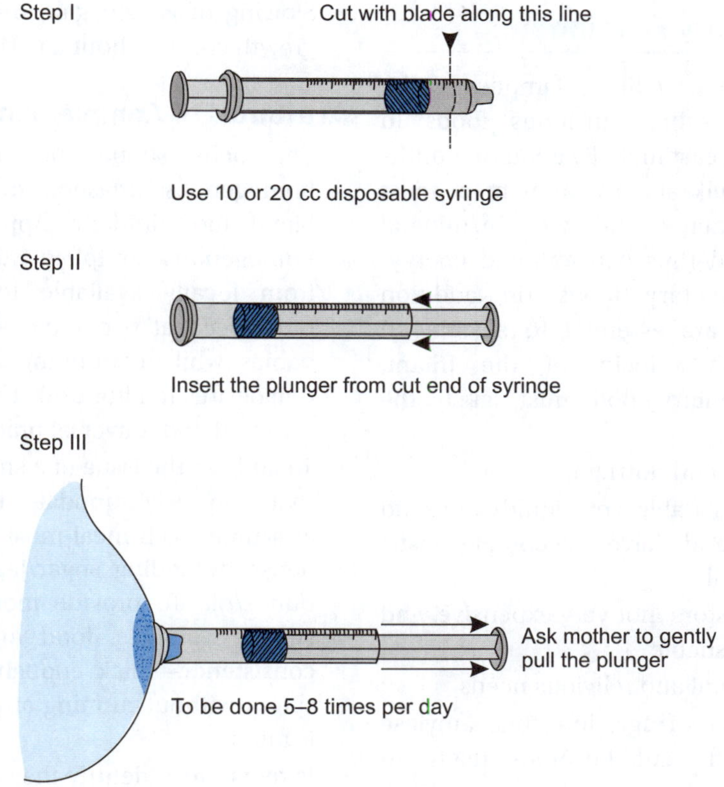

Figure 6.4 Syringing technique for treatment of inverted nipple.

- Certain drugs can be secreted in the breast milk and they can affect the baby adversely. Breastfeeding must be avoided if the mother is taking cytotoxic/anticancer drugs (cyclophosphamide, methotrexate), antithyroid drugs, anticoagulants, and antidepressants. Radioactive compounds such as gallium-67 (^{67}Ga), indium-111 (^{111}In), iodine-131 (^{131}I), and technetium-99m (^{99}mTc) may lead to secretion of radioactive substance in breast milk and are a contraindication to breast-feeding.
- Despite breast milk being the best for a baby, there may be few situations where an alternate milk feeding becomes necessary (such as adopted infant, critically sick mother, triplets, working mother who may be unable to breastfeed). Any milk (dairy milk such as standard/cow milk) may be given by a cup or spoon to the infant without any dilution. Sugar can be added to the milk as per baby's liking. Bottle feeding should be strictly avoided.
- Feeding by a cup or katori is better than bottle feeding and the cup or katori is easier to clean than the bottle. The baby should be held upright or semi-upright on the attendant's lap and a spoonful of milk should be held and brought near the baby's lip. Do not pour the milk into the baby's mouth; and let the baby touch the spoon and take it himself/herself. When the baby has enough milk, he/she will close the mouth and will not take more.
- Dried infant milk formulas can also be used instead of dairy milk with proper and hygienic dilution (one level measure of powder dissolved in 30 mL of preboiled warm water) but it is costly.

Complementary Feeding

Complementary feeding implies the introduction of other nutritious foods in addition to the breast milk. By about 6 months of age, breast milk alone cannot meet most babies' total energy and vitamin/mineral requirements and thus concentrated energy-dense complementary foods (in addition to breast milk) are essential to sustain an adequate growth velocity of the infant. Good complementary food must satisfy the following criteria:

- Rich in energy and nutrients
- Should be palatable, of liquid/semisolid consistency, and have acceptable taste, color, and smell.
- Easy to cook, store, not very expensive, and not easily perishable
- Fulfilling cultural and religious needs

By 4–6 months of age, intestinal amylase matures, and the gut becomes ready to accept cereals and pulses (legumes). Gum hardens prior to tooth eruption and the baby enjoys gumming semisolids. Thus, the body is "biologically" ready to accept semisolids by 4–6 months of age. Early introduction of complementary feeds poses the risk of infection to the child. Diluted foods also lead to infection due to malnutrition, whereas late weaning leads to growth faltering and malnutrition.

Six months is the ideal age for the introduction of semisolids as at this age, the infant starts to have eruption of the teeth and develops biting movements. The infant is thus ready to eat soft and mashed foods.

Signals Indicating Readiness for Complementary Feeding

- Being unsatisfied after full milk feed
- Demanding frequent and increasing quantity of milk feeds
- Baby able to control head movements
- Baby attempting to put things in his/her mouth
- Slowing of weight gain or leveling out on growth chart without a period of illness

Attributes of Complementary Feeding

- The baby should be started on soft, homogenous (mashed or strained), and bland food initially. Appropriately thick, homogenous complementary foods made from locally available foods should be introduced at 6 completed months to all babies while continuing breastfeeding as one desires (ad libitum). This should be the standard and universal practice.
- To address the issue of a small stomach size that can accommodate limited quantity at a time, each meal must be made energy dense by adding sugar/jaggery and ghee/butter/oil. To provide more calories from smaller volumes, food must be thick in consistency—thick enough to stay on the spoon without running off when the spoon is tilted.
- Parents must identify the staple homemade food consisting of cereal–pulse mixture (as these are fresh, clean, and cheap) and make them caloric and nutrient rich with locally available products.
- The complementary foods should be offered when the baby is hungry by replacing the milk feed. One food item should be given at one time and parents/caregivers should watch for its acceptance and tolerance before introducing another item.
- When the infant has well accepted the soft initial foods, different tastes, thicknesses, and textures should be gradually introduced in the diet. Small chopped pieces are a good option to mix in the complementary feeds later.
- The feeds should be adequate to provide all the nutritional requirements of the infant with respect to the energy, proteins, vitamins, and minerals.
- These foods should be prepared from cereals such as rice, wheat, maize, pulses, and milk in variable combinations.

- Addition of sugar, oil, and other fats increases the energy density of the complementary foods and improves the taste of the food.
- Hygienic practices are essential for food safety during all the involved steps, viz., preparation, storage, and feeding. Freshly cooked food should be consumed within 1–2 hours in hot climate unless refrigerated. Hands should be washed with soap and water at critical times—including before eating or preparing food and after using toilet.

Diets for Complementary Feeding

- The food should be "balanced food" consisting of various (as diverse as possible) food groups/components in different combinations. As the baby shows interest in complementary feeds, the variety should be increased by adding new foods in the staple food one by one. Easily available, cost-effective, seasonal, uncooked fruits, green and other dark-colored vegetables, milk and milk products, pulses/legumes, animal foods, oil/butter, and sugar/jaggery may be added in the staples gradually.
- Of total energy, 8–10% should be obtained from the proteins of good quality. Addition of small quantity of proteins of animal origin such as milk or eggs is usually sufficient to provide limiting amino acids in cereal-based diets.
- Foods can be enriched by making a fermented porridge, use of germinated or sprouted flour, and roasting of grains before grinding.
- Iron-fortified foods, iodized salt, vitamin A–enriched food, etc., should be encouraged. Soups and purees of green leafy vegetables are a good source of iron and vitamin A.
- Consistency of foods should be appropriate to the developmental readiness of the child in munching, chewing, and swallowing. Avoid foods that can pose choking hazard. Introduce lumpy or granular foods and most tastes by about 9–10 months. Missing this age may lead to feeding fussiness later. The details of food including texture, frequency, and average amount are enumerated in Table 6.3.
- As a general guideline, when the first complementary food is introduced to the child, a small amount of a single food is begun initially and then gradually increased to two to three times daily. The infant should be fed slowly and patiently.
- Traditional home-made foods in India are well-cooked gruel such as khichdi (made from three parts of rice, one part of moong dal, and some added curd) and this works as a satisfactory complementary food.
- Commercially available cereal-based foods are also available, but these are expensive and offer no added benefits over fresh home-prepared complementary foods.

TABLE 6.3 Amount and Frequency of Complementary Feeds

Age	Food	Frequency	Amount at each meal
6–8 months	Start with soft porridge, well-mashed foods. Add other mashed food later	Two to three meals per day plus frequent breastfeeding	Start with two to three tablespoons
9–11 months	Finely chopped or mashed food that baby can pick up	Three to four meals along with breastfeeds and one or two snacks between meals	1/2 of 250-ml cup/bowl
12–24 months	Family foods, chopped or mashed if needed	Three to four meals and, based on appetite, one to two snacks between meals	3/4 to one of 250-ml cup/bowl

- Adequate total energy intake can also be ensured by addition of one to two nutritious snacks between the three main meals. Snacks are in addition to the meals and should not replace meals. They should not be confused with foods such as sweets or other processed foods.
- Young children should be encouraged to take feed by praising them and their foods. Self-feeding should be encouraged despite spillage. Each child should be fed under supervision in a separate plate to develop an individual identity. Forced feeding, threatening, and punishment interfere with the development of good/proper feeding habits. Along with feeding, mother and caregivers should provide psychosocial stimulation to the child through ordinary age-appropriate play and communication activities to ensure early childhood development.
- A skilled help and confidence building is also required for complementary feeding during all health contacts and at home through home visits by community health workers.
- Some guiding principles recommended by the World Health Organization (WHO) for complementary feeding are shown in Box 6.2.

The energy (caloric) and protein content of commonly consumed prepared/cooked foods is shown in Table 6.4.

Dietary Assessment

Assessment of nutritional intake is important to determine whether there exists a gap between the child's dietary intake and his/her requirements that may be responsible for malnutrition or being overweight.

- The 24-hour dietary recall method is a common method used for this purpose when the parents are asked to recall the actual intake (quantitative and qualitative) both before and after the onset of illness.
- The energy value of food is expressed as calories or joule (1 kcal = 4.18 kJ) but calories are more commonly used for diet calculation. Once the diet has been calculated, one should then analyze whether the child is consuming the recommended amount as per his/her age or not.
- Dietary history and frequency of consumption of different food items should supplement the 24-hour dietary recall method to find out the qualitative aspects of the diet.
- An infant up to 1 year needs 100 cal/kg/day and thus at 1 year the requirement (10 kg body weight) is 1000 cal/day. As an average, the child needs additional 100 cal for every year of age. For example, a 5-year-old child needs 1000 + 400 = 1400 cal.
- Children require approximately 1.2–1.7 g/kg protein per day.
- An example of dietary assessment is shown in Table 6.5.

Box 6.2 Guiding principles for complementary feeding

- Continue frequent, on-demand breastfeeding until 2 years of age or beyond.
- Practice responsive feeding (e.g., feed infants directly and assist older children; feed slowly and patiently; encourage them to eat but do not force them; talk to the child and maintain eye contact).
- Practice good hygiene and proper food handling.
- Start at 6 months with small amounts of food and increase gradually as the child gets older.
- Gradually increase food consistency and variety.
- Increase the number of times that the child is fed: two to three meals per day for infants 6–8 months of age and three to four meals per day for infants 9–23 months of age, with one to two additional snacks as required.
- Use fortified complementary foods or vitamin–mineral supplements as needed.
- During illness, increase fluid intake including more breastfeeding, and offer soft, favorite foods.

TABLE 6.4 Calorie and Protein Content of Cooked/Prepared Foods in Household Measures

Prepared food	Calories (Kcal)	Proteins (g)
Cow/dairy milk (200 mL: one glass)	134	6.4
Buffalo milk (200 mL: one glass)	234	8.6
Cooked white rice (one small *katori*)	100	2
Cooked dal (one small *katori*: 25 g)	100	5
Roti (phulka, one: 30 g)	100	3.5
Khichdi (one small *katori*)	100	3.5
Vegetable (one small *katori*)	100	1
Puri (one)	50	1
Bread (one slice)	70	2
Idli (one)	50	2
Upma (one small *katori*)	150	3.5
Dalia (porridge; one small *katori*)	100	3
Banana (one, medium)	110	1.3
Apple (one)	60	0.3
Biscuit (one)	20	0.5
Tea 1 cup	60	1
Boiled egg (one)	80	6
Mutton (lean; 100 g)	200	18
Sugar (one spoon)/jaggery	20	–
Ghee/butter (one spoon: 5 g)	45	–

Measures: 1 *katori* (small) = 100 ml, 1 *katori* (medium) = 1 cup = 150 ml, 1 *katori* (big) = 1 glass = 200 ml, 1 tablespoon = 15 ml, 1 teaspoon = 5 ml.

TABLE 6.5 Dietary Assessment for 18-Month-Old Child (11.5 kg)

Meal	Food item	Calories	Proteins (g)
Breakfast	Milk (100 ml)	67	3.2
	Sugar (10 g: two tsp.)	40	–
	Biscuit (two pieces)	40	1
Snacks	Banana (one)	110	1.3
Lunch	Rice (one small *katori*)	100	2
	Dal (one small *katori*)	50	2.5
	Ghee (one tsp.)	45	–
	Vegetable (half small *katori*)	50	0.5
Snacks	Bread (one slices)	70	2.0
	Butter (5 g)	45	–
Dinner	*Chapati* (two)	200	4
	Khichdi (half small *katori*)	50	1.7
	Vegetable (half small *katori*)	50	0.5
Bedtime	Milk (100 ml)	67	3.2
	Sugar (one tsp.)	20	–
	Biscuit (two)	50	1.0
Total		1045	22.9

Present intake (total in 24 hours), 1045 cal (expected 1060 cal); proteins 22.9 g (expected 20 g).

Evaluation

- The child is taking adequate calories (1045 kcal/day) as against his/her requirement being 1060 kcal.
- He/she is taking adequate proteins (22.9 g/day) as against his/her requirement of approximately 20 g/day.
- He/she is receiving all groups of food items.
- Right feeding practices are being followed.

Decision

Diet and feeding practices of this child are normal.

Action

The child–mother duo requires no intervention. Parents should be praised for following right dietary practices.

KEY POINTS

- Diet has a close relationship with health and disease.
- Breastfeeding provides all the nutrients that the baby needs and is the best feeding practice up to 6 months of age.
- Breastfeeding should be continued for up to 2 years of age and semisolids should be introduced to the infant's diet at the age of 6 months.
- An adequate dietary assessment and healthy feeding practices are helpful tools in planning a balanced diet and guiding and counseling the family for the prevention of malnutrition and obesity.

CHAPTER 7

The Neonate

Paresh A Thakkar, Niranjan Shendurnikar

The infant in the first 28 days of life is called a neonate. A neonate is vulnerable due to the structural and functional immaturity of various organs and systems and is therefore at increased risk of morbidity and mortality. Just as children are not mini-adults, neonates are also not mini-children. Approach to a newborn is a unique challenge as very limited history can be obtained, symptoms and signs are often nonspecific and different, and examination also poses a great challenge. Important terminologies for neonates are given in Box 7.1.

The All India Institute of Medical Sciences (AIIMS), New Delhi, defines a normal newborn as one who fulfills the following criteria:

- Birth weight greater than 2.5 kg and gestation of 37 weeks or more
- Birth weight between the 10th and 90th percentiles for the corresponding gestational age, as per intrauterine growth charts
- Absence of maternal illness or intrapartum event that may put a newborn at risk of illness such as gestational diabetes and antepartum hemorrhage
- Normal Apgar scores and no need for resuscitation at birth

Box 7.1 Definitions and terminologies in neonatology

- *Low birth weight (LBW)*: A neonate weighing less than 2500 g at birth is termed LBW.
- *Very low birth weight (VLBW)*: A neonate weighing less than 1500 g at birth is termed VLBW.
- *Extremely low birth weight (ELBW)*: A baby weighing less than 1000 g at birth is termed ELBW.
- *Adequate for gestational age (AGA)*: If the weight of an infant at birth is between the 10th and 90th percentiles for the corresponding gestational age, then the infant is termed AGA.
- *Small for gestational age (SGA)*: If the weight of an infant at birth is below the 10th percentile for the corresponding gestational age, then the infant is termed SGA.

  Most of the time, SGA and intrauterine growth retardation (IUGR) terminologies are used interchangeably. IUGR is a clinical entity, while SGA is a mathematical definition for identifying babies with IUGR.
- *Large for gestational age (LGA)*: If the weight of an infant at birth is above the 90th percentile for the corresponding gestational age, then the infant is termed LGA.
- *Prematurity*: If a baby is born before 37 completed weeks of gestation, then that baby is termed preterm.
- *Postmaturity*: A baby born after 42 weeks of gestation is termed postmature.
- *Birth asphyxia*: The National Neonatology Forum of India has defined birth asphyxia as "gasping or ineffective breathing or lack of breathing at one minute of life."
- *Neonatal death*: It refers to death occurring in the first 28 days of life.
- *Early neonatal death*: It refers to death occurring in the first 7 days of life.
- *Late neonatal death*: It refers to death occurring after the 7th day and in the first 28 days of life.
- *Perinatal period*: Perinatal period extends from 28 weeks of gestation to the 7th day of life.
- *Perinatal mortality rate*: It refers to the number of deaths of babies after 28 weeks of gestation (or weight more than 1000 g at birth) and up to the 7th day of life per 1000 live births (late fetal deaths plus early neonatal deaths).

- No postnatal illness such as sepsis, respiratory distress, dyselectrolytemia, hypoglycemia, or polycythemia

History Taking in Newborn

Maternal health and events during the antenatal period, intrapartum events, and immediate care at birth have profound effects on the health and well-being of the baby. Thus, a detailed enquiry/information of perinatal factors and events is essential. The approach to maternal history with reference to neonatal examination broadly includes the following:

- All the basic information about the newborn including age in days/hours after birth, sex, birth weight, and gestational age, and information about parents including education, occupation, and economic status should be recorded.
- Socioeconomic status: Mothers belonging to lower socioeconomic class, due to associated poor nutritional status and vitamin and mineral (particularly iron) deficiency, are more likely to give birth to small-for-gestational-age (SGA) and preterm babies.
- It is important to note maternal age, as teenage pregnancies/young mothers are likely to produce low-birth-weight babies. Also, babies born to elderly mothers are at increased risk of chromosomal defects such as Down syndrome (trisomy 21).

Past Obstetric History in Mother

- Gravidity, parity, stillbirths, abortions, and neonatal deaths, if any, should be recorded. *Gravidity* is defined as the number of all conceptions including stillbirths and abortions, while *parity* is defined as the total number of pregnancies reaching viable gestational age (including live births or still births).
- Try to enquire about the cause of any earlier/past neonatal death/morbidities if possible.
- Further details about low-birth-weight or intrauterine growth retardation (IUGR) babies, mode of delivery, and any significant morbidity in the mother and infant should be noted.

Pre-Pregnancy Health Status of Mother

- Maternal malnutrition is one of the important causes of IUGR and hence low birth weight. Criteria for identifying maternal malnutrition are height less than 145 cm, weight less than 40 kg, and midarm circumference less than 20.9 cm.
- Chronic systemic illness in the mother such as chronic renal failure and heart disease is associated with growth retardation in the newborn.
- Maternal diabetes is associated with fetal macrosomia (large-for-date babies).

Antenatal History

Enquire about the adequacy and quality of antenatal care. For community purpose, "minimum antenatal care" is defined as at least four antenatal visits and two tetanus toxoid injections received during pregnancy.

- Enquire about the number of antenatal visits, ultrasound examinations, history suggestive of preeclamptic toxemia, history of fever with rash (for TORCH [**T**oxoplasmosis, **O**ther {syphilis, varicella-zoster, parvovirus B19}, **R**ubella, **C**ytomegalovirus, and **H**erpes infections] infections), and any febrile illness in the mother.
- History of medications during pregnancy should be asked in detail. Exposure to teratogenic agents may lead to malformations in the newborn. Table 7.1 shows few teratogens leading to malformations in the newborn or fetus.
- It is important to enquire about the maternal blood group as Rh and ABO incompatibility can lead to jaundice (neonatal hyperbilirubinemia) in the newborn.
- Enquire about the weight gain during pregnancy; the mother should gain around 6–11 kg.
- Ask for the history of vaginal bleeding. Antepartum hemorrhage, which may be due

TABLE 7.1 Teratogens

Neonatal disorder	Teratogen
Limb defects	Thalidomide, haloperidol
Hypoplasia of nasal bones and stippled epiphysis	Warfarin
Neural tube defects	Valproic acid, clomiphene, carbamazepine
Cleft palate, cleft lip	Diphenylhydantoin, diazepam, imipramine
Cretinism, goiter	Antithyroid drugs, radioactive iodine
Ebstein anomaly	Lithium
Deafness	Quinine, streptomycin, chloroquine
IUGR	Smoking, alcohol

IUGR, intrauterine growth retardation.

to placenta previa or abruptio placentae, can lead to hypovolemic shock and anemia in a newborn.

- Oligohydramnios may be associated with postmaturity, renal agenesis, obstructive uropathy, and placental insufficiency. Polyhydramnios may be associated with obstruction in gastrointestinal tract such as esophageal atresia, duodenal atresia, jejunal atresia, anencephaly, multiple gestation, hydrops fetalis, and toxemia in the mother.
- History of maternal immunization: Enquiring about the number of doses of tetanus toxoid and hepatitis B vaccination status is important. If the mother is unimmunized against hepatitis B vaccine, it is pertinent to know her hepatitis B antigen status (HbsAg) as it has implications for perinatal prophylaxis of hepatitis B.

Natal History

Assess whether any risk factors for perinatal distress and sepsis are present.

- History of prolonged labor, obstructed labor, difficult delivery, instrumentation, or cesarean section may be associated with fetal distress.
- History of maternal fever, prolonged rupture of membrane (>18 hours), repeated per vaginal examination, foul-smelling liquor, and unclean vaginal examinations are risks for neonatal septicemia.
- Note whether it was a singleton pregnancy or multiple gestation. Presentation such as vertex or breech should also be noted as vaginal breech delivery may be associated with birth trauma and asphyxia.

Postnatal History

- Enquire whether the baby cried soon after the birth or suffered asphyxia. A history of delayed cry and need of resuscitation/oxygen to establish and sustain respiration at birth may signify perinatal asphyxia.
- Ask whether the baby was required to be kept in neonatal ICU or was handed over to the mother after delivery (rooming in).
- Enquire about the weight of the baby at birth.
- Ask about feeding history and overall activity during the initial few days.
- Ask about history of any prelacteal feeds and when the breastfeeding was started.

History of the Present Illness

- The mother or any other relative may have some complaints/contributory information or concerns related to the newborn's illness. These should be patiently listened to and should be recorded. Always give due importance to what the mother or the caretaker has to say.
- The newborn might have been referred by the obstetrician or pediatrician who attended the labor call. One should go through the referral notes and, if possible, enquire about the details of delivery and birth.
- The neonate's illness should be correlated with the given setting for the baby, such as weight, gestational age, perinatal asphyxia, and prolonged rupture of membrane.

Box 7.2 Nonspecific presenting complaints of sick neonates

- Lethargy
- Refusal of feeds
- Vomiting
- Excessive or inconsolable crying
- Fast/difficult breathing
- Chest indrawing
- Yellowish discoloration of skin
- Bleeding from any site
- Abnormal movements or convulsions
- Unexplained/excessive weight loss

Most of the neonatal illnesses present with few common symptoms which are not specific to a particular condition (Box 7.2). Early identification of a sick neonate is the key to successful management and improving the neonatal outcome. These are the neonates who would require additional support such as referral to a tertiary care center and therapy such as oxygen, intravenous fluids, and/or antibiotics.

Family History

Enquire about history of consanguinity in parents. Details of the siblings, any significant illness such as major congenital malformations (congenital heart diseases, renal and/or gastrointestinal anomalies, spina bifida, etc.) in previous siblings, and genetic diseases (hemophilia, G6PD deficiency, sickle cell anemia, cystic fibrosis) should be asked for.

Immunization History

Check for the status of vaccination. Vaccines that are given at birth and within 1 month include BCG, first dose of hepatitis B, and zero dose of oral polio vaccine.

Examination of Neonates

For examination of a newborn, certain basic principles should be followed. The baby should be completely exposed and placed at an appropriate height on a flat surface. There should be adequate illumination in the examination area.

Utmost care should be taken while examining any newborn so that the baby is examined while being kept warm (preferably under a radiant warmer) and proper hand hygiene should be taken care of to avoid the transmission of infection. The examiner's hands should be clean, warm, and completely dry before touching the baby. All throughout the procedure, care should be taken so that the baby does not become cold or hypothermic. If a warmer is not available, the neonate can also be examined in the mother's lap. The basic objectives of an initial neonatal examination are to determine the neonatal well-being and note the following points:

- Has the newborn made a successful transition from the intrauterine milieu to the external environment and developed spontaneous breathing?
- Are there any effects of maternal diseases and drugs on the newborn?
- Are there any congenital anomalies present in the newborn that would need immediate attention?
- Are there any signs or symptoms of illness in the neonate?

After this assessment/examination, most newborns who are healthy are roomed in with mothers, while those who are sick need to be transported to a nearby level II or level III facility (Box 7.3).

Weight and Other Anthropometric Parameters

The weight of an infant at birth is the most important parameter. Normal weight at birth is between 2.5 and 3 kg and the average weight of babies in India is reported to be 2.9 kg. Initially, the neonate loses weight for 5–7 days. This is usually up to 5% of birth weight but may be up to 10% for premature babies. IUGR (small-for-date) babies usually do not lose weight. After the initial weight loss, the baby gains at least

Box 7.3 Purpose of newborn examination at birth

Ideally all newborns should be examined at birth:

- To ensure that the neonate has established normal respiration
- To prevent and treat hypothermia
- To prevent and treat hypoglycemia (establish breast-feeding) (in a normal delivery, the baby should be breastfed within 0.5 hour of birth, while in case of a lower-segment cesarean section delivery, within 4 hours of birth)
- To record the birth weight and assess the gestational age
- For referral (babies who are sick [such as those with perinatal asphyxia, respiratory distress, refusal to feed, lethargy, and convulsions] or are at increased risk of morbidity or complications [such as extreme preterms, very low birth weight] should be referred to a nearby level II or level III facility)
- To rule out congenital anomalies

Box 7.4 Normal anthropometric parameters at birth

- Weight: 2500–3000 g
- Length: 47–52 cm
- Head circumference: 32–35 cm
- Midarm circumference: 9–11 cm

1–2% of the birth weight per day. Thus, a baby with weight 2.5–3 kg would gain weight at least 25–30 g/day. The anthropometric parameters of a newborn are shown in Box 7.4.

- The head circumference exceeds the chest circumference by 2–3 cm at birth and they become equal by 6 months of age after which the chest circumference exceeds the head circumference. Normally, the difference between head and chest circumferences is less than 3 cm. If it is more than 3 cm, it indicates asymmetric IUGR.
- *Ponderal index* is calculated by the following formula: (weight in grams)/(length in cm)^3 × 100. It is:
  - More than 2.5 in normal, term, adequate-for-gestational-age infants
  - Less than 2 in asymmetric type of IUGR (SGA) babies
  - Between 2 and 2.5 in symmetric type of IUGR babies

Gestational Age Assessment

- The most commonly used and easy method of gestational age assessment is to calculate as per the date of the last menstrual period.
- If available, first-trimester ultrasound dating can provide the most accurate idea about the gestation with an accuracy of ±1 day.
- If both are not available, physical and neurological examination of a newborn can be used to assess the gestational age clinically.
- There are various scoring systems available such as New Ballard Scoring system, Meharban Singh's scoring system, and Dubowitz scoring system.
- *New Ballard Scoring system* can determine gestational age ranging from 20 to 44 weeks of gestation; it is more elaborate and hence it is somewhat more time consuming. Details of the scoring are given in Table 7.2. The gestational age is assessed under two categories, namely: (i) neuromuscular maturity and (ii) physical maturity. Each category has a number of items that are scored as per the findings, and based on the total score, the maturity is estimated.
  - Physical maturity criteria: As the baby matures, skin becomes thick, breast nodule size increases, lanugo hairs become sparse, and the plantar creases become well developed. In genitalia in full-term neonates, scrotal rugosity is well developed in males and labia minora are covered by labia majora in female neonates (Figs 7.1–7.4).
  - Neurological maturity criteria: The points of assessment under neuromuscular maturity are mainly dependent on the tone of the newborn baby, and as the gestational age advances, the tone of the neonate improves. A full-term neonate will have a flexed posture (Fig. 7.5), while

TABLE 7.2 Maturational Assessment of Gestational Age (New Ballard Score)

	Score	–1	0	1	2	3	4	5
Neuromuscular maturity	Posture	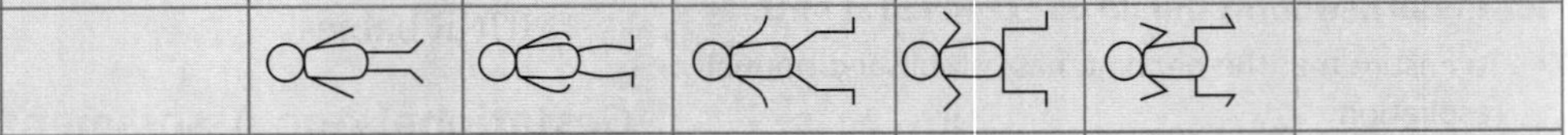						
	Square window (wrist)	 >90°	90°	60°	45°	30°	0°	
	Arm recoil		180°	140–180°	110–140°	90–110°	<90°	
	Popliteal angle	 180°	160°	140°	120°	100°	90°	<90°
	Scarf sign							
	Heel to ear							
Physical maturity	Skin	Sticky, friable, transparent	Gelatinous, red, transparent	Smooth pink, visible veins	Superficial peeling and/or rash; few veins	Cracking, pale areas, rare veins	Parchment, deep, no veins	Leathery, cracked, wrinkled
	Lanugo	None	Sparse	Abundant	Thinning	Bald areas	Mostly bald	
	Plantar surface	Heel–toe • 40–50 mm: –1 • <40 mm: –2	>50 mm, no crease	Faint red marks	Anterior transverse crease only	Creases over the anterior two-third	Creases over the entire sole	
	Breast	Imperceptible	Barely perceptible	Flat areola, no bud	Stippled areola, 1–2 mm bud	Raised areola, 3–4 mm bud	Full areola, 5–10 mm bud	
	Eye/ear	Lids fused • Loosely: –1 • Tightly: –2	Lids open; pinna flat, stays folded	Slightly curved pinna; soft, slow recoil	Well-curved pinna; soft, but ready recoil	Formed and firm, instant recoil	Thick cartilage, ear stiff	
	Genitals (male)	Scrotum flat, smooth	Scrotum empty, rare rugae	Testes in upper canal, rare rugae	Testes in descending, few rugae	Testes down, good rugae	Testes pendulous, deep rugae	
	Genitals (female)	Clitoris prominent, labia flat	Clitoris prominent; enlarging, small labia minora	Clitoris prominent, enlarging minora	Majora and minora equally prominent	Majora large, minora small	Majora cover clitoris and minora	

Maturity rating

Score	Weeks
–10	20
–5	22
0	24
5	26
10	28
15	30
20	32
25	34
30	36
35	38
40	40
45	42
50	44

Source: Lakshmanaswamy A. Clinical Paediatrics History Taking and Case Discussion, 4th ed. Wolters Kluwer India: New Delhi; 2017.

an extreme preterm neonate would be hypotonic. The popliteal angle, scarf sign, and heel to ear maneuvers are shown in Figures 7.6–7.8. Meharban Singh scoring system can determine gestational age ranging from 28 to 40 weeks of gestation and the accuracy is ±2 weeks.

The total of neuromuscular and physical scores should be added to give the maturity rating (Table 7.3).

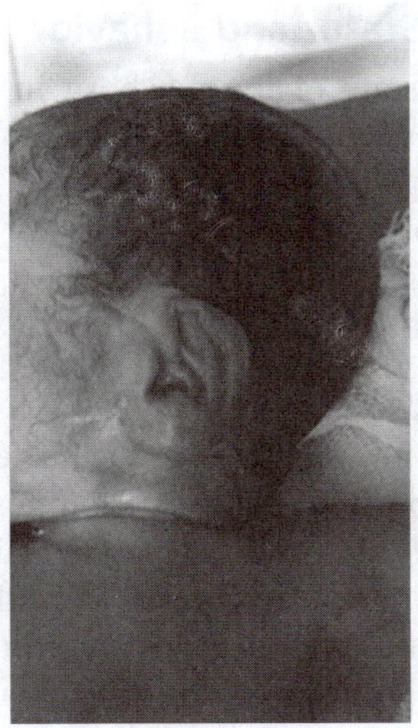

Figure 7.1 External ear—poorly formed cartilage in a preterm newborn.

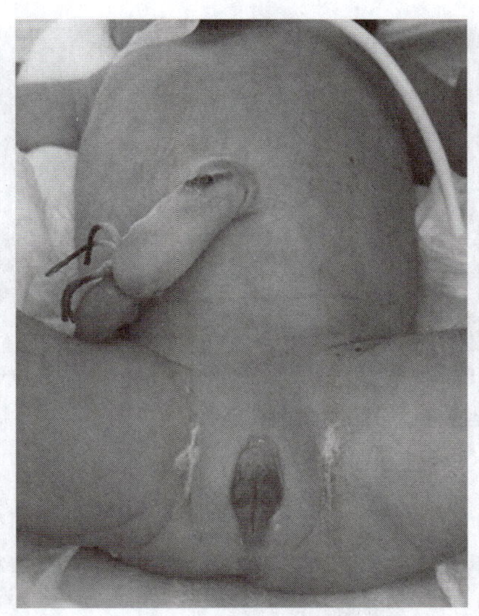

Figure 7.4 External genitalia—female.

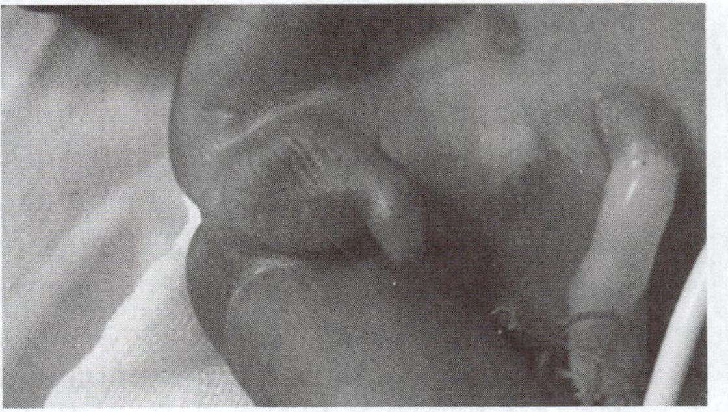

Figure 7.2 External genitalia—male, in a preterm newborn (lesser rugosities).

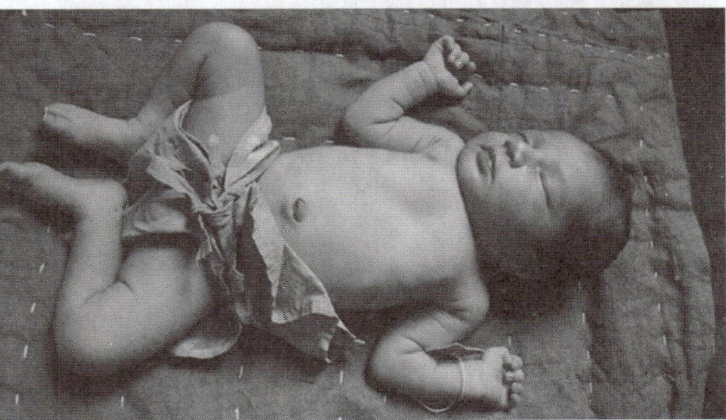

Figure 7.5 Normal flexed posture of a full-term newborn.

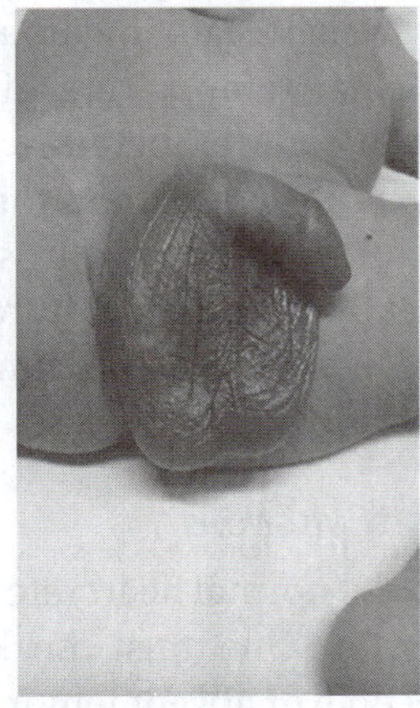

Figure 7.3 External genitalia—full-term male newborn.

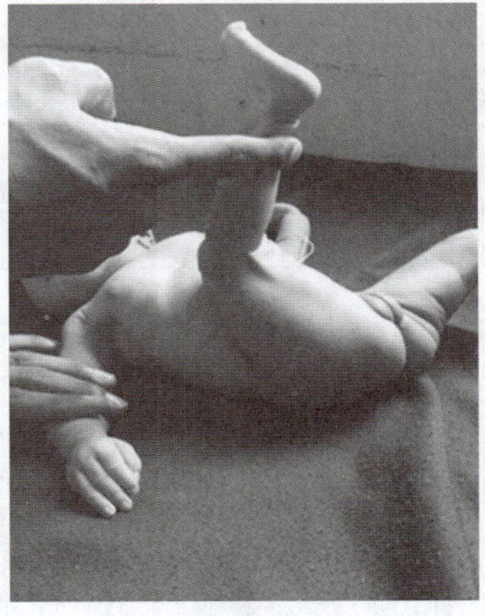

Figure 7.6 Checking for popliteal angle.

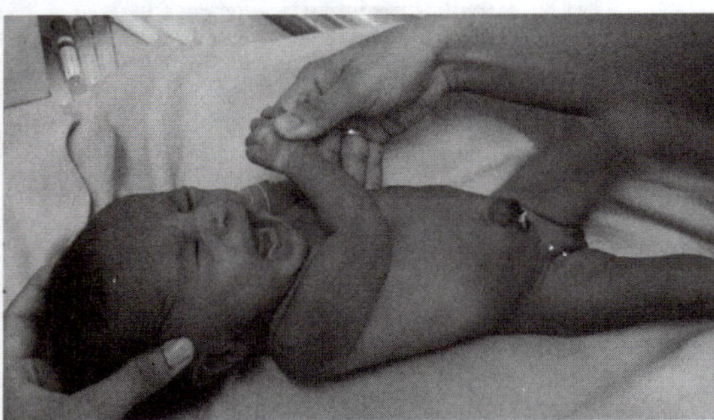

Figure 7.7 Scarf sign.

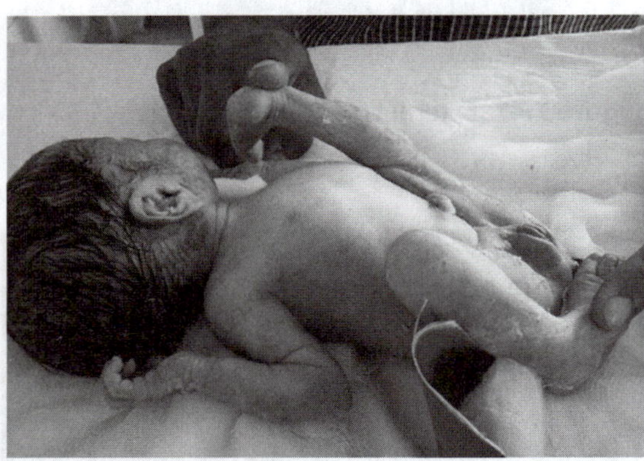

Figure 7.8 Heel to ear sign.

TABLE 7.3 Maturity Rating

Score	Weeks
−10	20
−5	22
0	24
5	26
10	28
15	30
20	32
25	34
30	36
35	38
40	40
45	42
50	44

General Status and Behavior

Note the state of the newborn in relation to wakefulness and alertness. A newborn who has been just fed would be drowsy or sleepy, but can be aroused.

Vital Parameters

Temperature

It is very important to note the temperature of a newborn. The normal temperature of a newborn is 36.5–37.5°C. Hypothermia is a more common response compared with fever in sick neonates, due to their larger body surface area that predisposes them to heat loss. The student has to use low-reading thermometers. Axillary temperature should be recorded and the thermometer should be kept for 3 minutes in the axilla. In a setting where thermometer is not available, temperature should be assessed by feel of hand.

In community setting, examine with the dorsum of hand and feel the temperature of the central area (trunk, abdomen) and extremities (palms and soles). If both are warm, the temperature is normal. If the central area is warm and extremities are cold to touch, then the baby is in cold stress. It is important to identify a newborn in cold stress to prevent its further progression into hypothermia.

Hypothermia significantly increases morbidity; it may be a sign of sepsis and also causes poor weight gain in otherwise stable newborns. Rectal temperature gives a closer estimate of the core temperature of the body. So, it would be useful in monitoring patients with significant hypothermia. It is not routine practice to take rectal temperature as it needs expertise and it may cause trauma to rectum and anal canal.

Heart Rate and Pulsations

In newborns, the normal heart rate is 140/min ± 20 (120–160/min). One must check for femoral pulsations. Feeble or absent femoral pulsations should raise the suspicion for coarctation of aorta and/or hypoplastic left heart syndrome.

Respiration

The normal respiratory rate is 40–60/min. Tachypnea in a newborn is defined as respiratory rate ≥60/min. Respiration should be assessed in a quiet baby and at least 30 minutes after feed. Postfeed tachypnea is common in neonates.

Periodic breathing is common in newborns: The baby would breathe faster for some time followed by a slower rate. Thus, for respiratory rate, respirations should be counted for full 1 minute and if the respiratory rate is ≥60/min, the rate should be determined again for confirmation. Flaring of alae nasi and subcostal and intercostal chest retractions are the signs of respiratory distress.

Blood Pressure

Normal blood pressure in a neonate is 60/40 mmHg (systolic BP 40–60 mmHg and diastolic BP 25–40 mmHg). Blood pressure should be measured with appropriate-sized cuffs. For recording blood pressure in neonates, noninvasive blood pressure monitors are available.

General Physical Examination

Head

- Examine for size, symmetry, and shape of skull.
- Look for evidence of molding, cephalhematoma or caput succedaneum, mark of forceps, sutural ridging, or suture separation.
- Caput succedaneum is a subcutaneous fluid collection of the scalp, seen as soft, boggy swelling at presenting part of the head. It is present at birth and usually disappears within 24 hours. It is not restricted by sutural lines (Fig. 7.9).
- Cephalhematoma is bounded by sutural lines, appears 24–48 hours after birth, and may persist up to 4–6 weeks. It is a tense collection of blood under the periosteum and is soft and cystic on palpation. It may be either unilateral or bilateral (Fig. 7.10).

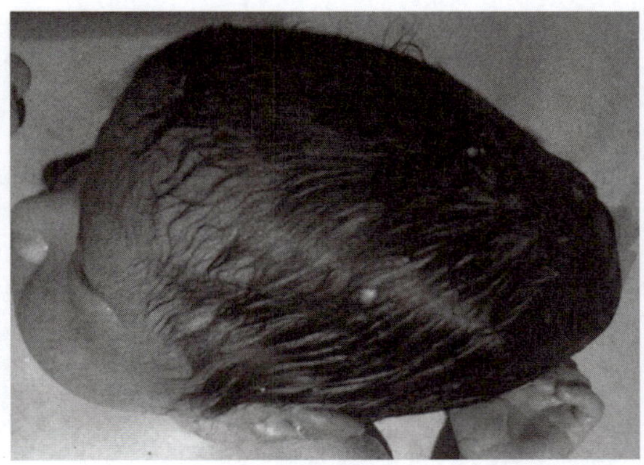

Figure 7.9 Caput succedaneum.

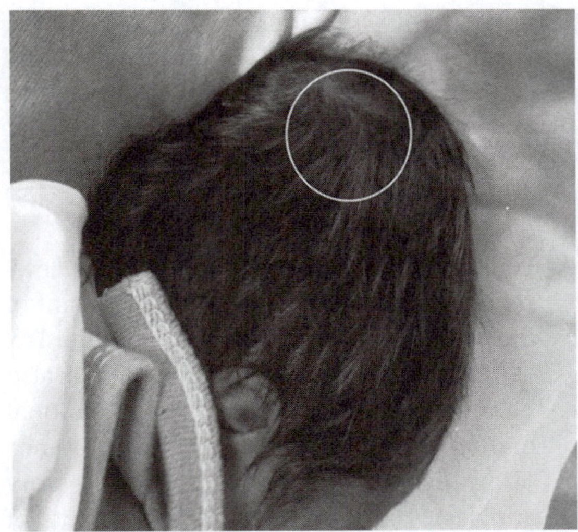

Figure 7.10 Cephalhematoma (area marked by circle).

- Sutural overriding in the first 24–48 hours after birth is normal.
- Examine anterior fontanelle, which usually is 3 × 3 cm in size. It is diamond shaped and should be measured diagonally. Status of anterior fontanelle should be checked. Bulging fontanelle is seen in conditions with raised intracranial pressure such as hydrocephalus, meningitis, and intracranial hemorrhage, while depressed fontanelle is seen with dehydration. Due to molding of the skull bones and the sutural overriding in the first 24–48 hours, examination of fontanelles is somewhat difficult during this period.

- Posterior fontanelle is a small-sized dimple placed between the sagittal suture and the lambdoid suture posteriorly.

Face/Ears/Eyes

- Look for evidence of abnormal or dysmorphic facies. The term dysmorphic is used to describe children whose physical features, particularly facial, are not usually found in a child of the same age or ethnic background.
- Bruising and forceps marks should be looked for.
- Marked facial asymmetry suggests facial nerve palsy.
- Flaring of alae nasi is a sign of respiratory distress and any nasal obstruction such as choanal atresia should be excluded.
- Look for cleft lip, cleft palate, retrognathia, micrognathia, and any abnormal and dysmorphic features.
- Look for abnormality of shape of ears, low-set ears, distance between two eyes, slant of the eyes, nose, lips, philtrum, and chin. Lax ear cartilage and/or overfolding of helix also helps in the assessment of the gestational maturity of the neonate. Note any presence of any preauricular ear tags (pits or accessory auricles). Hairy pinna is seen in infants of diabetic mothers (IDM).
- Examination of the eyes in the neonates needs patience and practice as their eyes are closed at most of the times due to physiological photophobia, and forcible attempts do not often yield positive results. The neonate can be rocked gently in the mother's lap or lifted with head propped up on the mother's shoulder to make his/her eyes open spontaneously. This thus allows for an inspection and a visual tracking of a bright red-colored object that the newborn can follow from side to side.
- Examine the eyes with a torch to look for evidence of congenital cataract and corneal haze. Subconjunctival hemorrhages in one or both eyes frequently occur following vaginal delivery even in normal newborns and may take a few days to resolve. Similarly, faintly blue sclera is most often normal in newborns and does not indicate any underlying disease.
- Normal newborns have clear cornea and equal-sized pupils reacting symmetrically to the light.
- Presence of any purulent discharge, corneal haziness or opacity, coloboma, or cataract should be noted.

Skin

As the skin of the newborn is thin, various internal changes and cardiorespiratory status may be reflected by changes in the skin.

- Pallor is seen with anemia, hypoxia, and poor circulatory status, while a newborn with polycythemia would look plethoric. Presence of plethoric skin is often associated with SGA babies and IDM.
- The epidermal layer of the newborn is thin, which makes it easy for it to appear pink due to the presence of oxygenated capillary blood beneath it.
- *Capillary refill time* (CRT) indicates the status of perfusion. Normal CRT of <3 seconds indicates that the neonate is well perfused. Prolonged CRT of ≥3 seconds is seen in shock/hypotension or hypothermia. For assessing CRT, press over forehead or sternum for 3–5 seconds and note the time in which the blanched area becomes normal after capillary refill (Figs 7.11 and 7.12).
- Acrocyanosis (cyanosis of hands and feet) is common and normal. It may be due to cold stress or hypothermia. Blood loss and circulatory shock imparts the skin a pale and an ashen gray color, while mottled skin is seen in newborns with sepsis, hypothermia, and circulatory insufficiency.
- Icterus is visible on the skin. There is cephalocaudal progression of yellow discoloration as the level of serum bilirubin rises. If the palms and soles are yellow, the bilirubin levels are likely to be more than 15 mg/dL. Jaundice should always be looked for in daylight to avoid any errors

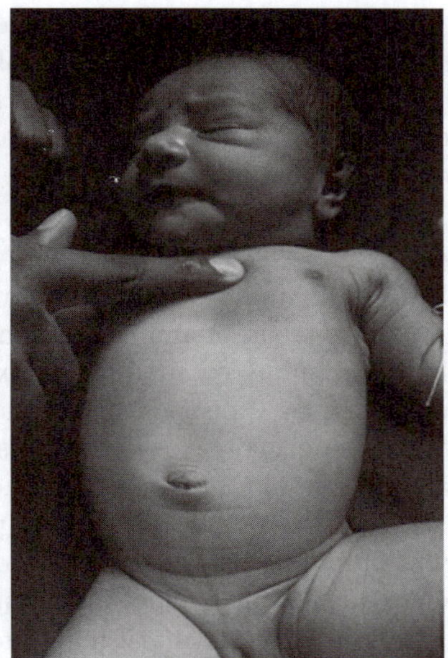

Figure 7.11 Examining for capillary refill time.

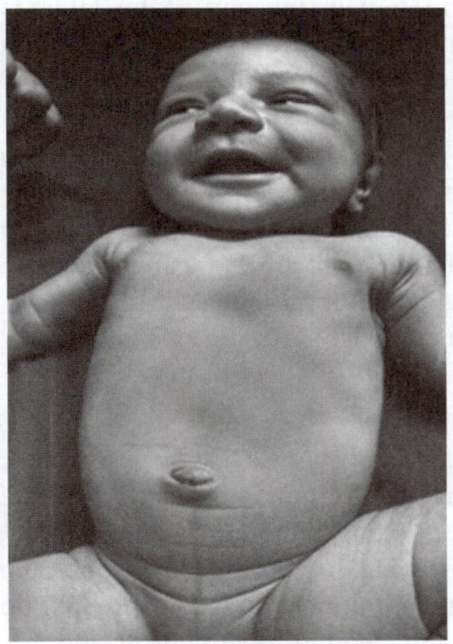

Figure 7.12 Look for blanching and note time for capillary refill (as seen on chest).

in clinical judgment. Due to physiological photophobia, it is extremely difficult to look for icterus in the eyes; instead, it should be looked for on the skin of face, trunk, and extremities.

- Look for evidence of cyanosis. Cyanosis over tip of nose, ear lobule, lips, and tongue would suggest central cyanosis, which is seen in cyanotic congenital heart diseases and respiratory distress syndrome with significant hypoxia.
- Also look for any evidence of birth marks, hemangioma, nevus, and rashes.
- Umbilical stump and nails should be inspected for chronic meconium staining that may have occurred in utero.
- Postmature neonates often have wrinkled and desquamating skin particularly over the creases of the hands and soles. Desquamation is also a feature of staphylococcal skin infections.

Chest

The clinical examination of the chest is limited in newborns due to the small size of the chest wall, periodic breathing, and soft, compliant chest wall. However, all the attempts need to be made to assess the cardiovascular and respiratory status to supplement a complete neonatal assessment.

- Observation is most important in assessing the neonatal respiratory status.
- Grunt is a respiratory sound that is produced to generate positive end-expiratory pressure; it occurs in case of hyaline membrane disease.
- Chest percussion is best avoided in the newborn as it rarely provides any meaningful clinical information and the newborn may not tolerate the procedure well.
- The breath sounds are harsh and have a bronchovesicular character due to better transmission across the thin chest walls as compared with those in older children.
- Check for air entry or any adventitious sounds such as crackles or rhonchi. Air entry is diminished in case of pneumothorax or pleural effusion.
- Presence of tachypnea, grunting, and subcostal indrawing may indicate not only a

respiratory disease but also a cardiovascular or a neurological problem.

- Auscultate for the rate, rhythm, quality of heart sounds, and the presence or absence of murmurs. Check the peripheral pulses (brachial and femoral). Look for femoral pulsation to exclude the possibility of coarctation of aorta. Easily palpable dorsalis pedis artery is indicative of wide pulse pressure, which is seen with opening of ductus arteriosus or patent ductus arteriosus.
- If heart sounds are better heard on the right side of chest, it may suggest dextrocardia in a quiet baby or pneumothorax or congenital diaphragmatic hernia in a baby with respiratory distress.

Abdomen

The abdomen is protuberant in the newborns and young infants, more so immediately after a feed.

- One should specifically examine the umbilical cord and/or the umbilicus of the neonate. If there is redness/induration in the periumbilical area or if there is foul-smelling discharge or pus, it suggests umbilical sepsis.
- Normally, the umbilical cord contains three vessels—two arteries and one vein. This should be specifically looked for at the time of birth to rule out a single umbilical artery that, at times, may be associated with certain anomalies of gastrointestinal tracts and kidneys.
- Look for meconium staining of umbilical cord, umbilical or inguinal hernia, umbilical granuloma, and exomphalos. Children who are born with respiratory distress and have a scaphoid abdomen may have diaphragmatic hernia in which bag and mask ventilation is contraindicated.
- Gentle palpation of the abdomen, starting from the lower quadrants and moving toward the upper quadrants, should be done. The right lobe of liver is normally palpable 1–2 cm below the costal margin as it is soft in consistency and the spleen tip can also be normally palpated in some newborns.

Genitalia

- Look for inguinal hernia, hydrocele, undescended testis, or ambiguous genitalia. Look for opening of urethra to exclude hypospadias or epispadias. Prepuce in newborn is normally non-retractable, and no attempt should be made to retract the foreskin in the newborn. Micropenis (penile length <2.5 cm) is seen with growth hormone deficiency as occurs in hypopituitarism.
- Usually, both the testes lie at the bottom of the scrotum in the term male babies but if they are not palpable or abnormally placed, it should be recorded and investigated. In term female newborns, the labia majora should completely cover the labia minora. A clear or occasional bloody vaginal discharge is normal in the first few days.
- If the genitalia are ambiguous, it is essential that the assignment of the gender should not be done immediately after birth and be deferred until further genetic, endocrinal, and genitourinary investigations have been performed.

Extremities

Look for anomalies such as single palmar crease (Down syndrome), polydactyly, syndactyly, clubfoot (congenital talipes equinovarus), and calcaneovalgus deformity. Postural talipes is not uncommon in the newborn period and does not require treatment if the feet are fully mobile.

Hips

One should exclude the possibility of developmental dysplasia of hip (formerly called congenital dislocation of hip) by modified Ortolani and Barlow maneuvers.

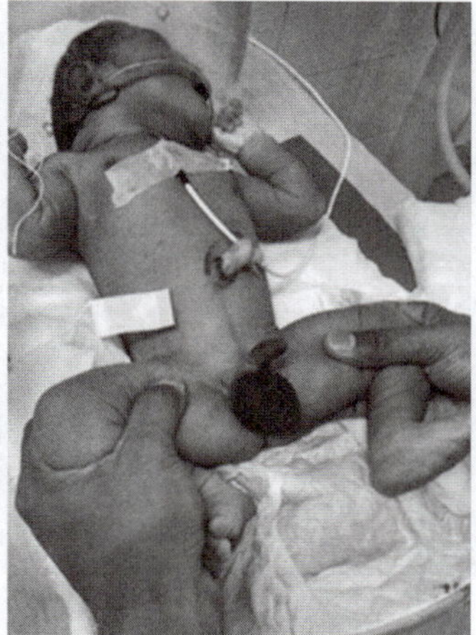

Figure 7.13 Modified Ortolani maneuver.

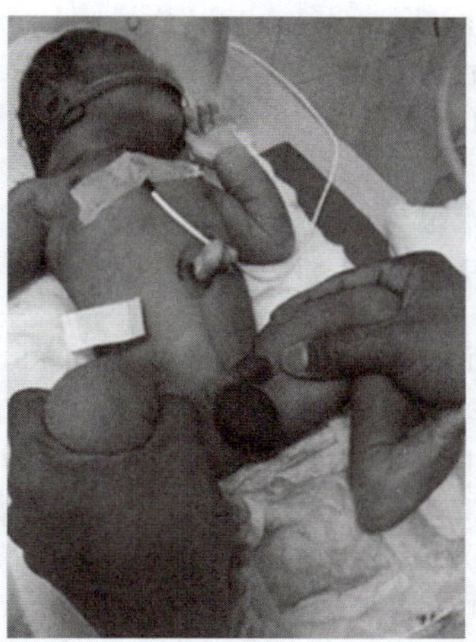

Figure 7.14 Modified Barlow maneuver.

Modified Ortolani maneuver

- Test one hip at a time with the infant lying supine with legs toward the examiner. The examiner tries to assess whether the hip is dislocated or prone to dislocation (Fig. 7.13).
- For examination of the left hip, stabilize the pelvis with the thumb of the left hand placed on pubic symphysis, and place fingers under the sacrum.
- Flex the left thigh and keep the knees bent. Use the right hand to grasp the left thigh of the infant by placing middle finger over the greater trochanter and thumb on the inner side of the thigh, opposite the lesser trochanter.
- In the modified Ortolani maneuver, the examiner tries to assess whether the hip is dislocated or not, for which pressure is applied over the greater trochanter with middle finger in an attempt to relocate the displaced femoral head.
- Movement of the head with or without a palpable or audible "clunk" suggests hip dislocation.
- If this is not present, the Barlow maneuver is carried out to look for the hip being prone to dislocation or subluxation of hip.

Barlow maneuver

- Barlow maneuver is done by placing the thumb on the inner side of the thigh. Backward and outward pressure is applied attempting to dislocate the hip. If femoral head is felt to move backward with or without a palpable or audible "clunk," then hip is prone to dislocation (Fig. 7.14).

Rule Out Congenital Malformations and Check All Orifices

- Certain obvious external malformations can be identified such as meningomyelocele, omphalocele, exomphalos, gross hydrocephalus, cleft lip, cleft palate, ambiguous genitalia, and congenital talipes equinovarus.
- Check for single umbilical artery that may be associated with internal malformation such as esophageal atresia, imperforate anus, and genitourinary malformation.
- Check all the orifices such as anal opening to rule out imperforate anus; pass infant feeding tube to rule out tracheoesophageal fistula. The most common variety of tracheoesophageal fistula is associated with esophageal atresia in which feeding tube cannot be passed to the stomach; it will

recoil and come back in the oral cavity. This can be confirmed by an X-ray that would show the coiling of the infant feeding tube.

Central Nervous System: Neurological Assessment

- Routine detailed neurological examination in a healthy term newborn is not necessary. A detailed neurological assessment is indicated in a sick baby or in a preterm/low-birth-weight baby to assess gestational age or in "at-risk neonates" as a part of neurodevelopmental monitoring. Hence, it must be remembered that the neonate's response can vary with his/her state of wakefulness and gestation also.
- Look for the state of wakefulness; usually, a newborn is drowsy or asleep after feed. An active or alert newborn usually indicates that the higher functions are intact. Examination of cranial nerves has limited usefulness.
- Look for the cry of the newborn—a normal healthy newborn's cry is purposeful, lusty, and generally pacifiable by the mother, while a sick newborn's cry would be unremitting, unmodulated, inconsolable, and often very persistent.

Special Senses

- *Vision*: Visual acuity of a newborn is 20/150. Check for pupillary reactions—the baby responds to bright light by blinking. Vision can also be assessed by examining whether the baby turns toward diffuse light or a moving red ball.
- *Hearing*: Look for response after a sudden sound stimulus. Response may be in the form of startle response, blinking eye, or change in activity.

Motor Functions

- *Spontaneous movements*: See whether the baby is moving all four limbs spontaneously or whether there is any paucity of movement involving the limb(s).

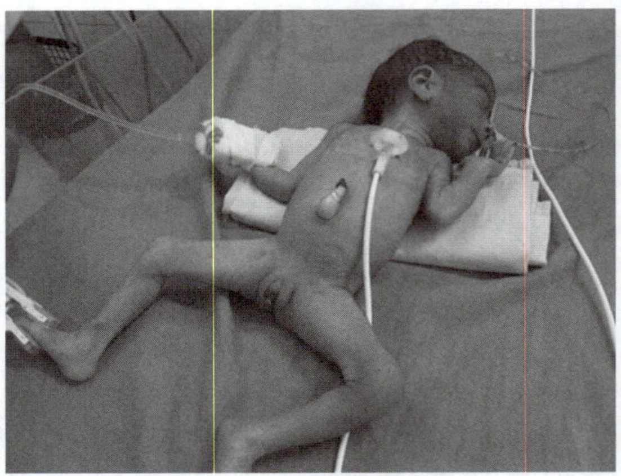

Figure 7.15 Hypotonic posture in a preterm newborn.

Muscle Tone and Tendon Reflexes

- A normal term baby has a good muscle tone in comparison to a preterm baby who is hypotonic. Hypotonia in a preterm newborn manifests as a posture in which the limbs are kept semiflexed and the baby assumes a frog-like position (Fig. 7.15). Another feature that suggests hypotonia in a newborn is abnormal head lag when the neonate is pulled to sit. The "pull-to-sit" maneuver is an important procedure in the neurological examination of the neonate and allows an appreciation of the baby's grasp, limb/trunk tone, and head control.
- Asymmetry of tone on either side is of localizing value. The neonate should have a symmetrical distribution of tone, power, and reflexes when the head is properly placed in the midline.
- Deep tendon jerks are variable and are rather difficult to elicit in neonates, except the knee jerks. An ill-sustained ankle clonus is normal in neonates, while a well-sustained ankle clonus (10–12 jerks, uninterrupted) is abnormal.

Neonatal/Primitive Reflexes

Neonatal reflexes are neurodevelopmental responses that are achieved at certain gestational ages. Most primitive reflexes disappear between 3 and 4 months of age and their persistence is considered as an early sign of cerebral palsy or brain damage. The examination of these reflexes forms an essential tool to complete a basic neurobehavioral assessment of any newborn and should be done in a quiet and alert state.

Moro Reflex

This is a vestibular reflex. It appears at 28 weeks of gestation and is fully developed by term age. It disappears by 4–5 months of age. Moro reflex is elicited by sudden drop of the infant's head by 30°. For this, the baby should be held in supine position over right hand and arm and the flexed head is suddenly dropped to about 30°. The positive response consists of rapid abduction and extension at shoulder and elbow joints, and extension of the arms, followed by adduction and flexion at elbow joint (known as embrace equivalent), and is often accompanied with crying (Fig. 7.16).

Response is depressed or absent in an infant with cerebral depression and exaggerated in an infant with cerebral irritability, such as in hypoxic brain injury, meningitis, and kernicterus. Incomplete Moro reflex suggests gestational age of less than 35 weeks. Asymmetric Moro reflex suggests brachial palsy and clavicle/humerus fracture or hemiparesis. In a newborn with kernicterus, sudden extension of arm is not followed by flexion but is accompanied by downward rolling of eyeball (setting sun) sign.

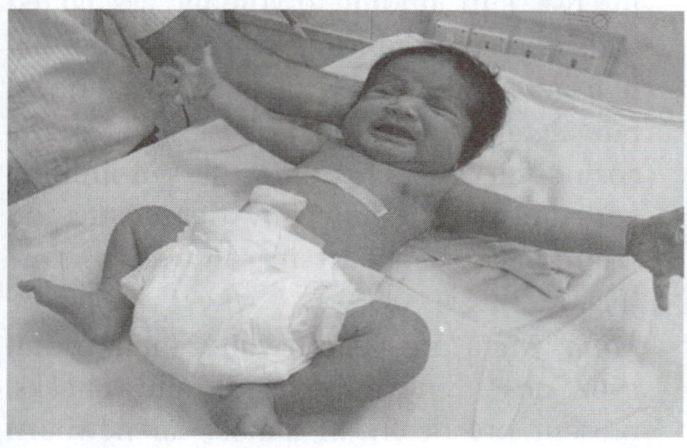

Figure 7.16 Moro reflex.

Startle Reflex

This is elicited by sudden noise and is equivalent to Moro reflex except that the elbows remain flexed and the hands remain closed. In Moro reflex, there are more outward and inward movements than in startle response.

Asymmetric Tonic Neck Reflex

When the baby's head is turned to one side, ipsilateral arm and leg get extended while contralateral limbs are flexed (Fig. 7.17). It disappears by 2–3 months of age. Persistence beyond 4–5 months may signify future development of cerebral palsy.

Rooting and Sucking Response

The rooting reflex helps the neonate to locate the mother's breast/nipple to initiate the breastfeeding. The reflex is elicited by stroking the cheek near the angle of mouth with a clean finger that results in the newborn turning his/her head to that side toward the contact. This reflex is fully developed by the gestational age of 34 weeks (Fig. 7.18). Placing a clean finger in the baby's mouth 2–3 cm inside would elicit a vigorous sucking response/reflex (Fig. 7.19). The reflex is depressed when the neonate is neurologically depressed, immature, or hypotonic.

Palmar and Plantar Grasps

The finger is placed on the palmar surface of fingers or plantar surface of toes of the baby to elicit grasp or flexion of digits

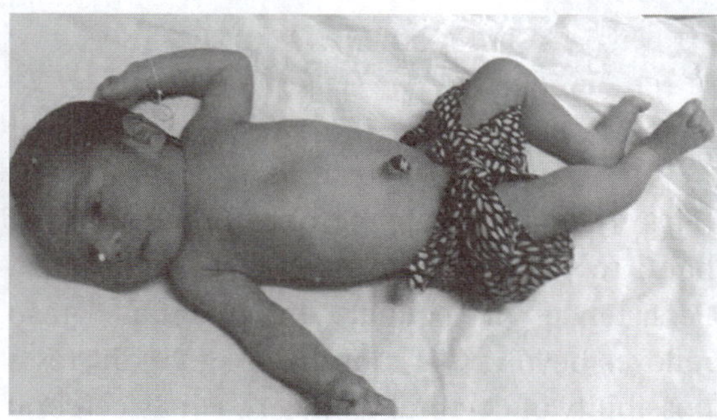

Figure 7.17 Asymmetric tonic neck reflex.

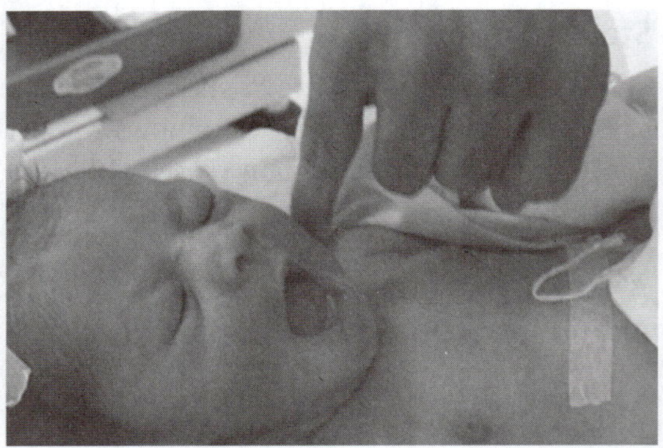

Figure 7.18 Rooting reflex.

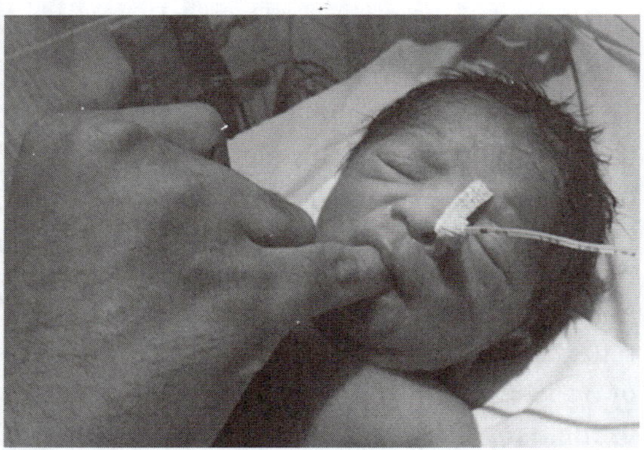

Figure 7.19 Sucking reflex.

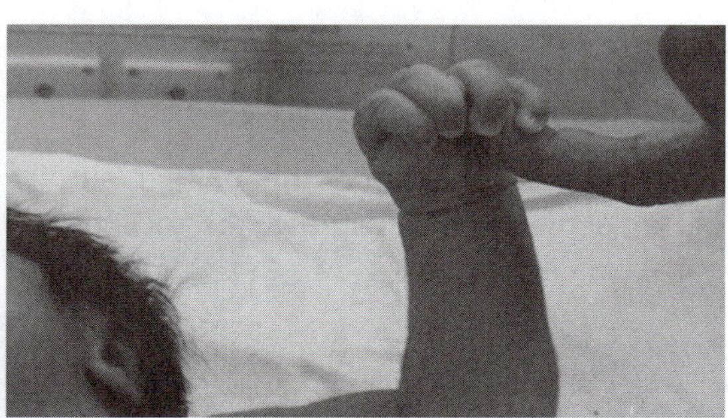

Figure 7.20 Palmar grasp.

(Figs 7.20 and 7.21). Stroke the dorsum of hand to persuade the baby to open the fist. Persistence of palmar and plantar grasp reflexes beyond 3–4 months of age indicates a possibility of cerebral damage such as cerebral palsy.

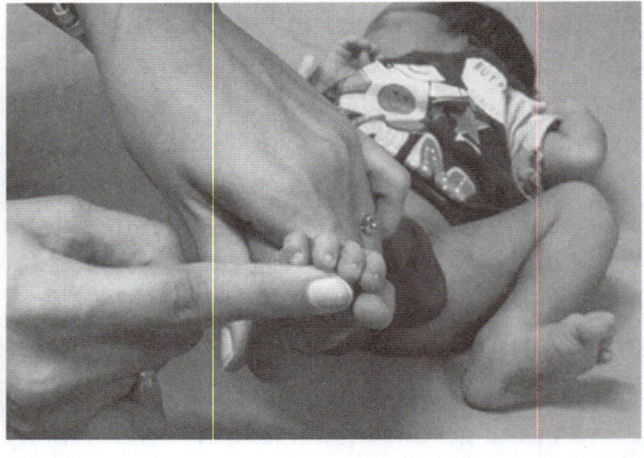

Figure 7.21 Plantar grasp in a newborn.

Other Reflexes

Other reflexes that can be elicited are glabellar tap and traction responses. Glabellar tap is a persistent blink response and is normally present from 32 to 34 weeks of gestation. Traction response is a primitive reflex that enables the child to hold on to the mother when being pulled.

Normal Variations in Newborn

- *Erythema toxicum*: It is a benign condition found in almost 50% of term newborns and is less common in preterm babies. It is characterized by the appearance of small, papular lesions with surrounding intense erythema that appear on the first or second day of life. Lesions are located on the trunk but can also be found on face and extremities sparing palms and soles. Intense surrounding erythema associated with this condition helps in differentiating it from pyoderma. Etiology is not known but scrapping from skin lesion shows eosinophils. This condition is self-limiting and does not require any treatment, and eruptions disappear in a week's time (Fig. 7.22).
- *Milia*: Milia are yellow-white spots found over nose, chin, forehead, and cheeks, present practically in almost all newborn babies, and disappear spontaneously. They

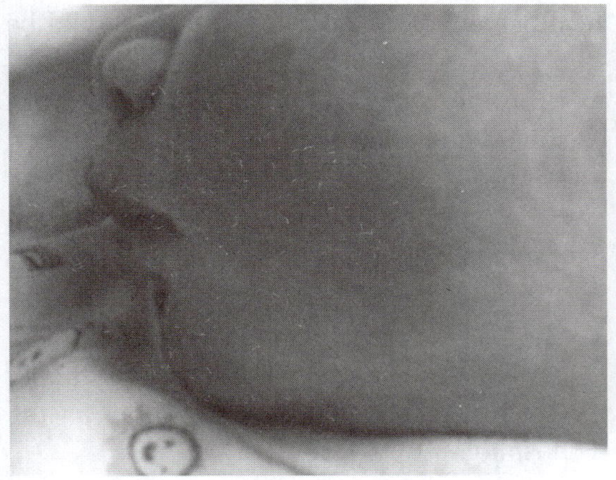

Figure 7.22 Erythema toxicum in a normal newborn.

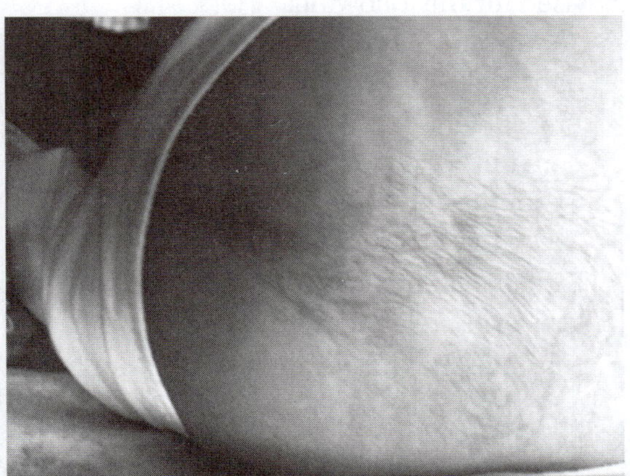

Figure 7.23 Mongolian spots.

are epidermal inclusion cysts (1–2 mm in diameter).

- *Mongolian blue spots*: They are commonly found on lumbosacral area and buttocks but can also be found on arms and lower limbs. They are bluish or slate gray macular lesions of variable size, much more common in Asian children (Fig. 7.23). They occur due to accumulation of melanocytes within dermis. They are benign lesions and disappear gradually in late infancy but may persist up to 2 years.
- *Epstein pearls*: They are epithelial inclusion cysts found on either side of median raphe of hard palate and are of no significance.

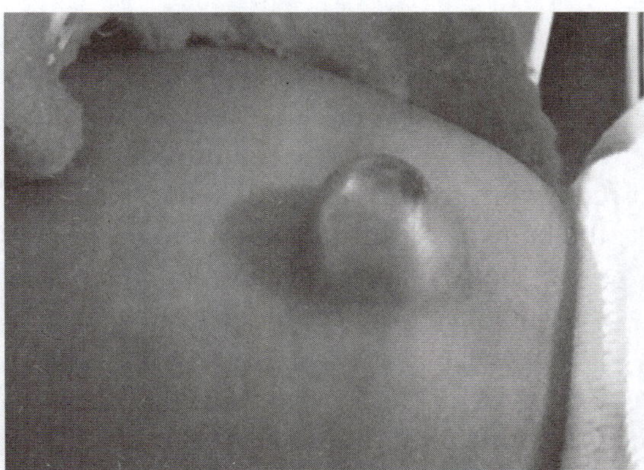

Figure 7.24 Umbilical hernia in a newborn.

- *Umbilical hernia*: This presents as a short swelling at umbilicus that becomes more prominent during crying or straining (Fig. 7.24). It is more common in infants having hypotonia such as in hypothyroidism, Down syndrome, and rickets. It disappears/reduces spontaneously in most of the infants by the age of 6 months to 1 year. Application of coins or bandages over hernia is not recommended. Surgical closure, rarely, is required if it causes strangulation or persists beyond the age of 4–5 years.

Minor Common Neonatal Problems

- *Failure to pass meconium*: Neonate should pass meconium within the first 24 hours of life. Meconium is black-colored stool passed by a newborn in the initial few days of life. Delayed passage of meconium is seen in conditions such as Hirschsprung disease, cystic fibrosis, and congenital hypothyroidism. Preterm neonates may also have slight delay in the passage of meconium. Failure to pass meconium is seen with imperforate anus. In any neonate presenting with a delayed passage of meconium (more than 24 hours), imperforate anus should be ruled out by a clinical examination and necessary investigations done appropriately for surgical management. Ideally, all orifices should be examined for any abnormality right at birth.

- *Failure to pass urine*: The neonate should pass urine within 48 hours of birth. In many cases, the baby passes urine at the time of birth that may go unnoticed. Another common reason is inadequate feeding—the baby passes urine after a proper feed or giving bolus of normal saline. If still the baby does not pass urine, it should be investigated for renal agenesis or obstructive uropathy.
- *Crying before urination*: Normally, babies pass urine 8–10 times per day or more. Few babies may cry before passing urine, which is normal and should not be confused with urinary tract infection. This is due to discomfort associated with a full bladder.

Essential Newborn Care (ENBC)

ENBC pertains to the basic care that should be provided to all neonates. There are four components of ENBC:

1. Care at birth including neonatal resuscitation (most of the babies cry immediately after birth, while few may need assistance for establishing respiration)
2. Prevention of hypothermia
3. Prevention of hypoglycemia by early initiation of breastfeeding
4. Prevention of sepsis

Discharge of Newborn from Health Care Facility

Usually the newborn is discharged after 48–72 hours of birth. Before discharge from healthcare facility following criteria should be fulfilled.

- A routine formal examination of the newborn should be performed and documented.
- Mother should be confident to take care of her newborn baby and all her queries are resolved.
- The adequacy of feeding is established.
- The newborn is hemodynamically stable and does not have any significant morbidity which needs a close observation in the hospital.
- Newborn has received the recommended vaccines.

At the time of discharge, mother should be advised for the following:

- To prevent hypothermia advise to cover the baby well.
- Breastfeeding every three hourly and on demand and exclusive breastfeeding for 6 months and to be continued till 2 years of age with other foods.
- Explain about hand hygiene to prevent sepsis and related morbidities.
- Nothing should be applied over umbilical cord.
- Regular follow-up for monitoring of growth and development and for immunization.
- Give the date of next follow-up and the date of next immunization.
- To report immediately if she observes any of the danger signs like refusal to feed, lethargy, poor sucking, yellow palms and soles, fast breathing, convulsions, etc.

KEY POINTS

- Neonates are vulnerable to various morbidities and are at increased risk of mortality and so need special attention.
- Every newborn should be assessed and examined at birth.
- History taking and examination of newborns is an art to be learnt with practice.
- All newborns must receive "Essential Newborn Care."

CHAPTER 8

The Gastrointestinal System

Niranjan Shendurnikar, Paresh A Thakkar, Tushar P Shah

Although the abdomen essentially refers to the conventional examination of the gastrointestinal system, it also includes the hepatobiliary system and the genitourinary tract. It thus becomes important to approach the examination of the abdomen to determine which system is involved, which organs are affected, and what the underlying cause for the disease is. This can be simplified by a systematic approach. In addition to the primary disorder related to intra-abdominal organs, abdomen may be secondarily involved in many other conditions in which primary disease is related to other systems.

Symptoms Related to Abdomen

Careful evaluation of the symptoms related to the abdomen is necessary as these could also be manifestations of extra-abdominal pathology. Very commonly, parents misinterpret symptoms such as excessive crying in their children to be due to abdominal pain. Although this is one possibility, it may not be the case always. As it is not always possible to obtain history from a pediatric patient, very careful approach is needed, and the symptoms should be evaluated in light of other associated symptoms and examination findings.

- Common constitutional symptoms related to abdomen include fever and loss of appetite.
- History of fever may be due to infective, inflammatory, or malignant conditions such as acute hepatitis, dysentery, urinary tract infection (UTI), abdominal tuberculosis, liver abscess, inflammatory bowel disease, or malignancy.
- Loss of appetite is a common complaint in many acute and chronic illnesses. Acute conditions such as gastroenteritis, dysentery, colitis, UTI, enteric fever, and hepatitis result in loss of appetite. In conditions such as acute hepatitis, loss of appetite often precedes nausea and vomiting and is of a relatively longer duration. Chronic conditions such as chronic liver disease, tuberculosis, chronic renal failure, malignancy, and malabsorption can also present with anorexia.
- Most of the mothers are not satisfied with the intake and appetite of their children and in fact "my child is not eating well" is a very common complaint by a large number of mothers. Thus, this needs careful evaluation and should be seen with respect to the growth pattern of the child. If the child's growth parameters are normal and the child is thriving well, the complaint is likely to be the mother's perception rather than be due to an organic cause.
- Increased appetite is seen in children with diabetes mellitus, those on steroid therapy, those having worm infestation, and those in recovery phase of hepatitis.

Abdominal Pain

This is a common complaint that needs careful evaluation to differentiate the cause of pain being organic or nonorganic. A great majority of abdominal pains in children are relatively benign but it is important to pick up on the cardinal signs that may suggest a more serious underlying pathological condition.

The pain in the abdomen may be acute or chronic, or it could be recurrent abdominal pain. One should inquire about duration, frequency, site of pain, intensity of pain, character of pain, onset, aggravating and relieving factors, and relation with meals, radiation, and associated symptoms.

Site of Pain

The knowledge of relevant anatomy and the location of intra-abdominal organs is important in relating the site of pain with the organ of origin.

Anatomically, the abdomen is divided into nine quadrants (Fig. 8.1) by two vertical lines from the midclavicular points on each side and two horizontal lines; the upper one connects the two lowermost points of costal margins and the lower line connects the tubercles of iliac crests on each side. The visceral contents of various abdominal regions are shown in Table 8.1. When the child is able to localize and pinpoint the site of abdominal pain precisely with one finger, it indicates that the pain has originated from a particular organ based on its anatomical location.

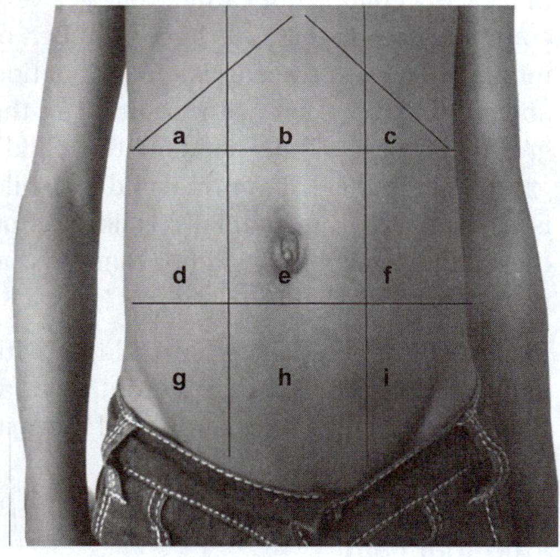

Figure 8.1 Diagrammatic representation of the regions of the abdomen: (a and c) right and left hypochondrium; (b) epigastrium; (d and f) right and left lumbar regions; (e) umbilical; (g and i) right and left iliac fossa; and (h) hypogastrium or suprapubic.

TABLE 8.1 Abdominal Contents and Their Regions

Region	Contents
Right hypochondrium	Liver, gallbladder, and part of colon
Epigastrium	Stomach, pancreas, and left lobe of liver
Left hypochondrium	Spleen, colon
Right lumbar region	Right kidney, large colon
Umbilical region	Small intestines
Left lumbar region	Left kidney, colon
Right/left iliac regions	Large intestines
Suprapubic region	Urinary bladder

- *Right hypochondrium*: Major organs in this area are liver and gallbladder. Common causes of pain in this area are acute hepatitis, congestive hepatomegaly, amoebic or pyemic liver abscess, cholecystitis, and right-sided pleurisy.
- *Epigastrium*: The commonest cause of pain in epigastrium is gastritis. Gastroenteritis is common in children. Certain drugs such as nonsteroidal anti-inflammatory drugs (NSAIDs), steroids, and antitubercular drugs can cause gastritis. Pancreatitis is relatively uncommon in children.
- *Periumbilical region*: It is the most common site of abdominal pain and in most of the cases the pain is nonorganic in which when asked, the child points at the periumbilical area. However, organic conditions involving small bowel and acute appendicitis can give rise to pain in this area.
- *Left hypochondrium*: The major organ in this area is spleen. Pain in this area can be due to splenic infarct, splenic enlargement, and left-sided pleurisy.
- *Lumbar region/flanks*: Pain in this region is usually of renal origin and there may be typical loin to groin radiation.

- *Suprapubic region*: Causes related to urinary bladder such as cystitis and bladder calculus can cause suprapubic pain.
- *Right iliac fossa (RIF)*: The pain of appendicitis is typically felt at McBurney's point in RIF (point between lateral one-third and medial two-third of the line joining umbilicus and anterior superior iliac spine).
- *Left iliac fossa*: Pain in this region can be related to fecal impaction, chronic constipation, or inflammatory bowel disease.

Referred Pain

The pain is said to be referred when it is felt at some other region having same segmental innervation as the site of lesion. This is more important for surgical conditions. The pain from appendix and ileum is referred to umbilicus. The pain of diaphragmatic irritation is referred to shoulder of the same side as diaphragm is supplied by phrenic nerve (C3, C4, C5). Similarly, pain due to pleural inflammation may be referred to upper abdominal wall.

Shifting of Pain

In appendicitis, the pain is around umbilicus initially that later shifts to RIF.

Radiation of Pain

The pain may radiate to a different site as seen in renal colic where the pain originates in the lumbar region and then radiates to the groin and the inner thigh. Similarly, pain due to pancreatitis also radiates to the back.

Timing of Pain

Pain at night that awakens the child from sleep is likely to be due to underlying pathological condition, whereas an episode of pain in morning in a school-going child may reflect anxiety and a reason to not go to school. Pain that occurs on an empty stomach and gets relieved by meals indicates dyspepsia or peptic ulcer disease.

The common causes of abdominal pain are shown in Table 8.2. While there are many causes of abdominal pain due to abdominal conditions, it must be remembered that there are extra-abdominal causes of abdominal pain also and a few of these include sickle cell crisis, abdominal migraine, abdominal epilepsy, diabetic ketoacidosis, lead poisoning, and Henoch–Schonlein purpura.

TABLE 8.2 Common Causes of Abdominal Pain

Medical	Surgical
• Gastroenteritis • Dysentery • Intestinal colic • Urinary tract infection, pyelonephritis • Acute hepatitis • Inflammatory bowel disorder • Functional • Chronic constipation • Henoch–Schonlein purpura	• Appendicitis • Meckel diverticulitis • Intussusception • Peritonitis • Intestinal obstruction • Malrotation/volvulus • Gastrointestinal perforation • Urolithiasis

Nature/Character of Pain

It is pertinent to find out the nature of the pain, that is, whether it is sharp, episodic gripping pain (colicky) as seen due to obstruction (e.g., bowel obstruction or a urinary calculus), burning in nature due to inflammatory conditions such as gastritis or esophagitis, or throbbing such as in cholecystitis.

Organic Versus Nonorganic Abdominal Pain

As nonorganic pain is common in children, it is important to differentiate it from organic pain. If pain is specifically pointed to a particular area, it is more likely to be organic. The characteristics of nonorganic pain are that it is generally periumbilical and diffuse, does not disturb the child's sleep/play, and occurs before going to the school.

Recurrent Abdominal Pain

This refers to episodic attacks of acute pain over a period of 3 months that interfere with the child's activity.

TABLE 8.3 Associated Symptoms in Abdominal Pain

Symptoms	Clinical relevance
Diarrhea	Gastroenteritis, inflammatory bowel disease
Blood in stools	Dysentery, ulcerative colitis, chronic constipation
Hematemesis	Esophageal varices, peptic ulcer, drug-induced gastritis
Bilious vomiting*	Small bowel obstruction
Jaundice	Hepatic, biliary, or hemolytic disease
Joint swellings	Henoch–Schonlein purpura, inflammatory bowel disease
Dysuria/hematuria	Acute nephritis, urinary tract infection

*Bilious vomiting, blood in the stools, significant weight loss, visceromegaly, and hemodynamic instability are considered red flag (alerting) signs in a child with abdominal pain.

Associated Symptoms

The associated symptoms for abdominal pain and their clinical correlates are shown in Table 8.3.

Vomiting

This is a common symptom of gastrointestinal disorders. Vomiting should be differentiated from regurgitation of feeds, which is a normal phenomenon seen in infants due to poor lower esophageal sphincter tone. Vomiting may be organic or nonorganic. It may be due to abdominal or extra-abdominal causes. Nausea is an early indicator of vomiting, seen mainly in appendicitis and hepatitis. The following points should be asked in relation to vomiting to find out the etiology:

- Type of vomitus: Bile stained or non-bile stained. Bilious vomiting is seen in obstruction distal to ampulla of Vater at second part of duodenum. History of any blood in vomitus should also be noted.
- Vomiting in relation to food intake: In pyloric stenosis, baby vomits immediately after taking feeds.
- Number of episodes per day: Profuse, persistent, and uncontrolled vomiting often suggests an intestinal obstruction.
- Nature of vomiting: Projectile or nonprojectile. Projectile vomiting is forceful vomitus where the vomitus falls far away; it is classically seen in pyloric stenosis and raised intracranial tension.
- The temporal relationship of vomiting with acute diarrhea must also be assessed. Most infants and young children have vomiting initially with the onset of diarrhea, but it should subside/resolve early, while diarrhea may persist for 7–10 days. Vomiting that persists longer is an alarming sign and indicates a possibility of another underlying systemic disease such as electrolyte imbalance, sepsis, or UTI.
- Associated symptoms: These include jaundice (hepatitis), loose stools (acute gastroenteritis), convulsions (raised intracranial tension), constipation (intestinal obstruction), abdominal pain (inflammatory bowel disease, renal stones), burning micturition (UTI), and weight loss in case of persistent vomiting or malignancy.
- Post-tussive vomiting, after a bout of paroxysmal cough, is common in children such as in children with pertussis. This is not likely to be associated with an underlying gastrointestinal disorder. The common causes of vomiting are shown in Table 8.4.

Diarrhea

Recent change in consistency associated with increased frequency of stool is called diarrhea in children. It is a common problem seen in children. Diarrhea should be differentiated from the normal change in the frequency of stool. Diarrhea in children is usually of viral origin. The following questions should be asked in relation to diarrhea to find out the etiology:

- *Onset*: Sudden (infectious), insidious (inflammatory bowel disease)

TABLE 8.4 Common Causes of Vomiting

Medical	Surgical
• Gastroenteritis • Hepatitis • Malaria • Urinary tract infection • Gastroesophageal reflux • Central nervous system infections • Diabetic ketoacidosis • Overfeeding (faulty feeding) • Uremia • Psychogenic • Drug induced • Post-tussive vomiting	• Congenital hypertrophic pyloric stenosis • Intestinal obstruction • Appendicitis • Intussusception • Perforation, peritonitis • Renal colic

- *Duration*: Short lasting (acute diarrhea lasting for <14 days), long lasting that is either persistent or chronic
- *Consistency and color of the stool*: Watery (viral diarrhea), rice watery (cholera), blood-stained (dysentery), bulky, frothy stools (malabsorption syndromes), clay-colored stools (cholestatic jaundice)
- *Relationship with food intake*: Possibility of food poisoning if food intake followed by diarrhea or, less commonly, may be due to an allergic component in the diet such as animal milk
- *Associated symptoms*: Fever (infectious such as bacillary dysentery, enteric fever), abdominal pain (inflammatory bowel disease, early stage of intestinal obstruction), perianal excoriation (lactose intolerance)
- *Tenesmus*: A clinical symptom where there is a feeling of constantly needing to pass stools, despite an empty colon
- *Diarrhea*: Can be of abdominal or nonabdominal origin (parenteral diarrhea, UTI, pneumonia) (the common causes of diarrhea in children are shown in Box 8.1)

Box 8.1 Common causes of diarrhea in children

- Gastroenteritis
- Food poisoning
- Antibiotic-associated diarrhea
- Lactose intolerance
- Cow milk protein intolerance
- Celiac disease
- Giardiasis
- Inflammatory bowel disease
- Irritable bowel syndrome
- Hyperthyroidism
- Systemic infections (parenteral diarrhea)

Constipation

Passage of hard stool associated with difficulty in passing stool or painful evacuation of stool is constipation. It is not just a passage of infrequent stools. The commonest cause of chronic constipation is dietary, related to low fiber and fluid content in the child's diet.

A normal child who is on exclusive breast-feed may pass stool every third or fourth day, but there is no difficulty in passing stool and the child has no discomfort. This does not need any treatment and the parents should be reassured. Babies on dairy milk or formula milk are likely to be constipated due to higher casein content of animal milk.

The following questions should be asked in relation to constipation:

- *Onset*: Sudden or acute (e.g., intestinal obstruction), insidious (Hirschsprung disease)
- *Duration*: Chronic (Hirschsprung disease, hypothyroidism)
- *Frequency of stools*: To differentiate from normal stool pattern in infancy
- *Relation to flatus*: Obstipation (inability to pass flatus, indicating intestinal obstruction, peritonitis) (most children who have intestinal obstruction have constipation associated with abdominal distension and vomiting)
- *Associated symptoms*: Pain and difficulty (dyschezia) during defecation (anal fissure, perianal excoriation), abdominal distension

Box 8.2 Causes of constipation in children

- Functional or dietary
- Hirschsprung disease
- Hypothyroidism
- Intestinal obstruction
- Cystic fibrosis
- Hypokalemia
- Anal stenosis
- Anal stricture
- Prolonged drug therapy, e.g., calcium and magnesium

(intestinal obstruction) (the causes of constipation are shown in Box 8.2)

Abdominal Distension

Abdominal distension may be due to multiple reasons such as flatus, fluid, feces, or fat in children. It may be physiological or pathological. Physiological distension is seen after ingestion of food and may also be due to accumulation of substances such as gas or fluid in toddlers. Visceromegaly (hepatomegaly/splenomegaly) and fluid (ascites) are the most common causes of abdominal distension in children in clinical practice. The following points should be inquired about:

- *Onset/duration*: Acute (intestinal obstruction), chronic (ascites, cirrhosis, liver disease)
- *Associated symptoms*: Post-diarrhea (hypokalemia), post-constipation (intestinal obstruction), vomiting (intestinal obstruction), abdominal pain (peritonitis)
- *Other causes (extra-abdominal) of abdominal distension in children*: Severe malnutrition and rickets due to abdominal wall hypotonia and electrolyte imbalances such as hypokalemia

Jaundice

- The patient may present with a complaint of yellowish discoloration of eyes and/or urine. Jaundice can be due to direct/conjugated or indirect/unconjugated hyperbilirubinemia. Indirect jaundice occurs due to hemolysis, while conjugated hyperbilirubinemia can be due to hepatic or posthepatic (obstructive) causes.
- As direct bilirubin is water soluble and gets excreted in urine, the urine turns dark yellow in color, while it remains unchanged in unconjugated hyperbilirubinemia. Furthermore, in case of obstructive variety of direct jaundice, the patient may have a history of passing clay-colored or pale stools. Thus, history of urine and stool color in case of jaundice is important and provides useful information about the type of jaundice. Itching may be an associated complaint in case of obstructive jaundice.
- Past history of jaundice is important; recurrent jaundice can be seen in hemolytic anemia such as sickle cell disease or there may be previous episodes of jaundice in cases of liver disorders or obstructive jaundice. It is important to ask about previous history of blood transfusion that might have been responsible for transmission of hepatitis B or C virus infection.
- Many a time, significant pallor can be misinterpreted as jaundice by the relatives, so it is important to ask whether the child is getting pale or yellowish. Apart from jaundice, dark-colored urine can be because of certain other causes also. Patients who are dehydrated, those with poor fluid intake, or febrile patients may pass concentrated yellowish urine. It can also be due to multivitamin supplementation and secondary to drugs such as rifampicin.

Gastrointestinal Bleeding

History of blood in vomitus or stool or passing black-colored stool may be indicative of bleeding from gastrointestinal tract. Coagulation factors are synthesized in the liver, so there is a state of coagulopathy with hepatic dysfunction. In chronic liver disease, there could be bleeding from the esophageal varices due to portal hypertension.

Melena

Passage of black, tarry stool is termed melena and suggests bleeding from upper gastrointestinal tract. The blood gets denatured and leads to black, tarry stool. This can also be seen with swallowed blood from oral cavity, nose, or upper respiratory tract. Patients who are on iron supplementation also have black stools, so it is important to ask whether the patients are on such supplementation or not. Hematochezia is the passage of fresh blood with the stools.

Hematemesis

Presence of blood in vomitus is called hematemesis and this should not be confused with hemoptysis, which is blood in sputum or coughing out of blood. Hematemesis is most commonly due to bleeding from esophageal varices in case of portal hypertension. This can also be due to severe gastritis (also drug induced), peptic ulcer, and severe raised intracranial tension.

Bleeding Per Rectum

It is important to differentiate whether the patient has fresh bleeding per rectum or has blood mixed with stool. In dysentery, it would be associated with change in consistency of stool and presence of pus along with blood.

Fresh bleeding per rectum can be due to hemorrhoids because of chronic constipation, portal hypertension, or rectal polyp, fistula, or fissure-in-ano. Passage of red currant jelly stool is seen in case of intussusception.

Other Relevant Points

- History of contact with a patient of tuberculosis is important when abdominal tuberculosis is suspected.
- Jaundice in mother could signify possibility of vertical transmission of hepatitis B or C.
- Family history of jaundice may be important as in case of viral hepatitis A and E and family members or even neighborhood might have acquired from a common source.

  This can also point to a possibility of inherited hemolytic anemia such as sickle cell anemia, G6PD deficiency, and hereditary spherocytosis particularly if there is a history of repeated blood transfusions also.
- Inquire about intake of hepatotoxic drugs such as rifampicin, isoniazid, pyrazinamide, valproic acid, and phenytoin. Rifampicin can also cause dark yellow or orange discoloration of urine.
- Past history of blood transfusion: This can be a source of transmission of hepatitis B or C or HIV. History of repeated blood transfusion might indicate possibility of hemolytic anemia, portal hypertension due to chronic liver, or other diseases.
- History of fever with rash in mother during antenatal period should be asked in a child suspected with TORCH (Toxoplasmosis, Other [syphilis, varicella-zoster, parvovirus B19], Rubella, Cytomegalovirus [CMV], and Herpes) infections. History of umbilical catheterization or umbilical sepsis in newborns is important in case of children having extrahepatic portal hypertension as it could have led to portal vein thrombosis.

General Physical Examination Relevant to Abdomen

- *Respiratory rate*: With significant abdominal distension, the child may be tachypneic or having respiratory distress. Massive distension can push up the diaphragm, compromising the lung volume. The child with respiratory distress may also develop gaseous distension of abdomen due to aerophagy. Tachypnea can also be due to fluid overload in case of renal failure.
- *Heart rate*: Tachycardia can be present in children with fever, fluid overload in case of renal failure, perforation, and appendicitis. A child with severe jaundice can have bradycardia.
- *Blood pressure*: A child with intestinal perforation and peritonitis may be hypotensive due to shock. Children with

glomerulonephritis and renal failure can have hypertension.

- *Eyes*: Look for signs of vitamin A deficiency such as Bitot's spots and conjunctival or corneal xerosis that can be seen in a child with obstructive jaundice or undernutrition. Kayser–Fleischer ring may be seen with torch light in Wilson disease, but can be better seen with slit lamp examination.
- *Icterus*: Look for icterus in upper part of sclera in natural daylight. It is seen in both unconjugated and conjugated jaundice, but it is usually not very deep in indirect jaundice as seen in hemolytic anemia. Absence of icterus does not rule out liver disease. It may be absent in cases such as Reye syndrome and liver abscess.
- *Pallor*: It is common in chronic renal disease due to lack of erythropoietin and in chronic liver disease due to occult blood loss. Children with malabsorption, worm infestation, and hemolytic anemia would have pallor.
- *Edema*: Look for pedal edema, periorbital puffiness, or generalized edema. This may be seen in children with chronic liver disease, congestive heart failure, and nephrotic syndrome. Sacral edema may be present in an infant or a child who is not ambulatory. Most often, the cause of edema is a decrease in the serum albumin levels causing reduction of plasma oncotic pressure. In chronic liver disease associated with portal hypertension, ascites may be out of proportion to the edema at other places.
- *Hydration status*: A child with diarrhea and/or vomiting should be assessed for signs of dehydration such as sunken eyeballs, poor skin turgor, thirst, lethargy, drowsiness, or altered sensorium in severe dehydration. A child with renal failure may show other signs of fluid overload in addition to presence of edema.
- *Nutritional status*: Anthropometry and assessment of nutritional status is important. Children with chronic liver disease, chronic renal disease, and malabsorption syndrome are usually malnourished. In addition, they can have multiple nutrient deficiencies. Look for evidence of deficiency of fat-soluble vitamins in children with obstructive jaundice.
- *Clubbing*: Clubbing can be present in children with chronic liver disease, ulcerative colitis, or Crohn disease.
- *Cutaneous bleeding*: Examine for the presence of petechiae, purpura, or ecchymosis. Cutaneous bleeds may be present in liver disease due to coagulopathy. They can also be seen in children with malignancy such as leukemia or lymphoma due to thrombocytopenia or at times due to altered coagulation.
- *Lymphadenopathy*: Generalized lymphadenopathy can be present in children with leukemia, lymphoma, or disseminated tuberculosis. Inguinal lymph nodes may be palpable due to some nonspecific infection involving lower limb or perineum.
- *Bony tenderness*: In case of leukemia, bony tenderness may be present.

Physical Examination of the Abdomen

This section proposes to discuss the routine physical examination of the abdomen including the gastrointestinal system and hepatobiliary system. The systemic examination needs to be carried out in a stepwise manner to assess the involvement of various organs, to detect the nature of the disease, and to logically arrive at a differential diagnosis. The steps of examination remain the same as for other systems, i.e., inspection, palpation, percussion, and auscultation.

Inspection

There are a few essential prerequisites for obtaining the best information from the examination of the child. The examiner should be standing or sitting on the right side of the

Box 8.3 Key information on inspection

- Shape of the abdomen
- Distension
- Abdominal movements
- Visible organomegaly/masses/scars
- Caput medusae (veins drain away from umbilicus); if present, then look for other signs of liver failure
- Umbilicus
- Visible gastric and intestinal peristaltic movements
- Hernial sites and genitalia

child who, in turn, should be lying supine on a firm surface with hips flexed. The child should be adequately uncovered in a comfortable environmental temperature to expose the lower chest, abdomen, and genitalia. The examiner's hands should be warmed by rubbing, especially in winters, to comfort the child. Infants and young children, if apprehensive, are best examined in their mothers' or attendants' laps. For an older girl child and adolescent female, a female attendant or nurse should be present by the side of the patient during examination, and utmost priority should be given to the privacy of the patient. The observations in Box 8.3 provide useful information on inspection.

- The normal shape of the abdomen is dependent on the age of the child. Children younger than 5 years have a protuberant abdomen commonly known as *pot belly*, which becomes further evident in an upright posture. However, it must be remembered that the abdominal fullness and/or distension can also be due to visceromegaly, the presence of fluid/ascites (Fig. 8.2), intestinal obstruction, and hypotonia due to vitamin D deficiency, malnutrition, and hypothyroidism. A full urinary bladder may be visible as suprapubic fullness.
- A visible lump can be seen after feeds in the epigastric region in a newborn and young baby with congenital hypertrophic pyloric stenosis. Flanks must be examined for their fullness as seen in children with ascites. Abdominal protuberance becomes further evident in an upright or standing posture due to exaggerated lordosis. Though very rare, distension of abdomen especially in an adolescent female or teenage female may be suspected as a teenage pregnancy.

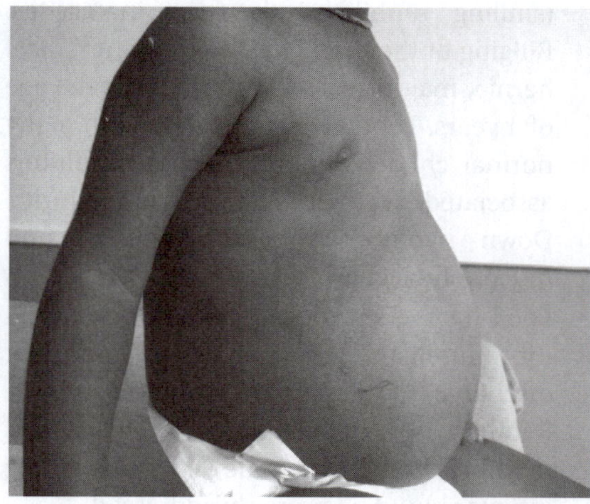

Figure 8.2 Distension of abdomen due to ascitis.

- Scaphoid abdomen is not normal in young children and is most often caused by severe malnutrition in children, and congenital diaphragmatic hernia and tracheoesophageal fistula with esophageal atresia in the newborn.
- A gap or defect in abdominal wall such as divarication of recti or an open defect such as an omphalocele and gastroschisis is obvious and should be observed carefully for extent and dimension. In such children with one congenital malformation of the abdomen and its viscera, other body systems need to be carefully examined to exclude involvement of other systems.
- Examination of the genitals and hernia sites is an extremely important step in the initial assessment. If the child is suspected to have undescended testis, the scrotum should be examined with the child standing, and then lying down and, if there is still uncertainty, in a squatting position that abolishes cremasteric reflex in cases of retractile testis.
- Umbilicus is normally inverted or flat in children. Transversely stretched umbilicus

(smiling umbilicus) is seen in ascites. Bulging of the umbilicus is due to umbilical hernia, majority of which resolve by the age of 4 years. Though commonly seen in many normal children, there are few conditions associated with it such as prematurity, Down syndrome, hypothyroidism, and mucopolysaccharidosis.

- Look for the signs of inflammation around the umbilicus, i.e., redness or purulent discharge, to exclude umbilical sepsis. Remnants of vitellointestinal ducts and umbilical granuloma in newborn and young infants should be properly addressed.
- Examination of back is very important and often missed and it may sometimes give important information such as scoliosis, kyphosis, and lumbar lordosis and gibbus as a clue to spinal tuberculosis. Infection of paraspinal area and bed sores should be especially looked for in chronic debilitating conditions.
- Movements: Normally, the abdomen rises with each inspiration and falls during expiration. The reverse (paradoxical) movements of the abdomen are seen during diaphragmatic paralysis. In peritonitis, there is restriction of abdominal movements and the respiratory movements become thoracoabdominal. Regional asymmetry of movements of abdomen indicates localized disease.

Palpation

It is of prime importance that the infant or child is relaxed while the examiner tries to palpate the abdomen. This needs patience, skill, and distraction techniques. Follow the given tips:

- Make the child lie supine with the hips flexed and the arms by the side.
- Place your hand and the fingers flat on the abdominal wall.
- Gentle palpation of the abdomen should be done initially followed by deep palpation of all the quadrants.
- Start with light or superficial palpation to get a feel of the abdomen such as its temperature (normal or increased), softness, tension or distension, and presence or absence of tenderness (local or diffuse).
- Avoid dipping the abdomen with your fingertips.
- It the child is crying, rest your palpating hand on the upper right quadrant and try to palpate between the cries, each time the child breathes in, rather than fighting it out against the resistance.
- *Guarding* is the voluntary contraction of the anterior abdominal wall muscles on palpation to guard the inflamed viscera within the abdomen. *Rigidity* is the abnormal muscle tension or the inflexibility of the abdomen seen in peritonitis and intestinal perforation.
- Deep palpation of the abdomen is done by dipping your hands on the abdomen.

Palpation of Liver

The palpation of liver should begin from the RIF. Use the tips of fingers or the side of the index finger on the abdomen, while allowing the respiratory movements of the abdomen to bring the liver in contact with your hand and fingers. Continue the palpation and proceed slowly upwards toward right hypochondrium to complete the palpation of liver (Figs 8.3 and 8.4). The following points should be noted:

- It is important to start palpation of the liver from RIF and slowly move upwards to avoid

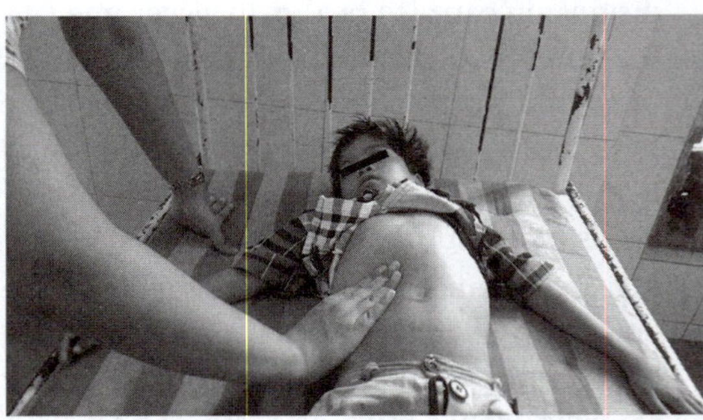

Figure 8.3 Palpation of the liver ascending up from right iliac fossa.

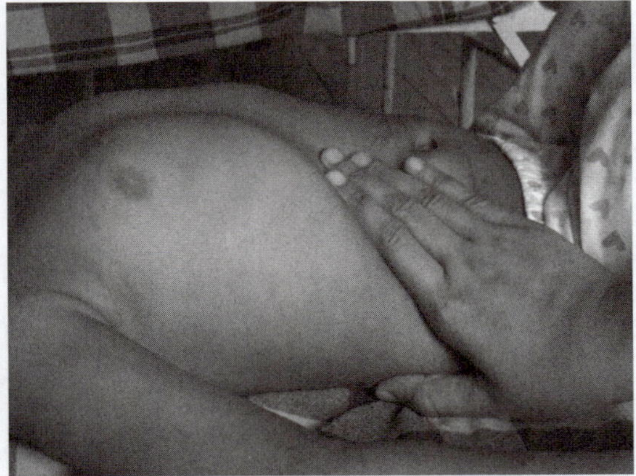

Figure 8.4 Palpation of the liver with fingers parallel to subcostal margin.

missing a massive liver enlargement up to RIF.

- A soft, nontender liver that is palpable 1–2 cm below costal margin is considered normal and is a common finding in normal healthy children. Liver span in such healthy children is normal.
- An enlarged liver is easily palpable in infants and it moves up and down with respiration.
- An enlarged liver may be firm and/or tender and is dull to percussion, and one cannot get above it.
- Once palpation of liver is completed, it needs to be decided whether it is a normal liver or abnormal/enlarged. The characteristic findings of a normal liver are tabulated in Table 8.5.
- Any variation in the findings given in Table 8.5 or combination should be carefully noted to assess the normality or abnormality. Enlargement of the left lobe of liver in epigastrium indicates a chronic hepatomegaly.
- Riedel lobe is a tongue-like, inferior projection of the right hepatic lobe beyond the most inferior costal cartilage. It is considered an anatomical variant of the right lobe of the liver. It has an incidence of 17.5% and is more frequently seen in females, with M:F ratio of 1:3. One should be aware of it because it can be falsely interpreted as mass from liver.
- Palpation of liver and pressing it firmly raises the blood column in external jugular vein for >30 seconds; this will occur in case of congestive hepatomegaly called positive hepatojugular reflex. This is seen in children with congestive cardiac failure.

TABLE 8.5 Normal Liver Characteristics

Liver characteristics to be noted	Findings of normal liver
Size	Liver span should be normal as per the age-specific limits (Table 8.6). Palpable liver 1–2 cm below costal margin in young children can be considered normal if other findings are normal
Surface	Smooth and regular
Consistency	Soft
Margins	Rounded
Tenderness	Absent

Broadly, hepatomegaly is considered whenever the liver size exceeds the limits beyond those specified for a particular age. Other points to be considered are as follows:

- While normal liver is soft, hepatomegaly is associated with a soft, palpable liver in conditions such as congestive heart failure, acute hepatitis, and kwashiorkor.
- Common causes of firm liver (as tip of the nose) are chronicity as in chronic liver disease, cirrhosis, kala-azar, chronic malaria, and congenital hemolytic anemia.
- Hard liver is rare in children and its presence is suggestive of hepatoblastoma and a secondary metastasis.
- Sharp/leafy margins are seen in cirrhosis and malignancy.
- Presence of tenderness on palpation indicates acute hepatitis/inflammation and congestive cardiac failure (CCF; due to congestion). While palpating the liver,

Box 8.4 Hepatomegaly and hepatosplenomegaly in children

- *Infections*: Malaria, enteric fever, kala-azar, viral hepatitis, tuberculosis, liver abscess, infectious mononucleosis, dengue, septicemia, infective endocarditis, brucellosis, TORCH infections, HIV
- *Hematologic/hemato-oncologic*: Hemolytic anemia (thalassemia, sickle cell anemia, congenital spherocytosis), leukemia, lymphoma, histiocytosis, hepatoblastoma, neuroblastoma
- *Chronic liver diseases*: Chronic liver diseases (chronic hepatitis B and C), autoimmune hepatitis, Wilson disease, alpha-1 antitrypsin deficiency and cystic fibrosis, portal hypertension
- *Connective tissue disorder/vasculitis*: Systemic lupus erythematosus, systemic juvenile rheumatoid arthritis (JRA), sarcoidosis, scleroderma, rheumatic fever, Henoch–Schonlein purpura, Kawasaki disease
- *Metabolic*: Glycogen storage disease, galactosemia, mucopolysaccharidoses, tyrosinemia, lysosomal disorders, lipid storage disorder (Gaucher disease), mitochondrial disorders
- *Miscellaneous*: Congestive heart failure, Reye syndrome, arteriovenous malformation, drug induced, e.g., isoniazid, rifampicin and valproate, neonatal hepatitis, biliary atresia

see whether the child winces with pain or not; avoid asking for presence of pain on palpation. If the tenderness is not evident on light palpation, try to elicit it on deep palpation.

- Palpable nodules and audible bruit over the surface of enlarged liver are distinctly rare in children. Auscultation over an enlarged liver can detect a bruit. Although rare, it is present in conditions such as arteriovenous malformation, hemangioma, and tumor.

The common causes of hepatomegaly and hepatosplenomegaly are enumerated in Box 8.4.

Palpation of Spleen

An enlarged spleen becomes palpable in left hypochondrium initially and, depending on the degree of splenomegaly, may even cross the midline. However, in newborns and infants, a small spleen may be normally palpable. Spleen must enlarge at least twice the size to become clinically palpable.

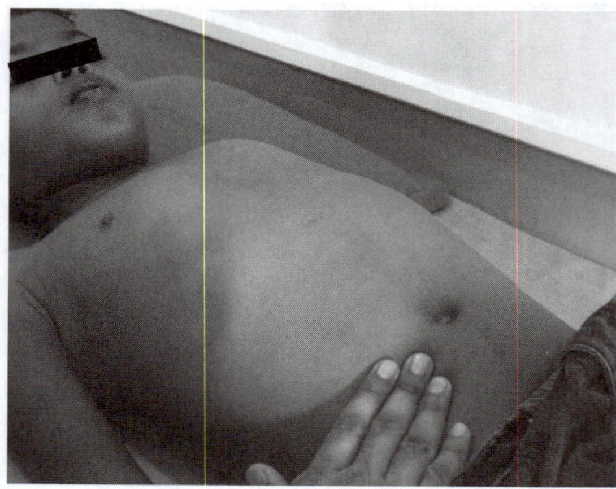

Figure 8.5 Approach to spleen from right iliac fossa.

- The examination of spleen should begin from RIF; otherwise, one can miss a massively enlarged spleen (Fig. 8.5).
- Palpate the spleen with the right hand over the abdomen with fingers pointing toward the left subcostal margin and slowly press the fingers a little into the abdomen with each breath (Fig. 8.6).
- The enlarged spleen moves with respiration, is dull to percussion, has a palpable notch, and one cannot get above it.

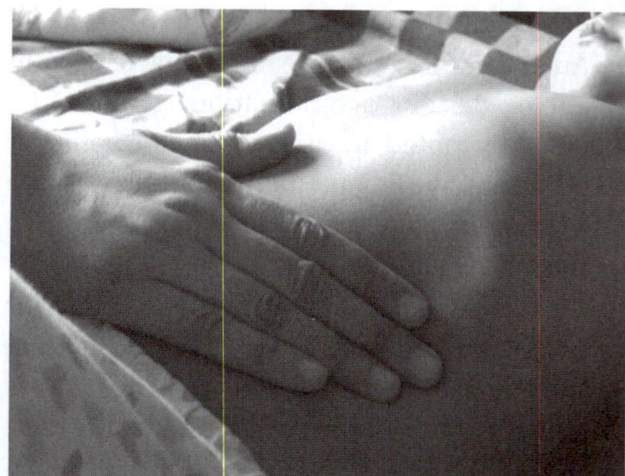

Figure 8.6 Palpation of spleen with fingers toward left subcostal margin.

Figure 8.7 Palpation of spleen in right lateral position.

- Try and feel for the lower end of the spleen as it comes and strikes your fingers at the peak of inspiration.
- If the spleen is not definitely made out on palpation, then make the child lie down on his/her right side and support the lower left rib cage with the left hand and palpate again while he/she continues to breathe in deeply (Fig. 8.7). This method is particularly useful to palpate a just palpable spleen.
- In the presence of massive ascites, palpation of spleen may be difficult. Palpate the spleen by dipping method by making the child lie in supine position while exerting sudden pressure by the palpating fingers to displace the fluid and palpate the enlarged organ.
- After you have palpated and identified, note its size, splenic notch, consistency, and tenderness.
- Size of the spleen is measured from the left subcostal margin in the midclavicular line to the tip along the direction of the enlargement. It is mildly enlarged if the tip is just palpable or up to 1–2 cm, moderate if up to 3–7 cm, and massive if more than 7 cm in size or crosses the midline.
- Note the consistency of an enlarged spleen. It is soft in enteric fever and firm in hemolytic anemia, malaria, and leukemia. Splenic notch is felt as an indentation at the lower medial border of the spleen and is easily appreciable in a moderately or massively enlarged spleen. The splenic notch can also become visible in cases of massive enlargement. The causes of splenomegaly are shown in Box 8.5.

Box 8.5 Splenomegaly in children

- *Infections*: Malaria, enteric fever, infective endocarditis, tuberculosis, infectious mononucleosis, kala-azar, septicemia, toxoplasmosis, cytomegalovirus infection
- *Hematologic/hemato-oncologic*: Hemolytic anemia (thalassemia, sickle cell anemia, congenital spherocytosis), leukemia, lymphoma
- *Congestive*: Cirrhosis of liver, portal hypertension, congestive heart failure
- *Storage disorder*: Lipid storage disorders such as Gaucher and Niemann–Pick disease, mucopolysaccharidoses such as Hurler and Hunter syndromes
- *Connective tissue disorder/vasculitis*: Systemic lupus erythematosus, systemic JRA
- *Miscellaneous*: Osteopetrosis, sarcoidosis, splenic abscess

Abdominal Lump

- In a child, when a lump or mass is palpable in the abdomen, try to identify the origin and nature of the lump. First, make sure that the mass does not pertain to an enlarged liver, spleen, kidney, or a full urinary bladder.
- Note the location of the lump in relation to abdominal quadrants.
- To know whether the lump is intra-abdominal or parietal, ask the child to lift his/her shoulders off the examination table or bed or ask him/her to raise both legs. This way, the muscles of anterior abdominal wall will be tightened. A parietal swelling would remain the same, while an intra-abdominal swelling would either disappear or become less obvious.
- Note the size, shape, margin, surface, and consistency of the lump.
- Check whether it moves with respiration or not. If swelling is arising from liver, spleen, and kidneys, it will move with respiration.
- Check for ballottement; renal lumps are ballotable.

- Note for tenderness and signs of inflammation such as erythema and warmth.
- Check for impulse on coughing.

Abdominal Wall Edema

Sometimes, there may be obvious marks of tight cloths indicating presence of abdominal wall edema. To look for abdominal wall edema, pinch the skin over abdomen for 10 seconds and check for pitting or indentation.

Abdominal Girth

In a child with abdominal distension, monitoring of abdominal circumference helps in assessing the progress. Abdominal circumference is measured at the level of umbilicus.

Percussion

Percussion of the abdomen helps in confirming some of the findings of palpation and tells about the presence and approximate amount of free fluid in the abdominal cavity. It is done with the child in supine position. The direction of percussion should be from above downwards and should follow the general rules of percussion. The normal note over the abdomen is resonant. The presence of free fluid in the peritoneal cavity would result in different findings depending on the amount of fluid present.

Puddle Sign

This sign is useful to detect presence of free fluid in the peritoneal cavity even when the amount is as low as 150–200 mL. In this, the patient is asked to remain in the knee–elbow position for 5 minutes (Fig. 8.8). The free fluid will get collected at the dependent periumbilical area in this position and there will be a dull note on percussion, while the same area will be resonant on percussion in supine position.

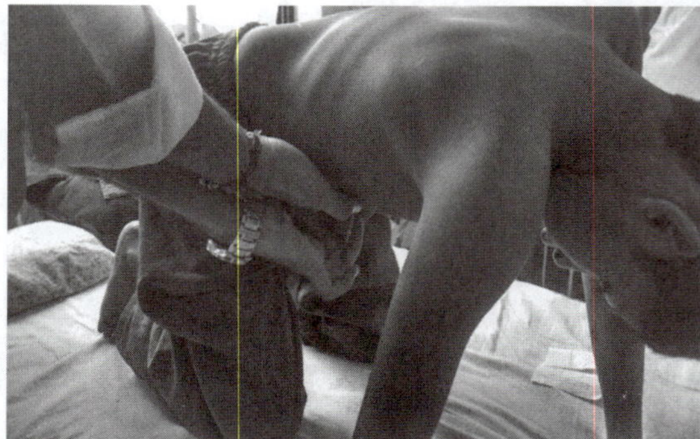

Figure 8.8 Puddle sign.

Shifting Dullness

This is a method to detect free fluid of about 500–1000 mL in the peritoneal cavity. Ask the child to empty the bladder as the dullness may be due to an underlying full urinary bladder. It will disappear if it is due to a full urinary bladder.

- Ask the child to lie supine; abdomen is then percussed from midline until the area of dullness is reached. From that point of dullness, go 1 inch above and percuss laterally from midline to flanks (Fig. 8.9).
- Once the dull note is noted in the flanks, the pleximeter finger is fixed and the patient is then asked to turn laterally to the opposite side (Fig. 8.10).
- After about 1 minute, the same area is percussed again. If the dullness in the flank is due to free fluid, it becomes resonant as the fluid will shift to the dependent area.
- Then the same flank is percussed again after making the child supine; presence of dull note again in the same area would indicate dullness due to shift of fluid.

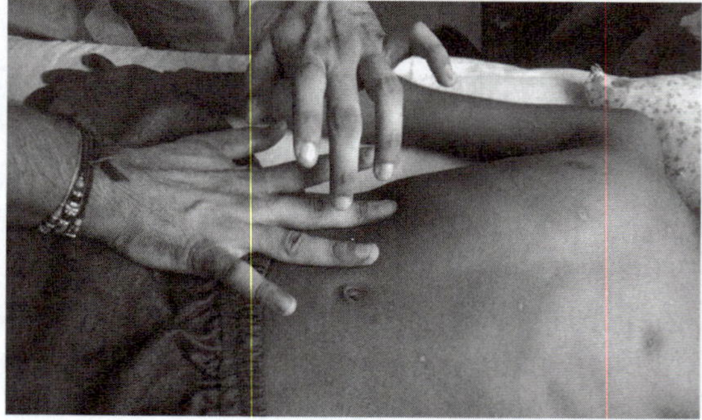

Figure 8.9 Percussion for shifting dullness from midline to flank.

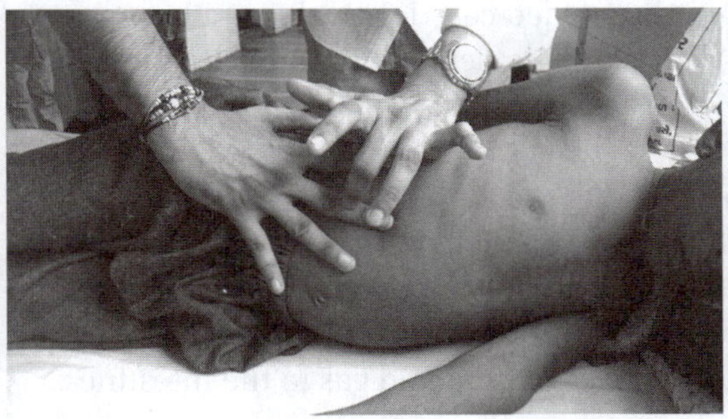

Figure 8.10 Demonstration for shifting dullness.

- Inability to demonstrate shifting dullness despite the presence of fluid can possibly be seen in a few situations such as massive ascites, loculated ascites, and obese patients.

Fluid Thrill

This is a method to detect massive fluid (more than 1000 mL) in the peritoneal cavity.

- In this method, ask the patient to lie in supine position. The ulnar side of the patient's hand or a third person's hand is placed vertically in the midline in order to prevent false transmission of wave directly through the abdominal wall.
- The hand should be placed firmly but not too tightly since tight pressure can prevent transmission of the thrill.
- Now the examiner places his/her one hand in one flank and taps the other flank with the fingers of the other hand. If free fluid is present in the abdomen, fluid thrill is appreciated on the opposite side of the tapping hand (Fig. 8.11).

Liver Span

The measurement of the distance between the upper and lower borders of the liver indicates its size and is referred to more popularly as liver span.

- To measure the liver, start percussion from the right second intercostal space in the right midclavicular line and proceed downward till the liver dullness is perceived.

Figure 8.11 Demonstration of fluid thrill.

TABLE 8.6 Liver Span at Different Ages

Age f children	Liver span
Infants	5–6.5 cm
1–5 years	6–7.0 cm
5–10 years	7–9.0 cm
10–15 years	8–10 cm

- The intercostal space in which the dullness starts is noted. The intercostal spaces are resonant till the upper border of the liver is reached, which usually lies in the fourth intercostal space.
- Confirm the lower border as described earlier and measure the distance between the two to determine the liver span.
- The normal liver span at different ages is given in Table 8.6. The total liver span is more important because the extent of liver only below the costal margin may not give the correct picture, as it may not be truly enlarged, but may be pushed down in conditions such as pleural effusion, pneumothorax, or emphysema.
- Liver span differentiates between true hepatomegaly and pushed liver. If there is pneumothorax or emphysema, the liver is pushed down and is palpable below the right costal margin. Here, the liver span would be normal, ruling out hepatomegaly.
- In the presence of right-sided pleural effusion or empyema, there can be a false impression of hepatomegaly due to a higher

level of dullness. This can be ruled out by doing tidal percussion. When the dullness is noted higher up in the intercostal space, and if the dullness shifts by at least one intercostal space with deep inspiration, dullness due to liver is indicated and pleural effusion or empyema is ruled out.

- The liver span may be reduced (less than normal), even though the lower edge is palpable, suggesting a chronic liver disease/cirrhosis.

Auscultation

The abdomen should be auscultated with a stethoscope to look for normal bowel peristalsis or to find out any abnormality in bowel movements and blood flow.

Bowel Sounds

- Bowel sounds are normally best heard near umbilicus toward RIF because of turbulence created by ileocecal valve.
- The frequency of sound is highly variable, maybe 6–8/min. The normal bowel sounds are metallic in nature; the abnormal sounds are high pitched and loud.
- The frequency of sound in small intestine is 10–15/min, whereas in large intestine, it is 3–5/min.
- Increased bowel sounds are seen in intestinal obstruction, diarrhea, and hyperthyroidism.
- Absent/decreased bowel sounds are seen in paralytic ileus, peritonitis, late intestinal obstruction, and hypokalemia.

Borborygmi

Increased frequency and intensity of sounds (gurgling sounds) often audible to the unaided ears are called borborygmi. It is caused by the movement of fluid and gas in the intestines.

Other Abnormal Sounds

- *Arterial bruit*: A bruit over the renal artery may be heard in patients with renal artery stenosis. Press the bell of the stethoscope deep into the abdomen over both the flanks to listen to the sound.
- *Venous hum*: Loud venous hum may be heard in cirrhosis of liver with portal hypertension in the midline between the umbilicus and the xiphoid. This is due to increased blood flow through narrow lumen of vein.

In a child presenting with primary abdominal condition, other systems also need to be carefully evaluated. The chest and the heart may be concurrently involved and in a child with ascites, there may be pericardial effusion due to polyserositis and hypoalbuminemia. Similarly, a pleural effusion may also be an associated finding in a child with primary abdominal disease.

KEY POINTS

- A detailed history and a carefully conducted physical examination are mandatory to analyze the child with an abdominal disease.
- Abdominal symptoms are not always manifestations of abdominal diseases but may be indicative of primary disease being present in other systems.
- A stepwise assessment is needed to find out which part is affected and what the nature of the disease is.
- After a systemic evaluation, the aim is to arrive at clinical diagnosis and differential diagnosis to plan an effective management.

CHAPTER 9

The Respiratory System

Baldev S Prajapati, Rajal Prajapati

The diseases of the respiratory system are one of the most common diseases affecting infants and children. The extent of the respiratory tract, which includes the nasal passage, the airways, and the lungs, makes it essential to obtain a history in detail. A relevant general physical examination is an essential component before the examination of the respiratory system. The examination of the respiratory system requires considerable skill on the part of the examiner, proper exposure of the child, and a quiet, warm, and comfortable room. The sequence of examination should be from least distressing to most distressing.

Box 9.1 Laid-down questions to elaborate each symptom

Evaluation of the symptoms

- Onset
- Duration
- Nature and type
- Diurnal variations
- Progress (increasing or decreasing)
- Associated symptoms
- Response to drug therapy
- Aggravating and relieving factors

History

The history of present illness should be ascertained in detail with special emphasis on onset (sudden, acute, subacute, or insidious), evolution of disease, and response to therapy. All the symptoms should be noted and listed in chronological order. Each symptom should be elaborated in detail with certain laid-down questions (Box 9.1). It will provide some clues that will help the clinician in further building up the story of illness.

- The common symptoms of respiratory system disorders include fever, cough, coryza (cold), sore throat, difficulty in breathing, fast breathing, chest pain, and rarely hemoptysis.
- The presence of fever favors an infectious etiology, which may be viral, bacterial, or a chronic infection such as tuberculosis.
- For each symptom, always ask about its onset, duration, nature, type, associated symptoms, and aggravating and relieving factors. This information tells the clinician how the disease started and whether it is acute, subacute, chronic, persistent, or recurrent.
- Recurrent infections are labeled depending on the episodes being separated with a period of resolution in between them.
- The nature and the type of the infection may be important clues for some specific conditions, associated symptoms, and aggravating as well as relieving factors, and thus will help to narrow down the possible conditions. One should find out in detail the medicines received by the patient and their effect on course of the symptoms.
- Respiratory infections (both upper and lower) are the most frequent respiratory illnesses in children and consist of combinations and permutations of varied symptoms such as cough, stridor, wheeze (also referred to as noisy breathing by parents), and poor or difficult feeding. In severe cases, there may be rapid breathing, grunting, cyanosis, restlessness, or drowsiness.

- Upper airway obstruction produces inspiratory stridor, while lower airway obstruction such as in case of asthma produces wheeze.

Cough

Cough is the most common presenting complaint in children presenting with respiratory illnesses. Even though in many instances it could be a trivial and innocuous symptom, it can be troublesome and interfere with the feeding in a young child and sometimes can be an emergency in conditions such as foreign body aspiration in the airways and the lungs.

- Cough is an explosive expiration. It is a protective reflex that results from stimulation of receptors by some irritant. It begins with deep inspiration, building expiratory pressure over closed glottis followed by explosive expiration.
- It must be checked whether the onset of cough is acute (less than 3–4 weeks) or chronic (more than 4 weeks).
- Also check whether the onset of cough is sudden or insidious. Sudden onset of cough in an otherwise healthy toddler (with or without history of choking) may be due to foreign body aspiration or viral croup syndrome.
- Many times, cough in children starts with an acute upper respiratory tract infection (URTI) of which viral infection (cold) is the most commonly prevalent. Even after the infection subsides, the cough (postviral cough) may remain for a few days to even a few weeks.
- Cough starting from very early in infancy with feeding difficulties may be an indication toward recurrent aspiration (gastroesophageal reflux disease [GERD]) or a congenital anomaly of the respiratory tract such as tracheoesophageal fistula.
- Intractable cough may be due to conditions such as rhinosinusitis, adenoidal hypertrophy, and viral infection or irritation/inflammation of tracheobronchial tree due to asthma and bronchitis.
- Nocturnal cough is common in a case of asthma, postnasal drip, and GERD.
- Cough is uncommon in neonates. Its presence in neonates indicates aspiration syndromes or chlamydial infection. In newborns, cough should be considered as an alarming symptom.
- Infants and toddlers (<3 years of age) cannot expectorate sputum and they often swallow it, which may be later brought out by vomiting.
- Barking cough is characteristic of laryngitis as it occurs in acute laryngotracheobronchitis. Paroxysmal and spasmodic cough occurs in pertussis and foreign body aspiration.

  Cough with expectoration is referred to by variable terms such as wet cough or productive cough and it may indicate chronic suppurative lung disease such as bronchiectasis, cystic fibrosis, and lung abscess. Although cough may be labeled as dry (in asthma) or wet (in pneumonia and suppurative lung conditions), its interpretation is somewhat difficult in infants and young children.
- Cough with expectoration (sputum) is an extreme rarity in infants and young children (till 3–5 years of age) as sputum is not seen and is swallowed almost always. However, the child may have a post-tussive vomiting with a bout of cough that brings out mucoid secretions and sputum.
- Inspiratory whoop is the hallmark of pertussis, but may occur in infections caused by *B. parapertussis*, adenoviruses, and *Chlamydia* (Table 9.1).
- Vomiting following an episode of cough (post-tussive vomiting) is a nonspecific symptom and can follow any bout of forceful cough, especially in young children.
- Helpful information can be obtained from the factors aggravating or relieving cough such as exposure to allergens (asthma). Postural changes exacerbating cough and expectoration indicate suppurative lung

TABLE 9.1	Cough: Attributes to be Noted
Onset	Sudden (foreign body), gradual, recurrent
Duration	Acute (viral), subacute, chronic (tuberculosis)
Nature	Dry (URTI, bronchial asthma), moist (pneumonia, bronchiectasis)
Type	Hacking (tracheitis), barking (viral croup, laryngitis), spasmodic (allergic, asthma), paroxysmal (pertussis)
Sputum	Amount, color, odor, blood
Severity	Disrupts activity, feeding, sleep (asthma)
Associated symptoms	Fever (infection), dyspnea (asthma, CHF), choking, gagging
Aggravating factors	Activity (exertional dyspnea), posture (postnasal drip in lying down position), diurnal, seasonal (bronchial asthma, allergic), nocturnal (bronchial asthma, postnasal drip, GERD)
Relieving factors	Medication, nebulization (bronchial asthma), spontaneous
Cough in neonates	Aspiration, chlamydia
Whoop	Pertussis, adenovirus, *Chlamydia*
Treatment taken	Effect of medicines on cough. ACE inhibitors may aggravate cough

ACE, angiotensin-converting enzyme; *CHF*, congestive heart failure; *GERD*, gastroesophageal reflux disease; *URTI*, upper respiratory tract infection.

conditions (bronchiectasis) or nonrespiratory conditions such as congestive heart failure.

Difficulty in Breathing

Children with difficulty in breathing should be evaluated in detail. Difficulty in breathing needs to be interpreted in its proper perspective. It should be checked whether the rate of breathing is faster than the normal rate for that age (tachypnea) or whether the child is having difficulty in his/her respiratory efforts (dyspnea). Both of these can be present in respiratory system diseases.

- Sudden onset of difficulty in breathing may be due to foreign body, asthma, or viral infection such as croup syndrome. The clinical diagnosis of childhood asthma should be guided by the family history, past history of similar episodes, and response to the bronchodilator therapy.
- Gradually increasing breathlessness indicates progressive diseases such as interstitial lung disease, cor pulmonale, or congestive heart failure. Level of intolerance will give an idea of its severity.
- Associated symptoms with breathlessness such as tightness of chest indicate asthma, while edema of feet, diaphoresis, palpitation, and cyanosis indicate breathlessness of cardiac origin.
- The presence of drowsiness, restlessness, irritability, and cyanosis indicates a severity of dyspnea and is due to the increasing degree of hypoxia. Presence of pain with breathing may be present in the early stages of pleural involvement and suggests pleural inflammation (Table 9.2).

Identifying tachypnea, retractions, and audible respiratory sounds can help indicate the site of pathology (Table 9.3). The respiratory sound is produced by some specific mechanism and its presence indicates a definite pathology.

TABLE 9.2	Difficulty in Breathing
Onset	Sudden, gradual
Duration	Acute, chronic
Severity	Level of intolerance on exercise/on routine activities, at rest, during sleep, inability to feed or speak in sentences
Associated symptoms	Fever, cough, chest pain, edema of feet, urine output, cyanosis
Aggravating factors	Position, time of day, exercise, allergens, irritants, infections, emotions
Relieving factors	Medicines, inhalers, oxygen
Treatment taken	Response to bronchodilators, drugs received such as antibiotics and steroids

TABLE 9.3 Respiratory Signs and Site of Lesion

	Extrathoracic airways	Intrathoracic airways	Pulmonary parenchyma
Tachypnea	+	++	+++
Retractions	++++	++	++
Stridor	+++	+	–
Wheeze	–	++	+++
Grunt	–	–	+

- Nasal snuffle indicates pathology at nostrils and it is characteristic of congenital syphilis.
- Nasal snoring is commonly due to adenoiditis.
- Stridor is produced due to extrathoracic airway obstruction or laryngitis.
- Wheezing is characteristic of lower airway obstruction.
- Grunting indicates a serious parenchymal lung disease. It is produced by the child by forceful expiration against partially closed epiglottis. It is an effort by the patient to keep the lung inflated in severe respiratory conditions such as hyaline membrane disease in preterm babies or severe pneumonia in older children.

Other Associated Symptoms

- Acute dysphagia may be due to acute pharyngitis, acute tonsillitis, diphtheria, or retropharyngeal abscess. Insidious dysphagia indicates any mediastinal mass or vascular ring.
- Hemoptysis is uncommon in children. It may be due to bronchiectasis, lung abscess, resolving pneumonia, pulmonary edema, mitral stenosis, pulmonary embolism, or tubercular cavity.
- Chest pain is also uncommon in children. The most common causes of chest pain in children are pleurisy, pneumothorax, pneumonia, pericarditis, herpes zoster, coronary insufficiency due to aortic stenosis, Kawasaki disease, GERD causing reflux esophagitis, etc. Some of the features that differentiate between different causes of chest pain are given in Table 9.4.

TABLE 9.4 Differentiating Features of Chest Pain

Skin pain	H/o local rash (herpes zoster) or pyoderma
Musculoskeletal pain	Increased with activity/movement
Pleuritic pain	Localized, catch in breath, aggravated by breathing and cough, sharp pain on deep inspiration that decreases laterally on the same side, nonpleuritic pain is not related to respiration
Esophagitis pain	Central/retrosternal pain; in small children, there may be arching and irritability related to food intake
Pericardial pain	Central with associated signs of pericardial disease; sharp, stabbing pain; intensifies during lying down and while breathing and coughing. Sitting up and leaning forward can often ease the pain

- A history of decreased appetite, reduced oral intake, and weight loss or faltered growth suggests chronicity of the underlying disease.
- Family history of tuberculosis and asthma should be routine points to be covered in history taking.
- The immunization status of the child should be enquired. It provides useful guidelines for exclusion or consideration of certain infections. BCG, vaccines against diphtheria, pertussis, measles, and *H. influenzae* type b, and pneumococcal vaccines offer protection from several respiratory infections.

TABLE 9.5 Common Respiratory Sounds and Their Site of Origin

Sound	Site of origin	Phase of respiration when heard
Snuffle	Nasal passages	Inspiration/expiration
Snore	Oronasopharyngeal airway	Inspiration/expiration
Stridor	Extrathoracic airways	Inspiration
Wheeze	Intrathoracic airways	Expiration
Grunt	Lung parenchyma	Expiration

General Physical Examination

Before starting the examination, spare some time to observe the child to assess his/her comfort and general appearance. In a child with dyspnea, one should note the use of accessory muscles of respiration, subcostal and intercostal recession, and flaring of alae nasi. Inspiratory dyspnea is due to obstruction of upper airways, while expiratory dyspnea is seen in children with obstructive lung diseases. Try to listen to audible respiratory sounds, if present. The characteristic of the sound indicates its site of origin, which is an important clue to the diagnosis (Table 9.5).

The signs of increased work of breathing (Box 9.2) and signs of acute respiratory failure (Box 9.3) should be noted. Increased work of breathing is manifested by suprasternal, intercostal, and subcostal recessions or indrawing. It gives a clue toward severity of disease. State of consciousness and nutrition of the child should be noted.

- Vital signs (temperature, pulse rate, respiratory rate, BP, and oxygen saturation by pulse oximeter) should be noted.

Box 9.2 Signs of increased work of breathing

- Tachypnea
- Flaring of alae nasi
- Retractions (suprasternal/subcostal/intercostal)
- Use of accessory muscles (sternocleidomastoid)
- Head bobbing
- Various sounds (stridor/wheezing/grunting)
- Cyanosis

Box 9.3 Acute respiratory failure

- Apprehension, anxiety, restlessness
- Tachypnea, dyspnea, chest retractions, cyanosis
- Possibility of severely compromised air entry to the lungs due to upper airway obstruction or marked bronchospasms (minimal or absent breath sounds on auscultation)
- Slow, shallow, gasping, or irregular respiration (may be due to CNS depression, neuromuscular disease, or terminally exhausted respiratory muscles)
- Decreased arterial oxygen saturation
  - <80% by pulse oximetry
  - $PaO_2 < 60$ mmHg
  - $FiO_2 > 0.6$
  - $PaCO_2 > 50$ mmHg

- Respiratory rate should be counted for full 1 minute with eyes at the level of the chest of the patient.
- Type of breathing and its character and depth should be noted. Cheyne–Stokes breathing and apnea occur due to depression of respiratory centers in brain due to various causes such as hypoxia, encephalitis, meningitis, raised intracranial pressure, and uremia. Cheyne–Stokes breathing occurs due to the involvement of cerebrum, hyperventilation occurs due to the involvement of midbrain and apnea, and apneustic breathing occurs due to the involvement of medulla oblongata.
- Anemia, cyanosis, and lymphadenopathy should be routinely checked.
- Ear, nose, and throat examination is a part of the respiratory system examination for URTIs such as acute tonsillitis, otitis media, and sinusitis.

- Frontal and maxillary sinuses should be examined for tenderness; these are not fully pneumatized until the age of 6–7 years.
- Chronic sinusitis is associated with nasal obstruction with persistent mucopurulent nasal discharge, puffy eyelids, and dark circles under the eyes. The important causes of chronic sinusitis are cleft palate, allergic rhinitis, Kartagener syndrome, immotile cilia syndrome, cystic fibrosis, Hurler syndrome, immunodeficiency disorders, etc.
- Examination of regional lymph nodes (cervical and axillary) should be performed and their size, presence or absence of tenderness, and consistency noted.
- Growth parameters should be noted (weight, height, and head circumference), and if these are affected, then a chronic disease should be suspected, e.g., progressive pulmonary tuberculosis and bronchiectasis.

Clubbing

Clubbing is thickening of the soft tissues of the terminal phalanges of fingers and toes. It is due to excessive growth of the connective tissues. The respiratory causes of clubbing include suppurative lung diseases (lung abscess and bronchiectasis from an underlying cause such as tuberculosis, cystic fibrosis), interstitial lung disease, and pulmonary hypertension.

Examination of the Chest

The respiratory system includes the entire respiratory tract consisting of nose, pharynx, larynx (via glottis), trachea, bronchi and their divisions, and lung (parenchyma, interstitium, and pleura). Certain anatomic and physiological variations in infants and children make them more prone to respiratory diseases as compared with adults.

- The pediatric airways are smaller and the soft tissues of larynx are softer and thus obstructive upper airway problems are more acute and severe in children.
- Right bronchus is straighter and shorter than the left bronchus. As infants are nursed more often in supine posture, aspiration pneumonia occurs in the right upper lobe of lung more commonly.

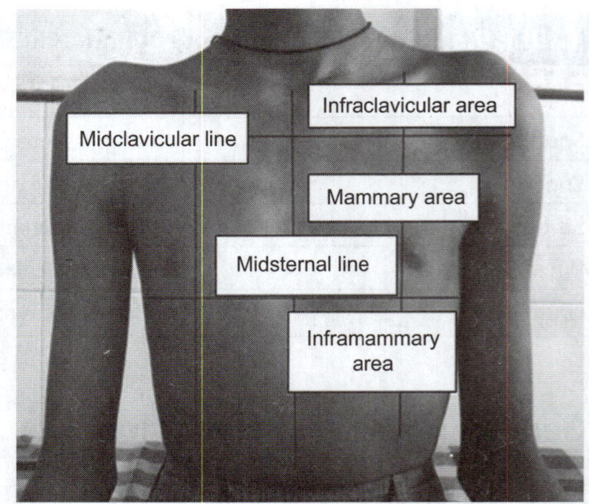

Figure 9.1 Diagrammatic representations of the areas of chest anteriorly.

- Infants are unable to localize the infections in the lungs as comprehensively as adults because the lymphatics in the lungs are not well developed.
- Beta-2 receptors in the smooth muscles of the airways up to bronchioles are in paucity and hence the response to the beta-agonists in obstructive airway disease is unpredictable.

The anatomical areas for clinical examination of the chest are as follows:

- *Anteriorly*: Supraclavicular, infraclavicular, mammary, and inframammary areas (Fig. 9.1)
- *Laterally*: Superior, middle, and inferior axillary areas
- *Posteriorly*: Suprascapular, interscapular, infrascapular, and basal areas (Fig. 9.2)

Anatomical Landmarks

- Angle of Louis (Ludwig's angle, sternal angle)
  - A transverse bony ridge at the junction of the body of sternum and manubrium sterni corresponds to the second intercostal space.
  - It corresponds to the bifurcation of trachea anteriorly and the fourth thoracic spine posteriorly.

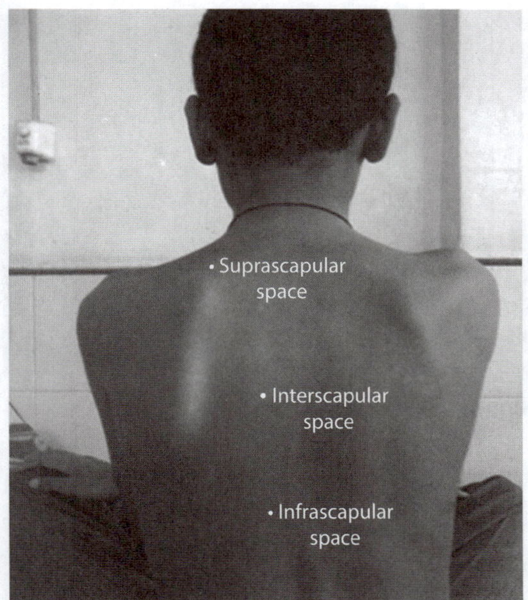

Figure 9.2 Anatomical areas on posterior chest wall.

  - The mediastinum is divided into superior and inferior at this level.
  - It corresponds to arch of aorta.
- A line drawn from the second thoracic spine to the sixth rib in the midclavicular line corresponds to the major interlobar fissure or upper border of lower lobe of the lung.
- The boundary between the upper and middle lobes is marked by a horizontal line drawn from the sternum at the level of the fourth costal cartilage to meet the major interlobar fissure on the right side of the chest.
- Upper (also middle on the right side) and lower lobes are accessible to physical examination anteriorly and posteriorly, respectively, while all the lobes are accessible in the axillary area.
- The costal cartilage can be counted from the angle of Louis (second rib at sternum) anteriorly and from the seventh cervical spine (most prominent) posteriorly.

Inspection of the Chest

Shape of the Chest

The conventional examination of chest proceeds as inspection, palpation, percussion, and auscultation; however, the scheme can be altered depending on the child's comfort, cooperation, and level of anxiety. The exposed area of chest should be inspected by standing at foot end or head end of the patient with eyes at the level of the chest (Fig. 9.3). In contrast, in supine position, make sure that the child is lying straight and flat on his/her back with arms on the side and facing upwards with the neck and face in a straight line and not turned to any side.

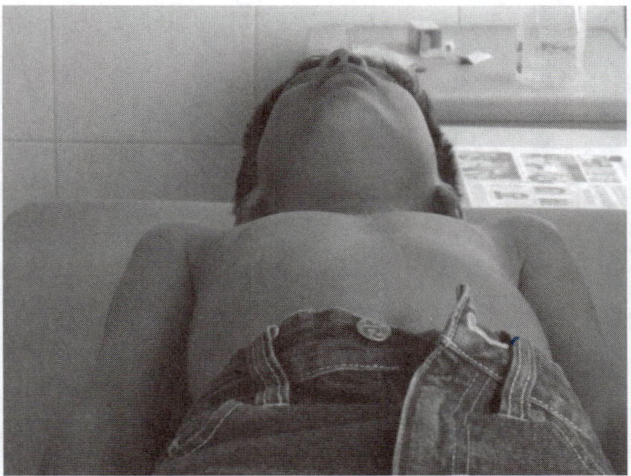

Figure 9.3 Inspection of the chest in supine position from the foot end.

The child can be examined in sitting as well as standing position with upper extremities by the sides. The chest should be uncovered from the waist up to the neck for complete examination and interpretation. It should be examined in a correct manner while avoiding partial and improper exposure of the chest (Fig. 9.4).

Shape of the Chest

- Adults and older children have an elliptical-shaped chest, which means that the transverse diameter is more than the anteroposterior diameter.
- Infants have a cylindrical or a circular-shaped chest.
- Barrel chest (emphysematous chest): The chest becomes barrel shaped, appears elongated with the shoulders being uplifted,

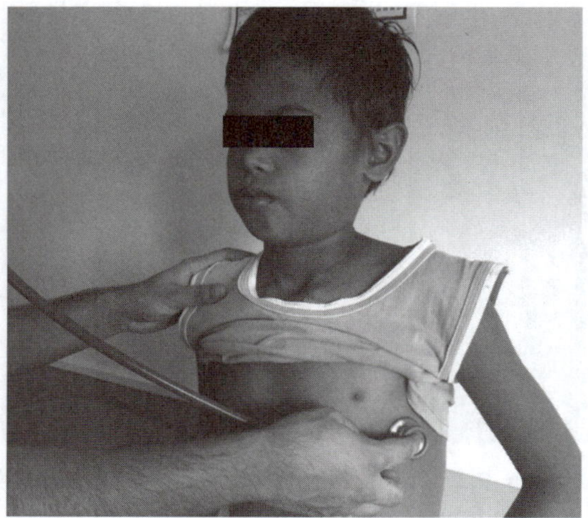

Figure 9.4 Incorrect method of chest examination (the correct method of examination is to completely uncover the chest, not to miss any important finding).

and is seen in chronic airway obstruction such as asthma.

- Pigeon chest (pectus carinatum): The sternum is prominent; this is caused by the anterior projection of the lower part of sternum and is frequently seen in children with rickets (Fig. 9.5).

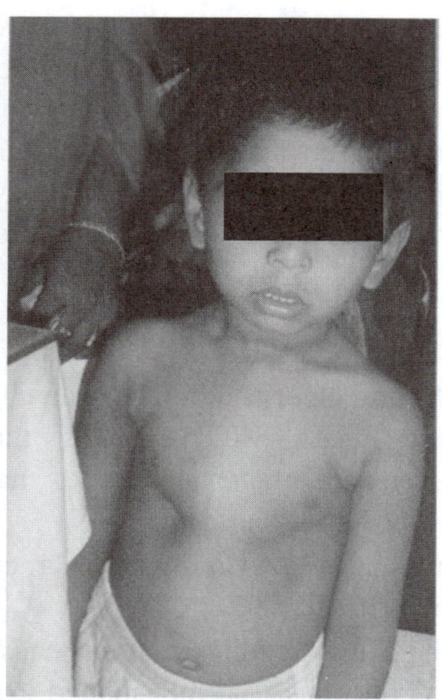

Figure 9.5 Pectus carinatum.

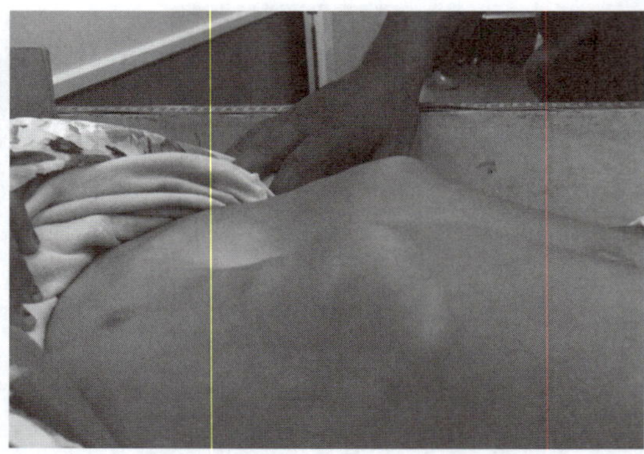

Figure 9.6 Pectus excavatum.

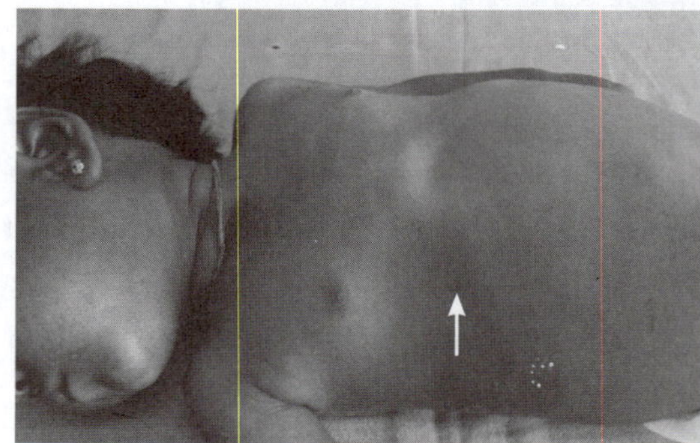

Figure 9.7 Harrison's sulcus in a child.

- Pectus excavatum (funnel shaped): The sternum is depressed and the central part of the chest is sunken (Fig. 9.6).
- Harrison's sulcus (Fig. 9.7) is the indrawing of the lower chest wall with the flaring up of the ribs. This is seen along the attachment of the diaphragm on a weak chest wall and is caused by the pulling of the diaphragm. Although it is commonly seen in rickets, the condition is often associated with chronic conditions such as left-to-right cardiac shunts and chronic airway obstruction.
- Kyphosis, lordosis, and kyphoscoliosis may give rise to abnormal shape of the chest.

Symmetry

- Look for the symmetry of the chest on both the sides. Inspection of the chest either from the foot end or from the sides (tangentially) is the best way to detect even a mild asymmetry of the chest.

- Note the distance of medial borders of both scapulae from midline on both the sides, which is useful to assess any asymmetry of the chest.
- Drooping of one shoulder may occur in patients with fibrocaseous tuberculosis.
- Look for any bulge that can be due to hyperinflation or pleural effusion or a retraction that is seen in lung collapse and fibrosis. A long-standing bulge may also be due to cardiomegaly.
- When empyema points through an intercostal space as a cystic swelling, which is reducible, and a cough impulse is present, it is called empyema necessitans.

Movements of Chest

- The type of breathing in infants is abdominal or diaphragmatic; in young children, the movements are abdominothoracic, and in older children after 7–8 years, the breathing is thoracic.
- Inspection also helps to observe the movements of the chest—whether these are equal or unequal, normal or diminished. Find out which side is affected.
- Indrawing of the upper part of the abdomen with each inspiration indicates paralysis of diaphragm of that side.
- Chest expansion is minimal or absent with paralysis of intercostal muscles.

Look for Indrawing

- Suprasternal recession is observed in obstruction of the upper airways, e.g., laryngeal diphtheria, acute laryngotracheobronchitis, and laryngeal or tracheal foreign body.
- Subcostal indrawing indicates airway disease, while intercostal indrawing is an indication for parenchymal lung disease.

Position of Trachea and Apex Beat, if Visible

- In a child with marked tracheal displacement, clavicular head of the sternomastoid muscle would be pushed forward and becomes visible as a bulge on the displaced side. This is sternomastoid sign or Trail sign.
- Normally, the trachea may be slightly on the right side. Trachea may be pulled toward the diseased side due to a collapsed lung, fibrosis, and thickened pleura. It may be pushed toward the normal side by pleural effusion and pneumothorax.
- Apex beat is normally located in the fourth intercostal space (ICS) in infants and young children or in the fifth ICS in children older than 7 years on the left side. It may be pulled toward the pathological side (collapse and fibrosis) or pushed toward the opposite side (pleural effusion or pneumothorax).

Palpation of the Chest

The findings of inspection should be confirmed by proper palpation.

Tracheal Position

- The position of trachea and apex beat should be confirmed. The trachea is examined in supine position or in sitting position with slight flexion of neck.
- Place the index finger into the suprasternal notch; gently push it backwards. The finger would touch the trachea in the midline in a normal child. If the trachea is deviated, the finger will slide into the tracheosternomastoid space.
- Place the ring and index fingers on the two sternal attachments of the sternocleidomastoid muscles. Gently pass the middle finger over the trachea to assess its relationship with the two fixed landmarks, and note whether trachea is central or shifted on either side (Fig. 9.8). Tracheal shift alone suggests an upper lobe pathology.

Chest Expansion

Determine the degree and symmetry of chest expansion with the following method:

- Place the palms on either side of the chest at the level of the nipples, gently opposing the thumbs in the midline. The expansion in normal school-age children is at least 3 cm. It is difficult to perform and often not suitable for infants.

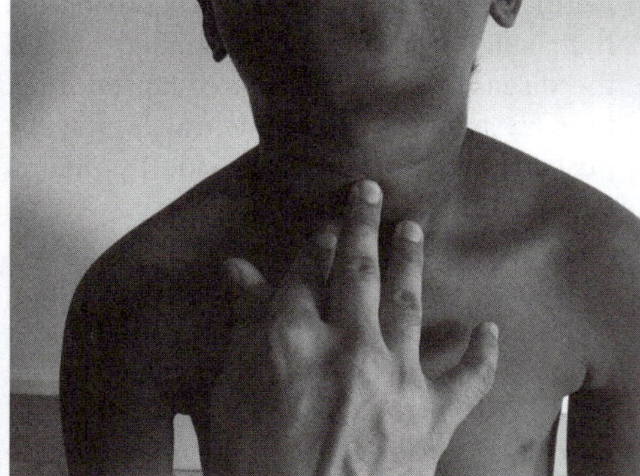

Figure 9.8 Palpation of trachea.

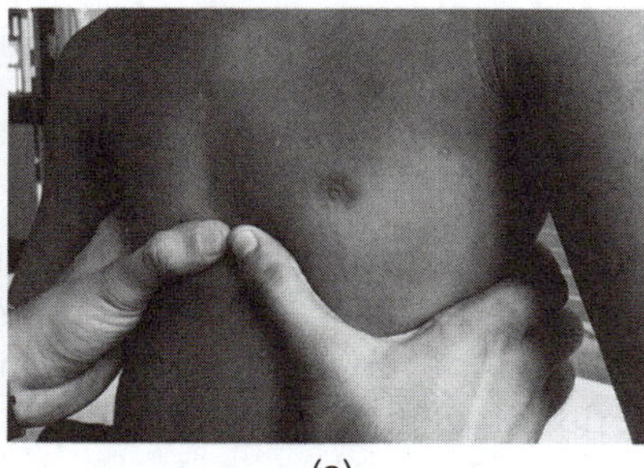

(a)

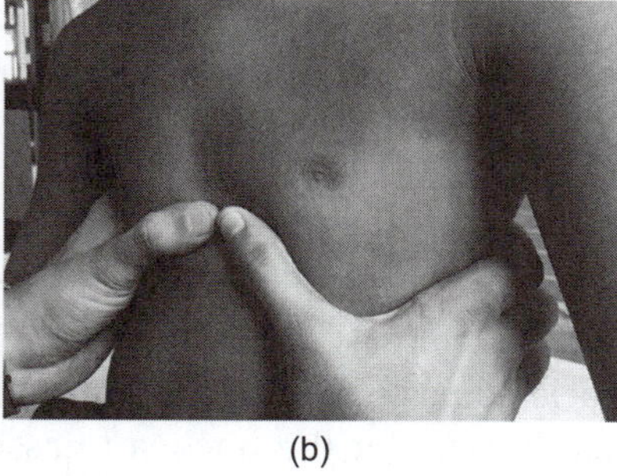

(b)

Figure 9.9 Chest expansion by palpation: (a) expiration and (b) inspiration.

- Ask the child to take in a deep breath and observe the movements of thumbs on both the sides (Fig. 9.9). It gives an approximate estimate of the degree of chest expansion and helps in assessment of symmetry. Only the thumbs should be moving, while the fingers and their tips must be kept firmly in contact with the chest wall all throughout the maneuver.
- The measurement can be taken posteriorly on the back also by hands placed over the side of the chest and thumbs opposed in the midline over the spine.
- The use of measuring tape would provide greater accuracy as it quantifies the chest expansion.

Chest Sounds

Feel for any abnormal sounds in chest (rhonchi, friction rub, and/or coarse crepitations).

- *Tactile vocal fremitus* is looked for by comparing tactile transmission of spoken words or cry in infants over identical areas on both sides of the chest. It may be normal, decreased (pleural effusion, pneumothorax), or increased (lobar pneumonia).

Percussion

Percussion should be performed gently by comparing the percussion notes on both the sides. If the child is old enough to understand, then inform him/her what you are going to do.

- Striking the chest wall with the fingers causes underlying tissues to vibrate and produce a sound. The resultant note (sound) depends on the type of underlying structure, whether it is solid or containing air, fluid, or both air and fluid.
- In infants and small children, it may be difficult to derive reliable inference due to a small chest.
- Chest percussion is an art and it can be best learned only by repeated and regular practice. Not applying the middle finger of the left hand firmly enough to the chest wall is one of the common errors to get a muffled note of percussion.
- Place the hand on the chest of the patient so that the middle finger is resting along an intercostal space. The other fingers should be off the chest.
- Tap the middle phalanx by the middle finger of the other hand. This action requires movement only of the wrist and not of the elbow or shoulder joint. The tapping finger is called plexor and the finger to be tapped is called pleximeter. Tapping should be sharp and at an angle of 90°. Lift the plexor

immediately off the pleximeter and listen to the note (sound) produced carefully.

- All the areas of the chest should be percussed and compared with contralateral side, immediately from above downwards.
- Direct percussion of the clavicle (tapping the middle clavicle) is done to percuss the lung apices.

Types of Percussion Notes

Resonant

The lung tissues contain air and percussion of the lung will give rise to a resonant note. The hyperinflated lungs may produce more resonance.

Hyperresonant

When there is excessive air between the chest wall and underlying lung tissues (pneumothorax), the note perceived is called a hyperresonant note. It is important to note that apart from being hyperresonant, loss of normal cardiac dullness on the left side and loss of liver dullness on the right side are important as well.

Dull note

When there is fluid or a relatively dense or solid structure (pleural effusion and lobar pneumonia), the sound produced is called a dull note. A less dull note is referred to as an impaired dull note.

Stony dull note

When the quality of a dull note is compared for consolidation and pleural effusion, the latter creates greater damping of vibrations and it is described as a stony dull note.

Transition in Percussion Note

Chest percussion on the right side, as one comes down from the second intercostal space to the fifth or sixth intercostal space, reveals a change in the note from resonant to dull. It indicates upper border of the liver. Similarly, percussion of chest on the left side, from lateral to medial, results in transition from resonant to dull note (cardiac dullness).

Auscultation

The Stethoscope

Before auscultations, ascertain that your stethoscope is functioning reliably.

- The stethoscope should be of sufficient length to examine the child comfortably. It should neither be too lengthy nor too short. A stethoscope with a pediatric diaphragm and bell is essential.
- The rubber tube should be soft, supple, and flexible.
- The earpieces should not be cracked or torn.
- Both the bell and the diaphragm should be able to conduct the sounds clearly.
- The perception and interpretative skill of the examiner is important for a good analysis of auscultation of the chest.

Method of Auscultation

- Deep breathing through the mouth by the patient generates a good airflow. The examiner should demonstrate breathing for older children to ensure that it is carried out properly. In an infant, the breath sounds are evaluated best not while the child is crying but when he/she stops crying for breathing in.
- Place the diaphragm of the stethoscope lightly but firmly over corresponding parts of the chest on both sides. Listen carefully to the breath sounds.
- All the areas should be auscultated in a systematic manner: supraclavicular, mammary, inframammary, axillary, infra-axillary, interscapular, suprascapular, and infrascapular on both sides.
- The findings should be described in terms of location, intensity, pitch, and timing.
- Terms such as diminished air entry should be avoided as it is not an appropriate way to describe auscultation.

Mechanism of Breath Sounds

Breath sounds are generated in the large airways. As the airflow becomes turbulent during passage through the airways and later during transmission through the alveoli, the quality of breath sounds continues to change. Turbulence is created by air that flows within tubes and encounters resistance that alters the flow dynamics. For example, air passing through trachea becomes turbulent when it encounters high resistance at the glottis due to the narrow orifice. The resistance causes the velocity of air to increase. When the air is distributed from trachea (single channel) to multiple small airways, considerable sound energy is lost. Besides flow and turbulence, the quality of sound is changed by its frequency. The sounds of varying frequencies take different pathways through the lungs.

In general, low-frequency sounds that pass through the lungs are directed toward the chest wall, while high-frequency sounds pass through the airways before being directed through alveoli and then the chest wall. The sounds need not be exactly symmetrical on both the sides even in a normal person.

Transmitted sounds are often heard in infants and toddlers and can cause confusion in auscultation. These are generated by the presence of mucoid secretions in the upper airways and are transmitted to the chest. These should not be confused with the abnormal adventitious sounds found in the diseases of the respiratory tract. It needs practice to listen to the chest and multiple attempts in a crying infant by listening in between the cries.

Breath Sounds

Vesicular Breathing

- The normal breath sound produced in alveoli is called vesicular breathing.
- The inspiration is loud, high pitched, and long, while expiration is low in intensity and short in duration.
- Inspiration is immediately followed by expiration.
- There should be no gap between inspiration and expiration.
- The breath sounds are best heard when the flow is maximal.

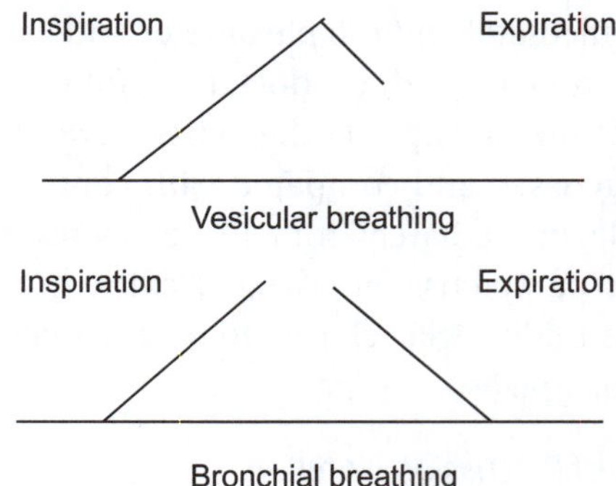

Figure 9.10 Types of breath sounds.

- The breath sounds are diagrammatically represented in Figure 9.10.

Bronchial Breathing

- Inspiratory and expiratory phases are equal.
- There is a pause (gap) in between the two phases of respiration. The pause in bronchial breathing is due to the fact that the air in the affected area is not able to reach alveoli and hence stops there.
- Bronchial breathing is heard over the area of consolidation and it is also heard just above the air–fluid interface in a case of pleural effusion.
- Bronchial breathing is considered as high pitched (tubular) as heard in consolidation, medium pitched (cavernous) as heard in small cavity and collapse with a patent bronchus, and amphoric (like blowing into a bottle with a narrow neck) as heard in a large cavity. It can be heard over a collapsed portion of the lung if there is an airway overlying the collapse.
- It may be normally heard over the neck, over trachea, anteriorly below the right clavicle, and in infants close to thoracic spine up to the fourth thoracic vertebra as these are the anatomical sites where the major airways come closer to the chest wall.
- Intensity of breath sounds may be normal, decreased, or absent on one or both sides.

In summary, the student should be able to decide whether the breathing and the breath sounds are normal, whether there are any additional/adventitious sounds, and whether they appear during inspiration, expiration, or both.

Adventitious Sounds

Rattling sounds

Upper airway sounds transmitted into the chest and heard during auscultation of chest are called rattling sounds. These sounds often make the auscultation in an infant somewhat difficult.

Wheeze (rhonchi)

Wheeze is produced by oscillations within the narrowed airways. It can be seen in conditions such as asthma or wheeze-associated lower respiratory tract infection (WALRI) due to narrowing of bronchi, and in cases of bronchiolitis due to narrowing of bronchioles. It is also seen in obstruction of large bronchi or trachea due to turbulent air passing through them. Unilateral or localized wheezing can be observed in foreign body inhalation or endobrochial tuberculosis.

When a large airway is narrowed or obstructed, the wheeze has a single frequency and pitch (monophonic wheeze). Narrowing of multiple smaller airways over a wide area of the lung creates sounds with varying frequencies (polyphonic wheezing). Wheezing is heard more often during the expiratory phase, since it is produced by limitation of flow. However, when airway obstruction is severe enough to limit airflow even during active inspiratory phase, wheezing can be heard during inspiration also.

Crackles

The terms crackles and crepitations are often used interchangeably. These are bubbling, interrupted wet sounds produced by passage of air through exudates collected in the alveoli. They are primarily inspiratory, rhythmic, and repetitive, usually not altered by coughing, sensitive to postural changes, and best heard in the dependent area of the lung.

There are two types of crepitations: fine and coarse. The resolving pneumonia and bronchiectasis give rise to coarse crepitations, while fine crepitations are caused by interstitial lung disease and pulmonary edema. Fine crackles are also described as Velcro sounds.

"Rales" is an old terminology and is no longer used.

Vocal resonance

- The child is asked to repeat some words (one, two, three) or made to cry. The sound generated from larynx passes through the airways and lungs; the high-frequency components get filtered. However, when there is consolidation, the relatively solid lung does not filter these frequencies and the sounds are transmitted to the chest wall. These sounds are heard by the examiner with the help of stethoscope kept over the chest wall.
- The intensity of vocal resonance may be equal/normal on both the sides.
- It is decreased or absent in pleural effusion, pleural thickening, pneumothorax, emphysema, and atelectasis.
- It is increased in consolidation.
- The increased vocal resonance may be so loud that it appears that sound is produced in the earpieces of stethoscope; this is called bronchophony and is found when there is a lung cavity.
- When the child is asked just to whisper certain words and still there is audible vocal resonance, it is called whispering pectoriloquy. It is found in bronchopleural fistula.
- The nasal twang of vocal resonance is called egophony and is heard at the upper level of pleural effusion due to a partially collapsed underlying lung.

Pleural rub

- It is produced by rubbing of visceral and parietal layers due to inflammation.
- It is a well-localized, superficial grating, creaking, or leathery sound.
- It is not altered by cough and is augmented by snug contact between the chestpiece of stethoscope and the chest wall.

- It is heard identically in both the phases of inspiration and expiration.
- It disappears when there is collection of fluid in the pleural space and two layers of pleura get separated.
- Pleural rub may be palpable.
- It may be associated with localized chest pain.

Succussion splash

Whenever pleural effusion is suspected, succession splash should be elicited to rule out hydropneumothorax. The chestpiece is affixed at the upper border of dullness and the child is suddenly shaken to elicit splash of fluid.

Coin test

A coin is placed in front of chest and tapped with another coin while chest piece of the stethoscope is placed at an identical spot on the back. A loud bell-like sound is heard in patients with pneumothorax.

Clinical Features (Signs and Symptoms) of Common Respiratory Diseases

Lobar Pneumonia (Consolidation)

- *Symptoms*: Fever, cough, dyspnea, chest pain, and rusty sputum (±)
- *Inspection*
  - Shape and symmetry of chest are normal.
  - Chest movements may be diminished on the affected side.
- *Palpation*
  - Trachea is central.
  - Chest expansion may be reduced.
  - Tactile vocal fremitus is increased.
- *Percussion*
  - Impaired or dull note on percussion
- *Auscultation*
  - Diminished breath sounds
  - Bronchial breathing
  - Crepitations (coarse)
  - Vocal resonance increased

Pleural Effusion

- *Symptoms*: Sudden or insidious onset, fever, cough, chest pain, and dyspnea. Onset may be sudden but is generally insidious.
- *Inspection*
  - The patient prefers to lie on the affected side.
  - Respiratory distress (tachypnea, dyspnea) may be present.
  - Chest may be bulging (especially intercostal spaces) on the affected side.
  - Movements are diminished on the affected side.
- *Palpation*
  - Trachea and/or heart are displaced toward the opposite side.
  - Expansion of chest is less on the affected side.
  - Tactile vocal fremitus is diminished.
- *Percussion*
  - Stony dullness on percussion
- *Auscultation*
  - Diminished or absent breath sounds on the affected side
  - Vocal resonance reduced or absent

Collapse or Atelectasis

Physical examination findings depend on whether an entire lung is involved or a single lobe is collapsed.

- *Symptoms*: History of foreign body inhalation and recurrent chest infections
- *Inspection*
  - Trachea and heart are pulled on the affected side.
  - Narrowing of intercostal spaces may be present on the affected side.
- *Palpation*
  - Shifting of trachea and mediastinum (apex beat) on the affected side
  - Diminished movement and expansion of chest on the affected side
  - Tactile vocal fremitus diminished or absent
- *Percussion*
  - Impaired note on percussion

- *Auscultation*
  - Breath sounds diminished on the affected side
  - Vocal resonance reduced or absent

Pneumothorax

- *Symptoms*: Sudden dyspnea and chest pain, cyanosis
- *Inspection*
  - Fullness of neck and upper chest may be due to subcutaneous emphysema.
  - Shifting of trachea and apex beat on opposite side may be seen.
  - Movements are reduced on the affected side.
- *Palpation*
  - Can feel subcutaneous emphysema, if present
  - Shifting of trachea and mediastinum on the opposite side
  - Diminished movements and chest expansion on the affected side
  - Diminished tactile vocal fremitus on the affected side
- *Percussion*
  - Hyperresonant on percussion
- *Auscultation*
  - Breath sounds are diminished.
  - Vocal resonance is reduced.
  - Coin test may be positive.

The salient physical signs in common respiratory diseases are summarized in Table 9.6.

TABLE 9.6 Common Respiratory Conditions with Salient Physical Signs

Signs	Consolidation (lobar pneumonia)	Pleural effusion	Collapse	Pneumothorax	Emphysema
Chest wall movements	Normal or decreased	• Reduced chest movements on the affected side • Bulging of intercostal spaces ±	Normal or minimal retraction of chest wall	• Hyperinflated (elevated) chest on the affected side • Reduced chest movements on the affected side	• Barrel-shaped, hyperinflated (symmetrical) chest • Chest expansion poor
Mediastinal shift	None	To opposite side	Same side	Opposite side	None
Tactile vocal fremitus	Increased	Diminished or absent	Normal/decreased	Diminished	Diminished
Percussion note	Dull	Stony dull	Impaired	Hyperresonant	• Hyperresonant • Liver and cardiac dullness might be lost
Breath sounds	Bronchial breathing	• Diminished or absent • Bronchial breathing may be heard at upper border of effusion	Absent/bronchial if bronchus is patent	Diminished amphoric (bronchopleural fistula)	Diminished with prolonged expiration

(Continued)

(Continued)

Signs	Consolidation (lobar pneumonia)	Pleural effusion	Collapse	Pneumothorax	Emphysema
Vocal resonance	Increased	Diminished or absent	Diminished	Diminished	Diminished
Adventitious sounds	Crepitations	Pleural rub may be heard in early stage of pleurisy	None	Succussion splash if there is hydropneumothorax	Rhonchi

KEY POINTS

- A detailed examination of respiratory system must include the entire respiratory system from the nose to the upper airways and the lungs.
- The completeness of the respiratory examination in infants and young children largely depends on patience on the part of the examiner, cooperation of the child, and a quiet and warm area to facilitate the auscultation.
- An integration of these findings goes a great length in helping the students to localize the disease with proper interpretation and becomes an essential prerequisite for discussion and clinical diagnosis in a respiratory case.

CHAPTER 10

The Cardiovascular System

Mukesh K Singh, Paresh A Thakkar

The history, clinical examination, and approach to a child with a suspected cardiac disease need to be accurate and should include a systemic assessment of the child to reach a logical conclusion and a working clinical diagnosis. The essential tools in cardiac assessment in children thus include relevant history, a physical examination that should include general physical examination and the systemic cardiac examination, an electrocardiogram, and a chest X-ray.

Thus, an adequate and complete history supplemented with clinical examination remains an important foundation in the clinical evaluation of a newborn, infant, or child with a suspected cardiac (congenital or acquired) disease. The information thus obtained can then be applied to determine:

- The type of the cardiac disease/lesion in the child
- Its severity and the presence and the absence of complications
- The need for investigations and the likely treatment required

History Taking

As in any other system, history taking forms a very important component of the evaluation of a child with a suspected cardiovascular illness. Thorough history should be taken, keeping in mind the age-specific presentations of heart diseases in children. Although it is often possible to follow a systematic approach in an older child, a flexible approach is more helpful in a young, sick, or anxious child to obtain valuable information during history taking and physical examination. A summation of good history taking and clinical examination paves a way to reach a working clinical diagnosis, its etiology, type, severity, and associated complications. Therefore, while taking history, the student should take note of the evolution of the symptoms, mode of presentation, duration, severity, aggravating factors, relieving factors, and the functional impairment, if any.

Antenatal and Natal History

Certain prenatal events are known to be teratogenic, especially if they occur early in the pregnancy.

- Certain infections, medications, and toxic substances such as alcohol are linked with congenital heart diseases (CHDs). Intrauterine viral infections such as cytomegalovirus, coxsackie B, and herpes virus are implicated to cause malformations including CHDs if they occur in early pregnancy.
- Maternal rubella infection in the first trimester is associated with patent ductus arteriosus (PDA) and peripheral pulmonary stenosis (PS), besides several other noncardiac malformations.
- Excessive alcohol intake during pregnancy has been associated with atrial septal defect (ASD) and ventricular septal defect (VSD). Lithium and benzodiazepine use during pregnancy may have a role in the causation of Ebstein anomaly. Anticonvulsant drugs such as phenytoin, valproic acid, and angiotensin-converting enzyme inhibitors are reported to cause multiple malformations including cardiac defects.
- Babies born to diabetic mothers have a high incidence of structural heart defects such as

transposition of great arteries (TGA), VSD, and PDA.

- Maternal lupus and other connective tissue disorders are associated with congenital heart block in offspring. Information about maternal age is useful as advanced maternal age is associated with Down syndrome, which in turn is associated with endocardial Cushion defects.
- The relevance of birth history is important as babies with birth asphyxia can have both persistent pulmonary hypertension and myocardial dysfunction.

These factors are now becoming more relevant as congenital cardiac lesions are increasingly detected on antenatal ultrasonography and/or echocardiography.

Birth Weight

Birth weight provides useful information regarding the nature of the cardiac condition. Babies may be small for gestational age due to intrauterine infections such as rubella or other TORCH infections and exposure to teratogenic agents. Macrosomic babies or large-for-gestational-age babies are seen in infants of diabetic mothers and have a higher incidence of cardiac anomalies such as TGA. The prevalence of CHDs in a baby of a diabetic mother is three to four times of that in the general population.

Prematurity

Persistence of the ductus arteriosus or PDA is a known complication that is seen in babies born preterm. Presence of respiratory difficulty/distress in a newborn is more often due to respiratory conditions such as respiratory distress syndrome than due to a cardiac disease.

Family History

Information about the family and siblings is important as few of the cardiac defects/diseases are inherited or genetically determined. Conditions such as VSD have an increased risk of recurrence in the siblings. In general, when there is one affected child with CHD in the family, the risk of recurrence in another sibling is increased to 3–5% and the risk increases further if two previous children are afflicted with CHD. If the mother has a CHD, then her offspring has a 15% risk of CHD as compared with 1% risk in the general population. Sudden death in the family might be indicative of hypertrophic obstructive cardiomyopathy (HOCM), malignant arrhythmias, or Marfan syndrome.

Presenting Complaints

Feeding Problems

Poor feeding or refusal to feed may be a presenting complaint in cardiac conditions associated with heart failure. Inadequate feeding and/or difficulty in feeding along with breathlessness become important factors toward the infant not gaining adequate weight and failing to thrive.

A young infant with congestive heart failure (CHF) may have a typical feeding difficulty that presents as "suck–rest–suck" cycle. This cycle indicates easy fatigability and is equivalent to exertional dyspnea in older children. Because of the heart failure, the infant gets fatigued after few sucks and starts sucking again after some rest. A history of sweating over forehead during feeding indicates fatigue in infants.

Fast or Difficult Breathing

In a child with CHF, the mother may complain that the child is breathing faster than normal or is having difficulty in breathing. Breathlessness remains a common symptom in a child with cardiac disease, although its manifestation and its severity tend to vary with the type of lesion/disease and the age. A newborn baby is rarely breathless due to CHD, while poor feeding and/or a difficulty in feeding is an expression of breathlessness in a young infant. An older child would become exercise intolerant due to increased cardiac work in a diseased heart.

Dyspnea and Reduced Exercise Intolerance

This can result from any significant cardiac disease such as moderate to large left-to-right shunt lesions, cyanotic heart defects, valvular lesions, and cardiac arrhythmias. A recent change in the child's daily activities such as walking and running is a useful assessment of the child's exercise intolerance.

Respiratory difficulty/dyspnea in cardiac disease is often a result of pulmonary vascular engorgement leading to a decrease in the lung compliance. It is usually caused by cardiac failure because of: (i) increased pulmonary arterial flow such as in VSD and PDA (or other left-to-right shunts), or cyanotic CHD with increased pulmonary blood flow, e.g., truncus arteriosus and single ventricle without PS; or (ii) pulmonary venous congestion as seen in mitral valve disease (mitral stenosis [MS] or mitral regurgitation [MR]), dilated cardiomyopathy, pericardial effusion, or pulmonary venous obstruction as in total anomalous pulmonary venous return (TAPVR).

The functional disability caused by dyspnea of cardiac origin is graded using the New York Heart Association Functional Classification (Table 10.1).

It is also important to note the relation of dyspnea with position in a child. Dyspnea occurring within minutes of lying down (orthopnea) indicates left heart failure.

Early form of orthopnea is paroxysmal nocturnal dyspnea in which a child develops breathlessness after approximately 2 hours of lying down.

TABLE 10.1 New York Heart Association Functional Classification

Class 1	No symptoms with ordinary physical activity
Class 2	Symptoms with ordinary activity; slight limitation of activity
Class 3	Symptoms with less than ordinary activity; marked limitation of activity
Class 4	Symptoms with any physical activity and even at rest

Cough

Cough is rarely a predominant symptom in infants and children with cardiac disease and is more commonly due to respiratory infections or hyperreactive airway disease, which are otherwise quite common in children. Persistent cough or wheezing, especially at night, may be an early sign of CHF, more so if other symptoms or signs related to CHF are also present.

Edema

A child with CHF may develop edema. This can even manifest as rapid weight gain in small infants. Small children who are not yet walking or are predominantly supine may not develop edema of feet; they may have sacral edema instead. Periorbital puffiness is rather a more common complaint. Edema and puffiness of eyes are a consequence of systemic venous congestion.

Recurrent Chest Infections

Recurrent lower respiratory tract infections are commonly associated with CHD and an increased pulmonary blood flow, especially left-to-right shunts such as VSD and PDA. This is believed to be due to increased mucus production because of increased blood flow that results in small obstructions and provides a nidus for infections.

Cyanosis

Acrocyanosis (peripheral cyanosis) is normal in newborns, which disappears soon after birth. It is also seen in conditions such as cold extremities and shock. The following details in the history should be noted:

- *Site*: If tongue, mucous membrane, and lips are blue, the child is having central cyanosis, which results from an increase in the deoxygenated hemoglobin.
- *Cyanosis in relation to cry*: Cyanosis that improves on crying is seen in bilateral choanal atresia.
- *Onset*: The presence or absence of cyanosis in a newborn, infant, or child with cardiac

disease is an important tool for evaluation with reference to the type of lesion (*cyanotic CHDs such as TGA and severe PS*, or acyanotic CHDs), complications (reversal of left-to-right shunts), and the severity of the disease (e.g., PS). In the early stages of CHD, the cyanosis may be mild/minimal and may often be detected and informed to the parents by their treating doctor.

- Central cyanosis, which indicates systemic arterial desaturation, is detectable only if there is more than 3–4 g/dL of deoxygenated hemoglobin in the skin capillaries, which corresponds to an arterial saturation of approximately 75% of hemoglobin of 12–16 g/dL. It may thus be difficult to detect whether there is associated anemia. Hence, low oxygen saturation is not generally apparent as clinically visible cyanosis until the hemoglobin saturation is <80–85%. Pulse oximetry alone can pick up this finding.
- It is important to differentiate peripheral cyanosis from central cyanosis. Peripheral cyanosis is mainly seen in the extremities, with the extremities being cold to touch, while in central cyanosis, both skin and mucous membrane are blue, and the extremities are warm to touch.
- It is important to ask about the onset of cyanosis. Cyanosis in a newborn can be caused by either (i) parallel systemic and pulmonary circulations, i.e., TGA, or (ii) lesions with reduced pulmonary blood flow, e.g., tetralogy of Fallot (TOF); some such babies having critical PS or atresia as part of the lesion are said to have a "duct-dependent" pulmonary circulation that relies on the blood flow across the ductus. In these babies, there is significant, even catastrophic, worsening of the cyanosis when the ductus arteriosus closes shortly after birth. Cyanosis is mild and may escape naked eye detection in conditions with abnormal mixing of the systemic venous and pulmonary venous blood, e.g., TAPVR without obstruction. In complex admixture lesions, cyanosis (typically mild) coexists with CHF—e.g., single ventricle without PS and truncus arteriosus.
- Depending on the severity and the complexity of the CHD, cyanosis of CHD may appear at birth or within 3–5 days when the ductus arteriosus closes. However, cyanosis usually becomes manifested a few days to weeks after birth such as in TOF, when gradually increasing right ventricular outflow tract obstruction leads to cyanosis. In children with complex admixture lesions, cyanosis can coexist with CHF.

History of "Cyanotic Spells"

Cyanotic spells are commonly seen in children with TOF. The parents should be asked about the time of appearance of the spell (on awakening in the morning, after feeding) and about the duration and frequency of the spell. Usually such spells are precipitated by activities such as exertion, excessive crying, feeding, and straining on defecation, resulting in hypoxia. The infant or the child may remain drowsy, cyanosed, and limp with fast breathing following the hypercyanotic spells. Previously attributed to the infundibular spasms, these spells are now believed to result from a complex interplay of factors such as acute changes in inotropy, oxygen consumption, systemic vascular resistance (SVR), and right ventricular preload contributing to acutely worsening hypoxemia.

It is also important to differentiate a true cyanotic spell from a breath-holding spell. This can be differentiated by asking whether the child was holding the breath or was breathing fast and deep during the spell.

Squatting Episodes

A child with cyanotic heart disease, particularly TOF, squats or takes a favorite body position (knee–chest position) when tired. History of such squatting episodes should be elicited. Squatting increases SVR and thus decreases the magnitude of the right-to-left shunt across the VSD.

Several other noncardiac causes of cyanosis in newborns/young infants include respiratory conditions such as hyaline membrane disease, meconium aspiration, congenital diaphragmatic hernia, failure of pulmonary vascular resistance to fall after birth (PPHN [persistent pulmonary hypertension of newborn]), septicemia, acidosis, and metabolic disorders.

Presence of clubbing and gum hypertrophy indicates that the cyanosis is of a long duration.

Palpitation

Palpitations mean subjective and undue awareness of one's own heartbeats. Generally, anxiety and phobia are more common causes of palpitation in children than cardiac disorders. Younger children may not be able to provide a history of palpitation. In few cases, the mother may report that the heart of the child is beating faster than the usual or that there is increased precordial activity or pulsations. Palpitations can occur in arrhythmias, in conditions with volume overload such as MR and hyperthyroidism, and with drugs such as salbutamol.

Chest Pain

Chest pain is not a common complaint in children and noncardiac causes are far more common than cardiac causes of chest pain. However, cardiac causes of chest pain could be due to:

- Pericarditis (acute rheumatic fever)
- Severe aortic stenosis (AS)
- Mitral valve prolapse (MVP)
- Anomalous origin of left coronary artery from pulmonary artery (ALCAPA)
- Kawasaki disease

Syncope

Syncope is loss of consciousness for a transient period due to an acute reduction in cerebral blood flow. This needs to be differentiated from other causes of loss of consciousness such as hypoglycemia, seizures, vasovagal shock, and postural hypotension. Syncope can occur in conditions such as AS, HOCM, heart blocks, and arrhythmias. Usually syncope in AS and HOCM is provoked by strenuous exercise. Vasovagal syncope can occur after prolonged standing, after acts such as micturition, and with emotional disturbances. Loss of consciousness on sudden standing can be because of postural hypotension.

Joint Symptoms

Arthralgia and arthritis are common presentations of acute rheumatic fever, which has a predilection to involve the joints and the heart most commonly. It is important to find more about the number of the joints involved, severity and duration of the symptoms, and whether the involvement is stationary or migratory. Characteristics of joint pain and swelling in rheumatic fever are the following: more than one joint is involved, pain and swelling are present in the large joints, and joint pain and swelling are migratory in nature. A preceding history of acute sore throat for 2–3 weeks is a helpful indicator of acute rheumatic fever in children.

Neurologic Symptoms

Neurologic symptoms such as stroke (limb weakness), convulsions, and syncope are more often observed as a complication of underlying cardiac diseases such as cyanotic CHD, infective endocarditis, and cardiac arrhythmias. These often occur as complications (thromboembolic phenomenon) of a preexistent congenital or acquired heart disease in a child.

Chest Deformity

Presence of a chest deformity and/or precordial bulge indicates a long duration of the cardiac disease. Some children with CHD can have associated skeletal abnormalities such as pectus excavatum (central chest depression), pectus carinatum (pigeon-shaped chest), and Harrison's sulcus.

Treatment History

Previous investigations (imaging and echocardiography), hospital admissions, interventions, and drug therapies during the

Box 10.1 Salient features for history in a child with suspected cardiac disease

- Antenatal, natal, and postnatal history
- Inadequate weight gain/failure to thrive
- Feeding and breathing difficulties
- Exercise intolerance
- Recurrent respiratory symptoms/infections
- Cyanosis, puffy eyes
- Palpitation, chest pain, neurologic symptoms
- Joint pains, swellings
- Presence of other congenital anomalies/syndromic/ dysmorphic features

course of illness or past/since the onset must be fully recorded.

Salient points for elicitation of history are summarized in Box 10.1.

General Examination

The importance of accurately recording the vital signs in a patient with cardiovascular disease cannot be emphasized enough. The pulse, respirations, and blood pressure are noted. Often, these provide valuable clues to the underlying disease. Also refer to Chapter 2 "General Physical Examination in Children."

Pulse

Commonly, pulse is assessed in the radial artery. Rate, rhythm, volume, character, and symmetry should be noted.

Rate

Younger the infant, faster is the heart rate. Common causes of tachycardia are febrile illnesses, anemia, and anxiety. Tachycardia is also seen with CHF and tachyarrhythmias. If heart rate is 200–220 bpm, tachyarrhythmias should be considered. Bradycardia is seen with hypothyroidism and bradyarrhythmias. Certain drugs such as beta-blockers (propranolol, atenolol) and digoxin also cause bradycardia in children.

The normal range of pulse rates in children is as follows:

- *Newborn*: 120–160/min
- *1 month to 2 years*: 80–140/min
- *2–6 years*: 70–120/min
- *>6 years*: 70–110/min

Rhythm

It should be noted whether the pulse is regular or irregular. Variation of pulse rate in relation to respiration is called "sinus arrhythmia." Here the pulse rate increases during inspiration and decreases during expiration. This is also referred to as respiratory sinus arrhythmia. It is a physiologic phenomenon common in children. Irregular pulse is seen with (i) arrhythmias, e.g., atrial fibrillation commonly associated with rheumatic MS and previous cardiac surgery, and (ii) conduction disturbances, e.g., heart blocks.

Volume

The volume of the pulse should be felt to note whether it is normal, low, or high. It depends on the difference in the systolic and diastolic blood pressures, i.e., pulse pressure: higher the pulse pressure, higher is the volume of the pulse. High-volume bounding, or a collapsing, pulse is classically seen in aortic regurgitation (AR) and PDA. To examine the collapsing pulse, the examiner grips the child's forearm with his or her left palm with sufficient pressure to feel the pulse. While keeping the same pressure, the examiner then lifts the child's arm suddenly with his or her right hand; on doing so, a sudden collapsing sensation would be felt if the pulse is bounding or collapsing. A combination of high-volume and rapid collapse pulses produces collapsing or water hammer pulse.

High-volume pulse can also be seen in high-output states such as anemia, fever, thyrotoxicosis, and beriberi. Low-volume pulse or thready pulse is seen with dehydration or hypovolemic shock. Here the low-volume pulse will be associated with tachycardia. Low-volume pulses are also felt in left ventricular outflow tract obstruction (AS) and large pericardial effusions. Alternate high- and low-volume pulse, "pulsus alternans," is a classical feature of a decompensated heart failure and is seen in left ventricular dysfunction with alternate strong and weak pulses that are regularly spaced.

Palpation of Peripheral Pulses

It is very important to palpate for femoral pulse, as weak or absent femoral pulsation in comparison with radial/brachial pulses strongly points to the possibility of coarctation of aorta. If femoral pulses are not easily felt, palpation of dorsalis pedis in feet excludes the coarctation of aorta. It is recommended that it should be looked for as part of normal neonatal examination at birth, to detect this anomaly early to avoid complications later. In rare cases of coarctation of aorta, if the narrowing is proximal to the origin of left subclavian artery, an inequality between the radial pulses may be observed.

Respiration

Observing the child's breathing and counting the respiratory rate for 1 minute when the child is quiet and not feeding and crying offers valuable clues in cardiovascular examination. Difficulty in breathing and labored breathing (use of accessory muscles of respiration) is often seen in children with heart failure, while the presence of Harrison's sulcus indicates the chronicity/long duration of the respiratory distress. Though rare, the presence of a stridor in a child with cardiac disease indicates the presence of a vascular ring leading to upper airway obstruction.

Blood Pressure

Conventionally the blood pressure is recorded with a sphygmomanometer. It is recommended that the width of the cuff should cover 40–50% of the circumference of the extremity. It is important to make the child comfortable and calm as white coat hypertension is common in children due to fear and anxiety of a doctor or paramedical staff. In a child with suspected heart disorder, it is important to take blood pressure in both upper limbs as well as in both lower limbs, i.e., all the four limbs.

Hill Sign

Normally the lower limb blood pressure is higher than the upper limb blood pressure by 5–10 mmHg. If the difference is more than 20 mmHg, then Hill sign is said to be positive. This is seen in case of AR. In case of coarctation of aorta, lower limb blood pressure will be lower than the upper limb blood pressure.

Significant differences in blood pressure and/or saturation can occur in the upper and lower limbs in certain conditions. These parameters are recorded in all four limbs (or in both upper limbs and any one lower limb) as part of a full examination.

Cyanosis

- *Central cyanosis*: It is commonly seen in lips, tongue, ear lobule, etc.
- *Differential cyanosis*: Cyanosis is limited to the lower limbs while upper limbs appear pink; this is seen in PDA with reversal of shunt.
- *Reverse differential cyanosis*: Cyanosis is present only in upper limbs while lower limbs appear pink; it is seen in complete TGA with PDA with severe pulmonary hypertension.

Clubbing

Apart from noncardiac causes, clubbing is also seen in cyanotic CHDs. Clubbing, conjunctival injection, and cyanosis indicate that the cyanosis is of a long duration. Apart from the cyanotic heart diseases, cyanosis is observed late in left-to-right shunts when the shunt gets reversed due to pulmonary hypertension (Eisenmenger syndrome).

Edema

In adults and older children with CHF, edema of the feet or pedal edema can be seen. In contrast, in younger children who are predominantly supine, pedal edema may not be evident but sacral edema can be seen. Puffiness of eyelids can also be commonly seen.

Jugular Venous Pressure (JVP)

It is an indirect measure of central venous pressure and reflects the pressure in the right atrium. It is expressed as the vertical height from the sternal angle to the pulsation in the internal jugular vein. Many times it is difficult to assess JVP in infants and young children.

Measurement of JVP

JVP is measured in the supine position with the head end propped up at 45°, head turned away to the opposite side, and neck relaxed. The sternal angle is taken as the zero point and the maximum height of pulsation in the internal jugular vein is measured. JVP more than 3 cm from the zero point is taken as abnormal.

Raised JVP indicates systemic venous congestion and causes are as follows:

- Right heart failure
- Tricuspid stenosis or regurgitation
- Pericardial effusion
- Fluid overload
- Superior vena cava obstruction

Hepatojugular Reflex

The right hypochondrial area should be pressed for 30 seconds. This may cause a transient rise in JVP up to 3 cm normally. If the rise is more than 3 cm or if the rise persists for more than 15 seconds, the hepatojugular reflex is said to be positive. This occurs in conditions like right heart failure or tricuspid regurgitation.

Hepatomegaly

Liver size, consistency, presence or absence of tenderness should be noted and mentioned under abdomen system examination. Liver is commonly enlarged and tender in right heart failure.

Other Relevant Findings

Other relevant findings on inspection during general examination that have a bearing on cardiac diseases are facies, dysmorphism, nutritional wasting, sweating, cyanosis, and clubbing, and these should be clearly described.

A full head-to-toe survey is performed to check for any associated dysmorphic features or signs of systemic diseases. CHD is often seen in many childhood syndromes, malformations, associations, and systemic diseases. Some of these are as follows:

- Trisomy 21 (Down syndrome): Endocardial cushion defect, VSD, and ASD
- Turner syndrome (45 XO): Bicuspid aortic valve, coarctation of aorta
- Chromosome 22q 11.2 deletion: Aortic arch anomalies, TOF
- William syndrome: Supravalvular AS, pulmonary artery stenosis
- CATCH 22 (cardiac defects, abnormal facies, thymic hypoplasia, cleft palate, and hypocalcemia) (DiGeorge syndrome)
- VACTREL association (vertebral, anorectal, cardiac, tracheoesophageal, radial, renal, limb anomalies): Left-to-right shunts, TOF
- Congenital rubella syndrome: PDA, peripheral artery stenosis
- Marfan syndrome: AR
- Maternal systemic lupus erythematosus: Complete heart block
- Infant of diabetic mother: Hypertrophic cardiomyopathy
- Maternal drugs including warfarin, valproate, carbamazepine, clomiphene, and maternal alcohol ingestion

Examination of Cardiovascular System

Inspection

While it is customary to proceed to examine the cardiovascular system in the order of inspection, palpation, percussion, and auscultation, it often becomes necessary to complete auscultation first if the child is likely to cry or become excessively irritable. Thus, the most valuable information must be taken as a priority to be completed but the clinical presentation should always follow the sequential pattern.

Shape of the Chest

- Precordium: It is the area of the anterior chest wall that overlies the heart. A precordial bulge can be best appreciated with the examiner looking up tangentially from the foot end of the bed with the child supine (Fig. 10.1). If visible, the location of the apical impulse is noted with respect to visual landmarks.
- The presence of a bulge on the chest (precordial bulge) with or without visible cardiac pulsations indicates chronic/long-standing cardiac enlargement.
- Sternal deformity such as undue protrusion or depression should be differentiated from precordial bulge. Pectus carinatum (pigeon chest), in which the sternum protrudes in the midline, is usually not a result of cardiomegaly.
- Pectus excavatum is undue depression of the sternum. Harrison's sulcus, which is a depression on the subcostal areas along with the attachment of the diaphragm, indicates poor lung compliance of prolonged duration.

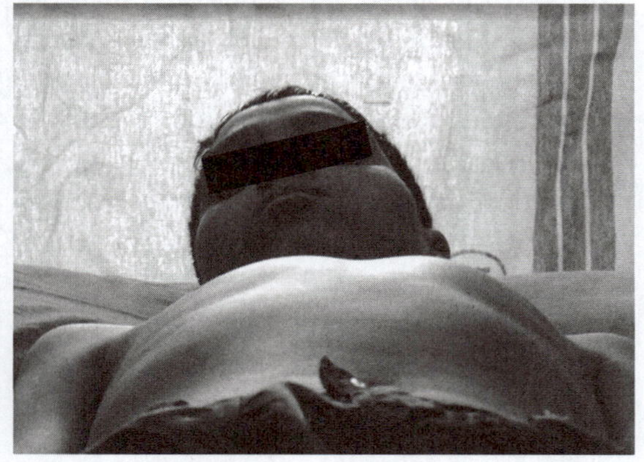

Figure 10.1 Inspection of chest for precordial bulge.

- The location of apical impulse is noted if visible.
- With cardiomegaly, it may be displaced downwards and laterally if the left ventricle is enlarged, and laterally if the right ventricle is enlarged.
- It may not be visible in pericardial effusion or severe cardiomyopathy.
- It may be normally undetectable in an obese patient or if the apical impulse is exactly behind a rib.
- Increased precordial activity/pulsations (hyperdynamic or active precordium) can become visible in the presence of cardiac enlargement resulting from volume overload, e.g., a large left-to-right shunt (VSD, PDA), or severe valvular regurgitation (AR, MR). It may be normal in a thin patient.
- Pulsations (of enlarged collateral arteries) may be found on the back in the region around the scapulae in older children with severe coarctation of the aorta. These can be identified more easily in tangential lighting, with the child bending forward while standing with the arms dangling by the sides.

Tracheal shift points to mediastinal shift as the cause of the displaced cardiac impulse. Scars (post-thoracotomy or poststernotomy) should also be looked for.

Palpation

The basic objectives of palpation of precordium are to:

- Identify the site and the type of apex beat and whether it is normal or abnormal
- Identify the presence or absence of abnormal pulsations over the precordium such as left parasternal area, epigastrium, suprasternal notch, and left second intercostal space
- Detect the enlargement of right and/or left ventricles and the dilation of the great vessels, i.e., aorta and pulmonary artery

Apex Beat

It is the lowermost and outermost point at which the cardiac impulse can be felt to impart a perpendicular thrust to the palpating finger. The apex beat is imparted by the anterior movement of the left ventricular apex during the early systolic contraction of the left ventricle. The initial step is to locate the position of the heart and then proceed for the precise localization of the apex beat. The steps for palpation and the localization of apex beat are shown in Figures 10.2–10.4. While palpating the apex beat, the finger pads are more sensitive than the tip of the finger.

- Confirm the location of the apex beat by palpating the sternal angle of Louis at the manubriosternal joint (which corresponds to the second intercostal space) and counting the intercostal spaces downwards obliquely.

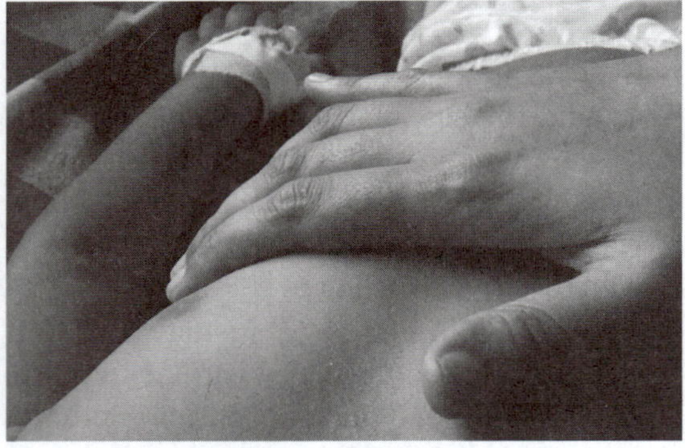

Figure 10.2 Palpation to locate the position of the heart.

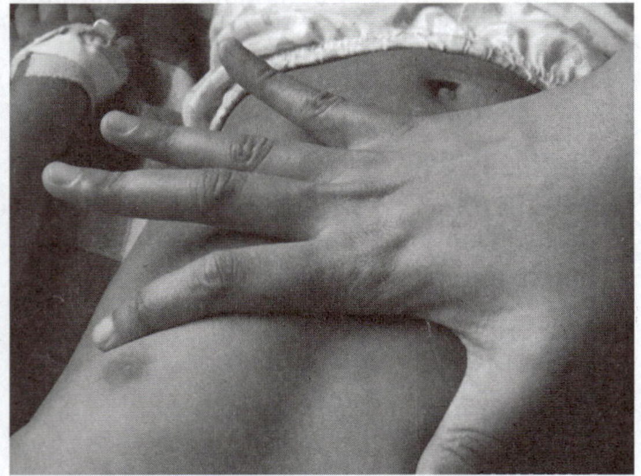

Figure 10.3 Palpation for the precise location of apex beat.

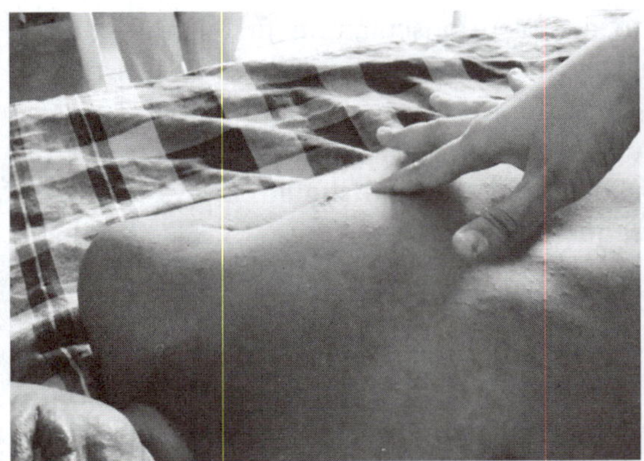

Figure 10.4 Localization of apex beat with the pad of index finger.

- It is described in relation to the midclavicular line (or in case of cardiomegaly, the anterior or midaxillary lines). If not found readily, the apex beat should be sought with the child in the left lateral position or in a sitting posture. The nipple is almost never in the midclavicular line and cannot be used as a landmark to locate the apex beat.
- The position of the normal apex beat is age dependent in children. In the first 3–4 years, it is in the fourth left intercostal space just lateral to the midclavicular line. Between the ages of 4 and 8 years, it is in the fifth left intercostal space in the midclavicular line, and beyond the age of 8 years, it is palpable in the fifth left intercostal space about 1 cm medial to the midclavicular line.
- It is well localized and gentle, and does not occupy more than a single intercostal space. If an apex beat cannot be found on the left side, it should also be checked for on the right side.
- A right-sided apical impulse may signify dextrocardia or left-sided thoracic space-occupying lesions (e.g., congenital diaphragmatic hernia).
- The apex beat is shifted to the left side in cardiomegaly, scoliosis, pectus excavatum, and contralateral pneumothorax and pleural effusion.
- The apex beat may be displaced laterally and downward (even up to the seventh

intercostal space) in patients with left ventricular dilatation (e.g., volume load such as MR, AR, or dilated cardiomyopathy). The character of apex beat is described next.

Hyperdynamic

The apex beat is forceful and has a rapid upstroke but is normal in duration, occupying one-third to half of systole. Hyperdynamic apex beat is also referred to as forceful apex beat.

The apex beat is produced by ventricular volume overload lesions such as regurgitant lesions (AR, MR) and left-to-right shunts (VSD and PDA). It is also produced by hyperdynamic high-cardiac-output states.

Heaving

Left ventricular hypertrophy (due to pressure overload lesions, e.g., AS, coarctation of the aorta, and systemic hypertension) results in an increase of the amplitude and duration of the normal left ventricular thrust, which becomes forceful and sustained impulse. In this apex beat, the palpating finger is elevated and remains so for a short period of time.

Tapping

In rheumatic MS, the apex beat has a sharp "tapping" character, i.e., brief and sharp. This is due to palpable mitral valve closure and the enlarged right ventricle forming the apex.

Point of Maximal Impulse (PMI)

The PMI is the point where there is a maximal impulse against the chest that can be felt. Most often, this is from the apex of the heart and thus PMI coincides with the apex beat.

However, in certain conditions, the apex of the heart does not cause the PMI. In a severe right ventricular hypertrophy and dominance, a left lower parasternal heave may be the largest impulse felt. This is in part from the right ventricular thrust against the anterior chest wall at the left parasternal region and partly from the enlarged right ventricle causing posterior displacement of the apex.

Left Parasternal Lift

Right ventricular hypertrophy often results in a sustained systolic lift, at the lower left parasternal area, which starts in early systole and is synchronous with the apex beat. This lift is best felt by placing the ulnar border of the examiner's palm vertically on the supine patient's left sternal border. It should be assessed for its force and duration. Right ventricular hypertrophy is seen in patients with pressure overload on the right ventricle, i.e., PS or pulmonary hypertension.

Epigastric Pulsations

The palpation for the epigastric pulsations (subxiphoid region) is done gently with the pad of two or three fingers of the right hand with a mild upward slant toward the xiphisternum (Fig. 10.5). Another way to look for epigastric pulsations is to gently press the thumb in the epigastric notch; the pulsations from an enlarged right ventricle are appreciated at the tip, whereas aortic pulsations are felt at the pulp. Epigastric pulsations are suggestive of right ventricular volume overload states such as ASD and tricuspid regurgitation.

Pulsations in Second Left Intercostal Space

The second heart sound may become palpable in pulmonary hypertension. This may suggest a dilated pulmonary artery, e.g., in ASD, VSD, PDA, and MS. Pulsations are best appreciated

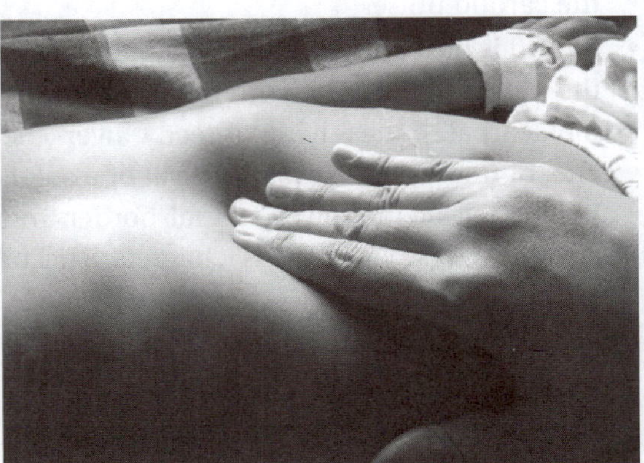

Figure 10.5 Palpation for epigastric pulsations.

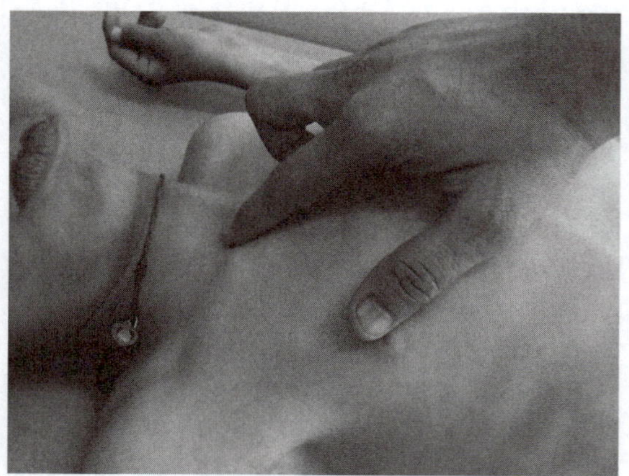

Figure 10.6 Palpation for suprasternal pulsations.

by palpating with the pulp of the fingertips (Fig. 10.6).

Suprasternal Pulsations

These are often seen and are palpable in suprasternal notch. They are commonly palpated during conditions such as PDA, AR, and coarctation of aorta.

Thrills

Thrills are the palpable vibrations associated with heart murmurs and their site coincides with the area of maximal auscultatory intensity of the murmur.

- The timing and localization of thrills should be carefully noted. The timing can be appreciated by comparing the thrills with simultaneous palpation of the apex beat or the carotid pulse.
- A thrill is best appreciated by palpating with the outstretched palm with the heads of the metacarpal bones lying directly over the area of interest. The systolic thrill of a small VSD is felt at the lower sternal border and an apical systolic thrill is characteristic of severe MR.
- A diastolic thrill at the apex is palpable in some patients with mitral valve stenosis.
- The thrill of AS is felt to the right of the sternum in the second intercostal space and that of PS to the left.
- The thrill of aortic valve stenosis is also palpable in the suprasternal notch and over the carotid arteries in the neck. The thrill in the suprasternal notch can also be due to PS, PDA, or coarctation of aorta.
- Rheumatic MR and tricuspid regurgitation produce a systolic thrill at the apical region and left fourth intercostal space, respectively.
- If a thrill is palpated and present, then the accompanying murmur on auscultation by definition becomes at least 4/6 in its intensity.

Percussion

- The structures that form the left border of the heart from above downwards are aortic arch, descending aorta, pulmonary artery, left atrial appendage, and left ventricle.
- The right border is constituted from above downwards by superior vena cava, right atrium, and inferior vena cava.

Percussion has a limited role in children. The left heart border normally coincides with the apex. The border of cardiac dullness is found outside the apex in pericardial effusion.

- The normal right heart border is retrosternal, so cardiac dullness to the right of the sternum signifies cardiac enlargement (usually involving the right atrium) or abnormal cardiac position.
- In a patient with a dilated pulmonary artery (usually with pulmonary hypertension), the second left intercostal space becomes dull to percussion.
- Rare causes of dullness in the second space are mediastinal mass and pericardial effusion.
- The percussion for the left cardiac border is started in the left midaxillary line in the fifth intercostal space and is moved medially toward the midclavicular line and the sternum. The point where the resonance of percussion note changes should be noted and then moving up the fourth space, the process should be repeated to delineate the left cardiac border (Fig. 10.7).

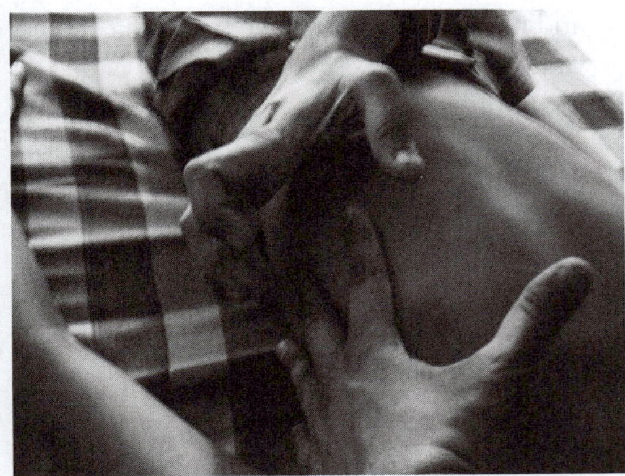

Figure 10.7 Percussion for the left cardiac border.

- Percussion is best performed by the pleximeter finger parallel to the expected cardiac borders, starting from the resonant areas and moving toward cardiac borders.

Auscultation

Cardiac auscultation is a skill that demands patience and practice. The diaphragm of the stethoscope is placed firmly on the chest for high-pitched sounds; the bell of the stethoscope is placed lightly on the chest for low-pitched sounds. The child should ideally be lying supine quietly and breathing normally; the infant may be examined in the mother's lap. Auscultation must be done in the four cardinal areas on the precordium, i.e., mitral, tricuspid, aortic, and pulmonary areas (Fig. 10.8). The areas for cardiac auscultation are shown in Table 10.2.

Apart from those mentioned in Table 10.2, other areas for auscultation include the third and fourth spaces close to sternum (for pansystolic murmur of VSD), infraclavicular regions (PDA and venous hum), left anterior axillary line (conducted murmur of MR) and both axilla, carotids, infrascapular and intrascapular areas (for coarctation—collateral murmurs), and femoral and brachial artery (AR).

The examiner should initially concentrate on the characteristics of the individual heart sounds, one at a time, and their variation with respiration and later proceed to focus on murmurs. The timing of a heart sound or murmur can be determined accurately from its relation with other observable events in the cardiac cycle—the carotid arterial pulse or the apical impulse. In addition, careful attention must be paid to the heart rate and presence of any additional sounds such as third heart sound and/or pericardial rub.

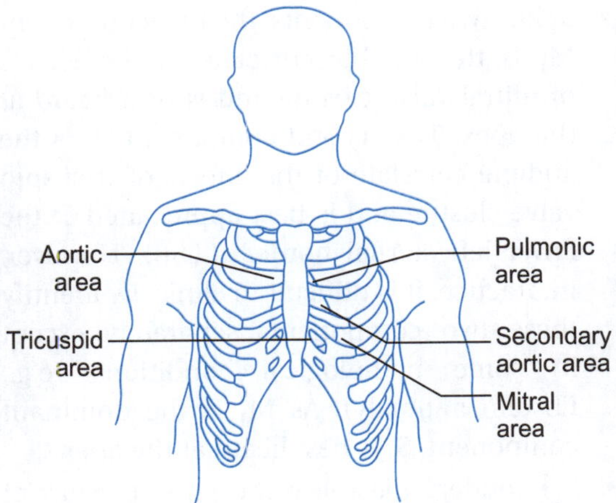

Figure 10.8 Cardinal areas for cardiac auscultation.

TABLE 10.2 Areas for Cardiac Auscultation

Area	Remarks
Apex (mitral area)	Fourth and fifth left intercostal spaces in midclavicular line
Tricuspid area	Fourth and fifth left intercostal spaces, just lateral to the lower end of sternum
Pulmonary area	Second left intercostal space close to sternum
Aortic area and second aortic area	Second right intercostal space near sternal border and third left intercostal space near left sternal border

The First Heart Sound (S_1)

The first heart sound (denoted as S_1) is caused by closure of the atrioventricular (AV) valves (mitral and tricuspid) as the ventricular pressure exceeds the atrial pressure at the beginning of the systole.

- S_1 has two components: the first component M_1 is the audible correlate of the effects of mitral valve closure and is best heard at the apex. The second component T_1 is the audible correlate of the effects of tricuspid valve closure and is best appreciated at the lower left sternal border (LLSB). However, in practice, it is difficult to clinically identify these two components separately except in some pathological conditions (e.g., Ebstein anomaly). As M_1 is the dominant component, S_1 is best heard at the apex.
- S_1 is louder if diastole is shortened because of tachycardia, if AV flow is increased because of high cardiac output or shunt lesions (e.g., a loud T_1 in ASD), if AV flow is prolonged because of MS, or in conditions with a short PR interval (AV conduction time).
- The loud S_1 in MS usually signifies that the valve is still pliable and that it remains open at the onset of isovolumetric contraction because of the elevated left atrial pressure.
- A soft S_1 may be due to poor conduction of sound through a thick chest wall (e.g., obesity), a long PR interval, or imperfect closure of the valve, as in MR. S_1 is also soft when the anterior mitral leaflet is immobile because of rigidity and calcification, even in the presence of predominant MS.

The Second Heart Sound (S_2)

The second heart sound (denoted as S_2) is caused by closure of the semilunar valves (aortic and pulmonary) at the end of ventricular ejection.

- S_2 has two components: the aortic component A_2 and the pulmonary component P_2.
- The aortic component A_2 correlates with the effects of aortic valve closure.
- The pulmonary component P_2 correlates with the effects of pulmonary valve closure. Normally A_2 precedes P_2 because left ventricular ejection ends slightly before right ventricular ejection.
- Unlike S_1, the physiologic splitting of S_2 can be appreciated clinically in normal children and its abnormalities have immense clinical value.
- S_2 should be assessed at the upper left and right sternal borders. During inspiration, the decrease in intrathoracic pressure results in increased filling of the right side of the heart, which leads to a longer right ventricular ejection time and thus relatively delayed closure of the pulmonary valve; therefore, physiologic splitting of the S_2 becomes accentuated during inspiration and decreases during expiration. S_2 may often appear to be single during expiration (Fig. 10.9).
- The S_2 is said to be widely split if the A_2–P_2 interval is prolonged and the split is easily appreciated during expiration also. Wide splitting will be heard in conditions that prolong right ventricular ejection time, such as ASD, total anomalous pulmonary venous drainage, PS, Ebstein anomaly, and right bundle branch block.
- Narrow splitting of S_2 occurs with early closure of the pulmonary valve (e.g., pulmonary hypertension) or delayed aortic valve closure (e.g., severe AS).
- A single S_2 occurs when there is a single semilunar valve (e.g., pulmonary or aortic

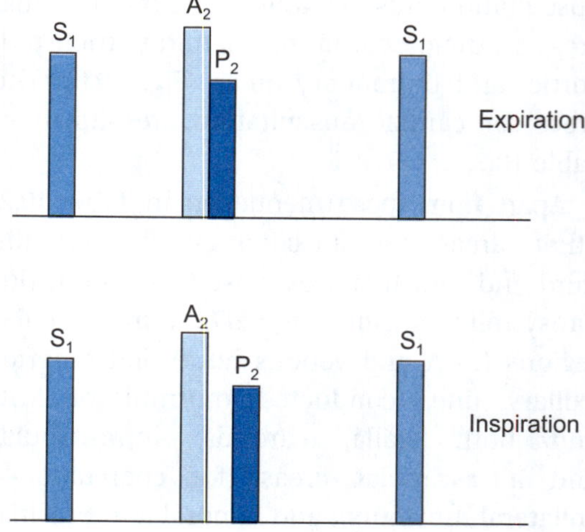

Figure 10.9 Diagrammatic representation of normal inspiratory splitting of S_2 on auscultation at left second interspace.

valve atresia, truncus arteriosus), an inaudible P_2 (e.g., TGA, with the aorta being anteriorly placed; or severe PS, as in TOF), delayed aortic valve closure (e.g., severe AS), or early pulmonary valve closure (e.g., pulmonary vascular obstructive disease in Eisenmenger syndrome).

- Paradoxical or reversed splitting occurs when the aortic valve closes later than the pulmonary valve (e.g., severe AS, large PDA, left bundle branch block).
- The split is said to be fixed if the A_2–P_2 interval does not vary with respiration. Wide and fixed splitting of S_2 is a characteristic of ASDs. In patients with an ASD, the proportion of right atrial filling contributed by the left atrium (across the ASD) and the great veins (normal systemic venous return) varies reciprocally during the respiratory cycle, so that overall right atrial inflow remains relatively constant. Therefore, the volume and duration of right ventricular ejection are not significantly increased by inspiration, and there is no appreciable inspiratory exaggeration of the splitting of S_2. This phenomenon of *fixed splitting* of the second heart sound is of great clinical value (Fig. 10.10).

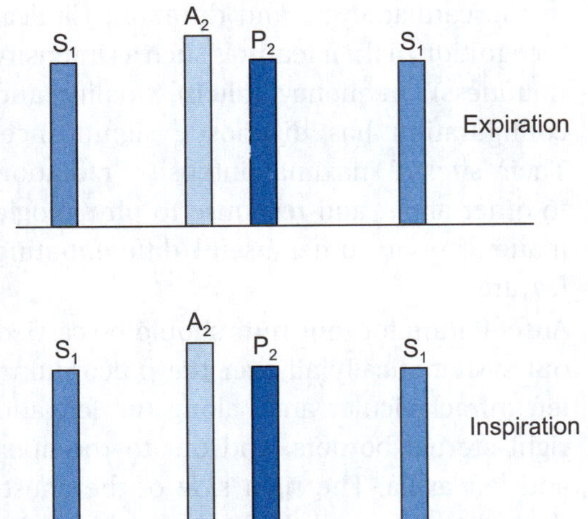

Figure 10.10 Diagrammatic representation of wide and fixed splitting of S_2 in a patient with ASD on auscultation at the left second interspace.

- Normally P_2 is softer than A_2. P_2 is loud in any condition with pulmonary hypertension, e.g., Eisenmenger syndrome.

Systolic Sounds

Ejection clicks

Ejection clicks, sharp high-pitched sounds heard in early systole closely following S_1, may be valvular or vascular in origin. Thus, they may be related to dilatation of the aorta or pulmonary artery or to a mildly to moderately stenotic semilunar valve.

- Aortic ejection clicks are best heard at the right second intercostal space and are constant in intensity with respiration. They occur in conditions in which the aortic valve is stenotic (e.g., bicuspid aortic valve) or the aorta is dilated (e.g., TOF, truncus arteriosus). An aortic valvular ejection click is often heard well at the apex too.
- Pulmonary ejection clicks, which are associated with mild to moderate PS, are best heard at the left middle to upper sternal border and vary with respirations, often disappearing with inspiration. A midsystolic click ("non-ejection click") heard at the apex, often preceding a late systolic murmur, suggests MVP.

Diastolic Sounds

The Third Heart Sound

The third heart sound (S_3) is a low-pitched diastolic sound produced in the ventricle, at the termination of its rapid filling.

- S_3 is frequently heard in normal children ("physiologic S_3") and in patients with high cardiac output.
- Thus, S_3 may be normal in an adolescent with a normal heart rate, but in a patient with the clinical signs of heart failure and tachycardia, its presence is pathological and may be identified as a "gallop." It indicates impairment of ventricular function (e.g., myocarditis, dilated cardiomyopathy), AV valve regurgitation (moderate or severe MR/tricuspid regurgitation), or other conditions

that increase the rate or volume (moderate or large left-to-right shunts) of ventricular filling.

- The left-sided S_3 (e.g., large VSD, severe MR) is best heard with the bell of the stethoscope at the left ventricular apex during expiration and with the patient in the left lateral position.
- The right-sided S_3 (e.g., large ASD) is best heard at the left sternal border or just beneath the xiphoid and is usually louder with inspiration. Third heart sounds often disappear with treatment of heart failure.

Fourth Heart Sound

The fourth heart sound (S_4) is a low-pitched, presystolic (i.e., end-diastolic, heard just before S_1) sound produced in the ventricle during ventricular filling; it is associated with an effective atrial contraction and is best heard with the bell of the stethoscope. S_4 is absent in patients with atrial fibrillation.

- The S_4 occurs when diminished ventricular compliance increases the resistance to ventricular filling usually in the presence of ventricular hypertrophy; it is frequently present in patients with AS, hypertrophic cardiomyopathy, long-standing systemic hypertension, and acute MR.
- The S_4 is loudest at the left ventricular apex when the patient is in the left lateral position.
- The right-sided S_4 is present in patients with right ventricular hypertrophy secondary to either pulmonic stenosis or pulmonary hypertension and frequently accompanies a prominent presystolic "a" wave in the JVP (in the presence of an intact ventricular septum).
- Sometimes with tachycardia, S_3 may merge with S_4, a finding known as a summation gallop.

Opening Snap

The opening snap (OS) is a brief, high-pitched, early diastolic sound, which is usually due to stenosis of an AV valve, most often the mitral valve. It is generally heard best at the LLSB and radiates well to the base of the heart. The A_2–OS interval is inversely related to the severity of MS. More severe the MS, higher is the left atrial pressure, and therefore earlier is the OS of the mitral valve.

Pericardial Knock

It is a sound that occurs earlier in the diastole than the usual S_3 and is higher pitched. It is found in patients with constrictive pericarditis, due to the restrictive effect of the adherent thickened pericardium, which abruptly halts diastolic filling.

Murmurs

In contrast to sounds that are brief, cardiac murmurs are a relatively prolonged series of auditory vibrations resulting from turbulence in blood flow in the cardiovascular system.

- Turbulence occurs when there is an abnormal (high) flow through a normal structure (e.g., pulmonary ejection murmur in high-output states) or normal (or high) flow through an abnormal structure (stenosed valve or narrow vessel) or a combination of both (regurgitant valve, septal defect).
- Murmurs are characterized by their timing in the cardiac cycle and duration. Clinical recognition of their features such as intensity (loudness), frequency (pitch), quality, and configuration has diagnostic significance. Their site of maximal intensity, radiation to other areas, and response to physiologic maneuvers are other useful differentiating features.
- Auscultation for murmurs should be carried out systematically all over the precordium, left infraclavicular area, along the left and right sternal borders, and out to the apex and left axilla. The right side of the chest, the right axilla, and the back should not be missed.
- The bell and chestpiece of the stethoscope are used to hear the low-pitched sounds

TABLE 10.3 Timing of Murmurs of Valvular Origin

Valve	Timing	
	Systolic	Diastolic
Atrioventricular	Regurgitation	Stenosis
Semilunar	Stenosis	Regurgitation

and murmurs and the diaphragm for the high-pitched ones.

- The precise time of onset and time of cessation of a murmur depend on the instant in the cardiac cycle at which an adequate pressure difference between the two relevant chambers/structures appears and disappears (Table 10.3).
- It is important to remember that the intensity of the murmur is no guide to the severity of the underlying disease or the hemodynamic disturbance.
- The term conduction of murmur refers to spreading of a murmur with the same loudness in an outward direction from its point of origin, while radiation of the murmur means that the intensity of the murmur becomes progressively less along a direction from the site of its origin.

The intensity of systolic murmurs is graded from I to VI as shown in Table 10.4.

TABLE 10.4 Grading of Intensity of Systolic Murmurs

Grade	Features
I	Barely audible
II	Medium intensity, easily heard
III	Loud but no thrill
IV	Loud with a thrill
V	Very loud but still requiring positioning of the stethoscope at least partly on the chest (e.g., if only the edge of the stethoscope is in contact with the chest)
VI	Loud that the murmur can be heard with the stethoscope off the chest

Systolic murmurs

Systolic murmurs are classified as ejection, pansystolic, or late systolic according to the timing of the murmur in relation to S_1 and S_2. Systolic ejection murmurs are due to forward flow across the left ventricular or right ventricular outflow tract, whereas systolic regurgitant murmurs are due to abnormal flow from a higher-pressure cardiac chamber to a lower-pressure chamber.

Systolic ejection murmurs

- These murmurs start a short time after a well-heard S_1, increase in intensity ("crescendo"), peak, and then decrease in intensity ("decrescendo"); they end before the S_2. Such a configuration has been called diamond-shaped due to the resemblance on diagrammatic representation (Fig. 10.11).
- Systolic ejection murmurs usually mean increased flow or stenosis across either of the ventricular outflow tracts. Aortic or pulmonary outflow obstruction, at the valvular (semilunar valve stenosis) or subvalvular level, produces a systolic ejection murmur.
- Most functional and innocent murmurs are also ejection murmurs.
- In infants with rapid heart rates, it is often difficult to distinguish between ejection and pansystolic murmurs. If a clear and distinct S_1 can be appreciated, the murmur is most likely ejection in nature.

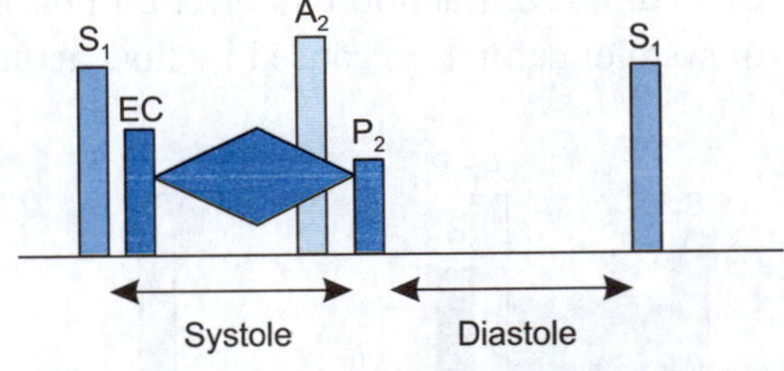

Figure 10.11 Diagrammatic representation of the auscultatory findings in a child with pulmonary valve stenosis, viz., an ejection click, widely split S_2 with soft P_2, and a long systolic ejection murmur. Note the diamond shape representing the crescendo–decrescendo configuration. *EC*, ejection click.

TABLE 10.5 Examples of Systolic Ejection Murmurs in Children

Aortic	
Valvular	• Bicuspid aortic valve with AS • Severe AR
Subvalvular	Hypertrophic obstructive cardiomyopathy
Supravalvular	Supravalvular AS in William syndrome
Pulmonary	
Valvular	• Pulmonary valve stenosis • Tetralogy of Fallot • ASD (due to increased flow)
Subvalvular	Tetralogy of Fallot

AR, aortic regurgitation; *AS*, aortic stenosis; *ASD*, atrial septal defect.

- Examples of systolic ejection murmurs in children are shown in Table 10.5.

Pansystolic or holosystolic murmurs Also called regurgitant systolic murmurs, these begin almost simultaneously with the S_1 (S_1-coincident) and continue throughout systole up to the S_2.

- Pansystolic murmur may mask S_1 and/or S_2 (Fig. 10.12). After closure of the AV valves (S_1), a brief period occurs (isovolumic contraction phase) during which ventricular pressure increases but the semilunar valves remain closed.
- Pansystolic murmurs (heard during both isovolumic contraction and ejection phases of systole) cannot be caused by flow across the semilunar valves because these valves are closed during isovolumic contraction.
- Thus, a pansystolic murmur implies a persistently large pressure gradient between the ventricle and another lower-pressure chamber throughout the whole of systole.
- Pansystolic murmurs are therefore related to blood exiting the contracting ventricle via either an abnormal opening (a VSD) or AV (mitral or tricuspid) valve regurgitation.
- A late systolic murmur begins well beyond the S_1 and continues until the end of systole. It does not mask either S_1 or S_2. Such murmurs may be heard after a midsystolic click in patients with MVP and MR.

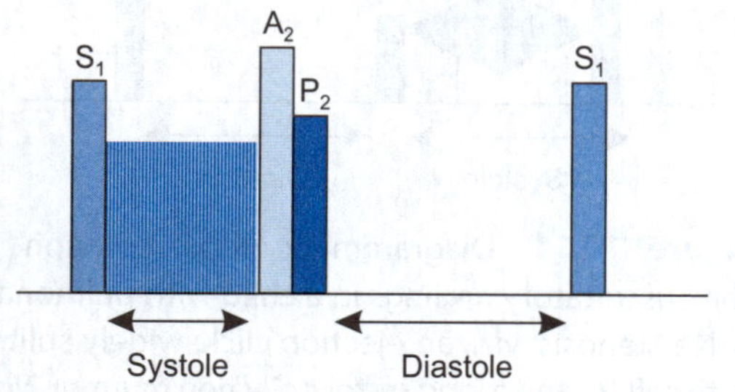

Figure 10.12 Diagrammatic representation of pansystolic murmur.

Diastolic murmurs

Diastolic murmurs are classified into early diastolic murmurs (diastolic regurgitant murmurs) and mid-diastolic murmurs (diastolic filling murmurs or "rumbles") according to their timing.

- Early diastolic murmurs are caused by regurgitation across an incompetent semilunar valve (AR or pulmonary regurgitation [PR]), while mid-diastolic murmurs are caused by forward flow across the AV valves.
- Early diastolic murmurs begin with S_2, as soon as the falling ventricular diastolic pressure falls below that in a great artery (aorta or pulmonary artery). The high-pitched murmurs of AR or of pulmonic regurgitation due to pulmonary hypertension are blowing and decrescendo. Their duration increases with increasing severity of AR or PR. The short (ending by mid-diastole), faint, high-pitched murmur of mild AR may be difficult to hear.
- With a cooperative patient sitting in a leaning-forward position and holding a breath in full expiration, the murmur of mild AR must be specifically sought by applying firm pressure with the stethoscope diaphragm over the left midsternal border. The murmur of AR is enhanced by handgrip. Presence of a "cooing dove" or musical

quality of the diastolic murmur usually denotes a rupture or retroversion of an aortic cusp.

- PR is found most commonly in the setting of severe pulmonary hypertension (e.g., Eisenmenger syndrome, idiopathic pulmonary artery hypertension) and dilatation of the pulmonary artery with incomplete coarctation of the leaflets of the pulmonic valve. The associated clinical findings help differentiate this functional murmur of hypertensive PR (Graham Steell murmur) from that of AR.
- When low-pitched, this murmur is associated with pulmonary valve regurgitation without pulmonary hypertension. Such a low-pitched diastolic murmur is typically found in patients with absent pulmonary valves and after certain surgical procedures performed to relieve obstruction of the right ventricular outflow tract in lesions such as TOF.

Mid-diastolic murmurs These are separated from their respective semilunar closure sound (A_2 or P_2) by a brief interval (the isovolumetric relaxation phase). These murmurs have a low frequency and are rumbling in character.

- They arise from stenosis of the mitral or tricuspid valves and occur during the phase of early ventricular filling. It is the duration of the murmur that is a more reliable marker of the severity of valve obstruction than its intensity. The diastolic rumble is prolonged when stenosis is marked.
- The intensity of the murmur depends significantly on the transvalvular flow and therefore is not an index of severity of stenosis. The murmurs can be soft or even absent despite severe obstruction if the cardiac output is very low; they can be quite loud in the presence of increased blood flow, although the AV valve may be normal or only mildly stenotic.
- When the stenotic mitral valve is mobile, the low-pitched, mid-diastolic murmur of MS characteristically follows an OS. It should be specifically sought by placing the bell of the stethoscope at the apex where it is best heard. It can be so well localized that it can be heard only at the site of the apical impulse localized with the patient in the left lateral position.
- In tricuspid stenosis (a rare condition), the mid-diastolic murmur is localized along the left sternal edge and, like other right-sided murmurs, it may be louder during inspiration. The presence of large "a" waves in the JVP can be an additional clue.
- Mid-diastolic murmurs may occur across the mitral valve in cases of MR, VSD, or PDA, and across the tricuspid valve in cases of tricuspid regurgitation or ASD. These murmurs are generated by the high flow across the AV valve, typically follow a third heart sound, and therefore suggest large left-to-right shunts or severe AV valve regurgitation.
- Longer duration and presystolic accentuation usually indicate organic AV valve stenosis, typically MS.

Austin flint murmur It is a mid-diastolic rumble heard best at the cardiac apex. It is thought to result from functional MS produced by the AR jet impinging on the anterior mitral leaflet.

Carey coombs murmur It is a short diastolic rumble produced by mitral valvulitis that may be heard during an episode of acute rheumatic fever. This rumble, especially in children and with fever and anemia, may be introduced by a third heart sound. This combination of an S_3 with a short rumble indicates that there is not enough obstruction to the valve to alter the characteristics of rapid early ventricular filling.

Continuous murmurs

- A continuous murmur is a systolic murmur that "continues" ("spills") across S_2 into diastole and implies similarly continuous, uninterrupted, and turbulent flow, such as in the presence of a PDA or other aortopulmonary communication. It need not be heard all throughout the cardiac cycle. It usually indicates a vascular cause.

- The murmur of PDA is the classic example and its quality has been described as "machinery-like." It is heard best in the left infraclavicular area and the second left intercostal space. It peaks in intensity at the time of S_2.
- A well-functioning surgical aortopulmonary shunt (e.g., Blalock–Taussig shunt between the subclavian and pulmonary arteries) also produces a similar murmur.
- A congenital or acquired systemic arteriovenous fistula or a localized narrowing of an artery (e.g., renal artery stenosis) can also have a localized continuous murmur ("bruit").

Venous hum Cervical venous hum is another common example of a continuous murmur. It is an innocent murmur caused by rapid blood flow, and can be very prominent in severe anemia. The venous hum is heard in the supraclavicular areas with the patient in an upright position. It is louder on the right than on the left side. It may radiate to the upper anterior chest. It disappears when the patient assumes the supine position. It can be abolished easily by light pressure on the internal jugular vein or by changes in head position. These maneuvers help differentiate it from the murmur produced by a PDA.

A continuous murmur should not be confused with a to-and-fro murmur, which is a combination of a systolic murmur (usually ejection type) and a diastolic murmur (usually early diastolic). The systolic component of the murmur ends at or before S_2 and the diastolic component begins after S_2 (e.g., AS with AR, PS with PR).

Innocent murmurs

Many murmurs are not associated with any significant hemodynamic abnormality. These murmurs have been called functional or innocent. If randomly checked, more than 30% of children may have an innocent murmur at some point; this percentage further increases when auscultation is performed under nonbasal circumstances (hyperdynamic circulation resulting from fever, infection, anxiety). Innocent flow murmur is often best heard at left sternal edge or pulmonary areas and does not radiate to other areas. The presence of a normally split second heart sound (S_2) makes murmur more likely to be an innocent one.

A murmur that has any of the following characteristics should never be labeled as innocent:

- Presence of any abnormal clinical cardiac findings
- Pansystolic murmur
- All diastolic murmurs
- Late systolic murmurs
- Loud murmurs
- Continuous murmurs (except venous hum)

Still's murmur The most common innocent murmur of childhood, Still's murmur is a medium-pitched, vibratory or "musical," systolic ejection murmur with a characteristic twanging quality. It is thought to originate from flow in the left ventricular outflow tract. It is heard best along the left lower and midsternal border or slightly lateral to this. It has no significant radiation. The murmur is heard most frequently in children between 2 and 7 years of age. The intensity of the murmur often changes with respiration and position and may be diminished in the sitting position.

The pulmonary ejection systolic murmur and the continuous cervical venous hum are other innocent murmurs. Functional murmurs found in states of high cardiac output (e.g., severe anemia, fever, exercise, thyrotoxicosis, peripheral arteriovenous fistula) usually originate from the pulmonary outflow tract.

Murmurs and Cardiac Disease

Prominent murmurs may be audible in the absence of a structural heart disease, e.g., with severe anemia or hypertension. On the other

TABLE 10.6 Dynamic Auscultation—Some Important Examples

Murmur	Maneuver	Effect on intensity	Mechanism
Right-sided murmurs	Inspiration	Increase	Increased systemic venous return to right heart due to negative intrathoracic pressure
Left-sided murmurs	Expiration	Increase	Increased pulmonary venous return to left heart
Mitral valve prolapse with MR	Inspiration	Increase	Decreased LV volume → increased valve prolapse
	Standing	Increase	
	Valsalva maneuver	Lengthens ± increased intensity	
Hypertrophic obstructive cardiomyopathy	Inspiration	Increase	Decreased LV volume → increased dynamic intraventricular obstruction
	Standing	Increase	
	Valsalva maneuver	Increase	
Aortic regurgitation	Handgrip	Increase	Increased systemic vascular resistance

LV, left ventricular; *MR*, mitral regurgitation.

hand, the absence of a precordial murmur does not in any way rule out a significant heart disease. Murmurs may be absent or be deemed insignificant in patients with many different congenital heart defects, e.g., TGA. In these cases, suspicion of heart disease is raised by other abnormal findings in the physical examination, viz., dysmorphism, failure to thrive, cyanosis, abnormal peripheral pulses, precordial impulse, and abnormal heart sounds. Auscultatory features suggestive of a high probability of heart disease include murmurs and are as follows:

- Pansystolic or late systolic
- Grade III or higher in intensity, harsh, located at the left upper sternal border, and associated with an early or midsystolic click or an abnormal S_2
- Diastolic and continuous murmurs, which imply pathological origin (with the notable exception of the venous hum in the neck veins)

Dynamic Auscultation of Murmurs

Characteristic changes in auscultatory findings occur in certain conditions with changes in posture, respiration, or certain maneuvers such as Valsalva or handgrip. Some important examples of dynamic auscultation are described in Table 10.6.

Pericardial Friction Rub

- Inflammation of the pericardial sac with a friction between its parietal and visceral layers with or without accumulation of fluid may cause a pericardial friction rub.
- These friction sounds are very high pitched, leathery, and scratchy in character. They seem close to the ear and are appreciated best with the patient leaning forward or in the knee–chest position.
- They are best audible with the diaphragm of the stethoscope in the second and third left intercostal spaces.
- The important causes of pericardial rub in children include acute rheumatic carditis and chronic constrictive pericarditis.
- They are heard transiently and can change over a few hours. The pericardial rub may have three components during each cardiac cycle but it is common to recognize only one or two.

Synthesis of Clinical Findings

At the end of history taking and the general and systemic physical examination, a clinical diagnosis is formulated, after considering all the relevant findings. A statement of the cardiac clinical diagnosis typically includes a mention of the following, as relevant to the case:

- Broad etiologic category: Congenital/acquired (e.g., rheumatic)
- In case of congenital structural heart disease, acyanotic or cyanotic
- Suspected lesion(s), e.g., MS, AR, VSD, and PDA
- Severity of the lesion(s) (mild/moderate/severe, or small/moderate/large as in VSD)
- Presence of heart failure, with New York Heart Association class
- Presence/absence of pulmonary hypertension
- Presence of sinus rhythm or otherwise (e.g., atrial fibrillation)
- Presence of active carditis/acute rheumatic fever/infective endocarditis
- Presence of systemic disease/dysmorphic syndrome, e.g., Down syndrome, Marfan syndrome, and mucopolysaccharidoses
- Comorbidities: Malnutrition, anemia, and respiratory infection
- Complications: Polycythemia and cerebral abscess
- Surgery/transcatheter intervention in the past, if any: For example, Blalock–Taussig shunt in TOF

Combining all the above-mentioned points offers valuable guidance to help the diseases in physiologic categories, reach a provisional clinical diagnosis, with or without associated complications/comorbidities, and plan for the medical and interventional management.

KEY POINTS

- A detailed history taking and a meticulous clinical examination are the bases for the correct diagnosis in the congenital and acquired heart diseases of the children.
- A flexible approach is often needed in the examination of the cardiovascular system in an infant and a young child who are apprehensive or sick for examination, making it difficult to gain the best information from the clinical observations and the physical findings. Irrespective of these circumstances, the presentation must be completed in a sequential manner.
- The synthesis of clinical findings is a key factor in presenting a clinical and/or differential diagnosis of any cardiac disease.

CHAPTER 11

The Nervous System

Sheela Bharani Chawla, Vaishali Chanpura

Pediatric neurology is one of the most challenging systems that includes the inherited, congenital, or acquired conditions involving nervous system, neuromuscular junction, or muscles. Besides neurological examination, it also includes developmental pediatrics. Varying ability depending upon the age of the child, developmental handicaps, inability to perform certain tests in young children and at times altered state of consciousness makes the task of neurological examination challenging. A comprehensive neurological evaluation with detailed history, physical examination, and judicious use of investigations is the key to reach the correct neurological diagnosis in children.

Objectives of Neurological Assessment

The purpose of neurological assessment is to come to a diagnosis. This includes not only making a neurological diagnosis, but also exclude non-neurological conditions which might mimic neurological illness. Neurological diagnosis has three components:

1. *Functional diagnosis* such as hemiplegia, acute flaccid paralysis, seizure disorder, etc.
2. *Anatomical diagnosis* refers to localization of lesion—central (cortical, capsular, or cord injury) versus peripheral (nerve injury).
3. *Etiological diagnosis* is finding out probable cause leading to illness and may include infection, perinatal insult/injury, vascular causes, etc.

History taking and examination of the central nervous system (CNS) in young children is difficult due to their anxiety, inability to communicate, and lack of cooperation and thus needs practice and patience.

- Unlike in older children, a lot of findings can be gathered just by observing a child. Translating the positive findings to localize the anatomical location and nature of the lesion is at times difficult due to fluctuating or evolving course of the illness and at times due to the presence of false localizing signs, like abducens nerve palsy in raised intracranial tension.
- Quite often, when child presents with acute emergency, events are either not narrated adequately or they are exaggerated. This is commonly seen in cases of convulsions, altered sensorium, and acute flaccid paralysis.
- At times, the events have not been observed by the person who brings a child to the emergency department. On the other end, developmental delay and slowly progressive condition in a child may not be recognized earlier by the parents and may cause delay in offering timely management.

History

- Basic information of a child such as full name, sex, and exact age should be noted. History of presenting complaints and detailed history should be taken. There are a few signs/symptoms that can point to the involvement of the CNS in a child. Common symptoms that are useful in establishing the involvement of the CNS in a child are shown in Box 11.1.

Box 11.1 Common symptoms in CNS disease

- Seizures and seizure-like events (syncope)
- Abnormal behavior and/or altered sensorium/mentation
- Headache
- Localized or generalized limb weakness
- Abnormal posturing, and/or involuntary movements (e.g., chorea, tremors)
- Speech/articulation problems
- Gait disturbances/clumsy movements
- Abnormal/altered sensations
- Vertigo or giddiness
- Visual and/or hearing deficits (such as diplopia)
- Developmental delay, mental subnormality, or progressive deterioration
- Asymmetry/abnormality of head shape and size

Common Symptoms Related to CNS

Seizures/Convulsions

A *seizure* is a transient occurrence of symptoms or signs due to an excessive abnormal or synchronous neuronal activity in the brain. When it is associated with motor components, it is called *convulsion*. Traditionally *epilepsy* is defined as occurrence of two or more episodes of seizures 24 hours apart. Current definition of epilepsy also includes one or more unprovoked seizures with predisposition to get recurrent seizures or seizures that are part of an epilepsy syndrome.

Convulsions in a child are one of the most frightening symptoms for the parents. When the child is brought to the health facility, the convulsions may have subsided. Thus, the treating doctor rarely has chance to witness the episode of convulsion. Sometimes the episode may not have been witnessed even by the parents; they might have received the information about the episode from another observer who witnessed the event. The crucial information might have been distorted in this process of transfer of information.

Seizures versus non-seizures

- Most "spells" are not seizures; they can be other paroxysmal disorders or seizure mimics such as syncope. Syncope is often misdiagnosed as seizures, as the child may be stiffened at the end of an episode of syncope. A few other examples of such episodes include breath-holding spells, syncopal attacks, benign paroxysmal vertigo, migraine, and shuddering attacks. These are termed nonseizure paroxysmal events or seizure mimics.

Careful analysis of history is important to differentiate convulsions from seizure-mimicking conditions. Whenever possible, it is very valuable to see a video clip of the paroxysmal event. If the parents have not taken the video clip, they should be asked to do so if such an event recurs.

The detailed history should be obtained and should include the following points:

- Has this episode occurred for the first time? Parents may not come out with this history until specifically asked. A child with epilepsy will have repeated episodes of seizures.
- Does any family member have similar episodes? In many genetic epilepsy syndromes, there may be positive family history of seizure disorders.
- Age: The causes of seizures are different at different ages. Febrile seizures typically occur in the age group of 6 months to 5 years and very rarely the child develops first episode of febrile seizure after 3 years. Causes of seizures in neonatal age are different (Box 11.2) and may need further evaluation accordingly.

Box 11.2 Common causes of seizures in neonates

- Hypoglycemia
- Hypocalcemia
- Hyponatremia, hypernatremia
- Hypoxic ischemic encephalopathy secondary to perinatal insult
- Bacterial meningitis
- Intraventricular hemorrhage
- Cerebral dysgenesis (malformations)
- Inborn errors of metabolism

Seizure episodes and associated characteristics are given in the next subsections.

Preictal or preseizure phenomena

Presence of aura and automatism preceding the episode of seizure occurs in complex partial seizures. Aura is usually an unpleasant feeling or a stereotypical visual or auditory hallucination or abdominal discomfort. The first feature of the seizure can be automatic behavior or a staring look. Automatisms are involuntary motor activities occurring during, or after, an epileptic seizure and they are usually followed by amnesia. In a given patient, automatic behavior tends to be similar from seizure to seizure. Such automatic behavior can be grimacing, chewing movements, and even running or walking.

Ictal phenomena

- *Type of convulsion*: It is important to know the type of seizure, focal versus generalized. Frequently, the seizures are focal/partial at the onset and they are secondarily generalized. The parents would describe them as generalized until specifically asked about the onset of the seizure. This is important to know, as these focal seizures may be indicative of some underlying structural lesion that may require neuroimaging for precise diagnosis and treatment.
- *Nature of movements*: The various seizure types could be tonic, clonic, tonic–clonic, or myoclonic.
- *Duration of episode*: Duration of simple febrile seizures is usually less than 10 minutes. Status epilepticus is defined as 5 or more minutes of either continuous seizure activity or repetitive seizures with no intervening recovery of consciousness.
- *Other associated features*: During the episode of convulsions, a child may have uprolling of eyeballs and urinary or fecal incontinence. The child is unresponsive during the episode and eyes are open during seizure activity at least at the onset of seizure. This helps to differentiate epileptic seizures from psychogenic, non-epileptiform seizure mimic.

Postictal/postseizure phenomena

After an episode of seizure, the child may have postictal drowsiness, weakness, confusion, or headache. Along with detailed description of seizure episodes, it is also important to identify provoking factors if any and its association with fever.

- *Provoked versus unprovoked*: Seizures occurring during the acute illnesses are called provoked or acute symptomatic seizures. Such illnesses can be febrile seizures, hypoglycemia, hypocalcemia, meningitis, encephalitis, etc. If the child is already on anti-epileptic medications, check for drug compliance, as missing few doses could have precipitated seizure.
- *Association with fever*: In a child with convulsion, it is important to ask history of fever. Fever and convulsions may indicate possibility of CNS infections such as meningitis or encephalitis but can be more commonly due to *febrile seizures*, which usually carry a good prognosis. Febrile seizures are a common cause of seizures in children. They are defined as "A seizure in a child between the age of 6 months to 5 years in association with a febrile illness, in the absence of CNS infection or acute encephalopathy." A typical description of a simple febrile seizure is: a seizure occurring with fever in a child in the above-defined age group that is generalized tonic–clonic, lasting less than 10 minutes without any postictal deficit. If such an episode is partial or prolonged, more than 10 minutes, or if there are multiple episodes in a day, it is called complex febrile seizure.

Common causes of convulsions in children are shown in Box 11.3.

Altered Sensorium

Alteration in sensorium implies significant alteration in the awareness of self and of the environment with varying degrees of

Box 11.3 Common causes of seizures in children

- Febrile seizures
- Metabolic causes
  - Hypoglycemia
  - Hypocalcemia
  - Hyponatremia
  - Hypernatremia
- Epilepsy
- CNS infections: Viral/bacterial/tuberculous—meningitis/meningoencephalitis, brain abscess
- Intracranial space-occupying lesions: Brain tumor, tuberculoma, brain abscess
- Vascular: Hemorrhage, thrombosis (e.g., sickle cell anemia)
- Neurocutaneous syndromes: Tuberous sclerosis, Sturge-Weber syndrome, neurofibromatosis
- Inborn errors of metabolism
- Structural abnormalities of the brain, e.g., lissencephaly
- Encephalopathy
  - Hypoxic ischemic encephalopathy due to perinatal insult
  - Hepatic encephalopathy
  - Hypertensive encephalopathy (e.g., acute glomerulonephritis)
  - Uremic encephalopathy (e.g., chronic kidney disease)
  - Toxic substances (e.g., lead)

Box 11.4 Alteration of sensorium

- Epilepsy
  - Status epilepticus
  - Postictal state
  - Epileptic encephalopathies
- Infectious
  - Meningoencephalitis: Bacterial, viral, tuberculous
- Metabolic
  - Hypoglycemia
  - Hyponatremia
  - Hypernatremia
  - Diabetic ketoacidosis
  - Inborn errors of metabolism
- Systemic disorders
  - Hepatic encephalopathy
  - Uremic encephalopathy
  - Adrenal insufficiency
- Complicated migraine
- Drugs
- Toxins: Neurotoxic snake bite, substance abuse
- Trauma: Post-traumatic brain injury
- Vascular
  - Cerebrovascular stroke
  - Intracranial hemorrhage
  - Hypertensive encephalopathy
- Increased intracranial tension
  - Brain tumors
  - Hydrocephalus

wakefulness. This is a medical emergency in which the child is brought with complaint of unresponsiveness or decreased responsiveness. Lack of responsiveness is not always lack of consciousness. For example, there may be transient lack of responsiveness in a child with psychogenic spells.

Common causes of alteration of sensorium or coma in children are shown in Box 11.4.

Obtain the following history carefully:

- Onset, duration, and progress of alteration of sensorium
- History of acute change in behavior such as agitation, confusion, delusions, or hallucinations (such changes of delirium in children are likely due to organic encephalopathy)
- History of convulsions in present or past
- History of limb weakness
- Exposure to drugs or toxins
- History of head injury or fall
- Personal or family history of epilepsy, migraine, or encephalopathy
- History of fever or other symptoms suggestive of systemic illness or CNS infection
- Headache, visual disturbances, and vomiting since they may suggest a possibility of raised intracranial tension or intracranial tumors
- History of severe diarrhea (severe diarrhea may lead to electrolyte imbalance causing seizures and severe dehydration can lead to cortical venous thrombosis)

Headache

It is one of the common neurological symptoms that can be due to a variety of causes ranging

Box 11.5 Headache in children

- Migraine headache
- Cluster headache
- Tension headache
- Febrile headache in viral illnesses, malaria, etc.
- CNS infections
- Raised intracranial tension, intracranial space-occupying lesions
- Sinusitis
- Headache secondary to tooth or ear diseases
- Refractive errors
- Trauma
- Post-lumbar puncture
- Following an episode of seizure

from benign nonorganic causes to organic causes such as brain tumor. Younger children may not be able to complain about and describe headache. Parents may just report about irritability in a child. It is important to elicit history in detail so that the benign causes are not overinvestigated, and more serious causes are not missed. Delay in diagnosis can be fatal in conditions like subarachnoid hemorrhage or raised intracranial tension.

Common causes of headache are shown in Box 11.5.

The questions given in the next subsections should be asked with relation to headache to know the etiology.

Onset

Ask whether the onset is acute, insidious, or chronic. Hyperacute onset is seen with subarachnoid hemorrhage. Headache in migraine and cluster headache are usually acute and recurrent. Tension headache and psychogenic headache are usually insidious in onset and usually present as chronic headache.

Location

It is important to know whether headache is generalized or localized to some area.

- Generalized headache occurs in conditions such as hypertension, CNS infections such as meningitis and encephalitis, and intracranial tumors or increased intracranial pressure (ICP) due to any cause.
- Localized
  - Frontal headache occurs in tension-type headache, sinusitis, and refractive errors.
  - Temporal headache occurs in migraine.
  - Occipital headache occurs in tension-type headache.
  - Headache occurs around the orbit in cluster headache.

Character

Headache in migraine is pulsating/throbbing in character, while it is band-like or dull in tension headache, boring or stabbing in cluster headache, and thunderclap in subarachnoid hemorrhage. Patients with subarachnoid hemorrhage describe their headache as the "worst headache of their life." Continued early morning headaches after awakening are suggestive of intracranial space-occupying lesions.

Duration and frequency

Migraine and cluster headaches are episodic; the duration of headache in migraine ranges from 4 to 72 hours and cluster headache usually lasts for 30 minutes to 3 hours. The patient may experience recurrent episodes of headache with a period of no pain in between. Chronic daily headache is seen in tension headache. Slowly progressive or worsening headache may indicate serious intracranial disease such as intracranial space-occupying lesion that is often accompanied by projectile vomiting. Any headache that disturbs or interferes with the child's sleep must be assessed.

Unilateral versus bilateral

Unilateral or side-locked headache is seen in classical migraine while bilateral headache occurs in common migraine, tension headache, and other intracranial diseases.

Precipitating and aggravating factors

Attacks of migraine get precipitated by stress, sleep deprivation, and certain food items. Headache due to raised ICT gets aggravated by coughing and straining and decreases after an episode of vomiting.

Functional impairment

Typically, a patient with migraine cannot continue to work and headache gets worse if ignored. A patient with migraine prefers to take rest and sleep in a dark room. In contrast, in cases of patients with tension headache, no functional impairment is caused, the patient can continue to work, and headache also does not disturb the sleep.

Associated factors

Look for the associated symptoms with headache:

- *Nausea, vomiting, photophobia, phonophobia, and visual auras*: Migraine headache
- *Fever*: Febrile headache and CNS infections
- *Limb weakness, blurring of vision, projectile vomiting, and altered sensorium:* Raised intracranial tension
- *Nasal discharge and nasal block*: Sinusitis

Neurological Evaluation Based on History

The initial assessment of the child should determine the child's general condition and the severity of sickness and whether it requires immediate treatment or not. Any child who is convulsing needs to be stabilized and treated for convulsions and then evaluated in detail later. The history and the evaluation should begin with the points to address the issues given in the next subsections.

Age of Onset

The age of the onset can offer information about a disease: an early onset may be linked to perinatal events such as asphyxia, malformations, and neonatal infections. Febrile convulsions are extremely rare before 6 months and after the age of 5 years.

Type of Onset

Is the onset acute, subacute, or chronic? Acute onset is seen in conditions such as infections (acute bacterial meningitis), vascular conditions (complication of cyanotic congenital heart disease, infective endocarditis, sickle cell disease), or traumatic events. Subacute presentations may be seen in partially treated bacterial meningitis, while chronic and insidious presentations are seen in tubercular meningoencephalitis (TBME) and intracranial space-occupying lesions (tumors, neurocysticercosis, neurodegenerative diseases, myopathies).

Onset of the Symptoms

Ask for sequence, duration, and the progress of symptoms. As an example, if a 2-year-old child presents with a high-grade fever of 1 day and seizures of few minutes' duration followed by 10 minutes of postictal altered sensorium and then regaining normalcy, the clinical diagnosis of febrile convulsions is extremely likely. But in another child of same age who presents with a fever of 3–4 days and persistence of altered sensorium with a single seizure of 10 minutes, there is a high probability of a CNS infection, which needs a prompt diagnosis and an immediate hospital admission and treatment. The most common presenting symptoms in children with CNS diseases are altered sensorium, convulsions, and paralysis or paresis.

Associated Complications

Associated complications should be thoroughly examined for. A child with TBME may have noncommunicating hydrocephalus at the time of presentation. A child may also have scholastic deterioration due to a progressive neurological condition such as degenerative diseases and epilepsy.

Prior Status

Information about the child being normal/abnormal prior to the illness in the aspects of past history, development, and scholastic performance is essential. A child with cerebral palsy would have developmental delay, while a child with autism would have prior history of speech delay and stereotyped repetitive behavior.

Evolution of the Disease

The disease being static, improving, progressive (or becoming worse), or episodic can provide important information about the disease. Cerebral palsy is a static insult to a growing brain while progressive neurological disorders are neurodegenerative diseases such as white matter disorders (e.g., leukodystrophies), gray matter diseases (mucopolysaccharidosis [MPS], progressive myoclonic epilepsies), extrapyramidal conditions (inborn errors of metabolism), and cerebellar disorders (ataxia telangiectasia). Patients with cerebral palsy would have developmental delay while patients with neurodegenerative disorders have a typical history of regression of acquired milestones. The examples of episodic illnesses in children are migraine and epilepsy.

Development and Neurological Status

Although the child's development and neurological examination are complementary to each other, it must be remembered that developmental assessment is the acquisition of new skills while neurological examination tends to ascertain the integrity of CNS and then to make a neuroanatomical diagnosis of the site of the abnormality.

Localization of the Lesion

This includes history suggesting involvement of higher cortical functions, cranial nerves, raised intracranial tension, cerebellum, or peripheral nervous system. This helps to narrow down the probable diagnosis and plan the investigations and therapy. This is discussed in the later part of the chapter to facilitate a better understanding.

Table 11.1 gives some examples of a combination of symptoms with probable clinical conditions.

Clinical Clues on History

- The history helps to decide about the site of the dysfunction. A child with seizures or altered sensorium represents involvement of cerebral cortex rather than involvement of nerves or muscles unless it is a combined lesion, which is seen quite rarely.
- The history of head injury, poisoning, drowning, drug overdose, and bites gives immediate clues for the diagnosis. Also inquire about history of fever, starvation,

TABLE 11.1 Symptomatology and Probable Clinical Conditions

Symptoms	Clinical conditions
Vomiting and severe headache with altered sensorium (drowsiness, irritability, or unconsciousness)	Raised intracranial pressure (ICP) or pseudotumor cerebri
Personality behavioral changes, reduced attention span, scholastic backwardness, regression of milestones	Progressive degenerative disease or some mass lesion
Abnormal movements, frequent falls, falling objects from the hands	Movement disorders, weakness (loss of muscle power), or ataxia
Difficulty in getting up from sitting position from the floor/climbing stairs	Proximal muscle weakness
Paucity of movements on one side of upper and lower limbs/both lower limbs	Hemiparesis/paraparesis/monoparesis
Root pains, paresthesia	Spinal cord, nerve roots, nerve pathology
Developmental delay in the form of "not yet learnt to sit, walk, speak, poor attention span, hyperactivity, slow learner"	Neurodevelopmental problems, e.g., cerebral palsy, mental retardation, attention deficit hyperactivity disorder
Back pain + bladder/bowel involvement	Spinal cord/nerve roots involvement

medication or trauma which could have precipitated the illness.

- Overdose of phenytoin or theophylline can give rise to seizures and improperly prepared oral rehydration solutions may result in hypernatremia in the young infants, giving rise to brain insults.
- The presence of any signs and symptoms suggestive of any systemic disease or other organs (infective endocarditis, hypertension, chronic liver disease) should be noted. A child with deep icterus and altered sensorium suggests acute fulminant liver failure.
- Recurrent paroxysmal events of similar types favor the diagnosis of epilepsy, migraine, and seizure mimics.

Perinatal History

Perinatal events such as intrauterine infections (TORCH), maternal illnesses (e.g., eclampsia), polyhydramnios/oligohydramnios, perinatal asphyxia, birth injury, prematurity/low birth weight, neonatal infections, neonatal seizures, neonatal hyperbilirubinemia, and malformations (e.g., spina bifida) are important aspects in neurological evaluation. Most of the congenital malformations involving the nervous system can now be identified with prenatal ultrasound imaging.

Developmental History

One should be aware of age-appropriate major milestones to identify the developmental delay and whether any area is affected specifically or globally. A well-elicited developmental history can help differentiate psychomotor retardation (developmental delay) from psychomotor regression. Here a child progressively loses the milestones and abilities he/she had achieved, and suggests the possibility of neurodegenerative disorders.

It may not be possible to complete a thorough developmental assessment due to time constraints but a good developmental history and a brief examination in developmental fields (gross and fine motor, social and language) should be carried out.

Immunization History

Encephalopathy following pertussis vaccine and demyelinating insult following influenza or rabies vaccine, though rare, can occur. Such history of vaccination should be obtained. History of childhood immunization is important as many of the childhood immunizations help in preventing diseases that can affect CNS and leave permanent sequelae. These include BCG vaccine that is known to prevent CNS tuberculosis, pertussis (encephalopathy), Hib (meningitis), and measles (viral encephalitis) in particular.

Family History

This is important and relevant for consanguineous marriages (autosomal recessive diseases) and diseases with multifactorial inheritance such as epilepsies, degenerative disorders, and migraine. History of contact with tuberculosis and HIV status of parents in relevant cases can prove to be extremely useful.

General Physical Examination

General examination can provide helpful clues for further neurological evaluation. It should include examination of general appearance, mental status, nutritional status, and posture of the child along with the anthropometry and vital parameters.

Detailed head-to-toe examination should be carried out, including head size and shape (microcephaly and macrocephaly), premature closure of sutures (craniosynostosis), neurocutaneous markers (café au lait spots, hypopigmented lesions), face and hair abnormalities, MPS, eye examination by slit lamp (Kayser–Fleischer ring for Wilson disease), cataracts (galactosemia and TORCH infections), and spinal abnormalities. Abnormalities/dysmorphic features should be looked for such as Down syndrome and MPS.

Neurological Examination

The neurological examination must be tailored according to the child's condition and age, and the setting where the evaluation is conducted. In a child with a history of recurrent seizures/epilepsy who is otherwise apparently looking and behaving normally, history may be more rewarding than examining for motor examination and sensory system. Additionally, the pattern and scheme of neurological examination can be modified for infants and toddlers while older children (>5 years of age and adolescents) can be examined in a traditional manner.

- Observation of the child during initial history taking unobtrusively yields important information such as general appearance, abnormal movements (e.g., tremors, tics), and gait. In general appearance, look at the young child for alertness, irritability, quality of cry, dull look, restlessness, anxious or sick look, color texture, response, hydration status, etc.
- Common instruments needed for CNS examination include torch, percussion hammer, measuring tapes, tuning forks, spatula, stethoscope, cotton wisps, and a red-colored ball.
- A broad scheme for neurological examination is shown in Box 11.6.

Box 11.6 Neurological examination for older children

- *Higher mental status*: General behavior, appearance, level of consciousness, orientation, speech and language, memory, cognition, and release reflexes
- *Cranial nerve examination*: First to 12th cranial nerves
- *Motor system*: Bulk of the muscles, tone of the muscles, power, coordination, abnormal/involuntary movements, and gait
- Superficial and deep reflexes
- *Sensory system*: Touch, pain, temperature, joint position, vibration, Romberg's sign, cortical sensation tests
- *Meningeal signs*: Neck rigidity, Kernig's sign
- *Cerebellar signs*: Tremors, truncal ataxia
- *Autonomic signs*: Hypertension, tache cerebrale, palmar erythema

Mental Status

Consciousness has two components: awareness (content) and arousability (wakefulness). One cannot check cognitive functions (content) of cerebrum if a child is not awake. In altered sensorium and/or coma, there is disturbance in the functioning of cerebral cortex and/or the reticular activating system of the brainstem. Altered sensorium is graded easily by using "AVPU" pediatric responsive scale (A, alert; V, response to voice; P, response to pain; U, unconscious), when one wants to evaluate a critical child in a short period of time. Glasgow Coma Scale (GCS) (with its modifications for children) is used for assessing the severity of coma in infants/children and is shown in Table 11.2.

In a conscious child, other higher functions such as orientation, memory, and cognitive abilities must be assessed depending on the age and the presenting condition of the child. The posture or the decubitus of the child should be noted and can be correlated with different neurological conditions (Table 11.3).

Higher Mental Functions

The testing of higher functions begins with a state of consciousness in the child, which means that the child is capable of perception of the self and the environment. To an extent, this also depends on the mental and the developmental status. In a younger child, it may be difficult to conduct an assessment of higher functions due to the presence of anxiety or lack of cooperation. For these reasons, the neurological examination in children younger than 5–6 years differs from a conventional approach like that done in adult neurological examination.

The spectrum of higher functions includes consciousness, cognition, memory, and

TABLE 11.2 Glasgow Coma Scale (GCS) for Children

Age (4–15 years)	Age (<4 years)	Score
Eye opening		
Spontaneous	Spontaneous	4
To verbal command	To speech	3
To pain	To pain	2
No response	No response	1
Best motor response (verbal command and painful stimulus)		
Obeys	Obeys or spontaneous	6
Localizes pain	Localizes pain	5
Withdrawal	Withdrawal	4
Abnormal flexion	Abnormal flexion (decorticate posture)	3
Extension	Extension (decerebrate posture)	2
No response	No response	1
Best verbal response		
Oriented and converses	Oriented to sounds, smiles appropriately	5
Disoriented and converses	Irritable cry, fewer words	4
Inappropriate words	Cries only on pain	3
Incomprehensible sounds	Moans or grunts to pain	2
No response	No response to pain	1

Note: Painful stimulus can be given either by a strong pinch or by applying pressure above the supratrochlear notch above the medial end of upper margin of the orbit. A score of GCS <8 indicates coma.

TABLE 11.3 Typical Postures in a Child with CNS Disease

Type	Location/conditions
Curled-up lateral position, hips and knees are flexed, neck extended, or head and neck arched backwards (due to inflamed meninges)	Meningitis/meningoencephalitis
Decorticate: Arms rigidly flexed over the body, lower limbs extended	Diffuse cerebral hemispheres
Decerebrate: All four limbs are rigidly extended and internally rotated. The head arches backward, toes point downward	Midbrain/upper pons
Opisthotonus: Rigid, arching the back with head thrown backward, hyperextension of the neck	• Tetanus, during tonic seizures, meningitis, encephalitis, kernicterus, infantile Gaucher disease, rabies • Brain tumor, severe head injury
Scissoring	Spastic quadriplegic, diplegic cerebral palsy
Hemiplegic: Upper limb flexion at elbow, wrist with internal rotation, hyperextension of lower limb of affected side	UMN—hemiplegia
Lordotic posture	Duchenne muscular dystrophy/other muscular dystrophies

CNS, central nervous system; *UMN*, upper motor neuron.

Box 11.7 Higher mental functions

- Consciousness
- Orientation
- Memory
- Intelligence
- Speech and language

speech/language assessment (Box 11.7). Given the pattern of neurological diseases in pediatrics, it may not be possible to evaluate all these components completely in certain children.

Consciousness

- Consciousness has two components: arousability (wakefulness) and awareness (content of consciousness, i.e., cognitive functions). Cognitive functions mean the construction of thought process that includes remembering, problem solving, and decision making, which evolves through childhood to adolescence to adulthood; an example of cognition is asking a 7-year-old child the following: What would you do if there is an outbreak of fire in your classroom at school? Cognition would involve remembering that fire is risky, solving the problem to use the fire extinguisher, and decision making in informing the fire brigade on phone.
- Other mental functions are tested in an alert, awake child. If the levels of arousal are reduced, then awareness is also reduced. One cannot evaluate awareness (content) in an unarousable/unconscious child.
- The normal state of consciousness comprises the state of wakefulness and awareness in which the child performs routine functions. A child is said to be in a vegetative state (coma vigil) when the child has spontaneous eye opening but is not aware of the surroundings and does not respond (e.g., after TBME, severe head injuries). This is due to diffuse bilateral cerebral dysfunction and is a state of wakeful unawareness.
- Altered states of consciousness have a variety of clinical stages depending upon the severity such as confusion, delirium, lethargy, obtundation, stupor, and coma.
- Altered level of consciousness may be due to diffuse dysfunction of the cerebral cortex, abnormality of the ascending reticular activating system located in the brainstem, or dysfunction of both.
- Lethargy is a state of drowsiness; the child is disinterested, has slower reaction to stimulation, and eyes are closed. In stupor, only vigorous and repeated stimuli arouse the child momentarily followed by an immediate relapse to the unresponsive state; it precedes coma. In stupor, the child can localize the pain and tries to remove the stimulus. In *coma*, one finds prolonged, profound unconsciousness (total unawareness), inability to arouse, and eyes are closed.
- In delirium, the child presents with confusion, disorientation with disordered thinking, delusions, motor restlessness, irritability, fearfulness, and sensory misperception in the form of hallucinations and illusions.
- Locked-in-syndrome is a condition in which child is unable to speak or move due to severe paralysis, but the child is fully conscious. So it is not an altered state of consciousness in true sense.
- AVPU pediatric response scale (which is not development dependent) and GCS are the two commonly used scales for clinical evaluation of coma. For children and infants, modified GCS is used that considers the normal phases of development in the earlier few years of life.
- GCS full-scale score gives the predictive value, is reliable, and is easily applied in traumatic and nontraumatic cases. Lesser the score, more is the risk of mortality or adverse neurological outcome.

Orientation to Time, Place, Person

The assessment of orientation should be age sensitive and questions should be tailored for the patient's age. It is important to ask age-appropriate questions, e.g., a 3- to 4-year-old alert child should be able to tell his/her name and gender, and identify his/her parents. An older child may be able to tell the names of few of his/her friends.

Memory

The evaluation of immediate, short-term, and long-term memory should be done systematically. Immediate memory is tested by naming three to four objects and asking the child to repeat the same shortly after. Short-term memory is tested by asking simple questions such as what the child had for breakfast in the morning of the same day or what homework he/she got the previous day. Long-term memory is tested by asking the child to tell a story, events, name of the school he/she is studying in, address of his/her house, names of his/her friends, telephone numbers, etc.

Intelligence

Judgment, reasoning, perception, abstract thinking, and vocabulary should be tested by asking age-appropriate simple questions. For an example, one can ask a 7-year-old child the following: What will you do if your friend falls from the bicycle and injures himself/herself? Formal assessment of IQ is time consuming and rigorous and is done by clinical psychologists particularly if the child has problems such as developmental delay, speech/language problems, seizure disorders, behavioral problems, and scholastic backwardness or/and has suffered from any significant CNS disease in the past.

Speech and Language

Speech should be evaluated for quality of voice, articulation, and language milestones should also be evaluated. Language includes testing speech, reading, and writing.

- Language is a system of words or signs that people use to express thoughts and feelings in the form of speech, gestures, sign language, or written symbols. Speech is a motor skill and consists of a system of oral sound sequence used to express inner language.
- Speech and handedness: Language is lateralized to the dominant hemisphere, which is generally the left hemisphere for a right-handed child and vice versa. Because of this, left hemispheric lesions frequently cause aphasia in right-handed individuals. Interestingly even amongst left-handed individuals, majority (70%) are still left hemisphere dominant, only 13% are right hemisphere dominant, and the remaining 17% are mixed.
- Loss of language: Aphasia/dysphasia means loss or impairment of language. This could be receptive (Wenicke's aphasia) or expressive (Broca's aphasia) or global. This should be differentiated from dysarthria (difficult or unclear articulation) and dysphonia (difficulty in speaking due to disorder of mouth, tongue, or vocal cords). Dysarthria or disturbances in articulation are suggestive of extrapyramidal disorders.
- Abnormality or absence of speech by 18 months of age and inability to make meaningful sentences by the age of 3 years is abnormal and indicates possibility of autism, mutism, or aphasia.

Cranial Nerves

- Examination of cranial nerves helps to localize the lesion.
- Sensory nerves may be difficult to examine in newborns, infants, children younger than 4–6 years, and uncooperative and mentally challenged children.
- Most cranial nerve nuclei are in the brainstem except the first and second cranial nerve nuclei.

- If a cranial nerve is affected, try to find out whether the lesion is of supranuclear (upper motor neuron [UMN]) or infranuclear (lower motor neuron [LMN]) type.
- The corticobulbar tract innervates cranial motor nuclei bilaterally except for lower facial part of VII cranial nerve, and XI and XII cranial nerves that are innervated unilaterally by the contralateral cortex.

Olfactory Nerve, I Cranial Nerve

Neonates, infants, and toddlers can detect olfactory stimuli and can express with facial expression but cannot express it verbally. Olfactory nerve is a purely sensory nerve and it is often not tested in routine CNS examination unless some problem is suspected. However, it can be tested in children above the age of 5 years by testing the ability to smell (with the eyes closed); a substance like peppermint or lime can be used separately for each nostril. Irritants should be avoided as they may stimulate the trigeminal nerve and give false impression of a sensation. Anosmia (absent) or reduced perception (hyposmia) can occur due to cribriform plate damage following meningitis and head injury.

Optic Nerve, II Cranial Nerve

Optic nerve is a sensory nerve. The testing for optic nerve involves five components as suggested in Box 11.8.

Visual acuity

- At birth, the vision is about 20/400 but matures to 20/20 by 12–24 months of age. The purpose of this examination is to find out the impairment of vision.

Box 11.8 Testing of optic nerve

- Visual acuity
- Color vision
- Field of vision
- Pupillary reactions
- Fundus examination

- Visual fields are clinically tested by the confrontation test and grossly by locating and reaching out for the objects. If a child can follow a moving object, it suggests that he/she has intact cortical vision.
- Menace reflex demonstrates gross vision and is done in infants, uncooperative, mentally subnormal children, and children in vegetative state. A finger is suddenly brought toward the patient's eye. Response is blinking of the eyes suggestive of grossly normal vision.
- Formal testing is done with a Snellen chart, which is possible in older and cooperative children.

Color vision

Color vision can be tested in children older than 3 years by using pseudoisochromatic charts of Ishihara. The Ishihara test is a diagnostic test of color perception for red–green color deficiencies and is carried out using pseudoisochromatic plates. A child gains the ability to recognize different colors around 18 months and starts noticing shapes, textures, and sizes. A child can name at least one color by the age of 3 years.

Field of vision

Visual field defects are labeled as homonymous when the same part of field is affected in both the eyes, e.g., a right homonymous hemianopia means that there is field defect in the temporal field of the right eye and the nasal field of the left eye, whereas a bitemporal hemianopia is a heteronymous visual field defect. Visual field is clinically tested by confrontation test.

Confrontation test

- Here the visual field of the child is compared with the visual field of the examiner.
- The examiner sits at about 50 cm distance and in front of the child (confront) (Fig. 11.1).
- Both eyes are tested separately and in all four quadrants.

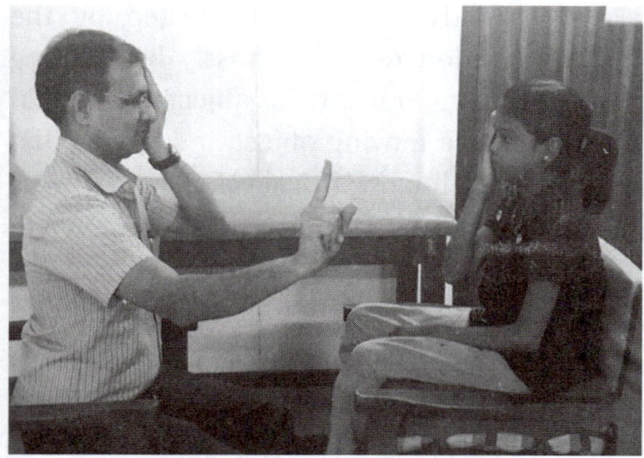

Figure 11.1 Confrontation test.

- For testing the child's left eye, his/her right eye should be occluded, and left eye of the examiner should be occluded.
- The child is asked to look directly into the examiner's eye.
- Examiner holds his/her finger outside his/her visual field in the middle of one quadrant and moves the finger slowly to the central field. The child is instructed to say "yes" when he/she starts seeing see the finger. A white or red pin of 10 mm can also be used instead of finger.
- If field defect is found clinically, the child should undergo a perimetry assessment by an ophthalmologist.

Pupillary reaction

- Testing for pupillary light reflex (both direct and consensual) should be done in a dimly lit or a dark room by shining the light suddenly with a torch from the side of the eye after asking a child to look at a distance (showing some attractive toy). Both the eyes are tested. The test is essential in children with coma, head injuries, brain tumors, and stroke. The reflex consists of optic nerve as afferent, center in pons (pretectal and Edinger–Westphal nucleus of oculomotor nerve), and the efferent being oculomotor nerve.
- *Direct reflex*: It shows constriction of the pupil in the same eye.
- *Consensual reflex*: Constriction of the pupil in the opposite eye is due to a bilateral innervation of Edinger–Westphal nucleus of the III nerve.

Fundus examination

It is a skilled task and is generally not required at basic level; a person trained to examine the fundus should be sought.

- Papilledema is suggestive of raised intracranial pressure and is a contraindication for lumbar puncture.
- Cherry red spot in retina is seen with storage disorders like Tay Sachs disease, Niemann Pick disease, and in central retinal artery occlusion.
- Other findings on fundus could be optic atrophy, retinal infarcts, or retinal hemorrhages.

Oculomotor, Trochlear, and Abducens Nerves (III, IV, and VI Cranial Nerves)

These are pure motor nerves and as they control the movements of the eyes (upper eyelid, eyeballs, and pupils), these are tested together.

- Inspect the eyelids for ptosis, position of the resting eyeball, squint, pupils, spontaneous movements of eye, nystagmus, or any other abnormal movements, e.g., opsoclonus.
- Movements of both the eyes when they move in the same direction together are referred to as conjugate eye movements and are controlled by the centers in the frontal lobe cortex, pons, and midbrain. Paralysis of these supranuclear regions gives rise to the supranuclear gaze palsies. In contrast, infranuclear lesions lead to paralysis of muscles of the eye or group of muscles.
- Conjugate movements are elicited by command, follow, or reflex doll's eye maneuver (in a comatose child, or in a newborn).
- Doll's eye phenomenon: After ruling out cervical spine injury in an unconscious

child, in this test, the head is rapidly rotated to one side; the eyes temporarily deviate to the opposite side. Both horizontal (turning head on right or left side) and vertical (head flexion or extension) conjugate eye movements can be tested. In a conscious child, the cerebrum would interfere with the doll's eye phenomenon.

- If brainstem is intact, the eye movement will be conjugate in the direction opposite to that of the head movement. Conjugated eye movements are absent in a lesion of brainstem or in the paths of supranuclear lesion. Associated motor paralysis and other cranial nerve affection help to locate the lesion, whether it is in the cortex or in the brainstem.
- All extraocular muscles except superior oblique (fourth cranial nerve) and lateral rectus muscles (sixth cranial nerve) are supplied by the third cranial nerve.
- The causes of palsies of these nerves include cerebral palsy, increased ICP (sixth nerve palsy as a false localizing sign), brainstem tumors, postmeningitis, and Guillain–Barré syndrome.
- An overview of third, fourth, and sixth cranial nerve assessment is shown in Box 11.9.

Box 11.9 Third, fourth, and sixth cranial nerves

- Check eyelids—ptosis and lag.
- Check pupils—size, shape, asymmetry, and reaction to light (direct, consensual) in dark/dim light. Check for accommodation reflex.
- The examiner moves the pointer (a pen or a finger) in all directions—right, left, horizontally, and vertically after fixing the head.
- Observe any failure to move fully in a particular direction/s, lag, diplopia, or nystagmus.
- Check for voluntary saccades and pursuit movements by performing the finger test.
- In cases of diplopia, first determine in which direction the double vision is greatest.

III nerve palsy

- Drooping of eyelids: Ipsilateral ptosis occurs due to involvement of levator palpebrae superioris muscle.
- Dilated pupil: The pupil on the affected side is fixed and dilated with loss of accommodation reflex.
- Divergent squint: The affected eye has loss of all movements except downwards and outwards due to unopposed action of the VI cranial nerve.
- Diplopia occurs.
- If third nerve palsy is associated with unconsciousness, it suggests temporal lobe (uncal) herniation due to raised ICP.
- Ptosis may also be present in Horner syndrome, but the ipsilateral pupil is small and reactive instead of being dilated. Ptosis without pupillary involvement is seen in ocular myasthenia and Miller Fisher syndrome, usually bilateral.

IV nerve palsy

- Isolated IV nerve palsy is rare.
- There is an upward deviation of the affected eye in the abducted position due to the unopposed action of inferior oblique muscle.
- Diplopia may occur on attempted downward gaze while climbing down the stairs.
- There may be compensatory torticollis.

VI nerve palsy

- Paralysis of lateral gaze (lateral movement) of the eye
- Convergent squint as the affected eye tends to deviate medially
- Diplopia on looking toward the affected side
- Compensatory torticollis

Trigeminal Nerve (V Cranial Nerve)

The fifth cranial nerve is a mixed nerve and is tested for its sensory components and motor components. Sensory component is responsible for the sensations of the face while motor component supplies the muscles of mastication.

Sensory component is tested for pain, touch, and temperature sensation over face. Its three branches are ophthalmic, maxillary, and mandibular nerves.

Follow the following general rules of testing sensory component of the V nerve:

- Eyes are closed.
- Lightly touch by a cotton wisp or nail polish brush.
- Touch both sides—scalp, cheek, and chin—at six areas (2 × 3) randomly.
- Test pain sensation by using a safety pin/toothpick point/some hammer that is having a needle and a brush.
- Test sensation of buccal mucosa by a spatula.
- In the children of younger age group, examine touch by tickling the nose and face with a piece of cotton: the child will respond by bringing the hand to the site of stimulation.
- Sometimes a sneeze is elicited when the nose is stimulated.
- Pain elicits withdrawal and crying in newborns and infants.

Interpretation: A normal child perceives sensations equally on both sides. If touch or pain sensation is impaired, test temperature by using cold and hot test tubes. The task is difficult in a young, uncooperative child.

Corneal reflex

- The test elicits sensations from the cornea in the ophthalmic division of the fifth cranial nerve and the motor part (efferent part) of the reflex is via both facial nerves to cause bilateral blinking normally. The test should be explained to the conscious child and should be performed in the end as the task is anxiety provoking in a child. Corneal reflex is a brainstem reflex and the center lies in pons.
- Before checking, ensure that the child is not wearing contact lenses.
- On looking up at the ceiling or other side, the cornea is touched on the lateral side with a sterile cotton wisp to avoid visual blink. Take care not to wipe or touch the central part of cornea as it can damage the cornea. Take care not to touch eyelashes or conjunctiva. Test on both the sides. Normal response consists of the child blinking bilaterally. If the fifth cranial nerve is affected, neither eye blinks as opposed to unilateral facial nerve involvement in which the normal eye blinks.
- Unilateral loss of corneal reflex with loss of pain sensation suggests V cranial nerve involvement.

Motor division

The motor division of the V cranial nerve innervates the muscles of mastication. Ask the child to clench his/her teeth and feel the bulk of masseter and temporalis muscles. Ask the child to open the mouth and to move lower jaw side to side to check for pterygoid muscles. Observe for the deviation of the jaw or asymmetry of muscle contraction. A unilateral lesion results in the deviation of the jaw to the affected side.

Jaw jerk

Fifth cranial nerve is both afferent and efferent for jaw jerk. To elicit, ask the child to slightly open the mouth. Place your finger over child's chin. Strike your finger with reflex hammer. Normally there is no appreciable movement or there is slight upward movement of jaw. Jaw jerk is exaggerated when there is clearly visible movement of the jaw (closure), indicating supranuclear lesion of trigeminal nerve. In nuclear or infranuclear lesions, jaw jerk is absent.

- Isolated affection of this nerve is uncommon. Involvement of the fifth cranial nerve is seen with other cranial nerves in conditions such as tuberculous meningoencephalitis, brainstem glioma, fracture of base of skull, herpes zoster, demyelinating conditions, and cavernous sinus thrombosis.

Facial Nerve (VII Cranial Nerve)

The facial nerve is mainly a motor nerve and has two divisions, namely, motor and sensory. The motor division supplies the muscles of facial expression of the whole of the face. The sensory division conveys the taste sensations from the anterior two-thirds of the tongue.

- Unilateral facial weakness is observed by the asymmetry of the face, with the loss of nasolabial fold, dropping of the corner of the mouth (orbicularis oris weakness), and drooling of the saliva (due to buccinator muscle weakness) on the affected side.
- Asking the child to wrinkle the forehead by looking upwards tests the frontalis muscle. If the muscle is paralyzed, then the child is unable to wrinkle his/her forehead.
- Ask the child to close the eyes and shut them tightly; the examiner tries to open them to test the orbicularis oculi. If the muscle is weak/paralyzed, then the child is unable to close the eyes. The weakness also manifests as a widened ipsilateral palpebral fissure.
- Asking the child to smile and show and clench the teeth can reveal the facial muscle weakness of orbicularis oris and levator angularis oris. In case of facial nerve paralysis, the affected side does not move out like the other/normal side and the nasolabial fold is obliterated on the affected side. The angle of mouth is also pulled toward the normal side.
- Ask the child to hold the air in the mouth; if there is facial nerve paralysis, then the air escapes through the ipsilateral side due to the weakness of buccinator muscle.
- These maneuvers are shown in Figure 11.2.
- In newborns and young children, the acts of smiling and crying provide a gross estimate of the function. Mouth pulling to the normal side with crying or smiling can be seen.
- Facial weakness can be due to lesion because of supranuclear causes (UMN) or due to nuclei, nerve, and muscles supplied by the seventh cranial nerve (LMN).
- In UMN lesion, upper part of the face will be spared so the wrinkling of the brow, eye closing, and blinking are unaffected, due to bilateral corticobulbar innervations.
- LMN lesion of the facial nerve (lesion from the facial nerve nucleus in the brainstem to anywhere along the nerve) affects the whole of the face, i.e., both the upper and lower halves on the ipsilateral side.
- In LMN lesion, one finds Bell's phenomenon: corneal reflex is lost, and weakness is accentuated when the child cries or smiles. It is seen on the same side of the lesion.
- As the facial nerve has a parasympathetic division, which supplies the lacrimal gland, and hence its affection, it can cause reduction in tears.
- Try to distinguish emotional movements from voluntary type in a supranuclear facial palsy lesion. In UMN lesion involving corticobulbar fibers, weakness is seen more on volitional movements but is seen less on emotional movements such as crying and smiling, which is called volitional facial palsy (a type of dissociated facial weakness).
- The sensory division supplies the taste sensation to the anterior two-thirds of the tongue, but it is rarely tested.

Common causes of unilateral facial nerve involvement

- *Unilateral UMN*: This includes lesions such as stroke, demyelination, and mass, and lesions at the cerebrum, cerebral peduncle, or upper pons at levels above facial nerve nuclei along with hemiplegia of the same side.
- *Bilateral UMN*, though rare, is seen in affection of corticobulbar tract involvement due to bilateral hemisphere affection as seen in progressive neurodegenerative disorders, bilateral strokes, either together or sequential, and severe head injury.
- *LMN*: Birth injury may occur due to forceps delivery, prolonged labor, Bell's palsy, meningitis, Kawasaki disease, vascular

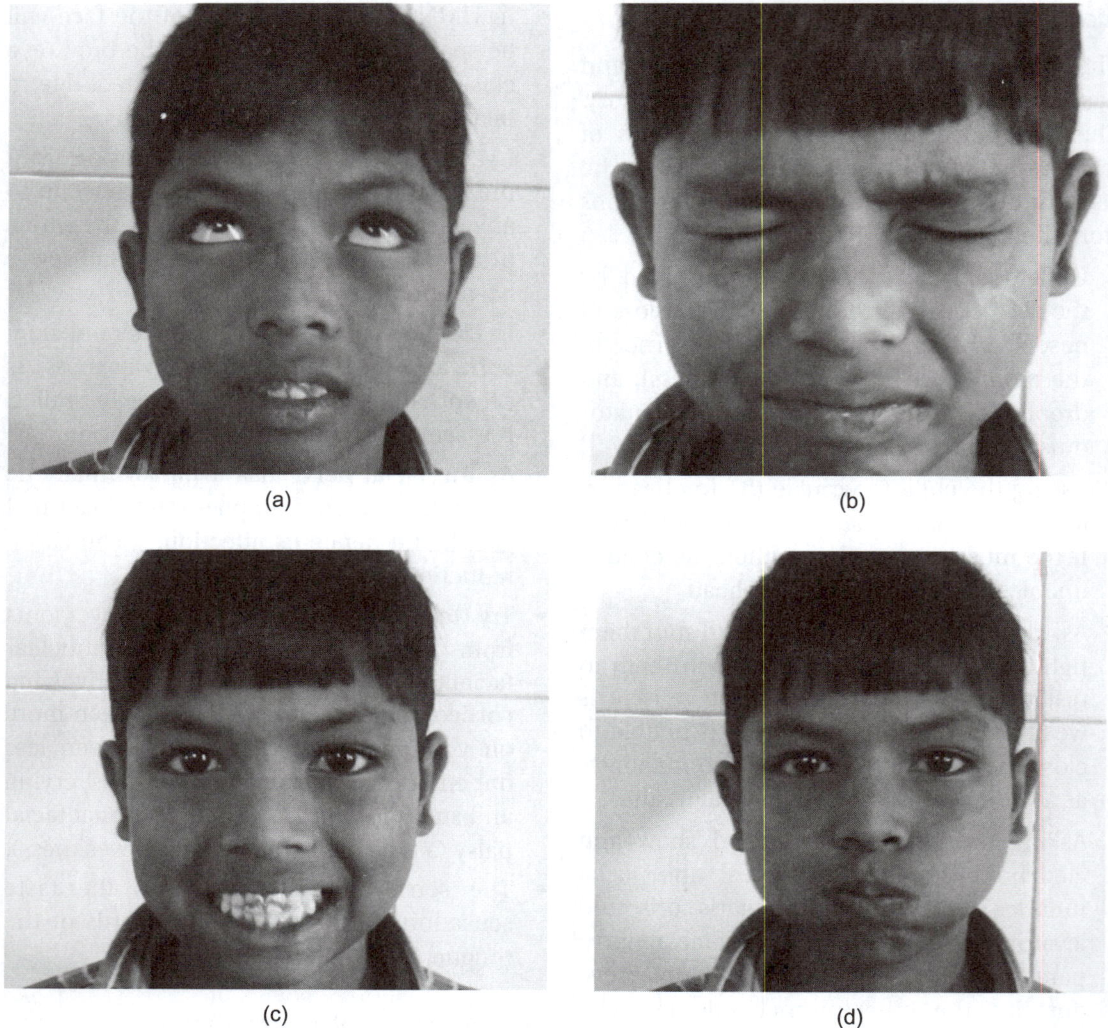

Figure 11.2 Testing the motor functions of facial nerve. (a) Testing for frontalis, (b) testing for orbicularis oculi, (c) testing for orbicularis oris, and (d) testing for buccinators.

accidents, tumor at pons, infection in the middle ear, trauma to parotid region, Guillain–Barré syndrome, myasthenia gravis, and Möbius syndrome.

- One should differentiate the seventh cranial nerve affection from the congenital absence of depressor angularis oris in which the corner of the mouth is moved toward the normal side and the lower lip moves downward and outward. Nasolabial fold will not be affected.

Vestibulocochlear/Auditory Nerve (VIII Cranial Nerve)

- Two divisions: Cochlear and vestibular components of this nerve are tested for hearing impairment and for equilibrium (labyrinthine function), respectively. This is a sensory nerve.
- *Vestibular function* is not tested routinely but in cases of dizziness, vertigo, nystagmus, and coma, patients are checked for intact brainstem. Caloric test may be done after confirming intact tympanic membrane.

- A rotational test may be done by keeping the child sitting erect, head tilted forward by 30°, and turning him/her several times (10 rounds in 20 seconds) in a full circle on a revolving chair. This test cannot test each ear individually. Observe deviation of the eyes and nystagmus.
- Normally, on rotation, the fast component of nystagmus is on the side of rotation and the slow phase of nystagmus is in the opposite direction. On stopping rotation, direction of fast and slow phases of nystagmus is reversed.

Hearing assessment

- Check tympanic membranes if hearing defect is suspected.
- Newborns respond to a loud sound by startle response, crying, or showing a changed behavior.
- An infant aged ≥3 months should be observed for turning to sounds produced by objects such as a bell or rattle. For an older child, observation is made by checking response to a ticking watch, finger rub, snapping the fingers with thumb, or whispers (commonly used words/numbers) used from behind the back of the child. The child should be asked to repeat the whispered words or numbers. Start snapping the fingers at 10 cm from the child's ear and ask him/her on which side the sound is heard.
- The sound stimulus should not be visible to the child. If the child does not respond, the tuning fork tests should be performed.
- Hearing loss in the very early period of life can affect speech.
- Rinne test and Weber test can be done by using a tuning fork of 256 Hz or higher to test hearing loss. Compare the hearing on both the sides.
- Rinne test: The tuning fork stem is held against the mastoid bone for testing bone conduction till the sound is not heard and then the vibrating end is held near the external ear of the same side for the air conduction test. Normally, air conduction is better than bone conduction; if a reverse of that relationship is found, it is suggestive of conduction abnormalities in the middle ear. In sensorineural affection, both air and bone conduction are reduced.
- Weber test: The stem of the vibrating tuning fork is placed at the vertex or glabella of forehead and the patient is asked to localize the sound, whether occurring in one ear or equally in both the ears. Normally, sound is heard equally in each ear. Lateralization of the sound to the side of decreased hearing indicates that it is a conductive hearing loss, while in nerve deafness, the sound is lateralized toward the normal side.
- Schwabach test: The child's hearing by bone conduction is compared with the examiner's hearing by placing the stem of a vibrating tuning fork against the child's mastoid process and then against the examiner's. If the examiner can hear the sound after the patient has stopped hearing it, then one can say that a hearing loss is present.
- If time is limited, it is not worth performing these tests and the child can be sent for audiometry if hearing impairment is suspected from history or by testing.
- For more detailed testing of hearing, brainstem auditory evoked potentials and audiometry may be needed in a child with hearing impairment. Hearing screening is mandatory in the high-risk-group babies and the goal is to identify hearing loss before 3 months of age.
- The risk factors for hearing loss/deficit in children include the following: preterm and/or low-birth-weight babies, particularly those less than 1500 g at birth, hyperbilirubinemia needing exchange transfusion, craniofacial anomalies, perinatal asphyxia (severe)/birth trauma, congenital rubella, cytomegalovirus, other perinatal infections, bacterial meningitis, ototoxic drugs such as aminoglycosides, and genetic and familial causes.

Glossopharyngeal and Vagus Nerves (IX and X Cranial Nerves)

- Glossopharyngeal nerve carries the sensation from nasopharynx and taste sensation from posterior one-third of tongue (not tested) and the motor part of this nerve supplies the stylopharyngeus muscle for swallowing. Vagus nerve controls the pharyngeal constrictor action, palate elevation, and vocal cord action and carries a part of sensation in the external ear canal, pinna, and behind ear (overlapped from other cranial nerves—V, VII, IX).
- Both the nerves are tested together by inducing the gag reflex and observing the symmetrical retraction of soft palate.
- Ask the child to open his/her mouth. By throwing light with a torch and depressing the tongue (as with the throat/tonsils examination), examine the soft palate movements by watching the uvula while saying "Ah." Palate should move upwards and backwards equally on both the sides.
- The gag response demonstrates contraction of the pharyngeal musculature, brief elevation of the soft palate, and elevation of the tongue. The child may get the sensation of retching. Look whether it is equal on both the sides. The response is consensual, meaning that the soft palate is elevated and symmetrical, regardless of the side touched. Absent reflex suggests peripheral nerve involvement. The afferent limb of the gag reflex is mediated through IX cranial nerve and the efferent is through IX and X cranial nerves.
- Next, ask the child to cough. Weak cough indicates that the vocal cords are affected.
- Hoarseness of voice, stridor, nasal regurgitation, nasal quality of voice or difficulty with guttural sounds, drooling, and difficulty in swallowing and whispering are important clinical clues to indicate the involvement of these nerves.
- In newborns and infants, look for swallowing and gag reflex.
- In unilateral IX cranial nerve involvement, there will be no response on touching the affected side. In unilateral vagus nerve affection, regardless of which side of the pharynx is touched, the palate fails to rise, and the uvula deviates toward the normal side during palatal movements.
- Isolated involvement of the IX cranial nerve is rare, but unilateral X cranial nerve involvement produces weakness of soft palate on the same side and hoarseness of the voice due to vocal cord palsy.
- Common conditions affecting these nerves are diphtheria, botulism, bulbar palsy variant of Guillain–Barré syndrome, polio-like illness due to non-polio viruses, posterior fossa tumors, trauma, demyelinating diseases, encephalitis, TBME, and Mobius syndrome.
- A child can be said to have bulbar palsy if the bulbar nerves (9th to 12th cranial nerves from medulla) are involved, and pseudobulbar palsy if there is bilateral involvement of corticobulbar fibers to bulbar nuclei presenting with exaggerated gag reflex seen with spastic quadriplegic cerebral palsy, high brainstem tumors, severe head injury, encephalitis, infantile Gaucher disease, and neurodegenerative disorders.

Spinal Accessory Nerve (XI Cranial Nerve)

- Spinal nerve (pure motor) supplies trapezius and sternocleidomastoid muscle.
- The nerve is tested by asking the child to shrug/lift the shoulders and feeling for the contraction/strength of the trapezius. If the muscle is affected, then the child is unable to perform this action.
- Another test is to place one hand against the right side of the child's face. Ask the child to turn the head against the hand; the left contracting muscle will stand out at the same time and can be palpated. Compare on both the sides. Another way to test this muscle from both the sides simultaneously is by placing a hand on the child's forehead,

asking him/her to bend forward, and observing the prominence of the muscle on both sides. Function of this muscle is to rotate the head to the opposite side.

- In the newborn, sternomastoid strength can be indirectly evaluated by observing head flexion on the traction response, by observing the resting head posture, and by spontaneous head rotation.
- Involvement is seen in dystrophies, spinal muscular atrophies (SMAs), polyneuropathy, poliomyelitis or polio-like illness due to non-polio viruses, and myasthenia gravis.

Hypoglossal Motor Nerve (XIIth Cranial Nerve)

- The XII cranial nerve supplies the muscles of the tongue and is a motor nerve. It can be examined by observing the tongue in resting position on the floor of the mouth followed by asking the child to protrude the tongue from the mouth.
- Look for fasciculations (muscular twitching involving the simultaneous contraction of contiguous groups of muscle fibers), atrophy, asymmetry, and any deviation.
- Look for movement by asking the child to move the tongue in and out, push the tongue side to side against the cheek, and produce lingual speech sounds.
- If the nerve is affected on one side, the protruded tongue will deviate to the same side of weakness. It is due to unopposed action of normal genioglossus muscle to push the tongue to the opposite side. In bilateral affection, protrusion of tongue is weak/absent. UMN lesions of the XII cranial nerve are extremely rare and may be seen in conditions such as cerebral palsy.
- Fasciculation in the tongue is seen in SMA.

Motor System Examination

The components for examination of the motor system include bulk of the muscles, tone, power of the muscles, and testing for coordination and involuntary movements.

Informal examination of posture and spontaneous movements (gross and fine motor), handedness, gait disturbances, presence of involuntary movements, limb growth retardation or deformity, localized or generalized wasting, and localized or generalized hypertrophy of the muscles should be done before formal testing for confirmation.

Muscle Bulk

Motor system examination should begin with the observation of the bulk of the muscle. Consider the patient's age, built, constitution, and obesity before examining the muscle bulk. The bulk may be difficult to assess in healthy infants and toddlers as they have a large amount of subcutaneous fat.

- Put the limbs in the symmetrical position and look for the atrophy (wasting) of the muscle(s) by inspection and palpation to check which muscles are smaller and floppy on contraction.
- Measure the circumference of the muscle(s) that represents maximum bulk, not crossing the joints and at clearly stated points with reference to a bony prominence, e.g., 10 cm above the medial malleolus of lower end of tibia, and compare both the sides.
- Difference of 1 cm in muscle girth or limb length is significant.
- The loss of muscle bulk (atrophy/wasting) may be due to LMN disease or disuse atrophy, or may be a part of generalized wasting. Wasting is more marked in proximal muscles in muscular dystrophies and poliomyelitis, while it is seen more markedly in distal muscles in peripheral neuropathies.
- Localized muscle wasting is an important finding for the neurological conditions such as nerve injuries, old poliomyelitis, old spastic hemiplegia, and spina bifida.
- Hypertrophy of the muscles can be either localized or generalized, and may be true of pseudohypertrophy. Pseudohypertrophy is seen in Duchenne muscular dystrophy and Becker muscular dystrophy involving

calves. Generalized hypertrophy is seen in myotonia congenita and in Kocher–Debre–Semelaigne syndrome (syndrome comprising pseudohypertrophy of muscles and hypothyroidism).

Muscle Tone

Muscle tone is the resistance to passive stretching and movement when the muscle is at rest. It can be normal, increased, or decreased. If the tone is reduced or increased, it is called hypotonia and hypertonia, respectively. It is essential to differentiate hypotonia and increased mobility due to neurological causes from hyperextensibility of joints due to non-neurological causes.

Testing of muscle tone can be done with inspection, palpation, and measuring range of movements.

- *Inspection*: A limb with an increased tone may be held in an abnormal posture, for example, a spastic upper limb is held adducted against the trunk and even flexed at the elbow as is seen in a patient with spastic hemiplegia. Hypertonic lower limbs are often circumducted at hip and adducted due to the adductor spasm of thigh muscles. A frog-like posture of lower limbs (semiflexed and abducted) indicates hypotonia.
- *Palpation*: Palpating the muscle gives an impression about the tone and whether it is normal or loose (hypotonia) or stiff (hypertonia).
- *Range of movements*:
  - The testing for muscle tone is done by putting the major joints through their full range of movements and noting whether the full movements are possible or not.
  - Resistance to passive movements is tested and noted by asking the child to relax and not resist voluntarily. If the child is unable to completely relax, the attention may be diverted by talking or asking some questions.
  - Passive movements of the major joints in the upper limb (elbow and wrist) and the lower limb (knee and ankle) are conventional and reliable methods of testing for tone. Difference in the tone is noted at each joint and compared with normal.
- Tone can also be decreased by certain drugs (e.g., diazepam, midazolam), severe malnutrition, electrolyte imbalances, and systemic illnesses, e.g., renal tubular acidosis. It may also be increased falsely due to anxiety or pain.
- In addition, presence of reduced tone/hypotonia is seen in LMN lesions (e.g., Guillain–Barré syndrome, spinal shock, and cerebellar/basal ganglia lesions, e.g., rheumatic chorea).

Difficulties and fallacies in eliciting the tone

- Children are often frightened to get themselves tested and fail to relax the muscles. Once a child gets convinced that it is painless and harmless, re-examination may be permitted by him/her.
- Minor degree of hypotonia is difficult to interpret.
- Voluntary resistance is commonly encountered, and misinterpreted as increased tone.
- If contractures are present, the tone is difficult to assess.
- Involuntary movements interfere in eliciting the tone and at times it is found to be variable.

Types of hypertonia

Hypertonia can either be clasp knife spasticity which results from pyramidal tract lesions or lead pipe/cog wheel rigidity which results from extrapyramidal lesions.

- *Clasp-knife spasticity*: There is initial resistance to a fairly rapid passive movement with sudden giving way toward the end of the movement (flexion or extension). This is a velocity-dependent resistance to the muscle stretch; if the passive movement is performed slowly, there may be a little resistance, but if the movements are done quickly, then an increased resistance is perceived easily. The muscles at rest do not have excessive tone but any brisk stretch of a muscle group will result in a "catch" at about mid-length of the muscle followed by a sudden release of the catch and relaxation of the muscle. The last two components, the catch and the release, have been likened to a closing pen knife, which is the origin of the term "clasp-knife" spasticity. Spasticity is felt easily in the flexor group of muscles of the arms and the extensors of the leg.

- *Rigidity*: There is equal resistance in agonist and antagonist muscle groups at any point giving rise to same degree of hypertonia on passive movements. It is not velocity dependent. Rigidity is classically described as *cogwheel* if the resistance noted is stepwise or as *lead pipe* if the resistance noted is uniform to passive movement.

Apart from the tone disturbances in limbs, tone can also be assessed in the trunk by observing whether there is head/neck lag when the child is pulled to sit from supine position or if the infant slips from the examiner's hands in axillary suspension suggesting hypotonia.

Muscle Power

Power is defined as the force of contraction that can be generated by an active contraction of each muscle or muscle group. Power (strength) can be judged in an older child by the methods described next and is graded on a scale of 0–5 as described in Box 11.10.

Box 11.10 Grades of muscle power by the Medical Research Council

- *0*: No contraction/movement
- *1*: Flicker or trace of contraction present
- *2*: Active movement with gravity eliminated
- *3*: Active movement against gravity
- *4*: Active movement against gravity and some resistance
- *5*: Normal power

Examining muscle power

- Individual muscle or muscle groups should be formally tested in children above the age of 5–6 years.
- In clinical practice, individual muscles are difficult to examine.
- Informal testing of muscle strength can be done by observing the child if he/she is ambulatory and playing with a ball, transferring the object from one hand to other, walking, running, jumping, hopping, getting up from supine to sitting position and from sitting to standing, or climbing steps.
- In toddlers and in preschool children, sometimes the strength is observed by taking some object (toy) away from the child. Children often resist giving away an object that they are holding.
- Identify age-related motor milestones.
- In older children, muscle strength can be tested by two ways (active and passive).
- Give commands with gesture to save time.
- Start distally, move proximally, and compare the two sides.
- Account the patient's age, to say as "normal" power.

The child is asked to perform a movement (e.g., flexion, extension, supination, pronation) by contracting a group of muscles at a specific joint using maximum power while the examiner tries to prevent it by using a greater force. For example, ask the child to flex the elbow, and the examiner will try to prevent that movement.

In this method, the group of muscles are put in the final position by completing the movement; a child is asked to maintain the same position while the examiner tries to oppose that motion. For example, here the child keeps the elbow flexed and tries to keep it flexed while the examiner tries to extend it. Each movement (function) should be tested against resistance.

Muscle power is tested at all major and small joints, testing all movements occurring at that joint. Testing movements means testing a group of several muscles at a time.

After checking the position, the patient must be told to do the specific movement by demonstrating it to him/her, e.g., flexing elbow. It must be in an extended position before. Ask the patient to flex it, and then ask to repeat with resistance. Few of the tests for determining muscle power are given as follows:

- The test for biceps in upper limb is done by asking the child to flex the elbow with his/her palm facing upwards. In contrast, triceps can be tested by asking the child to extend the arm.
- Asking the child to raise arms above the head tests the deltoid muscle.
- The test for quadriceps is to ask the child to extend the knee while he/she is sitting on the edge of the bed.
- When the child pushes down the examiner's palm with the sole of the foot, it tests the power of gastrocnemius and soleus muscles.
- The ability to stand up from the lying down posture requires good power in both the pelvic girdle and leg muscles.
- Identify muscle weakness and try to find out whether it is UMN or LMN type. Identify neurological deficit (mono, hemi, para, quadriplegia/paresis) after combining with other abnormal neurological findings.
- In a comatose child, raise both arms and let them fall back; this is followed by checking the legs by flexing the knee with soles of feet touching the bed together, and then letting them fall back. Observe the difference. Paralyzed limb(s) will fall rapidly than normal limb.
- Gower sign is elicited to test proximal weakness of pelvic girdle muscles and muscles of lower limbs by asking the child to get up from a prone position or squatting position. The child uses his own hands as support, and "climbs on himself" to get into an upright position. This sign is typically positive in Duchenne muscular dystrophy.

Coordination

- Coordination is not only a part of motor testing but also a combined function and outcome of smooth and correct movements for a definitive act made possible by intact motor and sensory systems including muscle function, cerebellar function, sensory system, and proprioception.
- Incoordination is seen in pyramidal and extrapyramidal disorders of motor control, sensory system involvement, and cerebellar disorders. Ataxia is the commonest manifestation of incoordination, which results due to affection of cerebellum and the paths involved, e.g., cerebellar ataxia, or due to altered proprioceptive sensations (sensory ataxia).
- To test coordination, one judges speed, rhythm, and accuracy of repetitive movements.
- Coordination is informally tested in the limbs and trunk by observing the gait during walking, playing, buttoning/unbuttoning, wearing shoes, writing, and drinking water with a glass or eating with a spoon.
- In a child aged 6 years and beyond, it is tested formally.
- Besides cerebellar diseases, coordination can also be impaired by poor visual acuity and sensory losses.

Coordination testing in upper limbs

Finger-to-nose test is the test of choice for checking coordination in upper limbs. Ask the patient to fully extend and abduct the arm and then to touch the tip of his/her own nose rapidly with the index finger with hand position in midprone. Observations are made of the accuracy with which the tip of the nose is touched by the child. This test should be done from both sides with eyes open and closed. This is followed by the nose–finger–nose test, in which the second target (point to be touched) is the tip of the examiner's finger. By doing this test, one can also find tremors. In cerebellar disease, the child overshoots the tip of nose. If this test is abnormal, look for other cerebellar signs.

It is a soft neurological sign that may not be correctly performed by a child up to 7 years of age. Informally, for a child aged between 1 and 6 years, some attractive object or torch may be used as a target to do this test.

Dysdiadochokinesis is the inability to perform rapid alternative movements (such as pronating and supinating the forearm quickly) and it is indicative of a cerebellar lesion.

Coordination in lower limbs

Heel-to-shin(-knee) test is most commonly performed when the patient is lying on the bed in a supine position. The patient is asked to raise one leg and bring the heel of the foot of that leg down accurately onto the knee of the resting leg and, after touching it, move the heel smoothly down the shin to the foot and back again. In cerebellar disease, the heel may overshoot the knee, movements will be slow and irregular, and the heel may fall off the shin. Ask the patient to repeat this test with eyes closed for evaluation for sensory ataxia.

Other tests for testing coordination in lower limbs such as Romberg test and tandem walking (walking on a straight line with one leg in front of other) can be performed after due consideration of physiological variation up to a certain age.

Involuntary Movements

These may be physiological such as shivering, sleep myoclonus, or pathological, originating from extrapyramidal system or due to involvement of other parts of the CNS. Involuntary movement caused by involvement of extrapyramidal system almost disappears during sleep and may present with variable tone or posture.

Observe the movements in the state of wakefulness, at rest, and during voluntary actions. Often parents capture videos of these movements if they occur infrequently or intermittently. The different types of involuntary movements are as follows:

- *Chorea*: These are rapid, sudden, and jerky movements, nonrepetitive and quasi-purposive, which may be generalized or one sided (hemichorea). These involve the proximal joints more than the distal joints and increase with stress and anxiety but disappear during sleep. The causes of chorea include rheumatic fever (Sydenham chorea), side effect of anticonvulsant drugs, Wilson disease, and Huntington chorea. The le on is in the caudate nucleus.
- *At etosis*: These are slow, involuntary, nonrhythmic writhing movements of axial rotation with hyperextension in the limbs. These are due to the involvement of basal ganglia and can be caused by rheumatic fever and Wilson disease. The lesion is in the putamen.
- *Ballismus*: These are rapid, violent, flinging, repetitive, and irregular movements affecting proximal joints and have a constant location, commonly presenting proximally at shoulders and hips. Unilateral ballismus (hemiballismus) is common with the lesions in contralateral subthalamic nucleus.
- *Dystonia*: These movements are spontaneous and involuntary sustained muscle contractions that force the affected parts of the body into abnormal twisted movements and posture, sometimes with co-contraction of agonist and antagonist muscles. These are rapid with slow relaxation. These occur due to involvement of the extrapyramidal system.
- *Tremors*: These are involuntary, very rhythmic, to-and-fro, alternating movements that resemble trembling movements or continued oscillations. These may happen at rest or when the child is reaching out to objects (intentional tremors of cerebellar disease). These can also be caused by anxiety, hyperthyroidism, or drugs such as salbutamol.

- *Tics*: These are seen in face, neck, and shoulder regions and are habit spasms and thus do not interfere with voluntary movements. They are stereotyped, repetitive, rapid, transient at the same location or restricted to a muscle group, and increased by stress. These manifest as head nodding, frequent eye blinking, or shoulder jerking.
- *Myoclonus*: It is a very sudden, rapid, jerk-like, and often repetitive contraction of a single muscle or a small muscle group. This may be generalized, localized, or flexion spasm of myoclonic epilepsy.
- *Fasciculations*: These are rapid involuntary contractions of one or more units of muscle and are visible just as a flicker on the skin. These are caused by inflamed, degenerating anterior horn cells.

Examination of Reflexes

- The reflexes are grouped as primitive reflexes (originate from the more primitive parts such as brainstem), superficial reflexes (cutaneous), and deep reflexes (tendon stretch).
- Reflex is an involuntary motor response to a sensory stimulus or muscle stretch. For the elicitation of a reflex, the spinal reflex arc should be intact. Spinal reflex arc is formed of receptors, afferent nerve fibers carrying signals from the sensory limb, an integrating center (link to motor neurons), efferent nerve fibers carrying signals from the anterior horn cells to the muscle, and the effector muscle innervated by the efferent nerve fibers that carries out the response.
- Primitive reflexes are also called developmental reflexes that are included in Chapter 7 "The Neonate." The significance of these reflexes is that most reflexes appear at birth and they disappear with time or are replaced by voluntary movements as the cortical control occurs. Persistence of these reflexes is the early marker of cerebral palsy/cortical dysfunction. Absence of primitive reflexes at the time of birth is also considered abnormal.

Deep Tendon Reflexes

- These are also known as stretch reflexes. When a normal muscle is passively stretched, its fibers resist stretching by contracting. Exaggerated DTRs (grade 3 or 4) are seen with UMN lesions such as cerebral palsy (which may present as spastic quadriplegia, hemiplegia, diplegia), cerebrovascular stroke, CNS trauma, and spinal cord lesions (demyelination, compressive pathologies). Exaggerated deep tendon reflexes (DTRs) are usually associated with other findings of UMN lesions such as spasticity, extensor planter response, and paralysis. In hypotonic cerebral palsy, the deep tendon reflexes (DTRs) are exaggerated even in the presence of hypotonia. Exaggerated reflexes sometimes may be normally seen in an anxious child. Pendular knee jerk may be observed in cerebellar lesions. Absent or diminished reflexes may be observed in LMN lesions like neuropathies, Guillain–Barré syndrome, spinomuscular atrophy, and in a state of spinal shock. In absence of other abnormal findings, sometimes symmetrical hypoactive grade I reflex may be considered normal.

  Important points to be noted while eliciting the DTRs:
- The child should be comfortable, relaxed, and properly positioned and the area to be examined should be properly exposed.
- By performing the test, one can find out whether the reflex is normal, absent, or exaggerated and it may be graded accordingly.
- Certain points should be observed such as position of the limbs to be examined, position of the examiner's hand, force of the stroke, place of the stroke, movements at the wrist, and holding of a hammer. The hammer strike should be quick, crisp, sudden, and forceful as necessary. Palpate the tendon for the correct point. Reflexes

should be tested on both the sides and compared simultaneously.

- Look at the contraction of the muscle and not only at the movement at the joint.
- Use of reinforcement methods (such as Jendrassik maneuver) is done if the reflex (knee jerk) is not elicitable. Here the child is asked to hook his/her hands together with flexed fingers and pull them apart as hard as possible and then the DTR is tested.
- The grading of DTRs is shown in Table 11.4.
- The methods of eliciting the DTR and their normal responses are shown in Table 11.5.
- Figures 11.3 and 11.4 illustrate the methods of eliciting the DTRs.
- In infants, the predominant flexor tone of early infancy makes the elicitation of triceps and ankle jerk difficult. The knee jerks are most easy to elicit and the triceps most difficult to elicit in children.
- Knee jerk can also be elicited by another way by asking the child to sit at the edge of a table supporting upper leg with the hand beneath the knee, knee flexed at 90° hanging loosely, keeping one hand on the quadriceps

TABLE 11.4 Grading of Deep Tendon Reflexes

Grades	Reflex
0	Absent
+1	Present but diminished
+2	Normal response
+3	Brisk/exaggerated/hyperactive
+4	Markedly hyperactive with clonus present

TABLE 11.5 Method of Elicitation of Some Important Deep Reflexes and Their Normal Response(s)

Name of the reflex	Spinal nerve roots	Method	Interpretation of normal response
Biceps	C5–C6	The patient's arm should be partially flexed at the elbow. Percuss with hammer on a finger placed over the biceps tendon in the antecubital fossa	Visible contraction of biceps muscle or flexion of the elbow
Triceps	C7–C8	If the patient is lying down, flex arm at elbow up to 90° and hold it close to chest or if the patient is sitting, keep the arm by the side of the body. Percuss the triceps tendon directly above the elbow	Visible contraction of triceps muscle or extension of the elbow
Supinator reflex (brachioradialis)	C5–C6	Flex the child's arm and rest his/her slightly pronated forearm on your forearm. Strike 1–2 inches above the wrist	Supination and flexion of the forearm, contraction of brachioradialis
Knee reflex (patellar)	L3–L4	If the patient is lying down, flex his/her knee. The knee should be at an angle of around 130°. Keep your one hand below both knees, supported by forearm, and percuss the tendon (not patella) directly with hammer	Note contraction of the quadriceps and extension of the knee. In an infant up to 6–7 months old, one may find crossed adductor response (adduction of other extremity)
Ankle reflex (Achilles)	S1–S2	Externally rotated the legs of the child, with knee and hip slightly flexed. Dorsiflex foot at ankle. Percuss Achilles tendon	Look for plantar flexion at the ankle and contraction of the calf muscle

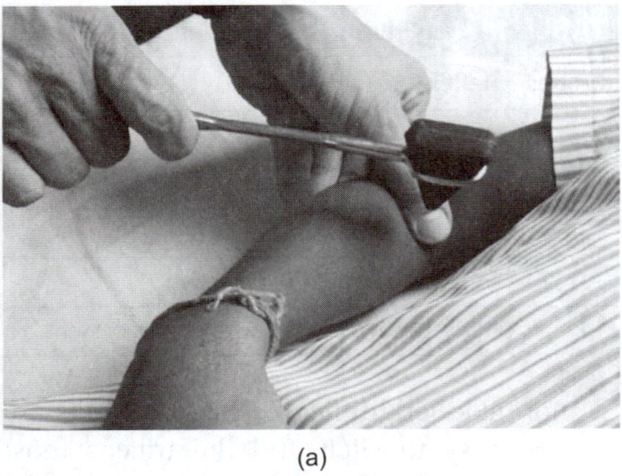

(a)

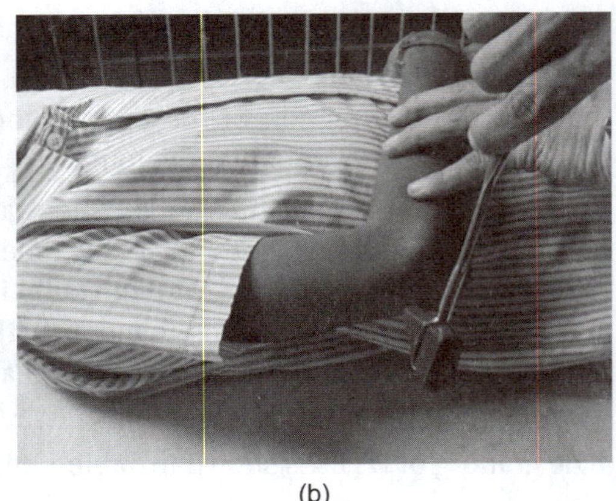

(b)

Figure 11.3 (a) Biceps reflex and (b) triceps reflex.

(a)

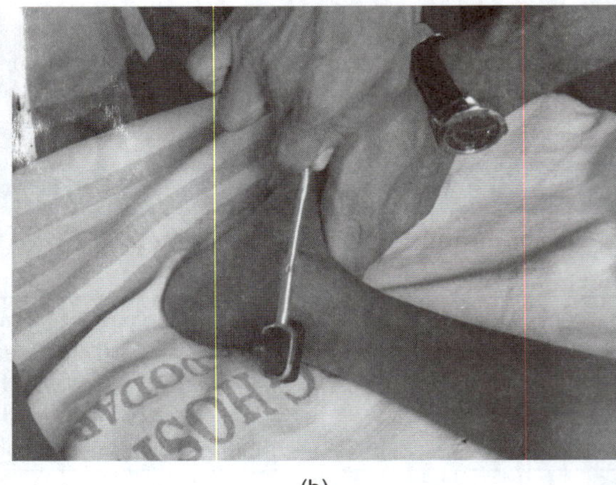

(b)

Figure 11.4 (a) Knee reflex and (b) ankle reflex.

so that the contraction can be felt, and percussing the tendon.

- Ankle clonus is elicited by bending a knee in a partly flexed position, Take the foot in your hand at the distal end and quickly dorsiflex with finger/s and maintain in the same position. Look for the rhythmic oscillations at the ankle joint. More than six beats or oscillations are termed sustained clonus.
- Clonus is a reflex response that indicates UMN lesion. Bilateral ill-sustained clonus may sometimes be normally seen in the newborns or in the young infants.
- Patellar clonus is elicited in a supine child and with extended lower limbs. The upper end of patella should be grasped with one end while the other hand should steady and fix the leg below the knee joint. A brisk downward thrust to the upper end of patella can lead to rapid patellar movements if the reflex is positive.
- The interpretation of DTR should be done in light of other findings of UMN lesion such as spasticity and plantar extensor response. DTR may also be transiently absent in spinal shock due to UMN lesion, but the plantar response remains extensor.
- *Hoffman sign*: It is one of the latent reflexes that appear in spasticity as in cases of corticospinal tract lesions. Hold the child's hand at the wrist with the palm facing downwards and hanging loosely. The tip of

middle finger is grasped with the examiner's thumb and index finger and the nail of the middle finger is given a snap with the examiner's thumb. The normal response is the absence of any thumb movement but in pyramidal tract lesion, there is flexion of the thumb in the palm.

Superficial Reflexes

- Superficial reflexes include corneal and conjunctival reflex, the abdominal reflex, cremasteric reflex, anal reflex, and plantar reflex. These are described in Table 11.6. Superficial reflexes (polysynaptic reflexes) are diminished or lost in UMN lesions and planter response is extensor. Superficial reflexes are different from muscle stretch reflexes in that the sensory signal has to not only reach the spinal cord, but also the brain. The motor limb then has to descend the spinal cord to reach the motor neurones. These reflexes are therefore lost in conditions that interrupt the pathways between brain and spinal cord and in case of any breach of the reflex arc affecting nerve or muscle.

Sensory System Examination

Sensory system examination is a difficult part of the CNS examination as the tests are subjective and require cooperation from the child and hence a detailed sensory examination may not be possible to perform in every patient.

- Patient may have history of loss of all sensations (anesthesia), exaggerated sensation (hyperesthesia), abnormal pain sensation (dysesthesia), or perverted

TABLE 11.6 Some Important Superficial Reflexes and Their Normal Response(s)

Name of the reflex	Spinal nerve roots	Method	Interpretation of normal response
Abdominal reflex*	T6–T12	Stroke the skin lightly over the abdomen from lateral to medial side with a key or blunt end of hammer across all quadrants	Underlying muscle contracts and umbilicus will move in that direction
Plantar reflex†	L5–S1	Stroking the lateral aspect of the sole from heel to little toe, and then medially from the base of the toes to the big toe with the tip of a hammer	• Flexor plantar response; plantar flexion of the great toe; often accompanied by flexion and adduction of other toes • Extensor planter response; extension (dorsiflexion) of the great toe, often with extension and abduction ("fanning") of the other toes. This is also called as Babinski response. Remember planter reflex may be normally extensor in infants, however assymetric response should be considered abnormal.
Cremasteric reflex (in males)	L1–L2	Stroke a line along the medial aspect of upper thigh, watching the movement of the scrotum	Elevation of testis on the same side
Anal reflex	S3–S4	Stroking the perianal area	Contraction of the anal sphincter

*Abdominal reflexes when absent with brisk deep tendon reflexes are seen in pyramidal tract lesions. In contrast, the retention of upper abdominal reflexes and the loss of lower abdominal reflexes indicate the level of spinal lesion.

†Gordon sign: Squeezing the calf muscles and noting the response of great toe in plantar reflex can also be performed and the fanning of the great toe is considered as abnormal.

sensations such as tingling, numbness, burning (paresthesia). If involvement of peripheral nerve, sensory root, spinal cord, thalamus, or sensory cortex lesion is suspected, a thorough sensory examination should be carried out. This may help to identify the location of the lesion.

- Peripheral neuropathy is the most common cause of sensory loss in children. All the sensations travel via peripheral nerves and sensory root to spinal cord. Thus, a peripheral nerve or root lesion will cause loss of all sensations to the area it supplies.
- Lateral spinothalamic tracts carry pain and temperature sensations while ventral spinothalamic tracts carry crude touch sensation and firm pressure, to thalamus and then to parietal cortex (sensory area). Dorsal column including tracts of fasciculus gracilis and cuneatus carries the sensations of fine touch, vibration, and sense of position.
- The procedure should be explained to the child and the test be demonstrated to him/her with the eyes open. The child should be asked to close the eyes during the actual testing.
- An examination is required to test touch, pain, temperature, vibration, or joint position.
- Light touch testing is done by using a cotton wool/wisp and asking the child to say yes when he/she feels the touch. Pain can be tested with the sharp and the blunt end of a ball pin and it should be tested after testing for touch sensation. Never use a needle to test the pain.
- Start with the area that is impaired and go proximal and distal to find the boundaries.
- Compare the sensations on both the sides, distally and proximally, to see if the loss is symmetrical or asymmetrical.
- If superficial touch and pain sensations are impaired, then check for the temperature by using cold and hot test tubes. Deep pain is tested by squeezing the calf, trapezius muscles, or Achilles tendons. Pressure is tested in a way similar to testing touch with firm pressure with the examiner's finger or thumb.
- Sensory deficit of pain, touch, and temperature suggests peripheral neuropathy.
- Table 11.7 shows the areas affected and their dermatomes.

TABLE 11.7 Areas of Sensory Loss and the Dermatomes

Surface	Dermatome
Lateral surface of upper arm	C5
Tip of the thumb	C6
Medial surface of upper arm	T2
Medial surface of lower arm	T1
Middle of anterior thigh	L2
Medial aspect of knee	L3
Medial side of calf	L4
Lateral side of calf	L5
Sole of the foot	S1

Cortical sensations are two-point discrimination, stereognosis, graphesthesia, point location, extinction phenomenon, and barognosis.

Vibration Sensation (a Proprioceptive Sensation)

- It is tested by putting the stem of a vibrating lower-frequency tuning fork (128 Hz) on the bony prominence starting from distal part such as big toe, medial malleolus of tibia, and radial and ulnar tuberosities (others are patella, iliac crest, spinous processes, sternum, and skull). The patient should be explained the difference between touch and vibration sensation of the tuning fork by putting the fork first on the forehead.
- Ask the child if he/she perceives vibration. If yes, then ask him/her to tell you the point and when he/she feels the cessation. Compare with yourself. If you still perceive and the patient does not, then one can say that vibration sensation is impaired.

- Sensations of vibration and position are lost in subacute combined degeneration of spinal cord, Friedreich ataxia, and familial spastic paraplegia.

Sense of Joint Position (a Proprioceptive Sensation)

- Hold the joint you want to test, e.g., hold the great toe by the thumb and index finger, and move from side to side while the proximal part is held fixed and the distal part is moved.
- Explain the different joint positions such as neutral, down, or up by demonstration.
- Ask the child to close the eyes and repeat the tests by moving in one position and ask him/her about the position.
- Return the digit to the neutral position before moving in the same or other direction randomly. The patient should tell you the correct position. Test both the sides and if normal, then there is no need to test each and every joint.
- Romberg sign, which also assesses proprioception, can be tested in children older than 4–5 years.

Cortical Sensations

The tests measure contralateral parietal lobe function. Ask the child to close both the eyes and perform each test after explanation.

- *Graphesthesia (soft sign)*: This may not be a conclusive test for children up to 8 years of age. Explain the child with eyes open, and then play a game with him/her after the eyes are closed. Ask him/her which number is written on his/her palm. Write it twice on palm. It is an ability to identify written numbers or letters on the patient's skin. If peripheral sensations are lost, even this cortical sensation will be also lost.
- *Stereognosis (soft sign)*: This may not be a conclusive test for children up to 5 years of age. The testing utilizes common objects such as coins, keys, or small balls. After closing the child's eyes, he/she is asked to identify the object given by using only his/her hands.
- *Two-point discrimination (soft sign)*: This test is inconclusive for children up to 6 years of age. This test is best done with the use of a special caliper manufactured for that purpose, but a paper clip can be used with two tips whose separation can be varied. Distal fingers and lips are very sensitive and can discriminate 3–4 mm of separation.
- *Sensory extinction*: Two stimuli are applied to two identical points on each side. Ask the child to describe how many spots are being touched. Normally, both sides are felt but with sensory lesion, the individual will sense only one.
- *Barognosis*: It is the ability to appreciate the difference of the weight on both the sides by putting two similar objects with same size and shape but different weight. To test, the child is given the objects and asked if they weigh the same or different.
- *Point location (topognosis)*: It is the ability to localize the stimuli given at different parts of body with eyes closed.
- The patterns of sensory loss are such that while a cortical lesion generally produces a hemisensory loss, a bilateral spinal cord lesion results in a complete bilateral loss below the level of lesion.

Cerebellar Signs

Any child who is found to have incoordination should be checked for cerebellar signs to detect cerebellar involvement and to localize lesions within the cerebellum (midline or hemispheric function) on the basis of clinical findings.

- The cerebellum is responsible for maintenance of balance, coordination, and tone.
- Dysfunction of the cerebellum is indicated by a presence of the signs given in the next subsections.

Ataxia

Ataxia refers to impaired control of posture or movement of the limbs and trunk.

- *Truncal ataxia*: The patient is unable to maintain his/her balance while sitting upright. This is manifested in the form of swaying or falling while trying to sit upright. In young infants, it is manifested as bobbing of the head (titubation). It is seen in lesions of vermis of the cerebellum.
- *Gait ataxia*: The patient is unable to maintain balance while walking and standing. It is tested by the following signs:
  - *Romberg sign*
    - This is actually a test of proprioception and maintenance of balance based on vision, vestibular function, and proprioception and it provides evidence of ataxia due to proprioceptive sensory loss.
    - The child is asked to stand with his/her feet close together. The patient will sway and tend to fall toward the side of lesion in case of unilateral cerebellar lesions. In case of bilateral cerebellar lesions or lesions of the vermis, the patient will tend to sway backwards. A broad-based gait is often seen in cerebellar involvement.
    - If the patient can maintain his/her posture with eyes open, but falls or sways with eyes closed, it is called positive Romberg sign. It is a sign of lesion of the proprioceptive pathway (sensory ataxia).
  - *Tandem walking (soft sign)*: This test may be inconclusive till the child is 7 years old. The patient is asked to walk in a line in such a way that one foot is placed exactly in front of the other. In cerebellar lesions, the patient will tend to sway and fall toward the side of the lesion.
  - *Dysmetria*: The patient is unable to gauge the exact distance for a particular action and this results in overshooting or past-pointing. The tests used to assess dysmetria are finger-to-nose and heel-to-shin tests.
  - *Tremors*: Usually, intention tremors are present. When the child tries to reach for an object, coarse, slow, side-to-side oscillations of the hands appear that increase in intensity as the goal comes nearer. Sometimes the tremors of head, fingers, and hands may be present at rest also.
  - *Dysarthria*: The following speech abnormalities are seen in cerebellar lesions:
    - *Scanning speech*: Each syllable of a sentence is carefully enunciated and separated.
    - *Staccato speech*: Speech is jerky and explosive.
  - *Rapid alternating movements (dysdiadochokinesia)*: This is a soft sign and cannot be tested with regular speed and rhythm till 10 years of age.
  - *Nystagmus*: This is defined as a periodic rhythmic oscillation of the eyes. The oscillations may be of approximately equal amplitude and velocity (pendular nystagmus) or, more commonly, with a slow initiating phase and a fast corrective phase (jerky nystagmus). Apart from the cerebellar causes, nystagmus can also be caused by vestibular lesion, brainstem dysfunction, and ocular lesions.
  - *Hypotonia*: It is defined as decreased resistance to passive movements of the limbs. It is different from hypotonia of LMN origin as there is no associated weakness.
  - *Rebound phenomenon*: An examiner suddenly releases the resistance when the child is attempting to flex the elbow and pulling his/her forearm against the resistance offered by the examiner. The child's hand inadvertently strikes the face.
  - *Pendular knee jerk*: The child is positioned in sitting at the edge of the table, with legs dangling. On eliciting a knee jerk,

one finds two to three oscillations of legs at knee joint moving like a pendulum.

The common conditions causing cerebellar ataxia are acute viral infections, drugs such as phenytoin and benzodiazepines, neuroblastoma, lead encephalopathy, tumors of cerebellum and brainstem, congenital malformations such as Chiari malformation, hydrocephalus, and vascular insults to cerebellum.

Signs of Meningeal Irritation

The meningeal signs are present when the meninges are inflamed due to infection or presence of blood. They are often present in conditions such as pyogenic meningitis and TBME but may be absent in newborns, in young infants, and in the advanced stage of the diseases. It is important to note that these signs are not always caused by meningitis.

- Meningism is the presence of meningeal signs and is a reflex to avoid painful extension resulting in stiff neck and back. It is commonly seen in cases of inflamed meninges such as meningitis and subarachnoid hemorrhage.
- Meningismus is a meningism (presence of neck stiffness) in the absence of meningeal inflammation, e.g., right upper lobe pneumonia.
- The different tests used to elicit the meningeal signs produce tension in the inflamed and hypersensitive spinal nerve roots and the resulting signs are protective muscle contractions and postures that minimize the stretching of the meninges and the nerve roots.
- Neck rigidity, positive Kerning sign, and positive Brudzinski sign constitute the triad of meningitis. It indicates meningeal irritation, which is most commonly due to bacterial meningitis or TBME. These are also caused by subdural hemorrhage, brain abscess, and rarely spinal cord tumors.

Neck Rigidity

- If the child is conscious, he/she is placed in sitting position. He/she is asked to flex his/her head voluntarily and touch his/her chin to his/her chest. The sign is considered positive if flexion of neck is associated with considerable pain or resistance.
- If the child has altered sensorium, he/she is placed in supine position. One hand is placed behind the head of the child and the neck is gently flexed. If there is considerable resistance to flexion of neck, the sign is considered positive (Fig. 11.5).
- In an uncooperative young child, neck stiffness is elicited by bringing the head beyond the edge of the table and supporting his/her head with your hand while trying to flex the head.
- Before performing this test, always confirm absence of cervical spine injury/trauma.

Kernig sign

- To elicit the Kernig sign, the patient is made to lie down in supine position, hip and knee are flexed to a right angle, and then the knee is slowly extended by the examiner. The appearance of resistance or pain during extension of the patient's knees beyond 135° constitutes a positive Kernig sign (Fig. 11.6). The inflamed and hypersensitive nerve roots are stretched, which leads to a reflex spasm of the hamstring muscles.

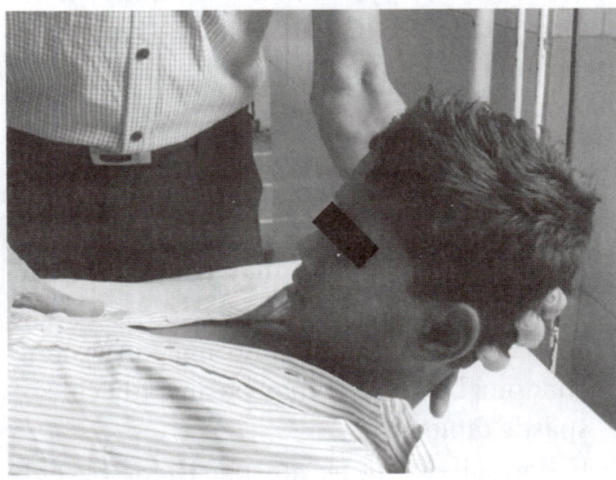

Figure 11.5 Neck rigidity.

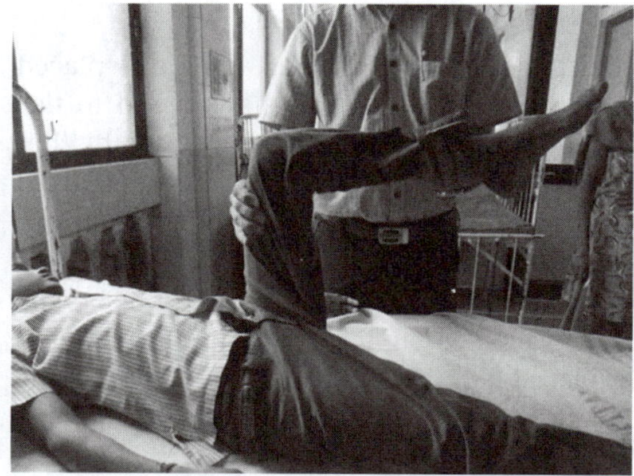

Figure 11.6 Kernig sign.

Brudzinski sign

- *Brudzinski neck sign*: It is performed with the patient in supine position. To elicit this maneuver, the examiner keeps one hand behind the patient's head and the other hand on the chest to prevent the patient from rising. Reflex flexion of the patient's hips and knees after passive flexion of the neck constitutes a positive Brudzinski sign.
- *Brudzinski leg sign*: When one leg is passively flexed, there is reflex flexion of the opposite leg.

Gait Examination

Examination of gait is very important in pediatric age group as it reveals abnormalities related to the cerebral hemispheres, extrapyramidal system, cerebellum, LMN lesions such as Guillain–Barré syndrome, myopathies, muscular dystrophy, and neuropathies.

- It is important to observe the child walking to and fro (sometimes running also) for a distance of a few feet in the examination room. Climbing stairs may be observed in selected cases.
- Toe walking may be normal in young children; however, it may be an early clue of spastic diplegia.
- If normal variations are persistent beyond the expected age limits or are asymmetric, or if there is any evidence of a neurological disease, then one should search for the cause. For example, if the child is walking on tiptoes, then check that there are no contractures by demonstrating the normal range of passive dorsiflexion at the ankle joint.
- The major varieties of abnormal gait seen in children are as follows:
  - *Scissoring/spastic gait*: Children with scissoring/spastic gait have tightness of adductor muscles of the lower limb, which leads to scissoring of the limbs. They also have stiffness or contractures of the Achilles tendon because of which instead of their entire foot, only their toes touch the ground while walking. Scissoring/spastic gait is commonly seen in children with spastic cerebral palsy.
  - *Broad-based gait*: In this type of gait, the patient tends to walk with the feet separated so that their base becomes broad. He/she sways from side to side when he/she is standing. He/she is not able to walk with heel-to-toe action in a straight line. Broad-based gait is normal up to 2 years of age. After this, children walk with their feet close together. Broad-based gait is seen in lesions of cerebellar hemispheres (cerebellar ataxia).
  - *Hemiparetic gait (circumduction gait)*: When one side of the body is paralyzed, the patient stands with unilateral weakness on the affected side, arm flexed, adducted, and internally rotated. Leg on the same side is in extension with plantar flexion of the foot and toes. When walking, the patient will hold his/her arm to one side and drag his/her affected leg in a semicircle (circumduction) due to weakness of distal muscles (foot drop) and extensor hypertonia in lower limb. This is most commonly seen in cerebrovascular accidents (stroke). With mild hemiparesis, loss of normal arm swing and slight circumduction may be the only abnormalities.

- *Waddling gait and lurching gait*: When there is affection of the hip girdle, the normal movement of the pelvis does not occur. In order to clear the opposite limb from the ground, the patient bends on the normal side and there is exaggerated lumbar lordosis. The opposite side of the pelvis drops when the lesion is unilateral; it produces a lurching gait. Affection of hip girdle on both sides leads to waddling gait. This is seen in muscular dystrophies such as Duchenne muscular dystrophy and SMA.
- *Neuropathic gait (high stepping gait, slapping gait)*: It is seen in patients with foot drop (weakness of foot dorsiflexion); the cause of this gait is an attempt to lift the leg high enough during walking so that the foot does not drag on the floor. On bringing the foot to the ground, toes touch first than heel. This is seen in peripheral neuropathies, spina bifida, and L5 radiculopathy.
- *Crouch gait*: One finds this type of gait in diplegic cerebral palsy with lower limbs flexed at hip, flexed knee, and ankle in equinus position.
- *Equinus gait (toe walking)*: The child is walking on the toes, which is seen in spastic cerebral palsy and Duchenne muscular dystrophy.

Autonomic Nervous System

- This comprises the sympathetic (T1–L2 thoracolumbar), parasympathetic (craniosacral), and enteric nervous system that acts as an efferent system affecting vital signs, pupillary reaction, lacrimation, salivation, gastrointestinal motility, bronchodilation, sweating, and sphincter functions.
- Peripheral autonomic nervous system is mainly involuntary motor-type response and is regulated by central autonomic network.
- Examination of autonomic system is not routinely carried out as part of CNS examination. However, it should be done when clinically indicated. Look for the temperature difference, postural hypotension (fall in systolic blood pressure of >20 mmHg with change from supine to standing position), tache cerebrale, punctate erythematous spots on palms, variation in perspiration, salivation, and tears. One may find sudden gross changes in vital signs, paroxysmal hypertension, and variable heart rate response to changes in posture and respiration.
- Conditions affecting autonomic systems are hereditary sensory and autonomic neuropathies, prematurity, mitochondrial disorders, and some chromosomal disorders. Common secondary (acquired) causes are TBME (tache cerebrate, erythematous spots on palms), Guillain–Barré syndrome, thyroid disorders, and some neoplasms, e.g., pheochromocytoma.

Integration of Clinical Signs and the Localization of the Lesion in Neurological Disease

The important clinical issues in a child with neurological disease are to collate the history and the examination findings to help arrive at the localization of the lesion, determine the time course of the disease (paroxysmal, acute, subacute, or chronic), and formulate a diagnosis (infective, metabolic, vascular, neoplastic, and/or degenerative). As the problem can be anywhere in the neuronal axis, it is important to differentiate first between UMN and LMN (Table 11.8).

- Central nervous lesions include lesions at cerebral hemispheres, white matter tracts, basal ganglia, cerebellum, brainstem, and spinal cord (till cranial nerve nuclei/anterior horn cells).
- UMN includes the brain and spinal cord extending from motor cortex in cerebrum,

TABLE 11.8 Upper and Lower Motor Neuron Lesions

Features of upper motor neuron lesion	Features of lower motor neuron disease
Weakness	Weakness
Paralysis affects movements rather than muscles. Can present as hemiplegia, paraplegia, quadriplegia, diplegia	Single muscle or group of muscles affected
Spastic paralysis (hypertonia)	Flaccid paralysis (hypotonia)
Exaggerated deep tendon reflexes	Decreased or absent deep tendon reflexes
Loss of superficial reflexes	Absent superficial reflexes
Extensor plantar response	Flexor or absent plantar response
Muscle wasting—absent or delayed	Muscle wasting—severe
No fasciculations	Fasciculations can be present
Peripheral sensations—normal	Peripheral sensations may be lost

corona radiata, and internal capsule brainstem to spinal cord till the fibers synapse with the anterior horn cells.

- Following are the guidelines for localization of neurological disease:
  - *Cerebral cortex*: Hemiparesis on the side opposite to the lesion and its extent depend on the area involved. There is aphasia if dominant hemisphere is involved. There is loss of cortical sensations and there may be visual field defects if occipital lobe is involved. Other signs of cerebral dysfunctions are present such as altered sensorium (bilateral involvement), seizures, and conjugate gaze palsy.
  - *Subcortical/thalamus*: There is contralateral weakness with loss of primary sensations and homonymous visual field defect. There are no seizures or aphasia but there may be involuntary movements such as chorea, dystonia, and/or hemiballismus.
  - *Internal capsule*: There is dense contralateral hemiparesis with sensory deficits with UMN facial palsy. There is no aphasia.
  - *Brainstem*: There are motor/sensory deficits on the side opposite to the lesion as all the tracts cross the brainstem just above the spinal cord. There are cranial nerve palsies on the same side of the lesion. Respiratory and circulatory changes are often present and there may be nystagmus and skew deviation of the eyes. Third and 4th cranial nerves are involved in midbrain lesions; 5th, 6th, or 7th cranial nerves are involved in pontine lesion; and 8th to 12th cranial nerves may be involved in the lesions of the medulla.
  - *Cerebellum*: The signs of cerebellar involvement have been described earlier in this chapter. Paralysis is not a feature of cerebellar disease, though hypotonia is present. Ipsilateral signs (e.g., swaying toward the side of lesion, tremors) are seen in lateral lesions (hemispheric), while midline cerebellar involvement produces truncal and lower limb ataxia, nystagmus, and disturbances of equilibrium.
  - *Spinal cord*: UMN type of motor and sensory deficits is seen below the level of lesion while at the level of lesion, the deficits are of LMN type.

The patterns/distribution of losses in peripheral nervous system are shown in Table 11.9.

TABLE 11.9 Localization of Lower Motor Neuron Lesions

Site	Signs
Anterior horn cells	Loss of power, flaccidity, fasciculation, atrophy, loss of reflexes. No sensory loss
Nerve roots	Pain and paresthesias in the dermatomal distribution. Motor affection as per myotome
Peripheral nerves	• Mononeuropathy or polyneuropathy • Pattern of motor/sensory loss: Numbness, paresthesia (glove and stocking), and loss of vibratory and position sense in the nerve distribution • May be patchy/asymmetric, presenting with loss of power, flaccidity, loss of reflexes
Neuromuscular junction	Weakness progresses with exercise, fluctuating fatigability, diplopia, ptosis, dysarthria more frequently seen, especially in myasthenia gravis
Muscles	Proximal muscles are more involved than the distal ones. Deep tendon reflexes are well preserved until late, no sensory loss

KEY POINTS

- Unlike in adults, the CNS evaluation in infants and children is made complex by limitations due to age, their developmental status, and their apprehension.
- Neurological examination in children is a task that is learnt with practice, patience, and knowledge.
- The neurological diagnosis must address the neurological disease in terms of its onset, progress (static, recurrent, or progressive), topography (unilateral or bilateral and/or focal or diffuse), parts of neural axis involved, and likely pathophysiology and etiological factors.
- A thorough assessment of a child with a suspected neurological disease paves the way for an appropriate diagnosis and the management.

CHAPTER 12

The Renal System

Fagun Shah, Uma S Nayak

The symptomatology and signs of renal disease might be overt or subclinical even in advanced renal conditions. In neonates or infants, the symptoms may be pertaining to other organ systems. A high index of suspicion should be maintained and a thorough knowledge of subtle clues is essential to lead to clinical diagnosis, early detection, and effective management of renal disease.

In majority of children with renal involvement, thorough history, clinical examination, and urinalysis will help to broadly arrive at a diagnosis. In others, screening by urinalysis and ultrasonographic evaluation may help to pick silent issues.

History

- Age
  - Children with nephrotic syndrome commonly present between the ages of 2 and 6 years. Presentation after the age of 8 years is more likely to be due to significant underlying glomerular lesions.
  - Poststreptococcal glomerulonephritis (PSGN) commonly affects children between the ages of 5 and 12 years and is rare below the age of 3 years. Congenital nephrotic syndrome can present in newborns or within 3 months of age.
  - Urinary tract infection in a younger child necessitates more investigations/workup to rule out anatomic abnormalities of urinary tract.
- Sex
  - Urinary tract infections are more common in females due to proximity of urethra to anal canal.
  - Nephrotic syndrome is more common in male children.

Common Symptoms

Edema

- Common causes of edema related to renal disorders are nephrotic syndrome, acute glomerulonephritis, acute renal failure, and chronic renal failure.
- Classically, renal edema starts with puffiness of eyelids, typically more in morning.
- When periorbital puffiness or generalized edema tends to reduce as the day progresses, it points commonly to renal etiology such as nephrotic syndrome or acute glomerulonephritis. The edema being more in the early hours is attributed to the fact that the periorbital tissues are loose and hence fluid accumulates initially in these spaces.
- The progression of edema is very gradual in nephrotic syndrome, while edema in glomerulonephritis develops very fast (due to salt and water retention)—a couple of days. Nevertheless, persistence of edema throughout the day without diurnal variation may signify chronic kidney disease and fluid overload states.
- In chronic liver disease associated with portal hypertension, ascites may be out of proportion to the edema at other places, while in renal diseases, ascites is more

often a delayed appearance of a generalized anasarca.

- In congestive heart failure, edema increases as the disease progresses. In ambulatory and older children, it usually starts with pedal edema, while in infants and young children, there may be sacral edema in the early stages.

Urinary Volume

- While oliguria or anuria is a frequent manifestation in children with renal diseases, in a subset of patients, polyuria forms an important symptom in the pediatric age group. Children with nephrotic syndrome have decreased urine output due to decreased intravascular volume.
- Oligoanuria is an indicator of either a dehydrated state or intrinsic renal conditions such as glomerular involvement, acute tubular necrosis, or postrenal obstructive conditions.
- Polyuria points toward conditions that cause defects in renal tubular concentrating mechanisms, e.g., diabetes insipidus, chronic renal tubule disease, interstitial diseases (dysplastic kidneys, polycystic kidneys), renal tubular acidosis (RTA), and Bartter syndrome. It is always associated with polydipsia. Typically, the mother would complain of the child drinking water out of proportion during day as well as nighttime.

Urine Color

- Passage of red-colored urine is most commonly due to hematuria. Other causes of red-colored urine are hemoglobinuria, myoglobinuria, porphyria, or some drugs (rifampicin, desferrioxamine) or food items (beetroot and black berries). Rifampicin produces orange-colored urine and desferrioxamine causes red-colored urine in patients with iron poisoning.
- The common causes of hematuria in children are acute glomerulonephritis, urinary calculi, and urinary tract infection (Box 12.1).

Box 12.1 Hematuria in children

- Acute glomerulonephritis
- Urinary calculi
- Renal vein thrombosis
- Urinary tract infection
- Renal trauma
- Acute pyelonephritis
- Thrombocytopenia
- Disseminated intravascular coagulation
- Wilms tumor
- IgA nephropathy
- Sickle cell disease
- Hypercalciuria
- Drugs: Cyclophosphamide causing hemorrhagic cystitis, NSAIDs

- Bright red-colored urine indicates blood either from interstitium as in acute interstitial nephritis (e.g., following nonsteroidal anti-inflammatory drug [NSAID] toxicity) or from calyces, ureters, bladder, or urethra (e.g., renal/ureteric/bladder calculi, renal cysts/tumors, bladder growth or tumors), or in bleeding tendencies and renal vein thrombosis. Most of the times, a thorough history and examination can easily point to a specific etiology. For example, red urine and severe pain in loin point toward renal or ureteric calculi.
- Cola-, tea-, or brown-colored urine signifies pathology of glomerular origin, most common being postinfectious glomerulonephritis.
- If microscopy does not show RBCs or disproportionately less RBCs in comparison to the deepness of color, it points to hemoglobinuria or myoglobinuria. However, ingestion of certain food substances such as beetroot or certain medicines such as pyridium or rifampicin may give red or reddish orange color to urine.
- Very white frothy urine points toward protein in urine as in nephrotic syndrome.
- Cloudy whitish urine having a foul odor is due to pyuria and signifies urinary tract infection.

- Rarely, certain inborn errors of metabolism may give specific color to urine such as pink in disorder of urate metabolism.

Pattern of Micturition

- History of burning micturition or dysuria, urgency, frequency, and straining signifies lower urinary tract involvement (cystitis).
- Poor stream or thin stream points toward bladder outlet obstruction as in severe phimosis, urethral stricture, posterior urethral valves in males, and bladder calculi.
- Poor stream and dribbling in infants may be due to ectopic insertion of ureter distal to bladder neck. It could also be due to bladder dysfunction because of neurogenic causes.
- Severe pain during micturition at the tip of penis straight away points to either urethral calculi or calculi at bladder trigone; it can also be seen in few cases of urethritis.

Fever

- Children with urinary tract infection commonly present with fever. Acute pyelonephritis is commonly associated with high-grade fever with chills and/or rigors.
- An attack or relapse of nephrotic syndrome is precipitated by infections such as respiratory tract infection or urinary tract infections; thus, fever is a common symptom in such children.
- Fever can also be present in collagen vascular diseases such as systemic lupus erythematosus with renal involvement.

Abdominal Pain

- Pain radiating from loin to groin points to renal or upper ureteric calculi. Similarly, severe colicky pain in lumbar region signals calculi in mid or lower ureter.
- Suprapubic pain may be due to bladder involvement such as calculi or cystitis.

Skin Rashes

History of presence of skin rashes bears an important clue to a variety of diseases of the kidney. Type of rashes, site and timing of occurrence, and timing of onset of renal disease in conjunction with skin rash denote specific glomerulopathies. PSGN may occur following skin lesions such as pustules or boils. A malar rash, often a prominent clinical feature, is seen in older children and more commonly in girls with systemic lupus erythematosus with renal involvement.

Other Symptoms

- A positive history of presence of hearing issues or defective vision may indicate congenital renal disorders. For example, high-pitched hearing loss and vision problems in a child with hematuria denote hereditary nephritis (Alport syndrome).
- Similarly, failure to thrive, polyuria, polydipsia, and deafness are present in primary distal RTA.
- Cystinosis presents with proximal RTA and vision defects in early childhood.
- Lowe syndrome has a triad of RTA, vision abnormalities due to retinal detachment, and developmental delay.

Alarming Presentations

Breathlessness

- In patients with renal failure, breathlessness is commonly due to pulmonary edema and fluid overload or left ventricular failure due to hypertension.
- Severe acidosis may also present with tachypnea as in renal failure.
- In patients with massive abdominal distension, diaphragm may be pushed up, compromising the lung volume and thus leading to breathlessness and cardiorespiratory embarrassment.
- In patients with anasarca, there may be associated pleural effusion.

Convulsions and Altered Sensorium

- In patients with renal involvement, convulsions and/or encephalopathy may be due to a variety of causes such as dyselectrolytemia mainly pertaining

Box 12.2 Symptoms suggestive of chronic renal disease

- Failure to thrive is very common in patients with chronic kidney disease, recurrent urinary tract infection, renal tubular disorders, renal hypoplasia/dysplasia, and posterior urethral valves.
- Resistant rickets and short stature are found in chronic kidney disease, renal tubular acidosis, vitamin D-dependent rickets, and hypophosphatemic rickets.
- Developmental delay is found along with congenital renal conditions such as renal dysplasia, congenital nephrotic syndrome, and certain congenital renal tubular disorders.

to sodium levels, hypocalcemia, severe hypertension, or uremia.

- It is now rare for patients with postinfectious glomerulonephritis to present with hypertensive encephalopathy. However, any child with acute nephritis can present with transient hypertension, which may be alarming during the course of illness.

The symptoms that are useful pointers toward the chronic renal disease are shown in Box 12.2.

Antenatal History

- Oligohydramnios may point to the possibility of renal anomalies such as polycystic kidneys, absent or ectopic kidney, and unilateral or bilateral hydronephrosis in a fetus or newborn.
- Congenital renal anomalies such as renal agenesis (unilateral or bilateral) and polycystic kidneys often result in oligohydramnios with features of Potter sequence with characteristic facies, limb deformities such as clubfoot, and pulmonary hypoplasia. Many of such affected babies may not survive beyond the neonatal period.

Family History

Many renal disorders run in families. It becomes imperative to thoroughly inquire regarding renal issues in families or any early deaths due to kidney diseases. The examples include:

- Alport syndrome, which is inherited from the maternal side
- Metabolic disorders such as idiopathic hypercalciuria, which may lead to formation of renal calculi and may have either of parents affected
- Autosomal dominant polycystic kidney disease, congenital nephrotic syndrome (FSGS [focal segmental glomerulosclerosis] or Finnish variety), vesicoureteric reflux (VUR) having siblings or parents affected, etc.

Past History

- In patients with acute glomerulonephritis, a preceding history of sore throat or pyoderma or any febrile illness 10–20 days before the present illness is an important indicator of the diagnosis.
- Similarly, in Henoch–Schonlein purpura, history of typical rashes helps to confirm the diagnosis.
- History of ventriculoperitoneal shunt for hydrocephalus implicates shunt nephritis.
- Recurrent episodes of edema suggest nephrotic syndrome. These episodes are often precipitated (as a relapse) by intercurrent illnesses and infections such as upper respiratory infections and urinary infections.
- History of prolonged administration of NSAIDs, penicillamine, aminoglycosides, etc., may be found in patients with acute renal failure.
- In a child with recurrent episodes of urinary tract infections, underlying structural anomaly of urinary tract or conditions such as VUR should be ruled out.

Drug History

Rifampicin can cause dark yellow or orange discoloration of urine, which may be confused with hematuria. Also inquire about the intake or administration of nephrotoxic drugs such as aminoglycosides, vancomycin, cyclosporin, angiotensin-converting enzyme inhibitors,

NSAIDs, amphotericin B, anticancer drugs, and penicillamine.

General Examination

A thorough general examination is warranted in all the patients as subtle markers or findings may give an important clue to clinch the diagnosis. The salient findings in general examination pointing to a specific renal condition are mentioned next.

Vital Signs

- *Heart rate*: Tachycardia in left ventricular failure/shock leading to kidney injury; bradycardia with uremia, hypokalemia, or hypocalcemia
- *Respiratory rate*: May be increased in patients with pulmonary edema, left ventricular failure, and RTA
- *Blood pressure*: Hypertension in renal parenchymal disease, renal artery stenosis, chronic kidney disease, and renal scarring

Growth

Anthropometry and assessment of nutritional status is important. Delayed growth, failure to thrive, short stature, and delayed puberty are important elements of chronic kidney disease. Failure to thrive and short stature are also found in renal tubular disorders and dysplastic/hypoplastic kidney disease. The term *renal osteodystrophy* refers to the bony and mineral changes seen in chronic kidney disease caused by secondary hyperparathyroidism.

Genitals

Examination of genitals is important in a child suspected to have involvement of renal or genitourinary system.

- Tight phimosis or vulvar synechiae may be responsible for recurrent urinary tract infections.
- Ambiguous genitalia may be seen in 21-hydroxylase deficiency leading to dyselectrolytemia, acidosis, and shock.
- Hypospadias and anorectal malformations are associated with structural disorders of kidney and urinary tract.

Edema

Look for pedal edema, periorbital puffiness, and scrotal edema or generalized edema. This is commonly seen in children with nephrotic syndrome, nephritis, renal failure, liver failure, and congestive heart failure. Typical morning puffiness seen in periorbital region and pitting lower limb edema subsiding in evening typify renal origin and point to nephrotic syndrome/acute glomerulonephritis. Sacral edema may be present in an infant or a child who is not ambulatory.

Pallor

- Anemia in chronic kidney disease can be due to nutritional cause or erythropoietin deficiency. The anemia in chronic renal diseases is often normocytic and normochromic.
- Sudden-onset pallor and fall of hemoglobin with hemoglobinuria with acute kidney injury is found in hemolytic uremic syndrome, G6PD deficiency after intake of offending drugs, and complicated malaria with severe intravascular hemolysis.

Skin

- Photosensitive butterfly rashes on cheeks are seen in systemic lupus erythematosus.
- Petechial or maculopapular rashes are seen in connective tissue diseases with vasculitis.
- The rash in Henoch–Schonlein purpura manifests as palpable purpura appearing in crops and seen on buttocks and legs.
- Pyoderma is associated with PSGN.
- Petechiae and pallor with acute kidney injury can be seen in hemolytic uremic syndrome.

Spine and Bony Deformities

- Meningomyelocele, anal dimple, tuft of hair, and nevus on back, all point to spinal dysraphism leading to neurogenic bladder and recurrent urinary tract infection.

- Resistant rickets in chronic kidney disease can be due to renal osteodystrophy, RTA, Fanconi syndrome, vitamin D–dependent rickets, and hypophosphatemic rickets.

Eyes and Ears

- Posterior subcapsular cataracts occur due to steroid toxicity.
- Cystine crystals in cornea occur in cystinosis, which can cause proximal RTA.
- Lenticonus and high-pitched hearing loss occur in Alport syndrome.
- External ear malformations or preauricular tag is associated with congenital abnormalities of kidneys and urinary tract such as dysplasia and cystic kidney diseases.

Systemic Examination

Systemic examination is important as there is almost always secondary involvement of other organs and systems due to renal diseases that needs to be addressed along with the renal issue in question. All the systems should be examined in a systematic manner as described in the respective chapters. The relevant points are described and/or emphasized here.

Abdominal Examination

Abdomen should be examined in a systematic manner with inspection, palpation, percussion, and auscultation. Children with nephrotic syndrome or nephritis commonly have anasarca and ascites. Kidneys may be palpable in conditions such as tumors of the kidneys, gross hydronephrosis, and congenital anomalies of the kidneys. In a child with pyelonephritis, renal angle tenderness may be elicited.

Inspection

In case of ascites, abdominal fullness and transversely stretched/smiling umbilicus may be noted. Marks of the tight cloths may be noted if there is abdominal wall edema.

Palpation of Kidneys

As kidneys are in the deeper plane in abdomen, they are not very easy to palpate compared with liver and spleen.

- *Renal angle tenderness*: Renal angle is formed in the back by lower border of the rib and outer border of erector spinae muscle. Check for tenderness in renal angle with the patient in sitting position and bending forwards (Fig. 12.1).
- *Renal lump*: Renal lump is palpable in conditions such as Wilms tumor, gross hydronephrosis, congenital anomalies of kidney, and perinephric abscess.

  It needs experience to palpate renal lump as it may be difficult to appreciate for the beginners. It is difficult to differentiate renal lump from the spleen, especially in cases where spleen is enlarged. The points to differentiate renal lump from spleen are shown in Box 12.3.

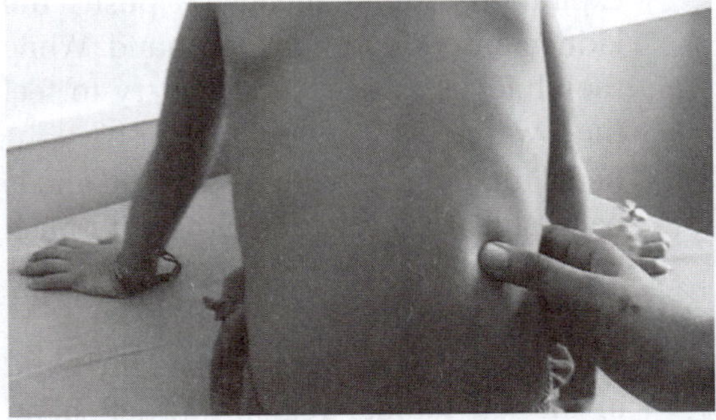

Figure 12.1 Looking out for renal angle tenderness.

Box 12.3 Differentiating factors between renal lump and enlarged spleen

- Spleen enlarges in the direction of right iliac fossa.
- It is not possible to insinuate fingers between spleen and costal margin, while upper border of renal lump can be felt.
- Renal lump does not cross the umbilicus, but huge spleen can cross the midline.
- Kidney can be bimanually palpated, while spleen cannot be palpated in such a manner.

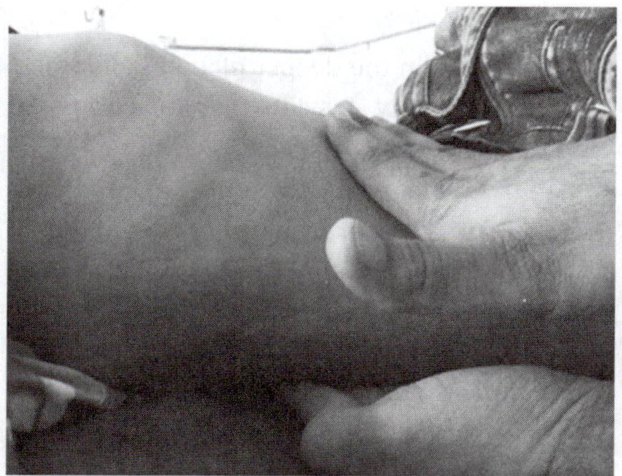

Figure 12.2 Bimanual palpation of kidneys.

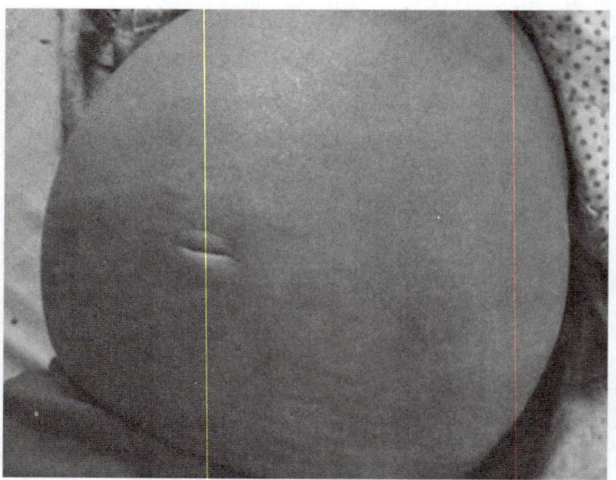

Figure 12.3 Abdominal wall edema indicated by stretch marks.

- *Bimanual palpation of kidneys*
  - For palpation of right kidney, place right hand over the right lumbar region and left hand at the right renal angle at the back (Fig. 12.2). Try to push kidney posteriorly by pressing the right hand deep into the abdomen during expiration; simultaneously, push the kidney anteriorly by the left hand. While the child takes deep breaths, try to feel the lower pole of kidney.
  - Renal lump moves with respiration and is ballotable. To check for ballotability, push kidney down with right hand and feel with left hand and vice versa.
  - To palpate left kidney, keep right hand in the left lumbar region and left hand posteriorly in the left loin and palpate in a similar way. One may stand on either right or left side of the patient.

Suprapubic Lump

A lump in the suprapubic region may be palpable due to a full bladder or a distended bladder and can be secondary to urinary retention in patients with bladder outlet obstruction such as posterior urethral valve or in neurogenic bladder.

Abdominal Wall Edema

To look for abdominal wall edema, pinch the skin over abdomen for 10 seconds and check for pitting or indentation. Obvious marks of tight cloths indicate presence of abdominal wall edema (Fig. 12.3).

Abdominal Girth

Abdominal circumference is measured at the level of umbilicus. Monitoring of abdominal circumference helps in assessing the progress in a child with abdominal distension.

Percussion

Percussion of the abdomen helps in confirming some of the findings of palpation and also tells about the presence and approximate amount of free fluid in abdominal cavity. Depending on the amount of free fluid present in the peritoneal cavity, different signs may be elicited. The signs of free fluid in abdomen are puddle sign, shifting dullness, and fluid thrill.

Auscultation

A bruit over the renal artery may be heard in patients with renal artery stenosis. Press the bell of the stethoscope deep into abdomen over both the flanks to listen to the sound.

Other Systemic Examination

Cardiovascular System

- Left ventricular failure due to hypertension can be present in a variety of renal disorders.
- Cardiomyopathy leading to cardiogenic shock may develop in chronic kidney disease.
- Congestive cardiac failure can be due to severe anemia in chronic kidney disease.
- Pericardial rub or distant and soft heart sounds may indicate the possibility of pericardial effusion in chronic kidney disease due to uremia.
- Missed beats or tachycardia can occur with hyperkalemia.

Respiratory System

- Decreased air entry can be due to pleural effusion in nephrotic syndrome.
- Pulmonary edema causing fine basal crepitations may occur in fluid overload or left ventricular failure.

Central Nervous System

- Altered sensorium, blindness, irritability, and seizures can be due to hypertensive encephalopathy.
- Unconsciousness and seizures can also be due to uremia/uremic encephalopathy.
- Hyponatremia or hypernatremia and hypocalcemia can also occur.

KEY POINTS

- Changes in urinary and micturition patterns, hematuria, and presence of edema are common indicators of renal diseases in children.
- Chronic kidney diseases are one of the important causes of failure to thrive, growth failure, and short stature in children.
- Careful history and examination of a child with suspected renal etiology is very essential in the diagnosis, which can be aided by certain investigations to arrive at the final diagnosis and for timely management.

CHAPTER 13

The Skeletal System

Ketan Shah, Habib Bhurawala

The examination of the limbs, bones, and joints is generally considered under the skeletal system examination in children. Although the involvement of musculoskeletal system is common, the features and the manifestations of its involvement are often varied and may show multisystem involvement (e.g., sickle cell anemia, rheumatoid arthritis, and acute leukemia).

The skeletal system is an integral part of disease manifestations. Hence, a proper examination, assessment, analysis, and interpretation of the skeletal system go a long way in the appropriate management of any child with disease affecting the muscles, bones, and joints. Among the musculoskeletal diseases, those affecting the joints (both acute and chronic) remain among the common morbidities affecting this system; hence, these are presented in elaborate details.

History

Important and practical points to be noted during history taking are the following:

- Presence of antecedent events such as sore throat (acute rheumatic fever) must be inquired. Constitutional symptoms such as fever, malaise, anorexia, and weakness are present in a patient with acute arthritis but may also herald the onset of a chronic and systemic disease.
- Certain conditions such as sickle cell disease predispose the child to osteomyelitis due to vascular insufficiency caused by infarcts in the shaft of the bone(s) that act as good media for bacterial growth.
- The symptoms that point to the involvement of bones and joints in children include pain, swelling of one or more joints, diminished or absent movements of the affected parts, limping, deformity, weakness, and fatigue.
- The age and the sex of the child can be a helpful pointer to the disease.
  - Scurvy (vitamin C deficiency), which may present with painful limbs due to subperiosteal hemorrhages in long bones and weakness of movements, is more likely in infants and young children.
  - The incidence of osteomyelitis is more common in boys than in girls and more than 50% of cases occur before the age of 5 years.
  - Systemic-onset juvenile idiopathic arthritis (JIA) is more common at a younger age.
  - Hemophilic arthropathy and malignancy such as Ewing sarcoma are more common in boys. Girls are more likely to have polyarticular JIA.
  - A sick neonate with neonatal sepsis can develop osteomyelitis due to bacteremia and spread of infection to bones through hematogenous route.
- A musculoskeletal injury with post-traumatic inflammation may manifest with pain, spasm, and swelling such as seen with transient synovitis or post-traumatic effusion in the joint.
- Catheterization of femoral vessels is also known to be a risk factor for the development of osteomyelitis.
- Gait is an important pointer for the involvement of musculoskeletal system. A child can present with a limp; this could

TABLE 13.1 Mechanisms of Limping

Mechanism of limping	Clinical characteristics and conditions
Pain	Child takes minimum support on the painful limb and there is compensatory increase in weight bearing on the other limb. This can be due to infections, trauma, inflammation, or neoplasm involving bones, joints, or soft tissues
Structural abnormality	Asymmetrical limb length, deformity, and muscle contractures cause this limp. This may occur in congenital (osteogenesis imperfecta) or acquired diseases
Neuromuscular disease	Limping occurs due to muscle disease (dystrophy) or due to lesion in nervous system causing loss of proprioception or muscle control (cerebellar disease)

be either painless or painful, acute or chronic. Hence, a proper evaluation of gait can provide useful information for further assessment. The different mechanisms for limping are elaborated in Table 13.1.

- Musculoskeletal pain in young, healthy children may not always be pathological. Limb pains, which generally occur during night, are bilateral, improve with massage, and disappear in the morning, are frequent in children and are referred to as growing pains.
- It must be remembered that a child with musculoskeletal involvement may initially present with difficulty in walking or limp. It is important to find out whether the limp is painful (such as in osteomyelitis, transient synovitis, trauma, acute slipped upper femoral epiphyses, acute leukemia) or painless (developmental dysplasia of hip, Duchenne dystrophy, Perthes disease, or cerebral palsy).
- The mode of onset and progression such as acute and migratory onset of joint symptoms (arthralgia or arthritis) suggests acute rheumatic fever, while slow, gradually progressive, and persistent involvement is suggestive of juvenile rheumatoid arthritis. The term "rheumatologic diseases" in children suggests a chronic and recurrent inflammatory process of the connective tissues throughout the body.
- Other conditions that can lead to acute onset of arthritis in infants and children include septic arthritis, trauma to the joint, collection of blood in the joint space (hemarthrosis seen in hemophilia), reactive arthritis as seen following viral infections, inflammatory bowel disease, and Kawasaki disease.
- It should be noted whether there is involvement of single joint or multiple joints. Few common causes of a single joint involvement in children include tubercular arthritis, early oligoarticular rheumatoid arthritis, and septic arthritis.
- It is pertinent to find out the relationship of pain with routine activities—pain of rheumatoid arthritis improves with activity, while mechanical musculoskeletal pain (trauma, hemarthrosis) increases with activity.
- History of remissions and relapses needs to be asked for in any child presenting with chronic joint and limb symptoms.
- It is important to ask about the pain, its severity, and the factors that lead to its exaggeration. It is equally important to find out which part of the limb is painful. Pain in the knee joint may be referred from the hip joint and the pain to the hip/thigh from the lower back.
- Other important pointers include presence of rashes (such as erythema marginatum in rheumatic fever), macular and malar rash in systemic lupus erythematosus (SLE), nodular rash of erythema nodosum in inflammatory bowel disease, renal abnormalities (hypertension, hematuria) in Henoch–Schonlein purpura (HSP), and hepatosplenomegaly in sickle cell anemia and acute leukemia.

- Chronic joint involvement may present with deformed joints or be associated with wasting of the surrounding muscles due to disuse atrophy.
- Disease variability often confuses a clinician about approach and diagnosis. Rheumatologic diseases in children are different from in adults. There is no dividing age between adults and children. Disease pattern does not change abruptly after a certain age. However, certain diseases never occur in childhood such as gout and osteoarthritis. Certain diseases occur only in childhood such as Kawasaki disease and oligoarticular arthritis with uveitis.
- A child having hypermobile joints may have joint pain, but it is mechanical pain rather than actual inflammation.

Physical Examination

- General inspection and the observation of the child, attempting to assess the degree of pain before actual examination, and observing the child while walking and in supine posture can offer vital clues to the well-being of the child. Always observe the active movements before any attempt to make a passive movement to avoid causing pain.
- The scheme of general assessment of skeletal system on physical examination is shown in Box 13.1.
- The physical examination should help to identify and confirm the presence or absence of pain and the limp and, if possible, to localize the site and origin of the pain.

Box 13.1 General assessment and examination of the skeletal system

- The sequence of examination should be the following: Look (inspect), feel (palpate), move, and, lastly, take the measurement if required.
- Look for any redness, swelling, subcutaneous nodules, and any scars.
- Look for deformity of the joint such as flexion deformity, spinal deformity, valgus deformity (knock knees), muscle wasting, and/or contractures.
- Look for any visible shortness of a particular limb.
- Observe the child's walk without shoes and after uncovering the affected limb or the joint.
- Observe whether the child can get up from floor and stand up. Inability to do so indicates proximal muscle weakness.
- Palpate the joint for skin temperature with the back of the hand.
- Palpation for tenderness should start away from the affected area and toward the involved part. Palpate gently and see the child's expression.
- Palpate for joint enlargement (effusion in acute arthropathy and synovial thickening in chronic arthropathy). This is easily perceptible in major joints such as the knee joint.
- Ask the patient to attempt active movements of lower limbs in supine posture: dorsiflexion (normal up to 20°) and plantar flexion (normal up to 50°) of the ankles, and bending the knees and the hip. Decide whether the movement is normal or restricted.
- Check passive movements of lower limbs such as internal rotation of hips with hip and knee flexed to 90°, extension of knees, and inversion and eversion of the foot.
- Movements in upper limbs are best checked with the child sitting up: Arms straight up above the head, then behind the head, and then toward the lower back checks the abduction and the extension of the shoulder. Full extension of wrist is checked in prayer/Namaste position with forearms parallel to the floor.
- With the child standing upright, examine the spine (such as scoliosis, cervical spine extension, and lateral rotation).
- Check the limb measurements—anterior superior iliac spine to medial malleolus (true leg length) and umbilicus to medial malleolus (apparent leg length)—and measure 10 cm above and below knees for muscular atrophy.

- Presence of hepatomegaly and/or hepatosplenomegaly with associated limb/joint pains is a valuable marker for the likelihood of a disorder such as acute leukemia, sickle cell disease, or a rheumatoid disorder.

Skeletal System and Related Diseases

This system involves muscles, skin, soft tissues, bones, and related structures such as ligaments and blood vessels. Secondary effects of the primary disease on major organs are observed. The rheumatologic conditions can be classified as follows:

- *Chronic arthritis*: For example, ankylosing spondylosis, JIA, and psoriatic arthritis
- *Systemic vasculitis*: For example, Takayasu arteritis, HSP, and Kawasaki disease
- *Systemic connective tissues diseases*: SLE, mixed connective tissue disorders, and autoinflammatory disorders of infancy
- *Primary and acquired disorders of bone and connective tissue*: Rickets, endocrinal diseases with rheumatologic manifestations, and hematological diseases such as leukemia, hemophilia, and sickle cell disease that manifest with rheumatologic features
- *Arthritis related to infections*: Rheumatic fever (following acute poststreptococcal sore throat—now less common), acute septic arthritis, tuberculous arthritis, etc. (they are not rheumatic diseases but important differential diagnoses)
- *Myopathies*: Viral myositis and dermatomyositis
- *Scleroderma*: Localized and/or generalized scleroderma
- *Noninflammatory musculoskeletal pain*: Fibromyalgia and growing pains
- *Immunodeficiency with rheumatologic manifestation*: For example, HIV with arthritis, congenital immunodeficiency with arthritis, and recurrent infections

Some Important Points

- Several systemic diseases present with bony pains, arthritis, and connective tissue disorders, e.g., leukemia.
- Many rheumatologic diseases have extra-articular manifestations such as renal, pulmonary, and ophthalmic and are not limited to the musculoskeletal system.
- Identification of musculoskeletal emergencies, e.g., bacterial arthritis and macrophage activation syndrome (MAS), is important to diagnose and manage.
- It may not be possible to give diagnosis at the first visit as several diseases evolve over a period of weeks to months and manifest their florid clinical picture, e.g., lupus (SLE).
- Pattern recognition is an important component of the diagnosis. For example, symmetrical rash on limbs with arthritis in young age is likely to be HSP.

When to Suspect Rheumatologic Disease

A few questions during history taking can be helpful in arriving at some conclusion. During history taking and examination, the student should try to get information regarding the following:

- Is it arthritis/arthralgia?
- Is any associated muscle involvement present?
- Is any associated vessel involvement present?
- Is there any associated organ involvement present?
- Is it primary disease or secondary to some primary disease (e.g., leukemia)?
- Is it really an organic/pathological symptom?
- Is it congenital or acquired type?

The difference between arthritis and arthralgia is given in Table 13.2.

TABLE 13.2 Difference Between Arthritis and Arthralgia

Arthritis*	Arthralgia
Signs of inflammation should be present and evaluated: • Redness • Tenderness • Range of movement • Swollen joint • Nearby structures affected or not • The part of joint that is affected more, e.g., synovium, bone, articular surface	Restriction of movement may be present, but signs of inflammation are absent

*Arthritis is inflammation of joint. Inflammation includes swelling, pain, redness, and decreased joint movement. Arthralgia refers to pain in joint. There is no associated swelling and the child may have decreased range of movements.

Joint Examination

After considering it as joint swelling, few questions need to be addressed. The following factors help to classify chronic arthritis:

- The duration of time since the joint was first affected
- The number of affected joints during the first 6 weeks (according to definition, JIA has to be more than 6 weeks old)
- The presence of various extra-articular signs
- Onset before the age of 16 years
- Presence or absence of rheumatoid factor

Is it Chronic Arthritis or Acute Arthritis?

The defining criterion for chronic arthritis is persistence of a symptom in the joint for more than 6 weeks. A patient coming with swollen joint, pain, and other systemic findings (may or may not be present) is categorized as having chronic arthritis. Subsequent discussion will follow for the chronic arthritis.

Is the Involvement Articular or Nonarticular?

Articular structures include synovium, synovial fluid, articular cartilage, intra-articular ligaments, joint capsules, and juxta-articular bones. Nonarticular structures include supportive ligaments, tendons, bursas, muscles, fascia, bones, nerves, and overlying skin. Pain, limitation of range of motion, and joint tenderness indicate articular disease. Associated swelling due to synovitis, joint effusion, bony enlargement, instability, locking, crepitus, and deformity signify articular involvement. Hyperpigmentation signifies long-standing deformity.

Nonarticular pain (periarticular pain) has point tenderness and pain on active movement rather than on passive movement, and range of motion is preserved. It is not associated with joint instability, crepitus, and deformity.

Is the Involvement Inflammatory or Noninflammatory?

Inflammatory disorder could be due to many causes such as infection, immune mediated, or idiopathic. Noninflammatory conditions usually have mechanical causes. Inflammatory disorders have systemic manifestations with positive laboratory evidence and consistent findings on examination, while noninflammatory disorders have variable clinical findings, affect mainly ankle and knee joint, and have no positive laboratory findings. Mechanical causes will lead to more pain after a physical activity that improves with rest and worsens as the day progresses, and these causes may have a chronic history. Swelling, warmth, and systemic features are absent, and laboratory parameters are normal. On examination, objective findings such as crepitus and restricted movement are in a certain plane only.

What is the Cause?

Causes of chronic arthritis are only few. They are mechanical, inflammatory, infectious, and rare miscellaneous disorders. Evaluation of joint symptoms, i.e., chronology of joint involvement, needs detailed history. The points discussed next will help the examiner to evaluate a joint.

Is the Involvement Over Hours, Days, Weeks, or Months?

Acute arthritis needs urgent treatment. It is likely to be septic arthritis. Bleeding because of hemophilia may present with acute arthritis. Chronic arthritis is defined as arthritis present for 6 weeks or more. This will have different differential diagnoses. One of them is JIA. Indolent infections such as tubercular arthritis, brucellosis, and rare miscellaneous disorders should be ruled out.

Is Axial or Peripheral Joint Involvement Present?

Axial joint involvement is rarely seen in SLE and vasculitis. It is one of the important manifestations of enthesitis-related arthritis (ERA), often called seronegative enthesopathy and arthropathy (SEA). However, it may occur 5–10 years after onset of the disease.

Is it Oligoarticular or Polyarticular?

Oligoarticular juvenile arthritis refers to arthritis with involvement of not more than four joints, and polyarticular arthritis refers to arthritis with involvement of at least five joints. This refers to joint involvement in the first 6 months of the disease onset.

Is the Involved Joint Characteristic of Some Disease?

Site of involvement is characteristic of many diseases, e.g., distal interphalangeal joint in psoriatic arthritis, bilateral temporomandibular (TM) joint in RF-negative polyarthritis, and hip joint in reactive arthritis.

Is the Involvement Additive, Migratory, or Intermittent?

This has important diagnostic clue. Additive involvement means that one joint is already affected and now another new joint is involved. This is seen in reactive arthritis. In migratory involvement, fleeting joint pain is present. From one joint, pain and inflammation spreads to another joint. In this type of arthritis, the first joint may start to feel better before pain starts in a different joint. This is seen in rheumatic fever. In intermittent involvement, after an episode of arthritis, there is a phase in which joint involvement is absent and after few months, pain reappears in the previously affected joint or a new joint. This pattern is seen in lupus.

What is the Distribution of Joint Involvement?

The joint involvement should be assessed for being symmetrical or asymmetrical.

- *Symmetrical*: This includes JIA (systemic, polyarticular), SLE, mixed connective tissue disease (MCTD), sarcoidosis, and infections such as viral infections and Lyme disease. In the beginning, a set pattern may not be seen, and this will cause limitation of diagnosis.
- *Asymmetrical*: This includes oligoarticular idiopathic arthritis (OIA), bacterial arthritis, and infective endocarditis.

Is the Arthritis Deforming or Nondeforming?

Deforming arthritis is seen in aggressive variety such as in RF-positive polyarticular JIA. This disease behaves like adult-onset rheumatoid arthritis. In oligoarticular JIA (OJIA), single joint damage leads to deformity and sometimes can also cause limb length discrepancy. Nondeforming arthritis is seen in SLE and in inflammatory bowel disease (IBD).

Is There Associated Enthesitis?

Enthesis is the connective tissue between the tendons, ligaments, or other points of attachment of skeletal muscles to the bone. Inflammation of entheses or the site where tendons or ligaments get inserted into the bones is called enthesitis. This is an important component of ERA.

Are any Extra-Articular Features Present and do they Contribute or Dominate Arthritis?

A complete examination is important. Any systemic examination finding will have diagnostic contribution. For example, uveitis is an important finding and complication of OJIA. Various types of rashes can point to specific disease. For example, vasculitis rash with arthritis is seen in HSP.

Relation to Age/Gender/Family History

Certain diseases such as OJIA are more common in females at the age of 1–3 years. ERA (SEA) is more common in boys after the age of 8 years. In late childhood and adolescence, polyarticular JIA is more common. SLE is more common in females than in males.

Associated Vascular System Involvement

To determine the extent of vascular involvement and identify the vessels involved:

- *Ask*
  - For pain while walking
  - For intermittent claudication
  - For pain because of an other system involvement
- *Look*
  - For vasculitis rash: Papules, blackish discoloration, and gangrene changes
  - For painless areas having poor vascular supply
  - For a nonhealing ulcer

Is it Localized or Part of Systemic Disease?

In case of SLE, multiorgan involvement may be seen. While in oligoarticular variety of chronic arthritis, only one joint involvement may be seen, in JIA or SLE, multiple joint involvement may be seen.

Is this Autoimmune Disease or Systemic Disease with Rheumatologic Manifestations?

This is a very important point for diagnosis. Like in leukemia, patients will have severe joint pain, swollen joints, anemia, low platelet, and/or high WBC count. Sickle cell disease may have multiple episodes of painful episodic crisis, often treated as rheumatologic conditions. Meniscus injury in a young athlete is treated as oligoarticular arthritis. Hodgkin lymphoma may have a manifestation like dermatomyositis. Thus, always try to find out whether any primary disease is present that has caused this manifestation. Origin, progress, and duration are the basics of history taking that are important. Progressive anemia with bone pain may be leukemia. Progressive anemia, with renal and skin involvement, is SLE. These are only few examples.

After a general assessment of a child presenting with musculoskeletal symptoms, the foremost objective is to decide whether the condition is purely a musculoskeletal disorder or is related to some systemic diseases. This has essential implications for the long-term management and the outcome of the condition. After this initial evaluation, the clinician will have some idea of a recognizable pattern. This clinical conclusion with laboratory investigation will classify the case.

Need for Laboratory Tests

Laboratory studies are a valuable adjunct to the care of patients with skeletal disorders. Laboratory investigations can:

- Help in screening patients for inflammatory disorders
- Help in confirming diagnosis
- Help in monitoring of disease activities
- Help in monitoring response of therapy
- Help in suggesting a prognosis
- Help in assessing the risk of morbidities

KEY POINTS

- The diseases affecting the joints (both acute and chronic) remain one of the most common morbidities involving bones, muscles, and joints in the children.
- Apart from the isolated musculoskeletal pathologies, bone and joint diseases are also a common manifestation of multisystem diseases in children.

CHAPTER 14

HEMATOLOGY

Sanwar Agrawal, Raghvendra Singh Kachhwaha

Hematological diseases such as nutritional anemia, hemolytic anemia, and bleeding and coagulation disorders constitute a fair proportion of pediatric morbidities. Anemia is a decrease in the red cell volume or total hemoglobin level below the normal range for that age and sex. Unlike adults, there are age-specific norms that need to be applied before one can tell normal from abnormal. What looks like anemia for an adult may be normal for an infant and what may be polycythemia for an adult may be normal for a neonate.

The WHO cutoff values for hemoglobin to define anemia are hemoglobin less than 11 g/dL in children between 6 months and 6 years of age and less than 12 g/dL between 6 and 14 years of age. Table 14.1 shows normal hemoglobin values at different ages.

This section deals with an approach to a child with anemia. It is important to explore and obtain answers to the following questions:

- Is the child anemic?
- What are the possible causes of anemia?
- What is the type of anemia?

A child may have clinical manifestations related to one or more constituents of the hematopoietic system—anemia, bleeding, and infections in isolation or in combination. It is very important to realize that these may be secondary to an underlying systemic disease, e.g., a child with chronic kidney disease may present to a clinician with pallor/severe anemia; similarly, bleeding manifestations in a sick child can be due to disseminated intravascular coagulopathy, which can be a complication of many systemic diseases and severe/fulminant infections. Many of the components and relevant issues related to the diseases in hematology have been discussed in individual systems elsewhere. This chapter provides a concise and practical roundup of salient features and an approach to a child with common hematological problems such as anemia and bleeding manifestations in addition to a simplified and basic interpretation of complete blood counts (CBC) and peripheral smear in these conditions.

TABLE 14.1 Hemoglobin and Hematocrit at Different Ages

Age	Hemoglobin (g/dL)	Hematocrit (%)
1 day	18	61
4 weeks	14.2	43
1 year	11.6	35
10–12 years	13	39

Common Symptoms of Anemia

- Pallor, tiredness, lassitude, weakness, easy fatigability, and shortness of breath are common symptoms observed in children with anemia. However, these symptoms are not specific to children with anemia and are also observed in congestive heart failure, hypothyroidism, renal diseases, vitamin deficiencies, and chronic respiratory diseases.
- Pallor is a common presentation of anemia; however, the skin color depends not only on hemoglobin levels but also on the status of circulation and the amount of skin pigmentation. Coexistent jaundice and cyanosis may mask the pallor of anemia.

- The symptoms of anemia depend not only on the severity of anemia and the underlying etiology but also on the rate of fall of the hemoglobin.
- Chronic nutritional anemia (iron deficiency anemia [IDA]), which is well compensated, may be relatively asymptomatic. A sudden and severe fall in hemoglobin (acute severe hemolysis, internal hemorrhage) can precipitate heart failure or shock in a child and untreated iron deficiency can lead to irritability, behavioral changes, and poor scholastic performance in a child.

History

- *Age of onset*: IDA generally begins in the second half of infancy due to the exhaustion of maternal iron stores. Congenital hemoglobinopathies also manifest around 6–7 months of age and present as an increasing pallor and abdominal protuberance while the presence of fetal hemoglobin prevents symptoms in early infancy.
- *Sex*: Anemia inherited by sex-linked transmission (G6PD deficiency) affects the males predominantly but rarely females may be affected.
- *Ethnicity and caste*: Congenital hemolytic anemias are the best example of the predisposition of caste and ethnicity in systemic diseases. Thalassemia syndromes are common in the Mediterranean and Middle East. Thalassemia is one of the commonest genetic hematological disorders in India and is more common in North and West India. There is an increased incidence in communities such as Sindhis, Punjabis, Muslims, and Gujaratis (Kutchis, Lohanas, and Bhanushalis). Sickle cell disease (SCD) is very common in tribal communities. G6PD deficiency inherited as an X-linked recessive disease is found more in Parsis.
- *Consanguinity*: Consanguineous marriages are common in a few communities. There are increased chances of birth of an affected offspring if there is a marriage (consanguinity) between the close relatives as seen in thalassemia syndrome.
- *Prior history of anemia*: In general, prior history of anemia indicates inherited forms, whereas previously documented normal blood counts in a patient suggest an acquired etiology. However, it must be remembered that certain inherited conditions such as sickle cell anemia and heredity spherocytosis can also present late for the first time/as a first episode. Constitutional (inherited) aplastic anemias (Fanconi anemia) also do not become apparent before the age of 5–6 years and present with evidence of bone marrow failure, congenital anomalies, and short stature.
- *Severity and initiation of symptoms*: Due to compensatory mechanisms, children with chronic anemia may not be as symptomatic as patients with acute anemia with similar hemoglobin values. A neonate with chronic fetomaternal blood loss is asymptomatic in contrast to a neonate with acute blood loss and with initially preserved hemoglobin levels.
- *Questions relating to hemolytic episodes:* Specific questions regarding changes in urine color, scleral icterus, or jaundice associated with the symptoms of anemia should be asked. In hemolytic anemia, because of unconjugated bilirubin, which cannot be excreted in urine, the urine retains its normal color; therefore, a simple history of diaper being stained yellow with urine points to the presence of conjugated bilirubin. Presence of cola-colored urine is suggestive of intravascular hemolysis (G6PD deficiency).
- *History of blood loss*: History of bleeding from the gastrointestinal tract, including history of bowel symptoms, changes in stool color, and/or blood in stools, should be reviewed. Detailed menstrual history in adolescent girls, including duration of periods, flow, and quantitation and saturation of tampons or pads, should be obtained. Black, tarry

stools in a child who is not on supplemental iron raises a possibility of gastrointestinal bleed. It may happen secondary to cow milk protein allergy, a polyp, or Meckel diverticulum.

- *Past medical history*: Enquiries should be made to exclude chronic infection or inflammation as a cause of anemia. Travel from endemic areas of malaria and/or kala-azar should be explored. A mild drop in hemoglobin may be common in acute infections.
- *Prior therapy for anemic episodes*: Earlier anemic episodes, duration, etiology, and resolution, as well as all prior therapy for anemia, should be reviewed. Patients with hemoglobinopathies (such as thalassemias) resulting in the production of small (microcytic) and pale (hypochromic) RBCs, may have a history of treatment on multiple occasions for an erroneous diagnosis of IDA, in which the RBCs are also hypochromic and microcytic.
- *Exposure to drugs and toxins*: Prior medications as well as environmental toxin exposure, including the use of well water containing nitrates, should be reviewed. Any history of oxidant-induced hemolysis should be obtained (e.g., in G6PD deficiency). Certain drugs can induce hemolysis in G6PD deficiency (e.g., primaquine, quinine, aspirin, sulfonamides, and quinolones). Some drugs have a propensity to cause marrow suppression and this possibility always needs to be addressed while evaluating a case of aplastic anemia.
- *Viral infections*: Infections such as Epstein–Barr virus, hepatitis B, hepatitis C, and HIV and cytomegalovirus (CMV) infections are also known to cause acquired aplastic anemias.
- *Lead exposure*: History of intake of indigenous or herbal medications should be undertaken because children receiving these preparations may be at risk for exposure to lead and other toxins. In addition, when evaluating a child with microcytic anemia, one should ask specific questions regarding environment, housing, paint exposure, cooking materials, and use of poorly glazed ceramic pots to evaluate for possible lead exposure.
- *Family history*: A family history of anemia, requirement of repeated blood transfusions, gallstones, splenomegaly, cholecystectomy, or splenectomy may help identify cases of hemolytic anemia.
- *Birth and neonatal history*: A neonatal history including infant and mother's blood type, any history of exchange or intrauterine transfusion, and a history of anemia in the early neonatal period should be obtained. Gestational age at birth is important, because premature infants may have iron or vitamin E deficiencies resulting in anemia. The presence of jaundice or need for phototherapy may signify the presence of an inherited hemolytic anemia. A prolonged hospitalization in the neonatal period is usually associated with multiple blood tests, which lead to decreased future iron stores. Microcytosis at birth should alert the physician to consider chronic intrauterine blood loss and/or alpha thalassemia.
- *Dietary history*: Questions should be primarily aimed at determining iron content in the diet and, to a lesser degree, folate and vitamin B_{12} content. The type of diet, type of formula milk (if iron fortified), and age of infant at the time of discontinuation of formula or breast milk should be documented. In addition, the amount and type of milk the child is drinking should be determined.
- *Pica*: Pica (particularly pagophagia, the eating of ice) is a useful clue to the diagnosis of iron deficiency and/or lead poisoning. A typical dietary history in an infant with IDA is of a child who consumes large amount of cow milk every day without an adequate introduction of semisolids in the diet. A strict vegan diet predisposes to vitamin B_{12} deficiency. A vegan mother may have a baby

with vitamin B_{12} deficiency due to the low maternal stores. Megaloblastic anemia is seen in children (more in rural) who are on goat milk diet that is poor in folate content.

- *Developmental milestones*: Loss of milestones or developmental delay in infants with megaloblastic anemia may signify abnormalities in the cobalamin pathway and folic acid malabsorption. Infants with infantile tremor syndrome have associated developmental delay or regression and have megaloblastic anemia.

Physical Examination

A general overview for relevant examination in relation to anemia and its causes in children is presented in Table 14.2. Besides these, anthropometry with reference to growth retardation (weight and height), evidence of an other system involvement (e.g., liver and kidney), and behavioral changes (e.g., reduced

TABLE 14.2 Physical Findings as Clues to the Etiology of Anemia in Children

Findings	Possible etiology
Skin	
Acral pigmentation	Vitamin B_{12} deficiency
Hyperpigmentation/café au lait spots	Fanconi anemia
Icterus	Hemolytic anemia, hepatitis, vitamin B_{12} deficiency
Cavernous hemangioma	Microangiopathic hemolytic anemia
Ulcers on lower extremities	Sickle cell disease
Facies	
Frontal bossing, prominence of the malar and maxillary bones, depressed nasal bridge (hemolytic facies)	Congenital hemolytic anemias, thalassemia major, severe iron deficiency
Eyes	
Microcornea	Fanconi anemia
Cataracts	Wilson disease with hemolysis
Mucosal/retinal hemorrhage	Acute leukemia
Blindness	Osteopetrosis
Mouth	
Glossitis, angular stomatitis	Vitamin B_{12}, iron deficiency
Hands	
Triphalangeal thumb	Red cell aplasia
Absent thumb, hypoplasia of thenar eminence	Fanconi anemia
Platonychia (flattening), spooning of nails (koilonychia)	Iron deficiency anemia
Lymphadenopathy	Leukemia, lymphoma, HIV
Height	
Short stature	Chronic renal failure, Fanconi anemia
Hepatosplenomegaly	
Visceromegaly	Hemolysis, hypersplenism, leukemia, lymphoma, complicated malaria

attention span and irritability [common in IDA]) remain essential components of physical assessment.

The clues from physical examination with respect to anemia are discussed next.

Isolated Anemia

- IDA
- Megaloblastic anemia (vitamin B_{12} and folate deficiency)
- Pure red cell aplasia
- Thalassemia minor
- Red cell enzyme defects (e.g., G6PD)

Anemia with Hepatosplenomegaly

- Congenital hemolytic anemia (thalassemia major and intermedia, SCD, heredity spherocytosis)
- *Infections*: Malaria and kala-azar
- *Connective tissues disorders*: Systemic-onset juvenile idiopathic arthritis (JIA), systemic lupus erythematosus (SLE)
- *Tumors*: Acute leukemia, lymphoma, and Wilms tumor (a child who looks sick and has anemia, out-of-proportion bleeding, and bone pains with associated hepatosplenomegaly and lymphadenopathy with abnormal blood counts is highly likely to have acute leukemia)
- *Miscellaneous*: Storage disease (Gaucher), hemophagocytic lymphohistiocytosis (HLH)

Anemia with Jaundice

- Hemolytic anemia (SCD)

Anemia with Petechiae and Purpura

- Immune thrombocytopenic purpura (ITP), aplastic anemia, and bleeding diathesis
- Disseminated intravascular coagulation
- Myelodysplastic syndrome

Anemia with Petechiae, Lymphadenopathy, and Hepatosplenomegaly

- Acute leukemia
- Disseminated infections (e.g., HIV)
- Myeloproliferative disorders (chronic myeloid leukemia, myelofibrosis)
- Infiltrative disorders

Clinical Approach to a Bleeding Child

Bleeding in a child may be an isolated event or part of a systemic illness. It is extremely important to discern whether the child is sick or not. By and large, localized bleeds in one area connote local issues.

The abnormal bleeding in a child is primarily because of one of the following two factors: a platelet disorder or a coagulation disorder. A detailed focused history many a time helps to differentiate between the two.

Clinical evaluation of a bleeding patient begins with a careful history, taking into account the child's age, sex, clinical presentation, past history, and family history. While the bleeding history is being elicited, attention should be directed to the type of bleeding present.

Bleeding into the skin and mucous membranes is characteristic of disorders of platelets and blood vessels (purpuric disorders) and may be manifested as petechiae and/or ecchymoses.

Bleeding into soft tissue, muscle, and joints suggests the presence of hemophilia or other disorders of coagulation. Salient differences are shown in Table 14.3.

Age and Sex of the Child

An inherited bleeding disorder should be strongly suspected when the onset of bleeding manifestations occurs in infancy or early childhood and is associated with a positive family history. However, a negative family history does not exclude an inherited coagulation disorder, as up to one-third of patients with hemophilia have a negative family history.

The following are examples of typical presentation:

- A male infant who is starting to walk and presents with a painful swollen joint after a fall has hemophilia until proven otherwise.

TABLE 14.3 Salient Differences Between Coagulation and Platelet Disorders

Clinical findings	Coagulation disorders	Platelet disorders
Skin—petechiae	Not usually seen	Characteristic
Ecchymoses	Common—large, one or more	Characteristic—small or many, scattered
Soft tissue hematoma	Characteristic	Rare
Joint hemorrhages	Characteristic—hallmark of the disease	Not usually seen
Delayed bleeding	Common	Rare
Bleeding from superficial skin abrasions	Uncommon	Common and persistent
Family history of bleeding	Common	Rare
Sex of the patient	Predominantly male	Predominantly female

- An adolescent girl who presents with excessive menstrual bleeding, recurrent nose bleeds, and pallor may have von Willebrand disease (vWD), the most common inherited bleeding disorder.
- A 5-year-old child who is not clinically ill but presents with moderate mucocutaneous purpura in the wake of a viral infection most likely has acute postinfectious ITP.
- A teenage girl with easy bruising and mild pallor presenting with a strong family history of autoimmune disorders (e.g., rheumatoid arthritis, systemic lupus erythematosus, or Hashimoto thyroiditis) may have chronic ITP.
- A 10-day-old infant with bleeding from the umbilical stump should be evaluated for factor XIII deficiency. Intracranial hemorrhage in an infant without other risk factors should also prompt consideration of this diagnosis.

Family History

The family history is helpful in formulating a possible diagnosis of an inherited disorder of coagulation. The presence of bleeding manifestations only in male siblings and maternal uncles is suggestive of X-linked recessive inheritance, such as that seen in hemophilia A or B.

In contrast, in autosomal dominant traits such as hereditary hemorrhagic telangiectasia (Osler–Weber–Rendu disease), an accurate pedigree will show affected individuals of both sexes for several generations. In autosomal recessive disorders, such as severe forms of the rarer coagulation factor deficiencies (e.g., factor VII or factor XI deficiency), the family history may be negative; consanguinity increases the probability of such disorders.

Medication

A thorough history of medication use is mandatory. Specific information should be sought about the ingestion of nonsteroidal anti-inflammatory drugs (NSAIDs). Such drugs impair platelet function and may exacerbate an underlying bleeding disorder. In addition, use of such drugs within 1–2 weeks of platelet function testing may cause abnormalities, which may lead to further expensive and unnecessary studies.

Complete Blood Counts

With the increasing availability of particle counters, the use of CBC has exponentially increased. A cursory look at the printouts is likely to miss important information.

- The automated machine measures total RBC count, hemoglobin, and MCV. It derives RBC indices such as HCt, MCH, and MCHC.
- The MCV in a neonate is around 100 fL. The lower limit of normal is given by 70 + (age in years) and the upper limit of normal is given by 84 + 0.6 (age in years), to define microcytes and macrocytes, respectively (corresponding adult values are 80 and 96 fL, respectively).
- The RDW is an index of the variation in cell volume within the red cell population. It is a measure of anisocytosis.
- RDW = ([standard deviation of red cell volume]/[mean cell volume]) × 100. Red cell populations with higher-than-normal RDW are termed *heterogeneous*; those with normal RDW are termed *homogeneous*.
- A combination of microcytosis and increased RDW is almost diagnostic of IDA, whereas microcytosis with normal RDW will suggest beta thalassemia trait.
- RDW is increased when there are lots of reticulocytes in the blood. This can happen in hemolytic anemia as well as following administration of hematinics in deficiency anemia. In dimorphic anemia, the anisocytosis will be marked, reflected by increased RDW. MCV may be near normal because of a mixed population of microcytes and macrocytes.
- A combination of increased RDW and MCHC is almost unique to congenital spherocytosis, whereas marked macrocytosis with increased MCHC may suggest autoimmune hemolytic anemia.
- Nucleated red blood cells are counted by all hematology analyzers (regardless of technique) as white blood cells. This is a common experience in cases of sickle cell anemia where the WBC count is reported to be very high.
- Reticulocyte count is an essential parameter in the evaluation of any anemia. However, routine reticulocyte count is not preferred because the number of reticulocytes is spuriously elevated as the number of RBCs falls in anemia. Hence, a corrected reticulocyte should be asked for. Hemorrhage, hemolysis, and iron therapy in IDA increase the reticulocyte count while aplastic/hypoplastic anemia, leukemia, and bone marrow infiltration decrease it.
- A low platelet count by the counter must be manually cross-checked. The counter also provides information regarding platelet size. Platelets with MPV >10 fL are regarded as large and when the marrow is active and producing platelets, the younger platelets that are larger in size will have a high MPV, thus giving a clue to peripheral destruction. When MPV is <6, it is suggestive of small platelet size and can be a feature of Wiskott–Aldrich syndrome, aplastic anemia, and TAR syndrome.
- A well-prepared and examined peripheral smear still retains an extreme value to help in the diagnosis of anemia and other hematological diseases.
- All the laboratory parameters and the results must be interpreted in the context of thorough history, physical examination, and previously prepared reports.

KEY POINTS

- Anemia in children often has widespread manifestations in children and may be either a primary presentation or a manifestation of an underlying systemic disorder.
- Although pallor remains a common symptom of anemia, very often the signs and symptoms may be nonspecific.
- A complete history and physical examination along with complete blood counts are essential tools for the diagnosis of anemia in children. A good peripheral smear is still extremely useful in the workup for anemia and other hematological diseases.

CHAPTER 15

Neonatal Resuscitation

Rinki H Shah, Paresh A Thakkar

More than 90% of babies have smooth transition from intrauterine to extrauterine life, with little or no assistance required. Only less than 10% of babies require some assistance and about 1% of these require extensive resuscitation. However, perinatal asphyxia is one of the leading causes of perinatal mortality in developing countries. Neonatal resuscitation is a lifesaving procedure. Every birth should be considered as a medical emergency. Adequate infrastructure and facilities for neonatal resuscitation at birth should be available.

Every birth should be attended by personnel who have been trained at initiating neonatal resuscitation and additional personnel would be necessary if full resuscitation is required. The American Academy of Pediatrics in collaboration with the American Heart Association has formulated guidelines for neonatal resuscitation, which were released in 2010 and last updated in 2015. The National Neonatology Forum (NNF) of India has made some necessary changes so that these guidelines can be followed even in a resource-limited setting.

Transitional Changes at Birth

The transition from being a fetus to a newborn is one of the most amazing events in human life but it is also one of the most stressful. Oxygen is needed for survival both during fetal life and after birth. Before birth, the oxygen to the fetus is supplied by its diffusion across the placental membrane from the mother's blood supply. During fetal life, the fetal lungs are filled with fluid and do not play any role in oxygenation of blood. After birth, the placenta is no longer a source of oxygen supply and the baby will have to depend on the lungs for oxygen supply. At the time of birth, with the first cry or with the few initial breaths, several changes take place whereby the lungs take over the function of respiration.

The following are the major changes that occur during "*normal transition*":

- The fluid in the alveoli of lungs gets absorbed and they get filled with air (Fig. 15.1).
- Clamping of the cord removes the low-resistance placental circuit and causes increase in systemic vascular resistance.

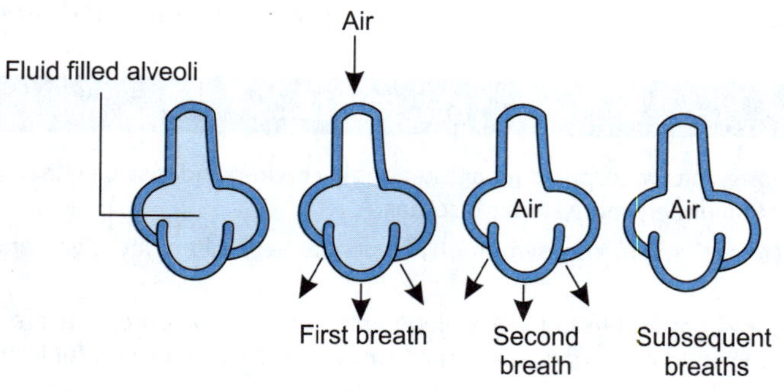

Figure 15.1 Fluid in the alveoli replaced by air.

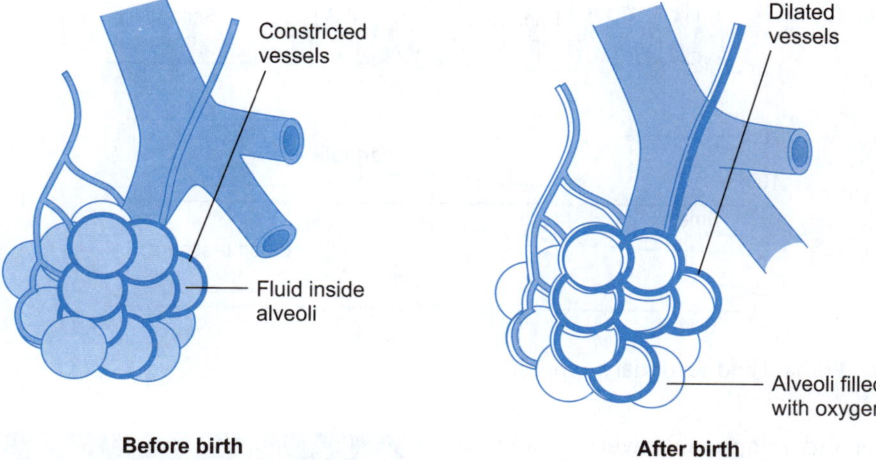

Figure 15.2 Dilatation of pulmonary arterioles due to oxygen in alveoli.

- Decrease in pulmonary vascular resistance causes an increase in pulmonary blood flow. This is due to increase in oxygen concentration in the alveoli that causes relaxation of pulmonary arterioles (Fig. 15.2).
- As the oxygen concentration in the blood increases, ductus arteriosus begins to constrict.
- The blood that was being shunted through ductus arteriosus now goes to pulmonary circulation and the oxygenated blood subsequently gets into systemic circulation (Fig. 15.3).

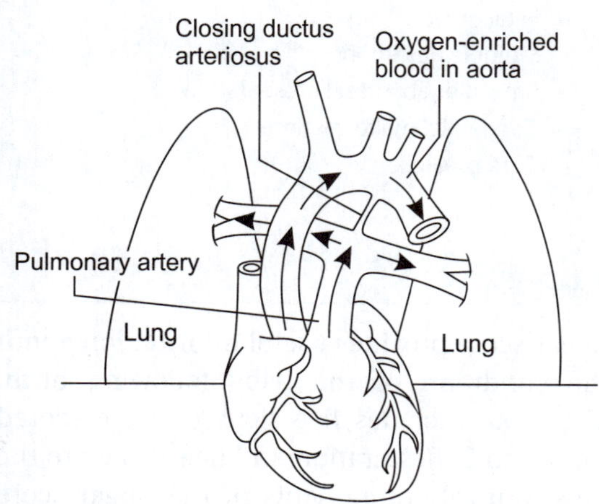

Figure 15.3 Closure of ductus arteriosus causing change in pulmonary circulation. *Source*: Reproduced with permission from Textbook of Neonatal Resuscitation: India, 2nd edn. National Neonatology Forum of India: New Delhi.

Perinatal Asphyxia

The term perinatal asphyxia is preferred over the term birth asphyxia, as this may occur before, during, or after birth. NNF India defines perinatal asphyxia as "gasping or ineffective breathing or lack of breathing at one minute of life." The asphyxiated newborn when deprived of oxygen passes through a series of events:

- There is rapid breathing and a fall in heart rate.
- If asphyxia continues, heart rate falls further and the baby enters *primary apnea*. Most babies will resume breathing in primary apnea when stimulated.
- Irregular gasping respirations occur and there is a further drop in heart rate and blood pressure.
- This leads to *secondary apnea*, which does not respond to tactile stimulation and needs assisted ventilation.

It is important to note that the apnea may be secondary to an asphyxia injury that could occur in utero, or during or just after birth. The infant might have gone through primary or secondary apnea while in utero. When the baby is born apneic, it is not possible to distinguish clinically whether it is primary

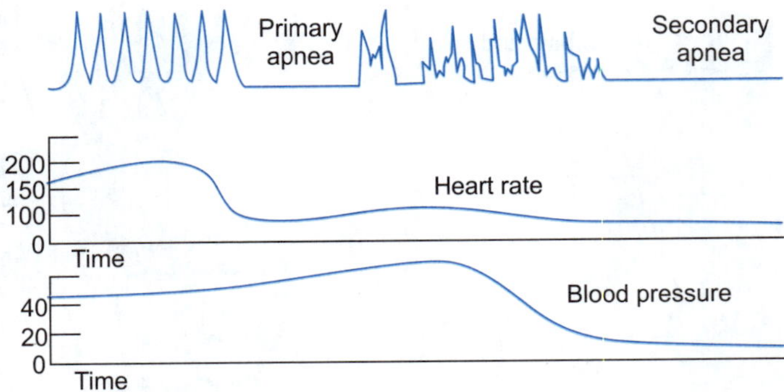

Figure 15.4 Primary and secondary apnea.

apnea or secondary apnea. However, response to physical stimulation may help differentiate the two: primary apnea will abort following tactile stimulation, whereas secondary apnea requires assisted ventilation (Fig. 15.4).

Preparation for Resuscitation

Every birth should be attended by at least one skilled personnel and if any complication is anticipated or already known before delivery, additional personnel are required. All necessary equipment should be kept ready in the labor room and should be functional. The risk factors requiring the need for resuscitation should be anticipated and are given in Box 15.1.

It should be kept in mind that up to half of the newborns who require resuscitation have no identifiable risk factors at birth. For the same reason, one should always be prepared for resuscitation in every delivery. A successful resuscitation thus depends on anticipation, adequate preparation, initiating the procedure promptly, and performing the procedure skillfully.

Equipment for Neonatal Resuscitation

The equipment for neonatal resuscitation should always be kept ready. This is shown in Box 15.2.

Box 15.1 Maternal and fetal risk factors

- **Maternal risk factors**
  - Pregnancy-induced hypertension or eclampsia
  - Meconium-stained liquor
  - Pronged labor
  - Obstructed labor
  - Oligohydramnios/polyhydramnios
  - Maternal infection
  - Maternal diabetes
  - Prolonged rupture of membranes
  - Premature labor
  - Placenta previa
  - Abruptio placentae
  - Bad obstetric history
  - Instrumental or operative delivery
- **Fetal risk factors**
  - Fetal distress
  - Multiple gestations
  - Breech or abnormal presentation
  - Congenital malformations
  - Cord prolapse

Apgar Score

Apgar score provides useful information about the condition of the baby following birth. The score includes five signs that are scored from 0 to 2. Respiration and heart rate are the most critical components of the Apgar score as muscle tone, reflex stimulus, and color are dependent on cardiorespiratory status and gestational maturity of the newborn. Thus, the total score ranges from 0 to 10. It is assessed at 1 and 5 minutes. If the 5-minute score is less

Box 15.2 Equipment for neonatal resuscitation

- Baby corner in labor room
- Radiant warmer
- Suction equipment such as bulb syringe, mechanical suction and tubing foot suction, mucus extractor, suction catheter
- Warm linens
- Stethoscope
- Self-inflating bag
- Face masks
- Oxygen source with flow meter and tubing
- Intubation equipment
  - Laryngoscope with straight blades
  - Extra bulbs and batteries
  - Endotracheal tubes 2.5/3.0/3.5/4.0
  - Tape
  - Laryngeal mask airway if available
- Drugs
  - Adrenaline
  - Normal saline
  - Ringer lactate
  - Soda bicarbonate
  - Dextrose 10%
- Syringes
- Needles
- For cutting umbilical cord
  - Sterile gloves
  - Scissors
  - Umbilical clamp
- Umbilical catheter
- Central oxygen supply
- Pulse oximeter
- Compressed air
- Transport trolley incubator for shifting baby to NICU

than 7, then extended Apgar is done every 5 minutes up to 20 minutes till the Apgar score becomes 7 (Table 15.1).

Limitation: Apgar score *cannot be used as a guide to resuscitation* since the score is not assigned till 1 minute and the resuscitation starts at 30 seconds. However, it is a basic and simple clinical tool to assess the condition of the baby at birth. Apgar score at 1 minute indicates need for resuscitation and 5-minute score indicates the adaptation of the baby to the external environment.

Resuscitation Procedures

The flow diagram for resuscitation is shown in Figure 15.5. Resuscitation begins with the birth of the baby.

Immediate evaluation: At birth, the baby should be evaluated for the need of resuscitation by answering the following questions:

- Term gestation?
- Breathing or crying?
- Good muscle tone?

If answer to all the above-mentioned three questions is "yes," then no active resuscitation is required. Such babies receive "routine care."

- The baby should be dried, covered with dry linen, and provided warmth by skin-to-skin contact with the mother.
- Clearing of upper airway can be done by wiping the baby's mouth and nose. Ongoing breathing and activity can be observed with the baby on the mother's chest and the breastfeeding can be initiated.

TABLE 15.1 Apgar Score

Sign	0	1	2
Appearance (color)	Blue or pale	Pink body, blue extremities	Completely pink
Pulse rate/heart rate	Absent	<100	>100
Grimace (reflex irritability)*	None	Grimace	Cry or active withdrawal
Activity (muscle tone)	Limp	Some flexion	Active motion
Respiratory effort	Absent	Gasping	Good cry

*Reflex irritability is assessed by inserting a catheter inside the nose.

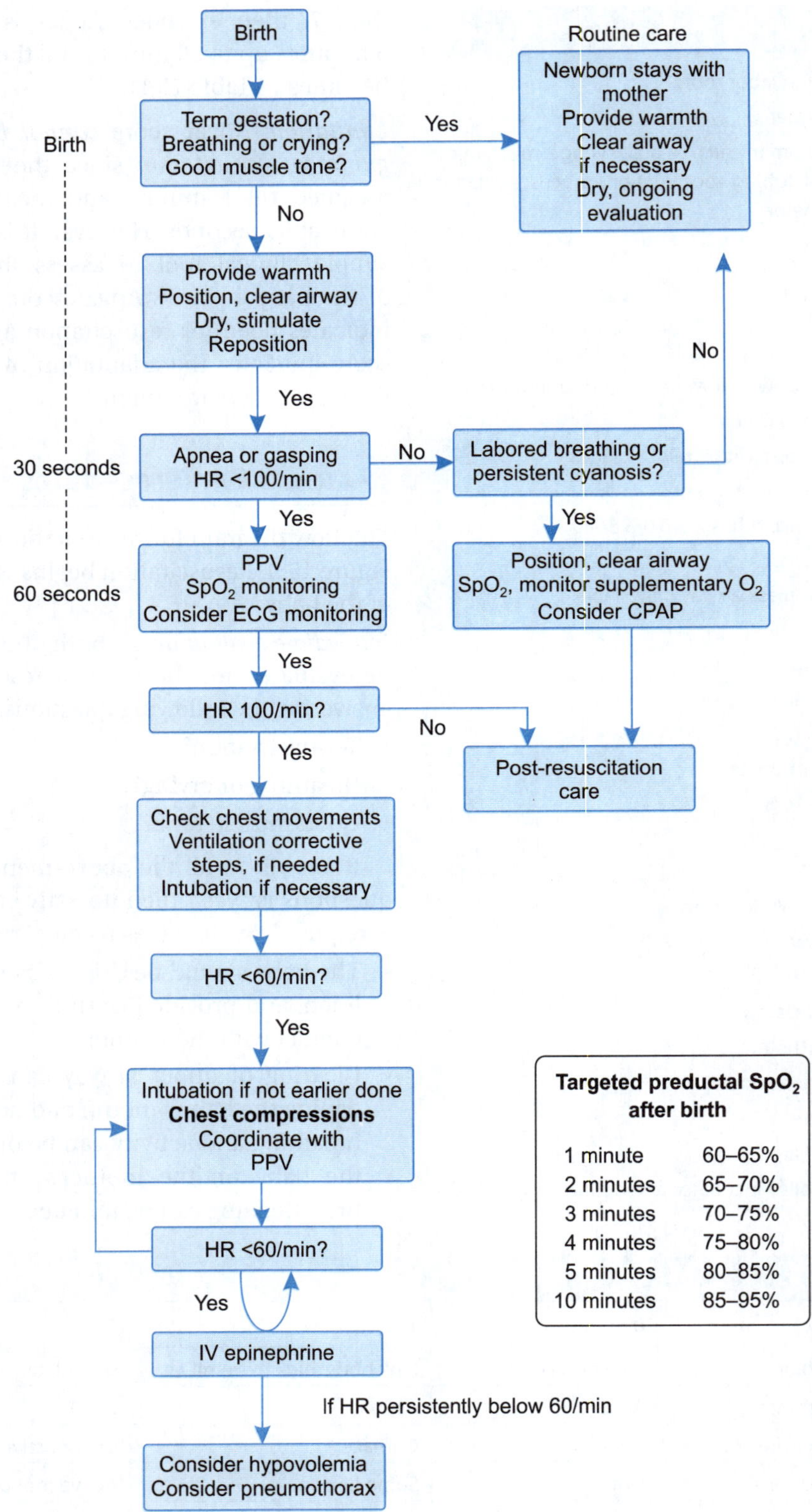

Figure 15.5 Resuscitation of the newborn (American Heart Association 2015 guidelines).

Box 15.3 Sequence of events during resuscitation

Step 1

- Initial steps of resuscitation
  - Providing warmth
  - Positioning
  - Clearing airway if necessary
  - Drying
  - Stimulation

Step 2

- Ventilation

Step 3

- Chest compression

Step 4

- Administration of medications (epinephrine/volume expansion)

If the answer to any of the above-mentioned three assessments is "no," then one should proceed for resuscitation as per the algorithm in Figure 15.5.

Preterm infants are given special attention owing to the fact that they have:

- Fragile skin
- Immature lungs
- Immature brain
- Fragile blood vessels of brain
- Immature tissues
- High risk of infection
- Less muscle mass and poor tone

Stepwise sequence of events has been described in Box 15.3.

Step 1: Initial Steps of Resuscitation

Once it is decided that the baby needs resuscitation, the "initial steps" should be initiated immediately and carried out in the correct sequence.

Provide Warmth

Cord should be cut immediately (without delay) for the babies who need resuscitation. The baby should be immediately placed under a preheated radiant warmer. This can be done by turning the warmer on for at least 20 minutes and using manual mode prior to delivery.

Other methods of maintaining temperature of a newborn in the delivery room include prewarming the linen, drying, placing the baby on the mother giving skin-to-skin contact, and covering the baby with a blanket. The baby's temperature should be closely monitored.

Positioning

The positioning should be done by slight extension of the neck. The baby should be positioned on his/her back, with the neck slightly extended in a sniffing position, because in this position, pharynx, larynx, and trachea are aligned in a straight line and facilitate unrestricted air entry to the lungs. To attain a correct posture, use a rolled blanket under the shoulder (shoulder roll) (Fig. 15.6).

Clear the Airway

The method for clearing the airway depends on whether the amniotic fluid is clear or meconium stained.

- *When amniotic fluid is clear*: Routine vigorous suction is not recommended in all babies. Vigorous nasopharyngeal suction can cause bradycardia. It should be done only for those babies who have obvious nasal or oral secretions. Suction should be done thoroughly, first from mouth and then

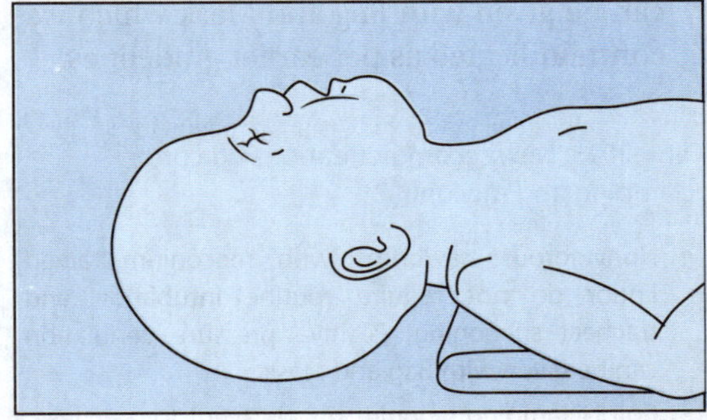

Figure 15.6 Positioning the baby by putting a shoulder roll. *Source*: Reproduced with permission from Textbook of Neonatal Resuscitation: India. National Neonatology Forum of India: New Delhi.

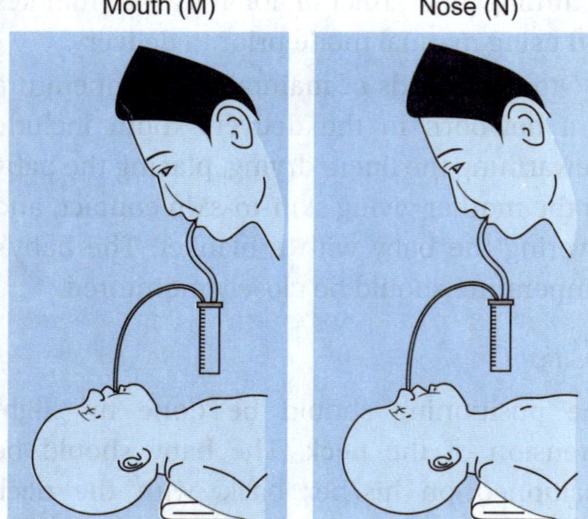

Figure 15.7 Suctioning the mouth and nose. *Source*: Reproduced with permission from Textbook of Neonatal Resuscitation: India, 2nd edn. National Neonatology Forum of India: New Delhi.

from nose either with bulb syringe or with suction catheter (Fig. 15.7).

- *When amniotic fluid is meconium stained*: In case of meconium-stained liquor, first suction mouth and posterior pharynx using a 12F or 14F catheter. In the earlier guidelines, direct suctioning of trachea by endotracheal intubation was recommended for nonvigorous babies. A nonvigorous baby is one who is limp, has labored breathing, and whose heart rate is less than 100/min. In the current guidelines of NRP 2015, direct suctioning of trachea is no longer recommended. Positive pressure ventilation can be given with Bag and Mask which was contraindicated as per earlier guidelines.

> **NRP 2015: New recommendations on cord clamping and meconium**
>
> - Nonvigorous newborns with meconium-stained liquor do not require routine intubation and tracheal suctioning. Positive pressure ventilation can be given with Bag and Mask.
> - Cord clamping should be delayed for at least 30–60 seconds for most vigorous term and preterm newborns. For babies who need resuscitation at birth and in conditions such as antepartum hemorrhage, the cord should be clamped immediately.

Dry, Stimulate to Breathe, and Reposition

- Once the airway is clear of the secretions, immediately dry the baby to prevent further heat loss. The baby is dried from head to toe with the help of a prewarmed clean towel. Drying and cleaning of airway by suctioning usually are enough to stimulate breathing. The baby needs to be repositioned to ensure slight extension of the neck.
- Tactile stimulation: Usually suctioning and drying provide stimulus to breathe. However, if breathing remains inadequate, tactile stimulation is given. This can be done either by gently flicking or slapping the sole of foot or by gently rubbing the back of the baby. Vigorous stimulations such as squeezing the rib cage and holding the baby upside down are inappropriate and can cause serious injuries. A newborn with primary apnea responds to tactile stimulation; failure to respond implies secondary apnea for which positive-pressure ventilation (PPV) should be started immediately without any delay (Fig. 15.8). Tactile stimulation should not be prolonged unduly or repeatedly after one or

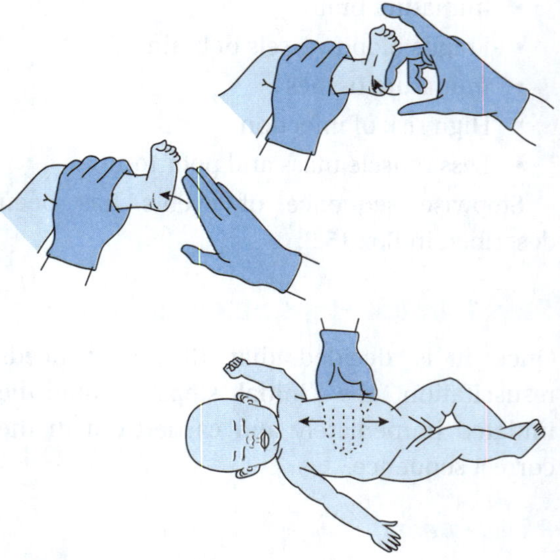

Figure 15.8 Appropriate methods for tactile stimulation. *Source*: Reproduced with permission from Textbook of Neonatal Resuscitation: India. National Neonatology Forum of India: New Delhi.

two attempts as valuable time may be lost to revive the baby.

Evaluation of Initial Steps

"The golden minute"/first 60 seconds are allotted for completion of initial steps, re-evaluating, and beginning ventilation, if required. The entire process of initial steps should not take more than 30 seconds. The parameters to be evaluated are respiration, heart rate, and status of oxygenation.

- *Respiration*: Check whether the baby has apnea or gasping respiration. The baby should have good respiration with good chest movements. In some babies, like in the case of a preterm baby, respiration can be labored, which might need additional respiratory support and monitoring.
- *Heart rate*: Assessment of heart rate can be done with a stethoscope or by palpating the umbilical cord at its base. Count heart rate for 6 seconds and multiply by 10. This gives a quick estimate of heart rate that whether it is less than or more than 100/min. Improvement in heart rate is a very sensitive indicator of a successful resuscitation or corrective step.
- *Status of oxygenation*: Check for the skin color and look for any evidence of cyanosis. Normally babies look pink in color. Status of oxygenation can be best determined by pulse oximeter if available.

2015: New recommendations on heart rate assessment

- Initial assessment of heart rate should be done with a stethoscope. Umbilical cord pulsations are less accurate as they may underestimate the true heart rate.
- Pulse oximeter can be used to assess heart rate.
- Use of electronic cardiac monitor is recommended for accurate assessment of heart rate while giving positive-pressure ventilation or chest compression.

Inference After Initial Steps

- If all three vital parameters are normal, i.e., respiration is good, heart rate is more than 100, and baby color is pink, then only "observational care" is required.
- If heart rate is more than 100 beats per minute but respiration is labored, and baby is cyanotic, administration of supplemental oxygen and continuous positive airway pressure (CPAP) should be considered.

Use of Supplemental Oxygen

Free-flow oxygen can be given to a spontaneously breathing infant, who appears cyanosed or has labored breathing. Use of supplemental oxygen should be guided by pulse oximeter, because both hypoxia and hyperoxia are dangerous to the baby.

Methods of giving supplemental oxygen

- Oxygen tubing held close to the baby's nose and mouth with cupped hand
- Oxygen mask (Fig. 15.9)
- Flow-inflating bag and mask
- T-piece resuscitator
- CPAP (preterm babies)

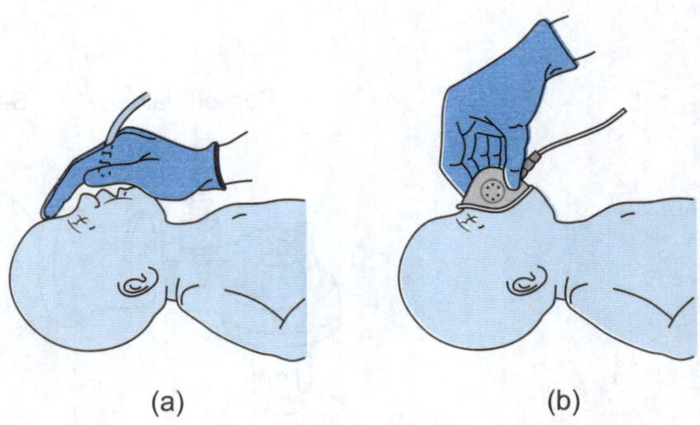

Figure 15.9 Supplemental oxygen: (a) with tubing and (b) with mask. *Source*: Reproduced with permission from Textbook of Neonatal Resuscitation: India. National Neonatology Forum of India: New Delhi.

NRP 2015: New recommendations on oxygen use

- In newborns ≥35 weeks' gestation, resuscitation should begin with 21% oxygen (room air) while in those <35 weeks' gestation, it should begin with 21–30% oxygen.
- If the baby is breathing and SpO_2 is not within the target range, administer free-flow oxygen, start oxygen concentration at 30%, and, if needed, increase and adjust the concentration of oxygen to achieve the target SpO_2.
- Trial of continuous positive airway pressure (CPAP) is indicated if a newborn has labored breathing and is not maintaining SpO_2 in the target range despite 100% free-flow oxygen.

Step 2: Positive-Pressure Ventilation

This is the most important and most effective step in neonatal resuscitation.

Indications

After completion of initial steps, PPV is indicated:

- If the baby is apneic or gasping
- If heart rate is less than 100 bpm

Methods of Delivering Positive-Pressure Ventilation

- Self-inflating bag—most commonly used
- Flow-inflating bag (anesthesia bag)
- T-piece resuscitator
- Laryngeal mask airway

Self-inflating bag

The self-inflating bag is the most commonly used device for providing PPV (Fig. 15.10). Due to elastic recoil, the bag remains inflated and does not require a constant gas source to remain inflated. It has a safety mechanism called "pop-off valve," which releases extra pressure that is usually set at 35–40 cm H_2O. There is a site for attachment of oxygen tubing and oxygen reservoir. However, in the absence of oxygen, this can be used with room air. For use in a newborn, it should be appropriately sized with volume ranging between 250 and 750 mL.

How to check functionality of self-inflating bag?

Each time, the functionality of the bag should be checked prior to use for resuscitation. For this, assemble the device correctly.

- Check for any visible cracks or break in the device.
- Squeeze the bag and release; it should inflate automatically.
- With squeeze, check for the airflow at the patient's end.
- Try to occlude the patient's end and check for the hissing sound and movement of pop-off valve.
- Check for the fish mouth valve; it should open and close.

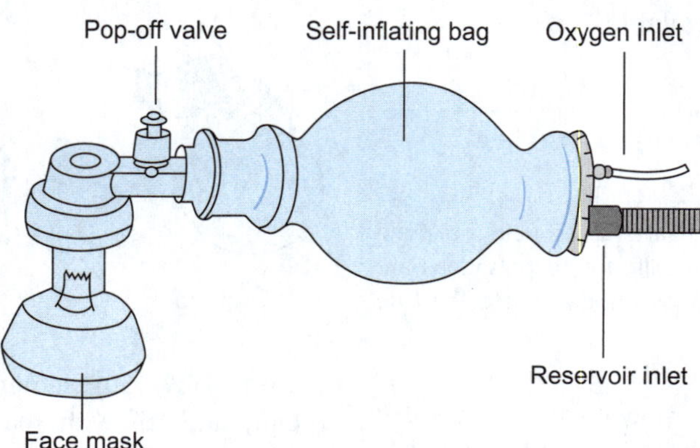

Figure 15.10 Different parts of self-inflating bag. *Source*: Reproduced with permission from Textbook of Neonatal Resuscitation: India, 2nd edn. National Neonatology Forum of India: New Delhi.

How to provide ventilation using self-inflating bag?

Positioning

- The baby should be put on a flat, firm, and clean surface.
- Position the head so that there is slight extension of neck; shoulder roll may be used.
- Rescuer should stand at the head end of the baby.

Application of face mask The face masks should be appropriately sized. They are available in a variety of sizes, shapes, and materials (Fig. 15.11). An appropriate face mask must form a tight seal around the mouth and nose but should not cover the eyes or overlap the chin (Fig. 15.12). Commonly, two masks for newborns are used, a preterm and a term mask. Masks with round shape and with cushioned rim are preferable.

- Apply the facemask firmly and gently to cover mouth, nose, and chin and achieve an air-tight seal.
- The mask is usually held with thumb, index, and/or middle finger encircling much of the rim by using the nondominant hand.

Providing ventilation

- Using the dominant hand, squeeze the bag between thumb and two fingers.
- Deliver breaths at the rate of 40–60/min.
- For this, one may speak loudly "squeeze, two, three."
- Deliver a breath when you speak "squeeze" and allow the bag to recoil during "two, three" (Fig. 15.13).

Assess the effectiveness and response to PPV

- Check for the chest rise and see for the improvement in heart rate.

Figure 15.11 Two sizes of face masks (1 and 0) used in newborns. *Source*: Reproduced with permission from Textbook of Neonatal Resuscitation: India, 2nd edn. National Neonatology Forum of India: New Delhi.

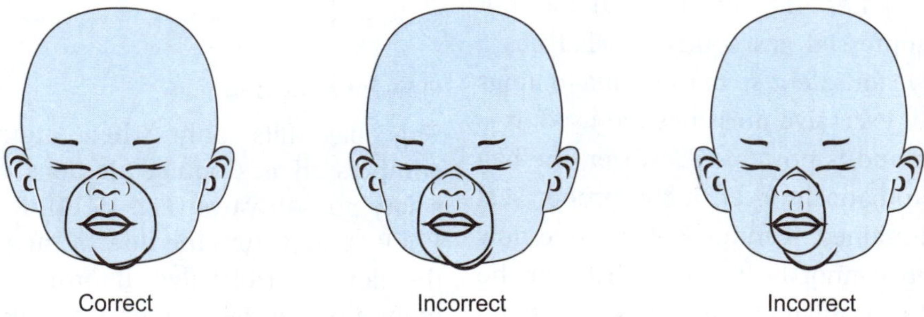

Figure 15.12 Application of face mask.

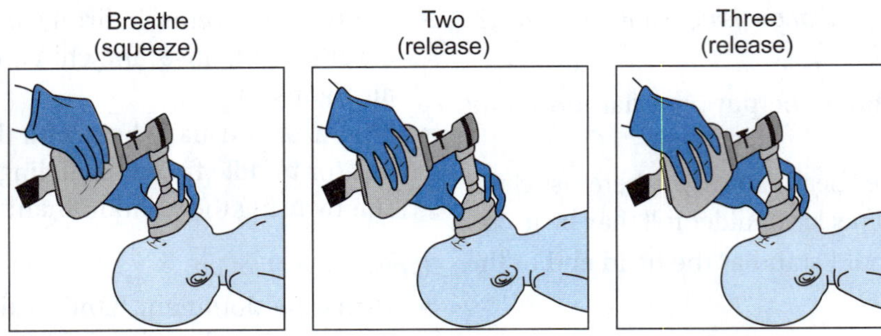

Figure 15.13 Delivering 40–60 breaths using self-inflating bag. *Source*: Reproduced with permission from Textbook of Neonatal Resuscitation: India, 2nd edn. National Neonatology Forum of India: New Delhi.

- Improvement in the baby's condition is indicated by increasing heart rate, improving color, spontaneous breathing (adequate chest rise with bilateral air entry), and initiation of active movements by the baby.
- Failure to improve may be due to inadequate seal, blocked airway, and not enough pressure being applied.

Evaluation after PPV

- If the heart rate is above 100 bpm and the baby is having sustained respiratory effort, then stop PPV and keep the baby under observational care with the mother.
- If the heart rate is more than 60 bpm but less than 100 bpm, continue PPV as long as the baby is showing improvement but ensure effective PPV.
- If the baby's heart rate is below 60 bpm despite 30 seconds of effective PPV, then start chest compressions.

The self-inflating bag has the advantage that it always reinflates after each use and does not need a compressed gas source. It also has a pop-off valve for safety, so barotrauma to lungs is avoided if excessive pressures are used. It is easy to use and is portable. However, the bag inflates automatically even if the proper seal is not maintained, cannot deliver free-flow oxygen, and cannot be used as CPAP in the absence of a positive end-expiratory pressure (PEEP) valve and compressed gas source.

Contraindications for Bag and Mask Ventilation

- Congenital diaphragmatic hernia
- Tracheoesophageal fistula

In babies who require PPV with bag and mask for longer than several minutes, orogastric (Ryle's tube) tube should be inserted and it is left in place, as air may cause stomach distension, preventing full expansion of lungs by the compressing diaphragm.

NRP 2015: New recommendations on positive-pressure ventilation

- A trial of PPV may be considered if the baby is breathing and heart rate is more than 100 bpm, but SpO_2 cannot be maintained within the target range despite free-flow oxygen or CPAP.
- When PPV is required for a preterm infant, it is preferable to use a device that can deliver positive end-expiratory pressure (PEEP); PEEP of 5 cm H_2O is recommended. Initial ventilation pressure should be 20–25 cm H_2O.
- For preterm infants, use of CPAP immediately after birth can be considered as an alternative to routine intubation and prophylactic surfactant administration.

Flow-inflating bag

This bag fills only when attached to a compressed gas source. It does not have a safety pop-off valve (Fig. 15.14). It can deliver PEEP by adjusting the flow of the gas through the flow control valve. If proper seal is not maintained at the face mask or if there is no or low flow of oxygen from the gas source, it will

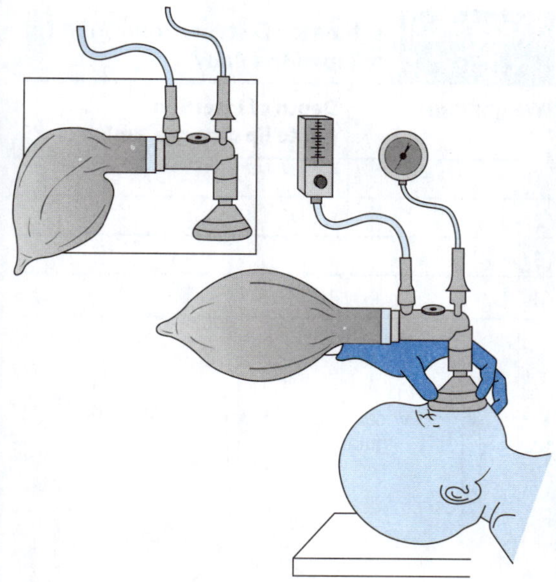

Figure 15.14 Flow-inflating bag. *Source*: Reproduced with permission from Textbook of Neonatal Resuscitation: India, 2nd edn. National Neonatology Forum of India: New Delhi.

get collapsed immediately and it will not be possible to deliver positive-pressure breaths.

T-piece resuscitator

It is a flow-controlled, pressure-limited ventilator device. Here, peak inspiratory pressure (PIP) and PEEP can be set. Inspiratory time or inflation time varies depending on the occlusion of the outlet hole.

Advantages

- It delivers PIP and PEEP consistently.
- It can be used to provide free flow of oxygen reliably.
- Provider does not get tired if ventilation is required for a longer duration.

Disadvantages

- It requires constant gas source and a blender.
- Pressures are required to be fixed before starting ventilation.
- Inspiratory pressure cannot be changed while using a T-piece resuscitator.

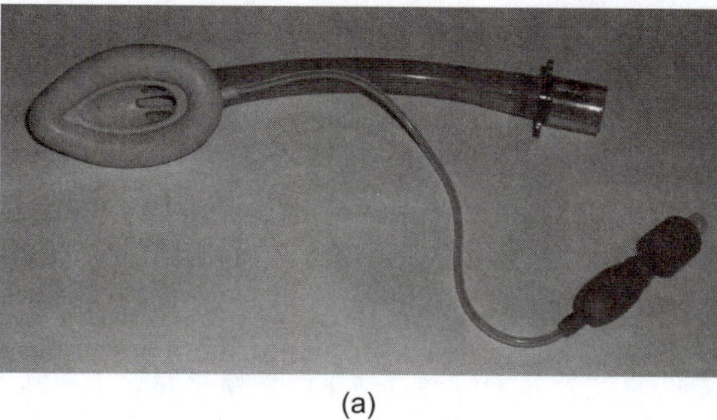

(a)

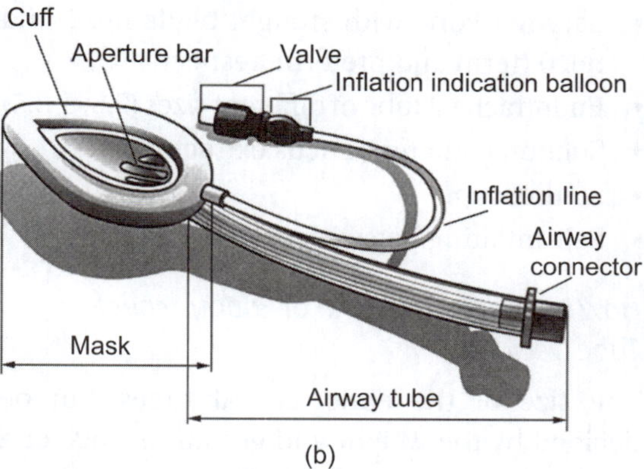

(b)

Figure 15.15 (a) Laryngeal mask airway. (b) Components of laryngeal mask airway. *Source*: Jacob R. Understanding Paediatric Anaesthesia, 3rd edn. Wolters Kluwer India: New Delhi, 2015.

Laryngeal mask airway

- It can be considered during resuscitation when face mask ventilation is ineffective and tracheal intubation is unsuccessful (Fig. 15.15).
- It fits over the laryngeal inlet and can be used for ventilating newborns ≥34 weeks of gestation.

Endotracheal Intubation

Endotracheal intubation may be indicated at several points during resuscitation.

Indications

- When bag and mask ventilation is ineffective or required for longer duration (more than 2 minutes)
- When chest compressions are performed for better coordination with PPV

- When PPV is needed and bag and mask ventilation is contraindicated like in suspected or proven case of congenital diaphragmatic hernia
- For extremely low-birth-weight babies (<1000 g) when appropriately fitting size of masks is not available
- For endotracheal administration of adrenaline

Equipment Used for Endotracheal Intubation

- Laryngoscope with straight blade no. 1 and no. 0 (term and preterm, respectively)
- Endotracheal tube of different sizes (2.5, 3, 3.5)
- Suction catheter/mucus extractor
- Stethoscope
- Self-inflating bag with oxygen reservoir

How are Size and Length of Endotracheal Tube Decided?

The size of the endotracheal tubes can be decided by the weight and gestational age of a newborn as shown in Table 15.2.

To decide the length of endotracheal tube to be inserted, calculate the "tip to lip distance" by adding 6 to the newborn's weight, e.g., if the baby's weight is 3 kg, then the tip of the tube should be inserted till 9 cm from the lip margin (Table 15.3). Endotracheal tubes also have a vocal cord guide, which should rest at the area of vocal cords. Vocal cord guide is seen as a black marking over the endotracheal tube (Fig. 15.16).

Noncuffed tubes are recommended for use in neonatal resuscitation. The tubes with a uniform diameter are preferred while tubes with tapering ends are not (Fig. 15.17).

TABLE 15.2 Size of Endotracheal Tubes

Weight (kg)	Gestational age (weeks)	Tube size (inside diameter, mm)
Below 1000	Below 28	2.5
1000–2000	28–34	3
2000–3000	34–38	3.5
Above 3000	Above 38	3.5–4

TABLE 15.3 Estimated Distance from Tube Tip to Lip of the Baby

Weight (kg)	Depth of insertion (tip to lip distance, cm)
1	7
2	8
3	9
4	10

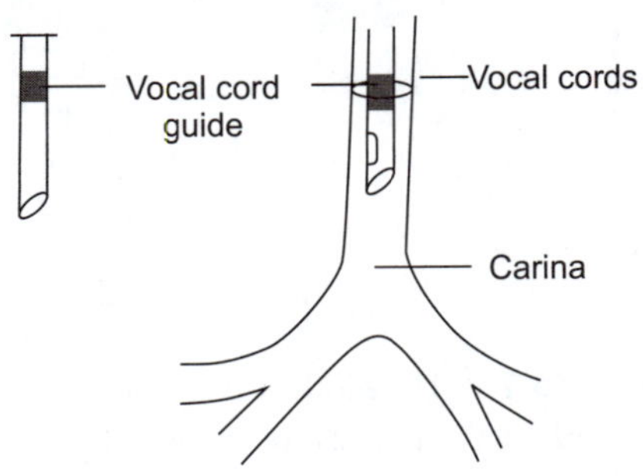

Figure 15.16 Vocal cord guide of endotracheal tube. *Source*: Reproduced with permission from Textbook of Neonatal Resuscitation: India, 2nd edn. National Neonatology Forum of India: New Delhi.

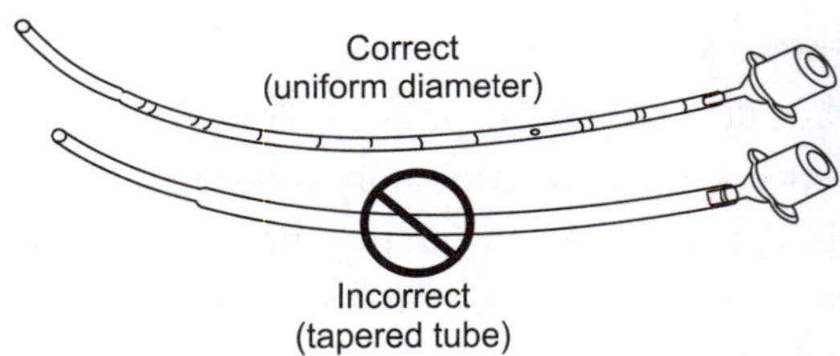

Figure 15.17 Endotracheal tube with uniform diameter. *Source*: Reproduced with permission from Textbook of Neonatal Resuscitation: India, 2nd edn. National Neonatology Forum of India: New Delhi.

Precautions While Performing Endotracheal Intubation

- Preoxygenate before attempting intubation.
- Deliver free-flow oxygen during intubation.
- Limit attempts to 20 seconds; if the newborn cannot be intubated in 20 seconds, then remove the laryngoscope and provide bag and mask ventilation and then try again.

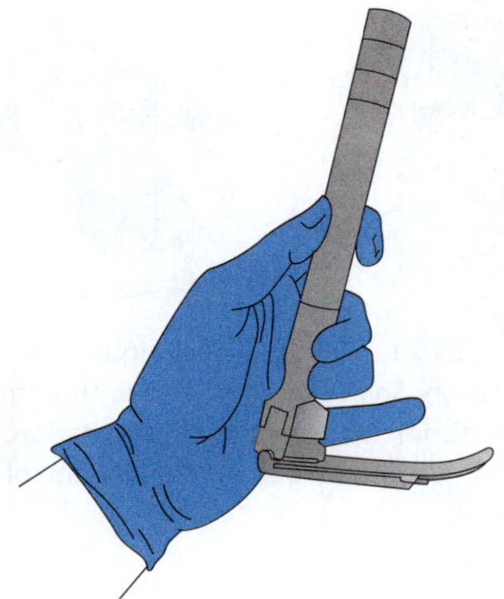

Figure 15.18 Correct method of holding a laryngoscope. *Source*: Reproduced with permission from Textbook of Neonatal Resuscitation: India, 2nd edn. National Neonatology Forum of India: New Delhi.

Procedure of Intubation

- Place the baby on a firm surface in a sniffing position, hold laryngoscope with a blade attached to it in your left hand (Fig. 15.18), and insert endotracheal tube through right side of tongue.
- Place the tip of the blade in the vallecula and gently compress the epiglottis against the base of the tongue, visualize the glottis, hold the endotracheal tube in your right hand, and insert it till the vocal cord guide through vocal cords.

Signs to Check Correct Placement of Endotracheal Tube

- Breath sounds heard on both sides of chest but decreased or absent over epigastrium
- No gastric distension
- Mist in the tube during exhalation
- Increase in heart rate and improvement in color of baby
- Symmetrical movement of chest with each breath
- CO_2 detection in expired air (end-tidal CO_2 measurement)

Common Problems and Complications Associated with Endotracheal Intubation

- Endotracheal tube gone too far into trachea or too less
- Endotracheal tube inserted in esophagus
- Hypoxia: Due to incorrect placements of tube and taking too much time to intubate
- Apnea: Due to hypoxia and vagal response from laryngoscope insertion
- Pneumothorax: Due to insertion of tube in right main bronchus and due to prolonged ventilation
- Injury to oral mucosa and tongue, gums, and airway
- Perforation of trachea or esophagus
- Obstruction of tube
- Infection

Step 3: Chest Compressions

Indications

- Heart rate is less than 60 bpm, despite 30 seconds of effective PPV.
- It is important to ensure that PPV is being delivered optimally before starting chest compression.
- Chest compression is required for improving myocardial function. As a result of persistent hypoxia and acidosis, myocardial activity decreases and due to poor cardiac function, blood does not enter the circulation. While giving chest compressions, heart is being compressed between the sternum and the thoracic spine; this will increase the intrathoracic pressure and pump blood into the circulatory system.

Site and Depth of Compression

Chest compressions should be delivered on lower one-third of sternum, avoiding xiphoid cartilage. The area to be compressed lies between the lines drawn between nipples and xiphoid cartilage (Fig. 15.19). Depth of compression is approximately one-third of anteroposterior diameter of chest (Fig. 15.20).

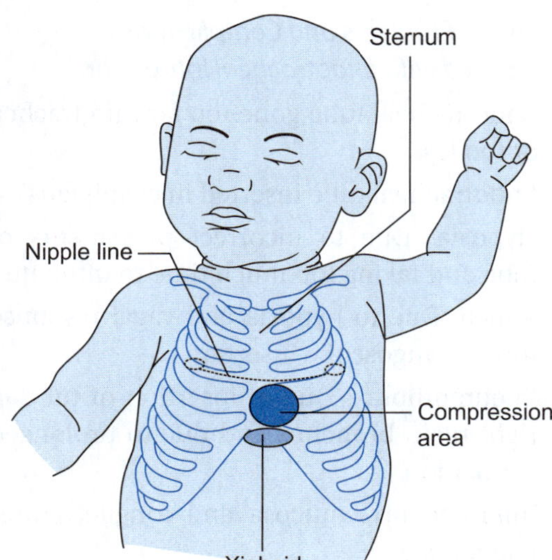

Figure 15.19 Site of chest compression. *Source*: Reproduced with permission from Textbook of Neonatal Resuscitation: India, 2nd edn. National Neonatology Forum of India: New Delhi.

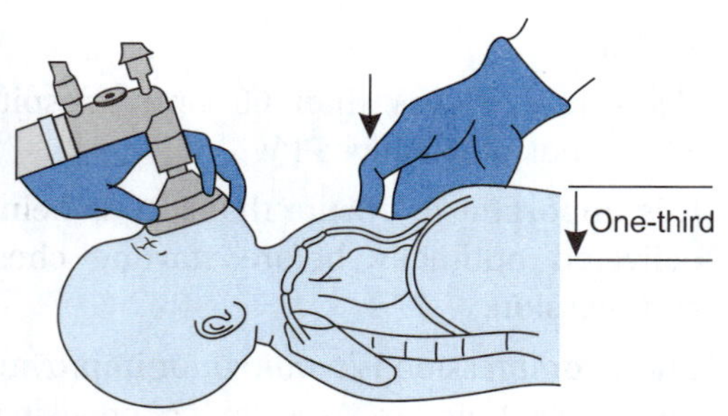

Figure 15.20 Depth of chest compression. *Source*: Reproduced with permission from Textbook of Neonatal Resuscitation: India, 2nd edn. National Neonatology Forum of India: New Delhi.

Improper placement of thumb and fingers can cause injuries such as damage to xiphoid cartilage, injury to internal organs such as liver, spleen, and lungs, and fracture of the ribs.

Technique of Chest Compression

There are two techniques of chest compression.

Thumb technique

In this technique, two thumbs are placed at compression area of sternum and both hands encircle the entire torso of the chest. The baby is firmly supported at back (Fig. 15.21).

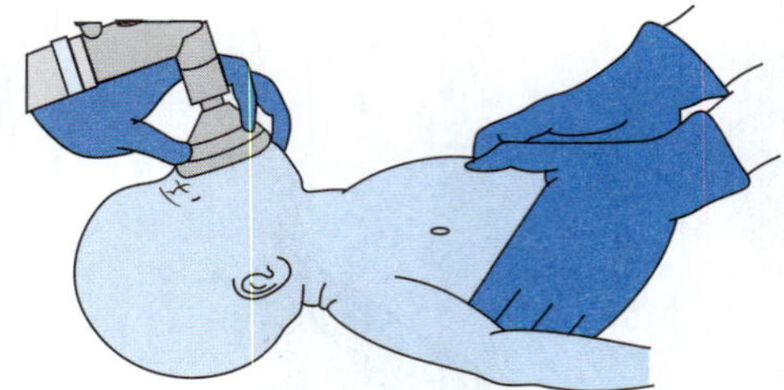

Figure 15.21 Thumb technique of chest compression. *Source*: Reproduced with permission from Textbook of Neonatal Resuscitation: India, 2nd edn. National Neonatology Forum of India: New Delhi.

- Advantages
  - Depth of compression is better controlled.
  - It generates high peak systolic and coronary perfusion pressure.
  - This method is less tiring, so it can be performed for a longer duration.
- Disadvantages
  - This method is not feasible if hands of the operator are small with respect to the size of the baby.
  - Access to the umbilicus is difficult if medications are required to be given.

Two-finger technique

In this technique, the tips of the middle finger and either the index finger or the ring finger of one hand are used to compress the sternum while the other hand is used to support the baby's back. Pressure should be applied vertically (Fig. 15.22). One should not lift the fingers off the chest as it will waste time in relocating the compression area (Fig. 15.23).

- Advantages
  - This method is helpful when the baby is large or when hands of the provider are small.
  - It is possible to have access of umbilicus when medications are required to be given by the umbilical route.

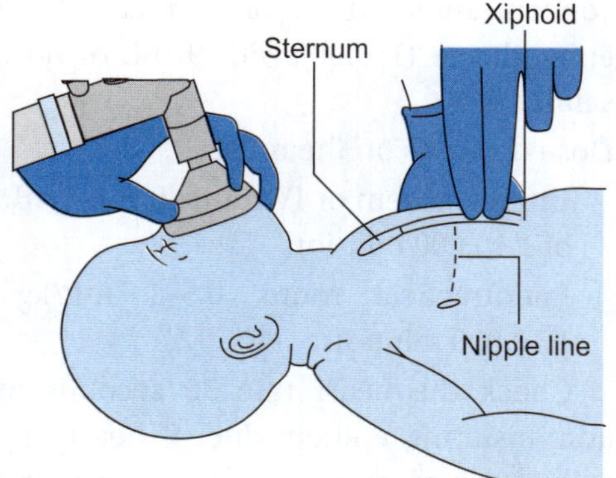

Figure 15.22 Two-finger technique of chest compression. *Source*: Reproduced with permission from Textbook of Neonatal Resuscitation: India, 2nd edn. National Neonatology Forum of India: New Delhi.

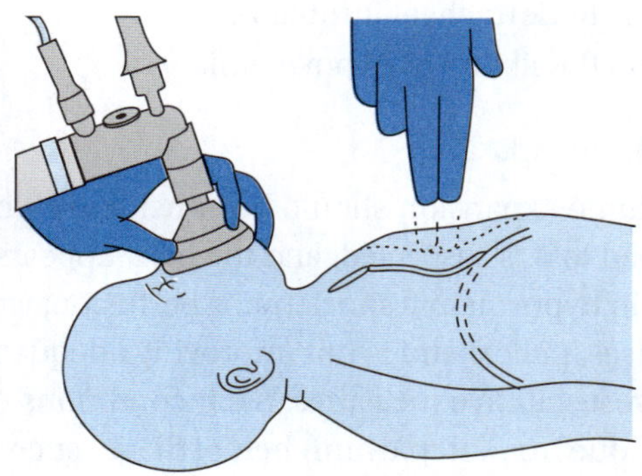

Figure 15.23 Incorrect method—fingers should not be lifted off the chest.

- Disadvantages
  - Control over depth of compression is not as good as that in thumb technique.
  - Precious time may be wasted in relocating the compression area.

Thumb technique is generally preferred over two-finger technique; however, both techniques should be learnt.

- Ventilations and compressions should be well coordinated to avoid simultaneous delivery. The ratio of compression to ventilation should be 3:1. In 1 minute, there would be total 120 events, out of which 90 compressions and 30 breaths would be delivered.
- Minimum two persons are required, one to provide PPV and another to give a chest compression. This should be well coordinated. After every three compressions, one breath should be delivered.
- The person who is compressing should call out the counting sequence of "one and two and three and breathe and." The person who is ventilating squeezes the bag during "breathe and" and releases during "one and ..." (Fig. 15.24).
- Endotracheal intubation at this stage helps in coordinating ventilation and chest compression.

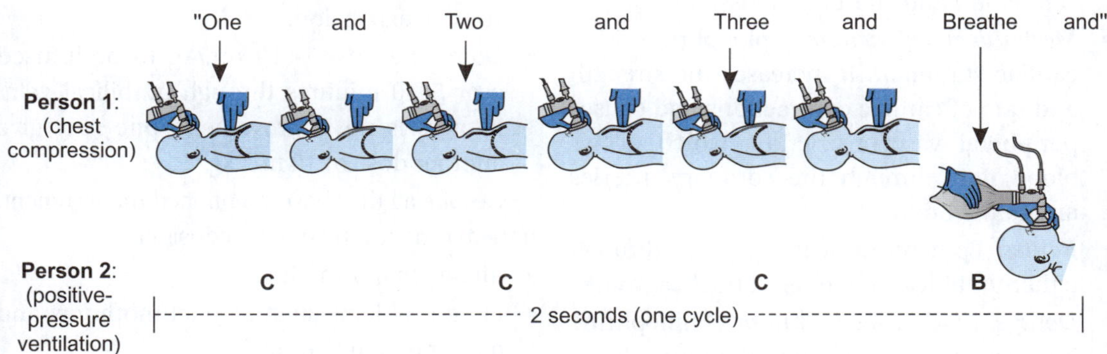

Figure 15.24 Coordinating ventilation and chest compression. *Source*: Reproduced with permission from Textbook of Neonatal Resuscitation: India, 2nd edn. National Neonatology Forum of India: New Delhi.

When to Stop Chest Compressions

- Assess after 30 seconds of coordinated chest compressions and ventilations.
- Stop chest compression if heart rate is more than 60/bpm but continue PPV at the rate of 40–60 breaths/min.
- Then gradually stop ventilation when heart rate is more than 100 bpm and the baby starts breathing spontaneously.

NRP 2015: New recommendations on chest compressions

- Intubation is strongly recommended prior to beginning of chest compressions.
- Chest compressions should be administered with the two-thumb technique.
- Heart rate should be assessed after 60 seconds of chest compressions.

Step 4: Medications

Medications are rarely required during resuscitation. Peripheral venous access is usually difficult during resuscitation, so umbilical vein remains the best intravenous route. Only two drugs are recommended for use in resuscitation in the labor room:

1. Epinephrine
2. Normal saline

Epinephrine

- *Indications*: Epinephrine is given if the heart rate remains below 60 bpm despite adequate ventilation and chest compressions.
- *Mechanism of action*: Epinephrine is a cardiac stimulant. It increases the strength and rate of cardiac contractions and causes peripheral vasoconstriction, which allows blood flow through the coronary arteries and to the brain.
- *Routes*: Epinephrine can be given through either umbilical vein or endotracheal route.
- *Dosage and concentration*: Epinephrine is available in 1:1000 dilution. It is recommended to be administered in 1:10,000 concentration. To make 1:10,000 concentration solution, mix 1 mL epinephrine (1:1000) with 9 mL of normal saline.

  Dose depends on the route:
  - Umbilical vein or IV route, 0.1–0.3 mL/kg of 1:10,000 dilution
  - Endotracheal route, 0.5–1 mL/kg of 1:10,000 dilution

  Check the heart rate 30 seconds after administering epinephrine. If heart rate is still <60 bpm or there is no improvement, repeat every 3–5 minutes till improvement occurs.

  If still the heart rate does not improve, then check for the following:
  - Ventilation
  - Chest compression
  - Endotracheal intubation
  - Possibility of hypovolemia

Volume Expansion

Volume expansion should be considered when blood loss is suspected, and the baby appears to be in hypovolemic shock (poor perfusion, weak pulses, pallor) and is not improving adequately to resuscitative measures. Such conditions can be due to antepartum hemorrhage such as placenta previa or abruption placenta or when there is blood loss from the cord.

- *Recommended fluids*: 0.9% NaCl (normal saline) is the solution of choice. Use of Ringer lactate is no longer recommended for volume expansion.
- *Dose*: The dose is 10 mL/kg to be infused over 5–10 minutes through umbilical vein. If there is no improvement, one may give another dose of 10 mL/kg.

Despite all the above-mentioned management, if there is no improvement, consider:

- Airway malformation
- Lung problems such as pneumothorax and diaphragmatic hernia
- Congenital heart diseases
- Meconium as mucus blockage

- Choanal atresia
- Pharyngeal airway malformations and Pierre Robin syndrome

There is no role of drugs such as sodium bicarbonate, aminophylline, and calcium gluconate during the labor room resuscitation.

NRP 2015: New recommendations on medications

- First dose of epinephrine can be given through endotracheal route. If the response is not satisfactory, subsequent doses must be given through umbilical route.
- For treating hypovolemia, use of Ringer lactate is no longer recommended.
- Sodium bicarbonate should not be routinely given to babies with metabolic acidosis.
- There is insufficient evidence to suggest safety and efficacy of using naloxone for respiratory depression in newborns born to mother with opiate exposure, as naloxone can cause pulmonary edema, cardiac arrest, and seizures.

Discontinuation of Resuscitation

If there are no signs of life (no heartbeat and no respiratory efforts) after 10 minutes of continuous and adequate resuscitative efforts, discontinuation of resuscitation is justified as this is associated with high mortality and severe neurodevelopmental disability.

Ethical Issues

There are certain situations when ethics and national legal practices do not mandate attempted resuscitation. Noninitiation of resuscitation may be considered appropriate in gestation below 25 weeks, anencephaly, and confirmed lethal genetic malformation/disorder such as trisomy 13 or 18. Parents are generally considered as appropriate decision makers for their own infants. For newborns with 22–24 weeks of gestation, parents should be involved in the decision-making process.

Recommendations of National Neonatology Forum of India for Neonatal Resuscitation

The NNF India has made certain minor changes in these recommendations to make them feasible to be used even in resource-limited settings.

- Instead of the initial three basic questions, the NNF India recommends only one question to start with, i.e., "Is the baby breathing or crying?"
- In a situation of labored breathing or persistent cyanosis, the recommendation is to do SpO_2 monitoring and consider CPAP after clearing the airway. NNF India recommends SpO_2 monitoring only if possible, and if it is not possible to start CPAP, then start supplemental oxygen and shift the baby to the NICU as soon as possible.
- The NNF India recommends starting PPV with room air and to assess the response in heart rate after five inflations.

According to the World Health Organization, an estimated 10% of approximately 120 million babies born every year worldwide need resuscitation. Perinatal asphyxia contributes to 20% of neonatal deaths globally every year. The stabilization, support, and the resuscitation of the neonates are thus an integral part of essential newborn care.

CHAPTER 16

Practical Pediatric Procedures

Baldev S Prajapati, Rajal Prajapati

Pediatric procedures and instruments form an important diagnostic and therapeutic tool in the management of sick infants and children. This chapter aims to provide the basic knowledge regarding common pediatric procedures as well as instruments and equipment required for them. It is very essential for every pediatric student to be aware of the basics of the common pediatric procedures. The procedures are best learnt by observation, performing the procedure under supervision, and repetitive performance. It should be practical, methodological, and safe for both the patient and the person who performs the procedure.

General Considerations

Before any pediatric procedures are performed, there are certain basic prerequisites and considerations that need to be followed properly. These not only are essential to carry out the procedure in a safe and methodical way but have also become important from a medicolegal point. These are as follows:

- *Counseling*: Explain the parents in detail regarding the procedure including its indications, its technique, and the potential complications. If the child is older and able to understand, talk to him/her in a simple language. Such a communication helps to increase the confidence between the parents and the medical person performing the procedure. It also decreases the anxiety of the parents and the relatives and the procedure can be performed smoothly.
- *Consent*: An informed consent is a process of communication that is ethically required before any procedure or treatment so that an educated decision regarding the intervention can be made by the patient or the parent. It is a must for all the procedures. In procedures such as lumbar puncture, pleural and pericardial taping, liver biopsy, renal biopsy, exchange transfusion, bone marrow aspiration (BMA), and biopsy or any other major procedure, it is prudent to get signed consent.
- *Containers*: Ensure availability of all the necessary instruments and equipment for the procedure and confirm that proper containers are available for collection and transportation of the laboratory specimens. Whenever feasible, sterile, disposable, or single-use instruments should be used to reduce the risk of cross-infection.
- *Sedation*: Children are afraid of procedures and react by crying, struggling, and giving a frightened appearance, which in turn can increase parental anxiety. It affects the performance of the person performing the procedure. It results in an increased rate of failure and complications related to the procedure. In this situation, sedating the child may help. Triclofos sodium 20 mg/kg/dose by oral route will suffice in most of the cases. Diazepam or midazolam (0.5 mg/kg oral or 0.1 mg intravenous or intramuscular [IM] or ketamine 0.5–1 mg/kg/IV).

- *Anesthesia*: Local anesthesia may be achieved by infiltrating tissues around the site with 0.5–2% lignocaine. The maximum dosage of 1% lignocaine that can be infiltrated is 0.3 mL/kg. An alternative is to apply lignocaine cream to a small area of the skin 60 minutes prior to performing the procedure, protected by adhesive dressing. Sedation or general anesthesia may be needed in certain cases.
- *Proper facilities*: Ensure adequate lighting and comfortable ambient temperature in the procedure room. A separate designated area for pediatric procedures is always preferable and the space should be spacious and comfortable to the patient and the team performing the procedure. All drugs and equipment of various sizes should be readily available. Properly restraining the child during the procedure is essential for both the successful performance of the procedure and minimizing the risk of injury. The child can be restrained by the paramedical staff physically (human restraint) or limb restraint can be applied by wrapping a wooden spatula in a gauze piece and encircling the limb with it for a short duration.

Handwashing

Handwashing is the single most effective infection control measure available in the intensive care units and general pediatric settings. The process of scrubbing the hands while washing is shown in detail in Figure 16.1.

A normal nonmedicated soap is good for handwashing.

The first wash should be at least for 2 minutes and subsequently one must wash before and after each patient contact for at least 15 seconds. After touching an infected patient or unclean fomite, a 2-minute wash is again required.

Asepsis

The physician should scrub hands and forearm using an effective cleaning agent such as 4% chlorhexidine or hexachlorophene before undertaking any procedure. Wearing of sterile gloves by the doctor is very important for both his/her and the patient's safety. The site of the patient's skin is then cleaned with 70% isopropyl alcohol and the surface allowed to dry; the surface is then again washed three times with 10% povidone iodine or 0.5% chlorhexidine gluconate in 70% isopropyl alcohol. It should be cleaned in a circular fashion from the center and outwards.

Waste Disposal

The biomedical procedural waste such as biological fluids, sharps, and others should be properly disposed of as per the waste disposal guidelines of the institute.

Documentation

Careful, complete, and timely documentation of the procedure is essential for medicolegal protection of the person performing the procedure, for the outcome of the procedure, and to ensure proper transport of the specimens to the laboratory.

Measurement of Body Temperature

The body temperature in children is recorded generally by two types of thermometers: clinical thermometers and rectal thermometers. Both have two components, a metallic bulb filled with mercury and a long, graduated glass tube. Oral thermometer has a long tip (Fig. 16.2), while rectal thermometer has a bulbous and rounded tip.

Precautions

- For measuring oral temperature, wait for 10–15 minutes after food or liquids have been taken. Hot or cold drinks should be avoided before measuring temperature.

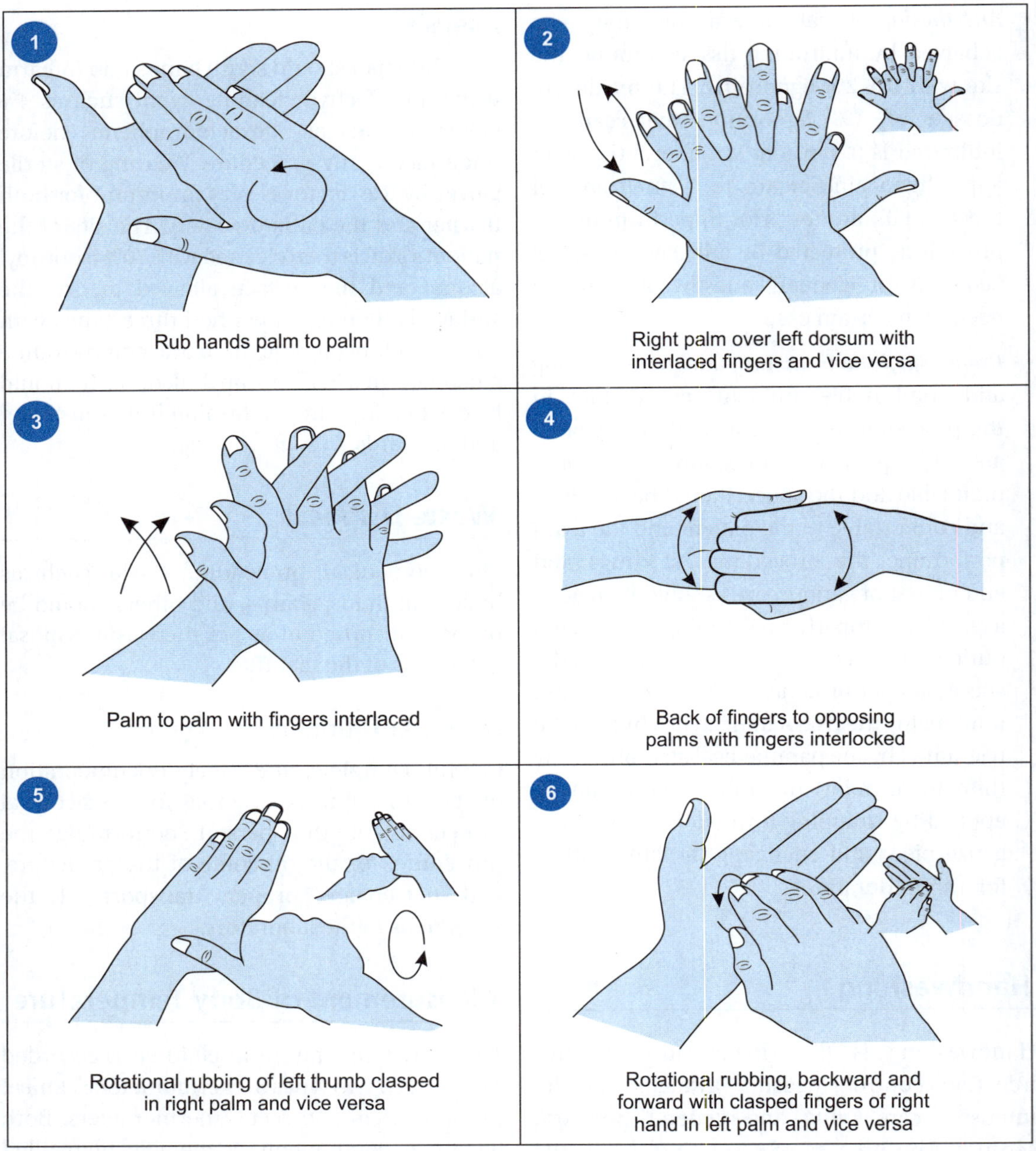

1 Rub hands palm to palm

2 Right palm over left dorsum with interlaced fingers and vice versa

3 Palm to palm with fingers interlaced

4 Back of fingers to opposing palms with fingers interlocked

5 Rotational rubbing of left thumb clasped in right palm and vice versa

6 Rotational rubbing, backward and forward with clasped fingers of right hand in left palm and vice versa

Figure 16.1 Six steps of handwashing. *Source*: Mathai SS. Armed Forces Medical College Paediatric Clinics for Medical Students, 2nd edn. Wolters Kluwer India: New Delhi, 2019.

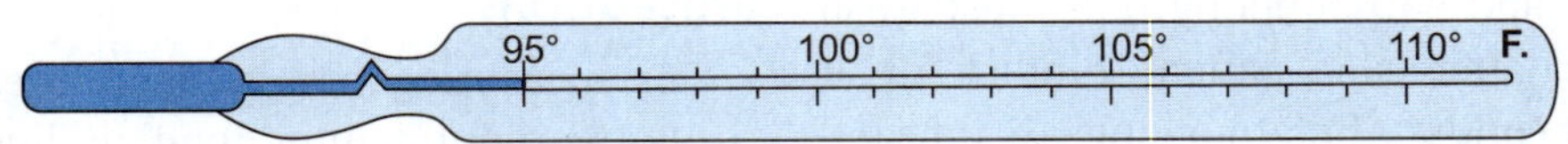

Figure 16.2 Clinical thermometer.

- The thermometer should be held by its upper end (opposite to the mercury bulb) and must be shaken to bring the mercury down below 37°C or 98°F.
- Below the age of 6 years, oral temperature should not be measured.
- In school-going children, oral temperature can be measured by placing the thermometer below the tongue and asking the child to breathe through the nose.
- Thermometer should be washed by cold water only.

Types of Thermometer

- Clinical thermometer: Mercury thermometer (95–110°F)
- Rectal thermometer: Low-reading mercury thermometer (30–40°C)
- Electronic thermometer
- Ear canal thermometer
- Forehead thermometer

Procedure for Recording Temperature

Axillary/Groin Temperature

These are common sites of measuring body temperature in children younger than 6 years of age. It is also the method for uncooperative, intellectually disabled, restless, or unconscious patients.

- Wipe the axilla or groin with cotton to make it free of moisture.
- Shake the thermometer to lower the mercury level. The thermometer tip should be properly and snugly placed after drying the area/body tissues for 3 minutes in either the axilla or the groin.
- Place the bulb of the thermometer in the hollow of axilla or groin with the stem pointing toward the patient's chest or abdomen. Bring his/her arm across the chest so that the bulb is in constant touch with the skin surface. If groin temperature is being taken, flex hip and support it. Allow the thermometer to remain in place for 3 minutes.

Oral Temperature

- In children older than 6 years of age, oral temperature can be recorded. The child should be cooperative and able to understand.
- Explain the procedure to the patient.
- The patient should not have taken anything by mouth at least 10 minutes before the procedure.
- Remove the thermometer from its tube and wipe with a swab from the bulb to the stem.
- Read and shake down mercury to below 95°F or 35°C.
- Place the thermometer in the patient's mouth under the tongue; lips should be closed. Teeth should not be closed and thermometer should not be pressed by teeth. Ask the child to breathe through the nose.
- Thermometer should be kept in the mouth for 2 minutes.
- Record the temperature.
- Wipe the thermometer with a swab from the stem to the bulb. Wash it with a soap solution. Wipe it again with a clean swab and return it to its tube.

Rectal Temperature

Newborn babies have not developed mature thermoregulatory mechanism. They are more vulnerable to develop hypothermia or hyperpyrexia according to the environmental temperature. The maintenance of a proper body temperature is very crucial for the newborns. Rectal temperature is more reliable in the newborns to know their core temperature. These differ from clinical thermometers on two counts:

1. These have a low reading range, i.e., less than 35°C, to detect hypothermia in newborns and sick infants.
2. They have a shorter round or pear-shaped bulb without constriction at the neck to minimize rectal injury. Only trained persons should be allowed to measure rectal temperature.

- Turn the baby in lateral position.
- Check the thermometer and lubricate its mercury bulb by Vaseline or simple edible oil (groundnut or coconut oil).
- Insert the mercury within the round bulb into the anus 2 cm deep in newborns and 5–7 cm deep in infants and older children. To avoid rectal perforation, the thermometer should be directed slightly posteriorly.
- Wait for 3 minutes.
- Remove the thermometer and wipe with dry cotton.
- Read and record the temperature.
- Wash the thermometer with soap water; wipe again with clean cotton and place it back in the container.
- Injury to anal canal and rectum has been reported if an untrained person carries out the procedure. Rarely, perforation of rectum is also reported. Routine rectal temperature recording should not be done.

Ear Canal Temperature

Ear canal thermometer records the temperature of the ear drum with a thermoscan, which works on the principle of infrared technology. Its reading is available within a second.

Orogastric Devices/Procedures

Nasogastric Tube Insertion

Nasogastric tube is passed for either aspiration of gastric contents or administration of feeds or therapeutic substances. Silastic and polyethylene tubes are being used because they have less tissue reactions. The appropriate sizes of the nasogastric tubes for different ages are shown in Table 16.1.

TABLE 16.1 Appropriate Sizes of Nasogastric Tubes

Age	Nasogastric tube size (Fr)
Up to 1 month	6–8
6 months	8–10
1–3 years	10–12
3–6 years	12
6–8 years	12–14
Above 8 years	14–16

Indications

- *Diagnostic*
  - Gastric aspirate test for diagnosis of neonatal septicemia
  - Shake test for lung maturity in preterm babies
  - Examination of gastric contents for acid-fast bacilli detection, poisoning
  - Assessment of upper gastrointestinal tract bleeding
  - Measurement of gastric volume
  - Diagnosis of esophageal anomalies such as esophageal atresia
- *Therapeutic*
  - Paralytic ileus, intestinal obstruction for gastric decompression
  - Enteral feeding
  - Administration of therapeutic substances

Contraindications

- Esophageal stricture
- Ingestion of corrosives (acid/alkali)—may cause esophageal perforation
- Head and neck injury preventing passage of tube
- Nasal fracture

Technique

- The head is raised in semiupright position.
- The distance from nose to earlobe and from earlobe to xiphoid process is determined to measure the length of the tube to be passed. The point is marked on the tube (Fig. 16.3).
- The more patent nostril is selected for passing the tube.
- The terminal part of the tube is lubricated with a lubricant. It is avoided in newborns

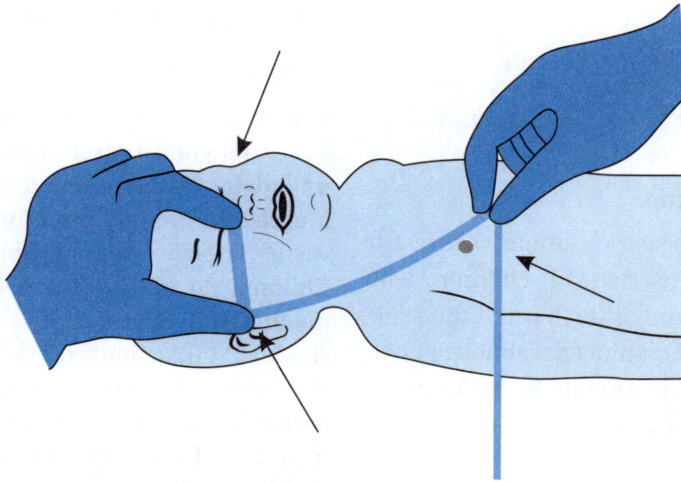

Figure 16.3 Insertion of nasogastric tube. *Source*: WHO Management of a Child with Serious Infection. World Health Organization: Geneva, 2000.

to prevent aspiration of an oily substance. In that case, it is moistened with water.

- The tube is passed into the nostril, its curve direct downwards. It is passed along the floor of the nose. In case of difficulty, it is tried in another nostril. Resistance is felt when it reaches the nasopharynx. Getting the patient to sip a little water helps to overcome it.
- With swallowing of the saliva or water by the patients, the tube is advanced into the esophagus.
- If the patient gags or the tube coils up in the mouth, the tube is withdrawn partly and again it is passed. If the child develops sudden cough or breathing difficulty, stop the insertion immediately as the tube is likely to have entered the airways instead of esophagus.
- The tube is passed up to the mark denoting the measured length of the tube to be passed.

Checking Placement

Confirmation of proper placement is done by the following tests:

- Aspiration of stomach contents on applying suction at the outer end of the tube with a syringe indicates that the tube lies in the stomach.
- Air is injected into the tube while epigastric area is auscultated. A sound is heard if the tube is in the stomach.
- Escape of air bubbles in the water on placing a tube in a glass of water indicates that the tube lies in the trachea.
- Placement of a radiopaque tube may be assessed by a chest X-ray, if needed.
  - The tube is fixed with a tape in a butterfly fashion around the tube or with vertical taping over the nose and the tube. The tape is fixed in such a way that the tube rests in the middle of the nasal lumen and not directly in contact with mucosa. It is not taped over the forehead as it may cause pressure necrosis of the nose.
  - The feed or drug should be allowed to go in the tube by gravity method. It should not be pushed by piston. The tube should be flushed with water periodically. It is prudent to check the tube position before giving each feed or drug and following vomiting as it might have displaced.
  - While removing the tube, pinch the tube end to prevent the spilling of the contents into the trachea.

Complications

- Pulmonary aspiration
- Gastric perforation
- Nasal necrosis
- Esophageal stricture

Instead of nasogastric tubing, orogastric tube should be inserted in children with facial trauma, fracture of the base of the skull, choanal atresia, and craniofacial abnormalities. Nowadays, orogastric tubing is preferred to avoid certain complications.

Gastric Lavage

It is useful in cases of poisoning to remove the toxic substances from the stomach. In case of corrosive and hydrocarbon ingestion, gastric lavage is contraindicated. In case of corrosive ingestion, passing the tube may cause perforation. Since passing the gastric tube is likely to induce vomiting, it increases the risk of aspiration of hydrocarbons into the trachea and lungs that causes pneumonia.

After passing the tube in the stomach as described in the section "Nasogastric Tube Insertion," lavage of the stomach using aliquots of normal saline is done in cases of poisoning. It is continued till the color of the lavage is normal.

Injections and Vascular Access Procedures

In children, injections are mainly used for administration of vaccines (intradermal [ID], subcutaneous [SC], and IM routes), drug therapy (SC, intravenous, and less often IM), ID skin test, and blood sampling. Disposable syringes and needles are mandatory to be used to reduce the risk of infection and transmission of hepatitis B and C and HIV infections. The injection site should be cleaned with isopropyl alcohol.

Intramuscular Injection

Common Sites

The basic principle of choosing an injection site is its good muscle mass and lack of any underlying major blood vessel or nerve. Muscles commonly used for IM injections are vastus lateralis, deltoid, and gluteus medius. Children do not have well-developed gluteus medius and therefore it is not the preferred site for IM injections. It has been documented that some vaccines such as hepatitis B and antirabies vaccines administered in the gluteal region produce a very poor antibody response and hence these sites should not be used in infants and children.

The bulk of vastus lateralis (anterolateral aspect of thigh) is the preferred site in infants. The site in vastus lateralis is the middle third of the area between the greater trochanter and the lateral femoral condyle.

In case of deltoid, the site for injection is midway between acromion process and deltoid insertion; it comes to 3–5 cm below the acromion process. This site may be used in children older than 5 years and adults. The quantity of drug should be less than 5 mL. Only watery injections with less viscosity should be injected at the deltoid region.

Technique

- The site of injection should be exposed well.
- For anterolateral aspect of thigh, the child may be laid supine or be held in the mother's lap. For deltoid, the child may be held in the mother's lap or may sit.
- The muscle selected for injection should be relaxed.
- The skin over the injection site should be cleaned with spirit. A circular motion of the swab is used proceeding from the puncture site and extending outward for 5 cm. Let the spirit evaporate and skin become dry; otherwise, the spirit entering tissues is painful.
- The syringe is filled with the medicine.

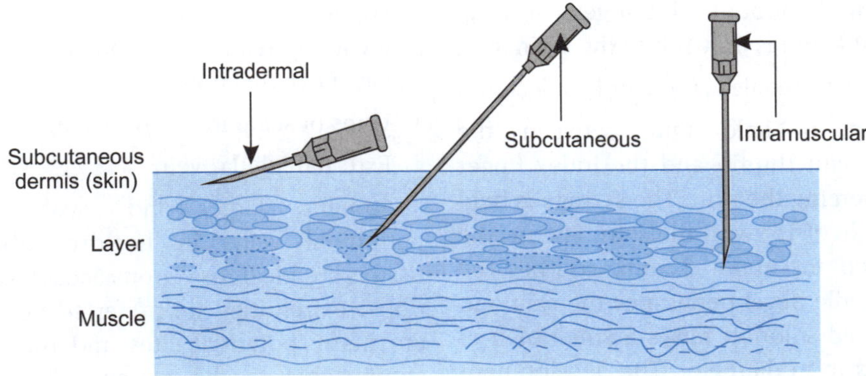

Figure 16.4 Position of the needle for different types of injections. *Source*: Reproduced with permission from Baldev P. Essential Procedures in Pediatrics. Jaypee Bros: New Delhi, 2003.

- In children, usually a 23G needle with 25 mm length is used for IM injections.
- Stretch the skin flat and push the needle down at 90° (Fig. 16.4).
- Aspiration before injecting the vaccine is not required.
- Inject the vaccine at the rate of 1 mL per 10 seconds.
- The needle is withdrawn, and the injection site is pressed for few seconds. Do not rub the injection site.
- The needle should be withdrawn smoothly with steady movement.
- Discard the needle and syringe as per standard guidelines.
- Vaccines should never be given into the gluteal region because of poor absorption and risk of damage to the sciatic nerve.

Subcutaneous Injection

Drugs (e.g., adrenaline) or vaccines (e.g., MMR) are injected subcutaneously when slow absorption and long duration of action are desired. Another indication of SC route is a coagulopathy that makes IM injection hazardous, for fear of development of IM hematoma. Insulin and heparin-like drugs as well as measles, MMR, and varicella vaccines are given by SC route.

Technique

- Common sites are arm, anterior abdominal wall, and thighs. Atrophic and infected areas are avoided.
- The skin is cleaned and disinfected with spirit.
- A 26G needle with 13 mm length is commonly used for SC injection.
- The skin is raised into a fold with thumb and index finger of the left hand.
- The midpoint of the fold is pierced with the needle held at 45° with its surface. The tip of the needle is advanced into the subcutaneous tissue.
- Aspiration is not required.
- Drugs or vaccine is injected, needle is withdrawn, and the site is pressed for few minutes.

Intradermal Injection

Indications for ID injections are BCG vaccination, Mantoux test, skin tests for allergy, and test for sensitization to certain drugs such as penicillin. Anti-rabies vaccine also can be given by ID route.

Technique

- Ventral (volar) aspect of forearm is commonly used for ID injection.
- Skin is cleaned with spirit or clean water.

- A measured amount of antigen or drug (usually 0.1 mL) is drawn into the syringe.
- A 26G or 27G needle is used for ID injection.
- The skin is held taut between the nondominant thumb and the index finger before piercing the skin. The syringe is held at an angle of 15° with the skin. The needle is inserted for about 2 mm, so that the entire needle bevel penetrates the skin and the injected solution raises a small bleb of about 5 mm in diameter. The development of perifollicular puckering (peau d'orange) indicates successful ID injection.
- The needle is withdrawn.
- The site is circled, and it is recorded in the patient's chart.
- The reaction is observed in the defined time.

Peripheral Intravenous Access

Peripheral intravenous access is one of the mainstays of therapeutics. It allows blood sampling and administration of medicines, fluids, nutrients, blood, and blood products. Intracaths (over-the-needle catheters) are commonly used and currently scalp veins are used very infrequently for this purpose. Generally, the venipuncture sites that are to be used should be prominent, should be easily visible, and should not interfere with resuscitation efforts and/or other diagnostic and therapeutic interventions. The peripheral venous access sites are easy to insert but have a limitation of being unsuitable for central venous pressure monitoring, as they can get dislodged/occluded and can contribute to tissue injury due to irritant drugs. Various sites for venous access are as follows in the order of preference:

- Veins on dorsum of hand
- Veins of the forearm, median cubital vein in antecubital fossa
- Superficial radial vein on radial aspect of wrist
- Superficial veins over volar aspect of forearm
- Superficial veins over dorsum of foot and great saphenous vein on medial aspect of leg above the ankle
- Veins of scalp in newborns and infants
- External jugular vein

Straight, large, and easily accessible peripheral veins in healthy subcutaneous tissues are ideal for venous access. Veins of the upper extremities are preferred because there are many potential sites and they are more comfortable to the patient. The distal and superficial veins are preferred as complications are more following extravasation and thrombophlebitis in proximal and deep veins. When the veins are not visible, they can be palpated at common sites and can be accessed. Other sites of peripheral venous access, e.g., femoral vein or external jugular vein, are rarely used considering the risk of concealed hemorrhage, extravasation, or spasm of neighboring artery in a femoral vein.

Scalp vein needles are hollow needles with a butterfly plastic handle and a plastic tube, at the other end of which a syringe or infusion set can be attached. These were used earlier for short-term peripheral venous access but are now largely replaced by intracaths. These are useful for venous sampling of blood and short-term use of intravenous route. A vein is counterpunctured very easily on movement of the limb.

Intracaths are plastic catheters over a hollow metallic needle (Fig. 16.5). The metallic needle projects just beyond the tip of the plastic catheter. It provides stiffness during insertion into the vein, after which it is withdrawn. The plastic catheter is then advanced further gently so that the vein is not counterpunctured. The plastic catheter is well tolerated. Intracaths and scalp vein needles are available in various sizes from 26G to 16G. In children, 26G to 21G needles are commonly used, depending on age of the child and requirement. These needle catheter sets (medicaths) are most commonly used because of the ease of fixation and the feasibility of prolonged use.

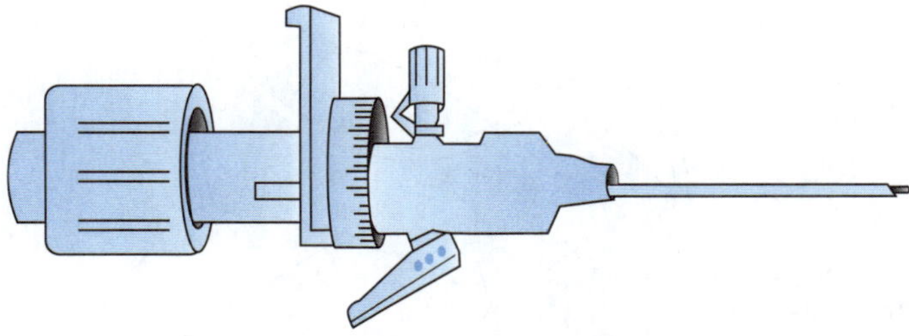

Figure 16.5 Intracath.

Technique

- A tourniquet is placed over the limb, 3–4 cm proximal to the site selected for venipuncture. The pressure should be such that it occludes venous flow, but arterial blood flow continues.
- Taping sharply over the vein causes mechanical reflex dilatation of the vascular walls. It should be light; otherwise, pain will cause vasoconstriction.
- Active or passive pumping of the extremity enhances blood flow and distends the veins.
- A warm moist towel may be applied to the site for several minutes. It causes venous dilatation.
- Aseptic precautions are mandatory.
- Methylated spirit is applied over 4–5 cm area at the planned site. It should be allowed to dry.
- The skin is pulled taut distally to stabilize the vein with the nondominant hand. It is punctured by the needle, bevel up at 15–30° angle, parallel to the vein. After entry into the subcutaneous tissue, the needle is aligned parallel to the skin surface and along the long axis of the vein. Its tip is depressed a little and is advanced until it penetrates the vein. Then, it is made parallel to the vein again and advanced until it is passed fully into the vein. Blood is collected if indicated and then the IV set is attached to it.
- The tourniquet is removed, and the infusion is started by releasing the clamp on the tubing. A hub of the cannula and IV set are secured to the skin with the adhesive plaster.
- For flushing the cannula, normal saline should be used and not distilled water. Distilled water causes pain at the intravenous site and it also causes hemolysis.
- If venipuncture is performed only for collection of blood, pull the needle gently after collecting the required sample and apply steady pressure at the site with a piece of spirit swab for few minutes.
- The site of IV cannulation should be checked frequently for any extravasation (diffuse swelling proximal or distal to the site), infection (tenderness or erythema), or blockage (slowed or stopped infusion).

Intraosseous Infusion

Peripheral percutaneous venous access is the fastest method of obtaining vascular access in children. However, during life-threatening emergencies, rapid access to venous compartment through peripheral or central venous route is occasionally a difficult or time consuming procedure for a pediatrician to perform. Small peripheral vessels in children often collapse during shock and efforts at setting up an IV line in a peripheral vein may fail. When IV access cannot be established within three attempts or 90 seconds time, intraosseous route should be used as per the recommendations.

Common Sites

- Anteromedial surface of the proximal tibia, one or two fingerbreadths distal to tibial tuberosity to avoid damage to epiphyseal growth plate

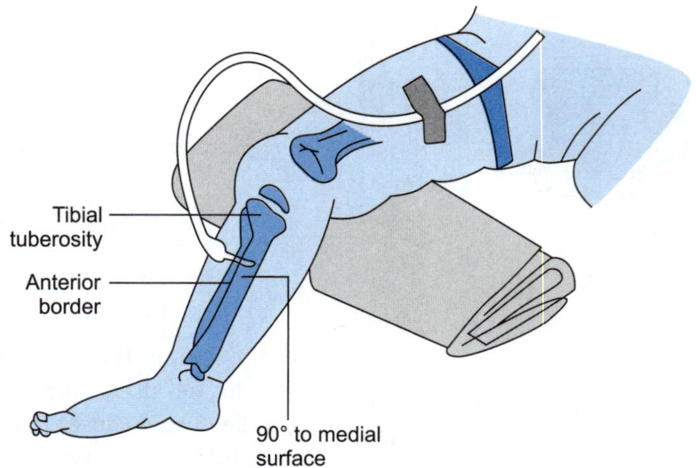

Figure 16.6 Site for intraosseous infusion. *Source*: Reproduced with permission from Baldev P. Essential Procedures in Pediatrics. Jaypee Bros: New Delhi, 2003.

- Two to 3 cm above the lateral condyle of the femur in the midline
- Medial surface of the tibia, proximal to the medial malleolus (Fig. 16.6)

Technique

- Specially designed needles available for intraosseous infusion should be used, if available. Hypodermic needle can also be used. Twenty to 16 G needles can be used for children younger than 18 months of age and 16–12 G needles for older children.
- Identify the site of placement.
- The patient's leg should be restrained; a small sandbag is placed behind the knee.
- The use of local anesthesia is optional, but is usually recommended as it may be more painful once the child is resuscitated.
- Aseptic precautions are a must.
- Insert the needle perpendicular to the skin, advance to the periosteum, and then with a screwing motion, penetrate the marrow. A distinct "give way" sensation indicates that your needle is in the marrow. Confirm that the needle is firmly embedded in the bone.
- Insertion of the needle to a depth of 1 cm is usually adequate as the distance from the skin to the cortex is rarely more than 1 cm in infants and children.
- The needle should maintain erect posture without support.
- Trocar is removed, and correct position is verified by aspiration of marrow and easy flushing with 5–10 mL of normal saline without signs of extravasations.
- The needle should be secured and sterile dressing should be applied over the site.
- It should be watched for local complications such as extravasations and infection.
- As soon as the peripheral IV route is established, intraosseous needle should be removed.
- Emergency drugs and fluids can be administered intraosseously with essentially the same dosage and rates as given by intravenous route.

Venous Cutdown (Venesection)

Venous cutdown is rarely resorted to in the present scenario of intravenous catheters and intraosseous access. It is mainly useful when routine intravenous access has failed in conditions such as shock or when large amounts of fluids have to be given for a long time as in total parenteral nutrition. The preferred site is saphenous vein near the ankle.

Umbilical Vein Catheterization

The main use of umbilical vein catheterization in newborns is to establish an access for the short-term administration of fluids, blood, and drugs, to perform exchange blood transfusion (although the preferred mode for exchange transfusion is by peripheral route), and to monitor central venous pressure. The umbilical vein spirals through the cord and is at 12 o'clock position at the level of abdominal wall. Here it turns cephalad and runs slightly toward right to enter the porta hepatis. It continues with left portal vein and then communicates with left hepatic vein and then with inferior vena cava. The umbilical vein is much wider than umbilical arteries.

Technique

- The child should be in supine position with gentle restraining. A padded crucifix splint is used to restrain the baby.
- Sterilize and drape the skin around the umbilical stump.
- The cord is then cut cleanly about 2 cm above the umbilicus and the umbilical vein is located at 12 o'clock position. The blood clot in the vein is expressed or pulled out by fine forceps.
- Mark the catheter for the correct distance to be inserted, which is about 20% of the crown–heel length.
- The catheter is passed into the vein slowly and gently, giving caudal traction on the cord stump till free flow of blood is obtained.
- Flush the catheter with heparinized saline.
- The free end of the catheter should be strapped to the abdominal wall.

Special Points

- If the cord is dried up, it can be excised flush with the umbilicus that can expose the orifice of the umbilical vein at 12 o'clock position. This can be gently dilated with Hagar's dilator and then catheterized.
- If both these methods fail, supraumbilical cutdown will become necessary.
- The catheter tip should be advanced up to the thoracic portion of the inferior vena cava.
- While passing the catheter, the resistance is felt at the ductus venosus. The catheter should be passed 1–2 cm beyond this point.
- Remove the umbilical vein catheter within 24–48 hours.

Complications

- Infections, such as septicemia
- Local trauma and/or perforation
- N crotizing enterocolitis
- Tl rombosis of portal vein with the de velopment of portal hypertension in future
- Cardiac arrhythmias

Umbilical Artery Catheterization

It is used for periodic monitoring of arterial blood gases and for constant monitoring of blood pressure in a neonate. There are two umbilical arteries and the lumen appears patent. The potential complications of this procedure are thromboembolism and necrotizing enterocolitis.

Radial Artery Catheterization

Arterial access is required for continuous blood pressure monitoring and repeated sampling of arterial blood gas samples and other blood samples in critically sick children. The radial artery is easily accessible at the wrist in the groove between the tendon of the flexor carpi radialis medially and the distal radius laterally.

Aspiration and Biopsy Procedures

Bone Marrow Aspiration

This is a very common procedure indicated in children with blood dyscrasias (such as aplastic anemia), unresponsive/refractory anemia, hemoparasitic infections (such as malaria and kala-azar), primary marrow disease and metabolic storage disease (Gaucher disease), malignancies, and undiagnosed infections and/or fevers. BMA and bone marrow trephine biopsy

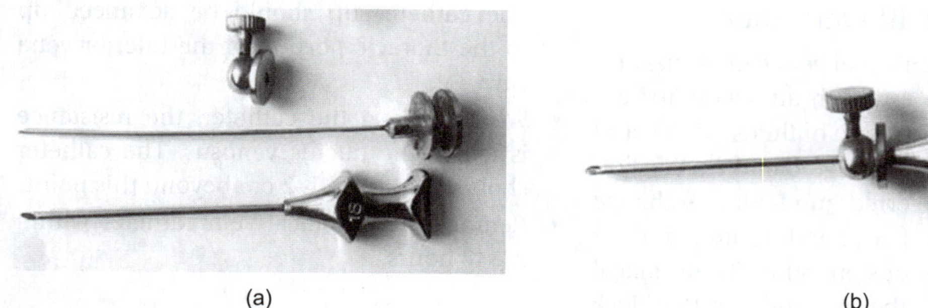

(a) (b)

Figure 16.7 (a) Bone marrow aspiration needle and (b) bone marrow biopsy needle (Jamshidi needle).

(BMTB) are the methods available for bone marrow examination (Fig. 16.7). BMA is most commonly done with a needle in most children but at times trephine biopsy is indicated when the BMA is dry.

BMA must be done with caution in the presence of hemorrhagic conditions or if the child is on anticoagulants. If essential, then factor replacement or stopping anticoagulants is needed before the procedure and the child should be monitored for the next 24 hours for any bleeding and complications. Severe thrombocytopenia is not considered a contraindication for the procedure if adequate and prolonged pressure is applied to the aspiration site to prevent any bleeding. The skin site for BMA should be free from any local infection before the procedure.

Common Sites

- *Iliac crest*: This is the most preferred site in children as it contains the most cellular marrow. The procedure is performed at 1 cm below the posterior iliac crest. The child should be lying in prone position for this procedure.
- *Tibia*: The upper end of tibia, just below tibial tuberosity on its medial aspect, is the preferred site of procedure in children younger than 2 years of age.
- *Sternum*: This is a site for biopsy/aspiration but should be avoided due to a risk of injury to the underlying heart and great vessels.

Technique

- Atropine should be given as premedication.
- Aseptic and antiseptic precautions are a must during the whole procedure. Drape the area with sterile linen. The child should be properly positioned and restrained.
- Ensure that adequate number of syringes, slides, and heparinized syringes are prepared and kept ready beforehand to collect the bone marrow aspirate for analysis.
- One percent lignocaine is locally infiltrated from skin to periosteum. In some irritable children, general anesthesia is desirable for successful outcome of the procedure. A small, 3- to 5-mm skin incision at the procedural site facilitates the entry and advancement of the biopsy needle.
- The trocar must be securely inside the needle.
- With a firm grasp, puncture the skin at 90° angle; advance to the periosteum, and then enter the bone marrow space with a twisting motion until the needle is firmly anchored in the bone. Once the needle enters the marrow space, a loss of resistance is felt.
- Remove the trocar from the aspiration needle and attach a 10- to 20-mL syringe to the needle hub and apply negative pressure to aspirate 0.5–1 mL of marrow in the syringe. This procedure is performed swiftly to obtain only bone marrow particles as slow, sluggish aspiration causes dilution of marrow with blood. To prevent dilution of marrow with blood, aspiration should be continued only till the material appears beyond the nozzle of the syringe.

- In case marrow is not aspirated at this point, the needle may be advanced further slightly with rotatory movements and aspiration attempted once again.
- Disconnect the syringe from the needle and place the aspirate on five to six slides for immediate preparation for further studies.
- BMA needle should be withdrawn with twisting movement followed by a firm pressure and sterile dressing over the site to prevent any bleeding.
- Along with smears of bone marrow, smears from peripheral blood should be prepared and sent for examination.
- BMTB can be performed through the same site if needed.

Complications

- Local pain and hematoma
- Infection, e.g., osteomyelitis
- Rarely, injury to deeper structures

Dry tap may be the result of an improper technique or severe marrow infiltration in malignancies. Trephine biopsy is indicated in such cases.

Lumbar Puncture

This procedure is performed to obtain cerebrospinal fluid (CSF) sample for analysis for diagnosing infections and other disorders of the central nervous system. It is also used for monitoring CSF pressure, intrathecal drug administration, and removing CSF in some cases of hydrocephalus.

Contraindications

- Marked raised intracranial pressure with closed fontanelle because of risk of herniation of brain substance through foramen magnum
- Local infection over the lumbar puncture skin site
- Cardiovascular and respiratory instability
- Bleeding/platelet counts less than 20,000/mm^3

Technique

The patient is placed on his/her side, at the edge of the table or bed, with the knee drawn up toward abdomen and the head flexed to get maximum flexion of the spine (Fig. 16.8). If the child is newborn or has respiratory distress, he/she should be firmly fixed at shoulders and buttocks only without flexing the neck and drawing up knees. In infants, sitting position allows easier identification of the midline. An experienced assistant has a vital role in positioning, restraining, and comforting the patient.

- Aseptic and antiseptic precautions are a must. Skin is prepared with surgical alcohol–povidone–alcohol and then draped.
- Routinely, local anesthesia is not used. But in older children who are irritable, local anesthesia may be useful for performing the procedure smoothly.
- Site of puncture is defined by palpating the iliac crest that corresponds to L3–L4. Hold the needle between index and middle

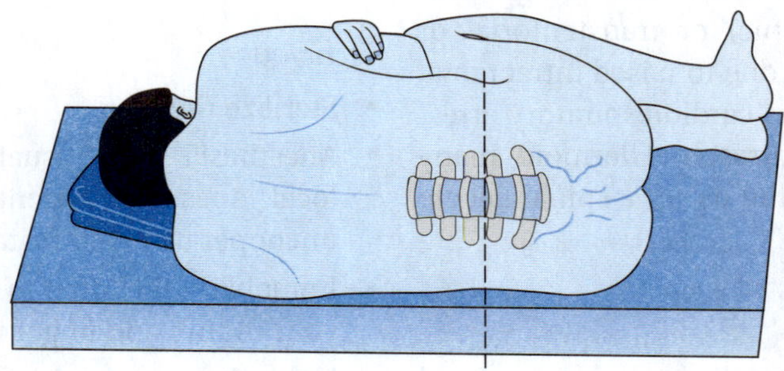

Figure 16.8 Technique for lumbar puncture.

fingers, the thumb acting as a guard at the open end.

- In children, instead of a lumbar puncture needle with a stylet, a simple hypodermic needle is commonly used. Twenty-two to 18 G disposable needles are well suited for infants and children. The best choice is to use a spinal needle (22G needle, 1–2 inches with a stylet).
- Gently introduce the needle in midline at the space mentioned earlier, needle being directed toward the umbilicus. Entry into the subarachnoid space is indicated by giving way sensation and free flow of CSF.
- Collect the CSF 0.5 cm^3 in an EDTA bulb for cell count and 1 cm^3 in a plain bulb for biochemistry. It should also be collected in a sterile bulb for culture. CSF for cell count should be examined first, usually within 30 minutes.
- Remove the needle and apply firm pressure for few minutes.
- Apply tincture benzoin seal at the puncture site.
- In case of raised intracranial pressure, head should be kept slightly flexed down to prevent herniation of brain through foramen magnum.
- Monitor the patient for some time after the procedure for pulse and respiration. Parents need to be instructed to keep the child in supine position to avoid post–lumbar puncture headache.

Complications

These are rare occurrences but can present as infection (iatrogenic) or transtentorial or cerebellar herniation due to raised intracranial pressure presenting as cardiorespiratory arrest and local inclusion (intraspinal dermoid) many years later following the use of a spinal needle without a stylet.

Subdural Tap

It is indicated for the diagnosis of subdural hematoma, effusion, and empyema in infants with open anterior fontanel. Before the procedure, an ultrasonography or CT scan of cranium is desirable.

Ventricular Tap

This procedure is indicated to diagnose ventriculitis, drain the CSF in noncommunicating hydrocephalus, and administer intraventricular drugs in the newborns. The procedure is performed by medical staff deemed competent in the procedure and is a sterile aseptic procedure. Prior to a ventricular tap, an ultrasound should be performed to confirm ventriculomegaly and measurements taken to confirm the depth and direction of needle insertion.

Fine Needle Aspiration Biopsy

Fine needle aspiration biopsy (FNAB) is very useful for cytological and bacteriological evaluation of masses or lymph nodes. It is minimally invasive and requires no sedation. It aids in tissue diagnosis and in determining the course of management.

Requirements

- One to 1.5 inch, 20–25 G needles (22 G, 1 inch length is the most commonly used size of a needle)
- Ten to 20 mL plastic disposable syringes
- Clean glass slides
- Seventy to 90% ethanol for routine wet fixation
- Containers for culture media whenever needed

Technique

- Sterilize the area.
- Anesthesia is usually not required; local anesthetic agent may be used in uncooperative and irritable children.
- Immobilize the lump to be biopsied between your thumb and finger with one hand.
- Hold the syringe in the other hand and insert the needle into the assigned area,

perpendicular to the skin surface, and position the needle within the target tissue.

- Pull the syringe plunger to apply negative pressure.
- While maintaining suction, make several passes through the mass or node.
- Release the negative pressure while the needle remains in the target tissue.
- Withdraw the needle.
- Detach the needle, draw 2–3 mL air into the syringe, reattach the needle, and blow the aspirates onto the slide.
- Apply pressure over the puncture site with a cotton swab for 5 minutes.
- Deep biopsies can be done with assistance of radiological imaging techniques such as ultrasound.

The following situations can give unsatisfactory yield during FNAB:

- When needle misses the lesion tangentially
- When central area is cystic, necrotic, or hemorrhagic and devoid of diagnostic material
- When there is a small malignant lesion close to a dominant benign mass
- When the target tissue is fibrosclerotic and poor in cells

Liver Biopsy

The indications for liver biopsy in children are to be obtain a histopathological diagnosis in several liver diseases such as chronic liver diseases (e.g., chronic hepatitis, metabolic liver diseases, infiltrative diseases, and cirrhosis), undiagnosed hepatomegaly, neonatal hepatitis, fever of unknown origin, and suspected malignancy (primary or secondary). Liver biopsy is done under ultrasound guidance rather than as a blind biopsy. Serial biopsies are indicated for the evaluation of therapeutic response in chronic liver diseases and in monitoring the liver following a liver transplant.

Contraindications

- Bleeding tendency: Prolonged prothrombin time (PT) with test >3 seconds over the control (international normalized ratio >1.6)
- Thrombocytopenia (platelets less than 50,000/mm^3)
- Massive and tense ascites
- Severe portal hypertension
- Suspected vascular malformation/hydatid disease of liver

Prerequisites

- Blood group, platelet count and PT, ultrasonography study of liver
- Premedication: Atropine 0.01 mg/kg IM 30 minutes before the procedure

Technique

- Vim Silverman needle, Menghini needle, and Tru-Cut needles are used for liver biopsy. A Tru-Cut needle is disposable, easy to operate, and having more success rate; thus, it is commonly in use.
- Informed written consent is a must.
- The patient is kept in supine position, near the edge of the bed or table with the right arm under the head and left arm by the side.
- The site of biopsy chosen is based on the liver span. If the liver is palpable, a subcostal approach may be used. However, a right lateral transthoracic approach is most common, in which the needle is inserted in the 10th intercostal space in the midaxillary line, after confirming liver dullness.
- The local area is prepared.
- Aseptic and antiseptic precautions are a must.
- One percent lignocaine is infiltrated into the skin, intercostal muscles, and Glisson's capsule. Wait for some time for good effect of the anesthetic agent. Some children may require sedation or general anesthesia.
- The Tru-Cut needle, 23G (Fig. 16.9), is introduced in a perpendicular manner under ultrasound guidance into the liver substance with the inner needle retracted.

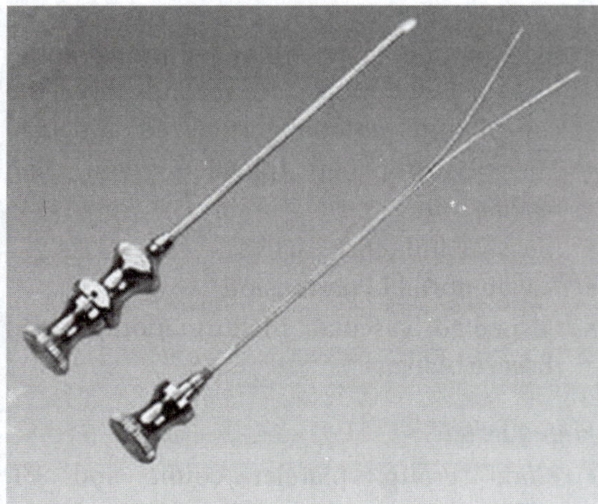

Figure 16.9 Tru-Cut liver biopsy needle.

The latter is then advanced, holding the outer cutting sheath steady. The outer sheath is then advanced to cut the liver in the biopsy notch. The whole apparatus is then withdrawn together quickly. The entire sequence should take only few seconds.

- The Vim Silverman needle has a trocar and bifid needle to cut the liver tissue. Menghini needle is rarely used for liver biopsy in pediatric practice.
- On removal of the needle, the puncture site is sealed with tincture of benzoin. The biopsy specimen should be collected and placed in 10% neutral buffered formalin for histopathological examination. The child should be watched for bleeding and abdominal distension and be monitored for vital signs for the next 24 hours.
- Complications: These include hemorrhage, hematoma formation, bile peritonitis, cholangitis, and precipitation of hepatic encephalopathy.

Renal Biopsy

Indications

- Steroid-resistant nephrotic syndrome
- Rapidly progressive glomerulonephritis
- Glomerulonephritis associated with conditions such as systemic lupus erythematosus and Henoch–Schönlein purpura
- Acute renal failure of unknown origin
- Renal allograft dysfunction

Contraindications

- Bleeding diathesis
- Solitary functioning kidney
- Ectopic/horseshoe-shaped kidney
- Severe uncontrolled hypertension

Prerequisites

- Bleeding time, clotting time, PT, APTT, platelet count
- Blood grouping and cross-matching
- Should control hypertension and uremia
- Informed written consent, which is a must

Biopsy Needles

Franklin-modified Vim Silverman needle and Tru-Cut needles were available since long for renal biopsy. Tru-Cut needle was relatively easy to use compared with Vim Silverman needle and had a lower failure rate. However, recently, gun biopsy needles are available, which are now being preferred over Tru-Cut needles due to their multiple advantages (Fig. 16.10). A gun biopsy needle offers a high-quality core specimen, has a very high success rate, and has significantly less risk of traumatic complications. The complex manual actions that are involved in the Tru-Cut biopsy are simulated by the gun biopsy needle, which makes the procedure much simple and eliminates the need of much experience of the operator.

Technique

- Atropine 0.01 mg/kg IM is administered 30 minutes before the procedure.
- The patient is placed in prone position on a firm bed. A pillow is placed under the patient's upper abdomen. This compresses and fixes kidneys to the posterior abdominal wall, bringing the kidneys closer to the skin

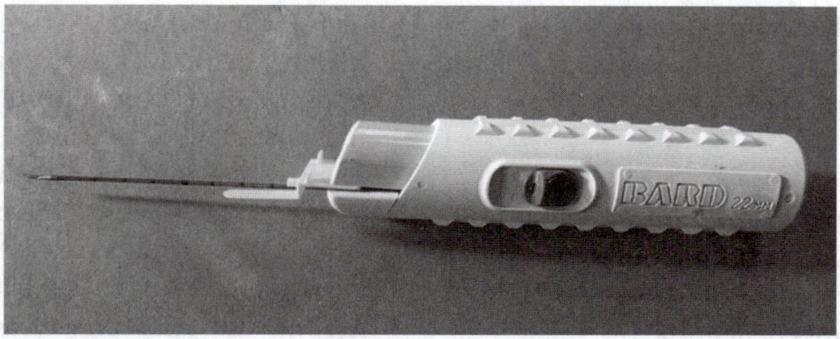

Figure 16.10 Gun biopsy needle for kidney biopsy.

and limiting possible ballottement of the kidney by the biopsy needle.

- With the help of ultrasonography, lower pole of kidney is marked on skin and depth of renal cortex is noted. The usual point of entry is the angle between the lower end of the 12th rib and the lateral border of the sacrospinalis muscle.
- The procedure is preferably carried out under short general anesthesia especially for young and irritable children. However, in older children, it may be carried out under local anesthesia.
- The area is prepared, and a local anesthetic agent is injected at the local site. A 23G exploring lumbar puncture needle is passed downwards and obliquely toward the lower pole of the kidney. A needle can be felt going through different structures and renal capsule. An experienced person feels giving way feeling on penetration of capsule of the kidney.
- The patient is asked to take slow deep breaths. If the needle is in the kidney, a characteristic pendular movement is seen with respiration; the hub of the needle swings through a wide arch, moving toward the head during inspiration and toward the buttock during expiration. If the needle is not in the kidney tissue, it is slightly advanced until it penetrates the kidney and moves characteristically on breathing. The needle is removed and depth of the kidney below the skin is measured on the stem of the needle.
- A small nick is made over the anaesthetized area with a scalpel. Then gun biopsy needle is loaded and pierced for the distance noted. Location of the tip of the gun biopsy needle just below the renal capsule is confirmed with ultrasonography and then trigger is activated. With this, the inner stylet pierces the tissue and the outer cutting cannula shears off the tissue, creating a high-quality core tissue specimen. Usually two such specimens are taken.
- The entire assembly is removed. Firm pressure is applied over the biopsy site for a few minutes and the site is sealed with tincture benzoin.
- Two good cores of tissue (8–10 mm long) are needed for adequate histological examination. One is immediately fixed in buffered formalin and the other in saline (for immune fluorescence study).

Postprocedure Management

- The patient is asked to remain in prone position for 2 hours and in bed for 24 hours.
- Monitor temperature, pulse, respiratory rate, and BP one hourly for 6 hours and then every 4 hours for 24 hours.
- Urine should be collected in separate bottles during each voiding and should be checked for hematuria.
- The patient is asked to take ample liquid orally.
- Diuretics may be given in case of oliguria to flush out any clot in the passage.

- If no frank hematuria is detected and vitals are normal, the patient can be discharged after 24 hours.

Complications

Transient hematuria for 24–48 hours is a common side effect, but other complications include:

- Persistent gross hematuria
- Perinephric hematoma
- Rarely, A-V fistula as a late complication

Suprapubic Bladder Aspiration

This procedure is performed to collect noncontaminated urine sample in neonates and infants. It is a safe and reliable way of collecting urine samples. It is easy especially in neonates as bladder is an intra-abdominal organ in these patients unlike a pelvic organ in older children and adults. The site of suprapubic aspiration is 1–2 cm above the pubic symphysis in the midline and the fullness of the bladder must be confirmed before the aspiration by either percussion or observing the dryness of the nappy for 1–2 hours. With asepsis, a 23G or 24G needle with syringe is inserted into the bladder perpendicularly with an angle of 10–20° cephalad. Gentle negative pressure in the syringe with slow advancement yields the return of urine after the bladder is entered.

Abdominal Paracentesis

Abdominal paracentesis is performed for diagnostic purposes in case of ascites, peritonitis, and hemorrhage and for evaluation of suspected peritonitis. In huge ascites, it is also done to relieve discomfort and respiratory embarrassment.

Technique

- The patient should be placed in supine position. If the patient is not comfortable in supine position or has respiratory distress due to huge collection, reclining or upright position is preferable.
- Site for paracentesis is selected in the midline, midway between umbilicus and pubic symphysis, or in the iliac fossa lateral to the rectus abdominis.
- The needle should never be advanced through a surgical scar because it can penetrate bowel adherent to the undersurface of the scar or lacerate an omental or mesenteric vessel.
- Aseptic and antiseptic measures must be taken and the surrounding area should be draped.
- Inj. atropine is given as premedication.
- One percent lignocaine is infiltrated under skin and into the deeper structures at the site selected for paracentesis. Wait for few minutes for good effect of the anesthetic agent.
- The hypodermic needle, 20 G, is attached to a 20-mL syringe. It is passed into the peritoneal cavity perpendicular to the skin. As the needle enters the peritoneal cavity, it gives way and ascitic fluid starts to drain through the needle.
- In a case of tense ascites, the needle should be passed obliquely, or skin should be retracted before insertion of the needle to produce a Z-track effect on withdrawing the needle so that needle tract after paracentesis gets sealed properly and persistent drainage can be prevented after removal of the needle.
- After removal of 10–15 mL of fluid for diagnostic purpose, the needle is withdrawn, and a seal of tincture benzoin is applied locally.
- If the paracentesis is for therapeutic purpose, the needle should be connected with an IV set and the regulator of the IV set should be adjusted in such a way that ascitic fluid is drained slowly. One liter of fluid may be drained over a period of 2–3 hours.
- The patient should be watched following the procedure.

Complications

- Intestinal perforation or laceration
- Peritonitis

- Hypotension, electrolyte imbalance, and shock due to massive drainage
- Precipitation of hepatic coma
- Pneumoperitoneum

Thoracocentesis (or Pleural Tap)

Thoracocentesis or pleural tap refers to temporary insertion of a needle or a catheter into the pleural space for removal of fluid or air from the pleural cavity. The fluid is collected for diagnostic purposes and in some cases, it is done for therapeutic purpose to remove fluid (effusion or empyema) or air that is in large quantity and causing respiratory embarrassment such as an emergency management of tension pneumothorax. Drugs such as antibiotics and steroids can also be instilled in the pleural cavity by this procedure.

Technique

- Inj. atropine must be used as a premedication.
- Site of insertion of needle can be decided by chest X-ray, dull note on percussion, and ultrasound study of thorax. The best way to perform the procedure is under ultrasound guidance (Fig. 16.11). The usual site chosen is the upper edge of lower rib in the seventh or eighth intercostal space in the posterior axillary line. For decompression of pneumothorax, second or third intercostal space in the midclavicular line is selected for the procedure.
- It should be performed with the patient in sitting position. The patient can lean forwards on the procedure table of a suitable height with head resting on his/her forearms.
- Strict aseptic and antiseptic measures should be taken.
- One percent lignocaine is infiltrated at the upper border of the rib below the space chosen. Anesthetizing a wide area and generous infiltration of local anesthetic agent for good anesthesia helps to get good cooperation of the patient, performing the whole procedure comfortably leading to successful performance with minimal chances of complications. Wait for some time for good effect of the anesthetic agent.
- A wide-bore needle (18–20G) is connected on one side of the three-way stopcock and opposite to it a syringe is attached. The three-way stopcock is arranged in such a way that there is a single track between the needle, stopcock, and syringe.
- The child can be asked to hold his/her breath and the needle is inserted into the chest in the same manner as for the anesthetic needle, finding the intercostal space and stepping over the lower rib with care, thereby preventing damage to the underlying structures. Slight suction is applied to the syringe, so that the fluid is aspirated with gentle suction in the syringe immediately as the needle enters the pleural space. The entry to the pleural space is felt by a sudden give way and decrease in the resistance.
- The fluid should be withdrawn slowly and steadily.
- Forceps should be attached to the needle at the skin level, which helps to prevent excessive deep insertion of the needle into the thorax.
- The fluid is aspirated in the syringe and then the three-way stopcock is turned to connect

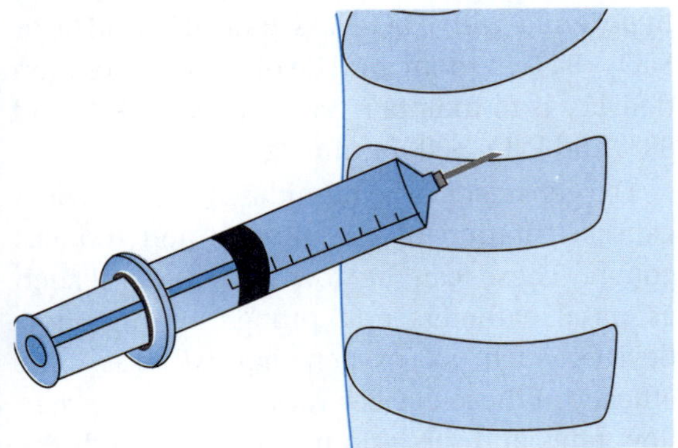

Figure 16.11 Site of needle for pleural fluid aspiration. *Source*: Reproduced with permission from Baldev P. Essential Procedures in Pediatrics. Jaypee Bros: New Delhi, 2003.

the syringe with the outlet that is attached to the IV set.

- Collect the fluid in EDTA and plain bulbs. It is also collected for culture. Smear should be prepared for Gram stain and Ziehl–Neelsen stain.
- The three-way tap is now turned again to connect the syringe with the needle and the pleural space; a further aspiration is carried out. It is expelled into the drainage bag by turning the three-way tap. The drainage bag or bottle should be placed well below the level of the patient's chest.
- As the fluid is removed, the lung expands, and this often makes the patient to cough.
- The needle is withdrawn, and the puncture site is covered with a benzoin seal. A sterile gauze is put over it and an adhesive tape is applied. The total aspirated volume in a single sitting should not be more than 5% of the child's body weight.
- In cases of empyema, intercostal tube thoracotomy is necessary for continued drainage of the purulent material.

Complications

- Pneumothorax
- Hemothorax
- Infection
- Traumatic injury to liver or spleen
- Subcutaneous emphysema
- Sudden lung expansion of the collapsed lung leading to unilateral pulmonary edema
- Fistula/sinus formation in tubercular effusion

Pericardiocentesis

The drainage of pericardial fluid is done for diagnostic purposes and therapeutic drainage of large collections and should always be done by a skilled operator under the continued monitoring of vital signs, ECG, and pulse oximetry. The procedure is a lifesaving intervention in cases of cardiac tamponade. Echocardiographic diagnosis is a must before performing the procedure. It gives an idea regarding the amount of fluid and also helps to determine the anatomical approach. The common complications include hemopericardium, vasovagal reactions, air embolism, infection arrhythmias, and cardiac arrest.

Peritoneal Dialysis

Dialysis involves the use of semipermeable membranes that permit the simultaneous passage of smaller-molecular-weight solutes and water while retarding or inhibiting the movement of large-sized particles. The basic principles controlling the transmembrane movement of solute and water are similar whether the membrane is artificial (hemodialysis) or natural (peritoneal dialysis [PD]). Few common indications for PD in children include life-threatening electrolyte imbalances (such as hyperkalemia with serum K >6.5 mEq/L), severe acidosis, pulmonary edema, blood urea >300 mg/dL, and drug intoxications such as salicylates and barbiturates.

Oxygen Delivery Systems

Delivery of oxygen is critical in sick newborns and children as the room air that provides about 21% oxygen is insufficient to correct hypoxia and meet the cardiopulmonary needs and hemodynamic stabilization. Administration of oxygen is indicated in documented or suspected hypoxemia with PaO_2 less than 60 mmHg or SaO_2 <94% in room air. The objective of oxygen delivery is to maintain SaO_2 between 94% and 99% and PaO_2 >60–74 mmHg.

Oxygen needs to be humidified as dry oxygen causes irritation of the airways and induces cough. These can be low-flow devices such as nasal catheters and prongs, or high-flow devices such as oxygen hoods/boxes. The efficacy of these devices varies with the oxygen flow rates and the amount of mixing with the environmental air.

- *Nasal catheter*: It is a simple rubber catheter with multiple side holes in its distal 2 cm and is passed through the nose after lubrication till the tip reaches nasopharynx just behind the uvula. The oxygen flow rate is generally 2–4 L/min.

- *Nasal cannula*: Nasal cannula with two prongs is a simple device and can be used to deliver a flow rate of 1–2 L/min (Fig. 16.12).
- *Face mask*: This is made up of a transparent PVC material with a connecting port and a face seal (Fig. 16.13). It delivers 35–60% of FiO_2 at a flow rate of 6–10 L/min. A minimum of 6 L/min should be given in face mask to prevent rebreathing of expired CO_2. Some modifications such as rebreathing masks and venturi masks are also available to deliver higher FiO_2.
- *Oxygen hoods/boxes*: These are made from a single piece of transparent plastic material. These are high-flow devices that can deliver 40–50% of FiO_2 at oxygen flow rates of 10 L/min. The oxygen tubing is attached to a nozzle at the upper/head end of the box, while a flexible shield near the neck end creates an effective seal around the baby's neck and prevents the entry of room air in the box. However, these devices are useful only for newborns and small infants.

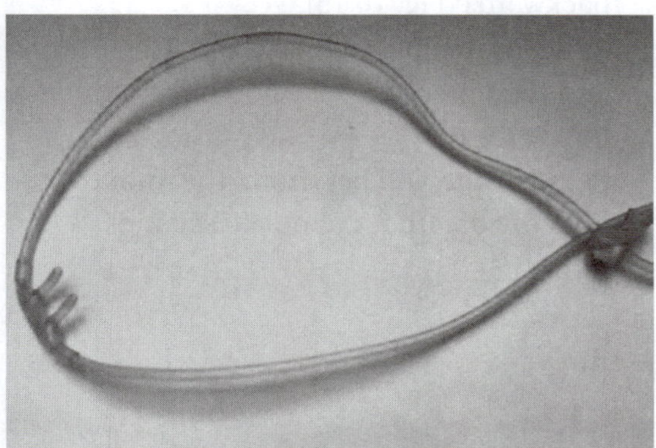

Figure 16.12 Nasal cannula.

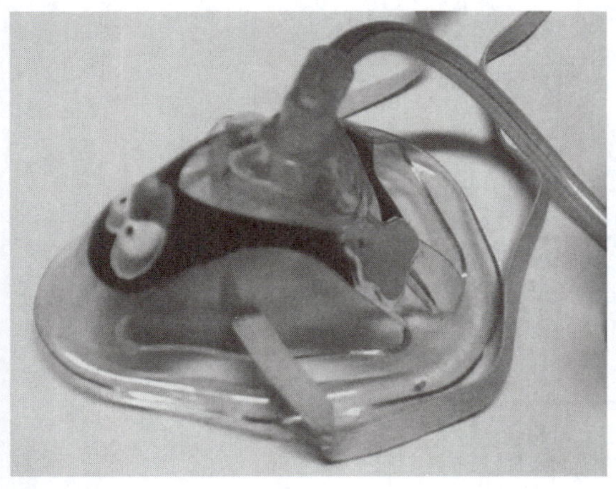

Figure 16.13 Face mask.

Aerosol Devices and Inhalation Therapy

In the treatment of asthma, the target site is the tracheobronchial tree. It is logical to use the inhaled route of drug administration in asthma as the drug can be delivered directly to the large surface area of the tracheobronchial tree. The drugs administered by inhalation route or by different inhalation devices have revolutionized the management of airway diseases. Only 10–15% of the drug reaches the lower airways by these devices, which is sufficient for a clinical response. There are many benefits of this route:

- With direct delivery of the drug, rapid action is obtained.
- Smaller doses are required.
- Systemic side effects can be avoided or minimized.
- Self-administration of the drug is possible.

The drugs that are commonly administered by this route include short- and long-acting bronchodilators, corticosteroids, 3% NaCl, and antibiotics. Depending on the age of the child, several modalities are available for inhalation therapy.

Uses of Inhalation Therapy

- Bronchodilators and steroids in bronchial asthma
- Bronchiolitis
- Vasopressin in enuresis
- Aminoglycoside (tobramycin) in cystic fibrosis

Inhalation Therapy in Asthma

A drug aerosol is basically a suspension of a drug (liquid droplets/solid particles) in a gaseous medium. For aerosol therapy to be effective, the drug must reach the lower airways and this requires a particle diameter <5 µm. Larger particles are mainly deposited in the upper airways or swallowed. To generate an aerosol with the correct particle size (<5 µm size), most metered-dose inhalers (MDIs) contain various propellants and surfactants. In contrast, dry powder inhalers (DPIs) use the patient's inspiratory force to generate the drug aerosol and are devoid of propellants. Only the drug particles along with an inert carrier such as lactose constitute the aerosol.

Devices Available for Inhalation Therapy

- MDI
- DPI (Rotahaler)
- Nebulizer

Metered-dose inhaler

MDI is a pressure-actuated device that delivers a fixed amount of medication in aerosol form each time it is activated. Inhaling as the medication is released delivers a metered dose of the drug to the airways. MDI is made up of two separate parts:

1. A pressurized aluminum canister with a valve and atomizing needle, which fits into
2. An outer plastic actuator sleeve with a mouthpiece. The valve allows only a fixed amount of the drug to be released and delivered after each actuation (Fig. 16.14).

How to use an MDI?

- Remove the mouthpiece cover and shake the inhaler.
- Breathe out gently.
- Place the mouthpiece of the inhaler in the mouth and seal lips around it, taking care not to bite it. Tilt your head slightly backwards (Fig. 16.15).
- At the beginning, take slow and deep breaths, and then press the canister and continue to inhale deeply.
- Remove the inhaler from the mouth and hold the breath for about 10 seconds.

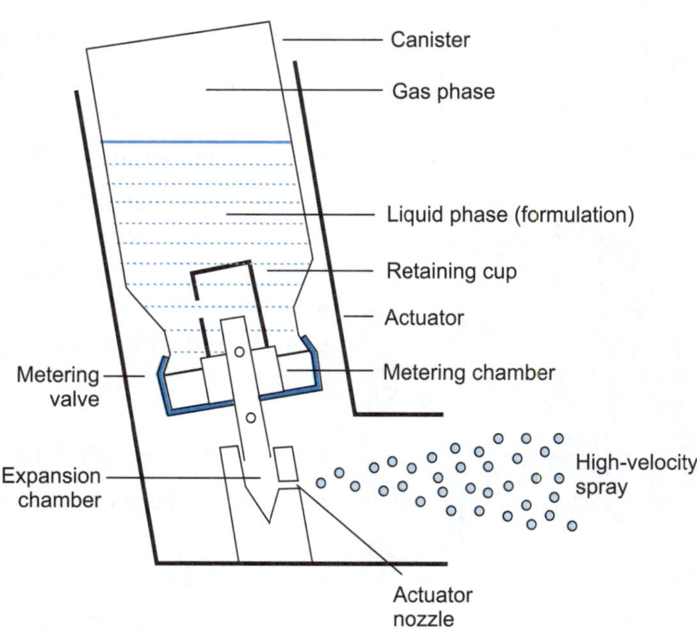

Figure 16.14 Metered-dose inhaler.

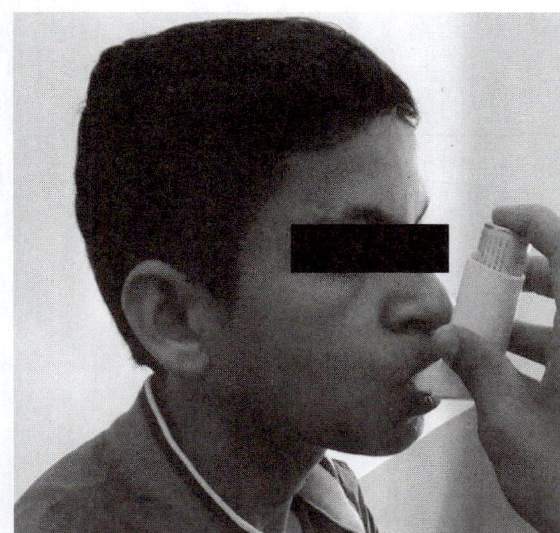

Figure 16.15 Proper placement of MDI in mouth.

Wait for at least 1 minute before taking another inhalation. Parents must assist and supervise the children using their MDI correctly.

Important points

- Appropriate coordination between press and breath is essential. The inhalation has to be timed to coincide with the discharge of drug from the canister. Young and preschool children cannot coordinate their breaths for effective inhalation; therefore, it is preferable to use a spacer and a mask for an effective delivery of the medicine.
- Holding the breath for 5–10 seconds after full inspiration ensures that the drug settles in the lower airways. After the inhalation of steroid-containing aerosols, the mouth must be rinsed with water to avoid local drug deposition and prevent secondary oral candidiasis.

Care of the MDI Clean the inhaler at least once a week.

- Gently pull the metal canister out of the adapter of the inhaler. Remove the mouthpiece cover.
- Rinse the adapter and the mouthpiece cover in warm water. Do not put the metal canister into the water.
- Replace the canister and mouthpiece cover correctly.

Spacers

Spacers are used as accessories to MDIs. A spacer acts as a temporary reservoir or chamber (10–40 seconds) for the aerosol released from the MDI. The child can then inhale from this chamber shortly after the drug is discharged from the MDI. He/she need not coordinate press with breath. Spacers are made up of two-piece compartments with a combined volume of 250–750 mL and are made up of antistatic polycarbonate/polyamide material with one inlet for MDI canister and another outlet as a mouthpiece (Fig. 16.16). A small-volume (250 mL) spacer is preferable for a younger child and a large-volume spacer (750 mL) is preferable for an older child. But a large-volume spacer can be used for all the age groups.

How to use a spacer device?

- Assemble the spacer.
- Remove the mouthpiece cover from the inhaler. Shake the inhaler well. Insert the inhaler into the spacer device.
- Ask the child to breathe out gently. Place the mouthpiece of the spacer in the child's mouth. Ask the child to seal the lips around the mouthpiece. Warn him/her not to bite it.
- Encourage the child to breathe in and out slowly and gently. Once the breathing pattern is established, press the canister and leave the device in the same position as the child continues to breathe several times. In infants and toddlers, a mask is fixed to the spacer device for the effective use of MDI.
- Remove the device from the child's mouth.
- If the child is able, ask him/her to hold the breath for 10 seconds or as long as it is comfortable to him/her. In a span of 15–30 seconds, most of the aerosol is inhaled.
- If the second dose is required, wait for at least 1 minute.

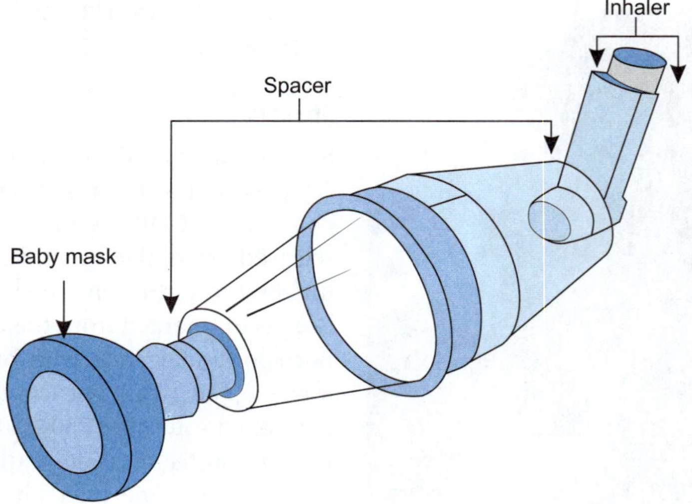

Figure 16.16 Spacer with MDI attached.

Care of the spacer and mask It is important to keep the spacer and mask clean. They should be cleaned regularly, preferably twice.

- Clean the mask and the spacer using a mild detergent and rinse thoroughly with warm water.
- Shake well to remove excess water; leave to dry.
- Store the mask and the spacer in a plastic container to keep them clean.

Important points

- The released drug stays suspended in the holding chamber for a short period (up to 5–10 seconds) during which the child commences inhalation and the drug is inhaled past a one-way valve. In a child unable to generate a sufficient inspiratory flow rate, tidal breathing is adequate. Exhalation into the mouthpiece leads to valve closure and escape of air through vents on the mouthpiece proximal to the valve.
- Reduction of oropharyngeal deposition of inhaled drugs leads to a decreased frequency of local side effects. Thus, oral thrush or dysphonia due to inhaled steroids and medicinal taste of agonists or cromoglycate are avoided or minimized. Systemic adverse effects on inhaled steroids that occur due to swallowing of the orally deposited drugs are also significantly reduced.
- It is recommended that a spacer be changed once every 6 months or so.

Dry powder inhaler

DPI/Rotahaler is a breath-activated device. It is considered as effective as MDI. In a Rotahaler, a capsule of the powdered drug formulation is inserted into the device and is broken into two halves by rotating the base relative to the mouthpiece. One half with the powder falls into the Rotahaler and the patient has to merely inhale though the mouthpiece (Fig. 16.17).

How to use a Rotahaler?

- Hold the Rotahaler vertically and insert Rotacaps, transparent end first, into the small raised square hole of the Rotahaler. Confirm that the top of the Rotacaps is at level with the top of the hole.
- Hold the mouthpiece firmly with one hand and rotate the base. The *fin* separates the two halves of the Rotacaps.
- The child is asked to breathe out gently. He/she is asked to grip the mouthpiece between the teeth and to seal his/her lips around it. The child should be warned not to bite it. Tilt the head slightly backward and

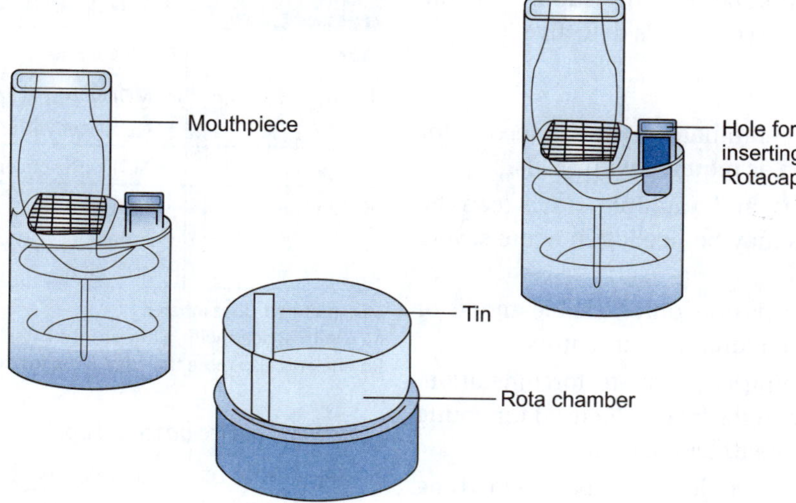

Figure 16.17 Rotahaler.

let the child breathe in the powder slowly and deeply. The sound of the Rotacaps shell rattling inside the Rotahaler indicates correctness of the technique.

- Remove the Rotahaler from the child's mouth and ask him/her to hold the breath for about 10 seconds or till he/she can do comfortably. In case any powder remains in the Rotacaps shell after the inhalation, repeat it till the Rotacaps is empty. Parents should assist and supervise the children, if they need help in using the Rotahaler correctly.

Care of the Rotahaler

- Wash the Rotahaler at least twice a week.
- Separate the two halves of the Rotahaler.
- Remove the empty Rotacaps shell from the raised square hole.
- Rinse the two halves in running tap water.
- Dry the Rotahaler thoroughly before reassembling it.

Nebulizer

Nebulizer is an electric device that converts a liquid drug into a fine mist that can be inhaled easily. Although there are two types of nebulizers (jet and ultrasonic variety), jet nebulizers are most frequently used in pediatric practice.

Principle of functioning of jet nebulizer Air from the compressor passes through a small hole (venturi). Rapid expansion of air causes a negative pressure that sucks fluid up the feeding tube system where it is atomized. Larger particles impact on baffles and the walls of the chamber and are returned for renebulization. Small aerosol particles are released continuously from the nebulizer chamber.

Important points

- Optimal volume of solution in nebulizer chamber should be 2–4 mL.
- Particle size should be 2–5 μm.
- Flow rate should be 4–6 L/min.
- Nebulizer should be oxygen or air driven.
- It should be electric 220 V AC or battery powered.
- Saline should be used as the diluent and not distilled water. With distilled water, hypotonic solution can lead to reflex bronchospasm.
- Drug should be nebulized over a period of 10–12 minutes. If the nebulization is taking longer than 15 minutes, either the chamber

is malfunctioning or the supply of the compressed oxygen/air is defective.

Advantages

- Nebulizer eliminates the need for coordination as required with MDIs.
- Larger doses and multiple drugs can be delivered as may be needed in acute severe asthma.
- Nebulization is the only feasible mode of delivery for children on ventilators.
- Tidal breathing is adequate for inhalation. Therefore, nebulizers can be used for young children or breathless patients.
- Nebulizer avoids reflex coughing occasionally experienced during inhalation from MDIs and DPIs.
- No chlorofluorocarbons are used (environment friendly).

Cleaning the nebulizer

After each treatment

- Disassemble the nebulizer completely.
- Rinse the tubing, medication cup, mouthpiece, or mask in warm water.
- Shake off excess water and allow it to dry. Avoid drying in dusty or smoky areas.

After each day

- Disassemble the nebulizer completely.
- Submerge the tubing, medication cup, and mouthpiece or mask in a mild detergent and warm water for a couple of minutes.
- Using a small bristle brush, scrub all parts to remove any sediment that may have accumulated.
- Rinse parts thoroughly after washing to remove all residual soap.
- Immerse all parts in acetic acid (one part white vinegar + three parts water—freshly prepared daily) disinfectant solution for 10 minutes.
- Remove all parts and rinse under a strong steam of warm water.
- Air dry parts between folded paper towels in a clean area.

TABLE 16.2 Aerosol Devices in Children

Age	Device options
Infancy to 3 years	• MDI with spacer and mask • Nebulizer with mask
3–6 years	• MDI with spacer
6–12 years	• MDI with spacer • Rotahaler • MDI alone

MDI, metered-dose inhaler.
MDI with spacer (with/without face mask) is preferred first.
Rotahaler is also more than adequate for day-to-day therapy.

Selecting a device based on age

- Selection of a device is based on age (Table 16.2).

Peak Flow Meter

- Peak expiratory flow rate (PEFR) is the measure of the greatest flow rate obtained on forceful expiration after complete inspiration to total lung capacity. It measures large airway function in children older than 5 years who can be trained to use a peak flow meter. It correlates well with FEV_1.
- The peak flow varies according to age, sex, and height. An asthmatic's normal peak flow should be within 20% of a person who is of the same age, sex, and height, but who does not have asthma.
- Peak flow meter is used to measure PEFR (Fig. 16.18). Commonly used peak flow meter is a mini-Wright peak flow meter, 20–25 cm long, made up of three parts:
  1. Detachable mouthpiece
  2. Main body of plastic with a graduated scale (liter per minute) to read PEFR

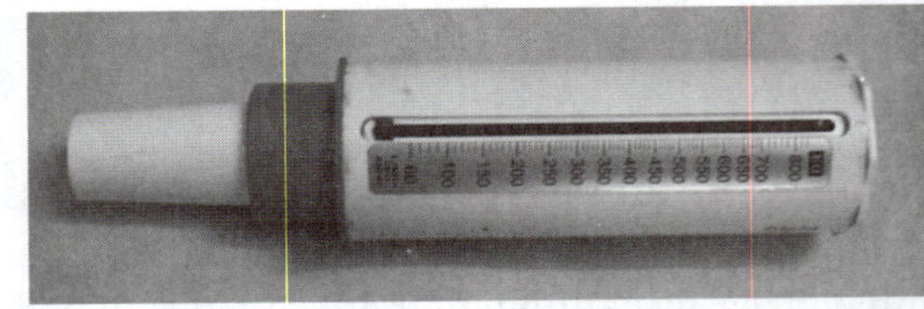

Figure 16.18 Peak flow meter.

3. Diaphragm inside the tube attached to the external pointer that moves on the main body's scale

How to Check Peak Expiratory Flow Rate

- Fit the mouthpiece to the peak flow meter.
- Confirm that the child stands up and holds the peak flow meter horizontally without restricting movements of the pointer.
- Adjust the pointer to zero.
- Ask the child to breathe deeply, as far as possible, with the mouth wide open.
- Place the mouthpiece in the child's mouth and seal his/her lips around it.
- Ask the child to blow out as hard and fast as possible. In case the child coughs, disregard that reading. Make sure that the child's tongue is not blocking the mouthpiece. Record the result. Repeat the procedure and record the highest of three readings.
- PEFR measurements are used to assess the severity of airway obstruction in an acute attack of asthma, to judge the therapeutic response to the drugs, and as a long-term monitoring of the course of the disease.

Resuscitation Devices and Procedures

The detailed approach to neonatal resuscitation has been described in Chapter 15. However, it is essential to be familiar with the commonly used equipment and the procedures in resuscitation that may be needed in a sick newborn or an infant/child with critical illnesses such as cardiac arrest, multiorgan dysfunction, trauma, and drowning.

Suction Devices

Suction catheters/devices are commonly required to remove the thick secretions that may be blocking the respiratory passages, and a sterile/disposable suction catheter that is attached to a central/portable suction device particularly in an intensive care setup suffices in most situations. Care must be exercised to ensure that the suction is gentle and intermittent and high pressure is not applied (not more than 80–120 mmHg and less than 30 mmHg in neonates to avoid mucosal trauma) and lowest effective suction pressure must be used. Care should be taken to avoid vagal stimulation that can cause bradycardia by forceful suctioning.

The most commonly used suction device during cardiopulmonary resuscitation in a newborn is a small, disposable, PVC suction device (DeLee mucus extractor) (Fig. 16.19) and it is made up of three parts:

1. Central bulb to hold and retain suctioned fluid such as mucus, meconium, and aspirated blood
2. A tubing with one end in the bulb and another end for the baby's mouth/nose suctioning
3. The user's end tube with an adapter for use for suctioning (with the suctioning done by the resuscitator, the fluid gets collected in the bulb/central chamber by the negative pressure); the device is simple, economical, easy to use, and disposable

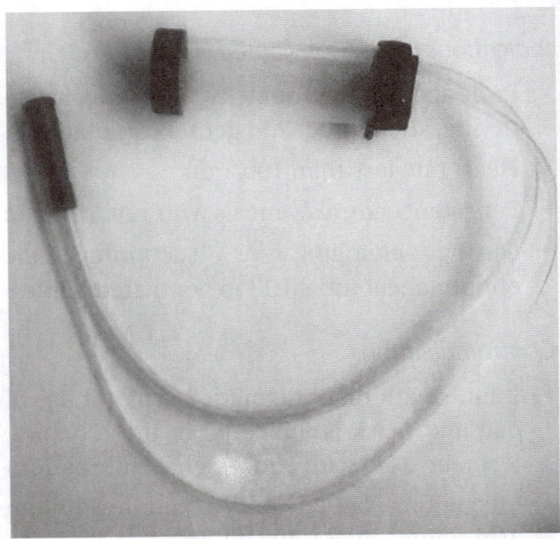

Figure 16.19 DeLee mucus extractor.

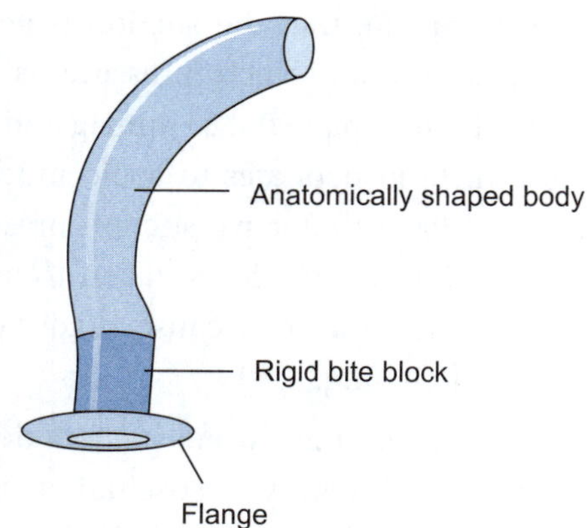

Figure 16.20 Oropharyngeal airway.

Oropharyngeal Airway

These are curved plastic or metal devices used to prevent glossoptosis and make the airways clear for suctioning in a child with impaired consciousness (Fig. 16.20). These should not be used in a conscious or a convulsing child to avoid the risk to traumatic injury.

Bag and Mask Ventilation

It is a very effective procedure for cardiopulmonary resuscitation of an asphyxiated patient when other measures have failed. Bag and mask ventilation is also included with reference to the newborns in detail in Chapter 15.

Indications in an Asphyxiated Newborn

- Prolonged apneic attacks unresponsive to drying, suctioning, and gentle stimulation
- Heart rate less than 100/min
- Persistent central cyanosis with 100% oxygen
- During changing or suctioning the endotracheal tube (ET) in ventilated babies

Contraindications

- Infants with diaphragmatic hernia (if use of bag and mask is indicated in these babies, it can be used with endotracheal intubation)
- Meconium-stained babies and meconium aspiration, unless meconium is sucked out from air passage

Self-Inflating Bag

- A self-inflating Ambu or Laerdal bag is more convenient to use. It inflates on its own as the grip on the bag is released. It does not require a compressed gas source to refill.
- The parts of the bag are air inlet, oxygen inlet, patient outlet, valve assembly, and the pressure gauge attachment site.
- The capacity of the bag for use in infants should not exceed 750 mL (250–750 mL) while larger (750–1500 mL) bags are used for older children. The air inlet is the largest opening, having a one-way valve, and is located at the rear end.
- The oxygen reservoir (a corrugated tube or a closed rubber bladder) must be attached at the air inlet to increase the concentration of oxygen being delivered to the infant. The oxygen inlet is located near the air inlet. It is a small nipple or projection to which oxygen tubing can be attached.
- The bag can be used in an emergency without attaching oxygen but it will deliver only 21% of oxygen contained in the atmosphere. The air–oxygen mixture is forced out from the patient outlet to which an appropriate-sized face mask or ET is attached. The patient receives approximately 40% of oxygen concentration by air–oxygen mixture.
- Applying an oxygen reservoir over the air inlets permits administration of 90–100% oxygen. The one-way valve assembly is positioned between the bag and the patient outlet. It allows delivery of oxygen to the outlet when the bag is squeezed but closes as soon as the bag is released so that exhaled air cannot reenter the bag. Due to the presence of valve assembly, the self-inflating bag cannot be used for free flow oxygen. The pop-off valve (pressure release valve) can be set to actuate when inflation pressure exceeds 30–35 cm H_2O. The pressure gauge allows a person to control the pressure of the air or oxygen being delivered to the patient.

Face Masks

The face masks of various sizes and shapes are available. Soft circular masks with cushioned rim are preferred as they can form an effective seal on the face and are less likely to leak or cause damage to the infant's eyes. The correct size of the mask for each infant should be chosen so that it covers nose, mouth, and chin of the infant. The siliconized rubber masks can be more easily cleaned and sterilized as they can withstand boiling and autoclaving.

Procedure

- The bag and mask assembly should be checked beforehand. The bag should be squeezed while making an airtight seal of face mask with the palm of the hand to assess functioning of valve assembly, pop-off valve, and leakage or tears in the bag. When the bag is filled, squeezing the bag should be able to force the pressure valve open and the valve assembly should be moving. The bag should reinflate quickly when the grip is released.
- The infant should be positioned supine and neck slightly extended by placing a thin roll of towel under the shoulders. After lifting the jaw, a properly sized mask is applied to snuggly enclose the nose, mouth, and chin of the baby. The mask is held in place by the left hand with the help of thumb and index finger while ring finger holds and lifts the chin of the baby. Pressure on eyes and trachea should be avoided. The face mask must establish an airtight seal with the face. Before starting compression over the bag with fingertips of right hand, oxygen source and oxygen reservoir should be connected.
- The rate should be 30–40/min depending on the age of the child. The force of compression should be adjusted to the size of the child and compliance of the lungs. There should be a noticeable rise and fall of the chest with each inflation. It should be associated with good air entry on both the sides of the chest and improvement in color and heart rate.
- To open up the collapsed alveoli, for few initial breaths, a pressure of 30–40 cm H_2O is recommended. For succeeding breaths, a pressure of 15–20 cm H_2O is adequate to keep the alveoli inflated. If the chest does not expand adequately, reconfirm that the face mask is forming an effective seal, airway is open, and enough pressure is applied on the bag without any leakage or tears.
- In case of a large tongue, glossoptosis, Pierre Robin syndrome, or bilateral choanal atresia, oropharyngeal airway should be inserted.
- If bag and mask ventilation is required for more than 2 minutes, an orogastric tube should be inserted to aspirate the contents of stomach. It also prevents distention of abdomen.
- If, rather than improvement, a newborn on bag and mask ventilation shows further deterioration (increasing respiratory distress and cyanosis), diaphragmatic hernia should be suspected. Bag and mask ventilation should be discontinued in such babies, an ET should be inserted, and bag and tube ventilation should be started.

Endotracheal Intubation

Endotracheal intubation is a procedure that every pediatrician and one working in intensive care units must be well conversant with. The critically ill patient often requires endotracheal intubation. It secures the patient's airway. It is a prerequisite for mechanical ventilation. Endotracheal suction can most efficiently be done through an ET. It is indicated when bag and mask resuscitation fails as is in a case of an asphyxiated newborn. Nasotracheal intubation is done when long-term ventilation is required. Postextubation stridor can be managed by nebulized epinephrine or steroids.

Indications

- In neonatal asphyxia
  - Failure of bag and mask resuscitation
  - Apparently stillborn baby after adequate suctioning of upper airways

 - Infants with diaphragmatic hernia
 - Meconium aspiration
- Cardiorespiratory arrest due to any cause
- Central nervous system depression in case of head injury or a comatose child
- Diseases of peripheral nervous system, poliomyelitis, Guillain–Barré syndrome, tetanus, organophosphorus poisoning, etc.
- Administration of general anesthesia

Equipment

- Laryngoscope—with a straight blade for neonates
- ETs for various sizes with/without stylet
- The approximate size of the ET tube: Internal diameter (ID) (mm) = age (years) + 16/4

Technique

- The patient is placed in a supine position. The operator stands beyond the patient's head. The patient's neck is slightly extended with the head in midline.
- Clear the oropharynx with gentle suctioning.
- Empty the stomach by nasogastric suction.
- Hold the handle of laryngoscope in left hand with thumb and first three fingers; stabilize hand with the fifth finger resting on the patient's cheek. The blade should be pointing away from oneself.
- Open the baby's mouth and push the tongue left with back of right forefinger and steady the head with the rest of the right hand.
- While visualizing, insert the blade midline until the tip is between base of tongue and epiglottis within the vallecula (Fig. 16.21).
- If the infant is making respiratory effort, free flow of oxygen with an oxygen tubing held close to the infant's mouth and nose should be provided during intubation.
- Open the mouth further by pulling on laryngoscope handle; simultaneously, tilt the blade tip upward slightly to elevate epiglottis and visualize glottis. Use base of tongue as pivot rather than maxilla.
- Suction is needed.

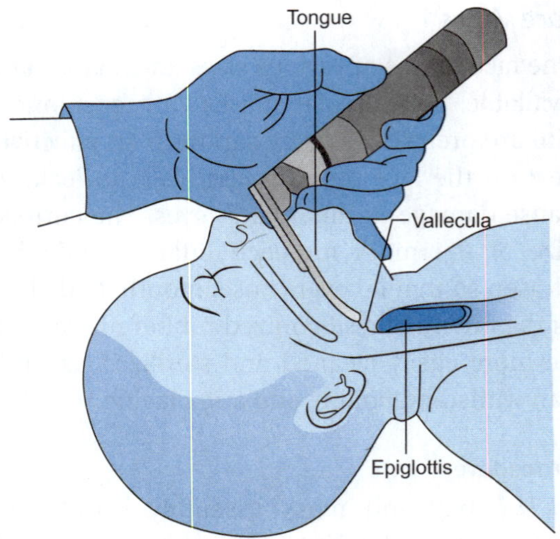

Figure 16.21 Position of laryngoscopic blade during endotracheal intubation. *Source*: Reproduced with permission from Gupta P. Textbook of Pediatrics, 2nd ed. CBS Publishers: New Delhi, 2019.

- Have the assistant palpate suprasternal notch with index finger, applying gentle pressure if desired.
- Hold the tube with concave curve anterior and pass it down the right side of the mouth, outside the blade, with maintaining visualization.
- As the patient inspires, pass the tube through cords 2 cm into trachea or until immediately after tip passes under the assistant's finger in suprasternal notch.
- The tube is then held firmly at the lips with the right hand and the laryngoscope and the stylet are carefully removed.
- Initially confirmation of the tube placement is accomplished by attaching a resuscitation bag with the connector and ventilating the infant. With a correctly placed tube, air entry is heard on both sides of the chest, breath sounds are of equal intensity, and air is not heard entering the stomach. While listening the breath sounds, the stethoscope should be placed at approximately the nipple line.
- Note the centimeter marks on the tube at the level of upper lips and then secure the tube to the infant's face.

- Final confirmation of placement of the tube can be obtained by chest film if it is needed.
- Attempts to intubate should not exceed 30 seconds. If one is unable to intubate within 30 seconds, abort and continue with bag and mask and then try again after a few minutes. Repeated attempts may cause serious glottic edema and bleeding.
- If you are unable to do so, please ask for help.
- Endotracheal route is also used for administration of some drugs such as epinephrine, atropine, and naloxone.

Complications

- Hypoxia
- Bradycardia
- Apnea
- Pneumothorax
- Trauma to epiglottis, larynx
- Infections

KEY POINTS

- Practical pediatric procedures form an essential and integral part in the diagnosis and the treatment of sick neonates, infants, and children.
- Every effort must be made to make the procedures safe and effective for children.

CHAPTER 17

Drugs and Dosages for Children

Niranjan Shendurnikar, Paresh A Thakkar

The list of the drugs that are included is by no means comprehensive but is largely meant to guide the students about the most common medications that are prescribed in general pediatrics and neonatology. As therapeutics is an evolving science and due to the availability of new data and ongoing developments, many drug doses continue to be modified with emerging and more recent information. However, best efforts are made to include essential information on the pediatric pharmacology, general dosing guidelines, common side effects/adverse reactions, and precautions with reference to drugs.

Antibacterial Agents

Before choosing an antibiotic in a given situation and for it to be effective in a given child, it is prudent to consider the following:

- Suspected microbiological agent and its likely sensitivity
- Site and the severity of infection
- Host factors such as the age, nutrition, and other associated morbidities in the child that may alter/affect the drug mechanism (e.g., renal and hepatic disease, drug allergies)
- Effective duration and route of administration. Severe morbid conditions such as acute bacterial meningitis, neonatal sepsis, and shock need to be treated aggressively with intravenous antibiotics for appropriate duration; an improper route and/or inadequate dose not only can contribute to therapeutic failure but can also increase the likelihood of antibacterial resistance; on the contrary, a narrow margin between the therapeutic and the toxic dose [gentamicin, amikacin] needs careful dosing and monitoring for their potential adverse effects

Penicillins

The penicillin group of drugs (benzylpenicillin, phenoxymethylpenicillin, penicillinase-resistant penicillins, broad-spectrum penicillins, antipseudomonal penicillins, and mecillinam) are bactericidal drugs and exert their action by inhibiting bacterial cell wall synthesis via a beta-lactam ring and killing bacteria by cell wall lysis. The different preparations of natural penicillins are shown in Table 17.1.

Penicillinase-Resistant Penicillins

- These penicillins are resistant to destruction/hydrolysis by the beta-lactamase produced by staphylococci and are thus antibacterials of choice for infections caused by penicillin-resistant staphylococcal infections.
- Their activity is based on the route of their administration and hence they should be used orally, intramuscularly, or intravenously (cloxacillin) or only as IV (methicillin and nafcillin). Their doses are shown in Table 17.2.

TABLE 17.1 Penicillins and Their Dosages

Penicillin	Route	Dose
Benzyl penicillin (penicillin G)*	Intravenous or intramuscular	50,000–100,000 units/kg/day divided every 4–6 hours
Procaine penicillin	Intramuscular only	50,000 units/kg/day, once daily
Benzathine penicillin	Intramuscular	6–12 lac units once every 3 weeks
Phenoxymethylpenicillin (penicillin V) (tablets 125 and 250 mg)†	Oral administration	30–50 mg/kg/day divided 6–8 hourly. Maximum dose is 3 g/day‡

The dose of benzylpenicillin to be administered is first tested by giving 0.1 mL of diluted solution intradermally and observing for itching, redness, or induration for 15 minutes. If none of these are present, then the full dose can be given. An emergency kit must be ready in anticipation of anaphylaxis.

*Intravenous route is most preferred in newborns and infants. Dilute the drug with 5% dextrose or 0.9% NaCl and administer over a period of 15–30 minutes.

†One milligram of penicillin V is equal to 1600 units of penicillin G.

‡The dose for rheumatic fever prophylaxis is 250 mg twice daily.

TABLE 17.2 Penicillinase-Resistant Penicillins

Drug	Dose
Cloxacillin*	50–100 mg/kg/day IV/IM/PO every 6 hours
Nafcillin	100–200 mg/kg/day IV or IM given every 6–8 hours

*To be diluted with 0.9% saline and best given as intravenous infusion because rapid bolus produces thrombophlebitis. Oral cloxacillin needs to be given on an empty stomach.

Other Penicillins

- Other drugs in the penicillin group including ampicillin and amoxicillin (commonly referred to as broad-spectrum penicillins) have a Gram-positive spectrum of penicillin but are also active against susceptible strains of Gram-negative organisms such as enterococci and *Listeria*.
- These agents are ineffective against penicillinase-producing bacteria unless combined with a beta-lactamase inhibitor. Amoxicillin is a derivative of ampicillin with a similar spectrum but with improved oral absorption. However, it cannot be substituted for ampicillin in the treatment of *Shigella* infections.
- Combination of amoxicillin with clavulanic acid (beta-lactamase inhibitor) extends the spectrum of amoxicillin against beta-lactamase–producing strains of bacteria, e.g., *Staphylococcus aureus, H. influenzae, E. coli*, and *Klebsiella* species.
- Commonly used broad-spectrum and extended-spectrum penicillins are shown in Table 17.3.

TABLE 17.3 Other Penicillins

Drug	Route	Dose
Ampicillin	Oral/IV/IM	100–200 mg/kg/day 6–8 hourly
Amoxicillin	Oral	30–50 mg/kg/day 8–12 hourly
Amoxicillin/clavulanic acid (co-amoxiclav)*	Oral/IV	30 mg/kg/day 12 hourly
Piperacillin	IV/IM	200–300 mg/kg/day 6 hourly
Ticarcillin	IV/IM	200–400 mg/kg/day 6 hourly

*The twice-daily oral dosage is preferred for treating children on an outpatient basis to improve the compliance, but it should not be used for severe infections and should be replaced with thrice-daily intravenous injections.

- Piperacillin and ticarcillin are extended-spectrum penicillins and are also referred to as antipseudomonal penicillins.
- Piperacillin, a ureidopenicillin, is available only in combination with a beta-lactamase inhibitor, tazobactam, while ticarcillin, a carboxypenicillin, is combined with another beta-lactamase inhibitor, clavulanic acid.
- These agents are highly effective against *Pseudomonas* and anaerobic infections but not against Gram-positive organisms, particularly methicillin-resistant *S. aureus* (MRSA).
- Piperacillin administration for intravenous preparation should be diluted with 5 mL of normal saline for each gram of drug, shaken well, and given slowly over a period of 3–5 minutes. Its reconstituted solution may be stored at room temperature for 24 hours and at 2–8°C maximally up to 48 hours.

Side Effects

- Hypersensitivity reactions are the most important side effects, and severe side effects of parenteral natural penicillins can be fatal; hence, any previous history of penicillin hypersensitivity is an absolute contraindication to its use.
- An intradermal sensitivity test must be done before the injections of parenteral natural penicillins. Other reactions such as urticaria, fever, angioedema, serum sickness-like reactions, and rashes can occur with oral/semisynthetic penicillins but anaphylactic reactions are rare.
- Other side effects include diarrhea (ampicillin, co-amoxiclav), antibiotic-associated colitis, thrombophlebitis at injection site, transient rise of liver enzymes (piperacillin), and, rarely, Stevens–Johnson syndrome.

Cephalosporins

- Cephalosporins are commonly used for the treatment of septicemia, pneumonia, meningitis, urinary tract infections, enteric fever, and intra-abdominal infections due to their broad-spectrum activity and relative lack of toxicity.
- Like penicillins, these are bactericidal agents and act by inhibiting bacterial cell wall synthesis. Based on their spectrum, these are divided into different generations (Table 17.4).
- The first-generation cephalosporins have an antimicrobial spectrum similar to that of penicillins, while the second-generation cephalosporins have an increased activity against Gram-negative organisms.
- Third-generation drugs have an extended coverage against Gram-negative bacteria, cross blood–brain barrier effectively, and hence are common agents to treat childhood meningitis.
- The fourth-generation cephalosporins extend the coverage of third-generation drugs to include *Pseudomonas* while retaining Gram-positive coverage. But like other cephalosporins, fourth-generation cephalosporins do not offer activity against most enterococci and MRSA.

The dosing schedule of cephalosporins is given in Table 17.5.

TABLE 17.4 Cephalosporins

	Common uses
First generation • Cephalexin, cefadroxil (oral) • Cephazolin (IV)	• Skin/soft tissue infections, upper respiratory infections, uncomplicated UTI
Second generation • Cefaclor, cefuroxime (oral/IV)	• Respiratory tract, skin infections, and genitourinary infections
Third generation • Cefotaxime, ceftriaxone, ceftazidime, cefoperazone (IV) • Cefixime, cefpodoxime, cefdinir (oral)	• Severe infections including acute bacterial meningitis • Gram-negative infections such as enteric fever, UTI, bacillary dysentery (cefixime), and cefpodoxime as an alternative in respiratory tract infections
Fourth generation • Cefepime, Cefpirome	

UTI, urinary tract infection.

TABLE 17.5 Cephalosporins: Dosing Schedule

Drug	Dose
First generation	
Cephalexin	25–100 mg/kg/day 6–8 hourly (oral)
Cefadroxil	30 mg/kg/day 12 hourly (oral)
Cephazolin	50–100 mg/kg/day 8 hourly (IV)
Second generation	
Cefaclor	30–40 mg/kg/day 8 hourly (oral)
Cefuroxime	• 100–200 mg/kg/day 8 hourly (IV or IM) in severe infections • 20–30 mg/kg/day 8 hourly (oral)
Third generation	
Cefotaxime	150–200 mg/kg/day 8–12 hourly (IV or IM)
Ceftriaxone*	50–100 mg/kg/day 12 hourly (IV)
Cefoperazone	100–150 mg/kg/day 8–12 hourly (IV)
Ceftazidime	100–150 mg/kg/day 8–12 hourly (IV)
Cefixime†	8–10 mg/kg/day 12 hourly (O)
Cefdinir	14 mg/kg/day 12 hourly (O)
Cefpodoxime	10 mg/kg/day 12 hourly (O)
Fourth generation	
Cefepime	100–150 mg/kg/day (IV)
Cefpirome‡	1–2 g IV infusion in children 12–18 years old

*Ceftriaxone may displace bilirubin from plasma albumin and thus should be avoided in neonates with unconjugated hyperbilirubinemia, hypoalbuminemia, acidosis, and impaired bilirubin binding to avoid the risk of kernicterus.

†Cefixime should be given in the dose of 20 mg/kg/day for the treatment of typhoid fever.

‡As the drug stability differs from drug to drug after reconstitution, it is mandatory to read the product leaflet regarding optimal storage duration of the solution and its appropriate dilution.

Side Effects and Precautions

- Cephalosporins are largely well-tolerated antibiotics but share cross-sensitivity with penicillin; thus, in children with a history of immediate sensitivity against penicillin, the use of cephalosporin is best avoided.
- Mild gastrointestinal side effects such as diarrhea are also known to occur.
- As most of the cephalosporins are principally eliminated by renal route, these drugs should be used with caution (reducing the total dosage and/or increasing the dosing interval) in children with coexistent renal diseases/damage and concomitant aminoglycoside therapy.

Carbapenems and Monobactams (Imipenem, Meropenem, and Aztreonam)

- Imipenem and meropenem are beta-lactam antibacterials, belonging to the group of carbapenems, with a broad-spectrum coverage against many Gram-positive, Gram-negative (including *Pseudomonas*), and anaerobic organisms but with no coverage against MRSA.
- These drugs are used intravenously in the treatment of severe hospital-acquired and/or polymicrobial infections. Although highly effective, these should not be used as monotherapy because resistance can rapidly develop while the child is undergoing therapy.
- Aztreonam is a monobactam agent with no significant activity against Gram-positive organisms and anaerobes but being highly effective against Gram-negative bacteria such as *P. aeruginosa* and most enterobacteria. The dosing schedule of these agents is shown in Table 17.6.

Side Effects and Precautions

- Imipenem is usually combined with cilastatin for administration (as it is partially inactivated in kidney by enzymatic activity, its combination with cilastatin, a

TABLE 17.6 Carbapenems and Monobactams

Drug	Dosing schedule
Meropenem	60–120 mg/kg/day 8 hourly (IV)
Aztreonam	90–120 mg/kg/day 6–8 hourly (IV)

specific enzyme inhibitor, blocks its renal metabolism) but this has been associated with high rates of seizures.

- Therefore, in a child with central nervous system (CNS) infections, meropenem is the preferred drug over this agent. Both these drugs need dosage adjustments in children with renal insufficiency.

Macrolides

- These antibiotics are mostly used orally and are a useful oral alternative to penicillin in penicillin-allergic children. Commonly used agents in this group include erythromycin (less often used), azithromycin, and clarithromycin and act by inhibiting bacterial protein synthesis by binding to the ribosomes.
- Common indications for their use include respiratory infections caused by Gram-positive cocci, pertussis, *Chlamydia*, and *Mycoplasma*, and skin infections.
- While azithromycin has been used in enteric fever and as a single dose to treat chlamydial genital infections, clarithromycin is used mainly to treat and eradicate *Helicobacter pylori* infections from gastrointestinal tract and as an adjuvant drug in combination with other antitubercular drugs to treat atypical mycobacterial infections.
- Spiramycin is also a macrolide agent and is mainly reserved to treat congenital toxoplasmosis in children and pregnant women (Table 17.7).

TABLE 17.7 Macrolide Antibiotics†

Drug	Dosage
Erythromycin	30–40 mg/kg/day 6–8 hourly
Azithromycin*	10 mg/kg/day (day 1), followed by 5 mg/kg/day on days 2 and 3, once daily
Clarithromycin*	15 mg/kg/day 12 hourly

*Azithromycin and clarithromycin have an advantage of once/twice-daily dosing, respectively, and cause much less gastrointestinal side effects than erythromycin.

†Avoid use in presence of liver disease or use with caution.

Aminoglycosides

- These antibiotics are active against a broad range of enteric Gram-negative bacteria and some are also active against *S. aureus*, but the different analogs differ in their antimicrobial activity.
- While all these agents are used via parenteral route, only neomycin is used topically and orally for gut sterilization.
- These are bactericidal drugs and inhibit protein synthesis. The most commonly used drugs in this group include gentamicin, amikacin, tobramycin, and netilmicin (Table 17.8). Streptomycin, a narrow-spectrum aminoglycoside, finds its most wide usage in the antitubercular therapy for children and adults. Once daily administration of gentamicin/amikacin is also practiced in few conditions, often in combination with other antibiotics.

Side Effects and Precautions

- As these agents have a narrow margin of therapeutic–toxic ratio, careful attention needs to be given for correct doses and duration of therapy.
- The most important side effects of aminoglycosides are nephrotoxicity and ototoxicity, and as these agents are almost entirely eliminated by renal route, their dosage must be adjusted with drug level monitoring even if there is a minor degree of renal dysfunction.
- Nephrotoxicity is usually reversible but is likely to occur in the presence of associated renal disease or concurrent administration of drugs such as furosemide, vancomycin, and amphotericin.

TABLE 17.8 Aminoglycosides

Drug	Dosage
Gentamicin	5–7.5 mg/kg/day 8–12 hourly (IV)
Amikacin	15–20 mg/kg/day 8–12 hourly (IV)
Tobramycin*	5–7.5 mg/kg/day 6–8 hourly (IV)

*Tobramycin is also used by nebulization/DPI for the treatment of *Pseudomonas* infection in children with cystic fibrosis.

- Ototoxicity may be irreversible if not detected early. Neuromuscular weakness is a very rare side effect.

Quinolones

- Quinolones are agents based on the structure of nalidixic acid. The experimental data in animals suggested a possibility of damage to the cartilage of weight-bearing joints, and their use in pediatric practice is thus limited.
- However, significance of these data in children is uncertain, but these agents do offer a benefit of activity against many aerobic Gram-positive and Gram-negative bacteria.
- Their indications for use in children are urinary tract infections, bacterial diarrheas, enteric fever resistant to other antibiotics, and as second-line drug(s) for childhood tuberculosis. Their doses are shown in Table 17.9.

Other Antibacterial Agents

Vancomycin and Teicoplanin

- These drugs belonging to the group of glycopeptide antibiotics are bactericidal against most Gram-positive bacteria including multidrug resistant staphylococci.
- These are used parenterally for serious infections (often with other drugs) such as endocarditis, septicemia, and osteomyelitis.
- Vancomycin is also given orally for the treatment of antibiotic-associated colitis caused by *C. difficile*.
- Teicoplanin is similar to vancomycin but due to longer duration of action is given once daily and is associated with a lower incidence of nephrotoxicity than vancomycin. Rapid infusion of vancomycin (in less than 30 minutes) can cause thrombophlebitis (rotate infusion sites) and histamine-like skin reactions (red man syndrome).

Linezolid

- Linezolid is a newer antibiotic and mainly effective against vancomycin/MRSA and penicillin-resistant *S. pneumoniae*.
- It is not active against Gram-negative bacteria.

Clindamycin

- This drug is effective against Gram-positive cocci and penicillin-resistant staphylococci and against many anaerobic organisms such as *B. fragilis*.
- It is reserved to treat intra-abdominal sepsis (e.g., perforated appendix and peritonitis) and staphylococcal arthritis and osteomyelitis.
- The drug should be stopped immediately if a child on treatment develops severe antibiotic-associated colitis as it becomes severe and potentially fatal. The doses are shown in Table 17.10.

Other antibacterial agents such as chloramphenicol, sulfonamides, trimethoprim–sulfamethoxazole combination (co-trimoxazole), tetracyclines, colistin, and nitrofurans have now very limited use in children. Tetracyclines, due to their propensity of drug deposition in bones and teeth, are not recommended for children younger than 8 years. They are useful in the treatment of cholera and plague. Sulfonamides and co-trimoxazole can cause severe Stevens–Johnson syndrome and

TABLE 17.9 Quinolones

Drug	Dosage
Nalidixic acid	50–55 mg/kg/day 6–8 hourly (O)
Norfloxacin	10 mg/kg/day12 hourly (O)
Ciprofloxacin	20–30 mg/kg/day 12 hourly (IV or O)
Ofloxacin	10–15 mg/kg/day 12 hourly (O)

Other agents such as pefloxacin and sparfloxacin are not indicated for clinical use in children.

TABLE 17.10 Other Antibacterial Agents

Drug	Dosage
Vancomycin	40–60 mg/kg/day 6–8 hourly (IV)
Teicoplanin	10 mg/kg 12 hourly (IV or IM)
Linezolid	20 mg/kg/day 12 hourly (IV or O)
Clindamycin	10–30 mg/kg/day 8 hourly (IV or O)

the latter is most often used for the prophylaxis of *Pneumocystis carinii* pneumonia in HIV-infected children. Nitrofurans (nitrofurantoin) are rarely used due to availability of better alternatives but are useful as urinary antiseptic as long-term prophylaxis in urinary tract infection given as a single dose of 2–2.5 mg/kg/day at bedtime.

Antiviral Agents

A large majority of viral illnesses/infections resolve spontaneously in otherwise healthy children. However, in case of immunocompromised children such as those with severe malnutrition, those with prolonged steroid therapy, and those on chemotherapy for cancer, these infections can become disseminated, complicated, and often fatal. Besides, certain viral infections are amenable to treatment with antiviral agents even in normal children and these include drugs for herpes simplex virus (HSV), varicella zoster infections, hepatitis B virus infection, influenza, and respiratory syncytial virus infections. The commonly used drugs in childhood viral infections and the doses are shown in Table 17.11.

Antiretroviral Drugs

HIV is an enveloped RNA virus belonging to the group of retrovirus family. Anti-HIV drugs are indicated for treatment of patients infected with HIV and to prevent perinatal transmission of HIV from mother to child. These drugs inhibit the viral multiplication and decrease the viral load. There are three major groups (Table 17.12).

Dosage and Adverse Effects

The dosages and adverse effects of antiretroviral drugs are shown in Table 17.13.

General Principles of Antiretroviral Therapy

- Treatment is lifelong and requires strict adherence to the schedule.
- Treatment depends on age, clinical staging, immune status, and the viral load of the patient.

TABLE 17.11 Antiviral Agents

Drug	Dosage	Remarks
Acyclovir*	15 mg/kg/dose 8 hourly (IV or O)	• Used in herpes simplex infections (encephalitis, mucocutaneous and genital infections), varicella, and herpes zoster. Higher dose (30 mg/kg/dose) is used in newborns and a few protocols†
Amantadine	5–10 mg/kg/day 12 hourly (O)	• Influenza A infections (treatment and prophylaxis)
Oseltamivir‡	Oseltamivir (Oral) therapeutic dose: For < 1 yr dose is 3mg/kg/dose BD; For > 1 yr dose depends upon weight; <15 kg: 30 mg BD; 15–23 kg: 45 mg BD; 23–40 kg: 60 mg BD; >40 kg: 75 mg BD for 5 days.	• Influenza A and B, H1N1 infections (prevention and treatment)
Ribavirin	Oral: 10–15 mg/kg/day 8 hourly Parenteral: 15–20 mg/kg/day	• Severe respiratory syncytial virus infections (bronchiolitis). Can be given orally or in aerosolized form • Also used parenterally for chronic hepatitis C infection along with alpha interferon

*Acyclovir is also used a topical skin and ophthalmic ointment. Ganciclovir is related to acyclovir but is more active than acyclovir against cytomegalovirus infections. Foscarnet is reserved for resistant herpes simplex infections and retinitis caused by cytomegalovirus infections.

†The duration of therapies varies between 10 and 21 days for different conditions.

‡Oseltamivir for prophylaxis of H1N1 infections.

TABLE 17.12 Antiretroviral Drugs

Antiretroviral drugs	General mechanism of action
Nucleoside reverse transcriptase inhibitors (NRTIs)	
• Zidovudine (AZT) • Stavudine (d4T) • Lamivudine (3TC) • Abacavir (ABC) • Zalcitabine (DDC) • Emtricitabine (FTC) • Didanosine (DDI)	These are all prodrugs and undergo intracellular phosphorylation to become activated. Active form of drug is triphosphate, which competes with viral nucleoside triphosphate and gets falsely incorporated into the growing viral DNA chain by reverse transcriptase enzyme and results in termination of the growing DNA chain. Thus, these drugs prevent infection of newer cells rather than treating already-infected cells
Non-nucleoside reverse transcriptase inhibitors (NNRTIs)	
• Efavirenz (EFV) • Nevirapine (NVP) • Delavirdine (DLV)	They bind to the catalytic site of viral reverse transcriptase, causing enzyme inactivation and inhibition of complementary DNA synthesis
Protease inhibitors (PIs)	
• Saquinavir (SQV) • Indinavir (IDV) • Nelfinavir (NFV) • Amprenavir (APV) • Fosamprenavir (FPV) • Ritonavir (RTV) • Lopinavir (LPV)	They competitively inhibit the viral protease enzyme and prevent the cleavage of *gag–pol* genes necessary for virion production. They block the maturation process of the virus. They are active against HIV-1 and HIV-2 infections

- Triple combination therapy is recommended.
- Commonly prescribed regime for children is two nucleoside reverse transcriptase inhibitors (NRTIs) plus one non-nucleoside reverse transcriptase inhibitor (NNRTI).
- The most commonly used NRTIs are stavudine (or zidovudine if Hb >9) and lamivudine.
- The most commonly used NNRTI is nevirapine.
- Efavirenz is substituted for nevirapine in children older than 3 years who are receiving antitubercular drugs, as hepatotoxic effects of nevirapine and rifampicin are additive.
- Protease inhibitor (PI)-based regime is two NRTIs plus PI, i.e., lopinavir–ritonavir combination or nelfinavir or amprenavir.

Antiretroviral Therapy in Prevention of Parent-to-Child Transmission (PPTCT) of HIV

- As per national guidelines, pregnant women who are found to be HIV positive are initiated on lifelong ART irrespective of CD4 count and WHO clinical staging. Their newborn (HIV exposed) babies are initiated on 6 weeks of syrup Nevirapine (2 mg/kg/day) immediately after birth so as to prevent transmission of HIV from mother to child. This duration is extended to 12 weeks if the mother has been on ART for less than 24 weeks.
- This regime reduces the perinatal transmission by 50%.

Antitubercular Drugs

Tuberculosis caused by *Mycobacterium* tubercle bacilli is an important cause of childhood morbidity and mortality. Tubercle bacilli are slow-growing bacteria with a doubling time of 24 hours. They are very resistant to phagocytosis due to their cell wall composition (mycolic acid), intracellular location (slow growing), and slowly dividing (spurters) and dormant nature of the bacilli (persisters). Before the pre-chemotherapeutic

TABLE 17.13 Drug/Dosages of Antiretroviral Drugs

Drug	Recommended dose	Maximum dose (mg)	Adverse effects	Remarks
Nucleoside reverse transcriptase inhibitors (NRTIs)				
Zidovudine Didanosine Abacavir Lamivudine Stavudine	360 mg/m² 180 mg/m² 16 mg/kg 8 mg/kg 2 mg/kg	600 400 600 300 80	• Hepatomegaly, hepatic steatosis, lactic acidosis, pancreatitis, peripheral neuropathy, myopathy, bone marrow suppression, headache, nausea, rash	• Metabolism of Zidovudine is increased by Rifampicin and it is decreased by Cimetidine, Fluconazole, and Valproic acid • Trimethoprim/Sulfamethoxazole increases the levels of Lamivudine • Lamivudine decreases the chance of Zidovudine resistance when given in combination with Zidovudine
Non-nucleoside reverse transcriptase inhibitors (NNRTIs)				
Nevirapine Efavirenz	300–400 mg/m² 15 mg/kg	400 600	• Hepatotoxicity, granulocytopenia, rash, Stevens–Johnson syndrome, psychosis	• They are active against HIV-1 only • Nevirapine is a moderate inducer of CYP3A4 and may increase its own clearance • Efavirenz is used in children older than 3 years and given on empty stomach, once-a-day dosage
Protease inhibitors (PIs)				
Lopinavir Ritonavir Nelfinavir	460 mg/m² 700 mg/m² 110–150 mg/kg	800 1200 2500	• Lipodystrophy, hyperglycemia, hyperlipidemia, osteoporosis, bleeding tendency, hepatic enzyme inducer • Saquinavir is associated with cardiac conduction defects and prolonged QT interval	• Metabolized by cytochrome P450 system and they cause significant reactions with the other drugs • PIs approved for pediatric use are amprenavir (>4 years), lopinavir (>6 months), nelfinavir, and ritonavir (>2 years) • They are more resistant to development of drug resistance. The only combination of PI used for HIV-1 and HIV-2 infections is lopinavir + ritonavir

era, the morbidity and mortality of tuberculosis were very high, which improved dramatically after the introduction of drugs against tubercle bacilli. Now with increasing resistance against antituberculous drugs and due to its common occurrence along with HIV infection, treatment of tuberculosis has become challenging. Drugs are required for a longer duration and in order to avoid resistance, combination therapy is started in tuberculosis.

Classification of Antitubercular Drugs

- First-line essential drugs
  - Isoniazid (INH)
  - Rifampicin (R)
  - Pyrazinamide (Z)
  - Ethambutol (E)
  - Streptomycin (S)
- First-line supplemental drugs
  - Rifabutin
  - Rifapentine
- Second-line drugs
  - Fluoroquinolones: Ciprofloxacin, levofloxacin, gatifloxacin, ofloxacin, moxifloxacin
  - Aminoglycosides: Amikacin, kanamycin
  - Polypeptide antibiotics: Capreomycin, viomycin

- Ethionamide, prothionamide
- Para-aminosalicylic acid
- Cycloserine
- Thioacetazone, terizidone
- Newer drugs
  - Linezolid
  - Clofazimine
  - Amoxicillin plus clavulanate
  - Imipenem plus cilastatin
  - Clarithromycin/azithromycin

First-Line Essential Drugs

Isoniazid (isonicotinic acid hydrazide)

- INH is the most powerful bactericidal drug and has structural resemblance with pyridoxine.
- The drug acts by the inhibition of the synthesis of mycolic acids. It is active against intracellular and extracellular bacilli. It mainly inhibits the rapidly multiplying bacilli. It does not act on dormant bacilli. It is active in acidic and alkaline media.
- It is well absorbed orally, metabolized in liver, and readily distributed in pleural fluid, peritoneal fluid, and cerebrospinal fluid (CSF).
- There are two types of metabolism depending on the genes, rapid and slow acetylation. This metabolism may influence the INH toxicity but not the antitubercular response. Rapid acetylators have a short plasma half-life (1 hour) compared with slow acetylators (3 hours).
- Dosage: Daily dosage is 10 mg/kg/day OD.

Adverse effects

- *Peripheral neuritis*: More common with slow acetylators due to inhibition of pyridoxine kinase by accumulated INH
- *Hepatotoxicity*: More common with rapid acetylators due to fast metabolism of INH, which provides a high concentration of hepatotoxic metabolites
- Psychosis
- Minor adverse effects: Rashes, hematological changes, diarrhea

Rifampicin

- Rifampicin is the most powerful bactericidal drug active against persisters/dormant bacilli. It has a good sterilizing activity, i.e., the ability to kill all the bacilli in tubercular lesions as rapidly as possible.
- It inhibits DNA-dependent RNA polymerase. It is active against intracellular and extracellular bacilli.
- It is well absorbed orally and readily distributed in all tissues. It is excreted mainly through liver into bile and undergoes enterohepatic circulation. It is a potent enzyme inducer.
- Daily dosage is 10–15 mg/kg/day OD.

Adverse effects

- Hepatotoxicity
- Nephrotoxicity, which may cause renal failure
- Flu-like syndrome characterized by fever, chills, myalgia, and thrombocytopenia
- Abdominal syndrome characterized by nausea, vomiting, and diarrhea
- Cutaneous syndrome characterized by rashes
- Others such as purpura, hemolysis, and shock
- Potent enzyme inducer, so other drugs get metabolized faster
- Imparts red orange color to urine, which is otherwise harmless

Other uses

- Treatment of leprosy
- Prophylaxis against meningococcal and *H. influenzae* meningitis and treatment of carrier state
- Prosthetic valve endocarditis due to its action against *S. aureus*
- For treating brucellosis along with doxycycline
- Second- or third-choice drug for treatment of diphtheria and *Legionella* infections

Pyrazinamide

- Pyrazinamide is a bactericidal drug active against slow-growing intracellular bacilli. It has a good sterilizing activity. It is active at acidic pH.
- It inhibits fatty acid synthase I enzyme and disrupts mycolic acid synthesis needed for cell wall.
- It is well absorbed orally and distributed in all tissues (macrophages, tubercular cavities, and meninges).
- Daily dosage is 30–35 mg/kg/day.
- It should be avoided during pregnancy.

Adverse effects

- Hepatotoxicity
- Hyperuricemia
- Minor adverse effects: Nausea, vomiting, drug fever, malaise

Ethambutol

- Ethambutol is the only first-line drug with bacteriostatic activity.
- It inhibits arabinosyltransferase enzyme and in turn prevents polymerization of arabinogalactans and stops cell wall synthesis.
- It is well absorbed orally and distributed in all body fluids.
- Daily dosage is 20–25 mg/kg/day.
- The most common adverse effect is retrobulbar neuritis impairing visual acuity and red/green color blindness. It is a reversible side effect and hence periodic testing is required.

Streptomycin

- Streptomycin is the bactericidal drug active against extracellular rapidly multiplying bacilli. It was the first drug to exhibit an effective antitubercular activity. It is active mainly in alkaline media.
- It inhibits protein synthesis by binding to 30s ribosomes.
- The drug is ionized in solution, is not absorbed orally, is distributed only extracellularly, and does not penetrate brain or CSF. It is administered parenterally, i.e., intramuscularly.
- The daily dosage is 15 mg/kg/day
- The adverse effects include nephrotoxicity and ototoxicity.

First-Line Supplemental Drugs

Rifabutin

Rifabutin is a structural analog of rifampicin and has partial cross-resistance with rifampicin. It is a less potent enzyme inducer than rifampicin, has a longer half-life, and has a better activity against *M. avium complex*. The most important use of rifabutin is in the HIV-infected population because it is not a microsomal enzyme inducer. The dosage is 5 mg/kg/day. *Rifapentine* is identical to rifampicin in all aspects and is given as 600 mg once or twice weekly.

Second-Line Drugs

Second-line drugs are used in case of resistance to first-line drugs:

- *Fluoroquinolones*: Ciprofloxacin, levofloxacin, gatifloxacin, ofloxacin, moxifloxacin
- *Aminoglycosides*: Amikacin, kanamycin
- *Polypeptide antibiotics*: Capreomycin, Viomycin, only parenteral preparations available
- *Ethionamide, Prothionamide*: Tuberculostatic drugs
- *Para-aminosalicylic acid*: Structural analog of PABA (para-aminobenzoic acid) and inhibits folate synthesis
- *Cycloserine*: Acts by inhibiting cell wall synthesis, is mainly excreted in kidney, and hence is very useful in renal tuberculosis (its adverse effect is neurotoxicity, which is reduced by the administration of vitamin B_6 100 mg/day)
- *Thioacetazone*: No longer used because of its ototoxicity and hypersensitivity reactions

TABLE 17.14 Treatment Regimens for Tuberculosis

Category of treatment	Type of patients	Treatment regimen	
		Intensive phase	**Continuation phase**
Category I (new cases)	• New cases • Smear-positive PTB • Smear-negative PTB • Extrapulmonary TB	2HRZE	4HR
Category II (previously treated cases)	• Relapse • Drug defaulter • Treatment failure • Others	2HRZES + 1HRZE	5HRE

E, ethambutol; *H*, isoniazid; *PTB*, pulmonary TB; *R*, rifampicin; *S*, streptomycin; *Z*, pyrazinamide. The number before the letters indicates the number of months.

Box 17.1 Certain case definitions

- *New case*: A patient who has had no antitubercular treatment (ATT) or had it for less than 4 weeks
- *Relapse*: A patient who has been declared cured or who has completed therapy in the past and has incidence of recurrence
- *Drug defaulter*: A patient who has taken treatment for at least 4 weeks and comes after interruption of treatment for 2 months and has active disease
- *Failure to respond*: A patient with TB who fails to have bacteriological conversion to negative status, fails to respond clinically, or deteriorates after 12 weeks of compliant intensive phase, provided alternate diagnosis/reasons for no response have been ruled out

Treatment Regimens

For treatment of drug-sensitive tuberculosis, thrice weekly regimen were recommended earlier as per RNTCP 2012. Now as per RNTCP 2015, use of daily regimen is recommended. The treatment regimens are shown in Table 17.14 and case definitions as per RNTCP are given in Box 17.1.

Antifungal Drugs

The common conditions in children that call for the use of antifungal drugs include systemic and disseminated fungal infections and superficial fungal infections. Immunocompromised children are at an increased risk of fungal infections. Conditions such as superficial candidial and disseminated infections, cryptococcus in (HIV-positive) children, aspergillosis causing respiratory disease, and skin and nail infections need therapy with either intravenous or oral antifungal agents. Few of the antifungal drugs of importance are outlined in Table 17.15. Miconazole is used most commonly topically for superficial skin/nail fungal infections, while nystatin is most often used locally for mucocutaneous candidiasis (thrush).

Side Effects/Precautions

- Amphotericin B can cause fever with chills and can be nephrotoxic, while fluconazole can produce skin rash and must be used with caution in the presence of associated liver disease and in children younger than 6 months.
- Ketoconazole is known to produce CNS excitation, and griseofulvin can be responsible for side effects due to its drug interactions with phenobarbitone and warfarin. It can also produce a photosensitive rash and hepatotoxicity.

Antimalarial Agents

The drug treatment of malaria in children is based on the severity of the disease, i.e.,

TABLE 17.15 Antifungal Drugs

Drug	Dosage/route	Users
Fluconazole	6–12 mg/kg/day once 24 hourly (IV or O)	Oral, or esophageal systemic candidiasis and cryptococcal meningitis
Amphotericin B*	0.25–1 mg/kg/day and to be diluted in dextrose solution and given slowly over 4 hours once a day	Serious systemic fungal infections only
Ketoconazole†	5 mg/kg/day once a day (O)	Dermatophytosis and systemic fungal infections
Griseofulvin‡	10–20 mg/kg/day 12–24 hourly (O)	Tinea infections of skin, scalp, and nails

*A liposomal formulation of amphotericin that is less nephrotoxic is also used.

†Also available as cream and shampoo (for dandruff).

‡The duration of treatment varies on the site of infection. While *T. corporis* needs treatment for 2–4 weeks, *T. unguium* may need therapy for 3–6 months.

whether the disease is uncomplicated or complicated/severe malaria, and the patterns of drug resistance of the parasite. The antimalarial drugs based on the site of action and on the stages of parasite are as follows:

- Tissue schizonticidals, which act on hepatic phase and are used for chemoprophylaxis or radical cure of malaria
- Drugs acting on erythrocytic phase, which are used for the treatment of malaria but do not prevent relapse in *P. vivax* infection
- Gametocides, which destroy the gametes and hence prevent the transmission of the disease
- Sporonticides, which prevent the maturation of parasites

Different drugs used in the treatment of malaria are shown in Table 17.16.

Artemether/Lumefantrine

This combination (20 mg of artemether and 120 mg of lumefantrine) orally is recommended for treatment of chloroquine-resistant and multidrug-resistant uncomplicated *P. falciparum* infections. Lumefantrine is not available as a single drug and has not been used alone in the treatment of malaria. The dosage of this combination is a total of six doses (in two divided daily doses) in 3 days as follows: children weighing 5–14 kg, one tablet twice daily; children weighing 15–24 kg, two ablets twice daily; children weighing 25–35 kg, three tablets twice daily; and children weighing more than 35 kg, four tablets twice daily.

Antiprotozoal and Antihelminthic Drugs

The common conditions in childhood that require the use of these groups of drugs include amebiasis and different helminthic infestations (intestinal and systemic). Their uses are shown in Table 17.17.

Other Antiparasitic Drugs

Mebendazole

- Mebendazole is a broad-spectrum antihelminthic drug that is active against ascariasis (roundworms), threadworms (enterobiasis), hookworms (ankylostoma), and trichuriasis (whipworms). The mechanism of action is by the blockage of glucose uptake by the parasites.
- The dose is 100 mg twice daily for 3 days for children aged between 6 months and 18 years. Threadworm infestations can be treated with a single oral dose of 100 mg and if reinfection occurs, a second dose after 2 weeks is needed.
- The side effects include abdominal pain and, less commonly, diarrhea and urticaria.

TABLE 17.16 Antimalarial Agents

Drug	Dose	Use	Side effects
Chloroquine (base)*	10 mg/kg IV or oral followed by 5 mg/kg 6 hours later and then 5 mg/kg OD × 2 days	*P. vivax*, *P. ovale*, and sensitive strains of *P. falciparum* only	
Mefloquine	15–25 mg/kg as a single dose, oral. Dose >15 mg can be split into two doses (15 and 10 mg 8 hours later) for treatment and 5 mg/kg/ week for prophylaxis	Treatment and prophylaxis of resistant malaria	• Not to be used in convulsive disorders, psychiatric diseases, and children younger than 3 months • Gastrointestinal effects and dizziness are common side effects
Artesunate[†]	2.4 mg/kg IV or IM as the first dose and then at 12 and 24 hours, followed by once daily for 7 days	Treatment of chloroquine-resistant *falciparum* malaria	• No significant side effects
Quinine[‡]	IV loading dose 20 mg/kg in 4 hours in 5% dextrose saline, and then 10 mg/kg every 12 hours for 2 days. Switch to oral 10 mg/kg 8 hourly × 7 days	Resistant malaria	• Vertigo, tinnitus, hypoglycemia, and rarely cardiac arrhythmia • Hemolysis in G6PD deficiency • Do not give loading dose if drug received in previous 12 hours
Primaquine	0.25 mg/kg/day OD for 14 days in *P. vivax* infections, and 0.75 mg/kg as a single dose in *P. falciparum* infections	Radical cure in *P. vivax* infections and gametocidal action in *P. falciparum* infections	• Hemolysis in G6PD deficiency • Not recommended for infants as they relatively lack G6PD
Pyrimethamine	1.25 mg/kg (along with 25 mg/kg of sulfadoxine), single dose orally	Treatment of chloroquine-resistant *P. falciparum* infections	• Photosensitivity, rash, and folate deficiency

*For prophylaxis, 5 mg/kg 1 weekly. Chloroquine is also used as an alternate drug for juvenile rheumatoid arthritis and treatment of extraintestinal amebiasis.

[†]Other agents in artemisinin group are artemether and arteether.

[‡]Tetracycline, doxycycline, or clindamycin should be added to quinine therapy for 7 days as soon as the child can swallow in multidrug-resistant *P. falciparum* infections.

TABLE 17.17 Antiamebic Drugs

Drugs	Dose	Indications	Side effects/cautions
Metronidazole*	30–50 mg/kg/day 8 hourly IV or O for 10 days (acute intestinal amebiasis, extraintestinal amebiasis including liver abscess)	Used in amebiasis (ineffective in asymptomatic cyst passers), giardiasis, urogenital trichomoniasis infections, and systemic anaerobic infections	Metallic taste in mouth, loss of appetite, dizziness. Use with caution in presence of convulsions
Tinidazole[†]	50–60 mg/kg/day (maximum 2 g) once daily orally for 3 days	Treatment of amebiasis and giardiasis	Metallic taste and gastrointestinal discomfort
Diloxanide furoate	20 mg/kg/day 8 hourly for 5–7 days	Intestinal amebiasis including asymptomatic cyst passers	Nausea, vomiting, and skin rash

*The dose of metronidazole in giardiasis is 15 mg/kg/day orally for 5 days.

[†]Tinidazole for 5 days in amebic liver abscess.

Albendazole

- Albendazole is a broad-spectrum antihelminthic drug.
- The dose is 200 mg as a single dose in children younger than 2 years and 400 mg once orally in children older than 2 years. The treatment for strongylosis (*Strongyloides stercoralis*) for children aged between 2 and 12 years should be given as 400 mg once daily for 3 days.
- The drug is also effectively used for the treatment of neurocysticercosis, 15 mg/kg/day for 3–4 weeks, and hydatid disease (*Echinococcus*) for 4 weeks. It should be given along with steroids in neurocysticercosis.
- The side effects include leucopenia, liver dysfunction, and worm migration particularly in heavy roundworm infestation.

Piperazine Citrate

- Piperazine citrate is used for roundworm and threadworm infestations.
- The drug acts by causing a flaccid paralysis of the worms. Due to its capacity to relax worms, its use is mainly restricted for intestinal obstruction caused by roundworms.
- The dose is 75–100 mg/kg once daily at bedtime for 2 days for ascariasis and 50 mg/kg/day for 7 days for enterobiasis.
- The side effects include abdominal discomfort, vomiting, drowsiness, nystagmus, and rarely convulsions.

Levamisole

- Levamisole is used against roundworm and hookworm infestations. The drug also has an immunomodulatory action that makes it a useful adjunct in the therapy of steroid-dependent nephrotic syndrome. It exerts its action by causing spastic paralysis of the worms.
- The dose is 2.5–3 mg/kg (maximum 150 mg) as a single oral dose. In case of hookworm infestations, the dose may be repeated after 7 days.
- Side effects include gastrointestinal disturbances, dizziness, rashes, and rarely convulsions.

Pyrantel Pamoate

- The drug is a broad-spectrum antihelminthic agent and acts by causing spastic paralysis of the worms.
- It is used in roundworm, hookworm, pinworm, and *Strongyloides* infestations.
- The dose is 10 mg/kg as a single oral dose but needs to be given in the same quantity for 3 days for hookworms and to be repeated after 2 weeks in pinworm infestations.

  It is usually well tolerated but must be avoided in hepatic diseases.

Niclosamide

- The drug is used for intestinal tapeworm infections. It has a direct wormicidal action against *Taenia solium, T. saginata,* and *D. latum* infestations.
- The dose is 40 mg/kg oral dose (in two divided doses, one dose before breakfast and another 1 hour after it).
- Side effects include gastrointestinal upsets, rash, and dizziness.

Nitazoxanide

- Nitazoxanide is an alternative drug to treat amebiasis, giardiasis, cryptosporidiosis, and multiple infestations.
- The dose is as follows: 1–4 years, 100 mg; 4–11 years, 200 mg; and adolescents, 500 mg to be given 12 hourly for 3 days.

  Few other antiparasitic agents useful in specific conditions are listed in Table 17.18.

Corticosteroids

Corticosteroids are important therapeutic agents that have a wide range of indications and uses in different conditions in neonates, infants, and children. Few important aspects and general principles to be noted about

TABLE 17.18 Other Antiparasitic Drugs

Drug	Dosage/route	Indications	Side effects/cautions
Sodium stibogluconate (pentavalent antimonial compound)*	20 mg/kg/day (maximum 850 mg) IM divided once/twice daily for 30 days	Treatment of kala-azar	Hypersensitivity, myalgia, renal dysfunction, cardiac toxicity, and pancreatitis
Praziquantel	10 mg/kg as a single dose for tapeworm infections and 50 mg/kg/day 8 hourly orally for 10–14 days in cysticercosis	Used as a second-line drug in cysticercosis and tapeworm infestations. Also used in schistosomiasis	Side effects unusual and no serious effects reported
Diethylcarbamazine	6 mg/kg/day 8 hourly orally × 14–21 days for filariasis	Antimicrofilarial agent. Also used for tropical pulmonary eosinophilia	May cause drowsiness, vomiting, and rashes
Ivermectin	150 µg/kg as a single dose orally in children older than 5 years	Drug of choice in onchocerciasis and highly effective in treatment of scabies and head lice	Itching and allergic rash

*New lipid formulations of amphotericin B are now first-line therapy for visceral leishmaniasis, and pentamidine is also used in kala-azar.

steroids and their uses in children are as follows:

- The therapeutic doses and the duration of therapies vary widely in different diseases and clinical conditions.
- These drugs can be lifesaving in acute conditions such as anaphylactic reactions, status asthmaticus, and severe exfoliative dermatitis where high doses need to be given for a short duration. In such conditions, the benefits of the treatment outweigh the side effects of drug therapy.
- When required on a long-term basis for treatment of conditions such as nephrotic syndrome and autoimmune/chronic diseases, their maintenance dose should be kept as much low as possible, along with careful monitoring for their potential adverse effects.
- The choice of the specific steroid needs to be based on the therapeutic properties required in that condition. Hydrocortisone and cortisone have glucocorticoid effects but have relatively high mineralocorticoid activity. These are thus unsuitable for long-term use but are useful in emergency situations for short-term use.
- Prednisolone has a high glucocorticoid activity with less mineralocorticoid effect and is useful for longer-term therapy in chronic diseases. Betamethasone and dexamethasone, due to their insignificant mineralocorticoid action and fluid retention, are particularly suitable in conditions where the fluid retention is to be avoided.
- Children who have been receiving steroids for longer than 3 weeks should not stop the drug suddenly to avoid the risk of adrenal suppression; instead, the drug dosage should be gradually tapered over a few days.
- Adrenal suppression is also reduced by giving single daily morning/alternate-day dose (e.g., nephrotic syndrome) or by intermittent courses of treatment (e.g., chronic immune thrombocytopenic purpura).

Commonly used steroids in children include those given in the next subsections.

Hydrocortisone

- Hydrocortisone is used in the treatment of shock, anaphylaxis, and status asthmaticus, and as a replacement therapy in congenital adrenal hyperplasia and acute adrenal insufficiency.
- The dose is 10 mg/kg IV or more as a bolus in cases of shock (maximum 50 mg/kg/dose) and then every 6 hours for 2 days. The dose in status asthmaticus is 4–8 mg/kg IV as initial dose followed by 2–4 mg/kg/day IV or PO every 6 hours.
- The side effects include steroid effects such as hypertension, hyperglycemia, mood changes, and osteopenia on a long-term basis. Hydrocortisone should not be used in active and untreated infections.

Prednisolone

- Prednisolone is an intermediate-acting steroid mainly useful for its anti-inflammatory and immunosuppressive actions (nephrotic syndrome, acute asthma, rheumatic fever, and autoimmune conditions such as systemic lupus erythematosus).
- The dose is 1–2 mg/kg/day orally and should not exceed 60 mg daily. The frequency of daily administration and the duration depend on specific conditions and may vary from a single morning dose to two to three divided doses per day such as in the treatment of acute asthma and croup, and as a replacement therapy for adrenal insufficiency in congenital adrenal hyperplasia.
- The drug is also effectively used on a long-term basis for the treatment of inflammatory bowel diseases and infantile spasms, and as an adjunct in chemotherapy regimens in childhood cancers.
- The side effects including gastric intolerance, steroid effects (cushingoid facies, hypertension, hyperglycemia, immunosuppression), cataracts, mood changes, and osteopenia can occur with long-term use. As hypothalamopituitary adrenal axis suppression is known to occur, children who receive a prolonged therapy should be monitored for their growth (height gain). Use prednisolone with caution whenever nonsteroidal anti-inflammatory drugs (NSAIDs) are given along with steroids.

Methylprednisolone

- The drug is mainly reserved for use in acute conditions because of its anti-inflammatory and immunosuppressive properties and is used in hospital settings for treating conditions such as status asthmaticus, acute spinal cord injuries, and demyelinating CNS diseases as a short burst pulse therapy.
- The drug needs to be given as slow intravenous infusion over 30 minutes diluted with either 0.9% saline or 5% dextrose solution. The recommended dose is 20–30 mg/kg once daily for 3 days. As it gets deposited into the adipose tissue, its slow release helps to make it possible to administer 3- to 4-weekly doses for chronic steroid-responsive diseases.
- The side effects are similar to those of other steroids.

Betamethasone

The drug is a long-acting corticosteroid with a predominant glucocorticoid activity and is mainly used on a short-term basis both orally and as IV or IM.

- The usual dose is 0.1–0.2 mg/kg/day divided into two to three doses. The drug is also used topically as eye drops/eardrops and skin cream. It is used as 12 mg IM every 24 hours for a total of two doses in mothers antenatally to stimulate fetal lung maturation in preterm labor.
- The side effects are similar to those of other steroids.

Dexamethasone

- The drug is a long-acting corticosteroid.

- The usual dose is 0.2–1 mg/kg/day IV, IM, or PO.
- Its main uses are in cerebral edema and in childhood bacterial meningitis caused by *H. influenzae* type b where it is given every 6 hours for 3 days, starting before or with the first dose of antibiotics.

Inhaled Corticosteroids

Inhaled corticosteroids (ICS) are effective in the long-term management of asthma as they reduce the airway inflammation and their inhaled administration through either a metered-dose inhaler (MDI) or a dry powder inhaler (DPI; Rotacaps) reduces their doses and potential side effects while maintaining their therapeutic benefits. Few of these drugs are as follows:

- *Beclomethasone*: It is used as inhaler and Rotacaps as 100–200 μg/puff. It is also used for allergic rhinitis.
- *Budesonide*: It is used in long-term prophylaxis of asthma as 100–400 μg every 12 hours. The dose can be reduced with the therapeutic response.
- *Fluticasone*: It is a locally acting steroid given through MDI and nasal spray (for allergic rhinitis). It is used as 50–100 μg per dose every 12 hours. This agent has less effect than beclomethasone in the suppression of linear growth in children.

All the above-mentioned drugs can cause dysphonia and oral candidiasis, which can be prevented/minimized by rinsing the mouth with plain water after the inhalation is over.

Antipyretics/Anti-Inflammatory Agents

These drugs that belong to NSAIDs are commonly used to treat infants and children with acute febrile illnesses, trauma, and musculoskeletal pain to relieve pain, fever, and inflammation. The other groups of drugs that are more potent, such as opioid analgesics, are reserved for treating moderate to severe pain particularly originating from visceral involvement. Commonly used NSAIDs in children are given next.

Aspirin (Acetylsalicylic Acid)

- Although the drug is an effective analgesic/antipyretic agent, it is more often used in the treatment of rheumatic fever for its anti-inflammatory action and its antiplatelet effect in Kawasaki disease and other thromboembolic states. The drug exerts its action by inhibiting prostaglandin synthesis.
- The antipyretic dose is 75–90 mg/kg/day every 6 hours (maximum 4 g/day), while the antiplatelet dose is 3–5 mg/kg/day given as a single oral dose (maximum 75 mg/day). The dose in rheumatic fever is 75–100 mg/kg/day every 6 hours.
- The side effects are gastrointestinal irritation, bleeding, and bronchospasm, and hence aspirin should not be used in viral illnesses due to potential risks of causing Reye syndrome.

Paracetamol

- Paracetamol in therapeutic doses remains one of the safest analgesics/antipyretics in children but it has no demonstrable anti-inflammatory action.
- The exact mechanism of paracetamol is not clearly understood but it is supposed to act through the inhibition of cyclooxygenase-2 (COX-2) activity.
- The drug is available in tablets, suspension, injections, and rectal suppository forms for usage.
- Dose is 10–15 mg/kg given 4–6 hourly, not to exceed 90 mg/kg/day in children and 4 g in adults.
- The antidote for overdosage/hepatotoxity is *N*-acetylcysteine.

Ibuprofen

- Ibuprofen is a conventional and widely used anti-inflammatory agent and acts by

TABLE 17.19 Other NSAID Agents

Drug	Dosage	Usage	Remarks
Diclofenac	• 1 mg/kg/dose, one to two times daily (maximum 150 mg, IV or IM × not more than 3–4 days) • Oral: 1 mg/kg/dose 8 hourly	Used in musculoskeletal pain and for relief of postoperative pain	Not to be used in NSAID-induced hypersensitivity and gastrointestinal bleeding and not in children younger than 6 months
Indomethacin	1–2 mg/kg/day 12 hourly PO (maximum 150 mg/day) for anti-inflammatory action	• Rheumatoid arthritis • For closure of patent ductus arteriosus in preterm newborns, 0.1–0.2 mg/kg/dose IV 12–24 hourly for three doses	Avoid its use in children with renal dysfunction and/or coagulation defects
Naproxen	10–20 mg/kg/day 12 hourly PO	As a NSAID in rheumatoid diseases	Side effects include gastrointestinal and renal dysfunction. Not to be used in children younger than 1 year

NSAID, nonsteroidal anti-inflammatory drug.
Mefenamic acid is advised to be used only in adolescents for short-term use (7 days) and its safety/efficacy is not established in children younger than 14 years. Piroxicam is equally effective as naproxen with a longer duration of action (once-daily dose) but has more gastrointestinal side effects and should not be used as a first-line treatment.

decreasing the production of prostaglandins by inhibiting the enzyme cyclooxygenase.

- Apart from its short-term use, it is also used in chronic/systemic diseases such as rheumatoid arthritis and as a pharmacologic agent for patent ductus arteriosus (PDA) closure in preterm neonates.
- The dose is 8–10 mg/kg/dose every 8 hours.
- It is contraindicated in the presence of gastrointestinal bleeding and peptic ulcer disease.

Few other NSAID agents are shown in Table 17.19.

Opioid analgesics are used for the relief of moderate and severe pain usually of visceral origin and these drugs should be used with caution and be supervised by the specialist. Fentanyl is a commonly used drug of this group and is used as analgesia in intraoperative, perioperative, and palliative care, and in assisted ventilation. It is also useful as a transdermal self-adhesive patch for pain relief and must be changed every 72 hours.

The dose of fentanyl is 0.5–5 μg/kg/dose 1–4 hourly intravenously or may be given as a continuous infusion at a rate of 1–5 μg/kg/h. It should be avoided in children with respiratory depression and asthma, and in comatose children.

Antihistamines

These drugs (histamine H1 receptor antagonists) are used orally to treat various allergic conditions in children such as allergic rhinitis, urticarial rashes, pruritis, nausea, and vomiting occurring in case of migraine, and as an adjunct in angioedema and anaphylaxis.

- These drugs may be either sedating (chlorpheniramine, promethazine) or nonsedating (cetirizine, levocetirizine). Side effects such as drowsiness are more common with older antihistaminics than with the newer agents.

- These drugs should not be used in children with epilepsy, asthma, long QT syndrome, glaucoma, porphyria, and urinary retention.
- These drugs are best avoided in infants younger than 6 months (except chlorpheniramine).
- Cetirizine is given orally as 2.5 mg once daily to children aged between 6 months and 2 years, 2.5 mg twice daily or 5 mg once daily to children 2–6 years old, and 5–10 mg once daily to children older than 6 years.
- Hydroxyzine is given orally as 2 mg/kg/day in three to four divided doses and 0.5 g/kg/dose intramuscularly.
- Sedating antihistaminics are often marketed as cough suppressants in combination with many cough/cold preparations. However, their use is associated with drowsiness, drying up of the secretions, and dosing problems, and thus their use in infants and young children is without any proven scientific benefit.

Drugs for Gastrointestinal Disorders

H2 Receptor Antagonists

- The drugs belonging to this group act by histamine H2 receptor blockade, thereby reducing gastric acid output and promoting the healing of gastric and duodenal ulcers.
- These are used to treat acid peptic disorders (dyspepsia) and gastroesophageal reflux disease (GERD) (Table 17.20).

TABLE 17.20 H2 Receptor Antagonists

Drug	Dose/route
Ranitidine	1–2 mg/kg/dose 12 hourly in IV infusion and 5–10 mg/kg/day PO 12 hourly for GERD
Famotidine	1–2 mg/kg/day 12–24 hourly IV or PO

GERD, gastroesophageal reflux disease.

Proton Pump Inhibitors (PPIs)

- These agents inhibit the gastric acid secretion by blocking hydrogen potassium ATP enzyme system (proton pump) of the gastric parietal cells.
- Lack of acid in the stomach prevents ulcer formation; promotes healing of existing ulcers in the esophagus, stomach, and duodenum; and provides symptomatic relief.
- PPIs are often used for the prevention and therapy of gastric acid–related disorders such as GERD, erosive esophagitis, and drug-induced gastritis, and in combination with other drugs for eradication of *H. pylori* infections in stomach.
- The commonly used PPIs are shown in Table 17.21.

Side Effects/Cautions

PPIs should be used only for appropriate indications, lowest effective doses, and shortest durations.

- Common side effects include gastrointestinal disturbances such as flatulence and diarrhea and less frequent ones are dry mouth, dizziness, and sleep disturbances.
- Rebound acidity and dyspepsia may follow stopping a prolonged treatment with PPI.
- Chronic acid suppression can compromise the efficacy of drugs that need an acidic environment for their absorption.
- Other PPIs (rabeprazole, pantoprazole) are not yet effectively studied to be safely used in children.

TABLE 17.21 Proton Pump Inhibitors

Drug	Dose/route
Omeprazole	0.6–1 mg/kg/dose PO daily. May also be given 12 hourly. Maximum daily dose 40 mg/day
Lansoprazole	0.5–1 mg/kg/day once daily (maximum 15 mg) in children weighing <30 kg; 15–30 mg OD, PO in children weighing >30 kg

Drugs Used for Nausea/Vomiting (Antiemetics)

Before prescribing a drug for vomiting in children, it is prudent to determine the underlying cause of nausea/vomiting because unless this is done, it may delay the diagnosis of the underlying condition (e.g., acute bacterial meningitis, diabetic ketoacidosis, and drug toxicities such as digoxin). The use of antiemetics in children with acute gastrointestinal infections/diarrhea is seldom warranted.

Domperidone

Domperidone (and metoclopramide) is a dopamine receptor antagonist that promotes gastric emptying and intestinal transit.

- The dose is 0.3 mg/kg/dose 8 hourly PO.
- Although it can cause mild sedation, as compared with metoclopramide, it is less likely to cause drowsiness and dystonic reactions as it does not readily cross the blood–brain barrier.

Metoclopramide

- Metoclopramide is mainly useful as an antiemetic for vomiting associated with cytotoxic drugs, postoperative period, and radiotherapy. It is also used as a prokinetic drug orally in GERD.
- The dose is 0.1–0.3 mg/kg/dose IV 6–8 hourly. The oral dose is 1–2 mg/kg/dose.
- Extrapyramidal reactions are a known side effect.

Ondansetron

Ondansetron and granisetron are specific 5HT3 receptor antagonists that block these receptors in gastrointestinal tract and CNS. They are useful in treating emesis induced in postoperative conditions and antineoplastic chemotherapy.

- The dose of ondansetron is 0.15 mg/kg/dose IV in chemotherapy-associated vomiting and can be repeated 8 hourly. The oral dose is 4–8 mg/dose 8 hourly.
- It may cause QT interval prolongation and moderate to severe hepatic impairment.
- Granisetron is a newer drug that is 10 times more potent than ondansetron. It can be used in children older than 2 years.

Other agents such as prochlorperazine, cyclizine, and hyoscine are used for controlling nausea and vomiting associated with conditions such as migraine, motion sickness, and vestibular disorders.

Drugs for Constipation

While certain conditions/drugs are useful for treating habitual/chronic constipation in a child, it is essential to make certain that the complaint is not a secondary manifestation of an underlying and undiagnosed disorder. Few of the drugs that are used to treat constipation are shown in Table 17.22.

Antispasmodics

The anticholinergic and antispasmodic drugs are often used to treat spasms and cramps in the gastrointestinal tract and urogenital tract and during a few emergency/surgical procedures. They are often available in different combinations with paracetamol and antacids. Caution must be exercised in their use with reference to their combinations, dosing, indications, and appropriate duration. Simethicone is an antiflatulent used in combination with an antispasmodic.

- *Dicyclomine hydrochloride*: Avoid in infants younger than 6 months. The dose is as follows: 6–24 months, 5–10 mg/dose, three to four times per day, 15 minutes before feeds; and >2–12 years, 10 mg/dose.
- *Drotaverine*: The dose is 20 mg, three times a day, in children aged between 1 and 6 years, and 40 mg/dose in children older than 6 years. It is available in both oral and parenteral forms. The common side effects may be dry mouth, nausea, and vertigo.

TABLE 17.22 Drugs for Constipation

Drug	Dosage	Remarks
Bisacodyl	Younger than 2 years, 5 mg, PO (tablet) or rectally (suppository); and older than 2 years, 10 mg, once daily	Stimulates intestinal peristalsis. Not to be given with milk/antacids. Used in habitual constipation and for bowel cleansing prior to radiological procedures/surgery
Lactulose	1–5 years, 5–10 mL; 5–12 years, 10–20 mL; and >12 years, 30 mL PO in two divided doses. Further dose can be adjusted as per response. For hepatic encephalopathy, 30–50 mL, 8 hourly PO. Dose adjusted to produce two to three soft stools daily	Osmotic laxative. Side effects include nausea, vomiting, flatulence, and abdominal discomfort

Drugs in Cardiovascular Disorders

Many conditions in children with cardiovascular and related diseases need a therapy often in combination and a close monitoring of the therapeutic response and side effects. The drugs that are used are for improving the myocardial contractibility for their inotropic effects, to normalize an abnormal cardiac rhythm (antiarrhythmic) to treat hypertension (antihypertensive agents), and to treat congestive cardiac failure and hypertension (diuretics). These drugs are discussed briefly next.

Digoxin

- Digoxin is a cardiac glycoside (inotrope) that improves the myocardial contractibility and slows the sinus node automaticity.
- The drug can be given IV, IM, or PO but it has a narrow therapeutic index.
- The recommended doses are for those children who have not received any cardiac glycosides within the preceding 14 days.
- Dosage schedules are guidelines and careful monitoring is needed with serum digoxin levels.
- Even though digoxin is used in heart failure in children, it is more often used to treat/control ventricular rate in atrial fibrillation/flutter (supraventricular tachycardia) and arrhythmias secondary to heart failure.
- The dose is PO, 0.02 mg/kg given stat followed by 0.01 mg/kg after 8 hours and then 0.01 mg/kg at 16 hours (the total digitalizing dose [TDD] in 24 hours is thus 0.04 mg/kg).
- The maintenance dose is 0.01 mg/kg (10 μg/kg/day) divided 12 hourly from the next day onwards.
- For preterms, TDD is 0.02 mg/kg (20 μg), and for full-term newborns, it is 0.03 mg/kg (30 μg).
- IV dose is 75% of the oral dose.
- The drug is contraindicated in AV block, constrictive pericarditis, and aortic stenosis. As the drug is primarily removed by kidney, dose reduction is needed in renal impairment.
- Side effects include nausea, vomiting, cardiac arrhythmias, AV block, dizziness, and visual disturbances.
- Digoxin immune fab antibodies (Digibind) are antidote for digoxin toxicity.

Milrinone

- Milrinone is an inotropic drug with vasodilatory action.
- It is used for short-term inotropic support with low cardiac output states, more so after cardiac surgeries. It has a rapid onset of action (2–5 minutes) after IV infusion that is performed only in ICU.
- The dose is 50–75 μg/kg as a bolus over 15 minutes, followed by a continuous infusion of 0.25–0.75 μg/kg/min.

- The side effects include headache, ventricular arrhythmias, hypotension, hypokalemia, and thrombocytopenia. Rarely, milrinone can cause thrombocytopenia and bronchospasm.

Amrinone

- The drug is an inotrope with vasodilatory properties.
- It is used in the short-term management of congestive heart failure.
- The dose is 0.75 mg/kg as an IV bolus in 2–3 minutes and then 5–10 μg/kg/min IV.
- The drug can cause hypotension, cardiac arrhythmia, and thrombocytopenia.

Adenosine

- Adenosine is an antiarrhythmic agent and a drug of choice in treating supraventricular tachycardia.
- The drug slows down the AV nodal conduction.
- The dose is 0.05 mg/kg as an IV push and is increased by 0.05 mg/kg every 2 minutes till clinical response is obtained or a maximum dose (0.3 mg/kg or total 12 mg) is reached in children up to 12 years of age. The increments between the doses must not be done earlier than every 2 minutes and IV injection must be followed by rapid saline flush.
- The side effects include heart blocks (discontinue if severe bradycardia or systole follows), flushing of the face, dizziness, hypotension, and bronchospasm.

Amiodarone

- Amiodarone is a long-acting drug for cardiac arrhythmias in supraventricular and ventricular tachyarrhythmias, particularly not responding to other drugs. It is used in both IV and oral forms.
- The oral dose is 5–10 mg/kg/day given 12 hourly PO for children between 1 and 12 years of age.
- The side effects include hypotension, bradycardia, optic neuritis, and photosensitivity reactions. If optic neuritis occurs, the drug should be stopped, and an alternate regimen chosen.

Verapamil

- The drug is a calcium channel blocker and, apart from it being used in hypertension, it is also useful in preventing and treating supraventricular tachycardia in children.
- The dose is 0.1–0.3 mg/kg IV under ECG monitoring. The oral dose is 1–2 mg/kg/dose 6–8 hourly.
- The side effect includes heart block and the drug should not be used in children treated concurrently/recently with beta-blockers and digoxin to avoid the risk of adverse cardiac events.

Beta-Blockers

Beta-blocker agents act by blocking the beta-adrenergic receptors in the heart, peripheral vasculature, and bronchi. Their action is to slow the heart rates and depress the myocardium; hence, they should not be used in second- and third-degree heart blocks and should be avoided in children with a history of asthma/bronchospasm. These drugs are also known to affect the carbohydrate metabolism and thus cause hypoglycemia/hyperglycemia in children. Beta-blocker drugs are given in the next subsections.

Propranolol

- The drug is useful for the treatment of cardiac arrhythmia, hypertension, cyanotic spells in tetralogy of Fallot, and thyrotoxicosis, and for prophylaxis of migraine.
- It is a nonselective beta-adrenergic blocker.
- The dose depends on the indication and the duration of therapy. The usual maintenance dose is 1–2 mg/kg/day 8–12 hourly PO. Lower doses (0.2–0.5 mg/kg/day) are needed for migraine prophylaxis. The drug is used intravenously in the initial treatment

of cyanotic spells in tetralogy of Fallot and then PO for prevention.

- Side effects include postural hypotension, bronchospasm, fatigue, constipation, and sleep disturbances.

Labetalol

- Labetalol is a beta-blocker drug with an additional arteriolar vasodilatory effect lowering the peripheral vascular resistance.
- It is mainly used for the treatment of hypertension, including severe hypertension.
- The dose is 0.5–1 mg/kg/h IV and needs to be adjusted at 15-minute interval as per the response in hypertensive emergencies (maximum 3 mg/kg/h) and then 4 mg/kg/day 12 hourly PO.
- The side effects include hypotension, congestive heart failure, bronchospasm, and rarely rash.

Atenolol

- The drug is a cardioselective beta-blocking agent.
- The dose is 0.8–1 mg/kg/day 12–24 hourly PO.
- All these agents should not be stopped abruptly.

Angiotensin-Converting Enzyme (ACE) Inhibitors

The ACE inhibitors inhibit the conversion of angiotensin I to angiotensin II. These are valuable drugs in the treatment of hypertension and heart failure in the course of which they are often combined with a loop diuretic. These drugs are contraindicated in bilateral renal artery stenosis or stenosis of renal artery in single functioning kidney where reduction in glomerular filtration can cause renal failure. They should thus be avoided or used with caution in children with suspected/proven renovascular disease.

Captopril

- The dose of captopril is 0.2–0.5 mg/kg/dose (maximum 6 mg/kg/day) 8–12 hourly PO in infants and children.
- The side effects include hypotension with the first dose, hyperkalemia, proteinuria, oliguria, and persistent dry cough.

Enalapril

- The drug is used in hypertension and congestive heart failure in children.
- The dose is 0.1 mg/kg/day PO once daily and the dose may be titrated/increased gradually for the desired effect after 2–3 days (up to a maximum of 0.5 mg/kg/day). Intravenous preparation is also available but used infrequently in children.
- The side effects include hypotension, dry cough, and hyperkalemia.

Lisinopril

- There is a limited pediatric experience with the use of this ACE inhibitor.
- It can be used to treat hypertension in children older than 12 years in a dose of 10–20 mg/day once daily PO.

Other drugs useful to treat childhood hypertension are shown in Table 17.23.

Diuretics

These drugs are included in this section as they often form an important adjunctive therapy in children with cardiovascular diseases such as with heart failure, hypertension, and pulmonary edema. Although they are grouped into different classes, only two groups, i.e., loop diuretics (e.g., frusemide) and potassium-sparing diuretics (e.g., spironolactone), are more often used than other diuretic agents in children.

Frusemide/Furosemide

- Frusemide inhibits the absorption of sodium, potassium, and chloride from the ascending limb of loop of Henle.

TABLE 17.23 Other Drugs for Childhood Hypertension

Drug	Dosage/route	Side effects/caution	Remarks
Hydralazine (vasodilator)	• 0.75–1 mg/kg/day 8–12 hourly PO • IV dose is 0.1–0.2 mg/kg/dose (maximum 20 mg) 4–6 hourly as required	Palpitation, tachycardia, and lupus-like reaction	Used as an adjunct to other antihypertensive drugs
Methyldopa (centrally acting)	10 mg/kg/day 8 hourly PO	Fluid retention, edema, sedation, and positive Coombs test	
Clonidine (centrally acting and alpha-adrenergic agonist agent)	5–10 µg/kg/day 8–12 hourly PO (maximum 0.9 mg/day). Also available as IV	Dry mouth and constipation. Sudden withdrawal can lead to rebound hypertension	Also useful in attention deficit hyperactivity disorder, and for growth hormone stimulation test
Nifedipine (calcium channel blocker)	0.5 mg/kg/dose PO or sublingual, 6 hourly. Also available in sustained-release formulation	Headache, palpitation, flushing of the face	For a rapid effect in hypertensive crisis, the gelatin capsule (5 mg) can be bitten/squeezed and contents put sublingually for immediate effect
Losartan (angiotensin II receptor antagonist)	0.7–1 mg/kg/day once daily PO in children aged 6 years and above	Dizziness and hypotension	Useful as an alternative to ACE inhibitor

ACE, angiotensin-converting enzyme.

- The dose is 1–2 mg/kg/dose PO, two to four times daily. IV bolus can be given as 0.5–1 mg/kg over 1–2 minutes (maximum 40 mg).
- The dose/duration and the route of administration depend on the underlying disease and its severity.
- The side effect includes electrolyte imbalances (hyponatremia and hypokalemia) and prolonged therapy may cause nephrocalcinosis. Concomitant use with nephrotoxic drugs such as gentamicin/amikacin should be avoided or closely monitored.

Spironolactone

- Spironolactone is the most commonly used potassium-sparing diuretic and aldosterone antagonist in children.
- It is often used along with another diuretic to decrease urinary potassium losses. Other indications include treating edema and ascites in renal diseases such as nephrotic syndrome.
- The dose is 1–3 mg/kg/day in one to two divided doses PO. In older children up to age 12–18 years, a maximum dose of 9 mg/kg/day (or 400 mg daily total) may be given.
- The side effects include hyperkalemia and gynecomastia. The drug should not be used along with ACE inhibitors.

Drugs for Respiratory Disorders

Bronchodilators

The major group of drugs that find use as bronchodilators in children with asthma are selective beta-2 agonists (beta-2 stimulants, e.g., salbutamol and terbutaline), which are the safest and most effective short-acting bronchodilators for the treatment of childhood asthma. Short-acting agents (salbutamol) are used for acute symptoms and immediate relief, while long-acting beta-2 agonists (salmeterol) are used by inhalation for long-term control, along with ICS for chronic asthma.

Adrenaline, which has dual alpha and beta adrenoreceptor agonist actions, is used in the emergency management of:

- Acute asthma (0.01 mL/kg/dose, SC, not to exceed 0.5 mL of 1:1000 solution)
- Anaphylaxis and other acute allergic reactions
- Severe croup (as nebulized solution)

Salbutamol

- Salbutamol is a short-acting beta-2 agonist for acute/immediate relief of bronchospasm in childhood asthma. The drug is also used to reverse severe hyperkalemia.
- The drug is administered orally, by nebulization, or through MDI/DPI.
- The dose is 0.1–0.2 mg/kg/dose 8 hourly PO, while it is 0.15 mg/kg (0.03 mL/kg of 0.5% solution, with maximum single dose of 5 mg) through nebulization 4–6 hourly but can be given more frequently as per the need. For nebulization, the drug needs to be diluted with 0.9% NaCl and can also be mixed/coadministered with ipratropium bromide for nebulization.
- The MDI (100 µg/puff)/DPI (dry powder inhaler) can be given as one to two puffs, four times every day.
- The side effects are irritability, fine tremors, palpitation, and hypokalemia, which occur more often with long-term therapy.

Terbutaline

- The drug is a short-acting bronchodilator.
- The drug can be used orally, subcutaneously, and/or by nebulization. The dose is 0.05 mg/kg/dose 8 hourly PO and 0.01 mg/kg/dose SC (can be repeated after 15 minutes).
- The side effects are similar to those of salbutamol.

Salmeterol

- Salmeterol is a long-acting beta-2 agonist administered by inhalation (MDI). Being a long-acting drug, it should not be used for acute asthma.
- The drug is reserved for the long-term control of chronic asthma and nocturnal asthma. This drug is always used with ICS.
- The dose is 50 µg (one puff) every 12 hours as preventer in children older than 4 years.
- The side effects are similar to those of other beta-2 agonists.

Ipratropium Bromide

- The drug is an anticholinergic agent used as an adjunct to salbutamol for the relief of acute asthma in children.
- The drug is given through nebulization and its duration of action is 3–6 hours.
- The dose is 250 µg through nebulization (up to 12 years) every 20–30 minutes for the first 2 hours and then 6 hourly. For children older than 12 years, the dose is 500 µg initially every 6 hours.
- The drug produces anticholinergic side effects such as dry mouth, blurred vision, headache, tachycardia, and urinary retention.

Aminophylline

- Aminophylline is a salt of theophylline mixed with ethylenediamine, which renders it soluble in water.
- It is being used as a second-line drug in acute asthma but finds an increased usage in the treatment of apnea of prematurity.
- When used IV for acute asthma, the dose is 5 mg/kg/dose diluted and given by slow IV infusion (1 mg/kg/h) over 6 hours.
- The side effects include irritability, tachycardia, arrhythmias, and convulsions.

Theophylline is a xanthine derivative and is more useful as a sustained-release preparation in the control of chronic asthma along with inhaled steroids. The recommended dose is 8–10 mg/kg/day 12 hourly PO.

Montelukast

- These drugs (montelukast and zafirlukast) are leukotriene receptor antagonist agents and block the effect of leukotrienes in the airways and are useful in the management of chronic and exercise-induced asthma.
- Montelukast is given PO as 4 mg (2–5 years old), 5 mg (6–14 years old), and 10 mg (more than 14 years of age) once daily in the evening.
- The common side effects include dyspepsia, dry mouth, and headache.

Cough Suppressants/Expectorants

- Cough/cold is a common presenting symptom in children and before one prescribes a cough suppressant or an expectorant, it is essential to decide the underlying condition that is producing the cough. These may range from uncomplicated, self-limiting respiratory infections to more severe conditions such as asthma, gastroesophageal reflux, and aspirated foreign body.
- There is very little evidence of benefit from cough suppressants in children with acute conditions causing cough and who are otherwise ambulatory. Cough syrups that contain a combination of cough suppressants with a sedating antihistamine should be avoided in children.
- Coughing is a natural mechanism to clear airways of secretions and keep them patent. However, it is one of the most bothersome symptoms for parents. Antitussives can be harmful in children who have secretions in the airways. However, they may be useful for suppressing dry, irritating cough.
- Dextromethorphan and codeine are the commonly used cough suppressants.
- Dextromethorphan is a centrally acting narcotic analog (D-isomer of codeine analog). It is relatively well tolerated. It may be used as an antitussive in a dose of 1–2 mg/kg/day 8 hourly orally (not more than 60 mg/day) for a duration not extending 5 days.
- Mucolytic agents (guaifenesin) do not have a role to play in routine management of upper and lower respiratory tract infections. They have been recommended for conditions such as cystic fibrosis in large doses.

Drugs in CNS Disorders

The common conditions that need drug therapy in children with CNS diseases include seizures, epilepsies, bacterial meningitis, attention deficit hyperactivity disorder, migraine (prophylaxis), and Guillain–Barré syndrome. Only specific drugs are included here, while other therapies such as antibiotic therapies are included elsewhere.

Anticonvulsant Drugs

The main indications for use of anticonvulsant drugs in infants and children are as follows:

- Epilepsies and epilepsy syndromes
- Acute CNS diseases such as acute bacterial meningitis, cerebral malaria, acute encephalitis/encephalopathy, head injury, and hypoxic ischemic encephalopathy in neonates
- Chronic meningitis, e.g., tuberculous meningitis
- Static encephalopathy associated with convulsions, e.g., cerebral palsy
- Febrile convulsions
- Progressive neurodegenerative diseases, e.g., subacute sclerosing panencephalitis (SSPE)

Drugs Used in Epilepsies

The long-term therapy/management of epilepsy with drugs aims to control the seizures as much as possible with a single antiepileptic agent. The choice of the antiepileptic drug is decided by the type of the seizures, age of the child, associated morbidities, and other ongoing medications (i.e., drug interactions). The drugs given in the next subsections are used in childhood epilepsies.

Phenytoin

- The drug is effective in controlling seizures in status epilepticus (IV route) and for long-term management of epilepsies such as generalized tonic/clonic seizures, focal epilepsy, and neonatal seizures. It is not effective in absence seizures.
- The loading dose for acute seizure control is 15–20 mg/kg/dose IV slowly (at the rate of 1 mg/kg/min, preferably in 20 minutes and diluted in 0.9% NaCl). The oral dose is 5–8 mg/kg/day PO 12 hourly. IM route should not be used for the drug.
- The side effects include ataxia, nystagmus, confusion, diplopia, hirsutism, gum hypertrophy, coarsening of facial features, rickets, and lymphoid hyperplasia. The cosmetic effects are particularly noticeable in young and adolescent patients.

Phenobarbitone

- The drug is used for neonatal convulsions and status epilepticus, and now less commonly as a long-term control of epilepsy.
- The IV dose is 10–20 mg/kg/dose slowly at a rate of 1 mg/kg/min. The subsequent PO dose is 3–6 mg/kg/day 12 hourly.
- The drug may cause drowsiness, sedation, behavioral disturbances, and hyperactivity.
- The drug has interactions if coadministered with frusemide, theophylline, and phenytoin.

Sodium Valproate

- The drug is a broad-spectrum antiepileptic agent effective against many epilepsies including generalized seizures, absence seizures, and myoclonic seizures and is useful if indicated in long-term prophylaxis of febrile convulsions.
- The therapy is started with 10–20 mg/kg/day initially PO 8 hourly and then gradually increased if needed up to 60 mg/kg/day if there are no side effects. Sustained-release preparations are also available that are to be given twice daily PO.
- The side effects include hepatotoxicity, hyperammonemia, drowsiness, weight gain, and temporary hair loss. Very rarely, the drug can cause pancreatitis.

Carbamazepine

- This antiepileptic agent is a broad-spectrum agent used against generalized tonic and clonic epilepsy and focal seizures. Apart from these, it is also useful in the treatment of trigeminal neuralgia and the prophylaxis of psychiatric bipolar disorders.
- It is often a drug of choice for focal epilepsy but can exacerbate absence seizures and myoclonic epilepsy.
- The recommended dose is 10 mg/kg/day PO, which can be slowly increased every 5–7 days in small increments to get the desired effect up to 30 mg/kg/day 8 hourly PO (maximum of 800 mg/day). Sustained-release preparations (tablets) should be given on 12-hourly dosages.
- The common side effects include allergic skin rash, drowsiness, bone marrow suppression (including aplastic anemia), blurred vision, nystagmus, and ataxia. The drug induces its own metabolism and a therapeutic drug level monitoring may be required.
- Oxcarbazepine is an analog of carbamazepine and is used as a treatment for partial seizures with or without secondary generalization. The dose is 5–10 mg/kg 12–24 hourly PO (maximum 300 mg/day). The side effects are less as compared with those of carbamazepine.

Diazepam

- This drug, belonging to the group of benzodiazepines, is a short-acting anticonvulsant and is useful for acute termination of seizures (status epilepticus, febrile convulsions, acute poisonings), drug-induced dystonic reactions, preprocedural sedation, and control of spasms in tetanus and anxiety disorders.

- The dose for the control of seizures is 0.1–0.3 mg/kg/dose IV, diluted in normal saline and given over 3–5 minutes, and may be repeated after 5 minutes if needed. Rapid push must be avoided as it can lead to respiratory depression. The dose for procedural sedation should be given 45–60 minutes before PO/per rectally. The maximum dose is 10 mg. The IV preparation can also be used per rectally.
- The drug can produce drowsiness, muscle weakness, and ataxia. All the benzodiazepines can precipitate hepatic coma in children with preexistent hepatic dysfunctions and thus should be avoided in them.

Clobazam

- The drug belongs to benzodiazepine group.
- It is used as an adjunctive therapy for epilepsies (e.g., complex partial seizures) and used for intermittent/short-term prophylaxis of febrile convulsions in children younger than 5 years.
- The dose is 0.25–0.5 mg/kg/day PO 12–24 hourly.
- The side effects are similar to those of diazepam.

Clonazepam

- This antiepileptic benzodiazepine is used in the treatment of infantile spasms, myoclonic epilepsies, atonic seizures, and atypical absence seizures.
- The dose is 0.03–0.1 mg/kg/day PO 8–12 hourly.
- The side effects include drowsiness, which may be marked, excess salivation, ataxia, and behavioral problems.

Nitrazepam

- The drug is effective in myoclonic epilepsy, particularly in infantile spasms.
- The dose is 0.25–0.5 mg/kg/day PO 12 hourly.
- The side effects include drowsiness and nightmares.

Lorazepam

- The drug is used in acute seizure control and as an antianxiety agent.
- The dose is 0.1 mg/kg/dose IV (maximum as 2 mg) diluted in NaCl or 5% dextrose slowly and may be repeated after 15 minutes.

Midazolam

- This drug, a benzodiazepine, is used as an anticonvulsant and as a premedication for sedation in clinical procedures in children.
- The dose is 0.1–0.2 mg/kg/dose over a period of 1 minute with a maximum dose of 5 mg IV as an infusion in 5% dextrose or 0.9% saline and increased as per need if required. The drug is also given through IM and intranasal routes and is a useful drug for procedural sedation in children.
- The drug may cause respiratory depression if given rapidly.

Few other newer anticonvulsants that are used in long-term management of epilepsy are also available, but these must be used under specialist supervision (Table 17.24).

Vitamins and Hematinics

Apart from their recommended daily intakes, vitamin supplements are required in their deficiency states and as supplements in malnutrition, chronic/systemic diseases, and metabolic diseases.

Vitamin A (Retinol)

- This fat-soluble vitamin is required for the prevention and treatment of xerophthalmia.
- The WHO recommends that infants aged between 6 and 11 months should be given 1,00,000 IU of vitamin A PO (first at the time

TABLE 17.24 Newer Antiepileptic Agents

Drug	Dose	Side effects	Remarks
Lamotrigine	2–10 mg/kg/day OD or 12 hourly PO. Start with low dose (0.6–2 mg/kg) and step up every 15 days	Drowsiness, headache, and rash. Consider withdrawal if rash/hypersensitivity occurs	Broad-spectrum antiepileptic drug as an add-on drug in refractory multiple seizures types. Use with caution along with valproate
Vigabatrin	40 mg/kg/day 12 hourly PO, to be increased in 2–3 weeks to 80 mg/kg/day (maximum 150 mg/kg/day)	Limited pediatric data. Visual field defects known	To be used along with neurologist consultation
Topiramate	0.5–1 mg/kg/day once daily PO and may be increased up to 5 mg/kg/day	Dry mouth, loss of appetite, impaired cognition, and nephrocalcinosis. Abrupt withdrawal may precipitate seizures	Used alone or as an adjunct in generalized epilepsy. Also used for prophylaxis of migraine in children
Gabapentin	10–15 mg/kg/day. Increase slowly up to 30 mg/kg/day 8 hourly PO	Dry mouth, dyspepsia, dizziness, and weight gain	Limited data on use in children. Used as an adjunct drug with partial seizures (focal epilepsy)
Levetiracetam	5–10 mg/kg/day once daily PO. Increase slowly up to 30–40 mg/kg/day 8–12 hourly PO	Avoid abrupt withdrawal. Drowsiness, dizziness, ataxia, rash	Add-on antiepileptic drug for refractory focal epilepsy without secondary generalization

of measles vaccine at 9 months of age) and then 2,00,000 IU once every 6 months at 18, 24, 30, and 36 months of age.

- The deficiency state should be treated with a dose of 50,000, 1 lakh, and 2 lakh IU in infants younger than 6 months, 6–12 months old, and older than 1 year, respectively. The same dose should be repeated the next day and then 2 weeks later. Use half the oral dose if given by IM route (which may be needed in cases of corneal involvement).
- Overdosage can lead to anorexia, vomiting, and signs of increased intracranial pressure.

Vitamin B Complex

- *Vitamin B_1 (thiamine)*: The dose in deficiency state (beriberi) is 10–25 mg IV or IM initially for 1 week and then 5–10 mg/day PO for 6–12 weeks.
- *Vitamin B_2 (riboflavin)*: The recommended therapeutic dose in deficiency states (angular cheilitis, glossitis) is 5–10 mg daily PO.
- *Vitamin B_3 (niacin)*: The recommended therapeutic dose in deficiency state (pellagra) is 50–200 μg/day PO. Niacin is also needed as an adjunct therapy in certain metabolic diseases.
- *Vitamin B_6 (pyridoxine)*: Pyridoxine dependency, deficiency, and concomitant antituberculous treatment need pyridoxine supplementation. The usual dose is 50–100 mg/day. If the deficiency is associated with seizures, then pyridoxine is given as IV or IM.
- *Vitamin B_{12} (cyanocobalamin)*: The deficiency states (megaloblastic anemia) along with folic acid need the administration of IM dose of vitamin B_{12} 250–1000 μg on alternate days for a period of 1–2 weeks. This should be followed by 250 μg once a week till the blood counts are normal and then

a maintenance dose of 1000 µg once every 3 months.

- *Folic acid*: The therapeutic dose in megaloblastic anemia is 0.5–1 mg/day for 4 months followed by a maintenance dose of 200 µg/day. The dose is 1 mg in children with hemolytic anemia and metabolic disorders. It should never be administered alone in vitamin B_{12} deficiency as it may precipitate subacute combined degeneration of spinal cord.
- Biotin, another member of vitamin B complex, is used in metabolic disease (biotinidase deficiency and nutritional biotin deficiency) as 5–10 mg once daily PO.

Vitamin C

- The recommended therapeutic dose in deficiency state (scurvy) is 100–200 mg/day PO. It is also used for the acidification of urine in a dose of 500 mg 6 hourly. Prolonged administration of high doses increases the risk of renal calculi.

Vitamin D

- Vitamin D includes calciferol (vitamin D_2), cholecalciferol (vitamin D_3), and 1,25-dihydroxycholecalciferol (calcitriol—metabolically active form of vitamin D).
- It is used to treat nutritional rickets (cholecalciferol) as 60,000 units daily PO for 10 days. Other activated forms of vitamin D (1,25-dihydroxycholecalciferol) are used to treat other forms of rickets such as vitamin D–dependent rickets and hypophosphatemic rickets.
- The normal daily requirement in healthy children is 400 IU daily.
- The side effects include gastric disturbances, polyuria, and hypercalcemia.

Vitamin E

- Vitamin E (alpha-tocopherol) is used in preterms to prevent hemolytic anemia and intraventricular hemorrhage and as a therapeutic supplement in chronic liver disease, malabsorption syndromes, and hemolytic anemia (sickle cell anemia and thalassemia).
- The dose in preterms and as nutritional supplement is 25–50 IU daily PO and other conditions can be treated with 100–400 IU PO once daily.

Vitamin K

- Vitamin K_1 (phytomenadione) is used to prevent and treat hemorrhagic disease of newborns (HDN).
- It is also used to treat vitamin K deficiency states with fat malabsorption (biliary atresia and chronic liver diseases) and to correct antibiotic-induced vitamin K deficiency and anticoagulant-associated prothrombin deficiency.
- The dose of vitamin K to prevent HDN is 1 mg IM once after birth. In other conditions, it can be given either PO 1–2 mg OD or 5 mg IM.

Iron

- The oral dose of elemental iron for the prophylaxis of iron deficiency anemia (IDA) is 1–2 mg/kg/day and the therapeutic dose is 3–6 mg/day given 12–24 hourly in between the meals.
- The choice of iron formulation should be decided by the palatability, side effects, and the cost of the preparation. It is essential to know the elemental iron content of the preparation.
- The common side effects include the reversible staining of tongue and gastrointestinal upsets such as epigastric pain, nausea, diarrhea, or constipation.

Other Miscellaneous Agents

Atropine Sulfate

- The dose for general use is 0.01 mg/kg/dose, subcutaneously or IV or through an endotracheal tube, and may be repeated after 4–6 hours. In cardiopulmonary

resuscitation, it is administered as 0.01–0.03 mg/kg/dose, q 2–5 minutes for two to three doses (maximum 1 mg).
- The drug is a critical component of initial treatment of poisoning with organophosphorus compounds.

Baclofen

- The drug is used in the therapy of chronic spasticity of spinal and cerebral origin such as cerebral palsy.
- The dose is 10–15 mg/day given 8 hourly orally with a maximum daily dose of 40 mg/day for children younger than 8 years and 60 mg/day for children older than 8 years.

Iron Chelators

Deferasirox (DFO)

- This is an iron chelating drug used to treat iron overload in chronic hemolytic anemia such as thalassemia.
- The dose is 20–35 mg/kg orally as a single dose on an empty stomach and it needs to be titrated every 3–6 months, to maintain the serum ferritin level <500 ng/mL. The dose should be rounded off to the nearest whole tablet size.
- The drug is approved for use in children older than 2 years.

Deferiprone

- This is an oral iron chelator approved for use in children older than 6 years for conditions such as thalassemia, hemolytic anemia, and acute iron poisoning.
- The dose is 25 mg/kg/dose, given three times daily (maximum 100 mg/kg/day).
- Blood dyscrasia including agranulocytosis has been reported with the drug.

Desferrioxamine Mesylate

- The drug is an iron chelator used in acute iron poisoning and chronic iron overload.
- In chronic iron overload, due to repeated blood transfusions, the drug is used as 20–40 mg/kg/day, subcutaneously given over 8–12 hours using a battery-driven pump, 4–5 days a week. The drug gives reddish color to the urine.
- The drug is useful in acute iron poisoning and is given intramuscularly as 1000 mg stat dose, followed by 500 mg every 4 hours for two doses, and then subsequently 500 mg every 4–12 hours depending on clinical response (maximum 6000 mg in 24 hours).

Erythropoietin (Recombinant Human)

- This is used to treat anemia associated with prematurity and chronic renal failure.
- The dose is 25–100 units/kg subcutaneously/IV three times a week.
- The hemoglobin should be monitored twice a week for 4–6 weeks, while following dose adjustments and until hemoglobin is stabilized.

Flunarizine

- The drug is a weak calcium channel blocker and is used for the prophylaxis of migraine headaches in children.
- It is used as 5 mg once daily orally at bedtime in children older than 5 years.
- The side effects include dry mouth, sedation, constipation, and weight gain.

Heparin

- Heparin is commonly referred to as standard or unfractionated heparin to differentiate it from low-molecular-weight heparins that have a longer duration of action.
- It is used as an anticoagulant in prophylaxis and the treatment of thromboembolic conditions.
- As an anticoagulant, a dose of 50 units/kg is administered as a bolus dose IV and then maintained at a rate of 10–25 units/kg/h. The dose is then adjusted based on the monitoring of activated partial thromboplastin time (aPTT).

- For the prevention of thrombotic conditions, heparin is given as 100 units/kg (maximum 5000 units) twice daily subcutaneously.
- Warfarin is a more commonly used oral anticoagulant that antagonizes the effect of vitamin K and takes 48–72 hours for its action. The dose is 0.05–0.34 mg/kg/day and should be adjusted to maintain the targeted international normalized ratio of 2–3.

Hydroxyurea

- The drug is used to decrease the painful episodes in sickle cell disease and thus to reduce the frequency of crises and blood transfusions.
- It is started in the dose of 15 mg/kg/day once daily orally with an increment of 2.5–5 mg/kg every 8 weeks with a maximum dose of 35 mg/kg/day.
- The drug is myelosuppressive and hence blood counts need to be monitored every 2 weeks for 8 weeks and then once every 2 months.

Insulins

- *Conventional insulins*: Initially, available insulins were extracted from beef and pork pancreases. These preparations had problems of being allergenic and were not very stable.
- *Newer insulins*: Subsequently, highly purified preparations are available that are less antigenic and allergenic. Now, synthetic preparations of human insulins are available prepared by recombinant DNA technology. Human insulins are now replacing the conventional insulins.

Advantages of Newer Insulins

- They are less antigenic and so less allergenic.
- They are more stable than older insulins.
- There is less chance of lipodystrophy.
- Human insulins have a faster onset and a shorter duration of action and are the least allergenic.

Insulins are divided according to their onset and duration of action as short acting, intermediate acting, and long acting. Human insulins and their duration of action are shown in Table 17.25.

Preparations

They are available as 40 or 100 units/mL. Both vials and pens are available.

Premixed insulins

Mixtures containing 70% NPH and 30% regular insulins are available, commonly used in mixed insulin.

Storage of insulin

Insulin should be stored at 2–8°C, in a refrigerator, preferably in the middle or lower compartments where there is no danger of its freezing. If a refrigerator (or electricity) is not available, insulin can be wrapped tightly in plastic and kept in earthenware clay pots ("matkas") in a cool and airy part of the house.

Transportation of insulin

During the hot summer months, insulin should be carried in insulated carry cases with a coolant or thermos with a few cubes of ice.

TABLE 17.25 Human Insulins

	Type	Onset (hours)	Peak (hours)	Duration of action (hours)
Short acting	Regular	0.5–1	2–3	4–6
Intermediate acting	NPH	2–4	4–10	14–18
	Lente	3–4	4–12	16–20
Long acting	Ultralente	6–10	–	20–30

TABLE 17.26 Pharmacokinetics of Insulin Analogs

	Type	Onset	Peak	Duration of action (hours)
Rapid acting	Lispro/aspartame/ glulisine	<15 minutes	1–2 hours	4–6
Long acting	Detemir	1 hour	Flat, maximum effect in 5 hours	12–24
	Glargine	1.5 hours	Flat, maximum effect in 5 hours	24

Administration

Insulins are given subcutaneously and in emergency situations, they can be administered intravenously. They are given with an insulin syringe having a 26-gauge needle.

Uses

- Insulins are used subcutaneously to treat hyperglycemia, in patients with type I and II diabetes mellitus who fail to respond to oral hypoglycemia drugs.
- For emergency management of diabetic ketoacidosis, intravenous infusion of insulin is given.
- Glucose–insulin drip can be given to treat hyperkalemia.

Side effects

- The side effects include hypoglycemia, insulin lipodystrophy, insulin allergy, and the development of antibodies against insulin that later cause resistance to insulin action.

Insulin Analogs

These are now available. Insulin analogs differ from human insulin in the structure of amino acid sequence. They bind to the insulin receptors and act like insulins. For example, in insulin lispro, amino acid proline at position B28 is replaced by lysine and lysine in position B29 is replaced by proline. In insulin aspart, amino acid B28, which is normally proline, is substituted with an aspartic acid residue.

Advantages of insulin analogs over insulins are as follows:

- They are absorbed rapidly, so have a rapid onset of action.
- Because of the rapid onset of action, they can be injected immediately before meal, which makes them much more convenient for use in children due to their unpredictable meals.
- Chances of hypoglycemia are less.

Insulin analogs are likely to replace human insulins in the future.

Insulin analogs and their duration of action are shown in Table 17.26.

Methotrexate

- The drug is used as a disease-modifying agent in rheumatoid disorders (DMARD) and can be used in all the types of chronic juvenile idiopathic arthritis. It is also used as an immunosuppressive agent in systemic lupus, scleroderma, and malignant diseases.
- The dose in juvenile idiopathic arthritis is 5–10 mg/m^2 body surface area, orally once a week.
- The side effects include bone marrow suppression and hepatic toxicity.

Potassium Chloride

- The electrolyte is given as a potassium supplement either IV or orally.
- The oral dose is 1–2 mEq/kg/day every 8 hours.
- Give only when there is adequate urine output.

Thyroxine

- Levothyroxine is given orally to treat hypothyroidism as follows: newborns, 10–15 µg/kg; late neonatal period, 6–8 µg/kg; 3–24 months, 5–10 µg/kg; 2–12 years, 5 µg/kg; and 12–18 years, 50–100 µg/day, as a single oral dose in early morning and on an empty stomach.
- Monitor total thyroxine levels 4–6 weekly initially and then once every 3–6 months to achieve the goal of therapy.
- Carbimazole and propylthiouracil are antithyroid drugs and treatment should be given under a specialist care.

Zinc

- The common use of zinc is in acute and persistent diarrhea of infants and children.
- It is given orally as 10 mg/day in children younger than 6 months and as 20 mg/day in children older than 6 months for a period of 14 days.

KEY POINTS

- Drug therapy forms an essential part of childhood illnesses.
- It must be remembered that apart from the pharmacokinetics, several factors influence the drug therapy in children such as age, nutritional status, and the presence of associated systemic diseases, which may need dosage modifications.
- All such factors are needed to be considered before deciding an appropriate drug therapy for an individual child.

CHAPTER 18

Radiological Imaging in Children

Paresh A Thakkar, Baldev S Prajapati, Niranjan Shendurnikar

Imaging and X-rays form important tools in diagnosis and management of childhood disorders. However, it is essential that the X-rays and other radiological images must be interpreted in the context of the given history and clinical scenario and not viewed as isolated tools. Hence, it is essential to interpret these images in the background knowledge of available clinical and other investigative information. This chapter presents essential X-rays and radiological images commonly seen in childhood disorders.

The present chapter interprets and describes the radiological images, X-rays in particular, with reference to common pediatric disorders along with a brief description and discussion of the associated condition(s). It is recommended that the readers have a careful and analytical look at the radiological images initially and make an attempt to analyze the findings themselves and then go on to read the relevant text to supplement their knowledge.

Basics of X-Ray Chest

The X-ray chest provides useful information about the possible diagnosis related to various cardiac and pulmonary conditions. It provides information about the situs, cardiac size and configuration, pulmonary pathology, and pulmonary vasculature.

Good X-Ray Chest

A good X-ray chest is one that has proper centering and correct exposure, and is a proper inspiratory film.

Reading an X-Ray Chest

- *Proper centering*: If both the clavicles are at the same level and shadow of the spine is not rotated, the X-ray is properly centered.
- *Correct exposure*: The space between the second and third vertebrae should be visible in a correctly exposed film. If the whole spine is clearly visible, the X-ray is overexposed and the vasculature would be underestimated. On the contrary, if the spine is not seen, the X-ray is underexposed, in which case the vasculature would be overestimated.
- *Proper inspiratory film*: If the diaphragm is at the level of the ninth intercostal space, it is a proper inspiratory film. If the film is taken before full inspiration, the diaphragm would be higher up and the cardiac size would be wrongly overestimated.
- *Lung fields*: These are divided into three zones:
  - *Upper zone*: Portion above the anterior end of the second rib
  - *Middle zone*: Portion between anterior ends of the second and fourth ribs
  - *Lower zone*: Portion below the anterior end of the fourth rib

Look for opacity, lucency, air bronchograms, calcifications, fluid level, and cavities in both the lung fields. Also look at costophrenic and cardiophrenic angles, hilar regions, bronchovascular markings, and position of tracheal shadow to know the push/pull (shifting) of the mediastinum.

- *Diagnosis of situs*: In situs solitus—normal situs—the stomach air bubble is seen on the left side and the liver shadow is seen on the right side. The right dome of diaphragm is higher than the left dome. In case of situs inversus, the stomach air bubble is seen on the right side while liver shadow is seen on the left side.
- *Cardiac size*: Cardiothoracic ratio is calculated for the assessment of heart size. Thoracic dimension is the widest internal thoracic dimension. For cardiac dimension, from the middle of the spine, maximum cardiac shadow on the left and right sides is taken. A child is said to have cardiomegaly if cardiothoracic ratio is more than 50% for children, 55% for infants, and 60% for neonates. One should ensure that it is a proper inspiratory film, as an expiratory film gives a false impression of cardiomegaly.
- *Cardiac configuration*: Figure 18.1 shows the structures and chambers of the heart that form the cardiac borders radiologically. The right heart border is mainly formed by right atrium along with superior and inferior vena cava, above and below, respectively. The left heart border has shadows casted by aortic knuckle, pulmonary conus, and left atrial appendage from above downwards and major portion of the left border is formed by left ventricle.
  - In left ventricular enlargement, cardiac apex is shifted downwards and outwards, making an obtuse cardiophrenic angle.
  - In right ventricular enlargement, cardiac apex is lifted, resulting in an acute cardiophrenic angle.
- *Vascular markings of lung*: In suspected cardiac pathology, it is also very important to note the pulmonary vascularity. Certain cardiac conditions such as tetralogy of Fallot and other conditions with Fallot's physiology have oligemic lung fields. Conditions with increased pulmonary blood flow show hyperemic lung fields such as acyanotic conditions (e.g., left-to-right shunts, ventricular septal defect [VSD], and patent ductus arteriosus [PDA]) and cyanotic congenital heart disease (CHD; e.g., total anomalous pulmonary venous connection [TAPVC] and d-TGV [dextro-TGV]).

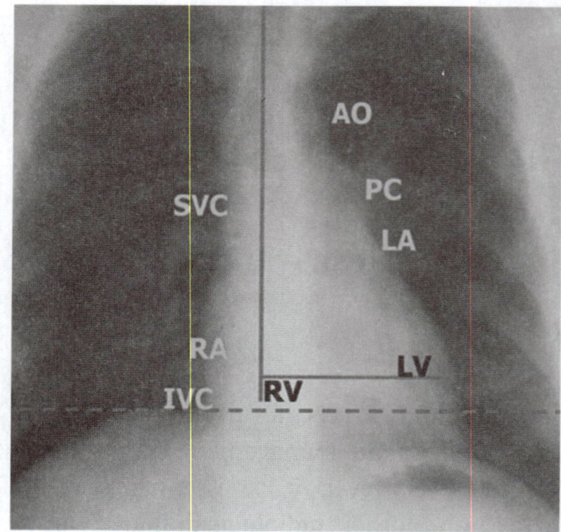

Figure 18.1 Components of cardiac borders to measure cardiomegaly. *AO*, aortic knuckle; *IVC*, inferior vena cava; *LA*, left atrium; *LV*, left ventricle; *PC*, pulmonary conus; *RA*, right atrium; *RV*, right ventricle; *SVC*, superior vena cava.

- *Ribs and spine*: Look for notching of ribs, costochondral beading, fractures.
- *Diaphragm*: Look for the level of diaphragm and gas under diaphragm.

Figure 18.2 shows an X-ray chest of a 10-month-old child who was brought to the hospital for fever, cough, and cold for 4–5 days. As his cough was worsening, an X-ray was advised. The X-ray chest showed an opaque shadow in the superior mediastinum.

The thymus (thymic gland) is often seen as a triangular sail-like shadow frequently toward the right of the mediastinum.

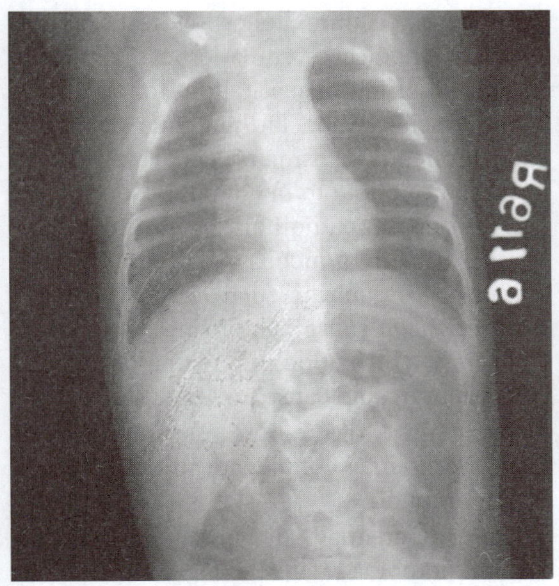

Figure 18.2 Normal thymic shadow.

- Commonly, radiographically, the thymus appears up to age of 2–3 years. At times, the normal thymus may be visualized even up to the age of 8–10 years.
- It gives several types of shadows, mimicking other pathological conditions.
- Various radiographic appearances include the following:
  - Covers the superior aspect of the heart like an umbrella and blends imperceptibly with the cardiac silhouette
  - Triangular in shape, producing "sail sign" (this sail sign on slight rotation may mimic pneumonic consolidation of upper lobe)
  - May appear as mediastinal mass because of blending with the cardiac silhouette
  - Bilaterally appearing normal thymus in superior mediastinum giving a mass-like configuration
  - Superior mediastinal widening
  - Thymic size decreased on inspiration and in response to stress, steroids, and cyanotic CHD, and absent in DiGeorge syndrome

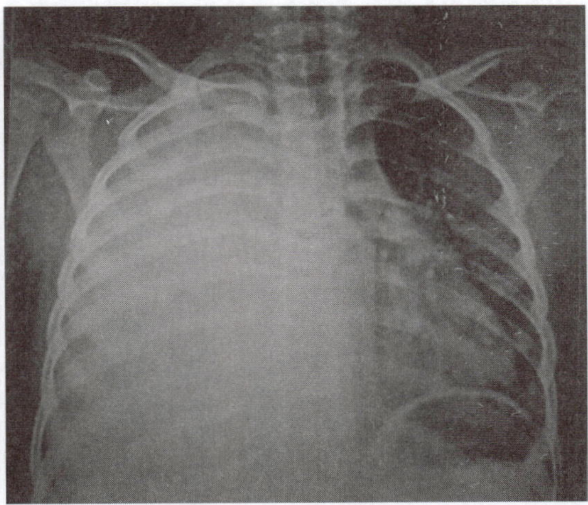

Figure 18.3 X-ray chest with opaque hemithorax (right).

Figure 18.3 shows a chest X-ray of a 5-year-old child who had fever for 15 days and progressive increase of cough and breathlessness over the past 4–5 days.

In this X-ray chest PA view, with homogenous opacity in right lung field and almost opaque hemithorax, costophrenic and cardiophrenic angles are obliterated. There is shift of mediastinum toward the opposite side. These findings are suggestive of right-sided pleural effusion.

- Clinically, there will be shift of mediastinum (trachea and apex beat) toward the opposite side, decreased air entry over the area of effusion, decreased vocal resonance, and sometimes bronchial breath sounds just above the level of effusion.
- Ultrasonography is helpful in detecting small amount of effusion, loculated effusion, and underlying consolidation, and also for guiding pleural tap.
- The diagnostic procedure to confirm the diagnosis is pleural tap.
- Pleural effusion can be transudative or exudative. Transudative pleural effusion can be due to causes such as nephrotic syndrome and congestive heart failure, while exudative pleural effusion can be due to bacterial infections including tuberculosis.
- Hemorrhagic fluid can be due to traumatic tap, tuberculosis, or malignancy.

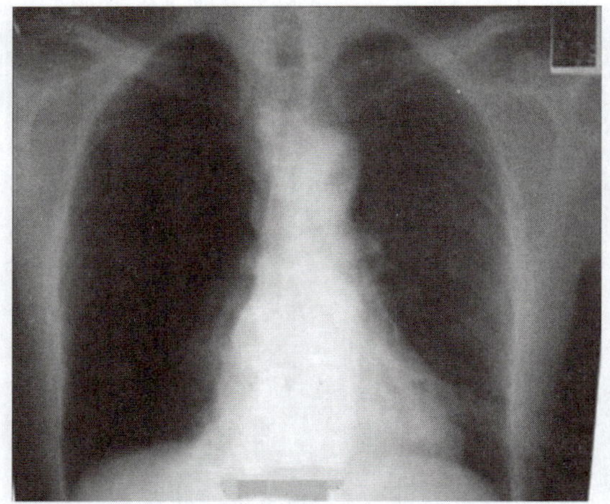

Figure 18.4 Hyperlucency on right side.

- When pleural effusion occurs secondary to consolidation, it is called parapneumonic or synpneumonic effusion.
- If the pleural tap drains pus, it is called empyema, which needs placement of intercostal drainage tube and antibiotics for 4–6 weeks.
- Surgical modality such as video-assisted thoracoscopic surgery (VATS) may be indicated in case of failure of medical therapy.

Figure 18.4 shows an X-ray chest of a child who presented with the sudden onset of breathlessness and respiratory distress.

The X-ray chest PA view shows hyperlucency in the right lung field. The increase in radiolucency is seen due to the accumulation of air anterior to the lungs. There is absence of bronchovascular markings on the right side. The shadow of collapsed right lung is seen and there is shift of mediastinum toward the left side, suggestive of right-sided pneumothorax. Cardiac shadow and left lung field are normal.

- Treatment of pneumothorax is emergency drainage by placing intercostal drainage tube and putting underwater seal.
- Pneumothorax can be primary spontaneous pneumothorax in normal lungs or it can be secondary to trauma, necrotizing pneumonia, cystic fibrosis, or iatrogenic causes. Iatrogenic causes can be postprocedure, following resuscitation or mechanical ventilation, overzealous efforts during resuscitation, or inserting endotracheal tube farther, thus placing it in bronchus causing selected ventilation and barotrauma to one lung. In such cases, right-sided pneumothorax is more common as right main bronchus is more in line with trachea. Organisms such as staphylococci or *Klebsiella* cause necrotizing pneumonia, leading to formation of pneumatoceles that can rupture and cause pneumothorax.
- Meconium aspiration syndrome in newborns may complicate to develop into pneumothorax.
- One differential diagnosis of tension pneumothorax is congenital lobar emphysema, which usually presents with severe respiratory distress in early infancy. X-ray shows hyperlucency in the lung field, which is usually accompanied by herniation of lung. Commonly, left upper lobe of lung herniates toward the right side.

A 7-year-old child presented with a history of fever for 1 month and breathlessness for 7 days (Fig. 18.5).

This X-ray shows homogenous opacity in left lung field; there is obliteration of costophrenic

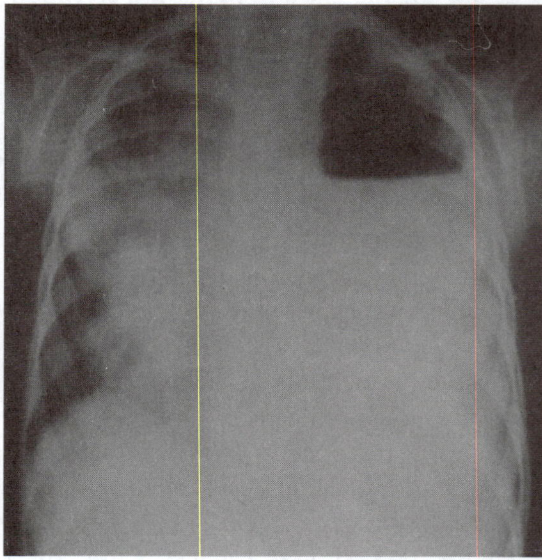

Figure 18.5 X-ray chest in a 7-year-old child.

and cardiophrenic angles. There is a shift of mediastinum toward the opposite side. There is sharp demarcation in the upper part and increased lucency in the left upper part of lung, suggestive of air–fluid level. This finding favors the diagnosis of hydropneumothorax on the left side. On the right side, there is opacity in paracardiac region with the presence of air bronchogram suggestive of right paracardiac consolidation. The presence of air bronchogram indicates the pathology of the alveoli and the conducting airways are patent with air.

- When serous effusion is associated with pneumothorax, it is called hydropneumothorax, and when pus is associated with pneumothorax, it is called pyopneumothorax.
- Organisms such as staphylococci and *Klebsiella*, which can cause necrotizing pneumonia forming pneumatoceles, can rupture and complicate pyopneumothorax. Patients with such a condition would also need placement of intercostal drainage tube and prolonged course of antibiotics.

Figure 18.6 shows an X-ray of a child who presented with a history of fever and cough of 4- to 5-day duration.

This X-ray shows opacity in the left lower zone in the paracardiac region, while the cardiac border is clearly visible. This indicates that the pathology is in the posterior basal segment. Similar opacity is also seen in the right posterior basal segment, suggesting consolidation. There is no shift of mediastinum.

- Common organisms causing pneumonia in children are *Streptococcus pneumoniae, H. influenzae, S. pyogenes, Staphylococcus aureus, Mycoplasma pneumoniae,* and viruses.
- Drug of choice for community-acquired pneumonia is amoxicillin or co-amoxiclav.

A 5-year-old child was brought to the hospital with a history of progressive weight loss, anorexia, and increasing cough over a period of 2 months. An X-ray chest was ordered as part of basic investigation (Fig. 18.7).

This X-ray shows presence of opacity in the right hilar region with convexity outside, suggesting hilar lymph node enlargement. Similar opacity is also seen in the right paratracheal region, suggesting right paratracheal lymph node enlargement. Thus, this is primary complex, a form of pulmonary tuberculosis.

- Primary complex, also called Ghon's complex, includes local infection at the portal of entry and involves regional lymph nodes such as hilar or paratracheal lymph nodes.

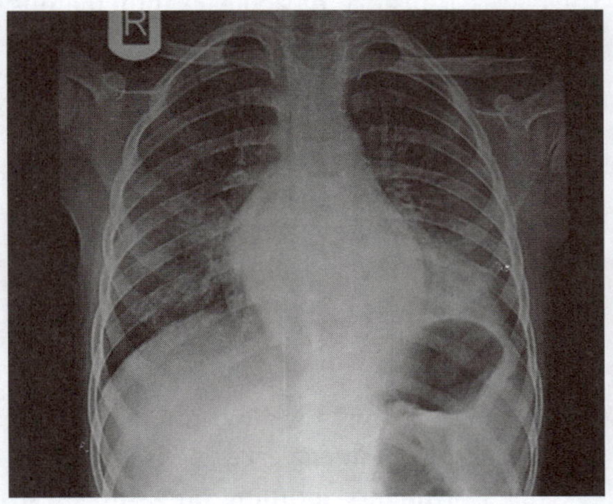

Figure 18.6 X-ray chest of child with fever and cough.

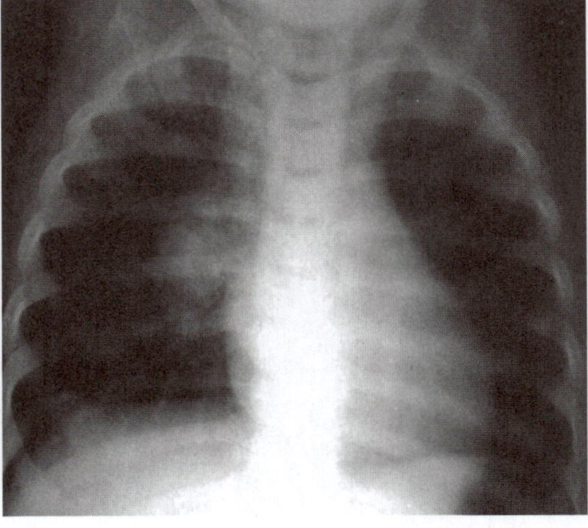

Figure 18.7 X-ray chest in a 5-year-old child.

- Fate of primary complex: It may heal by calcification or fibrosis, or it may progress to lead to the formation of large areas of consolidation or cavity, endobronchial tuberculosis, collapse, hematogenous dissemination leading to miliary tuberculosis, disseminated tuberculosis, and neurotuberculosis.
- Lymph node enlargement is common in childhood tuberculosis.
- Enlarged lymph node can press upon bronchus, causing paroxysmal or pertussoid cough. This may even lead to collapse of the affected segment of lung.
- It is important to ask for history of contact with an open case of tuberculosis.
- Positive Mantoux test indicates that the child has been exposed to mycobacteria; it has more significance for children compared with for adults.

Figure 18.8 shows an X-ray chest PA view depicting opacity in the right hilar region extending to upper part of lung field, having convexity outside likely to be right hilar lymph node enlargement. This lymph node is causing impingement over trachea. Additionally, the increase in transparency on the right side and widened intercostal spaces as compared with on the left side suggest air trapping, which can be due to partial bronchial obstruction. Whenever lymph glands cause impingement of trachea, it can lead to stridor and respiratory distress or paroxysmal/pertussoid cough in children.

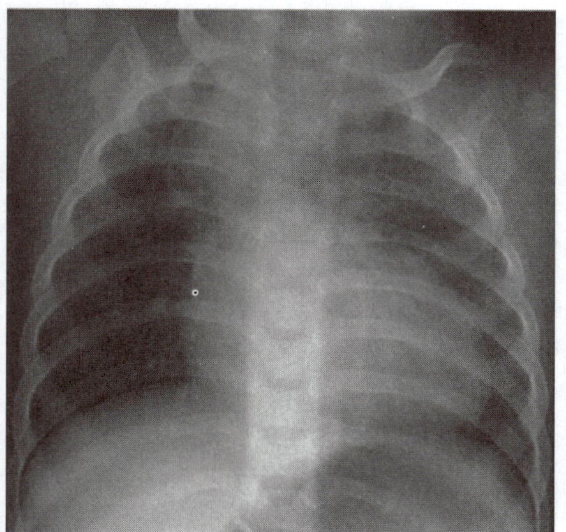

Figure 18.8 X-ray chest of a 4-year-old child.

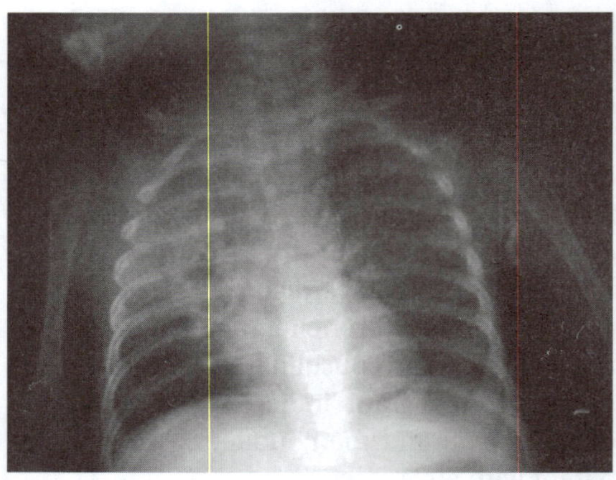

Figure 18.9 X-ray chest of a 5-year-old child.

Figure 18.9 shows an X-ray of a 5-year-child who presented with fever, cough, and breathlessness and was also undernourished. This X-ray chest PA view shows extensive nonhomogenous opacities involving right upper and middle lobes of lung. The likely cause is tuberculous pneumonia with hilar adenopathy.

Figure 18.10 shows an X-ray chest PA view of a child with a history of high-grade fever, cough, and breathlessness of 2-week duration. There was a history of acute exanthematous illness about a month ago.

The X-ray shows numerous small-sized, rounded opacities uniformly distributed in both the lung fields. These fine/small, millet-sized shadows seen in the entire lung field bilaterally are suggestive of miliary tuberculosis. The classical miliary mottling is usually very small, 1- to 2-mm-sized shadows, classically described as snowstorm appearance. Sometimes they are a bit larger, and occur when miliary shadows are too numerous and start to spread out to coalesce.

- Causes of miliary mottling on X-ray chest: The commonest is miliary tuberculosis; other uncommon causes are hypersensitivity

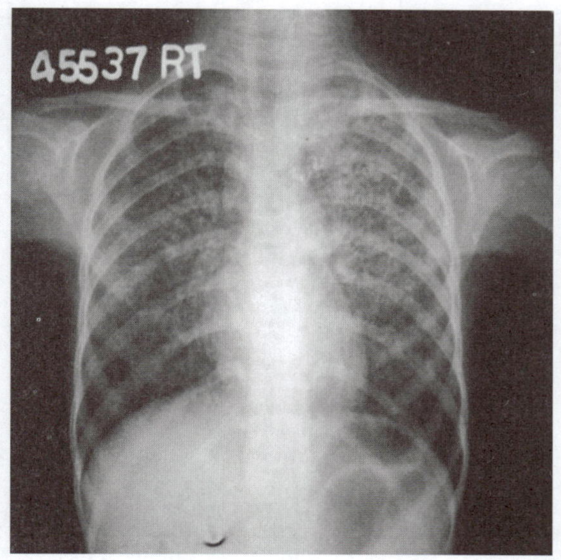

Figure 18.10 X-ray chest of a 4-year-old child.

pneumonitis, pulmonary hemosiderosis, pneumoconiosis, pulmonary alveolar proteinosis, miliary metastasis, and sarcoidosis.

- Miliary tuberculosis occurs due to massive hematogenous seeding of tubercle bacilli.
- The disease is more common in immunocompromised children such as in children after measles and those with severe malnutrition and HIV/AIDS.

Figure 18.11 shows an X-ray chest showing opacity in the upper and mid-zone of right lung. Air bronchogram is present, which suggests the presence of consolidation. There is a sharp demarcation with upward pull of horizontal fissure; there is shift of mediastinum toward the same side, suggesting associated collapse.

- Foreign body inhalation is one of the important causes of collapse in children.
- Other causes are tuberculous lymph node pressing upon bronchus, mucus plug causing obstruction, and endobronchial tuberculosis.

A newborn baby with low birth weight and history of premature delivery at the gestational age of 32 weeks developed respiratory distress within 2 hours of birth. The X-ray chest is shown in Figure 18.12.

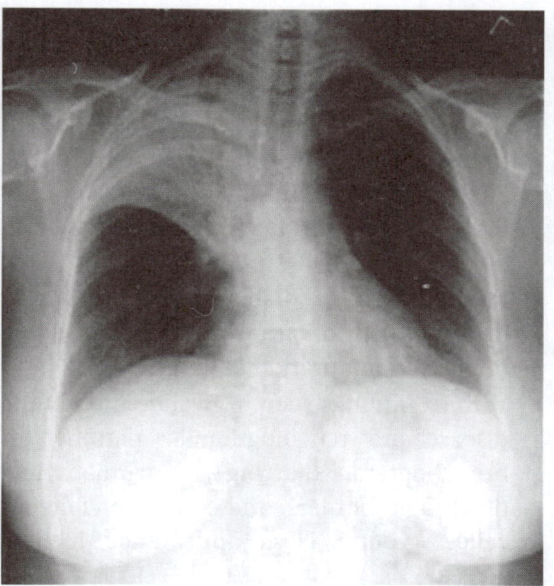

Figure 18.11 X-ray chest of a child with low-grade fever and pertussoid cough.

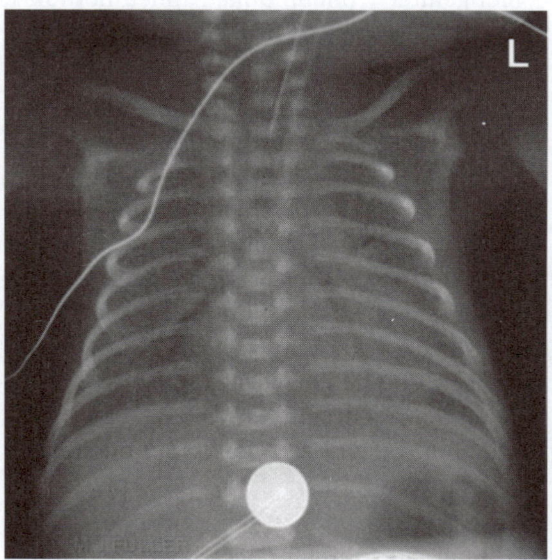

Figure 18.12 X-ray chest of a preterm baby with respiratory distress.

This X-ray chest PA view shows diffuse involvement of both the lung fields. Lung fields show reticulogranular pattern of opacities and presence of air bronchogram, suggesting consolidation. There is blurring of cardiac borders and borders of diaphragm.

Such findings are consistent with diagnosis of hyaline membrane disease in newborns.

- Hyaline membrane disease is caused by surfactant deficiency, which is due to immaturity of lung in preterm neonates. Such neonates present with respiratory distress soon after birth and usually within 6 hours of life.
- Infants born to diabetic mothers are at increased risk of surfactant deficiency, due to delayed maturation of lungs.
- Various findings seen in hyaline membrane disease are reticulogranular pattern, air bronchogram, blurring of cardiac and diaphragm borders, and complete whiteout called ground glass appearance in late stages.
- Other causes of respiratory distress in newborns are transient tachypnea of newborn, meconium aspiration syndrome, congenital pneumonia, pneumothorax, tracheoesophageal fistula (TEF), congenial diaphragmatic hernia, bilateral choanal atresia, and cardiac causes such as congestive heart failure due to PDA, TGA, or hypoplastic left heart syndrome.
- RDS due to HMD can be prevented by administration of antenatal steroids.

Another newborn presented with breathlessness and respiratory distress soon after birth. The X-ray chest is shown in Figure 18.13. The newborn was found to have a scaphoid abdomen, which is an abnormal finding, and decreased breath sounds on the left side.

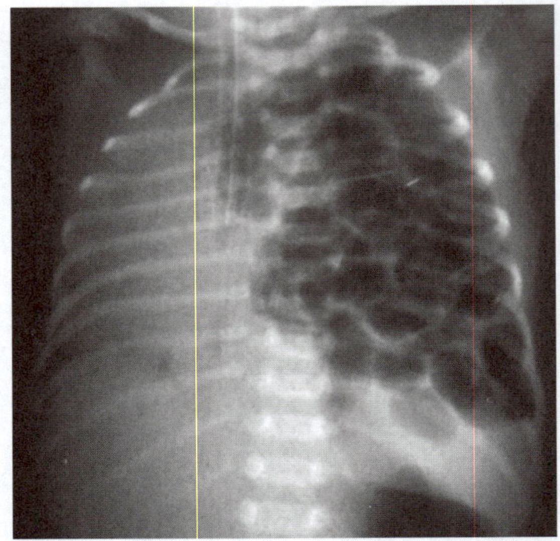

Figure 18.13 A full-term newborn with respiratory distress.

The chest X-ray shows presence of air-filled intestinal loops in left chest cavity. Left dome of diaphragm is not seen. Herniation of bowel loop in left chest cavity suggests diagnosis of congenital diaphragmatic hernia.

- Defect is more common on the left side. Herniation through posterolateral foramen of Bochdalek is more common than through anterior foramen of Morgagni.
- This anomaly can be picked up on antenatal sonography. If diagnosed antenatally, the delivery should be conducted in a tertiary care hospital with facility of neonatal ICU, mechanical ventilation, and other necessary equipment and facilities for management.
- Such a child usually presents with respiratory distress at birth and scaphoid abdomen. Bag and mask ventilation is contraindicated as it will worsen the condition.
- Usually, it is associated with hypoplastic lung and pulmonary hypertension.
- In severe cases diagnosed antenatally, ex utero intrapartum treatment (EXIT) procedure can be done.

Figure 18.14 shows an X-ray chest PA view depicting shift of mediastinum toward the right side. Diaphragm on the left side is pushed up, below which fundal gas shadow is seen, suggestive of eventration of diaphragm on the left side. There is no herniation of bowel loops; thus, it is not diaphragmatic hernia. It is important to note that all cases of eventration of diaphragm need not have mediastinal shift.

Figure 18.15 shows an X-ray of a baby who presented with frothing from mouth and choking episode immediately following breastfeeding soon after birth, followed by respiratory distress.

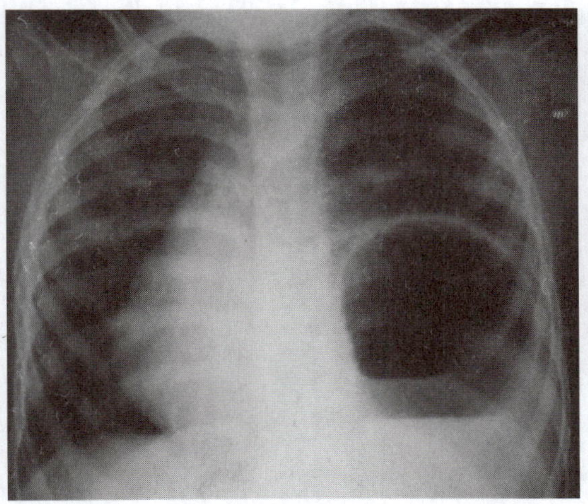

Figure 18.14 X-ray chest of a 3-year-old child.

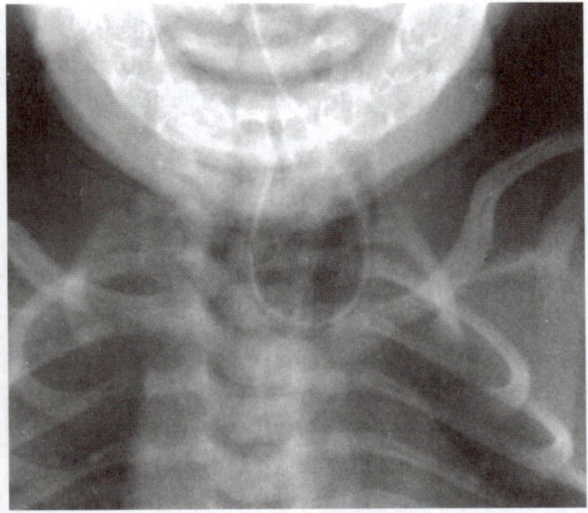

Figure 18.15 X-ray of a newborn with respiratory distress.

The X-ray shows a radiopaque tube in the neck region with coiling suggestive of esophageal atresia.

- Esophageal atresia can be isolated or can be a part of TEF.
- TEF can be associated with anomalies such as Down syndrome, duodenal atresia, or cardiac defects.
- It is associated with polyhydramnios in the mother. Thus, in all such pregnancies, esophageal atresia/TEF should be ruled out by inserting an infant feeding tube at birth. In a normal newborn, the tube can be inserted into stomach and can be clinically confirmed by pushing air with syringe and auscultating with stethoscope over stomach area. In case of TEF, the feeding tube will get coiled as the upper end of esophagus is a blind pouch and will come out from oral cavity. The diagnosis can be confirmed by demonstrating coiling using barium-impregnated feeding tube.
- There are five types of esophageal atresia, of which type III is the most common. In type III, the upper end of esophagus is a blind pouch and the lower part communicates with trachea.
- Absence of stomach bubble indicates either esophageal atresia without TEF or esophageal atresia with proximal TEF.
- A variety of TEF can present at a later age with recurrent pneumonia or LRTI.

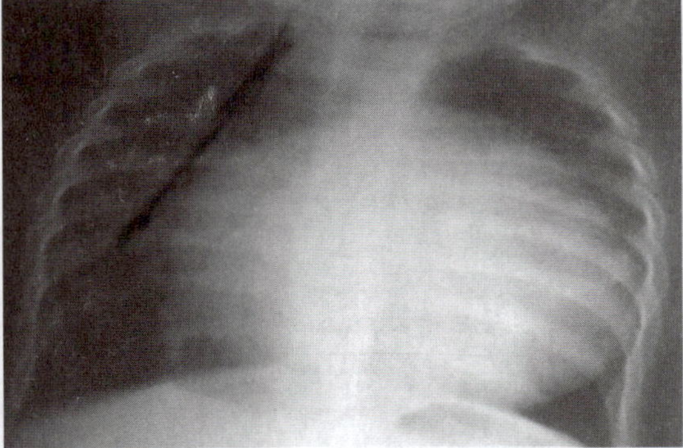

Figure 18.16 X-ray chest of a 2-year-old child.

Figure 18.16 shows an X-ray chest PA view with cardiothoracic ratio more than 50%, suggesting gross cardiomegaly. Here, the cardiophrenic angle is acute and not obtuse, suggesting right ventricular type of apex. Lung fields and vascular markings are normal.

- Common causes of cardiomegaly are left-to-right shunts such as VSD, PDA, hypertrophic cardiomyopathy, and valvular heart diseases such as aortic stenosis (AS), aortic regurgitation (AR), and mitral regurgitation (MR).

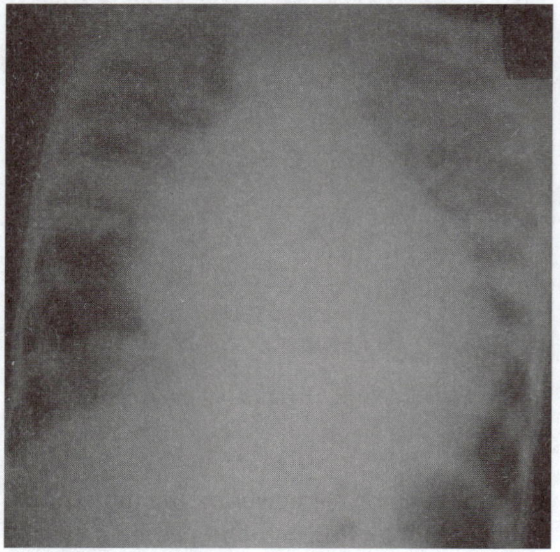

Figure 18.17 X-ray chest of a child with acute onset of breathlessness.

- Echocardiography is required for further diagnosis.

Figure 18.17 shows an X-ray of a 4-year-old boy who had a history of skin pustules 14 days back and was passing cola-colored urine since 5 days. He had a history of breathlessness since the past 24 hours.

The X-ray shows gross cardiomegaly. Bilateral lung fields are hyperemic; the opacities are spreading out from hilum. The vascular markings are much more prominent and extending to the outer third of the lung field, suggestive of pulmonary edema. This child had an earlier streptococcal skin infection following which he developed poststreptococcal glomerulonephritis (PSGN) and presented with acute left ventricular failure causing pulmonary edema. The classical X-ray picture has been described as "bat wing appearance."

- Left ventricular failure causes pulmonary edema; a child with such a condition presents with acute breathlessness and severe respiratory distress; at times, he/she has pink, frothy sputum.
- Intravenous frusemide is helpful in reducing pulmonary edema and thus respiratory distress.

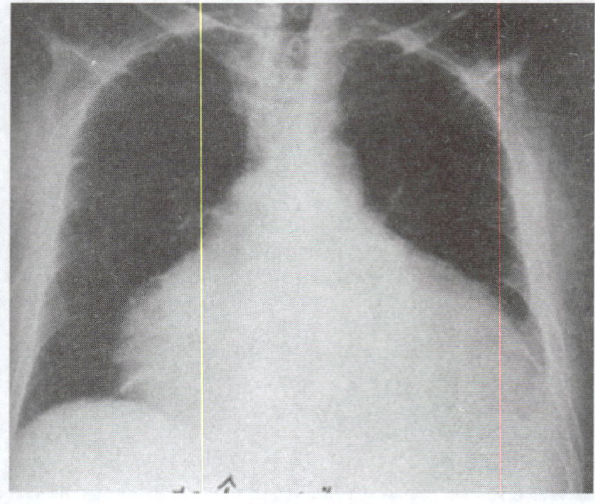

Figure 18.18 Pericardial effusion.

Figure 18.18 shows X-ray chest PA view depicting grossly enlarged and globular heart. The cardiac margins are very clear, which normally are somewhat blurred due to cardiac contractions. These findings suggest the possibility of pericardial effusion. The typical appearance is described as leather bottle appearance.

- Common causes of pericardial effusions are infections (viruses such as coxsackie B and EBV, and bacteria such as *Streptococcus, Staphylococcus,* and *Mycobacterium tuberculosis*), connective tissue disorders, beriberi, malignancy, and trauma.
- Corticosteroids are indicated if the condition is due to tuberculous pericarditis or pancarditis from rheumatic fever.
- If it is causing cardiac tamponade, then pericardiocentesis may be needed.
- Precordial pain that is sharp and stabbing, presence of pericardial friction rub, and muffled heart sounds are suggestive of diagnosis of pericardial effusion.

Figure 18.19 shows X-ray chest PA view depicting the apex of heart on the right side rather than on the left side, suggesting possibility of dextrocardia. One should also look for gas shadow of gastric fundus and shadow of liver, but here they are not clearly visible.

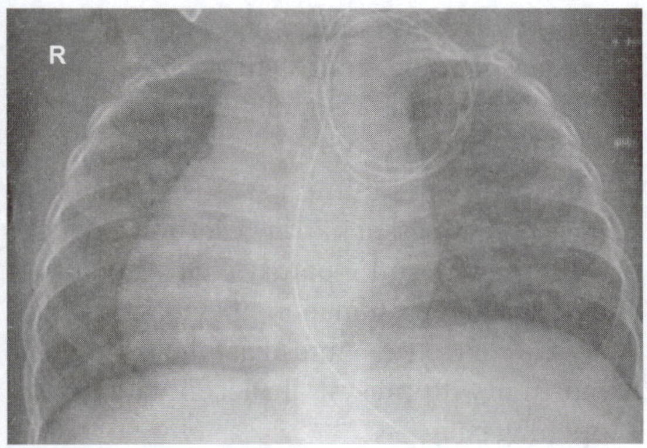

Figure 18.19 X-ray chest PA view.

- Dextrocardia may be associated with other internal cardiac malformation.
- It may or may not be associated with situs inversus.

Figure 18.20 shows an X-ray chest PA view depicting enlarged cardiac shadow with prominent hyperemic lung fields giving rise to typical figure of 8 appearance or snowman appearance, which is classically seen in TAPVC.

- TAPVC is a cyanotic CHD.
- Other cyanotic CHDs are tetralogy of Fallot, double outlet right ventricle, transposition of great arteries, Ebstein anomaly, tricuspid atresia, truncus arteriosus, and single ventricle with pulmonic stenosis.
- TAPVC is categorized as being with or without pulmonary venous obstruction. Nonobstructive presentation is more common, which, unlike other cyanotic CHDs, presents with congestive heart failure due to increased pulmonary blood flow. Usually, it is asymptomatic at birth and presents at 3–6 months of age. Obstructed variety presents in the neonatal period with marked cyanosis and respiratory distress.

Figure 18.21 shows an X-ray chest PA view of a 4-year-child who presented with breathlessness and central cyanosis and had marked clubbing. There was past history of such episodes of cyanotic spells.

The X-ray shows normal-sized heart and prominent oligemic lung fields. There is absence of shadow of main pulmonary artery as evidenced by concavity at area of pulmonary conus; apex is lifted up, giving rise to boot-shaped heart. These findings suggest possibility of tetralogy of Fallot.

- Tetralogy of Fallot is the commonest cyanotic CHD.
- Four components of tetralogy of Fallot are right ventricular outflow tract obstruction (infundibular pulmonary stenosis), right ventricular hypertrophy, overriding of aorta, and VSD.

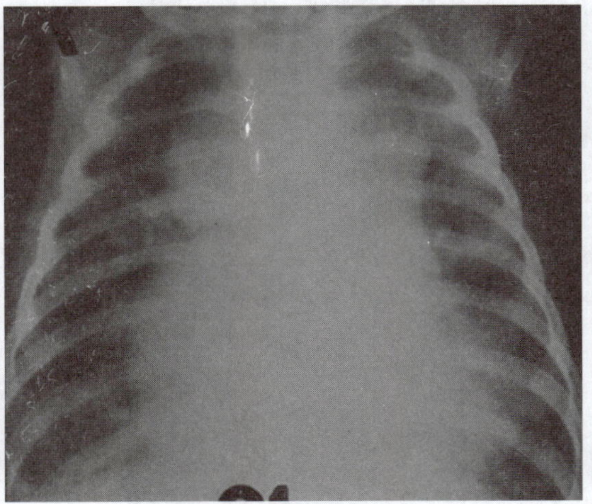

Figure 18.20 X-ray chest of a 4-month-old child with severe respiratory distress.

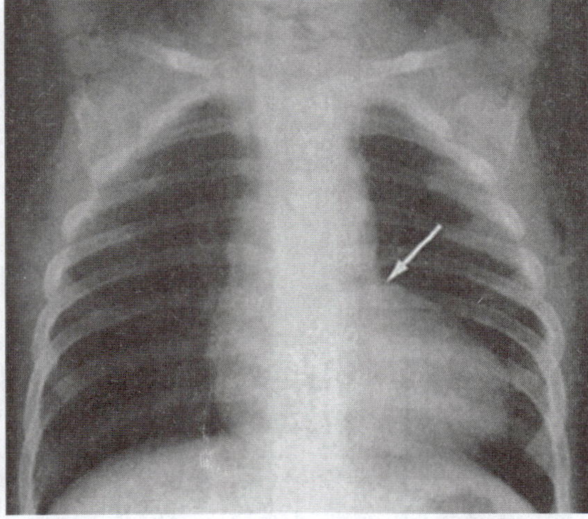

Figure 18.21 X-ray chest of a child with breathlessness and central cyanosis.

- Patients with cyanotic CHD present with central cyanosis, cyanotic spells, exertional dyspnea, effort intolerance, and squatting episodes. On examination, they have clubbing and ejection systolic murmur, and *S2 is soft and single.*
- Any sympathetic activity causes infundibular spasm, leading to worsening of cyanosis.
- Squatting position helps in increasing venous return and blood flow to right heart, increases oxygenation, and helps to decrease cyanosis. Such patients assume squatting posture repeatedly.
- Medical management includes use of β-blockers such as metoprolol or propranolol.
- Definite treatment is surgical.

Figure 18.22 shows an X-ray of a 14-year-old boy who was once admitted for polyarthritis 7–8 years back. He was advised some regular treatment that he defaulted. The child had complaints of effort intolerance, cough for 6 months, and nocturnal breathlessness for 2 months.

X-ray given in Figure 18.22 shows dilatation of pulmonary artery seen as prominent pulmonary conus with bulge at left atrial appendage causing straightening of left cardiac border. This area is normally concave. This is seen in mitral stenosis.

- Patients with mitral stenosis clinically have breathlessness on exertion, cough, orthopnea, and paroxysmal nocturnal dyspnea. On examination, they have tapping apex, loud P2, mid-diastolic rumbling murmur with presystolic accentuation, and opening snap.
- Left atrial enlargement is the early sign of mitral stenosis causing straightening of left heart border.
- Treatment is by balloon mitral valvotomy or valvuloplasty.

  Patients with rheumatic fever or rheumatic heart disease need penicillin prophylaxis, commonly benzathine penicillin.

Abdominal X-Rays

Figure 18.23 shows an invertogram that is done in case of imperforate anus to look for the level of intestinal gas it reaches. A radiopaque coin is placed at anus, the child is held inverted, and

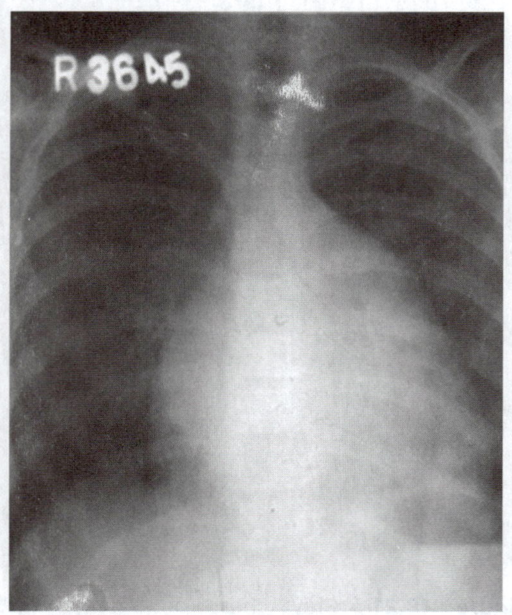

Figure 18.22 X-ray chest of a 14-year-old child.

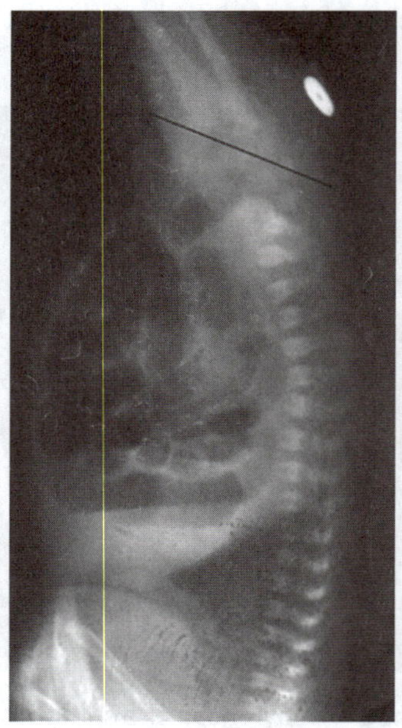

Figure 18.23 Invertogram.

X-ray is taken. It is taken usually after 18 hours to allow time for bowel gas to reach down. This X-ray shows absence of gas shadow in the anorectal region. It is likely to be high variety of anorectal malformation as there is no gas shadow below pubococcygeal line. Thus, this is a case of high variety of imperforate anus.

- This is a commonly missed congenital anomaly, which can be easily identified clinically at birth. All newborns must be examined at birth to look for patency of all orifices such as the anal canal.
- Mothers usually have polyhydramnios as in other cases of gastrointestinal tract obstruction and esophageal atresia.
- In a case of imperforate anus, one should look also for other anomalies as part of VACTERL (**v**ertebral anomalies, **a**nal atresia, **c**ardiac defects, **T**EF and/or **e**sophageal atresia, **r**enal and **r**adial anomalies, and **l**imb defects).
- Management is surgical, posterior sagittal anorectoplasty (PSARP), also called pull-through surgery. In certain high-variety cases, initially colostomy is done and later definitive repair is carried out.

Figure 18.24 shows an X-ray abdomen (standing) depicting multiple air–fluid levels suggestive of intestinal obstruction.

- Bilious vomiting or bilious gastric aspirates in any child should raise the possibility of intestinal obstruction. They are usually associated with constipation.
- Common causes of intestinal obstruction in children are obstruction due to adhesions following peritonitis or postoperative intussusception, congenital malrotation, atresia, and intestinal volvulus.
- It is an emergency condition requiring laparotomy and further management.

Figure 18.25 shows an abdominal X-ray film with a double bubble appearance in duodenal atresia due to the dilated stomach and the first part of the duodenum.

Figure 18.26 shows an X-ray abdomen of a newborn who developed vomiting and marked abdominal distension with poor peristalsis on day 5 of life.

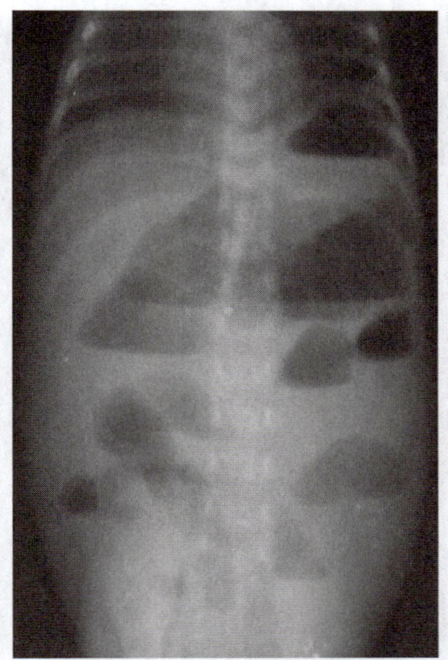

Figure 18.24 X-ray abdomen (in standing posture) of a child with bilious vomiting and constipation.

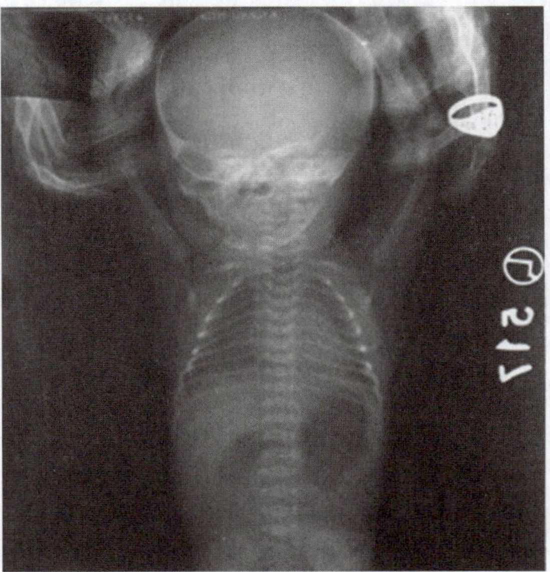

Figure 18.25 A newborn with bilious vomiting.

The X-ray abdomen (standing) shows dilated bowel loops, and there is presence of intramural gas (gas in the walls of the intestine,

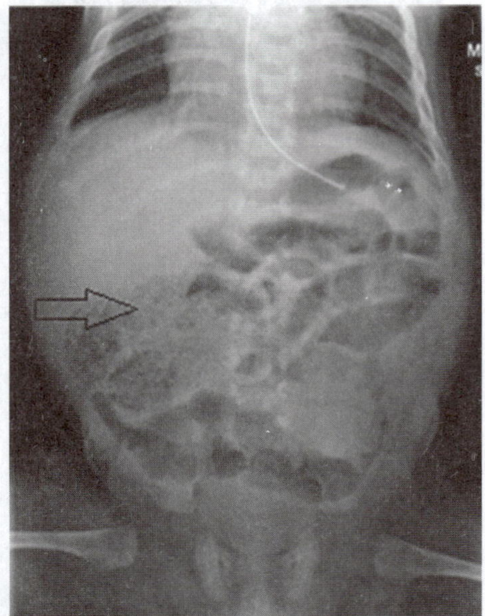

Figure 18.26 X-ray abdomen of a newborn with vomiting and abdominal distension.

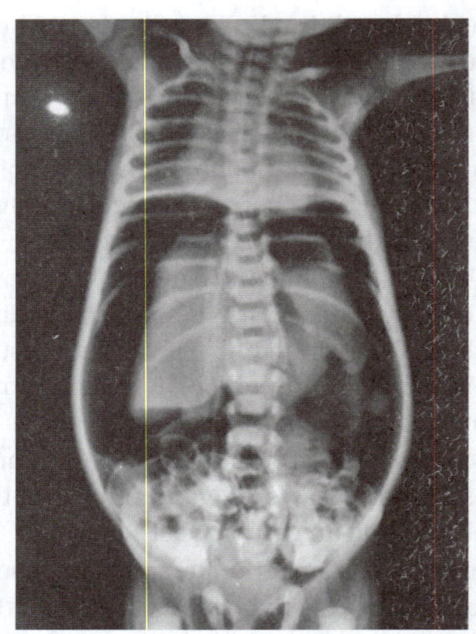

Figure 18.27 X-ray abdomen of a newborn with abdominal distension.

as shown by an arrow), which is suggestive of necrotizing enterocolitis (NEC).

- NEC is a known complication in preterm newborns.
- Risk factors for NEC are prematurity, hyperosmolar feeds, top feeds or formula feeds, septicemia, and bowel ischemia due to shock or perinatal asphyxia.
- Such babies clinically have feed intolerance such as high prefeed aspirates, abdominal distension, vomiting, and shiny skin over abdomen. They can also have apnea, lethargy, bradycardia, and hypothermia, so clinical picture resembles that of neonatal septicemia. In later stages, such babies can develop thrombocytopenia, bleeding, shock, acidosis, disseminated intravascular coagulation, and perforation of bowel.

Figure 18.27 shows an extensive presence of gas in the peritoneal cavity (pneumoperitoneum) in a newborn with NEC.

Figure 18.28 shows an X-ray abdomen (erect) in a 4-year-old child who had pain in abdomen and rigidity of the abdomen.

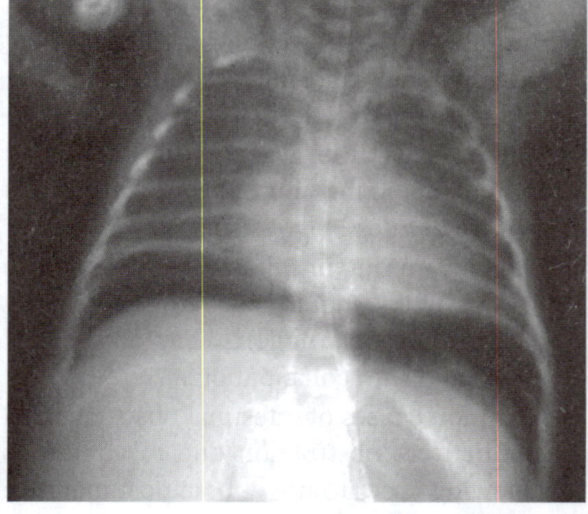

Figure 18.28 X-ray abdomen of a 4-year-old child with acute abdomen.

The X-ray abdomen in standing position shows the presence of gas under both the domes of diaphragm, which suggests pneumoperitoneum that is secondary to perforation in gastrointestinal tract.

- Common causes of perforation in gastrointestinal tract are ruptured appendix, enteric fever, NEC, trauma, and surgical complications.

- Clinically, such children present with acute abdomen, severe abdominal pain, and vomiting, and might develop shock.

Other Radiological Images

Figure 18.29 shows an X-ray film of a 15-month-old child, and Figure 18.30 shows a 10-month-old child who presented with wrist widening and frontoparietal bossing.

These X-rays show lower end of radius and ulna being concave (cupping). Normally, the lower end of long bones is a bit convex. There is break in continuity (fraying) and splaying at the lower end of radius and ulna. The distance between epiphysis and metaphysis is increased; there is generalized rarefaction (decreased in bone mineral density, manifesting as osteoporosis). These changes are suggestive of rickets. The increase in distance between epiphysis and metaphysis is due to loss of provisional zone of calcification.

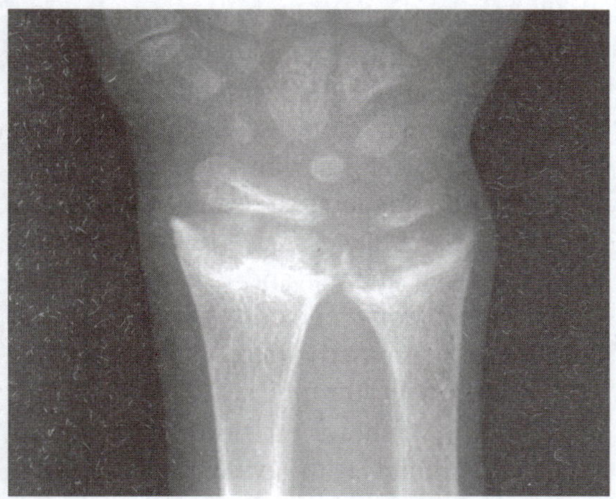

Figure 18.29 X-ray wrist in a 15-month-old child.

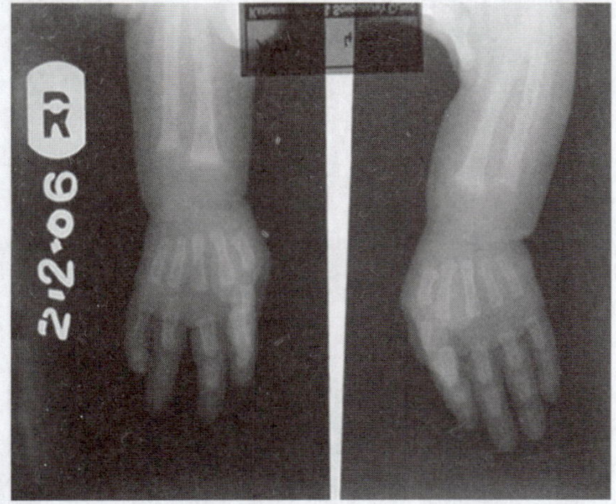

Figure 18.30 X-ray wrists in a 10-month-old child.

- The commonest form of rickets is nutritional rickets caused by vitamin D deficiency that causes nonmineralization of "growing bones." Rapidly growing bones of the body are commonly affected (wrists and knees).
- Sources: Fish oils, liver, egg yolk, milk, and fortified foods are main sources of vitamin D apart from sunlight.
- Vitamin D deficiency is increasingly common. Majority of the patients are asymptomatic. Clinical signs of rickets are frontoparietal bossing, wrist widening, bowing of legs, knock knees, coxa vara, delayed closure of anterior fontanelle, costochondral beading (rachitic rosary), Harrison's groove, pigeon chest, kyphoscoliosis, and pot belly abdomen.
- Diagnosis can be confirmed by estimation of vitamin D levels in blood.
- Treatment is conventionally given as 60,000 IU daily orally for 10 days. It can be given as single large dose of 6 lakh IU vitamin D either orally or IM (Stoss regimen).
- Changes of healing on X-ray are seen after 3–4 weeks.
- Causes of non-nutritional rickets are familial hypophosphatemic rickets, renal tubular acidosis, vitamin D–dependent rickets, and chronic kidney disease.

Figure 18.31 shows an X-ray knee joint of a 4-year-old child who presented with gum bleeding, and Figure 18.32 shows an X-ray of a 3-year-old child who presented with inability to move limbs due to severe pain.

These X-rays show changes seen in a child with scurvy. The changes seen are penciling

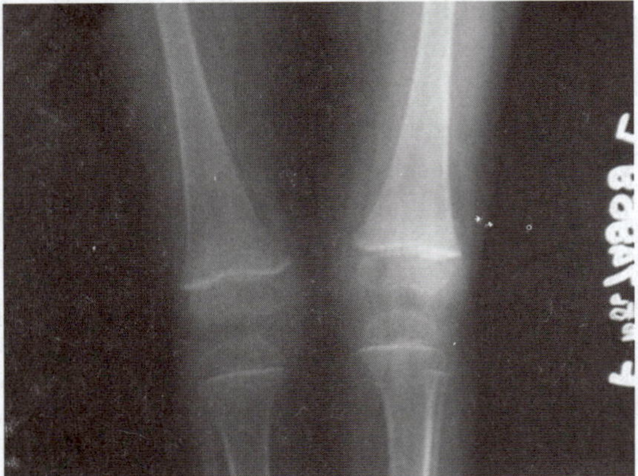

Figure 18.31 X-ray knee of a 4-year-old child with gum bleeding.

(thinning) of cortex and sharp outline of ring-shaped epiphysis (signet ring), with ground glass appearance (halo sign of Wimberger), white thick line at metaphysis (white line of Frenkel), Pelkan spur, subperiosteal hemorrhages (arrow, Figure 18.32), and increased Trummerfeld zone of lucency, and bones overall have ground glass appearance.

- Scurvy is caused by deficiency of vitamin C.

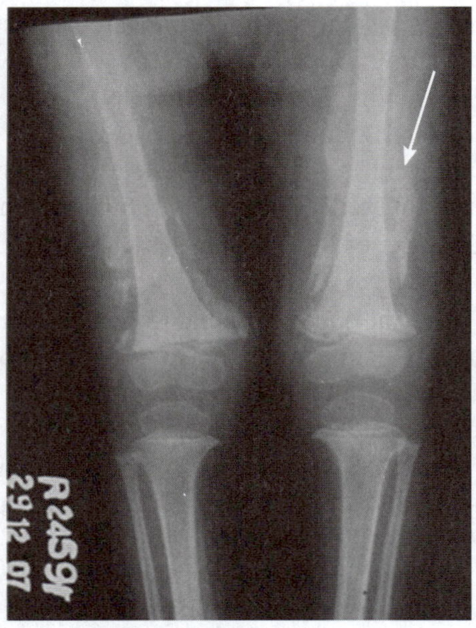

Figure 18.32 X-ray knee of a 3-year-old child with pseudoparalysis.

- Clinically, the child can present with irritability, gum bleeding, easy bruising, delayed wound healing, scorbutic rosary, and at times pseudoparalysis.
- Rachitic rosary versus scorbutic rosary: In rachitic rosary, the beads are semicircular, dome shaped, and nontender, while in scorbutic rosary, they are sharp, angular, and tender.
- Treatment is giving vitamin C orally, and there is dramatic response to treatment with vitamin C.
- Dietary sources rich in vitamin C are citrus fruits and vegetables including amla, lemon, oranges, and tomatoes. Leafy greens and germinating pulses also contain vitamin C.

Figure 18.33 shows a lateral view of an X-ray skull of a 5-year-old child with failure to thrive, chronic anemia, and hepatosplenomegaly. It shows typical hair-on-end appearance. Hair-on-end appearance can be seen in hemolytic anemias such as thalassemia and sickle cell anemia and can also be seen with chronic iron deficiency anemia. This is because of increased diploic spaces due to extramedullary erythropoiesis.

Figure 18.34 shows an X-ray skull (lateral view) of a child with evidence of chronic

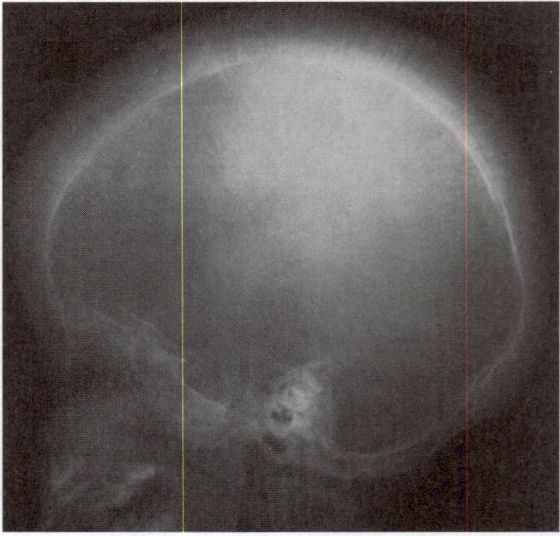

Figure 18.33 X-ray skull (lateral view) of a child with chronic anemia.

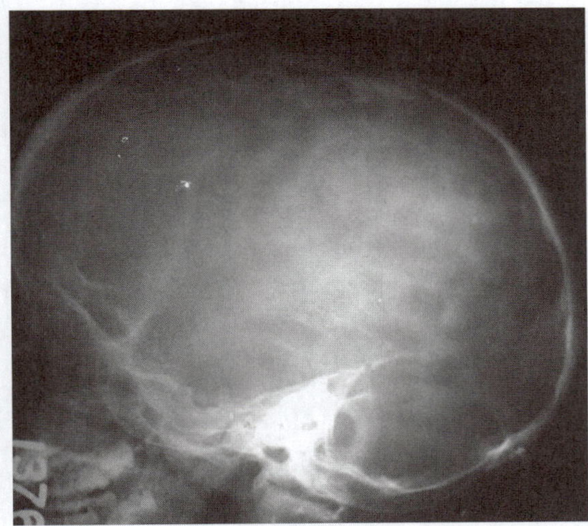

Figure 18.34 X-ray skull (lateral view) of a child with chronic headache.

increased intracranial pressure. The X-ray shows beaten copper appearance, also called beaten silver appearance, indicating possibility of conditions such as craniostenosis, obstructive hydrocephalus, and intracranial space-occupying lesion.

- Common causes for raised intracranial pressure in children include head trauma, CNS infections such as tuberculous or bacterial meningitis, intracranial space-occupying lesions, and/or hydrocephalous.
- Clinically, children with raised intracranial pressure will have complaints of headache and vomiting, and may have convulsions or alteration in sensorium. Signs include bradycardia, hypertension, irregular respiration (Cushing triad), tonic posturing, setting sun sign in eyes, papilledema on fundus, alteration of sensorium, and sixth cranial nerve palsy (false localizing sign).
- Neuroimaging is necessary for diagnosis and to find the cause.
- Aspiration of cerebrospinal fluid is contraindicated in conditions with raised intracranial pressure due to risk of herniation and sudden death.

Figure 18.35 shows an X-ray knee depicting absence of epiphysis of both femoral bones, which is normally present in a full-term newborn. This finding is suggestive of delayed maturation of bone. With the clinical background of coarse facies and umbilical hernia, this is very much likely due to hypothyroidism.

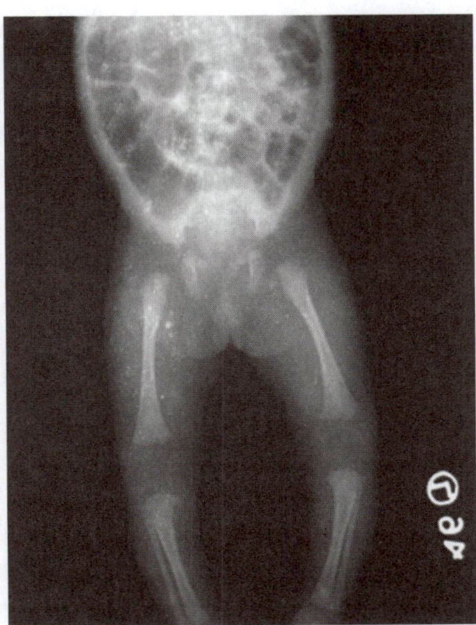

Figure 18.35 X-ray knee joint of a newborn with umbilical hernia and coarse facial features.

- Clinically, congenital hypothyroidism presents with coarse facies, umbilical hernia, persistent unconjugated hyperbilirubinemia, hypotonia, open posterior fontanelle, and developmental retardation.

Figure 18.36 shows a contrast study of micturating cystourethrography (MCUG). It shows dilated bladder and reflux in ureters and calyces on both sides. Ureters and calyces are grossly and bilaterally dilated (bilateral hydronephrosis and bilateral hydroureter). This indicates possibility of obstruction beyond the level of bladder, the commonest cause being posterior urethral valve in a male child leading to vesicoureteric reflux (VUR).

- The causes of bilateral hydronephrosis are posterior urethral valve, bilateral pelviureteric junction obstruction, stricture urethra, severe meatal stenosis, or phimosis.

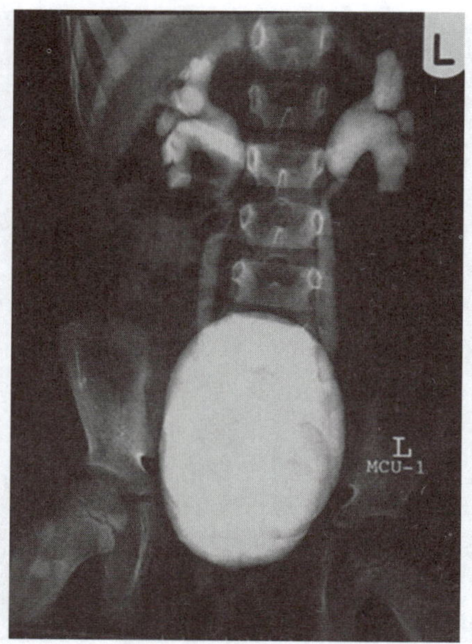

Figure 18.36 Contrast dye study in a child with recurrent urinary tract infection.

- The causes of unilateral hydronephrosis are unilateral pelviureteric junction obstruction, vesicoureteric junction obstruction, and unilateral obstruction due to calculi.

Figure 18.37 shows a neuroimaging film from a 4-year-old child who presented with a history of focal seizures.

This is a CT scan of brain with contrast showing ring-enhancing lesion in the left parietal region; there is presence of scolex inside favoring diagnosis of neurocysticercosis.

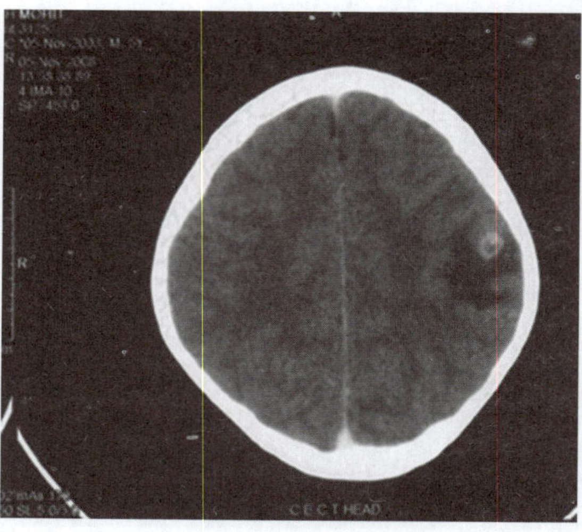

Figure 18.37 CT scan in a child with focal seizure.

The causes of ring-enhancing lesion in brain are tuberculoma, neurocysticercosis, fungal granuloma, and brain abscess. At times, it is difficult to differentiate tuberculoma from neurocysticercosis and it is very important as therapy would be different. Brain abscess usually is quite large and rarely causes confusion about the diagnosis. Few of the differences are listed in Table 18.1.

Figure 18.38 shows neuroimaging of a child with chronic meningitis (TB meningitis).

TABLE 18.1 Differences Between Tuberculoma and Neurocysticercosis

Neurocysticercosis	Tuberculoma
May be single but often multiple, may give rise to starry sky appearance	May be single or multiple but even if more than one, they are usually few
Scolex may be found within the ring, which is more likely to be picked up by MRI compared with CT	There is no scolex
Perilesional edema may or may not be present; even if it is present, it is unlikely to cause midline shift	Perilesional edema usually quite significant and may cause midline shift
Rings are smaller and have thinner walls	Rings are larger and have thicker walls
Basal exudates are not present	There may be presence of basal exudates
Usually supratentorial in location	Not necessary
More common in nonvegetarians, however can occur in vegetarians also	History of contact with patient of tuberculosis, other evidence of tuberculosis such as Mantoux test can be found

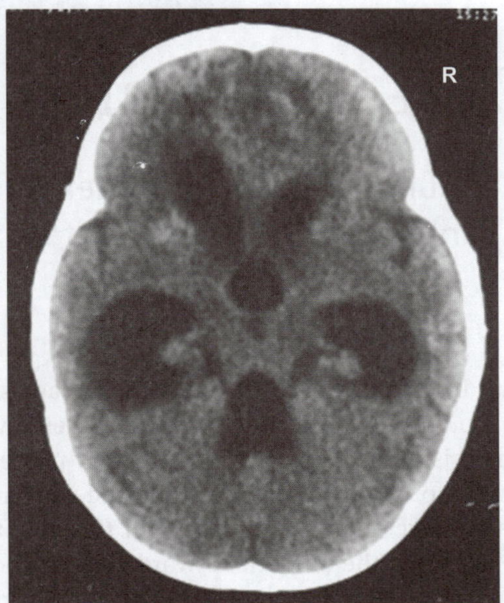

Figure 18.38 Postmeningitic hydrocephalous.

This CT scan image with contrast of brain shows moderate dilatation of frontal horns, bilateral temporal horns, and occipital horn of ventricles in brain. It also shows enhancement with contrast, suggesting the possibility of meningoencephalitis with postmeningitic hydrocephalus.

- Common causes of meningitis in children are bacterial meningitis and tubercular meningitis. Apart from this, it can be due to viral causes and, less commonly, fungal and amoebic causes in immunocompromised hosts. Cryptococcal meningitis caused by fungus *Cryptococcus neoformans* is seen in children with HIV/AIDS.
  - Clinically, a child with acute meningitis presents with high fever, vomiting, headache, later convulsions and altered sensorium, signs of meningeal irritation, signs of raised intracranial pressure, and focal neurological signs such as cranial nerve palsies and motor deficits. Focal neurological signs and hydrocephalus are more common with tuberculous meningitis. Tuberculous meningitis is commoner in children compared with in adults.

KEY POINTS

- Conventional X-rays and other imaging modalities are now essential tools in the diagnosis and treatment of children's diseases.
- The imaging procedures must be carefully considered and ordered so that they provide maximum benefit to the patients and help to answer a medical question, help in the management of the disease condition, and/or guide an invasive procedure (e.g., an ultrasound-aided kidney biopsy). All the imaging studies need to be correlated and interpreted with reference to the given clinical context.
- The analysis and interpretation of the radiological images should be a systematic approach with a careful observation and the search for pathology be deferred to the last till the basic preliminaries are completed.

CHAPTER 19

Clinical Case Scenarios

Niranjan Shendurnikar, Bakul B Javadekar,
Mukesh K Singh, Pankaj Agrawal, Sarah Morton

This chapter presents common clinical cases seen in pediatrics and outlines a systematic approach to the history, its initial analysis, clinical examination, inference and diagnosis, investigations, and principles of management. Common conditions are discussed, and an attempt is made to relate the importance of each component to reach a justifiable clinical diagnosis in a simplified and an easy-to-understand manner. Only the common conditions are included, and the approach is based on the child's presenting symptoms rather than any specific condition to avoid any bias in the diagnosis. The students are advised to go through the cases, attempt their own analysis after each section, and then proceed ahead to completely understand the case and its management. The objective of this chapter is to orient the students toward an analytical clinical approach and learn to analyze, interpret, and diagnose the symptomatology and clinical examination in a proper context. Each case scenario is followed by a brief discussion about the interpretation, provisional diagnosis, and practical insights about the clinical approach and case management.

Case 1: A Child with a Low-Grade Fever, Loose Stools, and Weight Loss

A 1.5-year-old girl child was brought to the hospital with complaints of low-grade fever for about 1 month, not eating well, and loose stools for the previous 15–20 days. The mother also noticed that the child appeared to have lost weight over the past 1 month and was appearing less active since the beginning of the illness. The family was socioeconomically poor.

On enquiry, the parents revealed that the child was a full term born to a gravida 3 mother with birth weight of 2 kg. She was started on breastfeeding on the third day of life before which she was fed with "batasa water," a kind of sugar solution. Afterwards, even as she was being breastfed, she was given water with a bottle to quench her thirst according to the parents. The mother had continued to breastfeed the child till now. The child was introduced to the semisolid diet at the age of about 8–9 months in the form of thin gruel made of wheat twice a day along with an occasional fruit such as banana.

The child was given two doses of DPT (Diphtheria, Pertussis, and Tetanus vaccine), hepatitis B vaccine (HBV), and oral polio vaccine (OPV) earlier but was not immunized subsequently with further doses. There was no record of the weight over the past few months, but the parents did notice that the child was not growing well in the past few months and had in fact seemed to have lost some weight in the past few days. There was a history of contact with tuberculosis in the neighborhood.

Analysis

- The presence of low-grade fever and weight loss of 1 month is suggestive of a possibility of a chronic infective process. One of the common causes of such a fever in an infant and a young child may be progressive primary tuberculosis. The other causes of fever in such a child may include a urinary tract infection, persistent diarrhea, occult middle ear infection, or chronic malaria.
- The fact that the child was a low-birth-weight (small-for-date) baby with incomplete immunization, improper and inadequate weaning, and mismanaged feeding poses an additional hazard to the health of the child. The child in view of incomplete immunization is at a particular risk of developing whooping cough and/or measles, which would further compromise the nutritional status of the child.
- A contact with tuberculosis in such a child is an important risk factor for the dissemination and severe forms of childhood tuberculosis.
- As there was no past record of the child's previous weight data, important opportunities for growth monitoring were missed to initiate early treatment interventions.
- Presence of diarrhea in this child may be due to intercurrent gastrointestinal tract infections or due to secondary lactose intolerance due to atrophy of intestinal villi. The associated deficiencies of vitamins and minerals with vitamin A in particular need to be considered in the context of the present illness.

Clinical Examination

- On examination, the child was conscious but lethargic. She weighed 5 kg; the length was 64 cm, head circumference 43 cm, and midarm circumference (MAC) 10.5 cm. As per the WHO classification, the child was falling in the category of severe wasting (<3SD weight for height) and severe stunting (<3SD height for age). The wasting grade and MAC placed her in the category of severe acute malnutrition (SAM).
- As per the IAP (Indian Academy of Pediatrics) classification, she was underweight and PEM (protein energy malnutrition) grade IV.
- General examination revealed sunken eyes, poor skin turgor, some pallor, angular stomatitis, severe visible wasting, cold extremities, poor capillary refill of >3 seconds, axillary temperature of 34.5°C, feeble and fast pulse, low blood pressure, and signs of vitamin A deficiency in the form of Bitot's spots.
- There was no fast breathing or chest indrawing. There was no pedal edema. Anterior fontanel was closed and there was no clubbing or cyanosis.
- Systemic examination did not reveal anything significant.

Inference and Diagnosis

The child had *SAM and severe dehydration* as per Integrated Management of Neonatal and Childhood Illness (IMNCI) guidelines. A child with severe wasting (weight for height/length less than $-3Z$ score or less than 70% of expected) or severe stunting (height for age less than $-3Z$ score or less than 85% of expected) is also considered to have severe malnutrition.

The other associated morbidities were vitamin A deficiency, nutritional anemia, shock, and probable sepsis. Children with severe malnutrition are known to be immunosuppressed, weak, and wasted and may not show clinical signs of infections. Thus, systemic infections cannot be ruled out clinically.

Investigations

Besides the routine investigations such as complete blood count (CBC) and urine microscopy, specific investigations to look for systemic infections such as blood culture and sensitivity, and urine culture and sensitivity should be ordered. X-ray chest may display consolidation even without clinical signs. Besides this, serum electrolyte to look for sodium, potassium, and bicarbonate disturbances should be ordered. Screening for tuberculosis should be done. Blood glucose should be done to rule out hypoglycemia.

The child's hemoglobin was 8.3 g% with MCV (mean corpuscular volume) 64 fL, RDW (red cell distribution width) 15%, TWBC (total white blood cell count) 11,000/mm^3, and blood culture sterile after 48 hours. The blood indices were suggestive of the presence of associated nutritional anemia due to iron deficiency. Urine routine and microscopy was also normal. There was evidence of hyponatremia and acidosis and X-ray chest showed no evidence of pneumonia or progressive primary tuberculosis. Mantoux test was negative.

Principles of Management

- The basic aim of the therapy of severe malnutrition is to reduce the mortality and accelerate the recovery and thus as per the guidelines of the WHO, the management should proceed sequentially in 10 steps. Thus, standard inpatient management of SAM involves two phases:
    1. Initial stabilization when life-threatening complications are treated. The management of hypoglycemia, hypothermia, infection, septic shock, electrolyte imbalance, dehydration, and the deficiencies of iron, vitamins, and other minerals forms Steps 1–6.
    2. Steps 7–10 are related to the dietary treatment and the nutritional rehabilitation when catch-up growth occurs, in the form of beginning of the feeding, energy-dense feeding, emotional and sensorial development, and subsequently transfer to home-based diets before the discharge in the rehabilitation phase.
- Children with severe malnutrition and without complications are managed on an ambulatory basis that promotes and provides ready-to-use therapeutic foods (RUTF). These RUTF are soft and crushable foods that can be consumed by the children from the age of 6 months and above without adding water. These foods can be safely used at home even without refrigeration.

Key Messages

- The assessment of the general condition of the child and the classification of the nutritional status are the initial steps to approach the child with malnutrition.
- The associated morbidities and the complications must be identified, and the treatment begun in a sequential manner.
- The nutritional rehabilitation and the treatment of micronutrient deficiencies must be continued after the discharge. The diet offered at home should be wholesome and nutritious, and should provide enough calories and proteins for the child's development.
- At home, the child should be referred to the community-based program, i.e., Village Child Nutrition Centre (VCNC), and should attend this center for a few hours during the daytime. If this is not available, at least anganwadi worker (AWW) or accredited social health activist (ASHA) workers should be kept in the loop for follow-up (every 2 weeks in the first months and subsequently monthly) of these babies till they lose all their wasting and become normal weight for height. This usually takes 4–6 weeks but may take longer.

Case 2: A 15-Month-Old Child with Delayed Complementary Feeding and Pica

A 15-month-old boy was brought to the hospital for mild fever and runny nose for 3–4 days. There were no other complaints. However, on asking retrospectively, the mother did inform that the child was not as playful as before, but no breathlessness or other complaint was noticed. He was a full-term newborn baby with birth weight 2.8 kg born to a gravida 2 mother out of nonconsanguineous marriage. There was no significant past and family history but there was a history of pica (clay/soil) and he had received his immunizations up to DPT, HBV, and OPV, three doses. He had not received his 9-month-scheduled measles vaccine.

The child had received exclusive breastfeed till the age of 7–8 months and was given complementary feeds in the form of about 600–700 mL of cow milk, diluted rice/pulse cereal, and occasional fruit juice. The family belonged to Class III of the modified Kuppuswami classification for socioeconomic status. The child had a normal motor and mental development.

Analysis

- The child had only minor symptoms suggestive of viral illness (fever and runny nose) of a short duration. The presence of pica (which means a persistent craving and compulsive eating of nonfood substances) is a pointer toward associated nutritional deficiency.
- A noncontributory personal and family history of affected siblings, blood loss, and transfusions is an important point to be considered along with the history of pica. The dietary history is suggestive of an excess intake of animal milk with lack of energy-dense foods.
- The delayed introduction of semisolid foods at 7–8 months of age puts the child at risk of developing both macronutrient and micronutrient deficiencies. If the child consumes excess amount of milk in the diet, the child is not sufficiently hungry to eat the semisolid/solid food.
- His not receiving the measles/MMR immunization at 9 completed months of age puts him at risk of measles infection along with its potential complications such as malnutrition and vitamin A deficiency.

Clinical Examination

The weight of the child was 9.2 kg (≤1SD), length 72 cm, and head circumference 45 cm. The heart rate (HR) was 116/min, respiratory rate (RR) was 34/min, and temperature was normal. The anterior fontanel measured 1 × 1 cm and there was no lymphadenopathy, jaundice, rash, pigmentation, edema, and/or clubbing. There was severe pallor noticed on the palms and the mucous membranes and the tongue was smooth. The liver was 3.5 cm and soft with a span of 7.5 cm, but there was no splenomegaly. Rest of the clinical examination was normal.

Inference and Diagnosis

The history of delayed introduction of complementary feeding, excess milk intake with complaints of pica, and severe pallor along with the absence of significant hepatosplenomegaly points to the diagnosis of *nutritional anemia (iron deficiency anemia [IDA])*, noted incidentally on the child's visit to the hospital for a minor ailment. Pica is the most important symptom of nutritional anemia in infants and young children, although it is also seen in children with mental retardation. It results from the altered brain functions owing to iron deficiency due to lack of iron at cellular levels.

A gradual onset of the iron deficiency and anemia may not produce any symptoms on a long-term basis unless the child develops a severe intercurrent illness that can lead to hemodynamic instability. Parents may fail to notice pallor and anemia; it may be coincidentally detected on clinical examination.

The most vulnerable age for the development of nutritional IDA is between the ages of 6 months and 3 years as the diet may be insufficient to meet the iron demands of the growing child along with the dietary lack of iron in the child's diet. In the absence of any major past illness, blood transfusions, and splenomegaly, other possibilities such as congenital hemolytic anemias (e.g., thalassemia major) are less likely. Mild hepatomegaly is a known feature of IDA. Other causes of anemia with such a presentation can include anemia due to ongoing/occult blood loss (cow milk protein allergy), certain infections in the past (e.g., malaria), anemia due to lead poisoning, and congenital and acquired red cell aplasia. Folate and vitamin B_{12} deficiency may be coexistent with IDA.

Investigations

The child's hemoglobin was 5.4 g/dL, with MCV of 64 fL, MCH (mean corpuscular hemoglobin) 18 pg, and RDW of 16.5%. The peripheral smear showed the presence of hypochromia and microcytosis and the serum ferritin done later after the febrile illness was <10 ng/mL (decreased). The test for stool occult blood was negative. Low MCV with an increased RDW along with low serum ferritin confirmed the diagnosis of IDA in the child.

Principles of Management

- Most of the children with nutritional IDA can be treated with dietary advice and oral iron supplementation.
- Response to the adequate dose and therapy should be monitored and failure to respond should lead to suspicion of other causes of anemia or any continued occult blood loss (e.g., due to worm infestations).
- Low-birth-weight babies should be supplemented with oral iron (3–6 mg/kg/day) beginning from the age of 4–6 weeks.
- Iron therapy needs to be continued for 3 months after the blood values have returned to the normal to replenish the iron stores in the body.
- Blood transfusion of packed cell volume (PCV) is rarely indicated in IDA unless the anemia is severe (Hb <4 g/dL) or the child is in congestive heart failure or if any severe infection is likely to interfere with the therapeutic medicinal response.

Key Messages

- Nutritional iron deficiency is the most common cause of anemia in children.
- The most common age for IDA is between 6 months and 3 years.
- IDA does not have associated organomegaly. Presence of splenomegaly in case of anemia usually points to hemolytic etiology.
- Promotion of supplementary foods rich in iron with the starting of complementary feeding is an effective prevention strategy for IDA.

Case 3: A 12-Month-Old Baby with Delayed Development and Unusual Features

A 12-month-old girl child who had not learnt to sit and stand was brought to the outpatient department with complaints of fever, cough, and noisy breathing since the past 2 days. The baby was born to a gravida 3 mother with two previous healthy children and her birth weight was 2.7 kg. There was no history of consanguinity and the mother's age was 30 years. The baby had a history of prolonged neonatal jaundice up to 3 weeks of age that subsided after the treatment with phototherapy.

There was a history of two earlier episodes of fever and cough (at the age of 6 and 10 months), which were treated on ambulatory basis. She was given a diagnosis of pneumonia and treated with antibiotics for 7 days in earlier episodes. An echocardiography was performed at 6 months of age and the parents were informed about her having a congenital heart disease (a hole in the heart) with a need for 6-monthly follow-up. The mother informed that the baby is a playful child but appeared loose and weak while handling and changing her clothes. She was unaware about any abnormal facial features till the baby was 6 months old and till she became ill for the first time. The baby's hearing and vision were reported to be normal by the parents.

Analysis

- The important points to be noted in the history are suggestive of delayed motor development as a child who does not sit unsupported by 9 months and stand independently by 12 months raises a concern about delayed development.
- The earlier episodes of fever, cough, and noisy breathing are important contributors to the history (recurrent pneumonia) due to an increased susceptibility to infections, which is possibly due to her underlying congenital heart disease as diagnosed at 6 months of age.
- The history of prolonged neonatal jaundice is also an important point to be considered in view of her development.
- Her unusual facial/dysmorphic features should offer helpful clues to the clinical diagnosis.

Clinical Examination

The child was weighing 7.5 kg, her length was 70 cm, and head circumference was 42 cm (<2SD). The temperature was 38°C, HR 100/min, and RR 44/min, and she was alert. She had an upslanted palpebral fissure (mongoloid slant), flat occiput, anterior fontanel of 3.5 × 3.5 cm, epicanthic fold (a fold of skin running across the inner margin of the palpebral fissure), depressed nasal bridge, protruding tongue, short neck, broad and small hands, clinodactyly of the fifth finger, single palmar crease, and sandal gap (increased distance) between the first and second toes. There was no cyanosis and clubbing.

The neurological examination showed generalized hypotonia and cardiovascular examination revealed the presence of grade 3/6 pansystolic murmur suggestive of ventricular septal defect (VSD). Rest of the examination was normal.

Inference and Diagnosis

The history and the examination show characteristic manifestations of Down syndrome (trisomy 21) along with the presence of a congenital acyanotic heart disease and delayed motor and mental development. The child's two previous episodes of recurrent respiratory infections were due to left-to-right shunt and due to an increased susceptibility to the infections.

As children with Down syndrome may have associated hearing impairment (due to secretory otitis media), visual impairments (cataract and squint), and hypothyroidism, a hearing assessment (brainstem evoked response audiometry [BERA]), ophthalmic evaluation, and thyroid screen are indicated. They should also be subjected to a formal assessment for their motor and mental development to plan their therapy for stimulation and development.

Investigations

The child's X-ray chest showed a left upper zone pneumonia. The thyroid profile showed increased thyroid-stimulating hormone (TSH) levels of 8.7 mIU/mL and low T4 level suggestive of hypothyroidism. The periodic evaluation of thyroid functions and other medical or surgical problems must continue throughout the childhood. Hearing and visual assessment was normal and developmental evaluation revealed a delay in mental and motor development.

The cytogenetic study confirmed Down syndrome (trisomy 21) with an extra chromosome as nondisjunction, which is the most common pattern of transmission.

Principles of Management

- The child was treated with oral antibiotics for pneumonia and also started on 25 µg of thyroxine once daily for hypothyroidism.
- There is no standard treatment for Down syndrome. Treatments are based on the individual's physical and intellectual needs as well as his or her personal strengths and limitations.
- Children with Down syndrome need an early intervention from a multidisciplinary team of professionals, which may include special educators, speech therapists, occupational therapists, physical therapists, and social workers.
- Prenatal diagnosis tests are available particularly with the risk of recurrence in the next pregnancy and genetic counseling must be offered to the family.

Key Messages

- Down syndrome is the most common chromosomal disorder and the most common genetic cause of mental retardation.
- Counseling, parent support, and a multidisciplinary team approach are the best modalities for management in the long term.

Case 4: A 4-Year-Old Boy Child with Short Stature

A 4-year-old boy was brought to the outpatient department with the complaint that he appeared short as compared with other children of his age. This was noticed when the child was admitted to a nursery school. The boy did not have any other complaints. He was a normal full-term newborn with a birth weight of 2.6 kg and was discharged from the hospital on the third day. He received all the immunizations on time and was fully immunized. The dietary and developmental history was also normal, and he had not suffered from any major illnesses since birth. There were no abnormal facial or limb features reported. As there was concern about his height, the parents brought him for checkup. The father, aged 27 years, on detailed inquiry gave a history of delayed onset of puberty and then accelerated gain in height.

Analysis

- The parents' concern about the child's height being less as per their perception will have to be properly addressed with appropriate growth monitoring and investigations so that a treatable cause is not missed.
- As no abnormal dysmorphic features were reported, there does not seem to be a likelihood of possible short stature being caused by skeletal dysplasia (e.g., achondroplasia) or dysmorphic syndromes (e.g. Down and Russell–Silver syndromes).
- Absence of chronic symptoms such as chronic diarrhea, constipation, polyuria, polydipsia, dullness, frequent lower respiratory infections, jaundice, chronic anemia, and cyanosis primarily at this stage suggests no underlying chronic and systemic conditions (e.g., chronic kidney diseases) causing his current symptom.

Clinical Examination

The examination showed that the boy was playful and the vital signs were normal including BP, which was 92/54 mmHg. The weight was 16 kg (at the 50th centile) and height was 91.2 cm (between –2SD and –3SD). The head circumference was appropriate for age and there were no abnormal physical features. The upper to lower segment ratio was 1.3:1. The limb length and limb and trunk proportions were normal. The father's height was 170 cm and the mother's height was 158 cm. Rest of the examination was normal.

Inference and Diagnosis

As the body and limb proportions of the boy are normal, causes of disproportionate short stature such as achondroplasia and mucopolysaccharidoses are excluded. Additionally, his normal upper to lower segment ratio also excludes short limb dwarfism.

Absence of features of any systemic and chronic illnesses and the weight being normal also exclude chronic systemic diseases as the likely cause of his being short.

The boy thus has a proportionate short stature as his height is below –2SD score for his age. This pattern is seen in malabsorption, chronic infections (e.g., tuberculosis), congenital heart diseases, renal failure, and endocrinal diseases (except hypothyroidism).

If the child with short stature is also thin and wasted, then it is likely to be due to an underlying systemic disease, but if he/she appears fat and short, then it is due to an endocrine condition causing short stature.

The history of father who had a delayed puberty offers a useful clue to the diagnosis for the short stature of this child. The clinical diagnosis is *constitutional growth delay (CGD)*. As the parents are of a normal height, familial/genetic short stature is excluded. Although children with growth hormone deficiency also have delayed puberty, the growth retardation is more severe (≤3SD).

Investigations

The evaluation should exclude chronic and systemic causes of short stature and growth velocity should be serially monitored, which should be 5 cm/year in this child (between the ages of 4 and 8 years). He had a normal thyroid profile. Any female child even in the absence of typical features of Turner syndrome needs to be evaluated to exclude this condition. This child had a delayed bone age on wrist X-ray, which confirmed the diagnosis of CGD.

Principles of Management

- If there is any underlying cause, it should be treated. But as this child does not have any underlying disease, he should be advised a diet rich in proteins and high in calories. Any underlying vitamin and mineral deficiency must be corrected.
- Serial growth monitoring is an essential tool so that the child follows his percentile curves and does not show any abnormal deviation from it.
- Catch-up growth, onset of puberty, and pubertal growth spurt are expected to occur later than average, resulting in a normal adult stature and sexual development.

Key Messages

- CGD represents a condition causing short stature with delayed maturation but with intact growth potential.
- All the children with short stature need a close follow-up and serial growth monitoring to judge the response of therapy (when needed) and to ensure catch-up growth.

Case 5: An 8-Year-Old Child with Abdominal Distension and Jaundice

An 8-year-old male child presented with complaints of abdominal pain and distension, vomiting, decreased oral intake, and anorexia with increasing jaundice and passing dark-colored urine over the past 1 month. The symptoms were progressively getting worse since the onset 1 month back. Since the past few days, he also started complaining about itching all over the body. He had no complaints of diarrhea, fever, or bleeding from any site. He had no complaints of swelling over the body or puffiness of face. There was no past history of recurrent jaundice, drug intake, or blood transfusions.

The family history was noncontributory. There was no major illness reported in the past and the child's dietary, immunization, and developmental history was normal.

There was no family history of chronic liver disease.

Analysis

- The child has a gradual onset of abdominal pain, vomiting, reduced appetite, and increasing jaundice, which are likely pointers to a gastrointestinal and possible liver disease.
- As the onset is subacute and there is no history of fever, an infective illness (e.g., viral hepatitis) involving liver parenchyma and causing its inflammation is less likely. Also, as the child has received his full earlier immunization including HBV, this should not be a hepatitis B infection.
- His abdominal pain may be a pointer to the progressive enlargement of liver/spleen particularly in the presence of an increasing jaundice, which is likely to be caused by a liver disease.

Clinical Examination

The clinical examination showed a weight of 23 kg and a height of 118 cm. The pulse rate was 100/min, RR 28/min, and BP 100/68 mmHg. The child was hemodynamically stable. He had deep tinge of jaundice in the eyes, with pallor but no signs of vitamin A deficiency. Scratch marks were present on his body. There was no cyanosis, clubbing, edema over feet, or palmar erythema. The presence of severe itching in this child is strongly indicative of cholestasis.

The abdominal examination showed a visible distension but no prominent or dilated veins over the abdominal wall. There was an enlarged liver 5 cm below the costal margin, firm, nontender with a well-defined margin. The liver span was 13 cm. The spleen measured 4 cm beyond the costal margin and was firm in consistency. Shifting dullness was suggestive of free fluid (mild ascites). Rest of the systemic examination including central nervous system (CNS) was normal.

The child was admitted to the hospital and was investigated for hepatosplenomegaly with jaundice and anemia. He received PCV transfusion and supportive therapy.

Inference and Diagnosis

Collaborating the history and the clinical findings, the child is a case of hepatosplenomegaly with jaundice with no significant past history. As discussed earlier, the onset and course of the disease does not favor the diagnosis of infectious causes of hepatitis but viral hepatitis (e.g., hepatitis B and C) can have a similar onset. Besides, absence of any fever and no illness in another family member or in the vicinity goes against the diagnosis of acute viral hepatitis (e.g., hepatitis A and E).

No history of exposure to toxins or drugs such as acetaminophen, isoniazid (INH), rifampicin, and anticonvulsants rules out toxic hepatitis. Other causes that can complicate hepatitis or can have hepatic involvement such as *Salmonella*, malaria, and liver abscess need to be ruled out. But absence of significant fever is against these infections. Chronic hemolytic anemia is excluded in view of decompensating liver disease (firm hepatomegaly with ascites) and absence of any past history of blood transfusions.

The clinical course and the findings are suggestive of chronic liver disease in the child, which results from long-term damage to the liver cell parenchyma from many causes that may include infective (hepatitis B, C, D), autoimmune (autoimmune hepatitis), and metabolic (e.g., Wilson disease [excess copper deposits], alpha-1-antitrypsin deficiency) causes, cystic fibrosis, and hemochromatosis. It must be remembered that these conditions, though chronic, can have an acute viral hepatitis–like onset. These have potential to develop into a chronicity leading to irreversible liver damage and cirrhosis. The final diagnosis needs to be confirmed by a battery of further investigations.

Investigations

These should include CBC with indices, peripheral smear, reticulocyte count, liver function tests (LFT) with serum proteins, prothrombin time (PT), international normalized ratio (INR), activated partial thromboplastin time (aPTT), and viral markers. These are likely to be abnormal in chronic liver disease. The final diagnosis is established by the liver biopsy.

Hemoglobin was 8.2 g%, and leukocytosis 20,670/cm with absolute neutrophilia. The peripheral smear showed macrocytosis and hypersegmented neutrophils. The reticulocyte count was 10% and this raised count suggested an ongoing hemolysis.

LFT showed total serum bilirubin of 18.8 mg% (direct 12 mg% and indirect 6.8 mg%). SGPT was 550 units/L and SGOT 170 units/L. Serum proteins were total 5.7 g (albumin, 2.3 g; and globulin, 3.4 g). PT was 41.7 seconds, INR 3.58, and aPTT 87.7 seconds. Serum alpha-fetoprotein was normal. Viral markers/antibodies for hepatitis B and C virus were negative.

The copper studies were found to be abnormal. Serum ceruloplasmin was 8.4 mg/dL (20–60 mg/dL normal). Twenty-four-hour urinary copper excretion was raised and abnormal (970.7 mg/L). Its normal range is 2–80 mg/L.

The ultrasonography of hepatobiliary system showed coarsened echo texture of liver with nodular surface and splenomegaly with ascites. There was no evidence of portosystemic collaterals.

The slit lamp examination of the eye did not find Kayser–Fleischer ring.

The final diagnosis was confirmed on liver biopsy as *Wilson disease* (an autosomal recessive metabolic disorder of copper deposition leading to excess copper deposition in liver, brain, kidney, and cornea).

Principles of Management

- Children with chronic liver disease need nutritional management in the form of high energy and moderate protein intake for growth (except during encephalopathy). Consider intragastric feeding if severe anorexia is present. There should be provision of adequate essential fatty acids, fat-soluble vitamins (A, D, E, K), zinc, iron, calcium, and sodium.
- Adequate dose of vitamin K and fresh frozen plasma may be required if acute episode of bleeding or coagulopathy is present.
- Pruritis causes significant morbidity. Ursodeoxycholic acid can be used and is the treatment of choice.
- The mainstay of therapy for Wilson disease is pharmacologic treatment with chelating agents such as D-penicillamine. Zinc salts act as inductors of metallothionein, which favor a negative copper balance and a reduction of free plasmatic copper.
- Evaluation and management for portal hypertension, endoscopy, and timely recognition and treatment of the complications are also crucial.
- Liver transplant is considered for children with acute liver cell failure or severe end-stage liver cell disease.

Key Messages

- A gradual onset of abdominal distension, appetite changes, and progressive jaundice is a useful pointer to a possibility of chronic liver diseases in children.
- Though chronic, many of the chronic liver diseases may present clinically like an acute hepatic viral infection.
- A timely diagnosis, assessment of degree of hepatic dysfunctions, prevention and treatment of complications, and supportive and specific therapy are essential steps of management.

Case 6: An 8-Month-Old Infant with Increasing Pallor for 1 Month

An 8-month-old infant girl was noticed by her parents to have increasing pallor since the past 1 month. She was apparently asymptomatic before this observation made by her parents except that the parents informed that she appeared dull looking since then. There was no past history of any acute or chronic illness, blood loss, jaundice, or breathlessness.

The infant was a normal newborn at birth and born of a second-degree consanguineous marriage. The breastfeeding was continued, and the complementary feeds were added at the age of 5 months along with multivitamins and hematinics by their general practitioner. The infant had one elder sibling (brother), 4 years old, who was reported asymptomatic and there was no relevant past and family history. Her immunization and developmental status was normal.

Analysis

- The noticeable pallor without any other associated symptoms such as irritability and breathlessness, which would have suggested cardiac decompensation, indicates that this anemia has developed slowly over a period of weeks to months. If it was acute and short in onset, the child may have gone into cardiac failure due to rapid fall of hemoglobin.
- As her age matches with the usual age of manifestation of nutritional deficiency anemia (IDA), this possibility needs to be considered. However, a history of breastfeeding with addition of complementary feeding and

iron supplementation earlier do not suggest a diagnosis of IDA unless the child had an ongoing and occult blood loss.

- Thus, if the deficiency and blood loss is ruled out clinically, then the cause of anemia has to be either chronic hemolysis or bone marrow aplasia. The latter is an uncommon occurrence at this age.
- Her being born of a consanguineous marriage raises the possibility of it being a congenital hemolytic anemia.

Clinical Examination

The infant weighed 6.1 kg (between –1SD and –2SD) with a length of 63 cm and was not sick looking. Her HR was 144/min and RR was 36/min, and she appeared severely pale. Anterior fontanel was 2.5 × 2.5 cm, the head was normal, and there was no icterus and pigmentation. There were no petechiae, ecchymoses, or bleeding from any site. There was no lymphadenopathy, koilonychias, edema, and bony tenderness. The infant remained comfortable in her mother's lap.

The abdominal examination showed a protuberant abdomen with a liver of 4 cm in the right hypochondriac region. The liver was firm and nontender with a smooth surface, and the liver span was 7 cm. The spleen was 3 cm and firm. CVS had the presence of soft systolic murmur grade 2/6 at the base of the heart. Rest of the examination was normal.

Inference and Diagnosis

The age of onset, presence of severe pallor, and hepatosplenomegaly point to a clinical diagnosis of congenital hemolytic anemia likely to be *thalassemia major*. The hepatosplenomegaly in this infant reflects a primary hematologic disease with the presence of severe anemia. As there is an absence of lymphadenopathy, bleeding manifestations, and prolonged febrile illness, this rules out hematologic malignancy (childhood leukemia) and bone marrow aplasia. Bone marrow aplasia also does not have significant hepatosplenomegaly.

Nutritional IDA is unlikely in view of the dietary history and gross hepatosplenomegaly. Mild hepatomegaly can occur in IDA. Other hemolytic anemias such as congenital spherocytosis are a very rare likelihood while G6PD deficiency is extremely infrequent in girls as it is an X-linked recessive condition. Although the infant's elder sibling brother is reported to be healthy, it cannot be categorically said that he may be completely normal. He may be an asymptomatic carrier. This child can be clinically diagnosed as *congenital hemolytic anemia (thalassemia major)*.

Investigations

The hemogram showed hemoglobin of 5 g%, MCV of 65 fL, and MCH of 21 pg, with peripheral smear of microcytosis, anisopoikilocytosis, target cells, polychromasia, and nucleated RBCs. The WBC count was 15,000 cells/mm^3 (P 55%, L 40%, M 3%, E 2%). Serum bilirubin was 2.1 mg% (indirect was 1.6 mg%) and the mild bilirubin level is due to ongoing hemolysis. High-performance liquid chromatography (HPLC) confirmed the diagnosis of thalassemia major. It showed HbF 93%, HbA2 4%, and HbA 3%. Both the parents had beta thalassemia trait on hemoglobin electrophoresis. Bone marrow examination is not generally required in the suspected case of thalassemia and hence was not performed.

Principles of Management

- Regular and repeated packed cell transfusions are needed to keep the hemoglobin level above 10 g/dL.
- Iron chelation to treat the iron overload from repeated transfusions must be instituted when the serum ferritin levels become above 1000 ng/mL.

- Regular growth monitoring is essential as the condition is an important cause of short stature.
- Bone marrow and stem cell transplant are curative options.
- Genetic counseling and antenatal diagnosis must be considered for future pregnancies.
- Screening for the carriers (HbA2) should be done in high-risk groups and community.

Key Messages

- Thalassemia forms one of the most common congenital hemolytic anemias in children.
- A diagnosis of thalassemia must be considered and excluded in any child with progressive and severe pallor presenting between the ages of 6 and 12 months.
- Regular transfusions and iron chelation form the mainstay of the treatment.

Case 7: A 12-Month-Old Infant with Fever, Cough, and Short-Duration Breathlessness

A 12-month-old, well-nourished infant is brought to the OPD with a history of high-grade fever for 2–3 days, along with cough and breathlessness of less than 1-day duration. He was apparently well 3–4 days back when he developed fever that gradually increased in intensity. The temperature was noted to be 102.6°F (39.2°C) before the parents brought him to the hospital. The infant also developed increasing cough since 1 day and breathlessness in the past 6 hours. The mother gave him oral paracetamol syrup at home and the child was able to take his feeds but with reluctance since the past few hours. The mother told that she was hearing some sounds from the child's chest.

The infant had no history of any past major illnesses and his dietary and developmental history was normal. He had received his earlier immunizations (BCG, three doses of DPT + HiB + HBV and OPV, and then measles vaccine at 9 months). Rest of the history was noncontributory.

Analysis

- The acute onset of fever followed by cough and then breathlessness suggests an acute respiratory infection. As there is no history of cold/coryza in the child or immediate family member and there is development of breathlessness, this is not likely to have begun as an upper respiratory infection. Hence, this is likely to be a bacterial illness, although a viral lower respiratory illness cannot be definitely excluded by history alone.
- Generally, bacterial infections appear to localize to one anatomical part (e.g., acute tonsillitis, acute otitis media, acute cervical lymphadenitis) while viral infections have a prodrome, rash, and involvement of multiple parts (runny nose, congested eyes, congested throat such as seen in measles and Epstein–Barr virus infections).
- As the infant has received his vaccine against *Haemophilus influenzae* type b (Hib), he is most unlikely to have an LRTI (pneumonia) due to Hib. However, there are other bacterial agents (such as *Streptococcus pneumoniae* and *Staphylococcus aureus*) that can present with similar manifestations.

- As the infant is a healthy child and has acquired the infection in his community settings, this is a community-acquired pneumonia (CAP) that occurs when a child gets an infection after exposure to bacterial agents outside of a healthcare setting. This is the most common type of bacterial pneumonia in children.

Clinical Examination

The infant was febrile (99.5°F) with a HR of 120/min and RR of 64/min, SpO_2 was 94%, and he was alert and conscious. The child had a fast breathing as per the WHO criteria. Anterior fontanel was closed; there was no cyanosis, pallor, rash, conjunctival congestion, or lymphadenopathy. Both the ears were normal and there was a mild congestion of throat. The child had respiratory distress with flaring of alae nasi and there were intercostal retractions.

The respiratory system revealed no chest bulge with equal movements on both sides of the chest. On auscultation, the breath sounds and vocal resonance were decreased on the right infrascapular region along with a bronchial breathing and few crepitations over the same area. The other side of the chest was normal with normal vesicular breath sounds. Other systemic examination was normal.

Inference and Diagnosis

The type of onset is suggestive of an acute bacterial infection with localization in the parenchyma of the right lung. Correlating the findings with surface anatomy of the lung, the findings are localized over the right infrascapular region, which is indicative of right lower lobe involvement. In contrast, if there is a pleural or an airway disease, the findings are more likely to be present across the lobes and not restricted to one particular area. The diagnosis is thus *consolidation due to acute bacterial pneumonia.*

Investigations

The CBC was normal except mild leukocytosis (total leucocyte count [TLC] of 18,500/mm^3) and the X-ray of chest showed right lower zone consolidation.

Principles of Management

- The treatment is guided by the clinical signs of hypoxia (oxygen) and rapid breathing and retractions are good correlates of hypoxia.
- The choice of antibiotic is decided by the suspicion and likelihood of the bacterial agent causing the disease.
- Adequate support for hydration, fever management, and feeding must be ensured. If the child is unable to sustain his/her adequate oral intake, then he/she may need intravenous fluids for a short duration.
- There is no proven benefit of cough syrups/suppressants in childhood pneumonias and hence their use is not recommended.
- An end-of-treatment X-ray is not required except in children in whom either the therapeutic response is delayed or unsatisfactory or an associated complication (e.g., cyanotic heart disease [CHD]) is present.

Key Messages

- Fever, cough, and breathlessness of acute onset are indicative of pneumonia in infants and children.
- CAP is a common cause of respiratory tract infections in infants and children.

Case 8: A 5-Year-Old Boy with Fever for 7 Days, Mild Cough, and Right-Sided Chest Pain for 2 Days

A 5-year-old previously healthy boy was brought to the hospital with a complaint of increasing intensity of fever for 7 days, followed by mild cough and pain in the chest on right side for 3–4 days that was increased by coughing. The fever was initially low grade but had become high grade over the past 2–3 days and while the cough did not worsen, the child developed right-sided chest pain aggravated by coughing. The parents also informed that the child had mild breathing difficulty. The child had received oral medications (probably antibiotics) in inadequate doses for 2 days before coming to the hospital. He preferred to lie on the right side. The child was also not taking well orally for the past 2–3 days.

Analysis

- The child had an acute onset of fever, cough, and chest pain that suggests a respiratory disease. The unilateral localization of the chest pain aggravated by coughing suggests pleural inflammation.
- The sequence of symptoms suggests an acute respiratory infection or illness (e.g., pneumonia).
- The increase in the intensity of fever, mild breathing difficulty, and reduced oral intake suggested an acute and ongoing illness with a possibility of a complication.
- The child's preference to lie on one side laterally suggests that he is avoiding chest movements on the affected side.
- Although some children with pneumonia can also complain of chest pain initially and discomfort, it should not progressively worsen over a few days but should subside or become less in intensity as the child gets better.
- Only a decrease in chest pain without other improvement should not be considered as a sign of recovery but a possible development of effusion within the pleural cavity.

Clinical Examination

The child appeared sick and toxic looking with a HR of 124/min, RR of 44/min, and temperature of 101°F, and SpO_2 was 88%. The anthropometric examination was normal. There was mild respiratory distress but there was no cyanosis, clubbing, or dehydration. Rest of the general examination was normal. A toxic appearance should be considered as an alarming sign.

The chest examination showed no fullness or bulge on the right side and there was no mediastinal shift noted. The chest movements were decreased on the right side as compared with on the left side and posteriorly the percussion note was dull in the infrascapular area. On auscultation, the breath sounds and the vocal resonance were diminished in the same area. There were no adventitious sounds. The other side of the chest revealed no abnormality.

Inference and Diagnosis

The acute onset and the progression of the symptoms along with the restricted chest movements, stony dull note on percussion, and ipsilateral decreased breath sounds localize the pathology to the right side. These findings indicate a collection of fluid in the pleural space on the right side. The toxicity, hypoxia, and mild respiratory distress favor a possibility of pyogenic infection (*empyema thoracis*).

The decreased breath sounds without any adventitious sounds are also a strong pointer to a pleural disease. The lack of mediastinal shift to the opposite side can be explained as the fluid (pus) collection in this case may not be large enough to push the mediastinum to the opposite side.

The differential diagnosis also includes tubercular pleural effusion that can sometimes have an acute onset, lung abscess, and an infected congenital lung cyst. A cavitary lung pathology without a communication with a bronchus can result in similar findings.

Investigations

The investigations showed a WBC count of 21,000/mm^3 with polymorphs of 80%, L 17%, M 3%, and E 1%. The erythrocyte sedimentation rate (ESR) was 80 mm FHR (first-hour reading). The chest X-ray revealed a haziness of lower zone and obliteration of costophrenic angle on the right side of the chest. Pleural tapping was done and it showed purulent material that on culture grew *S. aureus*.

Principles of Management

- Intravenous administration of antibiotics (vancomycin with ceftriaxone) along with an aminoglycoside for 14 days should be followed by oral antibiotics for another 2–4 weeks.
- Empyema needs to be drained by the placement of intercostal drainage till the drainage amount is less than 20–30 mL/day and there is no evidence of any air leak.
- Video-assisted thoracic surgery (VATS) is also a newer minimally invasive endoscopic option for the removal of pus particularly if there are adhesions or the pus is encysted. Thoracotomy is required in minimal cases only.

Key Messages

- An acute febrile illness with mild cough and breathing difficulty with localized chest findings without any adventitious sounds raises a strong possibility of an infective/inflammatory pleural disease such as empyema or lung abscess.
- Four to 6 weeks of antibiotic therapy is needed to ensure a total bacterial clearance.
- The modes of drainage and surgical management are determined by nature, extent, and the severity of the disease.

Case 9: A 7-Year-Old Child with Fever for 20–25 Days, Cough for 10 Days, and Increasing Breathlessness for 3–4 Days

A 7-year-old healthy boy was alright 20–25 days back and then developed fever that was high grade, intermittent, and relieved by medication initially. He also had cough since the past 10 days that was productive containing yellow sputum with no diurnal and postural variation. Since the past 3–4 days, he had some difficulty in breathing for which he was admitted to PICU.

On detailed history for these complaints, the child had consulted some local doctor for fever and cough but they were not relieved and then he had high-grade continuous fever that was not responding adequately to antipyretics. He developed some difficulty in breathing since 3–4 days and while he developed breathlessness, the cough did not worsen much. There was some chest pain 4 days back, mainly on the right side, relieved while sleeping on the right side, which decreased in the past 2 days. No investigations were done till date. On further inquiry, there was no history of trauma, vomiting, palpitations, abdominal pain, weight loss, and rash, and no similar complaints in the past. There was no history of contact with tuberculosis. Although the child was eating less, the family was not sure about the weight loss in the child.

Analysis

- The main symptoms are cough, high-grade fever, chest pain, and dyspnea, which favor a clinical diagnosis of pulmonary diseases, such as pneumonia, pleural effusion, and pneumothorax.
- The onset suggests an infectious etiology due to the presence of fever and a gradual progression of breathlessness, which suggests a decreasing lung compliance. This can be due to either parenchymal lung involvement (consolidation or collapse) or pleura (inflammation and collection of fluid/air—e.g., pleural effusion or a hydropneumothorax).
- Pneumothorax alone is unlikely to present in this manner without any antecedent complications, e.g., pertussis, asthma, cystic fibrosis, and chest trauma.
- Fever, wet cough, and then the breathlessness indicate a parenchymal or pleural disease rather than an airway disease (e.g., asthma). The onset is also not suggestive of asthma, which has a more sudden and acute onset.
- Although cardiac diseases can have similar presentations, absence of palpitation, significant past history, and no edema make it much less likely to be a congenital or an acquired heart disease.
- Persistent, high-grade, continuous fever rules out other diagnosis of fever with effusion such as dengue fever as there is biphasic fever and no other signs of generalized capillary leak (e.g., ascites).
- A simplified guide to the symptoms and their co-relation is given as follows:
  - *Airway*: Significant cough, often generalized signs
  - *Upper respiratory tract*: Dry, hacking cough, hoarseness, stridor, suprasternal retraction
  - *Lower large airways*: Wet cough → tachypnea, wheeze, subcostal retraction
  - *Lower small airways*: Tachypnea → cough (mild), e.g., bronchiolitis with mild or no chest retractions
  - *Lung parenchyma*: Cough not predominant, grunt, intercostal retractions, often localized signs (lobar distribution)
  - *Pleura*: Pain, tachypnea, no chest retractions, localized, pleural distribution of clinical signs
  - *Interstitium*: Mild cough, tachypnea, generalized signs
  - *Combined disorders*: (i) Generalized airway + lung + interstitium (viral infections) and (ii) localized—pleura parenchymal (bacterial infection)

Clinical Examination

The child was looking toxic and febrile, with an axillary temperature of 101°F. The pulse rate was 116/min, RR 40/min, and BP 100/64 mmHg. There were no intercostal and suprasternal retractions. There was no dehydration, clubbing, and cyanosis and no signs of heart failure such as edema feet and raised jugular venous pressure (JVP). The examination of throat and tonsils was normal.

On the examination of the respiratory system (inspection and palpation), there was no chest bulge or deformity but the chest movements were decreased on the right side and the trachea and the apex beat were shifted to the left side. There was no tenderness on palpation. The percussion note was stony dull on the right side posteriorly. On auscultation, the vocal resonance was diminished and the breath sounds were decreased in intensity over the same areas with bronchial breath sounds in the right interscapular region. Rest of the systemic examination was normal.

Inference and Diagnosis

The triad of symptoms of fever, cough, and breathlessness of a gradual onset and the findings on the respiratory examination favor a collection of fluid in the pleural space on the right side. The shift of the mediastinum to the left indicates that the amount of fluid in the space is considerable enough to push the mediastinum to the opposite side, i.e., left side. After systemic examination, it favors more toward pleural effusion than empyema, which occurs more commonly in a younger age group and has an acute onset of 3–5 days.

The condition is likely to be caused by progressive primary tuberculosis resulting in right-sided *pleural effusion*. It is likely that the primary focus of tuberculosis in the lungs may have enlarged and discharged its contents into the pleural cavity resulting in the effusion.

Unlike in this child, although many viral and bacterial infections can develop fluid collection in the pleural space during the course of infection (parapneumonic effusions), these are small in quantity, often self-limiting, and get better with the passage of time. Here, the course of illness has progressively worsened instead of improving and hence parapneumonic effusions should not be considered unless there are underlying complications such as severe malnutrition, atypical pneumonias, or HIV infection. Airway disease is ruled out due to the absence of any wheeze in the child. Rarely, a pleural or an extrapleural malignancy can have a similar presentation due to the collection of blood in the pleural cavity (hemorrhagic pleural effusion).

Investigations

The investigations showed a hemoglobin of 10.4 g% with a normocytic anemia and TLC of 22,000/mm^3 with P 70%, L 29%, and E 1%. The Mantoux test was positive with 15-mm, 48-hour induration, and the chest X-ray showed a uniform haziness of the right side (obliteration of costophrenic angle and mediastinal shift to the left side). The ultrasonography of chest revealed pleural fluid without any septations. The pleural fluid was exudative in nature with predominant lymphocytes and proteins of 1.2 g% in the pleural fluid. No acid-fast bacilli were detected by Ziehl–Neelsen stain.

Principles of Management

- The supportive care for nutrition, position (head up) with back rest, and oxygen as a drug are essential components of care.
- The administration of antitubercular drugs in their proper dosages and for proper duration forms the mainstay of therapy.
- Pleural tapping is often needed to provide relief from dyspnea and cardiorespiratory embarrassment and to establish the cause.
- The monitoring of the treatment for compliance, response, and any drug toxicity should be done.

Key Messages

- Cough, fever, and breathlessness with other negative history point to respiratory pathology with more so of alveoli or pleural space localization.
- An acute onset of chest pain localized to the right side, along with fever and cough, suggests pleural inflammation. As the pain decreases after few days, it is possible that the child has either developed pleural effusion or recovered from primary disease. But in view of persistent fever and increased breathlessness, it goes more in favor of pleural effusion.
- Systematic thinking leads the way for obtaining relevant history and performing focused physical examination.
- Structured analysis of symptom complex helps to define probable diagnosis in most cases—physical examination adds to fine-tune the final diagnosis; relevant laboratory tests can then be planned only to confirm diagnosis.

Case 10: An 8-Year-Old Girl with Recurrent Episodes of Cough, Breathlessness, and Wheezing

An 8-year-old girl child reported to pediatric emergency in late night with a history of runny nose and mild fever of 1-day onset, followed by development of increasing cough, tightness of the chest, and difficulty in breathing after her dinner at home. The fever was low grade, the cough was dry in nature, and the child was unable to go to sleep. The parents found her to have increased cough with discomfort and hence they brought her to the hospital.

The girl has had a few episodes of similar illness since the age of 3 years and, although initially these episodes occurred frequently, these now have become less frequent. In the past 6 months, she had only two earlier episodes that could be treated at home with the use of metered-dose inhaler (MDI) with the use of a spacer as advised by her pediatrician. In between these episodes, she has remained asymptomatic and has activities like any other normal child. There was no history of similar symptoms, allergies, or smoking in the family members. Rest of the history was normal.

Analysis

- The acute onset and short duration of increasing cough and breathlessness point to a disease affecting the lower respiratory tract most likely of the airways.
- The presence of mild fever does not always indicate a bacterial illness but rather it can be an inflammatory response or a mild viral infection transmitted through the droplets.
- Her being well in between the episodes of illness reflects the recurrent nature of her disease.
- The history suggests that in her earlier episodes, she has responded to the probable use of aerosolized drugs (bronchodilators) given through MDI for a short duration and this points to the lung airway disease rather than the parenchymal disease. Cough and breathlessness in varying combinations are a pointer to either the lung parenchymal or airway involvement.
- The family history of such an episode, though usually present, may not always be present in other siblings and the parents.
- Bacterial and other infective illnesses are very unlikely to have recurrences in an otherwise normal child with periods of normalcy in between. They can occur however in an immunocompromised, severely malnourished child, or in the presence of congenital malformation of the lungs.
- The condition appears to be a chronic inflammatory process affecting the airways associated with variable degrees of airflow obstruction, which often is reversible spontaneously or with treatment. This is likely to be childhood asthma in view of her previous episodes and the response to the treatment.

Clinical Examination

The girl weighed 27 kg (above the 50th centile) and her body mass index (BMI) was 17. She was alert and well oriented and her pulse rate was 96/min, RR was 40/min, and SpO_2 was 91% in the room air. Her body temperature was normal and there was no dehydration or cyanosis. The chest revealed mild lower chest wall retractions, with prolonged expiration and bilateral rhonchi. There were no crepitations and rest of the systemic examination was normal. Even though crepitations may be present sometimes, it does not necessarily indicate a bacterial infection or a justification to start antibiotic therapy.

Inference and Diagnosis

The mild fever, with runny nose due to a viral respiratory illness, has precipitated an episode of bronchospasm and bronchial inflammation in the child that has led to her further symptoms of cough, chest tightness, and breathing difficulty. Cough is almost never an initial disturbing symptom in a viral respiratory illness; here, it points to the progressive bronchospasm also manifesting as the tightness of the chest along with breathlessness. Any allergies, exercise, exposure to drugs, or smoke can precipitate such an episode. In a severe case of asthma, the child may be severely hypoxic, cyanosed, and disoriented, and the airflow may be severely restricted and the air compromised so that even wheezing may not be audible (silent chest). This constitutes acute life-threatening asthma and needs urgent and immediate management. The child has *acute asthma of intermittent variety*.

As this child has a classical presentation of acute asthma, other differential diagnoses to be considered include gastroesophageal reflux disease, foreign body aspiration, and allergic rhinosinusitis.

Principles of Management

- The detailed management of childhood asthma is beyond the scope of this chapter but the basic steps are to assess the severity of the acute attack and manage as per the severity.
- The mainstay of therapy remains aerosolized administration of short-acting and rapidly acting bronchodilators, or subcutaneous adrenaline and steroids if indicated.
- As childhood asthma is a recurring and chronic condition, long-term follow-up treatment plan, familiarity with the use of devices at home, and proper counseling must be ensured.

Key Messages

- Childhood asthma is an eminently manageable condition with good outcomes in majority of children.
- The classic triad of cough, breathlessness, and wheezing may not be present in all the children with asthma. Cough made worse by exercise or in night may be the only troublesome symptom in a few children.
- A good long-term plan must be ensured to keep the child symptom-free and to lead as normal a life as possible.

Case 11: A 5-Year-Old Boy with Recurrent Episodes of Fever, Breathlessness, and Failure to Thrive

A 5-year-old boy was brought to the OPD for a checkup by a pediatrician. The informants for this history were his parents who were illiterate. About 1 month ago, the parents had consulted the local doctor at their small town as the child had complaints of high-grade fever and cough. He started treatment and the child's fever and cough were relieved after 5 days. The doctor also insisted that they should consult specialist doctors at the general hospital within a week to get the boy checked up for heart disease. The parents brought the child for the checkup as advised by the local doctor.

In general, the child was well and there were no symptoms to report as per the parents. He had always been a "weak" child, but "gives no trouble." On (retrospectively) asking leading questions, they informed that the child had complaints of some breathlessness on prolonged exertion (e.g., playing hard). At times, he could not keep up so well with his peers in physical activity. He had a tendency for excessive sweating, which was very marked in infancy. His mother also said that she could feel excessively active heartbeats with her hand on his chest (and that this was not the case with his older and younger siblings).

There was no history of breathlessness at rest, chronic cough, bluish discoloration of lips or nails, and swelling over feet in the past. The past history

(Continued)

(Continued)

provided valuable information. During infancy, the baby had complaints of fast and labored breathing with excessive sweating. The baby was also slow to gain weight. The parents had been advised to consult a pediatrician at that time for suspicion of heart disease, but they did not do so. Over the years, there had been frequent (three to four) episodes of illnesses with cough and fever, generally resolving within 5–7 days with OPD-based treatment by the local doctor. These illnesses used to be noticeably more severe and prolonged in the earlier years than now. The child had been symptomatically better in the past few months than before. He never got admitted to any hospital earlier. There never had been any complaints of joint swellings or joint pains.

Analysis

- The child was referred to the city hospital as most likely the local doctor suspected a heart disease possibly on the detection of a murmur on auscultation.
- The parents' reference that the child was weak could indicate that the child was not growing and gaining weight well, implying that the child may have a failure to thrive (FTT). This is an important pointer to an underlying congenital, chronic, or systemic disease.
- When the parents refer to the child as not giving trouble, it indicates that the child may not be active and energetic with getting breathless on exertion unlike his peer group who would have normal play activities.
- Recurrent respiratory illnesses, most likely to be lower respiratory infections, may be due to several other reasons (gastroesophageal reflux disease, cystic fibrosis, congenital lung malformations). But there is a strong possibility of a congenital heart disease based on the symptomatic onset of fast breathing with excessive sweating in infancy, which indicates presence of heart failure.
- Rheumatic heart disease is most unlikely as it is extremely rare below 5 years of age.

Clinical Examination

The child was weighing 11.8 kg (<3SD) and height was 103 cm with a pulse rate of 116/min with regular rhythm and normal volume, and all the peripheral pulses were well palpable. There was no radiofemoral delay. Respiration and temperature was normal, and BP was 100/64 mmHg in right upper limb in supine position. SpO_2 was 98% in right upper limb. The child was comfortable and cooperative. There was some pallor but no cyanosis, clubbing, and neck venous engorgement. Rest of the general examination was normal.

The CVS examination showed a normal precordium and the apex beat was palpable in the fifth left intercostal space 1 cm outside the midclavicular line, indicating a mild cardiomegaly. It was well localized and hyperdynamic in character. There was no parasternal lift, and other pulsations were palpable. But there was a systolic thrill over the left third and fourth intercostal spaces. Epigastric pulsations could be felt on the pulp of the palpating thumb, suggesting aortic pulsations. The left cardiac border coincided with the apex and the second left space was resonant on percussion.

Auscultatory findings were as follows:

- The first heart sound was normal and appeared to be masked by the murmur. The second heart sound was normally split. It also appeared to be masked by the murmur.
- There was no third or fourth heart sound or click.
- A pansystolic murmur grade III/VI was heard just lateral to the left sternal edge. It was heard best at the left third and fourth intercostal spaces. The murmur was

uniform in intensity, and loud and harsh in character. There was no cooing or musical quality. There was no radiation to the axilla or back. There was no diastolic murmur.

Rest of the systemic examination was normal.

Inference and Diagnosis

This was a 5-year-old boy, suspected to have heart disease in early infancy, with suggestive features of heart failure. He had a history of recurrent respiratory infections. Over time, the severity of the symptoms was decreasing. The age of the onset, the progress of the disease, and the recurrent respiratory illnesses, mild cardiomegaly, and pansystolic murmur indicate a presence of left-to-right shunt, i.e., congenital acyanotic heart disease (VSD). There was no evidence suggestive of congestive heart failure at this time. The onset of symptoms in early infancy is a clue to the likely congenital nature of the lesion.

The severity of the symptoms has been decreasing in the long run, and the lesion is relatively well tolerated. This may be related to spontaneous decrease in the shunt across the VSD (in case of muscular and perimembranous VSDs). Other possible causes that result in symptomatic lessening include development of pulmonary stenosis (PS), aortic valve prolapse, or pulmonary vascular disease (Eisenmenger syndrome). Reversal of flow may indicate a paradoxical improvement but it indicates a development of pulmonary hypertension and cyanosis, which are ominous signs. Besides, a pansystolic murmur is present in only a limited number of conditions (VSD, mitral regurgitation [MR], and tricuspid regurgitation [TR]).

However, mild symptoms were persisting with a tendency of excessive sweating, breathlessness on severe exertion, and excessively active heartbeats felt on the chest. There is no evidence of shunt reversal and pulmonary hypertension as the second space was not dull, the second heart sound was normal, and there was no cyanosis.

Investigations

The chest X-ray showed a mild left ventricular hypertrophy (LVH) but there was no pulmonary plethora and the ECG confirmed LVH. X-ray chest and ECG can give useful clues but are not diagnostic. The magnitude of the changes depends on the size and the degree of the left-to-right shunt. Thus, synthesizing the findings and investigations (including echocardiography), a diagnosis of moderate-sized VSD was confirmed.

Principles of Management

- Medical management should include measures to prevent and treat congestive heart failure, infective endocarditis, and nutritional anemia. Regular follow-up is essential to ascertain the progress of the lesion as many of such lesions may close spontaneously.
- The need for surgical correction and closure is determined by multiple factors such as the anatomic subtypes and the size of the lesion, age at the diagnosis, associated comorbidities (e.g., heart failure), and to prevent permanent pulmonary hypertension and irreversible pulmonary vascular disease.
- Surgical closure is indicated in large defects if the heart failure is not controlled by medical management and if there is associated aortic incompetence, irrespective of the size of the defect.

Key Messages

- VSDs can have a wide range of presentations from an asymptomatic child with a heart murmur to recurrent chest infections, heart failure, and FTT.
- Regular follow-up and the assessment of the size and the severity of the lesion is an important guide to the likelihood of the spontaneous closure of the defect and/or the need for surgical correction.

Case 12: A Child Presenting with Cyanosis and Breathlessness

A 2-year-old male child was brought by his parents with complaints of increase in bluish discoloration of lips, nails, and body skin since the past 4–5 days. This event started after straining for defecation. There was also a history of child having fast and difficult breathing since the past 2–3 days. There was no history of fever, cough, vomiting, diarrhea, or convulsions.

In the past few months, the child had three to four similar episodes of bluish discoloration and breathlessness. The first episode was at around 6–7 months of age. The child was hospitalized 6 months back with similar complaints; oxygen and medications were given and the child discharged after 4 days. The parents did not have records with them of this hospitalization. They described that the child used to assume squatting posture and felt better in the same posture. The child used to look darker/blue even when he was stable. The perinatal and family history was not significant. The child was immunized for his age. The development was normal.

Analysis

- This child has a history of recurrent episodes of cyanosis and breathlessness. Both these symptoms can be due to involvement of either respiratory or cardiovascular system.
- Based on the symptoms, this child probably has disease related to cardiovascular system. This child does not have a history of fever; thus, an infective etiology is unlikely. Usually, central cyanosis in respiratory conditions will occur when there is significant loss of lung volume in lung parenchymal pathology or due to severe bronchospasm in case of asthma or hyperreactive airway disease. In such cases, a child will initially have complaints of cough and/or breathlessness, gradually progress to severe respiratory distress, and then develop cyanosis.
- In respiratory conditions, such events are unlikely to present as "recurrent" episodes of cyanosis. Recurrent episodes of cyanosis can be due to congenital cyanotic heart disease (CCHD). Squatting episodes are very typical of CCHD. By squatting, there is increased venous return to right heart, more blood would go to pulmonary circulation, oxygenation would improve to some extent, and the child would feel better.
- The child also appeared cyanotic even when there were no acute complaints. Children with CCHD remain cyanotic due to mixing of blood, which increases during "cyanotic spells." Such spells are commonly precipitated by exertion, feeding, excessive crying, or defecation. These cause sympathetic stimulation, which causes infundibular spasm compromising pulmonary circulation, and deepening of cyanosis.

Clinical Examination

In anthropometry, the child's weight and height were between −2SD and −3SD. He was conscious and oriented but irritable. The temperature was normal, the child had tachycardia and tachypnea, and the BP was normal. There was marked respiratory distress as evidenced by nasal flaring, prominence of sternomastoid muscle, and suprasternal and subcostal indrawing. There was presence of central cyanosis and grade III clubbing. The child did not have pallor; in fact, he appeared plethoric. The presence of conjunctival injection was noted. There were no signs of congestive heart failure or infective endocarditis.

The cardiovascular system showed that the shape of chest was normal and there was no precordial bulge. The apex impulse was not visible. In palpation, apex beat was located in the left fourth intercostal space just inside the midclavicular line, and was not forceful and not well sustained. There was no parasternal heave, diastolic shock, and thrill. In the percussion, the right heart border was retrosternal and the left border coincided with the apex. The auscultation revealed that S1 was normal; S2 was soft and single in pulmonary area. There was ejection systolic murmur grade III/VI, which was best heard in the second left intercostal space. Other systemic examination was normal.

Inference and Diagnosis

This child has cyanotic spells; there is deep cyanosis, tachycardia, tachypnea, and respiratory distress. There are no signs of congestive heart failure. Clubbing is seen with CCHD. Children with CHDs commonly have polycythemia; thus, they are commonly plethoric and not anemic. This is due to increase in erythropoiesis leading to polycythemia in response to chronic hypoxia. Iron deficiency can coexist, which makes the child more prone to get cyanotic spells. Conjunctival injection is seen with CCHD.

Patients with acyanotic CHD (VSD, patent ductus arteriosus [PDA]) commonly present with recurrent LRTI or heart failure, while patients with CCHD *usually* do not develop heart failure. (A child with CCHD develops cardiac failure only if there is significant anemia, infective endocarditis, or myocarditis.)

Finding of soft and single S2 is very important. It is seen in tetralogy of Fallot (TOF) and other conditions with Fallot's physiology. This is because P2 component of S2 is not heard due to pulmonic or infundibular stenosis making S2 soft and single. Ejection systolic murmur in pulmonary area is because of pulmonic stenosis. In TOF, there is no shunt murmur and the heart is of normal size.

Few cardiac lesions have a similar pathophysiology like that of TOF due to intracardiac mixing and restriction and obstruction to the pulmonary blood flow. Hence, these are grouped as Fallot's physiology (e.g., double outlet right ventricle [DORV] with PS, complete or corrected transposition of great arteries [TGA] with VSD and PS, and tricuspid atresia with PS). DORV has an aortic override of more than 50%.

Methemoglobinemia is also a condition that presents with central cyanosis and respiratory distress. Such patients will have normal cardiac examination.

The clinical diagnosis is CCHD and is most likely to be TOF. The differential diagnosis should include conditions of Fallot's physiology.

Investigations

The routine investigations should include CBC and peripheral smear. The chest X-ray shows oligemic lung fields and boot-shaped heart in TOF. The upturned apex due to right ventricular hypertrophy and absence of pulmonary artery (pulmonary bay) is responsible for the boot-shaped heart. It is important to note the vascularity of the lung fields. Patients with CCHD having decreased pulmonary blood flow such as TOF and TOF physiology will have oligemic lung fields while those having increased pulmonary blood flow such as total anomalous pulmonary venous connection will have plethoric lung fields.

The ECG shows right-axis deviation and right ventricular hypertrophy. The diagnosis is confirmed by right ventricular outflow tract obstruction, overriding of aorta, VSD, and right ventricular hypertrophy. Other CCHD can also be diagnosed with echocardiography. Cardiac catheterization may be rarely needed.

Principles of Management

Treatment of cyanotic spells includes:

- Hyperbaric oxygen
- Knee–chest position, or at least flexing the knees

- β-Blockers—Inj. metoprolol/propranolol, initially injectable and later oral
- Correction of metabolic acidosis
- Treating infection
- Correcting anemia if present
- Injection morphine

Definitive management consists of surgery:
- Palliative shunt surgery—Blalock–Taussig shunt, Pott shunt, Waterston shunt
- Definitive repair

Key Messages

- TOF is the commonest cyanotic congenital heart disease in children.
- CCHD commonly presents with cyanosis, squatting episodes, and clubbing, while heart failure is uncommon.
- TOF has single soft S2 and ejection systolic murmur.
- The palliative treatment consists of creating a communication (a shunt) between the systemic and the pulmonary circulation, while the definitive treatment consists of planned surgical corrections of the underlying defects.

Case 13: A 10-Year-Old Boy with Fever, Painful Swelling of Joints (Polyarthritis), and Breathlessness

A 10-year-old boy was brought to the hospital with complaints of fever for 15–20 days followed by joint swellings 3–4 days after the fever. Then he developed pain and swelling over both the knee joints, which made it difficult for him to walk. While the fever, which was moderate, persisted over the next week, his knee joint swellings became less but he developed painful ankles and elbow joints and became breathless over the past 4–5 days. He has also developed a mild cough over the past 3–4 days. The intensity of fever now has gone down since he went to district hospital about 4–5 days from where he was referred to tertiary care center but the family due to socioeconomic problems got delayed in reaching the hospital.

There was no history of similar illness in the past of any joint swellings, palpitation, breathlessness, skin rash, or abnormal movements. The parents did not notice antecedent throat infection in the past 3–4 weeks. The child, studying in the fourth standard, was otherwise a healthy child as per the parents before this illness.

Analysis

- The presence of fever, joint swellings, and breathlessness is indicative of a multisystem involvement, which has shown a changing clinical pattern.
- Progressive breathlessness in this child can be of cardiac or pulmonary origin. However, the breathlessness at rest points more to the possibility of it being of cardiac origin. This indicates the inability of the cardiac output to meet the oxygen needs of the body, indicating a gradual progression of left ventricular dysfunction. This thus suggests an impending heart failure.
- Congenital heart diseases are unlikely to present for the first time at this age.
- The presence of multiple joint swellings of migratory type raises the possibility of it being an acute rheumatic fever (ARF) with arthritis.

Clinical Examination

The child weighed 21 kg with a height of 123 cm and was poorly built and poorly nourished. The temperature was normal (98°F), HR 96/min, RR 30/min, and BP 104/60 mmHg in the right upper limb. The pulse was of regular rhythm and of good volume. There was mild pallor but no jaundice, cyanosis, clubbing, lymphadenopathy, and pedal edema. There was no rash, any palpable nodules, or abnormal movements. There was swelling or pain in the knee and ankle joints but there was mild swelling and tenderness of both the elbow joints. Other joints and the back/spine were normal. JVP was normal.

The CVS examination showed a mild bulge on the precordium and the apex beat was located in the fifth space 1.5 cm outside the left midclavicular line. It was hyperdynamic in character and well localized. There was a systolic thrill in the mitral area. The left second space was resonant on percussion and there was no dullness. The left border of the heart corresponded with the apex beat. There was grade IV/VI pansystolic murmur best heard in the mitral area and it was radiating to the axilla. There was no gallop rhythm.

The liver was 1 cm palpable, soft, and nontender and the spleen was not palpable. Other systemic examination was normal.

Inference and Diagnosis

The child has presented with fever and polyarthritis suggestive of ARF. In ARF, involvement of two or more joints is considered as polyarthritis. Although rheumatic fever is the most likely cause of migratory polyarthritis, similar joint involvement can be seen in conditions such as Lyme disease, extrahepatic manifestations of hepatitis B and C infections, gonococcal arthritis, and systemic lupus erythematosus.

The bounding pulse and the wide pulse pressure (low diastolic) suggest a valvular regurgitant lesion, and a well-localized apex beat of hyperdynamic type outside its normal position suggests a LVH. The mitral component of the first heart sound is masked by the pansystolic murmur, which radiates to axilla suggesting MR. The history and the physical examination point to a diagnosis of ARF (arthritis) in a case of established rheumatic heart disease (MR) with left ventricular hypertrophy without heart failure, without active carditis, and with normal sinus rhythm.

The child has manifestations of fever and polyarthritis but has no clinical evidence of cardiac involvement (carditis: such as pericardial rub, tachycardia, Carey Coombs murmur) in this episode of ARF. Hence, this MR can be explained on the basis of his previous attack of rheumatic fever. Even though there is no definite history of rheumatic fever in the past, established MR must be kept in mind as MR is the most common sequel of earlier rheumatic fever.

Investigations

The CBC showed a hemoglobin of 10.4 g% and TLC of 9000 mm^3, with P 68%, L 30%, M 1%, and E 1%. ESR was 60 mm and ASO (antistreptolysin O) titer was 660. The raised ASO titer goes in favor of acute rheumatic fever. X-ray chest showed cardiomegaly with left ventricular enlargement. Echocardiography confirmed the presence of MR. There was no evidence of infective endocarditis and active carditis.

Principles of Management

- Bed rest, penicillin (to eliminate the streptococci from the pharynx), and suppressive treatment in the form of aspirin or corticosteroids are used to treat ARF.
- Aspirin is preferred in the treatment of arthritis, while steroids are the preferred choice for the treatment of carditis.
- Congestive heart failure is a severe form of carditis in ARF, and is managed more aggressively, often needing corticosteroids, diuretics, digoxin, and occasionally inotropic agents.
- Rheumatic fever prophylaxis must be given to prevent further episodes of rheumatic fever.

Key Messages

- Rheumatic fever is one of the most common causes of acquired heart diseases in children.
- Although a firm diagnosis of rheumatic fever needs Jones criteria, based on the clinical judgment, ARF may be diagnosed even in the absence of these criteria if there is a high index of suspicion.
- Mitral valve involvement is the most common occurrence in chronic rheumatic heart disease with or without aortic valve involvement (aortic regurgitation).

Case 14: A 6-Month-Old Infant with Fever, Vomiting, Excessive Irritability, and Refusal to Feed

A 6-month-old infant was brought to the hospital with a short history of high-grade fever for 3 days, vomiting and irritability for 2 days, and not feeding well for 1 day. The mother was giving oral paracetamol to the baby for the past 2 days, but it made the baby feel slightly better only for 2–3 hours. As per the mother, the baby was unduly irritable since the early morning and was vomiting more frequently and that is why she brought the infant to the hospital. She was also doubtful that the baby also had a brief stiffening of the body just before leaving the home.

The infant was a normal newborn at birth with no significant past illness. He was still on breastfeed and the complementary feeds were introduced just a week ago. He had received all his due immunizations and had normal development till this illness. There was no history of contact with tuberculosis and there was no past history of seizure or trauma.

Analysis

- The infant has an acute presentation of febrile illness indicating an infective etiology and his excessive irritability is an alarming symptom for which he has been brought to the hospital.
- Persistent vomiting in the absence of diarrhea must be carefully evaluated as it can indicate an electrolyte disturbance, a surgical abdomen, or a CNS lesion causing increased intracranial tension.
- The episode of the stiffening of the body for a short duration can be a convulsive episode and should be taken into consideration for further investigations.
- Administration of paracetamol and/or antibiotics can alter the clinical presentation of serious conditions leading to an increased morbidity and complications.

Clinical Examination

The infant had a normal anthropometry and the HR was 140/min, RR 40/min, and temperature 39°C (102°F). The baby was crying inconsolably and appearing sick. The anterior fontanel was 3.5 × 3.5 cm and it was tense and nonpulsatile. There was no rash, petechiae, or cyanosis but there was some dehydration. The right middle ear examination revealed a congested tympanic membrane suggesting acute otitis media.

The systemic examination showed that the baby resisted the handling, the tone and power was increased in all the limbs, and the deep tendon reflexes (DTRs) were brisk (+++). There were no cranial nerve palsies. He resisted the flexion of the neck, suggesting the presence of neck rigidity. She also developed an episode of tonic posturing during the examination lasting for about a minute and was immediately given an IV anticonvulsant to terminate the seizure. Rest of the systemic examination was normal.

It is vital that the child should be hemodynamically stable at admission, the sensorium assessed, and the vitals should be stabilized before conducting a detailed examination.

Inference and Diagnosis

The acute presentation of a febrile illness with vomiting, irritability, and an episode of seizure highlights the possibility of an acute CNS infection, which is most likely to be *pyogenic (acute bacterial) meningitis*. Although the infant has neck rigidity, it may be absent in young infants and in late stages. The tense and nonpulsatile anterior fontanel is a strong evidence of an increased intracranial pressure (ICP) due to meningitis, which is also responsible for the episode of seizure (generalized stiffening of the body that occurred in the child). The other causes of seizure in this case could also be dyselectrolytemia or hypoglycemia.

Febrile seizure should not be considered in such a child due to tense anterior fontanel, even though febrile seizures are the most common cause of convulsions between the ages of 6 months and 5 years. Other differential diagnoses to be considered include acute viral encephalitis, brain abscess, and cerebral malaria.

Investigations

The investigations showed a leukocytosis of 25,500 WBC/mm^3 and the lumbar puncture was performed after the child was stabilized. The cerebrospinal fluid (CSF) examination yielded a hazy-appearing fluid, with 3700 cells/mm^3, most of which were polymorphs. The protein was 500 mg/dL and the CSF sugar (25 mg/dL) was low as compared with blood sugar of 80 mg%. Gram stain did not show any organisms in the CSF, and it was sterile on culture. The blood culture showed a growth of *S. pneumoniae*. Neuroimaging was not performed. Repeat CSF examination needs to be considered in cases of suboptimal clinical response, partially treated cases, and infections due to uncommon organisms.

Principles of Management

- Immediate intravenous administration of antibiotics (most often third-generation cephalosporins), even while pending the results of investigations, forms the core of management. Antibiotic therapy may be modified depending on the culture reports and the therapeutic response. Additionally, vancomycin is recommended in infections that are suspected to be caused by cephalosporin-resistant *S. pneumoniae* infections.
- In a child with meningitis between the age of 2 months and 5 years, steroids (dexamethasone) IV are given for initial 3 days in order to prevent complication of sensorineural hearing loss by *H. influenzae* meningitis.
- Measures to treat increased ICP, electrolyte and fluid imbalance, and anticonvulsants to control and treat the seizures should be given.
- Monitoring during hospital stay for the duration of therapy and subsequent follow-up after the discharge (including hearing assessment) are essential.

Key Messages

- Pyogenic meningitis must be strongly suspected in any febrile illness associated with excessive and inconsolable crying.
- The signs of meningeal irritation such as neck rigidity and Kernig sign may often be absent in young infants and in late stages of the disease.
- Early and appropriate intravenous antibiotic therapy forms the core of the treatment.

Case 15: A 2-Year-Old Child with Prolonged Fever, Convulsions, and Altered Sensorium

A 2-year-old child was referred from primary health center with complaints of low- to moderate-grade fever of 1-month duration, poor appetite and feeding, and onset of generalized convulsions followed by drowsiness of 12-hour duration. He had received some medications for the fever, the details of which were not known. The child was apparently well before the onset of illness and had no significant past history. He was third-born to a lower socioeconomic class family and there was a history of contact with tuberculosis with his uncle who had defaulted the treatment 6 months ago. He had normal motor and mental development and had received his vaccinations up to the age of 1.5 years.

When the child was brought to the hospital, he was in altered sensorium, was dehydrated, and appeared wasted. The child also had intermittent stiffening of the whole body. He was put on intravenous fluids and anticonvulsants, and stabilized in pediatric ICU.

Analysis

- The child has a chronic and progressive disease in view of his prolonged symptoms of a duration longer than 1 month. The disease is progressive because fever has been persistent along with poor appetite and there is deterioration in sensorium with the onset of convulsions after which the child has not regained his consciousness.
- From the history, the convulsion appears to be generalized tonic or tonic–clonic.
- The history of contact with tuberculosis in the relative is an important factor to be considered with regards to the history and the clinical diagnosis in this case.
- In view of the symptoms, the condition can be considered to be chronic meningitis (meningeal inflammation and the disease that persists for >4 weeks).

Clinical Examination

The child appeared wasted with his weight for length below –3SD. The HR was 90/min, RR 28/min, temperature 99°F, and BP 90/60 mmHg. There was some pallor, but there was no lymphadenopathy, clubbing, cyanosis, or edema. The child had some dehydration.

The child was in altered sensorium (modified Glasgow Coma Scale [GCS] of 8/15). On motor examination, there was generalized hypertonia (spasticity) but no involuntary movements or focal limb deficits such as monoparesis or hemiparesis. There was sixth cranial nerve palsy on the right side. DTRs were brisk (+++) with bilateral extensor plantars. Neck rigidity, Kernig sign, and Brudzinski sign were all positive. Rest of the systemic examination was noncontributory. Fundus examination revealed bilateral papilledema.

Inference and Diagnosis

The supportive evidence of prolonged fever followed by seizures and altered sensorium along with history of contact with adult tuberculosis with neurological findings of diffuse cerebral involvement points to a diagnosis of tubercular meningoencephalitis (TBME). History of contact can be traced in about 25–30% of cases of TBME. The most common age of occurrence of tuberculous meningitis in children is below 5 years. The involvement of the sixth cranial nerve (which occurs most commonly in TBM) is due to raised ICP. There may be associated hydrocephalus, which is of the communicating variety due to a blockage at the level of cisterns.

The differential diagnosis includes partially/inadequately treated pyogenic meningitis, viral meningoencephalitis (e.g., herpes simplex, measles, Japanese B, HIV), and uncommonly atypical infections such as fungal meningitis in an immunocompromised host. However, viral encephalitis generally has more acute onset of a shorter duration and hence is a remote possibility in such a case.

Investigations

Apart from the CBC and urine examination, Mantoux test was done (4 mm); X-ray chest showed bilateral hilar lymph node enlargement. CSF examination was clear on appearance with 150 lymphocytes/mm^3, proteins were 112 mg%, and CSF sugar was 45 mg/dL (with concomitant blood sugar of 75 mg%). CSF examination may be normal in 10–15% of cases with confirmed TBME. Definitive diagnosis of TBM can be done with detection of tubercle bacilli in CSF, polymerase chain reaction test in CSF, and specific antigen and antibody tests in CSF. CB-NAAT for *M. tuberculosis* is now a widely available and used test for the diagnosis of TBM in children. HIV testing must be recommended in any case of TBM including other forms of CNS tuberculosis.

CT scan was performed in the child and it showed the presence of basal exudates and hydrocephalus.

Principles of Management

- Early diagnosis and prompt treatment with antitubercular drugs for 9–12 months, along with steroids (4–6 weeks), anticonvulsants, and measures to decrease cerebral edema, have an important bearing on the outcome of the disease.

- Surgical treatment of hydrocephalus (shunt surgery) may be needed in cases of progressive hydrocephalus and/or worsening clinical condition.
- Prognosis of TBM is dependent on the stage at which it is diagnosed and treated. In stage I, almost all children survive without sequelae; stage II has 25% mortality and 50% of the survivors have sequelae; and in stage III, 50% of children die and almost 100% of the survivors have residual sequelae.

Key Messages

- Tubercular meningitis is a treatable condition with protean manifestations.
- CT or MRI showing basal meningeal enhancement with any degree of hydrocephalus is strongly suggestive of TBM.
- A high index of suspicion for an early diagnosis and treatment is necessary for a good outcome.

Case 16: A 9-Year-Old Boy with Acute Onset of Lower Limb Weakness

A 9-year-old boy was noticed to have developed an inability to walk and weakness over the past 2 days, followed by some weakness of the upper limbs few hours back. The child was reported well before he developed these symptoms but while preparing to go to school in the morning, the parents noticed that he was not able to get up from the bed. The boy told that his legs were feeling weak and limp and he was hardly able to stand up. The child was taken to a general hospital and was admitted and kept there for a day. Next day, it was noticed that he developed weakness of the right shoulder and had mild limb pains. The doctor there also noticed that the child also had deviation of the angle of mouth on one side and hence the child was referred for admission to a tertiary healthcare setup.

There was no history of trauma, fall, or intramuscular injections. There was no history of fever and bowel and bladder disturbances, and the child was able to drink fluids easily. There was a history of mild fever, runny nose, and mild cough with watery diarrhea 15 days ago for 2–3 days, which subsided on taking antipyretics and oral rehydration solution at home. The child remained well after that until he developed the present symptoms.

The child has had no significant past illness and had normal physical, developmental, and immunization history.

Analysis

- The onset of illness suggests an acute development of motor weakness in both lower limbs followed later by weakness in both upper limbs. The weakness in the upper limb was more proximal than distal.
- The absence of any fever and respiratory and feeding difficulty is notable and although it is not present yet, it can still develop due to the progression of the disease.
- The antecedent throat infection appears viral in nature and needs to be considered in correlation to the suspected diagnosis.
- An acute and sudden onset of weakness and floppiness is indicative of the child having developed acute flaccid paralysis (AFP).

Clinical Examination

The child was conscious and well oriented. His vital signs were normal. The general examination was also normal.

The neurological examination showed that there was infranuclear facial palsy, normal gag reflex, and hypotonia of all the four limbs but it was more evident in both the lower limbs as compared with in the upper limbs. The power in both the lower limbs was grade 3/5 in the distal part but proximally it was grade 1/5. The power in both the upper limbs was 2/5. Coordination could not be tested and there were no involuntary movements. The DTRs were absent and the plantar reflexes were not elicited. The child was able to feel the touch and pain sensations over the affected limbs and there were no signs of meningeal irritation. There was no urinary retention. Rest of the systemic examination was noncontributory.

Inference and Diagnosis

The child fulfills the criteria and the diagnosis of AFP as he has sudden onset of weakness in any part of the body and the further clinical diagnosis must be considered under the spectrum of AFP that can have a variable differential diagnosis.

As polio is eradicated from India and an ongoing surveillance is one of the most important strategies for polio eradication, all AFP cases must be reported, regardless of the clinical and final diagnosis.

The clinical history and the examination are quite compatible with the diagnosis of Guillain–Barré syndrome, which is an immune-mediated condition presenting as a lower motor neuron involvement. It must be remembered that the disease in this child can still evolve further and run a progressive course involving cranial nerve nuclei and also cause respiratory muscle paralysis needing ventilator support.

The differential diagnosis includes transverse myelitis, traumatic neuritis (extremely unlikely in this child as it would be restricted to one extremity), poliomyelitis, viral myositis, and periodic paralysis. Transverse myelitis is indicated by the definite motor and sensory level and the bladder involvement. Further investigations would be required to arrive at a final diagnosis.

Investigations

CBCs were normal. The CSF examination showed 15 cells (L)/mm^3 and 110 mg% of proteins with normal sugar. Neuroimaging was not indicated. Nerve conduction study showed reduced nerve conduction velocity suggesting acute demyelination. Stool samples were also transported for poliovirus isolation.

Principles of Management

- Notification to the district immunization officer must be done immediately.
- Early immunotherapy with intravenous immunoglobulin (IVIG) in a dose of 2 g/kg over 2–5 days forms the mainstay of management.
- Close monitoring to provide hemodynamic support is crucial.

Key Messages

- Guillain–Barré syndrome (GBS) is an important cause of AFP in children.
- Differentiation of the causes of AFP is guided by a thorough history and meticulous clinical examination.
- Symmetrical weakness (more proximal than distal) in a child is supportive of GBS.
- AFP cases must be reported, and necessary surveillance steps should be taken and followed up.

Case 17: A 15-Month-Old Child with Developmental Delay

A 15-month-old female child was brought by her mother to OPD with complaints of inability of the child to stand and walk or speak till this age. There was also history of feeding difficulties and drooling of saliva from mouth, and the child not gaining weight properly. There was no history of fever, convulsions, vomiting, and head trauma.

In the perinatal history, the mother had received antenatal care and had hypertension for which she received medications. The baby was full term and lower-segment cesarean section was done for fetal distress and tight loop of cord around neck. Birth weight of the child was 1500 g; the baby did not cry after birth and was kept in NICU for 6 days. She was required to be put on ventilator for 3 days, and the mother recalled that the baby remained limp and lethargic and had feeding difficulties even after she was handed over to her on the seventh day of life. She was tube fed initially and later was switched over to spoon feeding. The mother was also told that the baby had few episodes of convulsions while in NICU and blood pressure of the child was remaining low initially. Following discharge, they were going regularly for follow-up, and the child was receiving physiotherapy as per advice. The family history was not significant, and the child was immunized up to the age.

Developmental History

- *Gross motor milestones*: The mother is not able to recall when the child started holding neck. The child did not turn over abdomen, sit, stand, or walk.
- *Fine motor milestones*: The child was able to hold cube or similar objects when put in the hands but was not able to hold small beads or pellet-like objects.
- *Language*: The child was making cooing sounds at around 5–6 months and monosyllables such as ma, ba, da, and ah-goo sounds at around 12 months. The child was not able to speak bisyllables or any word.
- *Social/adaptive*: Social smile was achieved at 4 months and the child started to recognize the mother at approximately 6 months. The child did not learn to wave bye-bye and did not have stranger anxiety. She did not play with the toys like the children of similar age.

Analysis

- This child has developmental delay and it is global developmental delay (involving gross motor, fine motor, speech, and social domains). Any delay in two or more than two domains of development is labeled as global developmental delay.
- The child had severe intrauterine growth restriction (full term and very low birth weight). She had suffered significant perinatal insult in the form of perinatal asphyxia and hypoxic ischemic encephalopathy and also had seizures, feeding difficulty, limpness, and lethargy, which indicates that she had encephalopathy in the neonatal period. This is important contributory information on the perinatal history and has to be viewed and correlated with the child's delayed development.
- It is important to note whether delay in development is specific to a domain or global developmental delay. Children with only mental retardation will have delay in mental and social milestones and motor milestones will be normal. Children with hearing loss do not learn to speak, will present with only language delay, and may have normal motor milestones. A child with muscular or neuromuscular disorders can have motor delay and mental milestones can be normal.
- As the child has a delayed development from early infancy and has not lost any acquired milestones, this indicates a static

encephalopathy and not any progressive neurological diseases.

- Thus, this child has cerebral palsy (CP), which is a static disorder (static insult to the brain, but the clinical picture can be changing) that needs to be differentiated from the slowly progressive neurodegenerative or neurometabolic disorders in which the gained milestones are gradually lost. It thus reflects that the early brain insult in this child is of critical importance.
- Diagnosis of CP may not be made from a single examination, but by periodic and repeated evaluations.

Clinical Examination

The vital signs were normal. In the growth parameters (anthropometry), the child was having moderate malnutrition as per the WHO criteria (weight for height between –2SD and –3SD) and microcephaly (head circumference <–3SD). There were no dysmorphic features, head was small, mild pallor was present, and no neurocutaneous markers were present.

The neurological examination showed that the child was conscious and was not able to understand or follow verbal commands. Limited cranial nerve examination did not reveal any cranial nerve palsies; vision and hearing were present. In motor system, there was hypertonia/spasticity of all the four limbs; the child was able to move all four limbs against gravity. Deep tendon jerks were brisk (+++). Sensory system, gait, and cerebellar signs could not be tested. The child had dystonic movements and persistent asymmetric tonic neck reflex, and other systems were normal.

Inference and Diagnosis

The child had moderate malnutrition, which may be attributed to poor postnatal growth and feeding problems. She had microcephaly, which is likely to be secondary to perinatal insult. Sometimes, few children with primary CNS problems such as structural malformations and few genetic causes have microcephaly and such children also may not cry at birth manifesting as birth asphyxia. The child has spastic quadriparesis and persistent primitive reflex (asymmetric tonic neck reflex [ATNR]).

This child had suffered significant perinatal insult and had global developmental delay; there was no regression of milestones and no dysmorphism, abnormal tone, movements (dystonic) and reflexes involving all four limbs, and persistence of primitive reflexes, which favors the diagnosis of *spastic quadriparetic CP secondary to perinatal asphyxia.*

Diplegic CP, which is commonly due to periventricular leukomalacia following asphyxial injury especially seen in preterm babies, has involvement of all four limbs but predominantly lower limbs and lower trunk are involved. Mental functions are relatively spared. In hemiplegic CP, the child will have hand preference and difficulty in having motor skills involving one side of the limbs. Spastic quadriplegic CP has global developmental delay.

However, the child should be reassessed periodically to document the nonprogressive nature of CP or to look for any deterioration that would favor diagnosis of slowly progressive neurodegenerative or neurometabolic conditions.

Investigations

As CP is a clinical diagnosis, certain investigations would be necessary to rule out other conditions and for prognosis. This is especially true to identify and label a child with CP at an early age. Few other investigations would be necessary to find out other associated handicaps or morbidities.

- Developmental assessment tests: In a borderline case especially in the younger age, initially screening tests can be performed if delay in development is suspected. Baroda Developmental Screening Test (BDST) is a useful screening test. Trivandrum Developmental Screening Test (TDST) can be used in office practice also. Subjects who fail on screening tests are subjected to definitive tests such as Developmental Assessment Scale for Indian Infants (DASII). This child showed a delay in motor and mental development on DASII.
- Neuroimaging is recommended in evaluation of a child with CP if etiology has not been established, for example, by perinatal imaging, or if there is a family history of a similar disorder. MRI is preferred over CT scan. Neuroimaging may show evidence of perinatal insult, structural malformation of CNS, and hydrocephalus. This child was not subjected to neuroimaging. Neuroimaging can play an important role in prognosticating the course and progression of the condition.
- Genetic and metabolic testing should be done only in selected cases, if such cause is suspected. EEG should be done if there is an associated seizure disorder.
- Visual and hearing assessment should be done.

Principles of Management

The child with CP needs multidisciplinary management. Early developmental and physiotherapy intervention can lead to better outcome due to plasticity of neurons in early age.

- Management of spasticity
  - Physiotherapy: Crucial for spasticity and prevention of contractures
  - Neurodevelopmental techniques (NDT) (there are various NDTs; Bobath technique is most popular; it involves inhibiting abnormal reflexes and abnormal movement patterns with simultaneous facilitation of normal righting and equilibrium reactions)
  - Drugs: Oral—diazepam, baclofen, dantrolene
  - Intrathecal baclofen
  - Botulinum toxin injection
  - Phenol and ethyl alcohol—nerve block
  - Selective dorsal rhizotomy
- Occupational therapy
- Multisensory stimulation
- Speech therapy
- Aids and appliances
- Surgery—for contractures
- Management of associated morbidities such as epilepsy, hearing, vision, language problems, orthopedic complication such as scoliosis and hip subluxation, feeding problems such as constipation, drooling of saliva, nutrition, and growth
- Counseling

Key Messages

- The clinical hallmark of CP is the presence of motor dysfunction involving abnormal muscle tone, posture, and movement disorders.
- The severity of the manifestations depends on multiple factors such as type of the brain insult, its extent, and coexisting morbid conditions.
- A multidisciplinary team approach is most important for the management of a child with CP.

Case 18: A 5-Year-Old Child with an Episode of Seizure

A 5-year-old child presented to the pediatric emergency following a seizure (stiffness of body with abnormal movements and loss of consciousness) at home. By the time of assessment, he was afebrile, alert, and interactive. He had a similar episode about 15 months back and was shown to his pediatric consultant who advised the parents to get some investigations done but they did not follow up.

On a Sunday afternoon, the child was playing with his friends in his home garden. His friends saw him collapse suddenly to the ground; he started to shake with jerky movements of both his arms and legs with his eyes rolling upwards and frothing from mouth. He did not respond when his friends called his name loudly. He did not respond to skin pinching. After 2–3 minutes, shaking movements stopped but he was drowsy for almost 5 minutes. As soon as the parents knew about this event, they rushed him to the pediatric emergency. He was sleepy when his parents brought him to the emergency department. Twenty minutes later, he was awake and alert but complaining of slight headache. He did have runny nose and cough for the past 2 days but no fever. He did not complain of headache previously. He was eating and drinking normally till afternoon. There was no past history of trauma, drug ingestion, allergies, or similar episode in the past.

The child was born at term (40 weeks' gestation) via normal vaginal delivery, and cried immediately at birth with Apgar score of 9 at 1 minute and 10 at 5 minutes. The birth weight was 3.1 kg. The motor and mental development was normal except that he had speech delay requiring speech therapy when he was 2 years old. There was no history of previous hospitalizations. The child had received his complete immunizations. He attended preschool regularly. The child was studying in junior kindergarten. He was an only child of nonconsanguineous parents. The father had epilepsy in his adolescence for which he received antiepileptic medications, which he responded to well. He was otherwise well and continued the medications for 5 years, which were later stopped as he remained seizure-free.

Analysis

- This child developed a paroxysmal event at home with abnormal motor activity, impairment, and loss of consciousness for the first time in his childhood.
- It is important to confirm the event by asking whether it was a seizure. A complete description, its sequence, and its termination help to elucidate proper information. Absence of any precipitating event, tonic deviation of the eyes, and urinary incontinence are helpful pointers to it being a seizure. If the child goes off to sleep, it further points to its likelihood of a seizure.
- Taking a good history is key to distinguishing an epileptic seizure from a nonepileptic event. It is important to speak to the person who witnessed the event.
- From the description, it appears that this child had a generalized seizure. He did not have any antecedent factor that could have precipitated the seizure. Seizures occurring during the course of an acute illness due to an acute cause are labeled as provoked seizures (acute symptomatic seizures). Common conditions that can cause provoked seizures in children include febrile convulsions, head trauma, drug withdrawal, and metabolic disturbances (e.g., hypoglycemia and hypocalcemia). This child did not have a provoked seizure.
- This child had a second episode of seizure and thus this can be labeled as a recurrent seizure. The presence of family history of epilepsy in the father also lends credence to the recurrent seizures in the child.
- A seizure is a symptom and not a specific disease condition and hence a detailed history, clinical examination, and relevant investigations would be needed to determine its etiology.

- In view of the child having the first seizure episode 15 months back and remaining well for a long period in between and no progression and appearance of other symptoms, serious and progressive conditions causing this seizure are excluded.
- This should not be considered as a febrile seizure (which is the most common cause of seizures during the childhood, between the ages of 6 months and 5 years) as this child had no fever at the time of seizure.
- This can be labeled as a recurrent seizure at this stage as this was the second such episode in this child.

Clinical Examination

The child was alert and interactive and had normal vitals. He was pink and well perfused. The temperature was 37.2°C. HR was 110/min regular with normal volume. RR was 24/min. The BP was 92/60 mmHg. No rashes were noted and there were no neurocutaneous stigmata. Absence of skin features such as port-wine stain, facial angiofibroma, hypopigmented macules, or Shagreen patch suggestive of neurocutaneous syndrome was noteworthy in this child.

The child did not look dysmorphic. No bruises or injury marks were noted. The ear, nose, and throat examinations were normal. On neurological examination, pupils were bilaterally equal and reactive to light. Fundoscopic examination was normal. The cranial nerve examination was normal and tone, power, and reflexes were all within the normal range. No meningeal signs were detected and rest of the examination was normal.

Inference and Diagnosis

The clinical history and normal neurological and other systemic examination make this condition an unprovoked and recurrent seizure (second episode) of abnormal motor activity and altered consciousness. The description fits into the prototype of a generalized tonic and clonic seizure. As this was the second episode occurring more than 24 hours apart, this is diagnosed as *epilepsy (generalized seizures of tonic–clonic type)*. A generalized tonic–clonic seizure starts with continued tonic stiffening and is then followed by a clonic phase of rhythmic jerks of the body. The presence of epilepsy in the father (who earlier received antiepileptic drugs) further strengthens the diagnosis of epilepsy in the child as epilepsy can occur due to genetic predisposition. Absence of dysmorphic features and normal neurodevelopment exclude syndromic and progressive neurodegenerative diseases as the likely causes of epilepsy.

Other underlying causes of seizure are unlikely in this child as discussed earlier. However, certain conditions can mimic epilepsy and should be excluded if needed. These include breath-holding spells, syncopal attacks, migraine, and prolonged QT syndrome. The latter must be excluded if there is an exercise-induced syncopal attack mimicking epilepsy with a family history.

Investigations

Many children with epilepsy do not require investigations such as routine EEG, neuroimaging, and video EEG recording. The choice of investigations should be decided on the age of onset and seizure types (e.g., absence and myoclonic epilepsy, with typical EEG), to differentiate seizures from nonseizure activities and to localize the epileptogenic focus in intractable and difficult-to-control epilepsy. *EEG recordings reflect the* physiological manifestations of abnormal cortical excitability that underlie epilepsy. Neuroimaging (CT/MRI) is indicated in the presence of focal epilepsy or features of raised intracranial tension, or with a suspicion of an underlying space-occupying lesion.

This child was subjected to EEG, which showed the presence of bilaterally synchronous abnormal discharges on the recording.

Principles of Management

- The management aim is to control the occurrence of seizures in the future and thus assure a good quality of life.
- The decision to initiate the antiepileptic drugs depends on whether it is the first or a recurrent seizure, whether it is focal or generalized, and whether there is an associated preexisting neurological abnormality.
- Generally, absence seizures are treated from the first episode, while focal and myoclonic epilepsies require evaluation and treatment from the first episode. The long-term drug therapy from the first episode is withheld in generalized epilepsy except in few conditions such as first episode being status epilepticus or in the presence of neurological deficit or an underlying inflammatory granuloma. The treatment should begin with a single first-line drug for the seizure and then monitored for the response. Addition of another antiepileptic drug may be needed based on the seizure types, control, side effects, and the cost.
- The choice of antiepileptic medications is primarily based on the seizure types and epilepsy syndrome, and rational antiepileptic therapy should be offered to the child.
- Proper monitoring for the compliance, adverse drug effects, and response to the treatment are essential components of long-term management of epilepsy.
- The management must also address the family and the child to adjust and accept the diagnosis and the need for a long-term and continued care.

Key Messages

- The diagnosis of epilepsy is made if the child has had two or more unprovoked seizures more than 24 hours apart.
- A sequential history, patterns of abnormal movements, and their distribution help to establish the diagnosis of epilepsy. Investigations such as EEG and neuroimaging are often helpful.
- The aim of therapy should be to provide a rational antiepileptic therapy with the most appropriate drug for proper duration along with regular follow-up and monitoring.

Case 19: A 10-Year-Old Boy with Fever, Puffiness of Eyes, and Dark-Colored Urine

A 10-year-old boy was admitted to the pediatric ICU with a history of fever for 7 days, puffiness of the eyelids for 4 days, and generalized tonic–clonic convulsions for previous half an hour. He was having pain in abdomen and occasional vomiting in the past 4 days. He had earlier been seen by the family physician and given antipyretics and antiemetics 2 days ago but without much improvement. When he developed a sudden convulsion, he was brought into the emergency department of the hospital.

There was no history of any convulsions, headaches, or vomiting in the past. The mother had not noticed the color of the urine till now and did not know whether the child was passing adequate urine or not. There was no significant past history of a sore throat or pyoderma. On arrival in the hospital, the child was given an intravenous dose of an anticonvulsant and the vital signs showed a pulse rate of 98/min, RR 28/min, BP 170/124 mmHg (95th centile), and SpO_2 of 95%. Urinary catheterization yielded 200 mL of brown (cola-colored) urine, which was not earlier noticed by the mother. He was given IV nitroprusside and frusemide to control the blood pressure. After a few hours, he became fully conscious, although the blood pressure still remained above normal, 140/100 mmHg.

Analysis

- Although the child has a history of fever and puffiness of the eyes, the alarming symptom in this child is an episode of convulsion, which indicates a possibility of an underlying disease that has led to the convulsion. The BP of 170/124 mmHg was significantly high (>95th centile).
- Essential hypertension, unlike in adults, is rare in children and important causes of childhood hypertension include renal parenchymal disease (acute nephritic syndrome [ANS]), renovascular disease (e.g., systemic lupus erythematosus), tumors such as Wilms tumor, and coarctation of the aorta.
- It is important to determine whether the hypertension in the child is transient or persistent, the latter signifying a chronic/progressive disease. Renal diseases are the most common cause of hypertension in children.
- An acute presentation of hypertension seen in this child raises the possibility of it being a transient hypertension manifesting as hypertensive encephalopathy precipitating altered sensorium and seizures.
- Presence of fever may not always be due to an infective process but is likely to suggest an inflammatory response.
- The presence of puffiness of eyes is suggestive of fluid retention caused by renal disease, which is also suggested by the presence of cola-colored dark urine in the urine sample obtained by catheterization.

Clinical Examination

The child was drowsy with puffiness of the eyes and mild pitting edema of the feet. There was also presence of mild pallor but there were no boils/scars, purpura, petechiae, or bleeding from any other site. There were no signs of meningeal irritation and rest of the clinical examination was normal. The presence of pedal edema, facial puffiness, and probable hematuria with hypertension was now pointing toward a renal pathology rather than a CNS pathology that one thought earlier due to the convulsion.

Inference and Diagnosis

The child was a case of ANS, with hypertensive encephalopathy. This is the most plausible diagnosis due to the edema, cola-colored urine, and a hypertensive encephalopathy. Acute poststreptococcal glomerulonephritis (PSGN) is the most common cause of ANS in children. ANS is most commonly seen in children between the ages of 3 and 12 years. A child with ANS can also present with gross hematuria and oliguria, acute pulmonary edema, and, less frequently, acute renal failure. Other differential diagnoses to be considered in this case include:

- *Severe falciparum malaria with hemolysis*: This is a close differential diagnosis as the child was having a fever for 10 days, convulsions, and dark urine, which could be due to an intravascular hemolysis. The hypertension could be considered as a transient one due to CNS involvement.
- *Rapidly progressive glomerulonephritis (RPGN)*: This may also be present.
- *Nephritic onset of nephrotic syndrome (NS) (also known as non–minimal change nephrotic syndrome [MCNS] type of NS)*: Rarely, a non-MCNS could present with hypertension, hematuria, and proteinuria. However, a hypertensive encephalopathy would be extremely rare in this situation.

Investigations

- CBC: Hb 12.0 g/dL, TLC 15,500, platelets 252,000/mm^3
- Blood urea, 30 mg% serum creatinine, 1.2 mg/dL
- SGPT 20 units/L, PT 14.6, PTT 26.4
- Serum electrolytes: Na 142, K 4.8, Cl 110, serum HCO_3 18 mEq/L

- ASO normal
- Serum C3 low
- Urine: Protein +++, blood +++ with RBC casts and pus cells 10–15/high-power field (HPF)
- Posterior reversible encephalopathy syndrome (PRES) shown by MRI done on day 7 (this was visible as hyperintense shadows in the occipitoparietal region in patients with hypertensive encephalopathy; however, neuroimaging is rarely required in ANS)

Although acute PSGN is the most common cause of ANS, consider other causes of nephritis and consider a kidney biopsy if:

- Associated clinical features, viz., rash, purpura, arthritis, arthralgia, and abdominal pain, are present.
- ASO is normal or serum C3 remains persistently low at 8 weeks as in PSGN a low serum C3 returns to normal in 6–8 weeks.
- Hypertension, hematuria, and/or proteinuria persists for 3–4 weeks or longer.
- Azotemia is not only present but also disproportionate to the clinical features (this would suggest RPGN).
- Other causes of ANS are present, which include infective endocarditis, shunt nephritis, hepatitis B and C infections, vasculitis (systemic lupus, Henoch–Schonlein purpura), acute interstitial nephritis (drug induced), and IgA nephropathy.

Principles of Management

- *Supportive care*: Respiratory, HR, and blood pressure monitoring in an intensive care setup is essential. All care of an unconscious patient should be given and the airway, breathing, and circulation (ABC) supported.
- *Hypertension*: Drugs for controlling the BP should be started in proper dose and duration in the order of IV nitroprusside and followed by IV furosemide. Once the child is conscious, IV nitroprusside can be replaced by enalapril and nifedipine and furosemide tapered off in the next few days.
- *Edema/urine output (UOP)*: IV furosemide should be given in a high dose of 3–4 mg/kg/day in 6-hourly doses. The UOP should gradually increase over the next few days and as it increases, and the BP starts getting controlled, furosemide should be tapered off. Fluid and salt restriction are important aspects of management.
- *Benzathine penicillin*: It is given as a single intramuscular injection by most units to cover for the streptococci if still present.

Key Messages

- ANS presents most commonly with hematuria, oliguria, mild puffiness, and hypertension.
- ANS is the most common cause of hematuria in children.
- Uncommon causes of ANS apart from the most common cause, PSGN, need to be considered in the presence of unusual features.

Case 20: An 8-Year-Old Boy with Recurrent Generalized Anasarca with Proteinuria

An 8-year-old boy was admitted with a history of fever, cough, cold, and facial puffiness, and a decreased UOP since 2 days. He did not give a history of dark or red-colored urine and did not suffer from a headache or convulsions. He did not give a history of boils anywhere on his body. He gave a history of similar episodes of puffiness and decreased UOP frequently since the age of 5 years and was admitted twice in the past for these complaints. During a previous episode, he had swelling on his feet and abdominal distension too. On detailed enquiry, he did complain of pain in abdomen and had vomited twice in the past 24 hours and passed two to three loose stools too. No one in the family had suffered from such complaints. His one elder sister, 10 years old, was healthy. He was immunized for his age.

Analysis

- The significant complaint was of puffiness of the face. This complaint had been recurrent for the past 2 years and at times the child has had edema of the feet and abdominal distension too. Edema and decreased UOP suggest a renal origin of disease.
- The absence of hypertension, hematuria, and boils on the body points against the possibility of a nephritis. Recurrence strongly suggests the possibility of a NS.
- Fever and cough suggest the possibility of a respiratory infection being the probable cause of precipitating a relapse in this case.
- Abdominal pain, diarrhea, and vomiting in this patient may suggest the possibility of peritonitis as a complication.

Clinical Examination

On arrival, the child's vitals were stable and showed a pulse of 98/min and RR of 28/min, and the blood pressure on routine exam was found to be 110/80 mmHg.

The child had periorbital puffiness and facial fluffiness. He also had a pitting edema on both feet and an abdominal distension. He appeared waxy and pale and had no cyanosis. Respiratory system revealed few crepitations but no respiratory distress. The abdominal examination showed a distension, transversely stretched umbilicus (smiling umbilicus), and a fluid thrill. There was a vague tenderness on abdominal examination. On percussing the abdomen, a horseshoe dullness with a shifting dullness was present. All these signs suggested the presence of free fluid (ascites) in the abdomen. Genital examination (very vital for a suspected case of NS) showed a huge scrotal edema.

Inference and Diagnosis

This was a case of recurrent edema (anasarca) with a respiratory tract infection with ascites. Common causes of edema in children are:

- Renal (ANS, NS, and acute renal failure)
- Cardiac, mainly due to congestive cardiac failure (edema due to a cardiac case can be ruled out in this case by the absence of tachycardia, tachypnea, palpitations, and a known history of a cardiac disease)
- Primary malnutrition due to hypoproteinemia (although hypoproteinemia is the cause of edema in a case of NS, the clinical findings of primary malnutrition were not present in this case, making this cause less likely)
- Liver diseases, which can cause edema in children again due to hypoproteinemia (however, no other pointers toward liver disease in this child make it unlikely)

ANS is unlikely due to the symptoms and signs being recurrent in this case. PSGN, the commonest form of ANS, is almost always never recurrent.

NS is the most likely diagnosis as the condition is recurrent. Ninety percent to 95% of all NS are recurrent. MCNS is the commonest form of NS seen in 80% of all NS and is recurrent and relapses in 90% of cases. Other forms of NS are focal and segmental glomerulosclerosis (FSGS), which is seen in 10–15% of patients, and membranoproliferative glomerulonephritis (MPGN), which is seen in 5–10% of patients. One should consider the possibility of FSGS and MPGN when nephritic features are present such as hematuria, hypertension, and azotemia. Prognostically, MCNS does well and, with age, children outgrow the disease in adolescence in 85–90% of cases. FSGS and MPGN have a higher chance of going to end-stage renal disease (ESRD).

As this child has NS, it is important to remember its complications that may be present at the time of initial presentation also. These include:

- Recurrent infections such as pneumonia, meningitis, cellulitis
- Urinary tract infection and peritonitis
- Thromboembolic phenomena
- Complications of drug therapy (steroid toxicity)
- Hypocalcemic tetany

Investigations

- CBC: Hb 10.0 g/dL, TLC 15,700, platelets 212,000/mm^3
- Blood urea, 30 mg% serum creatinine, 1.2 mg/dL
- Serum electrolytes: Na 142, K 4.8, Cl 110, serum HCO_3 18 mEq/L
- Serum albumin 1.4 g% and serum cholesterol 375 mg/dL
- Serum C3 normal, suggesting the possibility of MCNS
- Urine: Protein ++++, blood nil with pus cells 10–15/HPF
- No growth yielded by urine c/s
- X-ray chest normal, and Mantoux test (MT) negative
- Free fluid shown by USG abdomen
- Peritoneal fluid: Proteins of 625 mg/dL, lymphocytes 10/HPF, and polymorphs 725/HPF
- Kidney biopsy: Indications
  - Suspected secondary NS
  - Steroid-resistant, steroid-dependent, and some cases of frequently relapsing NS
  - Persistent proteinuria for 6 months
  - Less than 1 year and more than 8 years
  - Non-MCNS features
  - Before giving alternative drugs

The urinary protein was ++++, serum albumin was <2 g/dL, and serum cholesterol was >200 mg/dL in the presence of generalized anasarca. The patient has had many relapses and has probably never been in good control or in remission. The peritoneal fluid shows infection with high proteins and cells. Thus, the final diagnosis was: *relapse of NS with LRTI and peritonitis.*

Principles of Management

- Supportive care and monitoring: Rest is advised for few days. Monitor 24-hour UOP, abdominal girth (AG) daily once/twice, blood pressure and urine albumin daily, and weight daily.
- Edema/UOP: IV furosemide should be given in a low dose of 1–2 mg/kg/day in 8-hourly doses. The UOP should gradually increase over the next few days and as it increases, the anasarca decreases and the patient loses weight. Furosemide should be tapered off when steroid-induced diuresis starts in the next few days.
- Antibiotics in the form of ceftriaxone or co-amoxiclav along with amikacin for the treatment of peritonitis and the respiratory infection should be given for 10–14 days. The antibiotics should be changed as per the culture reports.
- Steroids are the mainstay of treatment. Prednisolone is given in the dose of 2 mg/kg/day in three to four divided doses for 6 weeks followed by 1.5 mg/kg QOD (alternate day) as a single morning dose for the next 4–6 weeks. Steroids are tapered off over the next 4–6 weeks for the first attack and for infrequently relapsing patients in

most hospitals. For a frequently relapsing patient, like our case, 1.5 mg/kg QOD is given for a longer period like 12 weeks and slow tapering is done over 6–9 months.

- Alternative drug therapy should be considered in the following situations: steroid resistance, steroid dependence, and frequent relapses with steroid toxicity. Drugs used are cyclophosphamide, cyclosporine and chlorambucil, mycophenolate, or tacrolimus.
- Calcium supplements should be given to prevent hypocalcemia induced by steroid therapy.

Key Messages

- NS is a clinical condition characterized by massive proteinuria, hypoalbuminemia, edema, and hypercholesterolemia with or without hematuria, hypertension, raised blood urea, and deranged renal parameters.
- It takes a relapsing course and most children with MCNS outgrow the disease in adolescence.
- Prednisolone is the therapy that should be used in a controlled manner and followed up well to prevent relapses and to prevent/detect toxicity at the earliest.

Case 21: A 3-Year-Old Child with Fever, Pallor, and Painful Swelling Over the Joints for 7 Days

A 3-year-old boy from socioeconomically poor parents was referred by his family physician for fever, pallor, swelling, and pain over the hands and feet for the previous 7–8 days. The fever was of moderate grade and did not respond to the antipyretics and analgesics given by the family physician. Three to 4 days after the fever, the parents noticed the swelling over the child's both hands and the child was reluctant to move his limbs. He was also complaining of pain in feet and was able to walk with some difficulty. There was a history of similar complaints about 1.5 years ago when he was admitted to a district hospital for 7 days and treated with antibiotics, intravenous fluids, and 2 units of PCV. Although the parents had not noticed any pallor, the referring doctor told them that the child was pale looking and may need a blood transfusion.

The child was second-born with a birth weight of 2.4 kg born of a nonconsanguineous marriage. The other older sibling was reported asymptomatic. The child had received his primary immunizations but had not taken the booster doses at 1.5 years of age. He had two to three episodes of febrile illnesses without any other specific symptoms during the past year, which were treated by his local doctor. No long-term medications were prescribed.

Analysis

- The child has a triad of symptoms of fever, anemia, and joint involvement, which may be due to many conditions such as infective, hematologic, or rheumatoid etiologies.
- The past history of admission and receiving 2 units of PCVs is useful contributing information and should provide a valuable clue to the clinical diagnosis.
- In view of the possible multifactorial symptoms that point to different etiologies, clinical diagnosis can be arrived at only after a detailed clinical examination.

Clinical Examination

The child was febrile with the body temperature of 39.5°C and was appearing sick. The HR was 110/min, RR was 32/min, and BP was 90/60 mmHg. He had some palmar pallor and a mild icteric tinge in the eyes. There was no lymphadenopathy, rash, purpura or petechiae, or bleeding from any site. Hands and feet had a bilateral tenderness and mild swelling. Other joints and spine were normal. The liver was 5 cm, firm, and the spleen was 7 cm, firm and nontender. The chest showed few crepitations over the left infrascapular region with bilaterally equal air entry. Rest of the examination was normal.

Inference and Diagnosis

The age at the onset with a past history of a similar episode with severe anemia needs to be correlated with the present diagnosis. The pain and swelling in the hands and feet appears likely to be a painful crisis (hand–foot syndrome) resulting from vaso-occlusion and the microinfarctions of carpal and tarsal bones that could have been precipitated by any infection and dehydration in the child. Such a phenomenon is a common manifestation of a congenital hemoglobinopathy, one of them being sickle cell anemia (HbSS).

Even though there are different forms of sickle cell disease, children who are homozygous for HbSS (sickle hemoglobin) are more likely to manifest such symptoms and episodes of crisis (e.g., vaso-occlusive, splenic sequestration, and aplastic crisis). Dactylitis, often referred to as hand–foot syndrome, is frequently the first manifestation of pain in children with sickle cell anemia, occurring in 50% of children by 2 years of age. The presence of mild icteric tinge in the eyes is not due to hepatic disease (direct type of jaundice) but reflects an underlying hemolysis (indirect type of jaundice).

The differential diagnosis that needs to be considered includes acute leukemia but the P/H of a similar episode with a long period of wellness in between and absence of any bleeding manifestations rules out acute leukemia. Juvenile idiopathic arthritis (JIA) of systemic onset type should not be considered as the condition is rare below the age of 3 years, insidious in onset, and takes weeks to months to evolve and be labeled as JIA.

Investigations

The initial laboratory investigations showed a hemoglobin of 6 g/dL, WBC counts of 19,000/mm^3 (P 64% and L 36%), and ESR 50 mm/h. The platelet count was 1.2 lac/mm^3. The peripheral smear examination showed normocytic anemia and anisocytosis with target cells. The reticulocyte count was increased to 5%. Sickling test was positive.

The urinalysis was normal and chest X-ray showed infiltrations on the left side. Bone marrow aspiration was performed to exclude hematologic malignancy and was found to be reactive bone marrow with no other abnormality. On hemoglobin electrophoresis, HbS was 85%, HbF 13%, and HbA2 2%. Blood culture revealed no organism. The parents were screened for sickle cell anemia and both the parents were found to have sickle cell trait.

Principles of Management

- Sickle cell crisis is a medical emergency that requires prompt management.
- The treatment should largely be supportive, which includes correction of dehydration, transfusion if needed, and the treatment of infections that may have resulted in the present crisis.
- Pain management is required and severe pain itself requires hospital admission.
- Drugs such as hydroxyurea are used on a long-term basis to stimulate HbF levels and decrease HbS level.
- Folic acid supplementation, antibiotic prophylaxis with oral penicillin, and immunizations against encapsulated organisms are mandatory in such children.

Key Messages

- Sickle cell disease is a common congenital hemoglobinopathy seen in children.
- Sickle cell crisis should be handled as a medical emergency and needs hospitalization and prompt management.
- The goal is to achieve a normal life span with minimal morbidity. As therapy improves, the prognosis also improves.
- The patients and the family should be taught to seek urgent medical care in case of any of the following: persistent fever (>38.3°C), chest pain or shortness of breath, abdominal pain with nausea and vomiting, and persistent headache not experienced previously.

Case 22: A 4-Year-Old Girl with Bleeding Spots over the Body

A 4-year-old girl child was brought to the hospital with complaints of reddish-colored bleeding spots over the body over the past 3 days. The parents initially noticed a few pinkish-red-colored spots over the face and then on the upper limbs that then slowly increased in numbers and appeared at different places on her trunk and limbs. One to two light bluish-colored patches were also noticed over her body. She was reported to be healthy before the onset of this illness and there was no history of fever, trauma, drug intake, immunizations, and bleeding from any other site. The past and the family history was also noncontributory. The child remained well and comfortable at home.

Analysis

- Apart from the reddish-colored skin lesions and light bluish lesions, there is notable absence of any other alarming symptom. At this stage in a well-appearing child, this commonly rules out an immediate life-threatening illness. The absence of fever rules out an infective cause for this condition.
- Red-colored small spots over the body are likely to be purpuric lesions (between 2 and 10 mm in size) and the larger skin bleeds are likely to be ecchymoses. If the larger lesions seem to change color over a few days, they are confirmed as ecchymoses.
- Fixed drug eruptions can also lead to lesions appearing bluish black but then would fade away slowly.
- Presence of purpuric lesions and petechiae (<2 mm) in all likelihood indicates the presence of either a platelet or a vascular disorder, while ecchymoses can also be due to coagulopathy (e.g., hemophilia). Although coagulation disorders can present at any age, generally they would have an earlier onset and there would be a family history of bleeding. Besides, a coagulopathy such as hemophilia manifests as a deep-seated bleeding in a joint or muscle that can lead to crippling deformities if not diagnosed and treated properly.
- The bleeds being spontaneous and not precipitated by trauma also adds further information about it not being an inherited coagulopathy. If the child in any time in the past has undergone any surgery or dental extraction without any complication and excessive bleeding, then it suggests that the bleeding is acquired rather than an inherited one.
- This is also not a secondary coagulation defect such as seen in vitamin K deficiency, chronic diarrhea, and liver disease as there is no historical evidence of any of these.
- Thus, the condition most likely appears to be an acquired platelet disorder responsible for the purpura and ecchymosis in this well-looking child. Although it must be noted that this child has no mucosal bleeds, these can occur in both platelet disorders and inherited and acquired coagulation defects.

Clinical Examination

The girl is well nourished (18 kg and 98 cm), and looked comfortable and not sick with normal vital parameters. There was no pallor, lymphadenopathy, ulcers, other skin lesions, and mucosal bleeds. The throat and tonsils were normal; there were no mucosal bleeds, and oral cavity and gums were normal. The bones and joints were normal and there was no bony tenderness. There were multiple purpuric spots and a few ecchymoses all over the body. Systemic examination was completely normal.

Inference and Diagnosis

As discussed earlier in the analysis, the history and examination points to a defect involving either platelets or vascular endothelium. Given the history, apparent well-being of the child, skin bleeds, and absence of hepatosplenomegaly, this points to a most likely diagnosis of immune thrombocytopenic purpura (also referred to as immune thrombocytopenia [ITP]).

Other conditions such as bone marrow infiltrations/malignancy are almost ruled out as the child looks well and not sick, is not anemic, and there is no hepatosplenomegaly and lymphadenopathy. Antecedent viral illness precipitating ITP, though common, may not occur in all the children and hence its absence is not a strong point against the diagnosis of ITP.

Investigations

The hemoglobin was 10.5 g% and RBC and WBC counts were normal. The platelet count was 70,000 mm^3 (normal 1.5–4.5 lac) and platelet clumps were seen on peripheral smear. Bone marrow examination showed active marrow with large megakaryocytes confirming the diagnosis of ITP.

Principles of Management

- Majority of the children do not need any therapy with mild to moderate symptoms and bleeding.
- Treatment is generally indicated in the presence of platelet counts (<10,000/mm^3) or with significant mucosal and internal bleeding or suspected intracranial bleed, irrespective of platelet counts.
- The recommended modalities for treatment are IVIG, steroids, and anti-D globulin (only in Rh-positive children).
- Platelet transfusions do not benefit as these are destroyed rapidly by the antibodies. Splenectomy is reserved only for very few select cases of ITP.

Key Messages

- ITP is the one of the commonest causes of thrombocytopenia in children and is caused by the immune-mediated destruction of the platelets by the antiplatelet autoantibodies.
- ITP is a diagnosis of exclusion and hence a careful and meticulous attention must be paid to the clinical history, physical examination, and peripheral smear.
- Any atypical features must call for an alternate diagnosis and a mandatory bone marrow examination.
- The condition is usually self-limiting and the majority of the children become asymptomatic within 6 months of the onset of the symptoms. A very small proportion goes to become chronic ITP (persistence >12 months).

Case 23: A 5-Year-Old Child with Prolonged Fever of 15–20 Days, Abdominal Distension, and Easy Fatigability

A 5-year-old boy presented with a history of fever that was continuous, moderate, and not accompanied with chills and rigors. The intensity of the fever had remained same over the past few days without any good response to antipyretics that he received at the onset of illness for 4–5 days. Then he developed a gradual abdominal distension noticed over the past 15–20 days. The child had complaints of loose stools four to five times a day since 5 days, which were loose and not containing blood/mucus, and the child was also noticed to have had a reduced appetite. He was passing normal light-colored urine. There were no other complaints. The parents informed that the child was getting easily tired since the onset of his illness.

There was a history of gum bleed 2 days ago but there was no history of any other bleeding, vomiting, jaundice, headache, and swelling over the body. The past history and family history were also noncontributory, the child had his complete immunizations, and his dietary and development history was also normal.

Analysis

- The presence of prolonged fever, abdominal distension, and increasing fatigability that are progressively worsening are alarming symptoms. Most of the common causes of fever such as enteric fever and viral pyrexia would generally tend to get symptomatically better with the passage of time with or without specific treatment.
- The causes of fever in this child would need to be elicited beyond common infections and these may include disseminated tuberculosis, kala-azar, brucellosis, infectious mononucleosis, and other noninfectious causes of fever (such as connective tissue diseases, chronic liver disease, malignancy).
- The complaints of gradual distension of abdomen are a pointer to either a visceral enlargement (liver/spleen/both) or a collection of ascitic fluid. However, absence of history of jaundice and swelling over feet excludes liver disease causing ascites.
- The abdominal distension could be thus due to hepatosplenomegaly that may be caused by a variety of conditions such as infections (e.g., malaria, enteric fever), hemolytic anemia (sickle cell anemia), and infiltrations (e.g., malignancy). Acute malaria and enteric fever do not cause significant hepatosplenomegaly so as to cause abdominal distension.
- The cause of easy fatigability may be a constitutional symptom related to his sickness or the presence of anemia in this child that can reduce his work capacity.

Clinical Examination

The child had acute wasting with a weight of 12 kg (≤3SD) and his temperature was 37.9°F (100.2°F). He appeared sick looking with severe pallor with HR of 118/min, RR 36/min, and BP 90/60 mmHg. There was generalized lymphadenopathy with multiple cervical nodes that were nontender and firm on both the sides. There were also few bilateral axillary lymph nodes (>1 cm in size). There was no rash, purpura, or ecchymosis and the oral cavity was normal. The joints had no tenderness, but the child had tenderness on deep pressure on the sternum. The liver was enlarged 6.5 cm, firm, and nontender, and spleen was 5.5 cm, firm in consistency. Rest of the examination was noncontributory.

Inference and Diagnosis

The fever, anemia, bony tenderness, generalized lymphadenopathy, and hepatosplenomegaly should now be viewed and analyzed together to arrive at a clinical diagnosis. The clinical features are suggestive of a bone marrow infiltration and failure that produces anemia (fatigability and pallor), neutropenia (infections), and thrombocytopenia (petechiae and ecchymoses—not seen in this child). There is also evidence of infiltration of reticuloendothelial (RE) system in the form of lymphadenopathy, hepatosplenomegaly, and sternal tenderness. Rarely or initially, generalized lymphadenopathy and significant hepatosplenomegaly may not be detectable in early infiltrations. As the disease progresses, signs and symptoms of marrow and RE cell infiltration can become progressively more obvious with easy bruising, bleeding, and persistence of fever.

Collaborating the clinical findings, the clinical diagnosis is likely to be acute lymphoblastic leukemia (ALL). The other differential diagnoses include infectious mononucleosis, but it generally subsides in 4–6 weeks, non–Hodgkin lymphoma, JIA, and aplastic anemia. The latter does not have presence of hepatosplenomegaly and lymphadenopathy. Other organ involvement such as CNS infiltration and testes should be excluded but is more common during relapse.

Investigations

The CBC showed hemoglobin of 5 g%, with normocytic and normochromic anemia, TLC of 19,000/mm^3, predominantly lymphocytes, and platelet counts of 45,000/mm^3, and blast cells were seen on the peripheral smear. Lactate dehydrogenase (LDH) level was increased (550 units/L). The bone marrow examination confirmed the diagnosis of ALL with the presence of more than 40% blast cells. X-ray chest and CSF examination to exclude CNS leukemia were normal. Immunophenol typing by surface marking confirmed pre-B type of ALL.

Principles of Management

- The therapy includes specific chemotherapy for remission induction, consolidation, CNS prophylaxis, and maintenance therapy with a standard protocol.
- Supportive therapy to treat and prevent infections, nutrition, and blood component infusions are an integral part of the treatment.
- Hematopoietic stem cell transplant (SCT) is done in selective cases.
- The survival for standard risk ALL in India is 60–80%.

Key Messages

- Leukemia is the commonest childhood malignancy and accounts for up to 70–80% of all the childhood cancers.
- The clinical features of ALL are due to bone marrow infiltration and failure.
- A high index of suspicion can help in early diagnosis and better management.
- Favorable prognostic factors include age at diagnosis between 2 and 9 years and TLC <50,000/mm^3. Cytogenetic studies of the bone marrow at the time of diagnosis are important to identify specific prognostic factors.

Case 24: A 3-Month-Old Boy with Poor Growth and Sleepiness

A 3-month-old boy is seen for his well-child visit. The boy is the first child of his parents. The pregnancy was without complication, and 18-week fetal ultrasound was reportedly normal. Birth history was unremarkable with Apgar scores of 8 and 9 at 1 and 5 minutes, respectively. The birth weight was 3.0 kg. The infant did have prolonged jaundice that was noticeable till 4 weeks of age. He is on breastfeed but does not feed well and needs to be woken up for feeds. The mother reports that she has an adequate lactation and has no breastfeeding difficulty. As per her, the baby appears somewhat lethargic and less active. He had no history of abnormal or bloody stools, although he passes stools only once in few days. The family history is unremarkable.

Analysis

- The important concerns in this baby are his feeding problem, prolonged neonatal jaundice, and excessive sleepiness.
- From the history, it appears that the infant may be failing to thrive as the mother informs that the baby does not feed actively. If there is no breast milk inadequacy, this is an indicator of an underlying systemic problem. Mothers are keen observers of their baby's well-being and proper attention must be given to their feelings and observations even if they may appear minor.
- Infants with FTT include those with a weight <5th percentile or those who have had a decrease in two or more major percentile lines. The differential diagnosis for FTT includes inadequate oral intake, inadequate nutrient absorption, increased losses via urine or stool, or ineffective metabolic use of nutrients.
- Diagnosis of FTT should trigger thorough evaluation, including any psychosocial or behavioral barrier to feeding. Feeding schedule, adequacy of breastfeeding, and preparation of formula, if applicable, should

be reviewed. Growth chart should be studied for the onset of FTT.

Clinical Examination

On entering the room, the infant was noted to be a small child who was sleeping in his mother's arms. He had a puffy face and dry-appearing skin. Physical exam was notable for large anterior fontanel (6.5 × 5.5 cm), large tongue, umbilical hernia, and low truncal tone. No goiter was noted. His skin felt cold to touch. Otherwise, he had an appropriate physical exam for age. His birth weight was at the 50th percentile but his current weight was less than 15th centile. The head circumference was 38.3 (between –1SD and –2SD). The HR was 110/min, RR 34/min, and BP 60/40 mmHg in right upper arm. The oxygen saturation was 98%. Rest of the general and systemic examination was normal.

Inference and Diagnosis

With the evident FTT, prolonged neonatal jaundice, lethargy, large tongue, and hypotonia, the clinical diagnosis appeared to be congenital hypothyroidism. Most patients with congenital hypothyroidism have no symptoms at birth due to placental transfer of thyroxine. The presence of umbilical hernia, wide anterior fontanel, dry skin, and low tone make this the most likely diagnosis to explain his FTT. Infants with untreated congenital hypothyroidism are more likely to have prolonged jaundice, and later develop lethargy, constipation, and macroglossia. Some will also have cold skin. Often, their cry is noted to be hoarse. Other differential diagnoses to consider include:

- Immunodeficiencies: These are associated with repeated infection (absent in this infant). CBC can assess for leukopenia and lymphocyte subsets could be sent if a specific concern is present.
- Malabsorption can lead to FTT. For example, cystic fibrosis can also result in FTT due to malabsorption, usually associated with malodorous, voluminous stools. However, the onset of malabsorption (e.g., celiac disease, cystic fibrosis) is generally with chronic diarrhea (which is not present in this infant) in the later part of infancy and early childhood.
- Processes that increase nutrient requirements or decrease the ability to feed can also cause FTT. Cardiac disease can increase the work associated with feeding as well as the nutrient requirements for an infant. However, this is less likely due to his normal oxygen saturation, no increase in work of breathing described, and normal systolic blood pressures that vary less than 10–15 mmHg between upper and lower extremities. Chest X-ray, electrocardiography, and echocardiography could be used to formally exclude congenital heart disease if they are of concerns.
- Hypotonia or congenital anomaly leading to low intake should also be considered. Low tone due to hypoxic-ischemic encephalopathy, myopathy, or other causes can limit the amount of intake. This seems unlikely as the newborn was normal at birth. Congenital anomalies such as cleft lip or cleft palate can also make feeding more difficult.
- Metabolic disease can also lead to FTT due to inefficient nutrient utilization. Initial evaluation can include glucose, lactate, ammonia, and blood gas.

Investigations

The CBC showed hemoglobin of 14.2 g%, WBC 8300/mm^3, and platelets 192,000/mm^3. The serum electrolytes were Na 140, K 4.3, Cl 105, and HCO_3 21 mEq/L (normal). The TSH level was 23 mIU/L and T4 was 3 μg/dL (both of these are abnormal). Ultrasound of the neck demonstrated ectopic thyroid displaced to the suprahyoid area.

Principles of Management

- Thyroxine should be initiated on diagnosis with initial goal of T4 10–16 μg/dL. Patients in whom thyroxine is started at <30 days of life show much improvement in cognitive outcomes compared with those in whom it is started at a later age.

- Given the long half-life of thyroxine, TSH should be monitored every 2 weeks until stably <5 mU/L.
- The growth should be continued to be monitored closely until weight gain has stabilized in the normal range.
- Development should be tracked closely as a small proportion of patients with congenital hypothyroidism have cognitive or other difficulties despite hormone replacement. Undiagnosed and untreated hypothyroidism in infancy is an important and preventable cause of developmental delay and mental retardation in childhood.

Key Messages

- Hypothyroidism should be considered in infants and children with FTT, prolonged jaundice, constipation, or hypotonia as early diagnosis and therapy improves outcomes.
- Congenital malformations such as ectopic thyroid gland can present at birth, in the newborn period, or later in life.
- TSH needs to be serially monitored in patients receiving thyroid hormone replacement given the frequent need to change dose during infancy.

CHAPTER 20

Frequently Asked Questions

Paresh A Thakkar, Baldev S Prajapati, Mukesh K Singh, Abhishek Kulkarni

This chapter includes frequently asked questions (FAQs) to the students during their clinical case presentations, practical examination, and viva voce. These questions and answers are based on the current information and available medical literature and give a broad overview of common and relevant aspects of the system, disease, and related topics. These are by no means complete but include a large part of commonly accepted answers in a logical and systematic manner.

Neonatology

1. What are the complications/problems associated with premature babies?

A Due to immaturity of various organs, premature neonates may suffer from the following complications:

- Respiratory: Hyaline membrane disease (HMD), congenital pneumonia, apnea of prematurity, bronchopulmonary dysplasia
- Cardiovascular: Patent ductus arteriosus
- Central nervous system: Intraventricular hemorrhage, periventricular leukomalacia, neurodevelopmental handicaps
- Gastrointestinal: Feed intolerance, necrotizing enterocolitis, gastroesophageal reflux, feeding problems/intolerance, problems with coordinated sucking and swallowing, risk of aspiration
- Ophthalmic: Retinopathy of prematurity
- Neonatal septicemia/meningitis, vulnerability for sepsis
- Hypothermia
- Metabolic: Hypoglycemia, hypocalcemia
- Anemia due to frequent blood sampling and lower iron stores
- Increased risk of indirect hyperbilirubinemia
- Late metabolic acidosis due to renal immaturity

2. What are the complications/morbidities associated with term intrauterine growth restriction (IUGR) babies?

A These include perinatal asphyxia, meconium aspiration syndrome, hypoglycemia (due to low stores of glycogen), hypothermia, hypocalcemia, polycythemia/hyperviscosity, persistent pulmonary hypertension in the newborn (failure to achieve or sustain the normal decrease of pulmonary vascular resistance at birth), and pulmonary hemorrhage. Other complications that can occur later/subsequently include poor postnatal growth, neurodevelopmental sequelae, and higher incidence of diabetes (type II) and hypertension in adult life.

3. What are the criteria to discharge a newborn from hospital?

A The newborn can be discharged after 48–72 hours of birth if:

- He/she is hemodynamically stable.
- He/she is off the oxygen and supportive management.
- He/she is able to feed independently.
- The mother is confident in taking care of the newborn.

4. What advice would you like to give to a mother while you are discharging a newborn?

A While discharging a newborn, the mother should be advised for the following:

- Feeding: Exclusive breastfeeding for the initial 6 months, frequent feeding at least eight times in 24 hours, and ensuring night feeds
- Prevention of hypothermia, appropriate clothing, and kangaroo mother care (KMC) for low-birth-weight babies
- Prevention of sepsis, care with regards to hand washing, and maintaining hygiene
- For cord care, not applying anything over umbilical stump, and keeping cord clean and dry
- Immunization
- Regular follow-up in a well-baby clinic for monitoring of growth and development
- Danger signs and seeking medical help immediately

5. What is the best care for umbilical cord in the immediate neonatal period?

A The umbilical cord after the birth should be cleaned with normal saline/alcohol, allowed to dry normally, and kept clean and open. It should never be covered with any dressing and no local antibiotics or antiseptics are needed.

6. Which is the most common birth injury?

A Greenstick fracture of the clavicle is one of the most common traumatic birth injuries resulting from an excessive traction during the delivery.

7. Which are the extracranial bleeds that can occur in a newborn after a difficult delivery?

A These include caput succedaneum, cephalohematoma, and subgaleal hematoma or hemorrhage.

8. What are the danger signs in neonates?

A These include any of the following:

- Lethargy, refusal to feed
- Persistent vomiting
- Convulsions
- Fast/rapid breathing or difficulty in breathing
- Bleeding from any site
- Abdominal distension
- Yellow palms and soles

9. What is the normal range of temperature of newborns? Define cold stress and hypothermia.

A The normal range of temperature is as follows:

- *Normal temperature*: 36.5–37.5°C
- *Cold stress*: 36.5–36°C
- *Moderate hypothermia*: 32–36°C
- *Severe hypothermia*: Less than 32°C

In cold stress, the baby's trunk and abdomen remain warm but periphery becomes cold; thus, so while assessing a newborn's temperature by feel of hand, it is important to palpate both central area and the extremities to identify the baby in cold stress, so timely intervention can prevent further progression to hypothermia. In moderate and severe hypothermia, both trunk and periphery are cold on palpation.

10. How is hypothermia prevented and treated?

A Methods of prevention and treatment of hypothermia are as follows:

- KMC, skin-to-skin contact
- Covering the baby with warm linens, cap, socks, and woolen clothing
- Placing the baby under radiant warmer
- Keeping a 200-W bulb nearby the baby to provide warmth

11. Why are newborns more prone to develop hypothermia? What are the mechanisms of heat loss and heat production?

A The reasons for hypothermia are as follows:

- Newborns rapidly lose heat due to their relatively large body surface area.
- They have less subcutaneous fat and thus they are prone to hypothermia.
- Preterm and IUGR newborns are at increased risk due to lack of brown fat, which is responsible for heat production when exposed to a colder atmosphere.

12. What is "warm chain?"

A Warm chain is a set of 10 interlinked procedures carried out to ensure thermal stability in neonates. These measures would minimize the heat loss and would promote heat gain. These procedures are as follows:

1. Warm delivery room (25°C)
2. Warm resuscitation corner
3. Immediate drying and removing wet linen
4. Skin-to-skin contact, i.e., KMC
5. Breastfeeding
6. Postponing bathing
7. Appropriate clothing
8. Rooming in, keeping mother and baby together
9. Warm transport
10. Creating awareness of healthcare providers about prevention and management of hypothermia

13. What is kangaroo mother care? What are the advantages?

A KMC is a method to keep the baby warm, and is especially useful for low-birth-weight and preterm newborns. Here, the baby is kept on the mother's bare chest to provide skin-to-skin contact.

- *Position of mother*: The mother should either sit or lie in semirecumbent position.
- *Position of baby:* The baby is placed in between the breasts in a frog-like position. The baby's head should turn on one side and limbs are flexed. The baby's head should be covered with a cap and he/she can wear a diaper to prevent soiling; there should be direct skin-to-skin contact between the mother and the baby. Both the mother and the baby should be covered with a warm blanket.
- *Duration of KMC*: The mother can provide KMC as long as she wishes and at any time during day or night. Each session should last for at least 30–40 minutes, and minimum eight times a day. Apart from the mother, other family members such as father, grandmother, and others can also give KMC.
- *Advantages of KMC*:
  - Prevents hypothermia
  - Helps in establishing and promoting breastfeeding
  - Increases weight in low-birth-weight babies, so they can be discharged early
  - Prevents apneic episodes
  - Establishes better cardiorespiratory stability
  - Creates emotional bonding between mother and baby
  - Lowers the rate of infection

14. What are the poor prognostic factors in case of perinatal asphyxia?

A The following indicate poor prognosis in perinatal asphyxia:

- Apgar score of 3 or less at 5 minutes, failure to establish breathing by 5 minutes
- HIE (hypoxic ischemic encephalopathy) grade III, by Sarnat and Sarnat staging
- Onset of seizure within the first 12 hours, refractory seizures
- Multiorgan dysfunction, including acute renal failure
- Abnormal electroencephalography (EEG) or neuroimaging in post-asphyxia period

15. What are early onset and late-onset neonatal sepsis?

A If symptoms and signs of sepsis appear within the first 72 hours of birth, it is called early onset sepsis (EOS), and if they appear after 72 hours of birth, it is called late-onset sepsis. The source of organisms in EOS is usually the maternal genital tract or the delivery area, while late-onset sepsis is usually acquired from the community or hospital.

- Risk factors for EOS are as follows:
  - Prolonged rupture of membrane >18 hours

- Chorioamnionitis
- Multiple (>3) or unclean vaginal examination
- Colonization of maternal genital tract with group B *Streptococcus*

• Risk factors for late-onset sepsis are as follows:

- Low birth weight
- Lack of breastfeeding
- Frequent handling
- Mechanical ventilation
- Presence of central line
- Disruption in the continuity of skin with needle pricks and use of intravenous fluid

16. What is "sepsis screen" in neonates?

A Gold standard for diagnosis of neonatal septicemia is blood culture, but obtaining the report takes about 72 hours by the BACTEC method and 5–7 days by the conventional method of culture. Thus, usually, the decision for starting antibiotics is taken based on few laboratory tests called "sepsis screen." Sepsis screen is said to be positive when any two or more of the following five tests are positive and the baby is presumed to have sepsis; simultaneously, blood culture is sent to confirm or exclude the diagnosis of sepsis:

1. Total leukocyte count <5000 cells/mm^3
2. Absolute neutrophil count <1800 mm^3
3. Immature to total neutrophil ratio (I/T ratio) >0.2
4. Elevated C-reactive protein
5. Microerythrocyte sedimentation rate >15 mm/h

17. How is severity of jaundice assessed clinically by examination?

A Baby should be examined preferably in daylight. It is difficult to examine sclera of newborns for icterus, as they have physiological photophobia. Examine for jaundice by blanching the skin with finger and see for the yellow staining of the skin and subcutaneous tissue.

Due to varying thickness of the skin, there is cephalocaudal progression of jaundice with increasing levels of bilirubin. Kramer described the approximate level of serum bilirubin depending on the finding of icterus over body surface area, which can be used as a rough guide to determine the level of jaundice. Jaundice is seen in face when serum bilirubin is approximately 5–6 mg/dL. When palms and soles are yellow, bilirubin levels are likely to be more than 15 mg/dL. The cephalocaudal progression of jaundice is referred to as Kramer's rule (Table 20.1).

TABLE 20.1 Cephalocaudal Progression of Jaundice (Kramer's Rule)

Area of body with icterus	Level of bilirubin (mg/dL)
Face	5–6
Chest, upper abdomen	6–10
Abdomen, thigh	10–12
Legs	12–15
Palms, soles	>15

18. What is physiological jaundice?

A Physiological jaundice is quite common and occurs in healthy babies in the initial few days of life. It appears on the second or third day of life, peaks at 4–5 days, and disappears spontaneously without any treatment by 10–14 days of life; serum bilirubin level does not increase more than 15 mg/dL.

Physiological jaundice occurs due to the following reasons:

- Newborns have higher mass of red blood cells (RBCs) and life span of RBCs is shorter.
- Due to immaturity of liver, there is defective uptake by ligandin receptors.
- Conjugation is defective due to transient deficiency of glucuronyl transferase.

- Enterohepatic circulation is increased due to high activity of intestinal glucuronidase and paucity of gut flora.

19. What are the common causes of jaundice in a newborn?

A The causes of jaundice in newborns are as follows:

- Jaundice appearing in the first 24 hours of life
  - Blood group incompatibility—ABO, Rh
  - G6PD deficiency
  - Hereditary spherocytosis
  - Crigler–Najjar syndrome
  - Alpha thalassemia
- Jaundice appearing between 24 and 72 hours of life
  - Physiological jaundice
  - Polycythemia
  - Septicemia
  - Cephalohematoma
- Jaundice appearing after 72 hours of life
  - Septicemia
  - Hypothyroidism
  - Metabolic causes
  - Breast milk jaundice

20. How does breast milk jaundice differ from breastfeeding jaundice?

A Both breast milk jaundice and breastfeeding jaundice are different in the mechanism of occurrence. Breast milk contains 3-alpha-20-beta-pregnanediol. This substance inhibits hepatic glucuronyl transferase enzyme and Y acceptor protein. Thus, hepatic conjugation of bilirubin is compromised. The severity and duration of breast milk jaundice is variable. It may last up to 6–8 weeks. Despite this, the mother is asked to breastfeed the baby while continuing treatment and not asked to stop feeding.

Breastfeeding jaundice is seen among babies who are inadequately fed by their mothers or receiving less amount of feeding. This leads to dehydration of baby, which causes hypovolemia and jaundice.

21. What are the treatment options for neonatal jaundice?

A Treatment options are as follows:

- *Supportive measures*: Early feeding and maintenance of adequate hydration are useful to prevent hyperbilirubinemia. Hypoxia, hypothermia, hypoglycemia, and acidosis should be prevented.
- *Phototherapy*: Phototherapy light has a wavelength of 420–480 nm, which causes structural and photoisomerization of unconjugated bilirubin and converts it into water-soluble isomers of bilirubin, which get rapidly excreted.
- *Exchange blood transfusion*: Despite giving phototherapy, if bilirubin level remains high and exceeds more than 20 mg/dL, one may need exchange blood transfusion to prevent brain damage/kernicterus from unconjugated bilirubin. Indications for doing exchange depend on the level of bilirubin, weight and gestational age of newborn, day of life, and presence of risk factors such as ongoing hemolysis, asphyxia, sepsis, and acidosis.

22. How should babies be assessed for jaundice after their discharge from hospital?

A All the newborns who are discharged before the age of 24 hours should be seen again by 72 hours of age and babies discharged between 24 and 48 hours should be seen for jaundice at 96 hours of age. Babies discharged after 48 hours should be seen again at the age of 120 hours (5 days).

23. Which are the conditions that predispose a newborn to develop hypoglycemia?

A Newborns born to diabetic mothers, small-for-gestational-age and large-for -gestational-age babies, babies who are asphyxiated at birth, and babies with Rh incompatibility are more likely to develop hypoglycemia.

24. What are the common causes of respiratory distress in a newborn?

A The common causes are as follows:

- Respiratory:
  - Transient tachypnea of newborn (wet lung)
  - HMD
  - Pneumonia
  - Meconium aspiration syndrome
  - Pneumothorax
  - Pulmonary hemorrhage
- Cardiac: Congestive heart failure
- CNS: Perinatal asphyxia
- Metabolic: Metabolic acidosis
- Congenital malformations such as tracheoesophageal fistula, diaphragmatic hernia, and bilateral choanal atresia

25. What is transient tachypnea in a newborn?

A This condition, also called "wet lung syndrome," is common in full-term babies delivered by cesarean section, but can occur with vaginal deliveries also. It occurs due to delayed absorption of fluid from lungs after birth and it manifests within the first 6 hours of life and disappears by 24 hours. It does not require aggressive treatment.

26. What is hyaline membrane disease? How can it be prevented?

A HMD is caused by deficiency of surfactant due to immaturity of lungs in premature newborns. It is characterized by the triad of tachypnea, expiratory grunt, and intercostal retractions with or without presence of cyanosis. These symptoms begin at birth or within 6 hours of life.

Antenatal administration of steroids to the mother having threatened preterm delivery is a very effective intervention for the prevention of respiratory distress syndrome (RDS). This is done by giving betamethasone intramuscularly 12 mg, two doses, 24 hours apart.

Growth and Nutrition

1. When is a child considered as growth retarded/short statured?

A A child is considered as growth retarded if his/her height is less than the third percentile or less than 2SD below the mean for age and sex of the population reference standard. The child is considered as short statured if he/she shows a growth velocity of less than 25th centile on a velocity curve assessed over a minimum of 12-month duration.

2. What are the best feeding practices for infants?

A These include starting of the breastfeeding immediately after the birth, exclusive breastfeeding up to 6 months, and continued breastfeeding up to 1–2 years of age. Complementary feeds in the form of semisolids (hygienic, home-made recipes) should be started in addition to breastfeeds at the age of 6 months.

3. How does one know the adequacy of breast milk?

A A breastfed baby is getting sufficient milk if he/she gains adequate weight on serial follow-up, passes light yellow or colorless urine at least six times per day, and is playful and sleeps well after the feeds.

4. What is Holliday-Segar formula for the calculation of calories/energy for dietary advice?

A The formula for calculation is as follows:

- *Up to 10 kg of body weight*: 100 kcal/kg/day
- *Ten to 20 kg of body weight*: 1000 + 50 kcal for each kilogram above 10 kg
- *Above 20 kg*: 1500 kcal + 20 cal for each kilogram in excess of 20 kg

5. What are the common clinical features of rickets?

A Common clinical manifestations of rickets include enlargement of costochondral junction (rickety rosary), craniotabes (thinning of the outer skull layer resulting in a ping-pong sensation), delayed closure of anterior fontanel, frontal bossing, wrist widening, and bow legs. Genu valgum (knock knees) is not a feature of rickets.

6. What are the likely causes if a child with severe malnutrition does not respond to the treatment?

A If a child in spite of adequate dietary therapy does not respond and gain weight, then a hidden infection (such as tuberculosis or urinary tract infection) may be excluded and a proper dietary preparation and intake must be considered as the child may not be consuming the recommended amount.

7. What are the diagnostic features of kwashiorkor?

A The diagnostic criteria for a child with kwashiorkor include growth failure, presence of pitting edema, and mental changes.

8. What is ReSoMal and what are its contents?

A Children with severe malnutrition are deficient in potassium and have relatively higher levels of sodium. Thus, they need an oral rehydration solution (ORS) that has a higher content of potassium (40 mEq/L) and a lower level of sodium (45 mEq/L) in comparison to the standard WHO ORS. This is called ReSoMal (rehydration solution for severely malnourished children). It is made by dissolving one sachet of standard WHO low-osmolarity ORS in 2 L water (instead of 1 L) and addition of 50 g of sugar and 40 mL of mineral mix solution.

9. What are the causes of delayed dentition?

A The causes of delayed eruption of teeth include familial rickets, congenital hypothyroidism, Down syndrome, hypoparathyroidism, osteogenesis imperfecta, and ectodermal dysplasia.

10. What is the role and importance of folic acid?

A Folic acid is required for the synthesis of nucleoproteins and plays an important role in the cell division and development. An amount of 0.4 mg/day of folic acid should be taken daily during the periconceptional period for the prevention of neural tube defects during pregnancy.

11. What are the radiological changes seen in scurvy?

A There is a ground glass appearance of the shaft of long bones, with pencil thinning of the cortex, and there may be subperiosteal elevation due to underlying calcified subperiosteal hemorrhage. The changes seen at the epiphyseal end include white line of Frankel (thickened provisional zone of calcification), Pelken spurs (epiphyses extend as calcified line beyond the shaft), and signet ring appearance at the epiphyses.

12. Which are the radiological changes seen in vitamin D deficiency rickets? How is healing rickets observed?

A The X-ray changes seen in the wrist joint because of vitamin D deficiency include cupping and fraying (margin of metaphysis becomes blurred) and an increased epiphyseal and metaphyseal distance. Fraying and splaying (metaphysis is widened), cupping with decrease in bone density, and an indistinct cortex due to uncalcified subperiosteal osteoid are also seen. The healing is indicated by a white line of provisional calcification and an increased bone density.

Gastrointestinal System

1. What are the common causes of acute abdominal pain in children?

A Abdominal pain is one of the common symptoms in children that could have many causes and thus is one of the most misdirecting symptoms in children. The causes of abdominal pain are thus varied and can be due to acute conditions such as the following:

- Acute infections
  - Bacillary dysentery
  - Acute hepatitis
  - Peritonitis
  - Acute cholecystitis
  - Urinary tract infections

- Inflammation/obstruction
  - Acute appendicitis
  - Intussusception
  - Diverticulitis
  - Inguinal hernia
  - Renal calculi or extra-abdominal conditions such as sickle cell crisis

Other causes can be Henoch–Schonlein purpura, abdominal migraine, and lower lobe pneumonia leading to referred abdominal pain and, rarely, even diabetes ketoacidosis. It may also be a nonorganic pain (psychogenic).

The duration, location, severity of pain, appearance of the child, and other symptoms are helpful pointers toward the cause of pain. The important red flag signs that suggest that the pain is organic and there is some underlying cause for it are pain that awakens the child from sleep, location of pain other than at periumbilical region, bilious vomiting, visceromegaly, weight loss, and any other extraintestinal manifestations. The presence of fever does not always indicate a serious problem and a normal temperature can be seen with the more serious causes of abdominal pain.

2. Are there other helpful pointers on examination for acute abdominal pain?

A Abdominal pain that becomes aggravated on pressure is due to inflammatory conditions such as acute appendicitis and peritonitis, while pain that gets relieved on the application of pressure is due to intestinal colic.

3. What are the causes of chronic/recurrent abdominal pain in children?

A These are episodic attacks of pain spread over a period of 3 months or more and interfere with the child's activity. Few conditions that cause chronic/recurrent abdominal pain are gastroesophageal reflux disease (GERD), peptic ulcer disease (*H. pylori* infection), irritable bowel syndrome, inflammatory bowel disease (rare in children), parasitic infestations, and lead poisoning.

4. What are the red flag signs in children with recurrent abdominal pain?

A These include any of the following:
- Weight loss
- Faltering of linear growth
- History of gastrointestinal blood loss
- Unexplained fever
- Presence of other systemic symptoms and/or a family history of intestinal disease (e.g., inflammatory bowel disease)

5. What is infantile colic? How is it managed?

A It is a common complaint in early infancy. It is characterized by sudden bouts of crying spells in the evening. It usually starts a few days after birth, usually after 2–3 weeks of age. It is called "evening colic" as it occurs at nearly same time in the evening. There is sudden screaming with flexion of thighs and flushing of face lasting for few minutes to hours associated with excessive gurgling. The exact etiology is uncertain; it is possibly due to aerophagia. Holding the baby, rocking, prone positioning, cuddling, and taking him/her for a drive may provide temporary relief. This condition spontaneously resolves after 2–3 months of age.

6. What are the conditions that cause gastrointestinal hemorrhage?

A Many gastrointestinal and systemic conditions can cause gastrointestinal bleeding (hematemesis, melena, and hematochezia). These include esophagitis, gastritis (stress ulcers, drug induced, e.g., nonsteroidal anti-inflammatory drugs [NSAIDs]), esophageal varices, Meckel diverticulum, intussusceptions, polyps, inflammatory bowel disease, and systemic diseases such as vitamin K deficiency in liver diseases (e.g., hemorrhagic disease of newborn [HDN], hepatic cell failure in infants/children) and bleeding diathesis as seen in disseminated intravascular coagulation (DIC).

7. **Many young babies vomit/spit up after their feeds. Is it normal or abnormal?**

A Many newborns and young infants vomit/spit up some time after their feeds. Almost all infants regurgitate their feeds or a portion of it sometimes or the other. What differentiates normal regurgitation from abnormal regurgitation is how often the reflux/vomiting occurs, whether it is associated with discomfort, and whether it results due to other complications. These complications include poor weight gain known as "failure to thrive," breathing difficulties such as infrequent breaths or apnea, asthma symptoms such as wheezing, or a hoarse voice or cry. If any of these are the causes, then there is a possibility of the child having GERD.

8. **How is diarrhea defined?**

A Diarrhea is defined as passage of three or more loose or watery stools in a 24-hour period. For practical purposes, diarrhea is the recent change in the consistency and the character of the stool and its water content rather than the number or increased frequency of passage of stools. Exclusively breastfed babies normally pass several soft or semiliquid stools per day, which is considered normal. Thus, for breastfed infants, diarrhea is an increase in frequency or liquidity that is considered abnormal by the mother.

9. **What are the common causes of diarrhea in infants and children?**

A Most cases (70%) of acute diarrhea in children are viral in origin. The organisms causing diarrhea in children include rotavirus, enterotoxigenic *E. coli* (ETEC), *Shigella, Campylobacter jejuni, Vibrio cholerae*, and nontyphoidal *Salmonella*.

10. **What are the principles of management of acute diarrhea?**

A The broad principles of treatment of diarrhea include:

- General assessment of the child and evaluation of hydration status for the presence of dehydration
- Correction of fluid deficit, electrolyte abnormalities, and acid–base imbalance (such as acidosis) by the administration of appropriate fluids (oral rehydration/ intravenous fluid) for the prevention and treatment of dehydration
- Adequate feeding to provide normal nutritional requirements
- Zinc supplementation for a period of 14 days as zinc deficiency is common (preexistent and increased losses) in children with diarrhea
- Treatment of associated infections and antibiotics in bacillary dysentery, cholera, amoebic dysentery, and acute giardiasis (associated extraintestinal infections should be appropriately treated)
- Nutritional rehabilitation and health education for further prevention of diarrhea

11. **How is viral diarrhea suspected in a child?**

A Infants and young children are more prone to develop viral diarrhea, and the symptoms of viral infection include watery diarrhea, vomiting, and fever (temperature higher than 100.4°F or 38.0°C).

Persistent high fever (higher than 40°C or 104°F) and diarrhea that is bloody or contains mucus are more common with bacterial diarrhea.

12. **Is it necessary to give antibiotics in every case of childhood diarrhea?**

A No, it is not necessary, and it may be even harmful as it may lead to side effects and spread of antibiotic resistance in the community. Most acute diarrheas in childhood are self-limiting (10–14 days) and are caused by viruses such as rotavirus, and the antibiotics should be reserved for treating bacillary dysentery and cholera.

13. **What is antibiotic-associated diarrhea?**

A Antibiotics may also cause diarrhea by disrupting the normal bacterial flora of the gastrointestinal tract, and the diarrhea is usually mild and typically does not cause dehydration or weight loss. In most cases, antibiotics should not be stopped. However, pseudomembranous enterocolitis is the severe form of antibiotic-associated diarrhea and is best treated with a course of oral metronidazole.

14. What complications can result from acute diarrhea?

A Most cases of acute diarrhea are self-limiting and respond well to appropriately administered fluid therapy. However, few children can develop complications such as hyponatremia (due to intake of large amounts of plain water without electrolytes or incorrectly prepared ORS), hypokalemia, hypoglycemia (more common in children who have associated severe malnutrition), acidosis (large amount of loss of bicarbonate in stools), and, rarely, acute renal failure and hemolytic uremic syndrome due to toxins produced by enteroinvasive *E. coli* and *S. dysenteriae*.

15. What is the importance of chronic liver disease in children?

A Chronic liver disease (CLD) is a common cause of hepatosplenomegaly in children and is often the result of an ongoing liver cell injury and dysfunction from infection and inflammation, and, if left untreated, can lead to cirrhosis and its complications.

Unlike in adults in whom 6-month duration of symptoms is labeled as CLD, the criterion in children for CLD is a period of 3–6 months in view of irreversible liver damage that may occur at an earlier stage. Few causes of CLD in children include:

- Chronic hepatitis (B, C, and D)
- Autoimmune hepatitis
- Metabolic/genetic liver diseases (Wilson disease, glycogen storage disease types III and IV), storage disorders, e.g., Gaucher and Niemann–Pick diseases, mucopolysaccharidosis
- Vascular/chronic venous congestion such as Budd–Chiari syndrome, congestive heart failure, constrictive pericarditis
- Prolonged cholestasis such as biliary atresia, choledochal cyst
- Miscellaneous such as cystic fibrosis (CF) and polycystic disease of liver and kidney

16. What are the common causes of ascites in children?

A Although there are different mechanisms such as increased hydrostatic pressure (e.g., congestive cardiac failure) and reduced colloid osmotic pressure (CLD and nephrotic syndrome) that contribute to the development of ascites in children, it is seen in conditions such as advanced stages of CLD, congestive heart failure, nephritic syndrome, abdominal tuberculosis, pancreatitis, and venous obstruction such as Budd–Chiari syndrome.

Respiratory System

1. What are the most common causes of nocturnal cough in children?

A The most common causes of nocturnal cough in children include bronchial asthma, postnasal drip, and GERD.

2. What are the common causes of cough with expectoration in children?

A Expectoration in young children is not common as they frequently swallow the sputum but conditions such as bronchiectasis, lung abscess, and CF are important causes of cough with expectoration in children.

3. How is acute cough defined in children and what are its common causes?

A Cough is labeled as acute when it is present for a period of less than 3–4 weeks and is caused by upper and lower respiratory tract infections, pertussis and parapertussis, asthma, acute bronchitis, and foreign body aspiration.

4. What are the causes of chronic cough?

A Cough that lasts beyond 4 weeks is known as chronic cough and can be caused by postviral infection, GERD, childhood tuberculosis, asthma, psychogenic cough, and CF.

5. What are the causes of paroxysmal cough in children?

A The causes of paroxysmal cough in children include pertussis, parapertussis, asthma, foreign body inhalation, and certain respiratory infections such as *Mycoplasma* and adenoviruses.

6. Which are the conditions that can produce hemoptysis in children?

A Hemoptysis in children may be caused by bronchiectasis, lung abscess, pulmonary edema, pneumonia, mitral stenosis (MS), pulmonary embolism, and tuberculosis.

7. What are the common causes of chest pain in children?

A Pulmonary causes are more common than cardiac causes and include pleural inflammation, pneumonia, pneumothorax, pericarditis, aortic stenosis, anomalous origin of the left coronary artery from pulmonary artery (ALCAPPA), and GERD.

8. What are the different methods to measure digital clubbing?

A The ratio of the distal phalangeal diameter (DPD) to the interphalangeal diameter (IPD) or the phalangeal depth ratio is <1 in normal subjects but increases to >1 with digital clubbing.

The hyponychial angle is <180° in normal children but >195° in patients with clubbing.

The dorsal surfaces of terminal phalanges of similar fingers are placed together. In a case of clubbing, the normal diamond-shaped window at the base of nail beds disappears. It is called Schamroth sign.

9. What is the importance of sternal angle in the examination of the chest?

A Transverse bony ridge at the junction of the body of sternum and manubrium sterni is called sternal angle. It:

- Corresponds to the second intercostal space
- Corresponds to the bifurcation of trachea anteriorly and the fourth thoracic spine posteriorly
- Divides the mediastinum into superior and inferior at this level
- Corresponds to arch of aorta

10. What are the signs of an increased work of breathing?

A These include an increased rate of respiration (tachypnea), use of accessory muscles of respiration (sternomastoid), flaring of alae nasi, retractions (suprasternal, subcostal, and intercostal), head bobbing, various sounds such as stridor, grunting, and wheezing, and cyanosis.

11. Which is an early sign of hypoxemia in a child with a respiratory disease?

A Tachypnea is an early sign of hypoxemia in a child with a respiratory disease.

12. What is grunting?

A Grunting is a sign of severe pneumonia in infants and it is due to the effort generated by the lungs to create a positive end-expiratory pressure to keep the alveoli open. It is not observed in asthma or airway obstruction as there is already air trapping and peak expiratory pressures are already high.

13. Define tachypnea at different ages.

A The cutoff limits for tachypnea or fast breathing are respiratory rate (RR) >60/min (younger than 2 months of age), >50/min (2–12 months), and >40/min (1–5 years).

14. Which are the most common agents responsible for causing pneumonia in children between the ages of 2 months and 5 years?

A *Streptococcus pneumoniae* and *Haemophilus influenzae* type b (Hib) are the most common bacteria causing acute pneumonia in children between the ages of 2 months and 5 years.

15. What are the benefits of inhalation therapy in childhood asthma?

A The benefits of inhalation therapy in a child with asthma are as follows:

- The drug is delivered directly to the site of action and hence has a rapid onset of action.
- Negligible systemic absorption minimizes the side effects of the delivered drug.
- Much smaller doses are needed as compared with in oral routes.

16. Why is normal saline the preferred diluent over distilled water in nebulization?

A This is because distilled water is a hypoosmolar solution and can lead to bronchospasm if used as a diluent instead of normal saline.

17. How does a child with foreign body aspiration present?

A A sudden onset of respiratory difficulty in a previously healthy child is suggestive of foreign body aspiration, particularly in an infant and a young child between 1 and 3 years of age. There may be a history of sudden coughing and choking without any other features of respiratory infection.

Cardiovascular System

1. Which are some of the important cyanotic congenital heart defects?

A These include:

- Tetralogy of Fallot
- Transposition of the great arteries (TGA)
- Tricuspid atresia
- Total anomalous pulmonary venous return (TAPVR)
- Truncus arteriosus

2. What are the signs that can alert on the presence of cardiac disease?

A Presence of any of the following signs is an important finding to alert the clinician on the likely presence of a cardiac disease: increased precordial pulsations, heaves, or thrill; brachiofemoral delay and/or weak or absent femoral pulses; extra heart sounds such as S4, opening snap (OS), and pericardial rub; and very harsh, loud, or blowing murmurs.

3. Why is tetralogy of Fallot called so? What is the embryologic basis of this defect?

A Historically, the diagnosis of the defect that has come to be known as tetralogy of Fallot was made by recognizing the combination of four components, namely, a large malalignment-type ventricular septal defect (VSD), an overriding (dextropositioned) aorta, pulmonary stenosis, and right ventricular hypertrophy. Fallot was a French physician who correctly made the diagnosis in a living patient, hence the name. The basic embryologic abnormality is an anterior malalignment of the conal (infundibular) part of the interventricular septum relative to the trabecular part. This produces the well-known combination of anatomical and physiological abnormalities.

4. Which heart defects are typically found in congenital rubella syndrome?

A Patent ductus arteriosus (PDA) and peripheral pulmonary artery stenosis are the most common congenital heart diseases (CHDs) found in congenital rubella syndrome.

5. What are the different types of VSDs? Can some VSDs close spontaneously?

A Depending on their location within the ventricular septum, VSDs are classified as membranous (commonly called perimembranous), muscular, inlet, and outlet VSDs.

The natural history of a VSD depends on the location and size of the defect. About 30–50% of small VSDs close spontaneously, most frequently in the first 2 years of life. Small muscular VSDs close spontaneously in up to 80% of patients, and small membranous VSDs in up to 35% of patients.

6. What are the permissible exceptions to diagnose rheumatic fever without strictly fulfilling the modified Jones' criteria?

A The exceptions include chorea, indolent carditis, and some cases of recurrence of acute rheumatic fever.

7. What signs help diagnose carditis?

A The following signs are helpful in diagnosing carditis:

- Tachycardia disproportionate to the fever (sleeping heart rate is a good parameter to follow)
- Rapidly developing cardiomegaly
- Changing murmurs/appearance of new murmurs (of valve regurgitation)
- Carey Coombs murmur of mitral valvulitis
- Pericardial rub (may be heard very transiently only)
- Pericardial effusion (usually diagnosed on imaging)

8. Describe the effect of aspirin therapy in a patient with arthritis of acute rheumatic fever.

A The arthritis responds dramatically to aspirin therapy even in small doses; indeed, if a patient with arthritis suspected to have acute rheumatic fever does not improve in 48 hours, other alternative diagnoses should be sought.

9. Which are the valves commonly affected by rheumatic heart disease?

A The mitral valve is the most commonly affected valve by rheumatic heart disease, followed by the aortic valve. The tricuspid valve is involved rarely, and the pulmonary valve only exceptionally. Isolated (i.e., without mitral valve disease) aortic valve involvement is also uncommon.

10. How can the severity of mitral stenosis be assessed clinically?

A The combination of the following findings in a given patient can help to assess the severity of MS clinically:

- Symptoms such as paroxysmal nocturnal dyspnea and orthopnea point to severity.
- Atrial fibrillation is a hint to severity and chronicity.
- Right heart failure manifested by raised jugular venous pressure (JVP), peripheral edema, and hepatomegaly also serves as a marker of severity and chronicity.
- Evidence of pulmonary hypertension (e.g., parasternal lift or epigastric pulsations suggesting right ventricular hypertrophy, or loud P_2) also indicates severity.
- The best guide is the A_2–OS interval. The shorter the A_2–OS interval, the higher is the left atrial pressure, the higher is the pressure gradient across the mitral valve, and the more severe is the degree of MS.
- The longer the mid-diastolic murmur, the more severe is the MS.

11. Can the murmur of MS be inaudible even in the presence of severe MS?

A The intensity of the murmur of MS is related very significantly to the flow across the mitral valve and is thus not a reliable guide to the severity of the mitral valve obstruction. When there is a marked reduction in cardiac output resulting from severe mitral valve obstruction, the flow across the valve is also markedly reduced and may be associated with a soft murmur or absent murmur ("silent MS").

12. How does calcification of the mitral leaflets alter the auscultatory findings in a patient with severe MS?

A A loud S_1 and an OS are present only if the stenotic mitral valve is mobile. These sounds depend on the "OS" and closing (S_1) motion of the mitral leaflets. With calcification resulting in a rigid immobile mitral valve, these valuable signs are lost.

13. What is the mechanism of the presystolic accentuation of the diastolic murmur of MS?

A The murmur of MS may have a characteristic presystolic accentuation heard just before the S_1, conventionally attributed to increased flow during atrial systole (the last phase of ventricular diastole). This mechanism explains its causation only during sinus rhythm. More recently, another mechanism has been appreciated. The presystolic accentuation of the murmur may also be related to antegrade flow through a progressively narrowing mitral orifice (as the valve closes) during the end of the ventricular diastole, explaining this finding even in patients with atrial fibrillation.

14. Which rare condition can closely mimic valvular MS?

A The rare condition is left atrial myxoma. Clinical findings may vary significantly with posture if this tumor is pedunculated and therefore highly mobile. Constitutional symptoms and signs are also quite common. Echocardiography is diagnostic.

15. What are the causes of mitral regurgitation (MR) in children other than rheumatic valvular disease?

A These include the following:

- *Acute MR*: Infective endocarditis, chordal rupture (e.g., in MVP [mitral valve prolapse]), trauma
- *Chronic MR*: Atrioventricular canal defects, congenital isolated cleft mitral valve, MVP (myxomatous mitral valve), hypertrophic cardiomyopathy
- *Functional*: Myocarditis, dilated cardiomyopathy

16. What are the signs that help to assess the severity of aortic regurgitation (AR)?

A Normally, the systolic blood pressure in the lower limbs is higher (up to 20 mmHg) than that in the upper limbs. This difference is increased in the presence of AR (Hill sign) and correlates with its severity. In mild AR, it is 20–40 mmHg; in moderate AR, it is 40–60 mmHg; and in severe AR, it is >60 mmHg. The presence of florid peripheral signs of AR (aortic runoff) is a marker of severe AR.

17. Describe some important peripheral signs of AR.

A The peripheral signs of AR depend on diastolic aortic runoff (i.e., reversal of flow) and the resultant wide pulse pressure. They include the following:

- Water-hammer pulse/collapsing pulse
- Hill sign (vide supra)
- *Corrigan sign*: Dancing carotids
- *De Musset sign*: Head nodding synchronous with each heartbeat
- *Quincke sign*: Alternate flushing and blanching seen in the nail bed on pinching the fingertip
- *Traube sign*: Booming systolic sounds ("pistol-shots") auscultated over the femoral artery in the groin
- *Duroziez's double murmur*: A diastolic murmur auscultated over the femoral artery in the groin on distal compression (e.g., with the edge of the stethoscope), and a systolic murmur with proximal compression
- In very severe cases (chronically neglected), may also appreciate alternate flushing and blanching of the skin of the forehead, alternate pupillary constriction, dilatation synchronous with the heartbeat, pulsations of the uvula, liver, or spleen.

18. What are the cutaneous manifestations of infective endocarditis?

A The cutaneous manifestations of infective endocarditis include clubbing of the fingers (which can appear as early as a few weeks), splinter hemorrhaging of the nails, petechiae, Osler's nodes, and Janeway lesions. Splinter hemorrhage is linear and found in the distal third of the nail bed. Osler's nodes are small, reddish-purple, tender, raised lesions typically found in the pads of the fingers or toes. Janeway lesions are small, erythematous, nontender, flat lesions and involve the palms or soles.

Central Nervous System

1. **What is the difference between a seizure and epilepsy?**

A Seizures are defined as sudden, time-limited, transient, paroxysmal events having a tendency to recur, arising from the abnormal and excessive involuntary neuronal discharges from the brain that may manifest as abnormal motor activity, behavioral abnormality, sensory disturbances, or autonomic dysfunction that may or may not be associated with an impairment or loss of consciousness. Any acute or chronic insult to the brain can produce seizures. The motor manifestations of a seizure are known as convulsions.

Epilepsy is defined as an occurrence of two or more unprovoked seizures, 24 hours apart in any individual. If a person gets more than one episode within 24 hours, it is considered as single event.

2. **What are the common causes of fever with convulsions?**

A One of the most common causes of fever with convulsions in a child between the ages of 6 months and 5 years is febrile seizures.

Febrile seizures refer to convulsions occurring along with fever but with no evidence of intracranial infection or any defined causes and without any history of seizures.

Other common causes of convulsions with febrile illnesses include acute bacterial meningitis, tubercular meningitis (TBM), viral encephalitis, cerebral malaria, and head trauma.

3. **What is Cushing's triad?**

A The combination of slow or irregular respirations, bradycardia, and elevated blood pressure (increased systolic pressure) with a widened pulse pressure resulting from an increased intracranial pressure (ICP) makes the Cushing's triad.

4. **What is the cerebrospinal fluid (CSF) picture in bacterial meningitis?**

A Examination of CSF is essential for the diagnosis of acute bacterial meningitis. The differences between CSF values normally and those in acute bacterial meningitis are shown in Table 20.2.

TABLE 20.2 CSF in Acute Bacterial Meningitis

	Normal	Acute bacterial meningitis
Appearance	Clear	Turbid, hazy
Pressure	50–80 mm H_2O	Increased (100–300 mm H_2O)
Protein	20–45 mg/dL	100–500 mg/dL
Sugar	More than two-third of plasma sugar	Less than two-third of plasma sugar
Microscopic examination	5 cells/hpf. Mostly lymphocytes	10–10,000 cells/hpf. Mostly polymorphonuclear cells
Gram stain	Negative	Organism may be detected
Culture	Negative	Organism may be detected

CSF, cerebrospinal fluid.

5. **What is the significance of hypertension in a child with neurological disease?**

A High blood pressure is suggestive of hypertensive encephalopathy. Hypertension is also seen in raised ICP, Guillain–Barré syndrome (GBS), encephalitis, and posterior fossa lesions.

BP should be checked in supine and in an upright position in a patient with suspected vasovagal syncope and peripheral neuropathy to pick up orthostatic hypotension with a difference of >20 mmHg in systolic BP. It is seen as an autonomic dysfunction. Hypotension is an ominous sign and is frequently observed in shock, sepsis, and cervical spine injuries.

6. What are the complications of bacterial meningitis?

A These include raised ICP and hydrocephalus, while delayed complications include neurological sequelae (deficits) such as sensory neural hearing loss, developmental delay, visual impairment, behavioral and cognitive problems, and epilepsy.

Presence of a deep coma, raised ICP, respiratory depression, and shock are important predictors of mortality and morbidity.

7. What are the signs of raised intracranial pressure?

A The signs of raised ICP are the following:

- *In infants*: Bulging fontanel, large head size, setting sun sign, irritability, shrilled cry
- *In children*: Headache, vomiting, diplopia, strabismus, personality changes, decreased consciousness, papilledema, Cushing's triad, positive crack pot sign

8. What are the causes, apart from bacterial meningitis, of raised intracranial pressure?

A Apart from bacterial meningitis, other conditions that can cause increased ICP include brain abscess, viral encephalitis, subdural hemorrhage/empyema, neurocysticercosis, tubercular meningoencephalitis, and any other intracranial space-occupying lesion (ICSOL) such as medulloblastoma and other metastatic tumors.

9. What are the two varieties of hydrocephalus? Mention a few causes of each type.

A These are the following:

1. *Communicating*: As a sequela of bacterial and tuberculosis meningitis, posthemorrhagic, meningeal malignancy, and achondroplasia
2. *Noncommunicating*: Congenital aqueductal stenosis, Arnold–Chiari malformation, Dandy-Walker malformation, and posterior fossa tumor (e.g., cerebellar astrocytoma)

10. What is the staging of tubercular meningitis?

A TBM is divided into three stages:

Stage I: The child is conscious with nonspecific symptoms with no neurological signs.

Stage II: The child has signs of meningeal irritation with slight or no clouding of consciousness with or without minor neurological deficits (cranial nerve palsies or limb paresis).

Stage III: The child has severe alteration of sensorium, convulsions, and focal neurological deficits, with or without involuntary movements.

11. What is meant by serous TBM?

A This is a milder form of TBM seen especially in BCG-vaccinated children who present with fever and vomiting and may be conscious at the time of admission. The disease is mostly localized and the CSF examination is normal.

12. Apart from TBM, what are the other causes of increased protein levels in CSF?

A Increased protein level in CSF (normal 30–50 mg%) is a nonspecific finding that may be found in pyogenic meningitis, GBS, viral meningoencephalitis, cerebral hemorrhage, and degenerative white matter brain diseases.

13. What are the differential diagnoses of a child presenting with hemiplegia?

A These include: TBM, spastic cerebral palsy, ischemic stroke (as a complication of CHD by a clot formed in the heart and reaching the cerebral vessels), and sickle cell disease and the trauma that injures the large vessels of the brain and causes uncommonly brain tumors.

14. What is the difference between psychomotor retardation and regression?

A Psychomotor retardation is considered when a child is achieving developmental milestones at a slower rate (developmental delay), while in psychomotor regression, a child loses the milestones and abilities progressively that he/she had achieved in the past.

15. What is microcephaly? Mention a few causes of microcephaly.

A Head circumference <3SD of mean for a particular age and sex is known as microcephaly.

Common causes of microcephaly are intrauterine infections such as rubella, cytomegalovirus (CMV), and *Toxoplasma*. Hypoxic ischemic damage to the brain is commonly seen with perinatal asphyxia, chromosomal disorders such as Down syndrome, Edward syndrome, primary microcephaly in autosomal/X-linked recessive inheritance, and fetal hydantoin syndrome.

16. Which are the units comprising lower motor neuron (LMN)? Mention one condition affecting each unit that can lead to LMN type of paralysis.

A The following constitute the LMN units:

- *Anterior horn cells*: Poliomyelitis
- *Nerve root*: Compression by some tumor
- *Peripheral nerve*: GBS
- *Neuromuscular junction*: Myasthenia gravis
- *Muscle*: Myopathies or muscle dystrophies

17. Define acute flaccid paralysis (AFP). Enumerate the common causes of AFP.

A AFP refers to any paralysis occurring in children younger than 15 years of age, of duration <4 weeks, associated with flaccidity for which no obvious cause is found (such as severe trauma or electrolyte imbalance), or paralytic illness in a person of any age in which polio is suspected. The common causes of AFP are:

- GBS
- Transverse myelitis
- Traumatic neuritis
- Poliomyelitis (India has been certified polio free by the WHO in 2014)

Pediatric Endocrinology

1. What is the importance of endocrine system in body functioning?

A An intact endocrine system is integral to the fundamental body functions of growth, pubertal development, metabolism, and fluid and electrolyte homeostasis.

2. What are the common presenting features of congenital hypothyroidism?

A Large posterior fontanel, coarse features, prolonged neonatal jaundice, constipation, lethargy, and delayed milestones are cardinal features of congenital hypothyroidism. However, majority of the cases are asymptomatic at birth.

3. What is the underlying etiology in these cases?

A Most cases are secondary to gland dysgenesis or ectopia and the remaining are due to dyshormonogenesis.

4. How can this condition be detected early, treated, and its neurological sequelae prevented?

A Newborn screening with a blood sample drawn on day 4 of life, thorough evaluation of babies with thyroid-stimulating hormone (TSH) >10 μIU/mL, and subsequent treatment with thyroxine in doses of 10–15 μg/kg is the only way to detect and treat this condition timely, thus salvaging intellectual function of the infant.

5. How does acquired primary hypothyroidism manifest?

A The condition commonly manifests with coarse features, periorbital puffiness, lethargy, dry skin, constipation, and growth retardation. In an older child, delayed puberty could be an association. Hypothyroidism in childhood can be goitrous or nongoitrous.

6. What are the common underlying causes?

A Majority of the cases are due to autoimmune etiology. A few are due to other etiologies such as dyshormonogenesis, secondary to systemic disorders such as thalassemia, granulamatous disorders, drugs, and radiation.

7. How is the condition treated?

A TSH values of greater than 5.5 µIU/mL in the presence of positive thyroid antibodies and goiter and TSH values above 10 µIU/mL in the absence of the conditions mentioned above with or without low free T4 values should be thoroughly evaluated and treatment in dose of 2–6 µg/kg/day should be initiated.

8. How is short stature defined?

A Height below the third percentile or two standard deviations below the mean on sex- and race-specific growth charts is defined as short stature. In addition, a child is defined short also if his/her height is two standard deviations below the midparental height.

9. What are the common causes?

A Nearly 50% of all causes of short stature are physiological including familial short stature and constitutional delay of growth and puberty. Uncorrected systemic diseases such as chronic anemia secondary to hemoglobinopathies such as thalassemia, chronic kidney and liver disease, malabsorption, rickets, renal tubular acidosis, chronic infections, and inflammations remain a major cause of short stature in the pathologic group.

The remaining causes include endocrine disorders such as hypothyroidism, growth hormone deficiency, genetic syndromes, skeletal dysplasias, and small-for-gestational-age babies who fail to catch up.

10. Which clinical tools help us to differentiate between physiological and pathologic causes of short stature?

A A normal growth velocity, normal body proportions, and height centile falling within the midparental height centile range usually indicate a physiological cause of short stature. In constitutional delay of growth and puberty, the height centile may be below the midparental height centile range that eventually catches up.

11. What are the common causes of obesity in children?

A Exogenous obesity due to diet and physical activity mismatch is the commonest cause of obesity in children, although polygenic inheritance is being increasingly attributed to this form of obesity as well. Endocrine causes of obesity such as hypothyroidism, Cushing syndrome (typical features such as mooning, hump, striae, hypertension), and growth hormone deficiency are associated with growth failure. Syndromic causes of obesity such as Prader–Willi syndrome and Bardet–Biedl syndrome have distinct clinical phenotypes.

Monogenic causes of obesity manifest with pathologic weight gain in infancy itself. Hypothalamopituitary (H-P) lesions manifest with obesity in addition to features of disturbances of other hormones of the H-P axis.

12. How does one commonly differentiate between exogenous obesity and obesity secondary to endocrine, syndromic, or monogenic causes?

A Children with exogenous obesity usually have height on the higher centiles of normal, while obesity with underlying endocrine connotations is usually associated with growth velocity deceleration. An obese child who is short needs to be thoroughly investigated to rule out an endocrinopathy. Syndromic obesity is associated with characteristic dysmorphic features and occasionally neurological and ophthalmic features. Monogenic obesity often manifests with pathologic weight gain in infancy or the first few years of life.

13. How is diabetes in children defined?

A Diabetes is defined as sugar values of ≥200 mg% in the presence of osmotic symptoms ± weight loss or as fasting sugar values of 126 mg% and above and postprandial sugar values of 200 mg% and above.

14. **What are the common types of diabetes in children?**

A Nearly 90% of all pediatric diabetes is type 1, which is due to autoimmune destruction of the pancreas. With the increasing prevalence of pediatric and adolescent obesity, the incidence of type 2 diabetes due to insulin resistance is on the rise. Diabetes secondary to steroids, antiretroviral therapy, L-asparaginase, pentamidine, and other drugs needs a mention.

Children with genetic syndromes such as Down, Turner, and Klinefelter syndromes are at a higher predisposition to diabetes. Secondary diabetes due to inflammation, infiltration from systemic disease, and destruction of the pancreas must be surveillanced for when appropriate. Monogenic (including neonatal), mitochondrial, and syndromic diabetes are extremely rare in incidence but encountered in pediatric endocrine practice.

15. **How is diabetes in children treated?**

A Insulin therapy with the basal bolus regimen, regular self-monitoring of blood glucose, and prudent meal planning are the cornerstones of therapy in type 1 diabetes mellitus. Type 2 diabetes in children and adolescents is usually managed with a combination of metformin, diet, and exercise.

16. **When is puberty defined as precocious?**

A Onset of secondary sexual characters before the age of 8 years in girls and before the age of 9 years in boys is defined as precocious puberty. There are racial differences in normal ages of onset of puberty that need to be kept in mind while defining precocious puberty.

17. **What are the first events in the onset of puberty?**

A Thelarche (breast budding) in girls and testicular volume of 4 mL and above are the first signs of puberty.

18. **What are the common causes of precocious puberty?**

A Most of the cases in girls are central in origin, commonly idiopathic, and a few due to underlying abnormalities (hamartomas, adenomas, other tumors) in the H-P region. In boys, underlying abnormalities in the H-P axis are significantly higher in central precocious puberty than those in girls. Common causes of peripheral precocious puberty in boys are congenital adrenal hyperplasia, testicular tumors, and adrenal neoplasms. In girls, ovarian cysts, tumors, and occasionally severe primary hypothyroidism may present with peripheral precocious puberty.

19. **When is puberty defined as delayed?**

A Absence of thelarche by 13 years of age in girls and testicular volume <4 mL in boys beyond 14 years of age is defined as delayed puberty.

20. **What are the common causes of delayed puberty?**

A Constitutional delay of growth and puberty and untreated systemic disease leading to growth failure and associated delayed puberty are common causes of delayed puberty. Delayed puberty is classified as hypogonadotropic hypogonadism, which is due to abnormalities in the H-P axis (Kallmann syndrome, pituitary tumors, prolactinomas), and hypergonadotropic hypogonadism, which is due to primary insufficiency of the testis or the ovary (Turner syndrome, Klinefilter syndrome, gonadal dysgenesis).

Hematology

1. **What are the causes of microcytic anemia in children?**

A The most common cause of microcytic and hypochromic anemia in children is iron deficiency, which is the most common nutritional deficiency. Other causes of microcytic anemia include thalassemia syndromes, lead poisoning, sideroblastic anemia, and anemia of chronic diseases.

2. What is the usual complete blood count (CBC) in iron deficiency anemia (IDA)?

A Usually, the CBC shows microcytosis (mean corpuscular volume [MCV] will be low), anisocytosis (red cell distribution width [RDW] will be increased), and hypochromia (mean corpuscular hemoglobin [MCH] will be low) in a case of IDA. Most often, there is associated thrombocytosis. Total RBC count is low but may be variable.

3. What does red cell distribution width indicate?

A RDW indicates whether the RBCs are of same size and shape or are of different morphology. It is the coefficient of variation of red cell volume distribution. RDW is the objective documentation of subjective anisocytosis. Normal range of RDW in children is 11.5–15%.

4. How does RDW help in anemia?

A RDW can help classify anemia with low MCV, particularly in children. If RDW is high with low MCV, then it indicates IDA; if RDW is normal with low MCV, then it indicates thalassemia minor.

5. What is the recommended dose of iron to treat IDA?

A The therapeutic calculated dose is 3 mg/kg of elemental iron. The iron content of various salts differs and the most commonly recommended salt (ferrous sulfate) has 20% elemental iron. Higher doses are unnecessary and may produce increased side effects of therapy.

6. What is Mentzer index?

A The index is calculated from the results of a CBC. If the quotient of the MCV (in femtoliters) divided by the RBC count (in millions per microliter) is less than 13, thalassemia is said to be more likely. If the result is greater than 13, then IDA is more likely.

7. Why is corrected reticulocyte count important than plain reticulocyte count?

A Reticulocyte count is important in the evaluation of anemia and response to the therapy. However, it must be corrected for anemia as it is the percentage of total RBC count and is spuriously elevated when the number of RBCs falls in the child with anemia. It is calculated by the following formula:

$$\text{Corrected reticulocyte count} = \frac{\text{Actual reticulocyte count} \times \text{Packed cell volume}}{0.45\ (\text{normal PCV})}$$

8. What are the causes of macrocytic anemia in children?

A The most common cause of macrocytosis is megaloblastic anemia due to vitamin B_{12} and folate deficiency. Other causes include liver disease, hypothyroidism, hemolytic anemias (due to high reticulocyte count), and drugs such as valproate and zidovudine.

9. What are a few causes of normocytic anemia in children?

A Normocytic anemia in children is caused by bleeding disorders, anemia of chronic renal disease/chronic inflammation, and primary bone marrow disorder (e.g., aplastic anemia).

10. What is the significance of mean platelet volume (MPV) in a CBC report?

A It may be helpful in differentiating between central and peripheral causes of low platelets. When there is peripheral destruction, the marrow sends to circulation younger platelets that are larger in size, so the MPV will be higher. In bone marrow failure, there are older cells, smaller in size; hence, MPV will be low. In Wiskott–Aldrich syndrome, the MPV is low, while in platelet functional disorder with giant platelets, it will be higher.

11. What is the role of platelet transfusion in idiopathic thrombocytopenic purpura (ITP)?

A There is no role of platelet transfusion in ITP as the transfused platelets are also destroyed by the antibody.

12. What is the basic pathophysiology in disseminated intravascular coagulation?

A DIC is a process initiated by a variety of stimuli in which initiation of coagulation cascade leads to thrombi in microcirculation followed by consumption of coagulation proteins to result in bleeding tendency.

13. What are the common causes of neutrophilia in children?

A Increased neutrophil counts in children are commonly seen with acute or chronic infections, inflammation (rheumatoid diseases), stress, and trauma, and after surgery.

14. How is neutropenia defined?

A Neutropenia is defined as an absolute neutrophil count of less than 1500/mm^3. Severe neutropenia is defined as absolute neutrophil count of less than 500/mm^3.

15. What are the causes of neutropenia?

A Neutropenia is caused by viral infections (e.g., dengue, Epstein-Barr virus, and HIV), Gram-negative bacterial sepsis, fungal infections, drugs (e.g., NSAIDs), anticancer chemotherapy, and immune deficiencies.

16. What are the causes of eosinophilia in children?

A Eosinophilia (>400/mm^3) is indicative of allergic conditions (asthma, urticaria), skin diseases (eczema, psoriasis), parasitic infestations (roundworms, hookworms, and filariasis), prolonged steroid therapy, and hypereosinophilic syndromes.

17. What are the causes of thrombocytosis in children? What risk does it possess?

A Thrombocytosis is often a reactive change and is seen in conditions such as IDA, hemolysis, and Kawasaki disease, and following splenectomy. It can lead to blood clot formation in the blood vessels.

18. What are a few causes of thrombocytopenia in children?

A Thrombocytopenia is seen in children with ITP, viral infections (dengue, HIV), microangiopathic hemolysis (DIC, hemolytic syndrome), liver diseases, autoimmune disease, and bone marrow dysfunction.

19. What are the clinical features that suggest hemolytic anemia as a cause of anemia in a child?

A These include hemolytic facies (depressed nasal bridge, frontal bossing, maxillary prominence), jaundice (usually mild), pallor, dark-colored urine (due to urobilinogen), splenic and liver enlargement, and severe heart failure.

20. What are the complications of chronic overload due to iron in thalassemia?

A These include growth failure, congestive heart failure, endocrine disturbances such as hypothyroidism and diabetes, delayed sexual development, and progressive liver fibrosis and cirrhosis due to iron deposition.

Musculoskeletal System

1. What are the common/variant skeletal conditions in children?

A These are common conditions that are noticed by the parents and many of these resolve without any intervention, but if any of these are painful, severe, persistent, or asymmetrical, these would require proper evaluation and therapy.

2. What is the significance of bow legs?

A Bow legs (genu varum) are caused by the bowing of tibiae causing the knees to be widely separated while standing with feet together.

These are mostly normal in children up to the age of 3 years and most often do not need treatment.

An important cause of bow legs is rickets. One should check for other signs of vitamin D deficiency in a patient with bow legs.

3. Are knock knees normal or abnormal?

A In knock knees (genu valgum), the child has the feet wide apart while standing with the knees together. They may be seen in children between the ages of 2 and 7 years resulting in an intermalleolar distance at ankles of up to 5 cm. These do not need treatment usually and resolve with age.

4. What is the importance of flat feet in children?

A Flat feet (pes planus) are usual in the first 1–2 years of life. Young children learning to walk have flat feet due to the flatness of the medial longitudinal arch and the presence of pad of fat, which disappears later.

The arch can be demonstrated if the child is able to stand on tiptoes.

Though a normal variant in young children, marked degree of pes planus can be found in connective tissue disorders such as Ehlers–Danlos syndrome and hypermobility. It is important to check for flat feet during regular checkups as a persistent low arch could lead to joint misalignments and balance difficulty in some cases.

5. What is clubfoot?

A This can be talipes equinovarus (clubfoot), which is a complex abnormality in which the foot is short, forefoot is adducted, and the entire foot is inverted. This cannot be corrected completely and is often bilateral. This may be a feature of a malformation syndrome or of an underlying condition such as spina bifida.

Positional talipes is a common occurrence and is a result of intrauterine compression of the fetus.

This is mild and can be corrected to neutral position with passive manipulation.

Infectious Diseases and Immunization

1. What are the general sequelae of congenital intrauterine infections?

A The sequelae of congenital intrauterine infections in newborns that may be seen weeks to months later include microcephaly, mental retardation, hearing loss, visual defects such as cataract (rubella) and chorioretinitis (toxoplasmosis), and recurrent eye and skin infections (herpes virus).

2. How should the newborns born to mothers who are HBsAg positive be managed at birth?

A Such babies must receive hepatitis B immunoglobulin (0.5 mL intramuscular) and the first dose of hepatitis B vaccine at separate sites within 12 hours of birth to prevent the perinatal transmission of hepatitis B virus infection to the newborn.

3. When is the fever labeled as fever of unknown origin (FUO)?

A FUO, also called PUO (pyrexia of unknown origin), is defined as the daily presence of fever (rectal temperature >38°C) documented by a healthcare professional for which no cause is identified after 3 weeks of outpatient evaluation and after 1 week of evaluation as an inpatient that includes a careful history/physical examination and initial laboratory assessment.

4. Why should childhood vaccines not be given in buttocks?

A The gluteus maximus muscle is not a good site for vaccines as it is incompletely developed in infants and there is a risk of injury to the sciatic nerve. Besides, the efficacy of vaccines (rabies, hepatitis B vaccine) given in buttocks is less if they are injected into the fat and not in the muscle.

5. **Can multiple vaccines be given simultaneously?**

A Multiple vaccines can be given simultaneously if separate injection sites are used without compromising their efficacy and safety as the immune response to one vaccine generally does not interfere with the immune response to another vaccine.

6. **What schedule should be followed for a child who has missed his/her earlier immunizations?**

A The immunization schedule for an unimmunized child is shown in Box 20.1.

Box 20.1 Immunization schedule for an unimmunized child

- *First visit*: BCG*, DPT first dose (dT or TdaP if older than 7 years); OPV or IPV 1 (if younger than 5 years); Hib (younger than 5 years) and HBV first dose
- *Second visit (1 month after the first visit)*: DPT second dose (dT if age 7 years and above); OPV second dose; HBV second dose; Hib second dose (if younger than 15 months)
- *Third visit (1 month after the second visit)*: OPV 3 or IPV second dose; MMR vaccine
- *Fourth visit (6 months after the first visit)*: DPT third dose or dT (if older than 7 years); OPV 4 or IPV booster (till 5 years age) and HBV third dose

*BCG should be given only up to 5 years of age.

7. **Why are ophthalmic complications and blindness more common after measles infection?**

A This is due to the presence of vitamin A deficiency in the child that leads to persistence or worsening of the epithelial damage, and malnutrition further increases the risk of infection (i.e., keratitis).

8. **What are the complications that are likely to occur after a child is infected with measles?**

A The complications that can follow measles include bronchopneumonia, acute otitis media, reactivation of tuberculosis, precipitation of malnutrition, and meningoencephalitis.

9. **Which are the common viral skin infections seen in children?**

A The common viral infections affecting the skin are chicken pox, molluscum contagiosum, viral warts, and hand, foot, and mouth disease.

10. **What is the role of acyclovir in managing children with varicella?**

A Routine administration of acyclovir in otherwise healthy children for uncomplicated varicella is not recommended below 13 years of age. However, acyclovir needs to be given if the child is immunocompromised or if there is neonatal varicella infection.

11. **What is aseptic meningitis and what are its causes?**

A Aseptic meningitis is defined as clinical and laboratory evidence of meningeal inflammation (CSF pleocytosis and raised protein) without evidence of bacterial infection on either Gram stain or CSF culture. The common causes include viruses such as coxsackievirus, enterovirus, and echo virus. Aseptic meningitis can also be caused by inflammatory conditions such as Kawasaki disease.

12. **What are the reasons for a false-negative Mantoux test?**

A A false-negative Mantoux test is observed because of faulty technique, severe malnutrition, immunodeficiency, and severe forms of tuberculosis such as meningeal and military tuberculosis.

13. **Why and how does hydrocephalus occur in TBM?**

A TBM leads to the formation of basal exudates in the brain and this results in the obliteration of the cisterns, thereby leading to the interference to the CSF flow.

14. **What is the role of steroids in TBM?**

A Steroids are administered in the first 4–6 weeks along with antituberculous drugs and they help to decrease the incidence of complications by reducing the inflammatory response in the meninges and subsequent fibrosis.

Index

A

D

H

I

O

P

Q

R